£1.25

Lovers and Gamblers

Jackie Collins burst on to the publishing scene in 1969 with the first of a string of provocative and controversial bestsellers, *The World is Full of Married Men*. Since then she has written eleven novels, including the phenomenally successful *Hollywood Wives*, which rocketed to the top of the international bestseller lists throughout the world, and has now been made into a highly successful mini-series.

Jackie Collins lives in Los Angeles with her husband and three children and is currently working on a new novel.

Also by Jackie Collins
in Pan Books

The Bitch
Chances
Lovehead
Sinners
The Stud
The World is Full of Married Men
The World is Full of Divorced Women
Hollywood Wives
Lucky
Hollywood Husbands

Jackie Collins

Lovers and Gamblers

Pan Books London, Sydney and Auckland

First published 1977 by W. H. Allen & Co Ltd
This edition published 1978 by Pan Books Ltd
Cavaye Place, London SW10 9PG
39 38 37 36 35 34 33 32 31
© Jackie Collins 1977
ISBN 0 330 25651 3
Printed and bound in Great Britain by
Richard Clay Ltd, Bungay, Suffolk

For all the
Lovers and Gamblers
I have known.
Especially Oscar

book one

one

Al King slammed and locked the bathroom door. He ran the shower until it was pleasantly warm, then let the water cascade on his body for at least five minutes. He soaped himself vigorously, turning the shower onto ice cold and marvelling at the sudden shrinkage of his cock. Amazing. Never failed.

He climbed out of the shower and studied his nakedness in the full-length mirror. A week at a health farm had done him the world of good. The slight paunch he had suspected was gone, his stomach was flat as a pancake. Forty push-ups a day helped there. He turned sideways. Pretty good. The body was in fine shape. Lean, tanned, hairy, masculine. Al allowed himself a pleased smile, and leaned forward to study his face. Everything seemed in order except for an incipient blackhead lurking on his chin. He squeezed it carefully.

Yes, he still looked pretty goddamn good.

In fact he looked better than ever. The recent operation to remove the bags under his eyes had been an unqualified success, and the new teeth-capping job was excellent.

Physically he was in perfect shape for his forthcoming tour across America, an event he was looking forward to with mixed feelings. It was two years since he had been on the road, and although he wouldn't admit it to anyone he was worried that he could keep up the pace. Jesus Christ – so many cities – and every one of them would expect a peak performance. His voice was in pretty good shape, but the tour promised a gruelling schedule – and the press, the critics, would be the first to pounce if he wasn't up to his previous standard.

He opened the bathroom door carefully. The redhead and the blonde were both waiting, lolling on the bed in an advanced state of nakedness. He headed towards them. Time to play. Time to get it on.

An hour later his enthusiasm was turning to boredom.

'Al!' exclaimed the blonde for the tenth time, 'you are the

greatest!' She smiled a vacant pretty smile and concentrated once more on pleasuring him. Earlier in the day, when they had first met, she had promised him in a heavy southern drawl, 'I am gonna *pleasure* you honey, like you ain't *never* been pleasured before!'

He was still waiting.

'Al!' mumbled the redhead, mouth full, 'you are *too* much! Just too too much!'

Al wasn't really listening. He lay naked and relaxed in the shuttered hotel room, his arms casually behind his head. With his eyes half-closed he endured the attentions of the two women. He had no plans for getting involved or of even participating. Why should he? Let them do all the work. After all he was a star, wasn't he? They were lucky to be in his bed, his room, his life.

Al King was a rock-soul superstar. A singer who drove women mad the world over with his low throaty growl and his sexual gyrations. At thirty-seven he had reached the peak of his success. He had everything.

Money. Plenty of that. Off-shore investments, and lots of ready cash for the useful little things in life like a two hundred thousand pound house in London. A new red Ferrari, plus matching Rolls and Bentley.

Love. Well, he had a wife of sixteen years standing, a fair-haired sensible woman called Edna, who stayed out of the way because that was how Al wanted it. For more exciting sex there was always a selection of ready and able ladies. Any shape, size or specification.

'Al,' suggested the blonde, shifting so that her well-developed mammaries hung invitingly over his mouth, 'Al, baby, why don't we fuck?'

The redhead paused at what she was doing and expressed great interest in the blonde's suggestion.

Al grunted. Stick it into these two. They must be kidding.

'Just keep at it,' he pushed the redhead back into position.

Women had never been a problem. Always plenty to go around, even before he was famous. With the fame came the classy bits. Falling over themselves for a piece of Al King cock. And what ravers!

He could feel no sign of an orgasm. The trouble was that he just couldn't be bothered to make it with the casual pick-ups that crowded his bedroom. He started off thinking – yeah – great. And he ended up thinking – why bother? Lately it had to be a very special girl – and how many of those were there around?

It was four o'clock in New York. It was the middle of July, and hot. Of course the room was air-conditioned, but still it was a strange sort of coolness.

Al said, 'Get dressed, girls, I've had enough.'

They both chorused their disappointment. He hadn't even touched them.

'I could make you come,' the blonde said, 'if we got rid of *her*.' Scornfully she indicated the redhead.

Al got off the bed and headed for the bathroom. Whatever gave her the impression he would *want* to come with her? 'Dressed and out in five minutes,' he snapped.

'Hey . . .' objected the redhead.

Al took another shower, you couldn't be too careful. This time when he emerged from the bathroom the girls had gone. Good. Sometimes they stayed to argue. He pulled up the window shades, flooding the bedroom with sunlight.

He contemplated phoning his brother Paul, but he was with Linda, and she wouldn't be too pleased. Linda wasn't bad, too strong for Paul though, it wouldn't last. Anyway, she wouldn't stand a chance against Paul's wife, Melanie. Now she was a real little toughie. She liked the money, the big house, and all the perks of being Al King's sister-in-law. She would never stand for another woman in Paul's life.

Al yawned. Now *his* wife was another proposition. Sweet, faithful Edna. He had met her when she was sixteen, knocked her up, done the right thing and married her. Well, her father had been very persuasive, he had given Al two thousand pounds to set him up in a record shop. However, being shut up in a shop did not appeal to Al. What he really wanted to do was sing. He was well known locally. Whenever there was a wedding or an event people would say – 'Get Al to give us a few songs.' He made the odd five pounds here and there, but he would have done it for nothing.

Paul was the brains of the King family. He had just finished a course of business accountancy and was working for a chartered accountant. Al had persuaded him to leave his job and open up the shop with him. 'After all, it's just the two of us now,' he had said. Their parents had recently died within months of each other.

Soon the shop became the local musicians' hang-out, and a group called 'Rabble' invited Al to sing with them. Paul took over their management, and within two years it was 'Al King and Rabble'. Within four years it was just Al King, and the ride to superstardom had really begun.

Edna had never complained. They had started married life in one room. Al was out all day working, and then, when he joined 'Rabble', he was out all night too. Edna looked after the baby, helped out in the shop, cooked, cleaned, struggled to make ends meet. She had been a softly pretty girl when Al had met her. Now, at thirty-three, she was plump and matronly, and she stayed very much in the background of her husband's starry life.

Al's family was important to him. His sixteen-year-old son, Evan, received everything he wanted, although to Al's chagrin he never seemed to appreciate anything. He was a skinny, sulky boy with acned skin and greasy hair. '*You're* Al King's son?' People would question in disbelief when they first met him. He was a poor scholar and hated school. Al had promised that at the end of the present term he could leave and perhaps accompany him on his tour. Evan had shown unheard-of enthusiasm. Al had decided it would do the boy good to get away from his mother. Edna fussed round him too much, the boy was stifled.

As a boy Al had never been stifled. He had engaged in sexual relations at the ripe old age of thirteen with one of the local hookers. Evan, at the ripe old age of sixteen, never seemed to notice girls, let alone screw them.

Al had plans to change all of that. Get the boy away from his mother, show him what it was all about. Yes, it was about time he gave some of his attention to Evan. Get rid of those spots. Put some weight on the boy. Get him royally laid. Yes.

The hell with it, Paul should be at his disposal – not Linda's. He picked up the phone. 'Hey Paul baby, you want to shift your ass up here and discuss more important things than getting your rocks off?'

'What's up, Al? Can't it wait?'

'No. I need company.'

'Give me a few minutes.'

Al switched on the television.

Wrapped in a black towelling bathrobe he poured himself a bourbon and coke – fattening but favourite – and settled down on the bed.

He clicked the remote control dial. Quiz game. Western. Cookery. Chat show. He stopped there.

'Well,' said the interviewer, 'who shall we pick out to talk to next amongst this bevy of beauties?'

The camera switched to a group of about fifteen girls in swim-suits clustered together at the front of the audience. 'Miss Phila-

4

delphia,' continued the interviewer, 'would you like to step up here, dear.'

Miss Philadelphia was a skinny, nervous girl, with long legs and freckles. She smiled jumpily.

'Gee, honey,' said the interviewer, leering at his audience, 'I'm not going to *eat* you. What do you think your chances are of winning the "Miss Coast to Coast" title tonight?'

'I'd like to,' she replied breathily.

'What would you do if you did?'

'I want to travel. Then I guess I'd just like to settle down and be a good wife and mother.'

'Wonderful. Isn't that wonderful, everyone?' The audience obediently clapped.

'Bullshit!' exclaimed Al, and he was just about to change the channel when Miss Los Angeles stepped forward. She was wearing a black shiny bikini, and she had a body that stopped even Al in his tracks. Big bosom, long legs, finely muscled stomach, small waist. He dragged his eyes up to her face and it was not a disappointment. She was great looking, with a wide luscious mouth, and long streaked blondish hair which fell past her shoulders in soft waves.

'Not bad!' exclaimed Al out loud, and he felt himself slightly aroused, which was a good sign.

He would have her. He would get his brother to arrange it.

For Al King nothing was impossible. He could have any woman he wanted, and he usually did.

'Why do you always have to run whenever he calls?' demanded Linda.

'Because,' explained Paul King patiently, 'that's why Al and I have such a good relationship, and that is why we are still together.'

'Christ!' exclaimed Linda crossly, 'you make the two of you sound like an old married couple.'

'That's right,' agreed Paul, 'a manager and his star have a very sensitive relationship. It *is* sort of like a marriage, and Al and I have a good one.'

'God! You and your bloody marriages! It's not only your wife I have to contend with, Al is a lot more demanding than any woman.' Linda Cosmo climbed out of bed. She was a thin woman in her early thirties, with Elizabeth Taylor eyes, and straight black hair. She was strikingly attractive.

'Come back here,' demanded Paul.

'Why? For a quick one? You know I don't appreciate quick ones. Anyway, I thought you said he would be busy this afternoon – all afternoon. It's only just past four.'

'I expect he got bored, you know Al.'

'Yes. I know Al. He's a pain in the ass. I really don't know why you stay with him – you have plenty of money, you don't *need* Al King any more.'

'Cool it, Linda,' Paul followed her out of bed, 'you should understand.'

'Oh sure, I *do* understand. I understand about Al, and about your wife, and about your kids. What time does that leave for *me*? How often are we alone together?' She locked her hands behind Paul's neck, 'You know I love you,' she continued softly, 'but love needs attention too.'

He kissed her, running his hands down her naked body. She was right, he did neglect her. But what could he do? He had so many other commitments.

'How would you like to come on the tour?' He had blurted it out before really thinking about it.

She looked at him suspiciously. 'I'd love it – you know that. But how?'

'Officially, that's how. I'm appointing you tour photographer.'

'You're kidding!'

'I'm serious. Only stop giving me a hard time about Al.'

'You really mean it?' She wrapped her arms around him, kissing him long and hard. 'We can be together, and it's a terrific challenge. I always did get turned on by a challenge.'

She kissed him again, and he pushed her away, laughing. 'If I'd known I was going to get this good a reaction I'd have given you a job sooner! I feel like a Hollywood producer!'

She grinned. 'I'll join you on the casting couch later!' Then seriously she added: 'I won't let you down, I promise you that.'

'On the casting couch?'

'On the tour, you fool!'

'I know you won't let me down, you never do.'

He guided her back to the bed. 'Why don't we put the casting couch into action now?'

She laughed softly. 'Why not indeed? There's nothing I like better than screwing the man with the most beautiful cock in the world ...'

As usual it was the best for him. Linda Cosmo was the only woman that he genuinely liked making love to.

6

He had met her a year previously. New York. Opening night in cabaret for Al. Noise. People. Booze. Food. She had been sent by a magazine to photograph the event. Paul had seen her, fancied her, moved in before Al. He usually gave Al first crack, but that time it had been different.

They had been together on and off ever since. The on was when he was in America. The off was when he was in England.

He was pleased with the idea of bringing Linda on the tour. She was an excellent photographer, and they would be able to be seen together.

Later, as they dressed, Linda asked, 'Can I tell people?'

'Tell them what?'

'About the job?'

'Not yet. Let me cue Al in first. And I've got to break it to B.S. – you know what he's like, he may struggle a bit.' B.S., better known as Bernie Suntan – was Al's American publicity man – the best, but somewhat nervous and temperamental. He might object. Then again he might be delighted with the idea. Whatever he thought it was tough shit. Only Al could influence Paul's decisions.

The reasons that Paul and Al were in New York was because of the Al King Supertour. A spectacular odyssey across America. There were a few minor details to sort out – things that Paul could have really taken care of on the phone – but he had wanted to make the trip if only to be with Linda. Al had decided to come along at the last moment. Fresh out of the health farm he was ready for some action.

The tour was immensely important. In the last year Al's record sales had been slipping. Nothing desperate, just a slow, hardly noticeable slide. But Paul had noticed, and coupled with the fact that Al's last two singles had failed to make the top of the charts, he realized that it was time to bring Al back in front of the people. Too much time in television and recording studios created a vacuum between a star and his public. On stage Al was pure dynamite.

The trip was meticulously planned. Al would travel in his own lavishly equipped plane – that way all travel hassles would be taken care of.

So far Al had made no mention of bringing his wife, and Paul was sure that the matter would not come up. Paul was relieved because it gave him a beautiful excuse with his own wife. If Edna wasn't allowed on the trip, then Melanie certainly wasn't. Not that Paul would compare the two women. Edna was a doormat and Al treated her as such. Melanie was a sharp lady, which was why Paul had to play it very carefully with Linda. If Melanie got a whiff that he was serious about anybody – well . . . He didn't like to think about it.

He had been married to Melanie for ten years – since she was eighteen, and they had two young children. Melanie was an ex-dancer. She was very pretty, but oh what a bitch! And a nag. And somewhere in the back of his mind Paul knew for sure that she had slept with Al. He had no proof, knew nothing for certain, but he just had a feeling . . .

Linda was dressed and ready to leave. 'Later?' she asked.

'As soon as I'm free.'

'Come to the apartment, I'll cook dinner.'

'We may have to go out with Al, I don't know what he's got in mind but I can't leave him alone.'

Linda laughed sarcastically. 'The great Al King alone – never!'

'Watch it, you'll be working for him soon.'

'I don't understand it,' Linda mused, 'you're better looking, taller, and a whole year younger. Why aren't *you* the superstar?'

'Because I can't sing, and whatever you may think about Al he's got a bitch of a voice. Besides, I like being the manager, it means I score the best birds.'

'Oh, really?'

'Oh, really, yes. I got you, didn't I?'

'Yeah, you got me hooked like some stupid fish. There I was, looking for a stable relationship, and I get some dumb married man who spends his life wetnursing superschmuck!'

'You've got a big mouth, but I love you.'

'That's *why* you love me.' She glanced quickly at her watch, 'Hey – you're going to be late – better move it.'

'I'll call you later.'

'Fine, I'm photographing the "Miss Coast to Coast" competition tonight. It shouldn't take long. I'll call you.'

'Can't you cancel it?'

'No way, I need the bread.'

She left, and Paul finished dressing in a hurry. Out to the elevator, up two floors, and then he was knocking on the door to Al's suite. A waiter let him in.

'Where the fuck have you been?' Al asked rudely. 'I ordered you a steak sandwich, you took so fucking long I ate it.'

'I'm not hungry. What happened to your companions?'

'Jesus! Dogs! Horrible. I had them out of here in double time.'

'I warned you.'

'How would *you* have known? In the lobby they looked like two real little darlings. I'll tell you what though, I saw one I *really* fancy.'

How many times had Paul heard *that*. Growing up together had been a checkered path of fame, fortune, and women. Al had always fancied anything that moved and was female.

'Who is she?' inquired Paul, 'and where did you find her?'

'*You're* going to find her,' corrected Al, 'I don't know her name. I spotted her on television – there's some beauty competition to-night – she's in it.'

'Miss Coast to Coast?'

'Yeah, that's right. How did you know?'

'I'm a detective on the side. Only how do we find the girl if you don't even know her name?'

'Miss Los Angeles.'

'Dinner tonight. It's as good as done.'

two

Dallas licked already shiny lips. She stared at herself in the full-length mirror and adjusted the Miss Los Angeles sash. She wished that she could take it off, it ruined the whole effect of the leopard skin bikini.

Later in the evening, when she won, she would have to put on the stupid crown and cover herself with the fake ermine cloak. What a drag!

Dallas knew she would win. She had taken steps to make certain she would.

'You wearing a hair-piece?' Miss Long Island asked bitchily, craning to see herself in the mirror.

'Yeah,' agreed Dallas, 'around the crotch!'

Miss Long Island retreated angrily.

Dallas peered at herself once more in the mirror. She did look her absolute best. She deserved to win. There really was no con-test. Still, it was just as well that she had taken out insurance.

'The judges are being introduced!' someone shouted with excite-ment and the girls in the dressing-room crowded round the closed circuit television set in the corner.

A smile hovered round Dallas' mouth. Five judges, and she had taken care of three of them. On those odds she could afford to feel secure.

'First, the ladies', the announcer on television said, 'and I would like to hear a big round of applause for that wonderful screen star, Miss April Crawford.' April Crawford appeared, swathed in mink.

'Now, someone we are always reading about – leader of fashion and fun, Lucy Mabel Mann.'

'Isn't she *pretty*!' one of the girls exlaimed.

Yes, agreed Dallas silently. And I should know, for it was only this morning that I visited her in her Central Park West duplex, and gave her the greatest head job she has ever had!

'Now let's hear it for Ramo Kaliffe, the man with the million dollar eyes.'

Hello Ramo, thought Dallas. I took care of you last night, and you were more than grateful.

'Petro Lorenz, writer and television personality. And lastly, Ed Kurlnik, of Kurlnik Motors fame.'

Ed gave that short embarrassed smile that Dallas had grown to know so well over the last few months. She had been taking care of Ed for exactly sixteen weeks. Twice a week, Mondays and Fridays. It was no secret that he was a married man.

The girls were being summoned together and hustled out the door. The parade was about to begin.

Dallas shook out her mane of hair and strode confidently onto the stage.

Dallas Lunde, born twenty years previously at a small zoo her parents had off the main highway outside Miami. An uneventful childhood, no brothers or sisters, but plenty of animals to play with. Her parents didn't believe in school, so they never bothered to send her.

Sometimes, when he had the time, her father would tutor her in various subjects. He was particularly fond of geography and real life adventure.

The three of them lived a very tight life; her parents had no friends. They were some kind of religious maniacs – following a cult all their own – which made them reject any contact with the outside world. The animals they looked after were their whole life.

Dallas grew up alone. The zoo was off the beaten track, and the only other people she ever saw were the two-dollar-a-day visitors. Once a month her father went into town for supplies, and it wasn't until Dallas was sixteen that he took her with him. She would always remember that day. The shops, the people, the cars and the noise. Along with the supplies her father collected a young man called Phil, who was to come and help out at the zoo. Unbeknown to Dallas he had also been picked out as a husband for her. She was given no choice. On her seventeenth birthday she and Phil were married.

At the time it didn't occur to her to object. Her parents' words were law; she had never argued. She knew nothing of the world outside. She had never even seen television or movies. The only books she had ever read were about animals and wild life.

Phil was tall and nice-looking. He spoke softly. It was a shock when that evening he threw off her nightgown and violently deflowered her. The only sexual education she had received had been from observing the animals, but even they behaved with more gentleness than the man who was her husband.

Night after night Phil demanded his rights. He never kissed or caressed her, merely lifted her nightdress and thrust himself in. Dallas accepted this. She worked hard during the day, and at night she cooked and cleaned and suffered her husband's attentions, because this was the way she thought things were. When her mother became ill, her father decided they needed more help at the zoo, so he employed a young black couple named Burt and Ida Keyes. Dallas liked them immediately, they were always laughing and giggling, and they seemed so fond of each other. She couldn't help watching them. She noticed the way they kept on touching each other, and the secret smiley little looks they exchanged.

After several weeks she plucked up the courage to discuss this with Ida. 'You and Burt are always feeling each other, kissing, things like that. Do you like it when he does ... well ... you know?'

'Like it!' Ida make a sucking sound of enjoyment. 'I just couldn't live without it!'

Dallas studied Burt with new eyes. What made him so different from Phil? It couldn't only be his black skin. It wasn't long before she had the chance to find out. They were alone together one day cleaning out one of the cages, when Burt reached out and lazily pushed the hair off her forehead. Then he cupped her face in his hands, and kissed her long and hard. The feel of his tongue exploring her mouth created a vacuum of excitement in Dallas that she had never known before.

He undid the buttons on her blouse, and exposed her breasts. All the time he was whispering endearments.

Dallas could not have moved even if she had wanted to. She was powerless, thrilled, on the brink of a fantastic new discovery.

Burt bent his head to her breasts, and she leaned back hoping the moment would last forever. Then she saw the blood as it fell on her breasts from the cut above Burt's eye. She heard the cursing as Phil

11

lifted the stick to strike once more. She felt the shame sweep over her in a great wave.

She jumped up, covering herself. Oh God, how could she ever face her friend Ida again?

She ran back to the house and collected a few belongings, then she took twenty dollars from the dresser and fled.

She had no idea where she was going, she just ran.

On the highway she thumbed a ride, and it was only when she was settled in the front seat of the Ford car that she stopped to think.

'Where to, sweetie?' inquired the florid driver of the car, and he reached over and patted her on the knee.

'Miss Los Angeles. A beautiful young lady of twenty whose vital statistics come out at a staggering 39–22–36. Dallas by name, a model, whose life ambition is to marry a fellow American – because – and I quote the lady herself – American men are so big and strong and handsome. Wowee folks, that's *some* compliment.'

Dallas paraded across the stage. The spotlight felt hot on her almost naked body. Stomach in. Bosom out. Head high. Fixed smile. Walk tall.

She glanced briefly at the judges. Ed was regarding her like a proud father, and well he might. What was that sweet old-fashioned phrase? Sugar daddy. Yeah – that's what he was, her sugar daddy.

She had met him in Los Angeles, and he had transported her to New York and set her up in a very nice apartment. When she had heard he was to be a judge on 'Miss Coast to Coast' she had asked him to pull a few strings. He had done so, flown her to Los Angeles where she won the local contest, and now here she was. With connections it was as easy as that.

Ed Kurlnik could pull a lot of strings if he so cared. He was an important man, head of the Kurlnik Motor dynasty – a vast corporation almost as large as the Ford empire.

Dallas turned and flashed a smile at the television camera. Ed was most impressed at the fact that she was only twenty. He was sixty-one, and looked it. Money could buy most things, but it couldn't turn back the clock. Having a young girlfriend made him feel virile and alive.

'Honey-blond hair, green eyes, five foot seven inches of beautiful woman. Let's hear it for Miss Los Angeles – the lovely Dallas.'

She turned and smiled one last time, then she was off the stage, and running back to the dressing room.

She unhooked the top of her bikini, stepped out of the tiny

pants. Then, totally naked, she inched her way into a long green tube of a jersey dress. Nine hundred dollars worth, Ed had bought it for her. It fitted like a second skin, skimming her hips, clinging round her breasts, plunging back and front. She fluffed out her hair, licked her lips. She was ready.

She watched the other contestants on the closed circuit television. Some were pretty, some cute, but none could hold a candle.

'You sure think you're hot shit!' Miss Long Island hissed.

'Served your way. Right up the ass!' replied Dallas calmly. They were all jealous of her and well they might be. She was going to win. Of that there was no doubt.

The man in the car had taken her to a motel. She was grateful to him, she had nowhere else to go.

He was about her father's age. He wore a brightly patterned sports shirt, and baggy beige trousers.

'Say, girly, what ya gonna do to make an old man happy?' he asked.

Dallas sat quietly on the corner of the double bed. What was she going to do?

'Make yourself comfortable,' the man suggested, 'and I'll go and get us some beers.'

Dallas sat unmoving. She didn't know what to do. If she hadn't met this kind man she would still be out on the highway thumbing a lift. She had made the move, she couldn't go back. Phil would kill her. Her parents would never talk to her again, and as for Ida . . .

The man returned, carrying a plastic bag from which he produced a six pack of beer, and a box of Ritz crackers. 'We'll have ourselves our own little party.' He switched on the television, and drew the curtains. Then he snapped open a can of beer, and handed it to her. He was sweating a lot, small rivulets running down his face.

Dallas sipped from the can. She had never tasted beer before. Her eyes were glued to the television set. So much going on. So many new experiences.

'You gonna get undressed?' the man inquired, licking his lips and sticking a fat fist into the Ritz crackers.

'Why?' asked Dallas carefully, not at all sure what it was he wanted from her.

'Ha!' exclaimed the man, 'I'll take care of you, girly, don't worry on that score.' He unzipped his trousers and struggled out of them. He had sunburned thighs, and underpants that matched his shirt. 'Come on, girly,' he insisted, 'let's go.'

So this was the price of a bed. Dallas sighed. She knew what he

13

wanted now. Well, it couldn't be any worse than it was with Phil.

She felt nervous and unsure. But if it meant a bed for the night . . .

She had no money, no choice. The only alternative was returning home, and she couldn't do that. This man would look after her, he was a fatherly type, he had behaved kindly.

She stood up and removed her jeans, and the man moved forward and took off her pants. Then, sweating more than ever, he removed his own pants, and pushed her back on the bed. He was struggling with a rubber thing, fitting it over his penis.

Dallas closed her eyes, bit down on her lip and counted silently. With Phil she never got as far as fifty, with this man it only took to fifteen, and then he was grunting and heaving, and it was over. He hadn't been as rough as Phil. It was almost painless.

'You're a little beauty!' exclaimed the man, 'you been at it long?'

'Oh,' said Dallas vaguely, 'I guess so.' She went to the bathroom and put her pants and jeans back on. She stared blankly at herself in the mirror. Her eyes were tear-filled, but she couldn't cry, nobody was forcing her to do anything. Quietly she went back into the bedroom and settled on the bed in front of the television.

Half naked, the man was asleep, his snores hardly disturbing her.

In the morning she awoke with a start. She had fallen asleep in front of the television still in her clothes. She looked around for the man, but he was gone. On the beside table there was a note and a twenty-dollar bill. The note read – 'Vacate room by twelve, all paid for. Thank you.'

Where was he? Why had he deserted her? Maybe she hadn't pleased him. Why had he left twenty dollars? Did he know she had no money?

Puzzled, Dallas ate the rest of the Ritz crackers while watching television. Then, at twelve o'clock, she was back on the highway.

There were six finalists. Nervously they huddled together back-stage waiting for the results.

Dallas stood slightly apart, aware of the fact that a television camera was trained on them to catch every nuance of disappointment. She tried not to look too confident. She smiled slightly and parted her lips appealingly. Let all the guys in the audience drool. She knew she looked great. She knew she was a winner.

They were announcing the three winners now.

Miss Kansas City was third. She squealed with delight and kissed the girl nearest to her before rushing onto the stage.

Miss Miami Beach was second. 'Oh my God!' she muttered,

the colour draining from her face. And she had to be pushed onto the stage.

Here it comes, thought Dallas, here comes my little bit of fame – here comes my passport to better things. If any of those sonsof-bitches have double-crossed me . . .

'And now the winner – "Miss Coast to Coast" – The beautiful – Dallas! Miss Los Angeles!'

She pulled in her stomach, threw back her shoulders and walked confidently onto the stage.

Flashbulbs were popping, the audience was applauding and cheering. Maybe she would have won it without taking out insur-ance . . . She seemed like a popular choice.

The MC was grabbing her excitedly – 'Miss Coast to Coast! Miss Coast to Coast!' he kept on screaming.

She smiled towards the television cameras. The previous year's winner was placing the sash around her. Ramo Kaliffe was placing the crown on her head. 'Later,' he whispered.

'Maybe,' she whispered back. Maybe not – she thought. Wouldn't do to let Ed find out there were others . . .

Out of the corner of her eye she spotted Ed, he was smiling proudly. He had been smiling the first time she had met him, but that had been for different reasons . . .

Dallas thumbed a lift into Miami with a truck driver. He chewed gum and barely spoke to her. When he stopped the truck to let her out she had hesitated.

'Whassamatter?' he asked.

'I thought you might want to keep me with you . . .' she ventured.

'Aw, shit!' he spat on the sidewalk. 'I got daughters older than you. Go peddle it at the Fontainebleau.'

The truck drove off and she was left standing there. Go peddle it at the Fontainebleau – what did that mean?

'Excuse me?' she asked a woman at a bus stop. 'Is there a Fon-tainebleau Street?' The woman shook her head. 'Fontainebleau Hotel,' she suggested, 'but that's over on Collins Avenue.'

'How do I get there?'

The woman looked her over. 'Goin' for a job?'

'Er – yes.'

'Come with me on the bus, I'll tell you when we get there. Hadn't you better smarten up?'

'I will later,' agreed Dallas. She was wearing her standard clothes of old jeans, a T-shirt, and sandals. Perhaps she should brush her

15

hair and wash her face. She was beginning to feel extremely hungry.

The Fontainebleau Hotel seemed a large and formidable place. Dallas hung around outside for a while and watched the people emerging and collecting their cars. Two girls walked by in beach clothes, and Dallas fell into step behind them as they entered the hotel. The huge air-conditioned lobby seemed even more formidable, so Dallas followed the two girls into an elevator. They took it down to a lower level, and emerged into an arcade of shops. She smelled the restaurant, and wondered how much a sandwich would cost. While she stood outside wondering, a group of men appeared. They were middle-aged and jolly. They were shouting at each other in friendly tones, and clapping each other on the back.

'Excuse me?' Dallas asked the nearest one, 'how much is a sandwich?'

This question produced much hilarity, and they crowded round her, staring and laughing.

'What you doin' here?' one of them finally asked. 'You don't look like you belong here.'

'I'm . . . er . . . looking for a job.'

'What sort of a job?'

Dallas shrugged. 'Anything where someone will take care of me.'

'If you'll have a bath, I'll take care of you,' one of them suggested leeringly.

'All right,' said Dallas seriously.

'I think I just got lucky!' he joked to the others.

Dallas stared at him. 'What's your name?' she asked. This time she wanted to know, then maybe he couldn't run off in the middle of the night.

'Frank,' he said, 'you can call me Frankie.'

The others were walking off into the restaurant. 'I'll see you guys later,' volunteered Frankie.

'Make sure she takes a bath,' one of them said as a parting shot, 'don't want to carry anything back to Irma!' They all departed laughing.

Now they were alone Frankie lost some of his strut. 'You look awfully young,' he said, 'you sure you old enough?'

'Twenty dollars,' stated Dallas, 'and a sandwich.'

She was learning fast.

three

'I'm sorry,' said Linda firmly, 'but she wouldn't come.'

'Wouldn't come?' echoed Al and Paul in unison.

'That's right. You got it in one.'

'You didn't tell her it was me,' exclaimed Al in disgust.

'Of course I told her it was you. I said – Al King – the famous singer – would like you to be his guest for dinner tonight.'

'And?'

'And she smiled, flashed those lethal teeth, and said, that's nice but I'm busy.'

'Busy!'

'She probably *was* busy. After all, the girl just won "Miss Coast to Coast". There were horny little guys all over the place, I was tripping over them.'

Al shook his head in amazement. 'I guess she didn't believe you. I suppose she thought you were putting her on.'

'Maybe,' said Linda irritably, 'I don't carry an official document stating I am a certified pimp for Al King.'

'Perhaps you should,' said Al, 'that way you . . .'

'Come on, you two,' interrupted Paul quickly, 'the girl's probably married or engaged or something.'

'Since when has that made any difference?' asked Al, moodily.

'I have, however, managed to acquire a consolation prize,' stated Linda. 'Miss Miami Beach is waiting in the lobby for us, so *someone* believed me.'

'Fuck Miss Miami Beach!' said Al dourly.

'I thought that was the whole idea,' replied Linda. 'She's downstairs, gorgeously pretty, and creaming her white lace panties at the thought of meeting you!'

'Great!' exclaimed Paul. 'She came second, didn't she? Shall I get them to send her up, Al?'

'I thought we were going out to dinner,' said Linda coldly. She was fed up with the whole thing. She hated Paul when he was with Al, she wished that just once he would tell his brother to shut up.

'Tomorrow,' said Al, 'I'll have lunch with her tomorrow.'

'With who? Miss Miami Beach?'

'The original one – the piece that won – Dallas – that's her name.'

'*I* can't arrange it,' said Linda quickly.

'I wouldn't ask you to. Paul can take care of it, can't you, boyo? Come on, let's go, I fancy some Italian food. How does that grab everyone?'

Linda bit back a swift retort. It didn't grab her at all, in fact it was the last thing she fancied. But she had learned not to argue with Al. What Al wanted – Paul wanted – and she was not ready to put her relationship with Paul to the test. If it came down to the crunch, who would Paul side with? One day she would be ready to find out. But not now, not yet.

Miss Miami Beach waited in the lobby. She was a creamy-looking blonde with puffed-out hair and baby blue eyes. She leapt up at the sight of Al. 'Oh my goodness!' she exclaimed, 'this is like a wonderful dream!'

Al smiled and took her by the hand. 'Why didn't *you* come first? You're the prettiest.'

'Oh, thank you. I won two thousand dollars. I'm going to go to Hollywood for a screen test too. It's the most heavenly evening of my life. And now meeting you . . .'

'Are you wearing knicks?'

'Pardon me?'

'Knickers. Drawers. Panties.'

'I don't understand . . .'

Linda shot Al a cold look. 'He's joking,' she said, 'his sense of humour is sometimes obscure.'

Al laughed. 'Oh Linda. If only you and I had met first, what a couple we would have made.'

'Yeah,' agreed Linda sarcastically, 'a real fun couple.'

'What was the girl that won like?' Al turned his attention back to Miss Miami Beach.

She wrinkled up her nose. 'Horrible. Nobody liked her. She wasn't friendly at all.'

'But a great looker.'

'If you like that type. I never thought she would win. We were all hoping she wouldn't.'

'Naughty little girls. Were you mean to her?'

'*She* was mean to us. She was a – well she was a bitch.'

'We're going to eat spaghetti, with clams and meatballs. Then we're going to come back to the hotel and I'm going to let you breathe garlic sauce all over my cock. You do know what a cock is, don't you?'

'Oh. Er – yes.'

'Good girl. You and I are going to get along fine.'

*

Two hours later their table for four had swelled to ten.

'Al shouldn't drink,' Linda complained, 'who *are* all these people?'

'You know Al,' replied Paul, 'he likes to have people around.'

'I wish you'd stop saying – you know Al. Yes, I know him, and most of the time I find him a big fat pain.'

'I wish the two of you would get along. It would make *my* life a lot easier.'

'I can't help it, he just behaves so badly, bossing people around, intimidating that little blonde – he's done nothing but make obscene suggestions to her all night.'

'She loves it.'

'She doesn't love it. She's just too overawed to object. He makes fun of people – cruel fun.'

'You take things too seriously.'

'Maybe I do. Maybe it's because I hardly ever see you, and when I do I want us to be alone together. I want to cook for you, and make love to you. I don't want to watch you being a yes man to your brother.'

'Your bitching is starting to get on my nerves.'

'*So sorry.*' She felt tears sting the back of her eyelids and she fought for control. If only she didn't love Paul so goddamn much. If only she wasn't so jealous of him. When he left her he had another life neatly waiting for him. A wife. Two kids. A home. And what did she have? A lousy apartment and a half-assed career. It wasn't fair. She had so much to give to the right man. Was that man Paul? She was beginning to wonder.

'Take off your clothes,' said Al. He was sitting fully clothed on the bed in his hotel suite.

'Now?' asked Miss Miami Beach hesitantly.

'No – tomorrow,' Al replied sarcastically, 'Come on – strip off. Let's see the form that made you number two.'

'Can we turn the lights off?'

'I don't want the lights off.'

'I've got a scar.'

'What sort of scar?

'Appendix. It sort of embarrasses me.'

'Bullshit. Clothes off or out.'

Slowly she unzipped her dress and stepped out of it. She was wearing a flesh-coloured bra and lace briefs.

'Will you sign one of your albums for me?' she asked.

'I'll do better than that, get that felt pen from the dresser and come over here.'

She did as she was told.

'Take your bra off,' he instructed.

She did so.

Roughly he grabbed her left breast, and holding it steady he scrawled Al. He repeated the process with King on the right one.

She was breathing heavily, and her breasts signed with his name were featuring erect nipples.

'Get dressed,' Al sighed, 'go home. I'm tired.'

'But . . .' she began.

Why did they always have to argue? Wasn't it enough they had spent time with him, been seen with him?

'Out!' said Al sharply.

Miss Miami Beach snatched up her clothes, and turning her back she began to dress.

Al waited impatiently. Why were the majority of females quick as a flash at getting *out* of their clothes, and yet it took them forever to put them on again?

At last she was finished, and she turned towards Al. 'Was it something I did?' she asked meekly.

Al shrugged. Conversation she wanted now!

'Well,' she sighed, 'I guess I'll always remember tonight. Maybe I'll see you in Hollywood.' She waited for him to reply, but he had shut his eyes and was feigning sleep. 'Goodbye then,' she said softly, and tiptoed out.

He waited until he heard the door shut, then he got up, switched on the television, fixed himself a scotch and coke. It was four in the morning and he wasn't tired. He felt like a little action – a game of poker or craps. But this wasn't Vegas, and he didn't know where it would all be happening. On impulse he decided to phone Edna. There was no delay, so he got right through.

'Al?' questioned Edna sleepily, 'is anything wrong?'

Edna had a hangup about spending money. She still assumed that to go to the expense of telephoning from America meant instant disaster.

'Nothing's wrong,' assured Al, 'just thought I'd see how you were,'

'I'm fine. You only left yesterday. Are you *sure* nothing's the matter?'

Oh God. Why couldn't she just accept the fact that he had called for the pleasure of hearing her voice. 'Is Evan around?''

'He's asleep. Al, these calls are so expensive, I wish you wouldn't waste your money.'

It was always your money. Never our money. If Edna had her way they would still be living in one room. She had never learned to accept his success gracefully. She always predicted gloom. If the truth were known she was a miserable woman. He had to twist her arm to get her to go out and buy herself a new dress.

'Wake him up, Edna. I want to say hello.'

'He's got school tomorrow.'

'OK. So *don't* wake him up.'

'I'll tell him you phoned.'

'All right, tell him in the morning.'

'Goodbye, Al.'

'Goodbye, Edna.'

She couldn't wait to hang up. Waste not. Want not. Her favourite motto.

Edna probably would have been the perfect wife for a guy with no money. But as the wife of a superstar she was a total loss.

Al phoned room service. Bacon and eggs. Christ – but he must keep a sharp eye on the weight. Al knew what was happening every minute of the time. On stage he had to look great, and to look great he had to be thin. It was a lot easier to keep your weight down when you were twenty-seven. At thirty-seven, bulges appeared where they shouldn't, and they were hell to get rid of. However – one portion of bacon and eggs, some champagne to swill it down with. He would cut out breakfast. He would save himself for lunch.

Dallas – funny name for a girl. She was certainly a great looker. If he was lucky she just might be able to hold his interest for an afternoon.

Probably another dumb bitch though. They were all dumb. Starstruck pushovers. They would fuck for money. Fame. Power. Whatever happened to good old lust?

Bernie Suntan stretched in front of the Beverly Hills Hotel pool. 'Jesus H!' he exclaimed. 'If they were givin' out tickets for happiness this would be it!'

'Mr Suntan' a female voice boomed through the loudspeaker. 'Telephone for Mr Suntan.'

Bernie heaved himself up. Two hundred and sixty pounds of fifty-two-year-old flesh, every inch – except a few crucial ones – heavily suntanned. He wore white boxer shorts trimmed with a

Mickey Mouse motif, purple sunglasses, a white peak cap which bore the legend 'Everybody Likes It', and a lot of solid gold jewellery. Underneath the cap the dome of his head was totally bald, but halfway down his scalp a profusion of blond curls sprouted and luxuriated well past the back of his neck.

'I'm the oldest hippie in the business!' Bernie would often announce. And nobody ever argued with him.

En route to the telephone Bernie stopped to greet people. 'Hey, Rod baby, where's the kilt?' 'David Tebet – my favourite man – when did you get back? Good to see you.' 'Princess! How do you look! How does she *look*?'

He finally reached the phone and snapped into a rapid business dialogue. Apart from being the oldest hippie in the business Bernie Suntan had the reputation of being one of the top press agents. If you wanted action, call for Bernie. It would cost you, but it would be worth it. Right now he was setting up the public relations side of the Al King tour. And setting it up right. Every city had to roll past like clockwork. No riots. No trouble with the local police. No drugs. No bad publicity.

He didn't worry about Al too much, the only thing you had to watch out with him was the women and gambling. But the others on the tour could cause trouble, and by doing so give the whole caboodle a bad name.

For a start Bernie was doubtful about the three black girls who were to be Al's backing singers. The Promises. Three beautiful girls – if you liked spades – and frankly that wasn't Bernie's particular scene. So they sung up a storm, but what about their private lives? One of them married to a drummer who just drew three for dealing. One of them making out with a certain minor mafiosa. And the third young enough to be definite jailbait. Three ding-a-lings. Bernie wasn't happy about having *them* along.

Then he had also heard talk that Al was planning to bring his son. Well what was *that* all about? A sex symbol superstar dragging along his teenage son. Bad image. Very bad image. If he did come he would have to be pushed very much into the background. Like completely out of sight.

Bernie had big plans for Al in Hollywood. As far as he was concerned it would be the publicity pinnacle of the whole trip. The stars would be brought out in force to meet the great Al King. There would be parties, receptions, interviews. There was so much to get together before the start of the tour. Everything had to be planned down to the last detail. Nothing could go wrong. Bernie

22

was staking a lot on this tour – he had been offered an incredible deal that would take him out of the publicity business forever and into the heady world of production. If all went off without a hitch Bernie had no doubt the job would be his.

'Hey,' he yelled into the phone, 'I want the best. Everywhere we go – the best.'

four

Edna King sat in the kitchen with eyes downcast, trying to shut out the slightly hysterical voice of her sister-in-law.

'It's bloody disgusting!' shrieked Melanie. 'Honestly, Edna, I just don't know why you stand for it. *I* wouldn't, I'll tell you straight.'

'It's all lies,' muttered Edna, going over to the fridge, opening it, and staring vacantly inside.

'*You* know that. *I* know that. But don't think that everyone who reads it is going to think that. They'll eat it up. The public loves a bit of juicy gossip. What *are* you looking for?'

'Nothing.' Edna shut the fridge and came and sat back at the table.

'Anyway,' continued Melanie, 'what about Evan? It can't be much fun for *him* reading all this junk about his father.'

'I'll hide it from Evan.'

'The boys at school will show him.'

'Oh, Melanie!' Edna's eyes filled with despairing tears, 'What can I do?'

Melanie smiled triumphantly. 'You *know* what you can do, I've told you enough times. If you *really* want to put a stop to all the gossip and lies, you can go on the tour with Al.'

'But . . .'

'No buts. I know what you're going to say. Al likes to travel alone. He worries when you're along. He likes you in the background. Well, shit, Edna. If you want to put a stop to the gossip you *must* be seen by his side.'

'Maybe you're right . . .'

'Of *course* I'm right. And I'll come too, you won't be alone. Will you tell Al? Or do you want me to?'

'No.' Edna jumped up nervously. 'I'll mention it.'

'Don't mention it – *tell* him.' Melanie stood up. 'I've got to be off, hairdressing appointment. Now don't forget, when he gets home tomorrow *tell* him.'

Edna nodded unsurely.

Outside the house Melanie climbed into her new white Simca sports car. Edna wouldn't tell him. Edna was scared shitless of him. If only *she* was married to Al. Oh boy, but things would be different then. Unfortunately she had picked the wrong brother. Paul just basked in the aura of a star – what *she* needed was the real thing.

Al liked her, he had always liked her. In fact . . . Melanie smiled. If *she* was married to him he wouldn't have to spend his life whoring around. Edna was a drag. Fat and dreary, not even pretty. What on earth had Al ever seen in her?

Melanie wanted to go on the tour. She would give anything to go on the tour. But – and it was a big but – as long as Edna wasn't going there was *no way* she could be aboard. She had nagged and cajoled Paul, but he had pointed out that as long as Al wasn't taking Edna it would be impossible for him to take her. And of course Al had no desire to take Edna. It would restrict his activities.

So Melanie was stuck, and the only hope was to prod Edna into a little action – and that was a difficult task. Edna thought the sun shone out of Al's ass, and even if she actually caught him screwing some hooker she would have a mouthful of excuses ready on his behalf.

Melanie pulled up her car on the double yellow line outside 'Mr Capones' and got out. She was blonde and pretty, with slightly pointed features, fashionably thin in all the right places, with a reasonable-sized bosom, and long dancer's legs. It was her legs that had first attracted Paul's attention. It was her legs that first attracted *everyone's* attention. She remembered, with a little smile, Manny Shorto, *the* Manny Shorto – famous but elderly American comedian. He had started on her legs and worked his way up . . . But then the bastard had run out on her . . . And she had met Paul. She had been one of the dancers on an Al King television spectacular. Paul had invited her out, and a year later they had married. Materially she had everything she wanted. It wasn't enough.

She swayed into 'Mr Capones', throwing her jacket at the receptionist. Mr Capone himself stepped forward to do her hair.

'Hi there,' she smiled lazily, catching his attention with her eyes, and holding it.

Mr Capone responded with a lingering look of his own. He was all tight trousers and teeth. He ran his hands through her hair. 'What do you want today?' he inquired.

Melanie smiled. 'Paul's coming back tomorrow, so you'd better make it something fuckable!'

Edna didn't smoke or drink. Her weakness in times of crisis was eating. As soon as Melanie had departed she returned to the fridge and stared yet again at the contents. There was nothing she fancied. Nothing with chocolate or cream or pastry.

The maid came into the kitchen, and Edna shut the fridge guiltily. She could never get used to the servants. She hated having them around. A maid to do the work. A cook to prepare the meals. A chauffeur to take care of the shopping. What was there left for her to do?

'Can I get you something, madam?' asked the maid.

'Nothing, thank you.' Edna picked up the newspaper with the vitrolic gossip item that Melanie had brought over and left the kitchen. She wandered into the garden: it was a nice day, sunny and warm. She hoped that the good weather would last over the weekend. Al enjoyed sitting by the pool, it did him good to be able to relax.

Maybe Melanie was right. Maybe she should go on the tour. She didn't relish the thought much, doing anything with Al publicly was a frightening experience. But it *would* put a stop to all these terrible rumours . . .

Al had mentioned he might take Evan along. She didn't like *that* idea at all, the boy was difficult enough as it was. Bad tempered, lazy, untidy, rude. However, without Evan at home it would be so quiet, and she could handle him, she understood him. He was a growing boy and needed the presence of his mother close by.

Edna sighed. Perhaps she should have gone to the hairdressers with Melanie. She wanted to look pretty for Al, she had been trying to diet but it wasn't easy. Anyway he was always saying that he liked her just the way she was. 'I like something to grab hold of,' he would comment.

On the other hand Melanie was always nagging at her to do something with herself. 'You *must* lose weight,' she would insist, 'why don't you come to the health club with me?' Edna remembered her day at the health club with cringing embarrassment. Perfectly made-up girls in white mini dresses who looked like they had come straight from the hairdressers verbally pulled her to pieces. 'You're *very* overweight.' 'Your skin is in a neglected state.'

'Your hair is lifeless.' 'You need massage, sauna, scalp treatment, colouring, tinting, skin therapy, a professional make-up.'

Edna had got through the day somehow, and she had to admit that when she emerged she did look almost glamorous. But the price had been ridiculous, and Al had hardly noticed any difference. That had been three months previously and she hadn't bothered to go back.

'Do you want to swim, Mrs King?'

Edna jumped. It was Nelson, the odd job man, who also attended to the maintenance of the swimming pool.

'No thank you, Nelson.'

'You sure? Won't take me but a minute to get my equipment out.' He leered knowingly at her.

'No.' Edna shook her head. She didn't like Nelson, there was something not quite nice about him. He had only been with them six weeks, and when she had complained to Al about him he had said, 'Give him a chance. It's not that easy to get people to work for you today.'

Nelson was watching her, and she tried to avoid his penetrating stare. It was no good, she couldn't feel at ease in front of him. Abruptly she turned and went back into the house. Was it her imagination or could she hear Nelson laughing? She would really have to talk to Al about him again.

Evan King sat chewing on his fingernails in the back of the chauffeured Rolls. He huddled into the upholstery hoping as usual that not too many people would notice him. He was a very thin boy, with acned skin and greasy brown hair.

He resented the fact that every day he had to be ferried to and from school in a Rolls Royce. 'Why can't I take my bike?' he constantly demanded of Edna.

'It's not my decision,' she would reply. 'You know that your father insists on security.'

'Balls!' Evan would mumble in reply. He hated his bloody father. Bloody Al King. What a burden it was to go through school with someone like that for your father. The other kids gave him hell about it. Evan looked forward to the end of term with unconcealed joy. It was his *last* term, the end of school forever. He couldn't wait.

The Rolls dropped him off in front of the house, and Evan kicked at the gravel drive moodily. He anticipated his mother's questions. Hello, dear. Did you have a good day? What was for lunch? Who did you talk to? Is anyone coming over?

She bloody *knew* no one was coming over. They never did, except maybe once to check out Al King's house, and then to sneer. *Three* colour televisions. A *billiards* room. A *swimming* pool.

'Evan! Evan!' Nelson was calling to him from the side of the house.

'Yes?'

'Come here for a minute, got something to show you.' Evan followed Nelson to the shed he used. 'Seen these?' said Nelson, proudly thrusting a pile of magazines upon him.

Evan squatted down on the ground and leafed through the magazines. They featured titles like 'Sun Child', 'Birds of Nature' and 'Pussy'. They consisted entirely of females in various stages of undress.

'Where did you get them?' asked Evan, slowly.

'I found them. Nice, aren't they? Some lovely little birds in there, real tasty little pieces. Nice. Aren't they nice then? I'll sell you the lot for a quid.'

'OK,' agreed Evan quickly. He stuffed the magazines in his school satchel and fished in his blazer pocket for some money.

'I could get you the real thing for a tenner,' offered Nelson, slyly. 'Ever had the real thing?'

'Course,' said Evan weakly.

'Yes,' agreed Nelson, 'I expect your old dad passes a few your way.' He laughed knowingly. 'I bet he's got crumpet knee deep.'

'See you,' said Evan, and headed for the house. Now if he could only avoid his mother he could settle down and *really* get a good look at the magazines.

'Evan, dear.' Edna sprang at him from outside the kitchen. 'How was school today?'

'OK.'

'You father telephoned from New York last night. He sends you his love.'

'What did he want?'

'Just to see how we were.'

'Did he mention the tour? I *can* go on it, can't I?'

'I suppose so. Whatever your father says. I was thinking that perhaps I might come too.'

'*You*,' stated Evan scornfully, 'why would *you* want to come?'

'I just thought it would be nice for both of us to go . . .'

'That's a lousy idea. It stinks. I don't want to go if you're going.'

'Oh, Evan.' Edna bit her lip, 'why ever not?'

'Because you spy on me. You're always asking me questions. Anyway, I'd like to be with dad alone.'

Edna nodded miserably. Where had they gone wrong with Evan? They had given him everything, denied him nothing. Yet he was full of hostilities and resentments. 'Is anyone coming over?' she asked.

'No.'

'Do you want some tea?'

'Yes.'

Edna scurried off to the kitchen to prepare him a tray. He was going through a difficult time. It was his age. She understood. He was just a child. Although when *she* had been sixteen she had been pregnant, and shortly after, married.

Edna sighed. She wished Al was home, she hated it when he was away.

five

Things were beginning to grow hazy. She had won. She was a star. And prepared as Dallas had been, the fuss and activity around her was startling. Photographers. Television cameras. People. Men. And a sudden tinge of respect reserved for a person who was about to become a personality. Dallas liked it, in fact she loved it. But she wanted to get rid of the cheesy cloak and crown. Most of all she wanted a drink.

At last the photographers were finished, and she was escorted back to the dressing room to collect her belongings. The organizers of the contest seemed intent on taking her over. She was their 'Miss Coast to Coast', and as such they expected to make quite a bit of money promoting her for the year she would carry the title. She had won ten thousand dollars prize money, a screen test, and the chance of making a lot more money by accepting the various contracts to promote products that would be waved in her direction. For the time being she was being given a suite at the Plaza for a week, a car and chauffeur for the same period, and a list of immediate engagements that she would be expected to fulfil.

She was also being given a permanent escort, Mrs Fields, a middle-aged lady hired to keep a firm eye on the winner, and an even firmer eye on the winner's reputation. 'Miss Coast to Coast' was supposed to represent the young, good, clean image of American girlhood.

Dallas couldn't help giggling at *that* thought.

Dallas Lunde survived the hazards of staying in Miami with hardly any money, no permanent residence, and no job, for almost three months.

She quickly picked up the pattern of the way things were. No man was permanent. They came and they went, and the trick was to find one who wasn't just a one nighter.

The conventions were the best hunting grounds, and sometimes Dallas found herself with a man who might even stay as long as six or seven days.

She soon developed a routine. She got up late in whichever hotel room she had spent the night. Then she would order a substantial breakfast, watch television for a few hours, and if the man she was with had checked out, she would saunter down to the beach or swimming pool and look for a likely replacement. There was no shortage of replacements. She began to use make-up, bought herself some new clothes. In a way it was a whole exciting new life.

She had started to copy the way people talked on television. She loved the old Lana Turner movies, and moulded herself on the good time girl with a heart of gold.

It did not occur to her that the type of life she was leading might be wrong. Sexually she derived no enjoyment from her encounters with the mainly older men she slept with. They seemed more than delighted with her, and she tried to please. They didn't bother her, they didn't hurt her, and most of the time she was free to watch television which was teaching her so much about life.

Then one day she met Bobbie.

It had been a fairly normal week. A married man in his fifties had kept her in his room for three days. He was in from Chicago on a toilet tissue convention. On his last night he became restless. 'Know any other broads?' he questioned.

Dallas shrugged. 'Nope.'

'I fancy a sandwich, a nice thick juicy little sandwich. Rye one side, white the other. Can you handle that?'

Dallas smiled vaguely. She had no idea what he was talking about.

The man phoned the desk clerk and made some mumbled requests. Half an hour later Bobbie arrived. She was a tall black girl, wearing denim hot pants, boots, a lace-up sweater, and a curly wig. She had an incredible rounded jutting out ass, and a flashing dazzling smile.

She greeted the man with a friendly kiss, and a 'Hey baby sugar. We gonna have ourselves a *party!*' Then she requested a hundred dollars which she tucked safely into her boots. 'This your wife?' she asked, indicating Dallas. She had a habit of emphasizing the last word of every sentence.

'Just another hooker,' the man said, and a thick excitement was creeping into his voice.

Dallas sat watching bemusedly.

'Well!' exclaimed Bobbie, arms akimbo, 'watcha want, man? What's your pleasure?'

'Undress me. Both of you.'

'Sure, sweetie honey. Bobbie will do a job on you that you ain't never gonna forget.' She turned and smiled at Dallas. 'You gonna help out, sister?'

Dallas stood up. She was wearing a red bikini.

Bobbie grinned at her, 'We all gonna have ourselves a little fun. Good clean dirty fun!'

She wriggled out of her hot pants, revealing a thick bush of wiry pubic hair. 'Take your drawers off,' she instructed Dallas, 'let's get this dude really in the mood. I don't want no limp dicks come hangin' out at me when I peel down his pants.'

Dallas slipped off the bottom half of her bikini, and for the first time since Burt Keyes she felt a strange sexual stirring.

'Let's get this show shakin'. Lie down, mister, I'm a gonna give it to you good!' Bobbie slithered his clothes off him as he lay immobile. Dallas stood watching as Bobbie casually hoisted herself on top of him.

'Come on, baby,' Bobbie encouraged, 'show him your titties, sit on his face, do somethin'!'

The situation was strange to Dallas. She didn't know what to do. And all the time there was this strange building excitement. She unhooked her bikini top.

'Hey momma!' shrieked Bobbie, bouncing happily up and down, 'you have got yourself a real pair!' She climbed off the man, leaving him gasping. 'Wanna see a show, daddy? Wanna see a little female action?'

The man nodded, his face red, his eyes bulging.

'So!' stated Bobbie, and she smiled at Dallas. 'Watcha say, sister? You wanna be the fella? Or will you leave it all to big bad Bobbie?'

'I don't know . . .' stammered Dallas. This was one situation that television hadn't covered.

30

'Lie down,' said Bobbie with a wicked grin, *'I always did like virgins!'*

'You're a very lucky girl,' Mrs Fields said crisply, as they sat in the limousine whisking them to the luxury of the Plaza.

'Yeah,' replied Dallas in mocking tones, 'a lucky little girl.'

Mrs Fields looked at her sharply; she hoped this one wasn't going to be difficult. The previous year's winner had been a sweet child, but the year before that the girl had been a bitch and caused everyone a lot of trouble.

'There will be a photo call at nine thirty in the morning. Usual thing, sitting up in bed wearing a nightie and the crown. Then we're to go to the office for you to sign some contracts. Lunch will be with a representative of a wool firm, if they decide to sign you it could be most lucrative. In the afternoon you open a super-market, and in the evening you will go to the premier of *Guns at Dawn*. Do you have a boyfriend?'

'No.'

'Good. Much better that way. Boyfriends can get very jealous. This title will make a lot of difference to your life, you will be amazed at all the important people you'll meet. "Miss Coast to Coast" 1966 married a Senator. She was a lovely girl.'

'Was he?'

'Pardon?'

'Joke.'

'Oh. Well anyway, there are a few things you would do well to remember. You will be in the public eye for a year, and if you conduct your private life discreetly it will be much better for all concerned. A lot of men will be after you, but as far as this title is concerned morals are most important. My advice to you – and I have been looking after "Miss Coast to Coast" for thirteen years – is to not let it all go to your head. Remember your home and your family. Remember your grass roots.'

Dallas choked back a laugh.

'I shall be staying at the Plaza with you for a week,' Mrs Fields continued, 'during that time your year's reign will be planned, and we will find you a suitable place to live, and of course, after that, I will accompany you on any out of town trips, and I will always be available for help and advice.'

'Sounds like a heavy schedule.'

'"Miss Coast to Coast" 1972 made a hundred thousand dollars. She was dedicated. She worked hard and she never complained.'

31

Dallas was silent. A hundred thousand dollars was a lot of bread. Not bad. She had entered the contest for a joke, an ego trip. Now perhaps she should look at things more seriously. She would have to ask Ed's advice, he might not be too thrilled now she had won. She would ask him later at the party.

Dallas went to live with Bobbie. It was nice to have a proper home again after so many hotel rooms.

'Twenty dollars a lay!' Bobbie had scoffed, 'and all nighters too! Kid – you bin givin' it away! From now on you're with me, and we don't do nothin' under a hundred a piece. Stick with me, baby queen, and we will all get rich!'

Bobbie lived in an untidy one-room apartment with mice roaming the kitchen, shabby furniture, and a closet full of kinky outfits. She had connections with most of the hotel clerks and her phone never stopped ringing. Most important, she had television, colour, twenty-eight inch screen.

She taught Dallas everything she could. At first Dallas was a reluctant learner, but as her body responded to Bobbie she began to enjoy their relationship. Bobbie was the first person to come along that seemed to care about her.

Making love with men had never triggered any response, but with Bobbie it was different, and sex took on new meanings.

Bobbie organised their business engagements. She told Dallas what to do, what to wear. She taught her how to turn men on in exciting, new and inventive ways.

'You can fuck 'em shitless,' she advised Dallas, 'but it's only a job – keep it business like, never let them get to you. I'm the only one can get to you – right, sugar sweet? Right.'

Dallas agreed. But she didn't really agree. Deep down she knew that Burt Keys could have got to her.

Six months went by. Then one night there was a call from a motel on the highway.

'Shoes. Chocolate sauce on your tits. Raincoat.' Bobbie instructed. 'I know this old dude, all he wants to do is lick the sauce off and come in your shoes,' she giggled, 'he's old!'

Bobbie drove them to the motel in her battered Ford. She was laughing and chattering all the way.

Dallas felt strange with the chocolate stickiness on her breasts, and her nakedness sticking to the plastic raincoat.

The man was indeed old. Bobbie had forgotten to mention the fact that he would be wearing pyjamas with his shrunken penis hanging limply out.

'He must be about ninety!' Dallas whispered, 'I don't think I can stand it.'

Bobbie threw her a stern look. 'I never back out on a promise. I'll make it up to you later. Let's go.'

They took off their raincoats, and the old man's eyes shone with a long lost desire. He lay down, and Bobbie leaned over him, dangling her chocolate coated nipple over his mouth. Dallas did the same. The old man licked feebly.

After a few minutes Bobbie took off her shoe and held it over the old man's slightly aroused penis. 'Let's do it for mamma!' she crooned.

He started to come in great heaves and jerks.

Dallas turned away. Was that the moment she decided that this wasn't the life for her?

Suddenly there was a strange, groaning, rattling noise, then silence.

'Oh Holy God!' exclaimed Bobbie suddenly, 'the old bastard died on us. He died!'

Dallas turned slowly round. Surely Bobbie was making one of her usual jokes? But when she saw the old man lying there, she knew that he was dead.

Bobbie slapped him on the face. 'Wake up!' she commanded, 'wake up.'

'If he's dead,' stated Dallas blankly, 'what are we going to do?'

Bobbie gathered her raincoat up. 'Get the hell out of here, that's what we'll do.'

'But what about the police? They'll know we were here, the desk clerk called you, he'll tell them.'

'We didn't kill him.'

'I don't want to see the police.'

'I'm with you, sister. We'll get the hell out. Nobody will find him till the morning, we can be in LA by then.'

'Have we got enough money?'

'Sure and he hasn't paid us.' Bobbie looked for his bankroll, found it, started to peel off two hundred dollar bills, thought better of it and pocketed the lot. 'Let's go, sugar, baby. Let's get our asses out of here.'

Dallas was the star of the party, and she positively glowed in the limelight. Everyone wanted to talk to her, men and women alike.

Ed Kurlnik hovered nearby. He had to be cool, couldn't be obvious. Ramo Kaliffe flashed Arab white teeth in her direction. Lucy Mabel Mann smiled sweetly and invited her to lunch.

'Miami Beach has gone off to meet Al King,' Miss Boston volunteered, 'isn't *she* the lucky one.'

Dallas smiled, and vaguely recalled some photographer offering her the chance of a night with Al King. Who needed that scene? Stars were boring. Boring people. Boring fucks. All they did was talk about themselves and break a leg to reach the mirror first.

'I think I'll stay at the apartment tonight,' Ed managed to inform her.

'I thought you always had to go home on Saturdays?'

'Tonight will be an exception.'

She had only won a matter of hours earlier, and already Ed was prepared to make exceptions. 'I have to stay at the Plaza for a week.'

Ed raised his eyebrows, 'You don't *have* to.'

'But I think I will.'

Ed frowned. 'Why?'

'Why not? I've always wanted to stay at the Plaza.'

'Why didn't you say so before, we could have done so any time.'

'Any time, Ed?' He was scared to even walk down the street with her. If wifey ever knew she would clamp down on his seventy million dollars like a vice.

'If you like,' Dallas offered slyly, 'you could come and see me at the hotel later.' The thought of Ed Kurlnik sneaking into the Plaza to visit her brought tears of laughter.

'I can't do that,' replied Ed, outraged. 'You *know* I can't do that.'

They were interrupted by a photographer snapping random shots, and Ed nipped smartly out of the picture.

Dallas yawned, it had been a tiring day and she was exhausted. But so what? She was a somebody. She was 'Miss Coast to Coast', and she couldn't flake out on her night of triumph.

This was her night and she was determined to enjoy it.

SIX

Al woke late with a feeling of apprehension. He didn't feel that good, in fact he felt dreadful.

He lay in bed, opened his eyes, and did not feel like getting up at all.

He knew why he felt bad, it was fear, plain honest to goodness fucking nerves.

The forthcoming tour was bugging the hell out of him.

Why was he so nervous? He had tried to figure it out. It wasn't like he had never been on the road before, he had done many successful tours. But the last one had been two years previously, and two years was a long time between gigs. OK, so there had been the cabaret dates, the television spectaculars, the records. But basically what Al *liked*, what he *wanted*, was that contact with a huge live audience. Going out there and doing your thing was what it was all about. The ultimate high.

He had made so much money in the last few years. If he wanted to pack it in and never work again he would be more than set. So the records weren't selling so well, they tried to keep it from him, but he was well aware of every happening in his career. So what did the tour *really* mean to him?

It meant finding out how the people felt. Were the same fans who had been out there two years ago still going to be around? Were they still going to react with the same degree of enthusiasm? Was he still the tops? Or was he, at thirty-seven, a little too old for the adulation and hysteria? Would he now be regarded as just another establishment star?

He still looked great. He still sounded the same. Was that good or bad? Would they expect him to have changed?

And would his voice still be up to it? Would it survive the strain of God knows how many performances in vast stadiums?

Al coughed nervously. He wished the goddamn tour would start already. Every morning he woke up to the same fears and it was getting him down. He couldn't even discuss his thoughts with Paul, he didn't want to give voice to his doubts. Maybe when he got home he would tell Edna, but knowing her she would probably suggest that he cancel the whole tour and stay at home. Her secret dream was that they would lose all their money and move back into one room.

Edna was still the same sweet simple girl that he had married. She hadn't changed with his success. She hadn't grown.

In a way Al was grateful, but in another way he resented her. Why didn't she read more? Entertain? Wear beautiful clothes? *Improve* herself?

He had changed, and he was glad of it. When he had started in the business he had been very rough, a right layabout. Now he could go anywhere, meet anyone, and feel perfectly at ease.

Edna was more like a mother than a wife. Always there. Always uncomplaining. Hot meals. Clean shirts. She was the one who took his cock out to massage his balls because his stage trousers were too tight. That was about the only time she took it out too. He sighed. Every day the bridge seemed to get wider.

Of course he should never have got married. But then he would not have had Evan, and it was wonderful to have a son, even if the boy did need taking in hand.

How many happy marriages did he know of? How many that lasted longer than five years? In the world he moved in now – not many. At least he could trust Edna. She would never think of looking at another man. And she loved him for himself, the whole Al King bit meant nothing to her.

He sighed again. Then he remembered Paul was supposed to be arranging lunch for him with – what was her name – the beauty contest winner – Dallas. Yeah. Al grinned. Not a bad bit of crumpet.

He consulted his digital watch to discover it was eleven-thirty. He hauled himself out of bed, and launched into thirty push-ups. Christ, but they got more difficult every day.

Lunch with a girl called Dallas. What would she be like?

Like the rest. Pretty but dumb. Either posing in front of a mirror all the time, or allowing him to scrawl his autograph across her ripe and ready breasts. Women – they were all the same.

Disgust built in Al's gut. Disgust at himself for using women, and contempt for the women for *allowing* themselves to be used just because he was a star.

Fuck it. To hell with a girl called Dallas. He picked up the phone and dialled Paul's room.

Paul had not spent the perfect morning.

He had left Linda's place at 6 a.m. while she still slept. She had woken at seven and phoned to inform him that she was not pleased.

He was not pleased either. He had fought off a stoned mugger and been unable to find a cab for ten blocks.

Mental note. Get Linda an apartment on the better side of town.

Now he was going through one big hassle trying to arrange a lunch date for Al with 'Miss Coast to Coast'. He had finally convinced the organizers what a great coup it would be, but apparently Dallas felt otherwise.

Paul wondered who or what would placate Al. Turn downs were rare, in fact Paul could not recall the last one.

The phone rang. It was Al.

'Ah,' said Paul cherrily, 'how we feeling today?'

'In good shape. What's new?'

'Mention of the tour in all the columns. Bitch item in *Reporter*. Nothing heavy.' Paul was damned if *he* was going to mention the lunch. Maybe Al had forgotten.

'About that lunch I wanted you to arrange . . .'

'Oh, yes. Well, it's like this, she . . .'

'Cancel it.'

'Cancel it?'

'You heard me. Who needs it?'

'You're right. I'll wipe it out immediately.' Paul hung up relieved. He was off the hook. Now Al would never know he had been turned down.

Paul was very protective towards his brother. He liked things to go smoothly for Al, he always had. Even at the beginning Paul had only told Al the good things that happened. He never mentioned the recording companies and theatre managers who had not wanted to know . . . He spoke only with glowing enthusiasm of Al's future career, and he pushed and pushed until he made a crack big enough to send Al into orbit.

He had willed Al's success, and he had also worked his ass off to make it happen.

There was a knock on the door. 'Morning,' Linda said brightly, 'I was a bitch on the phone and I'm sorry.' She put her arms round his neck and stretched on tiptoe to kiss him.

The phone rang, and Paul went to answer it.

Linda lit a cigarette and wandered over to the window. She felt the usual tight feeling that she always got when Paul was leaving. He came into her life. He went out of her life. He was like the goddamn sea. It was most unsettling. She was just his New York girlfriend, someone to hump while he was away from his wife. She had made up her mind though that *something* would have to be settled on the tour, or that would be it.

'Trying to get hold of Bernie is impossible,' Paul complained, hanging up the phone.

Linda laughed, 'What about "Miss Coast to Coast"? Did you line her up for lunch?'

'Funny thing, she turned us down flat. Can you believe that? First time that happened in . . .' He was interrupted by the phone jangling. It was Bernie Suntan. He launched into a business conversation.

Linda was just lighting another cigarette when Al came in. He swooped down on her with a kiss and a hug. Standard Al King greeting, but it made her uncomfortable. He had a habit of thrusting a knee intimately between her legs. She had learned to automatically back away, but this time she was not quick enough.

'You smoke too much,' Al admonished.

'It's *my* cancer.' Linda replied defensively.

'Funny. Hope you're not laughing all the way to the grave.'

'So "Miss Coast to Coast" was *still* not available,' Linda snapped, 'hate to say I told you so!'

'What do you mean? *I* was the one who cancelled out on the lunch.'

'Oh come on, Paul told me she turned you down flat.'

Al's smile faded. 'Paul – what is this shit?'

Paul waved vaguely. He was busy on the phone and had not heard their conversation.

'He's talking to Bernie,' Linda explained.

'Fuck Bernie. When I want to talk to baby brother, I talk.' Al walked over and cut off the connection with a vicious slam of his hand.

'What the hell are you doing?' complained Paul, 'I've been trying to get hold of Bernie all morning.'

'Did you fix up that beauty queen bitch for lunch or did you not?'

'You said you didn't want to have lunch with her.'

'I know that. But was she coming?'

'I don't really know – I was . . .'

'Cut the shit . . . She said no. Right? As your girlfriend so nicely put it, she turned me down flat. Right?'

Paul glared at Linda, 'What does it matter? You didn't want to have lunch anyway.'

'I've changed my mind. Get her.' Al slammed his way out of the room.

'What can I say?' mumbled Linda.

'I think you've said enough. You *know* what he's like, why couldn't you just keep quiet?'

'I guess I'll go home.'

'I guess you should.'

Once again Al had come between them. Well screw him, she wasn't going to creep out. 'If you like,' she ventured, 'I'll see if I can fix something. I have some pictures I could drop by the hotel – maybe I could talk to Dallas.'

'Anything would help.' He softened. 'Look, I know it's no really your fault, I should have told you not to say anything.' He kissed her. 'I'll be waiting for your call, do what you can.'

seven

Her photograph adorned the front page of the newspapers, and she studied it intently. It was a thrill, a great big crazy thrill. On the same page there was an article about the President, and there was a picture of him also, a small picture, *much* smaller than the one of her. Suddenly she was *somebody*, no longer a faceless hooker, but a person whose photograph was larger than the President's!

She was staying at the Plaza Hotel and she didn't have to fuck anybody. She was a free agent. She had a cheque for ten thousand dollars, and she hadn't lain on her back to earn it.

She felt incredibly elated. She leapt out of bed, threw open the window, and admired the view.

'Check out the view, sugar baby!' Bobbie insisted when they flew into Los Angeles, 'Mind blowing!'

They went to stay with a friend of Bobbie's who was white, miserable, and addicted to heroin.

'I can't stand it here!' Dallas insisted after a few days. 'Aren't we going to get a place of our own?'

'Yeah,' agreed Bobbie, 'we gotta get back in action.'

So she found them an apartment off the Strip, and renewed her connections.

Things in Hollywood were different. No longer out of town schmucks set on getting laid. Instead, sophisticated, jaded people, who required much more than a simple fuck. Dallas started to complain immediately.

'Shit man!' exclaimed Bobbie, 'just shut your eyes an' think of nothin'. Their money is just the same.'

'No,' insisted Dallas, 'I won't do it.'

'OK,' agreed Bobbie, 'we'll only book you out to the straights.'

So Dallas found herself alone most of the time. She cleaned the apartment and did the cooking; it kept her busy while Bobbie was out working. She also learned to drive – an essential for California living.

But it wasn't long before she started to feel a revulsion at Bobbie's advances. At first it had been something new, but now, with Bobbie coming home from a twenty-handed orgy, it began to pall when she wanted to make love.

'You got yourself another girlfriend?' Bobbie asked accusingly.

'No, I'm just tired.'

The more she resisted Bobbie, the more the black girl started to do for her. She bought her presents and flowers and chocolates. She became like an attentive suitor.

One day Dallas packed her things and left. She was fed up with the whole situation. She moved into a bungalow at the Beverly Hills Hotel with an impotent writer who liked her to walk around naked. That was all he required of her, and he was quite friendly and nice. He didn't pay her, but she had free board and lodging at one of the best hotels in town, and the use of his Cadillac. It was a convenient arrangement, and occasionally Dallas would pull a trick on the side and make some extra money. There was one man who came to the hotel pool every day and offered her a thousand dollars to star in a porno film. Dallas declined. 'Why?' he had questioned affronted, 'ain't ya ever heard of Linda Lovelace?'

She had heard of her, but it wasn't the kind of stardom she wanted. In her mind she knew there was a better life for her somewhere. Television had shown her the American dream, and she saw no reason why there shouldn't be a piece of it for her.

Bobbie found her five weeks later. She was waiting when Dallas returned from a shopping trip. 'Get your ass packed and out of here!' she snapped.

Dallas stopped in amazement. How had Bobbie found her?

The writer, somewhat nervous, but smiling bravely, said: 'I think that you had better do what your – uh – friend says.'

'You goddamn right she better do it!' snapped Bobbie, tossing her wig impatiently, and tapping green-taloned nails on the table.

'Are you asking me to go?' Dallas inquired of the writer.

'Well – er – yes. I didn't realize that you were – that you had a – uh – well permanent sort of – er – friend.'

He was deeply embarrassed and would not look her in the eyes.

'I don't have to go,' Dallas stated flatly.

'Oh yes you do, sugar sweets,' interrupted Bobbie quickly, 'I got things to say to you that you ain't gonna want no-one to hear.'

Dallas packed. One suitcase of possessions was the sum total of her belongings.

'Goodbye,' she said to the man she had lived with for five weeks.

'Bye,' he mumbled, redfaced. God knows what Bobbie had told him.

'See ya!' yelled Bobbie cheerily, 'any time you wanna free one give me a call.' Under her breath she muttered, 'No balls, you sure picked a loser, kid.'

Outside, in the car Bobbie said: 'I bail ya outa the shit in Miami, give you a home, clothes, work my black ass off fuckin' pigs so that you can take it easy, and what happens? What the frig happens? Soon as I turn my back you all hightail it outa my life for what you think will be forever. Well, sugar baby, life just ain't that simple. I knew I'd find you, and I did.' She smiled triumphantly. 'Shoulda bin a friggin' detective.'

'What do you want? I didn't take anything.'

'I didn't take anything!' mimicked Bobbie sarcastically. 'Kid, you are green all the way up. You an me are together, a team. We know too much about each other to split up. You dig what I mean, baby doll? Cast your mind back to a certain motel and a certain old dude, a very old dude. You get it?'

'I get it.'

'Good girl. I knew you would understand once I explained it to you real simple like. Now we can get to work – you an' me. I think it's about time ya got used to the Hollywood way of life. Shit, baby – I am through protectin' you – from now on it's togetherness – all the way. You dig?'

The photo call was fun. Sitting upright in bed, low cut nightie, crown on the head, and fifteen guys struggling to get the best picture. Smile. Flash. Laugh. Flash. Sexy look. Flash.

Mrs Fields allowed them an hour, and then it was up and dressed and over to the offices of the organizers to sign some contracts.

Dallas wouldn't sign. 'I have a friend who I'd like to check them out with first,' she explained sweetly.

'Sure,' they agreed, but they were all pissed off.

'By the way,' Mrs Fields said, 'Al King, the singer, would like to take you to lunch. We could arrange it as a nice little publicity thing.'

'I thought I was supposed to be having lunch with some wool firm?'

'We could postpone that.'

'Don't. The more things I do as "Miss Coast to Coast" the more I'll like it.' Offhandedly she added, 'Let's face it, Al King's

41

probably only looking to get laid and really, I'm not that sort of a girl.'

'Quite,' agreed Mrs Fields, and she sighed, because suddenly she realized that it was not going to be an easy week.

'Now,' said Dallas brightly, 'have I got time to spend some money before lunch? I've always wanted to go into Saks and spend *my* money.'

Life with Bobbie was no longer the same. The black girl's easy-going friendliness was gone. Instead she was tough, flip, and businesslike. She spelled it out to Dallas in no uncertain terms. They had killed a guy, together, and because of that simple fact they were stuck with each other.

'You had better get used to it, kid,' Bobbie warned, ''cos if you run off again I'll find you, and next time I ain't gonna let you off so easy.'

So began a year of complete and utter degradation for Dallas. She had not believed that people with such devious and perverted tastes existed. Bobbie made sure that she came across every one of them.

'They're clients,' Bobbie would explain, straightfaced, 'it's just another job.'

It was a year of gradual hardening for Dallas. The only way she could face the things she did for money was to shut everything out. They could have her face, her body, but they could never get into her mind. She became as good and as practised at her job as Bobbie. And like the black girl who had been a hooker since was was thirteen, she became hard, cynical, tough and unfeeling. Unlike Bobbie, she wanted no other comforts, she didn't turn to women for a relationship, she cut that side of her life out completely. Sex was her profession, and that was all.

Bobbie and she lived together increasingly uneasily.

They did not resume any personal relationship, and Bobbie – who had always been into smoking pot, started on other little habits. By the end of the year she was into heroin, and Dallas knew she had to get away.

She waited for the right opportunity, and as soon as she set eyes on Ed Kurlnik she knew that this was a chance she mustn't blow.

Mrs Fields accompanied Dallas around Saks.

'I want this – this – and this,' Dallas snatched dresses off the racks. 'Oh and the black evening gown from the window, and does it come in any other colours? Great, I'll take it in every colour.'

'Your money won't last long at this rate,' Mrs Fields said warningly.

'I know,' laughed Dallas. But oh the thrill of spending her own money. She had a charge at Saks that Ed had opened for her, but buying this way was much more satisfying. She managed to spend three thousand dollars in half an hour, and she was giddy with excitement. She breezed through lunch with the wool firm representatives full of charm and laughter. They wanted her to sign to an advertising and promotion contract immediately. Mrs Fields was impressed. 'They usually take weeks to make up their minds.'

'I want double the amount they have paid before.'

'They'll never pay more.'

'Wanna bet, baby!' Dallas laughed, 'they'll pay, and be pleased to.'

'I'll tell the office,' said Mrs Fields, tight-lipped.

'By the way,' inquired Dallas, 'what's the fee I'm getting for opening the supermarket this afternoon?'

'I don't really know.'

'Find out, 'cos if it's not enough I'm not doing it.'

Mrs Field nodded. She had been right, this one *was* going to be difficult.

Ed Kurlnik and Dallas Lunde were side by side in their respective cars at the traffic lights. Dallas recognized him immediately, she had seen him on television only three days previously.

Ed Kurlnik. Head of the Kurlnik Motor dynasty. One of the richest men in America. Married. Two children. Sixty-one years old.

And here he was, driving a Kurlnik Leopard, completely alone. Dallas couldn't believe her luck.

The traffic lights changed, and his Leopard sprang away with surprising speed. Without hesitation Dallas slid into the lane behind him. She knew exactly what she would do.

He stopped at the next red light, and Dallas, in her battered old Buick, careered into the back of him. It wasn't a bad smash, but it was enough to dent her fender and break one of his rear lights. She slumped forward over her wheel and waited.

It was that easy.

He was concerned. He took her to his hotel for coffee.

'I must have fainted,' she explained.

He was kindly, fatherly. He asked her out for dinner. She told him she was a student. He took her out again. She told him she was a virgin. Another date. She became an orphan.

When he suggested the apartment in New York she hesitated at first. When he insisted she finally agreed. But what to do about Bobbie? She would never let her go, and if she did manage to get away, Bobbie would come looking for her, and then Ed would find out the truth and that would be that.

Dallas puzzled over what to do. This was her chance and she didn't want to blow it.

The answer when it came to her was incredibly simple – she would kill Bobbie.

'Not enough,' Dallas stated. 'If you want me to open supermarkets I get a thousand dollars.'

'They won't pay that.'

'Then I won't open them. It's that simple. Now I'm taking the afternoon off and I'll see you back at the hotel later. Don't worry, I'll be there in plenty of time for the première.'

She left Mrs Fields sitting rigid-faced in the offices of Beauty Incorporated Co. – the outfit that organized the 'Miss Coast to Coast' contest.

If they thought they had hold of another dumb girl to hustle and promote for a year, they were on the wrong track. She had her own idea of the way things should be, and that way was *her* way.

She took a cab over to the apartment in the hope that Ed would be there, but he wasn't. Probably pissed off about the previous evening. She phoned him on his private number at his New York office. He *was* pissed off.

'Listen, sweetie,' she cooed, 'it's just all been so exciting. I'm sorry about last night, were you lonely? Why don't you come over now and I'll surprise you.'

He wasn't hard to persuade.

She took a quick shower, and then surveyed her closet of Ed's favourite outfits. What would surprise him today? Something subservient, something apologetic.

She finally hit it. Martha the Maid.

Humming softly to herself she slid into the short black dress with the white starched collar and cuffs, the sheer black stockings, the neat black shoes, and as a final touch a small adornment of white lace ribbon in her hair.

One thing about Ed, he loved surprises.

eight

The stewardess smiled winningly. 'Everything all right?' she asked for the twentieth time.

Al ignored her.

'Perfect,' replied Paul, returning her smile.

'More champagne?'

'I think we're well topped up.'

'If you need anything just give me a buzz.'

'Wouldn't hesitate.'

She smiled and lingered. 'Mr King,' she said directly to Al, 'I *loved* your last record, I just had to tell you.'

Al looked her over. She was sleek and blonde with a well-developed bosom straining at the confines of her regulation blouse. 'Do you fuck?' he asked crudely.

She didn't even blush. 'It depends,' leaning forward slightly she added, 'Are you offering?'

Paul wished that he was somewhere else. Al was impossible when he was in one of his 'I hate women' moods, and that was the mood he had been in all day.

'When?' inquired Al.

'Tonight, tomorrow.'

'Screw tonight, tomorrow, I want it now.'

She laughed. 'I'm on duty.'

'All I want is a little service.'

Paul got up. He was not enjoying being in the crossfire of their conversation. He wandered over to the magazine rack.

A few minutes passed and then Al got up and vanished into one of the toilets, followed shortly by the stewardess.

Paul went back to his seat. Casual sex had never appealed to him, it gave him bad vibes. It always reminded him of the way animals went at it. Sniff Sniff – I fancy you. He preferred to get into a woman's head first, her body second.

He thought about Linda. She was all the woman he had ever wanted. Intelligent, attractive, independent. If he wasn't married to Melanie . . . But he was and somewhere along the way, she had changed. She had become one of life's grabbers. Gimme . . . Gimme . . . Gimme. Bigger house, bigger pool, bigger car. She demanded the best of everything, and nagged the hell out of him if she didn't get it. If it wasn't for the children . . . married man's lament, and he knew it. But they were both so young and vulnerable, and they needed him.

Al returned to his seat, strapped himself in, and resumed gazing out of the window.

'Only another two hours,' remarked Paul.

Al nodded. He had become completely uncommunicative ever since Paul had been unable to arrange lunch with Dallas. It was his way of showing disapproval.

He was a *star* for Chrissakes. If he wanted something, he should have it *immediately*.

Melanie King went to the airport in Al's white Rolls Royce to meet them. She enjoyed being the centre of attention, and some of the airport photographers took her photo.

Al and Paul came walking through from customs, and the photographers sprang into action.

Melanie darted forward and kissed Al, she followed this up with a quick peck for Paul, then hanging firmly onto Al's arm she walked with them both to the car.

'Edna's cooking dinner,' she volunteered, 'steak and kidney pud, she slung the cook out and she's having a ball.'

'She hasn't fired the cook, has she?' asked Al, alarmed.

'Oh no, just got rid of her for the night. The maid too. I don't know how she manages.'

'She enjoys it,' sighed Al. 'My wife the worker!'

Melanie squeezed his arm. 'Tell me about the trip, I want to hear all about it. I hope you two didn't get up to anything naughty,' she giggled, 'bet *you* did, Al. It's all right, I won't tell Edna.'

Edna opened the oven and prodded the sizzling potatoes with a fork. They were just the way Al liked them, cut into thin slices and covered with onions and herbs. The steak and kidney pudding simmered on the cooker, and all she had left to do was to whip the cream that would accompany the baked jam roll dessert.

All Al's favourite things, and yet she couldn't remember the last time they had eaten such delicious food. Al usually instructed the cook on what they would have for dinner, and it varied between steak, plain chicken, or fish, always with a salad. Al insisted that he had to watch his diet. 'Cholestrol,' he would mention ominously if Edna suggested so much as a cottage pie. In the old days they had lived on cottage pie, sausages, mashed potatoes, and chips. In the old days Al had loved his food, and for once Edna wanted to be sure that he got something he enjoyed.

She hummed softly as she busied herself in the kitchen. It

seemed such a long time since Al had been home, although in point of fact it was only a couple of weeks. New York, and before that the health farm.

Everything in the kitchen seemed in order, so Edna went upstairs and changed out of her pinafore dress into a long plum-coloured shirtwaister. She powdered her face, added lipstick, too much rouge, and blue eyeshadow which immediately streaked. She had never been much good with make-up, but Al liked her to try. She dabbed on some perfume, and brushed her short mousey brown hair. As she was surveying herself in the mirror Evan slouched in.

'What are *you* all dressed up for?' he asked sneeringly.

'I want to look nice for your father.'

'Well, you look awful. All that stuff on your face doesn't suit you. It looks stupid, I don't know why you bother, he *knows* what you look like.'

Edna frowned. Perhaps he was right, perhaps she did look ridiculous. But it was too late to do anything about it; she could hear a car pulling up on the gravel outside, and excitedly she ran downstairs.

Al got out of the car and Paul pulled Melanie back and snapped, 'Do we *have* to stay for dinner?'

'Yes,' snapped back Melanie, 'Edna's prepared it specially.'

'I wanted to see the children.'

'Nobody's stopping you. Pop over, kiss them goodnight, and come right back. I'll go in and make some martinis,-I shouldn't think Edna could cope with that.'

'All right,' agreed Paul. 'I'll be back in a minute.'

Al and Paul had adjoining houses. They had acquired the land at a reasonable price some seven years previously, and they had divided it neatly down the middle and built respective mansions. Al's was ranch style, Paul's white and modern. They both had swimming pools, garages large enough for four cars, billiard rooms, and saunas. Paul often thought it was stupid and nouveau riche to have both built swimming pools, but Melanie had *insisted*. 'I don't want to feel like a poor relation,' she had complained when he had suggested they didn't need one.

His children were sitting up in bed washed and scrubbed, and nanny was reading them a story.

'Hey, kids!' exclaimed Paul, 'did you miss daddy?'

They leapt excitedly out of bed and threw themselves at him, until he was a tangle of arms and legs and kisses. It was a good feeling. Love. Pure and unblemished. The only true kind.

Nanny got them off him and settled them back in bed.

'Mustn't get too excited,' she admonished, 'otherwise we won't sleep, will we?'

Paul knew when he wasn't wanted. Nanny hated having her routine screwed up. And Melanie bent over backwards to please nanny. 'Do you realize,' she had once informed Paul, her pretty face grimacing with horror, 'if nanny ever left us I'd have to look after the children myself!'

On impulse Paul went downstairs to his study, locked himself in, and direct dialled Linda's number in New York. She was there.

'I miss you,' he said.

'I love you,' she replied.

He wondered very seriously what Melanie would say if he asked for a divorce.

'Hello there, fatso!' Al walloped Edna on the behind. 'All tarted up. Are we going out?'

Edna blushed. He *had* noticed.

Melanie hung onto Al's arm. 'How about a delicious cold martini? Shall I fix us some?' She led Al into the living-room and called over her shoulder, 'Ice, Edna.'

'Where's Evan?' Al demanded. 'Funny kid, you'd think he'd be here to greet me.' He went to the foot of the stairs and screamed out, 'Evan!!'

The boy appeared at the top of the stairs, white-faced and pasty.

'Don't I get any sort of greeting?' demanded Al. 'Come down here,'

Evan walked slowly down the stairs and Al grabbed hold of him in a bearhug.

'How's it going, boyo?' he asked cheerfully, 'still the randiest little bugger at school!' He winked at Melanie. 'Just like his dad. I thought about nothing but girls when I was his age.'

'Have things changed?' giggled Melanie.

Al burst out laughing. Evan scowled.

Edna came bustling in with the ice. 'Where's Paul? Dinner's nearly ready.'

'He'll be right back, he just popped over to see the kids.' Melanie busied herself behind the bar.

'Was New York nice?' Edna asked.

'Not bad,' replied Al, 'business, business, business. I just want to relax now. Christ, but it's a noisy city.'

'I love it there,' interrupted Melanie. 'The shops, and the theatres. Wouldn't you love to go, Edna?'

'Not really . . .' she caught Melanie's look and added lamely, 'Well yes, I suppose I would.'

Al wasn't even listening, he was staring out into his garden. 'Who's been fucking around with my apple tree?' he demanded.

'Don't use that language,' said Edna, 'not in front of you know who.' She glanced stealthily at Evan. 'You know I don't like it.'

'Who,' said Al coldly, 'has touched my apple tree?'

'I did,' scowled Evan, 'I cut off a few rotten branches.' He turned to Edna. '*She* told me to.'

Edna blushed. 'I didn't think you'd mind. The bad apples were falling in the pool. I didn't think you'd mind . . .'

'Jesus H!' exclaimed Al. 'What the fuck do you think I employ a gardener for? It's too bad, Edna, just too bloody bad . . .'

Her eyes filled with tears. 'I'll see to dinner,' she mumbled.

'Martini!' said Melanie brightly, and she handed Al a glass.

Paul returned, and Al took him to one side. 'I've had a great idea.'

'Yeah?' questioned Paul with relief. At least Al was talking to him again.

'We finish off the TV special next week?'

'That's right. There's just the locations left to shoot.'

'Great. You know the number "Lady"?'

'The song you sing to Katy May?'

'Right. Where are we shooting it?'

'South of France.'

'Terrific. Now Katy just sits there, right?'

'We start off with a shot of you and her in an open car driving along the coastline, then the beach, swimming, fooling around. Should be fantastic.'

'Have you ever seen Katy in a bikini?'

'Why?'

'She's short. Oh I know she's cute and cuddly, and a lovely little singer, but . . .'

'And very popular.'

'I give you that.'

Paul sighed. He smelled trouble. 'What are you leading up to?'

'I don't think it's going to look right my singing "Lady" to Katy.'

'She's the only female guest on your show.'

'She doesn't have to be.'

'Who do you want? Raquel Welch?'

'I want "Miss Coast to Coast". Perfect little spot for her. She'll do it if we pay her the right amount. Call New York and arrange it. And Paul – this time don't fuck it up.'

'Dinner's ready,' called Edna. She had recovered her composure, and proudly set out all Al's favourite foods in the middle of the dining room table.

'When you get a hard-on . . .' muttered Paul.

'Humour me. After all, I *am* the star of the family. Evan! Come on, boyo, dinner's ready.'

Melon to start. Al liked melon. He wolfed it down, then got up from the table and said, 'None of this other crap for me, I've got to watch the old weight.'

'I've cooked all your favourite things,' wailed Edna. 'Al, you *must* eat.'

'Sorry,' said Al cheerfully, 'can't let the paying public down. Anyway, I'm not hungry. Evan, fancy a game of tennis?'

Evan scowled. That was the last thing he felt like doing.

Edna's eyes brimmed over with tears, and, streaked with blue eyeshadow, they fell silently down her cheeks.

One thing stardom had done for big brother, mused Paul, it had turned him into a right bastard.

nine

When Ed Kurlnik left, Dallas fixed herself a large vodka on the rocks. She put on a bathrobe, curled up in a chair, and nursing her drink, she mulled over the previous scene.

Ed Kurlnik. Powerful. Rich. Married

Ed Kurlnik. Little sixty-one-year-old boy who liked to play games. Naughty games.

She reached beneath the chair she was sitting on and fished out a recent magazine. Ed Kurlnik was on the cover with his wife, Dee Dee, a strong, respectable-looking woman with steely grey hair and icy blue eyes. A woman in her middle fifties – fifty-six the magazine said – who was still attractive in a lady of the manor way.

Dallas opened up the magazine and turned to a picture of two girls. The Kurlnik twins. The Kurlnik heirs. Rich bitches, with cool blond hair and wide-spaced grey eyes. Twenty years old. The same age as she was. One of them wore riding clothes, the other a neat skirt, sweater, and pearls.

Dallas laughed aloud. Pearls indeed! She would fuck their father wearing pearls, she would make him buy them for her. Or maybe he could borrow them from his daughter, now *that* would be a laugh . . .

She read the article through for the hundredth time. It was like reading about a stranger. And yet she knew him so well, or thought she did. 'Ed and Dee Dee Kurlnik are one of the happiest married couples on the island.' She read about their holiday home on Fire Island. 'There is nothing better Ed Kurlnik likes to do than pitch a barbecue and feed his family.' Dallas could think of many things he liked to do better than that. 'Ed Kurlnik has always been the perfect father. Work or play, he always puts his family first.' Did they still make love? Ed and the well-preserved Dee Dee. Dallas bit hard on her lip. She didn't want him making love to anyone else, she wanted to be the only one.

'The twins never bother or worry their father. Dana is studying nursing, and Cara is interested in social work.' Crap! No one family could be *that* perfect. Dee Dee was probably an old lush, and the twins raving nymphos.

Dallas stuffed the magazine back under the chair.

How would life have been if Ed Kurlnik had been *her* father? Would she have worn riding clothes and studied nursing? Would someone have *cared* what she made of her life?

She had left home at seventeen and *nobody* had cared. Nobody had come looking for her. She had become a hooker, a whore. Nobody had forced her to, she had just drifted into it. And nobody gave a shit. She wondered if her parents or her husband or even Burt and Ida Keyes had given her a second thought. Probably not. Life at the zoo had probably just kept going.

What would they all think of her now? A beauty queen, a title holder, girlfriend of one of the richest men in America. They still probably wouldn't give a shit. They were like that.

Dallas sighed. She had got over the hurt a long time ago. So they hadn't come looking for her. Big deal. They wouldn't even recognize her now, she had changed. Before she had been a pretty little nothing, now she was a beauty, a showstopper, a breathtaker, a winner.

She downed the rest of the vodka, dressed, and took a cab back to the Plaza.

Mrs Fields was waiting impatiently. 'Where have you *been*?' she demanded.

'Did my shopping arrive? I want to wear the black dress tonight.'

'I hung everything up.'

'How kind of you. Just like having a personal maid!'

Once the decision to kill Bobbie was made, Dallas fantasized hundreds of ways to do it. She hadn't been watching television steadily for four years without having learnt a thing or two. There were several workable methods.

Poison. Fire. Gunshot. Drowning.

Dallas finally picked on drowning as the neatest method. Bobbie had never been a very good swimmer, she attacked the water like a dog – thrashing around in all directions. 'I like the water, but it scares me,' she had confided to Dallas, 'I think my old man tried to do me in under a fire hydrant one hot and funky summer!' Pity he hadn't succeded.

Bobbie had become very dependent on her heroin, and because of her habit she was not insisting on such a vigorous professional schedule. That was a relief as far as Dallas was concerned. It gave her time to see Ed, and also time to plan what she was going to do. Her constant fear was that Ed might find out her line of work. He wouldn't want her if he knew, he would want nothing to do with a common hooker. She vetted every job Bobbie arranged. Who would be there? How many? What was involved?

'Don't start getting high hat again,' complained Bobbie, 'I need the bread.'

Half the time she was incapable of performing at all, and Dallas was tempted to leave, just vanish off to New York with Ed. Bobbie would never find her in the state she was in most of the time. But if she did it would blow everything . . . No, it was a risk Dallas couldn't afford to take.

She felt no remorse about what she was planning to do. The things that Bobbie had forced her into . . . The humiliations, the degradations, the sexual nightmares of beatings and animals and sadomasochist happenings . . .

She watched one night while Bobbie fixed herself up, then she produced good Mexican grass, turned on, and invited Bobbie to join her. She cooked a sensational dinner and made love to the black girl for the first time in a year.

'Wow!' Bobbie exclaimed, 'What's happenin', man? What'd I do?'

Dallas smiled. 'Like old times, huh?'

'Like – yeah sugar. Do that again.'

Dallas obliged, then later she suggested they go down to the communal pool and swim.

'Skinny dip?' inquired Bobbie, 'I love to feel that warm water go ridin' up my hot little pussy!'

'Sure,' agreed Dallas, 'only quietly. We don't want to wake everyone up.'

They twisted towels around their nakedness, and crept down to the pool.

Dallas slid in the water first. It was cool and dark. 'Come on,' she called to Bobbie.

'Hey, I'm cold,' Bobbie complained.

'It's lovely in the water, come on.'

Bobbie sat gingerly on the edge of the pool in the shallow end and dangled her legs in.

'Let's go, baby,' whispered Dallas.

'Aw – I think it's too cold.'

Suddenly Dallas gripped her by the ankles and pulled her sharply into the water. She kept a firm hold of Bobbie's ankles, raising them above the water so that the top half of the black girl's body was completely submerged.

There was no sound, just the sudden splash when she had first pulled Bobbie in. For seconds Bobbie was still, and then all at once she started to struggle, and it was like holding a fish. Dallas moved slowly back into deeper water, but Bobbie's struggling was becoming so intense that she managed to free one leg, and was kicking out with it. Dallas hung firmly on to the other one.

How long did it take to drown? How painful was it? Jesus Christ – what was she doing? This wasn't some TV film, this was life, this was happening, this was now.

Abruptly she let go of the struggling girl, and spluttering and choking, Bobbie surfaced. She thrashed her way to the side of the pool and crawled out. She lay by the side retching.

Dallas climbed silently out. She wrapped the towel around herself.

'You fuckin' bitch!' Bobbie groaned, 'you tried to kill me. You want me out of your life that bad you fuckin' got it. Get out of my apartment – and don't you never come back!' She started to retch again, and Dallas left her lying there. She went up to the apartment and packed her things.

Maybe she hadn't meant to kill Bobbie at all. Maybe she had just wanted to frighten her . . .

Yes, that was it. She had only wanted to frighten her and it had had the desired effect. Dallas nodded to herself. She wouldn't have hurt her, really she wouldn't.

•

Ramo Kaliffe was Dallas' arranged date for the première, and Ed would not be pleased about *that*. She froze him out of thinking there would be any action. Screw him. He had served his purpose. 'Did I not please you last time?' he asked in a hurt voice at the end of the evening.

'Please *me*?' she said incredulously. As far as she could remember she had spent three quarters of an hour going down on him, and he had kindly dipped his head to her for a fast two minutes. Not that she minded, sex was no turn-on whichever way it was served. Sex was a means to an end. Sex was Ed Kurlnik and pleasing *him*.

Back at the hotel someone had dropped off an envelope of photos, and she devoured them with her eyes.

They were ten by eight glossies of her taken at the 'Miss Coast to Coast' contest. Enclosed was a brief note, 'Dropped these by as souvenir – would like to get together and do some more. Please call Linda Cosmo.' And there was a telephone number.

It was still early, before midnight. Dallas picked up the phone and asked for the number.

Linda answered sleepily.

'Hi, this is Dallas – "Miss Coast to Coast". I got your note. I'd love to do some photos.'

Linda stifled a yawn, she had been fast asleep. 'Marvellous. When are you free?'

'Tomorrow morning?'

'Wonderful. About ten o'clock.'

'Couldn't be better. What shall I wear?'

'Can I look at what you have when I get there?'

'Sure.'

'See you tomorrow then.' Linda hung up and switched on the light. Too late for Al King, but it would be a good scoop to do some photos of the girl. She might be able to place them in *People* or *Newsweek*.

Dallas hung up the phone and flopped out on the bed. She felt drained, it had been a busy day. The first day of her new life. Beauty Incorporated were probably going to be furious that she had arranged her own photo session, but that was just too bad. For once in her life *she* was going to be the decision-maker, and doing a photo session with a female photographer appealed to her. Guys were always on the make, trying to hustle, making suggestive comments. It would be nice to have some good photos taken, sexy but decent. Not like the murky photos from her past. Photos where she had tried to keep her face out of the picture. And it had been easy really, it wasn't her face they were after. Gyno shots, Bobbie had called them – 'Snatch money! The easiest way to make it!' she had joked. But Dallas had hated posing for that kind of picture. What kind of sick people paid for that kind of photograph? Guys who couldn't get it up . . . Or maybe guys who didn't want to . . . Dallas finally fell asleep, surrounded by the glossy pictures of her as 'Miss Coast to Coast'.

ten

The sun at Nice airport was blazing down. Photographers were jostling for shots of Al as he disembarked from the Air France plane. Tourists were gaping. Officials were pushing forward to greet him.

He wore a white sports shirt, white trousers, and a thin black alligator belt that clasped together his initials in gold. His black hair was just long enough and carefully tousled. His black eyes hid behind grey tinted shades.

He had spent the previous week at his home in London lying by the swimming pool and acquiring a perfectly respectable golden tan. London had been having a heat wave, and Al had taken full advantage.

Paul, by his side, was more conservatively dressed. But the women, when they had stopped eyeing Al, turned their attention to him and wondered who he was. He was a couple of inches taller than Al, leaner, with finer bones and smokey eyes. The brothers were by no means plain.

Al was in a very good mood indeed. Dallas had been booked for the show, and everyone seemed pleased about it. The producer had been delighted, and the only person who was somewhat put out was Katy May.

The English press played the whole thing up to the hilt, with photos of Katy in a swimsuit looking dejected, and recent shots of Dallas.

Bernie Suntan had telephoned from California. 'Ace publicity – great starter.'

With Melanie's coaching Edna had finally said to Al that she would like to come to the South of France with him. 'Forget it,' he had replied, 'I'll be working all day, you'll be stuck in a hotel, and I'll be worrying about you.' That had been that. No Edna. No Melanie.

A convertible Cadillac met them at the airport and sped them off to the Hotel Voile D'Or, at St Jean Cap Ferrat.

'This is the life!' exclaimed Al. 'Give me the sun and I could become a real beach bum.' He admired the passing girls. 'Place is jammed with little darlings!'

He had not mentioned Dallas to Paul since the night he had told him to get her for the show. It was almost as if he had forgotten all about her, and when Paul had told him it was arranged he had just nodded. Paul understood. The girl had said yes and that was that. Al knew that he could have her, so the thrill was gone.

They arrived at the hotel, and Paul went off to meet with the director and camera crew. Al changed into white swim shorts and a short towelling jacket, and sauntered down to the pool. He enjoyed the buzz that went up when he appeared, but it was a sophisticated group and no one came running over for his autograph.

He acquired a beach bed and lay out. A girl in an orange bikini was openly staring at his crotch. The myth of Al King and his tight stage trousers was alive and well and bulging in his swim shorts.

The sun was delicious, burning into his dark skin and causing thin rivulets of sweat to moisten on his hairy chest.

He tried to empty his mind and think of nothing. But the tour kept on drifting uneasily into his thoughts, and his stomach turned mildly in anticipation of the ordeal. He had spoken to Edna of his fears. He had lain next to her warm comfortable body in the night, and confessed his terror. She had held him close and crooned, 'Don't go, stay with us, stay with Evan and me.'

That wasn't what he wanted to hear. He wanted encouragement. He wanted building up. And if Edna couldn't give him that, who could? Who else knew the real Al King? They all saw the strutting, cocksure, virile star. They didn't want to see just another man with insecurities. They wanted glamour. He gave them what they wanted. Why else did he force himself to diet, have plastic surgery to remove that extra chin, re-cap his teeth so that the famous Al King smile remained whiter than white.

Later Al hosted a dinner at an open air restaurant called 'The African Queen' for some of the crew, and an assortment of local talent rounded up on the Croisette in Cannes.

It was a boisterous evening, the wine flowing freely and food likewise. Around midnight Al got bored, and he brushed aside the girls swarming round him, and suggested to Paul that they split and carry on to Monte Carlo where they could indulge in a little gambling.

Paul was only too pleased to oblige. He discreetly settled the bill, and they escaped.

Al wanted to drive. He handled the Cadillac restlessly, and drove it too fast along the winding coastal road.

'Let's *get* there at least,' muttered Paul.

'You nervous?' laughed Al, putting his foot down harder, and nearly colliding with an oncoming Citroën.

'Cut it out,' mumbled Paul.

'Trouble with you is you don't want to live dangerously. You live a safe life – you're even faithful to your girlfriend! Didn't you fancy *any* of them tonight?'

'Didn't *you*?'

Al sighed. 'I don't fancy any of them any more. They're all a bunch of scrubbers. Get the clap as soon as look at them.'

'So don't look.'

'Do me a favour. You know the score. I've got them comin' out of my ears! Who has to look? They're grabbing at me before I even fart in their direction!'

They drove straight to the Casino in Monte Carlo.

Al could feel the adrenalin flowing. He headed over to the nearest roulette table and surrounded twenty-six and twenty-nine with fifty franc chips. Seventeen came up. He repeated the procedure, doubling his bet. Six came up. He piled some chips on black, and once again chevalled twenty-six and twenty-nine. Zero came up. He changed tables and piled chips on number five. He was lucky first time, and the croupier pushed stacks of chips in his direction.

'It's my night, boyo!' he gleefully told Paul.

Two hours later they left. Al was three thousand pounds down.

'It's a mug's game,' announced Paul.

'Horseshit. I'll come back tomorrow night and beat the shit out of 'em.'

eleven

Dallas sat on the Pan American jet, sipping champagne and marvelling at the events of the previous week.

So much had happened. So many exciting things.

Now here she was sitting on an aeroplane heading for Europe. She could hardly believe it.

A passing stewardess smiled in a friendly fashion and asked, 'Everything all right, Dallas?'

She nodded to indicate that everything was fine. In the space of a week people recognized her, they treated her with that special kind of deference reserved for the famous.

Getting the Al King show had been a terrific break – all she had to do in the show was look pretty – but it was a beginning, and everyone had to start somewhere.

The photos that Linda had taken of her were selling well, and Linda was nice, easy to work with, friendly, and someone to rap with. Of course Dallas wasn't into the confiding bag, she had too much to hide, but just discussing what was happening to her now was a relief.

Ed had taken her sudden rise to mini fame in a different fashion. He was used to having her completely available, and now that she was in the limelight it made things more complicated. Strangely enough, he was pleased when he heard about the trip to Europe. 'I'll meet you there,' he promised, 'I'm about due on a business trip to London, and I'll fly down to the South of France after.'

She had not been exactly thrilled, but then again why not? It was progress, and why was she with Ed Kurlnik if not to make headway in the affair? If he ever left his wife for her . . . Well, that would be worth more than all the transient fame could ever be.

The 'Fasten Your Seatbelts' sign was flashing on. They were due to land in London where Dallas had a one-day stopover to organize her clothes for the television special. She had managed to dump Mrs Fields. 'This whole chaperone scene is not for me,' she had flatly informed Beauty Incorporated. They had not been pleased, but Dallas carried the scent of success, and they stood to make a substantial amount in commissions, so for once they relaxed their rules. Mrs Fields had muttered ominously, 'This girl means trouble.' But money spoke louder than words.

At London's Heathrow airport Dallas was met by a bevy of photographers.

She was wearing a white suit, and she obligingly shrugged off the jacket, and posed provocatively in a tubular, strapless sweater, which clung like glue round her sensual unfettered breasts.

The picture was on the front of all the evening newspapers. In England she was an instant celebrity.

By the next morning she was on another plane to the South of France. Briefly she thought about Al King, wondered what he would be like. Linda – who knew him – had merely commented, 'Steer clear, he's a prick.' The way she had said it gave Dallas the impression that she didn't like him at all, but further questioning had produced nothing, so Dallas had dropped the subject.

She didn't much care anyway. They were all the same. Men. Sonsofbitches. Perverts. Sex-mad little boys.

And stars. The worst kind.

She should know, in her former business capacity operating in the heart of Beverly Hills she had met enough of them.

Case one. A hero of the West. Always the good guy, never the villain. What would his loyal faithful public do if they knew that in private he indulged in horseback activities that would *never* find their way onto the screen.

Case two. Baby-faced former child star. He liked nannies and governesses, and a good solid beating daily.

Case three. A football player. Adored by women the world over. Could *only* get it up when clad in women's clothes with a dildoe up his ass.

Dallas knew of many more examples. Where were all the *normal* people? *She* had certainly never come across any. But then of course she hadn't exactly led what could be termed as a normal life.

At Nice airport, things followed the same pattern. Photographers. A press agent to meet her. She posed, this time in a clingy red dress. God, but there was something mesmerizing about a camera lens. She could communicate with a small piece of engineering, much more so than with people. Mouth slightly parted, moisten lips, head back so that hair flowed, body muscles tensed. She had it down to a fine art.

'I'm Nicky,' said the television assistant who accompanied the press agent. He was a young man, with pimples and red hair.

Dallas smiled, and Nicky was immediately captivated.

'I'll take you to your hotel. They want to do a rehearsal after lunch. Was it a good flight?'

Dallas nodded. She was busy looking around her and taking in the strange sights and sounds. It was a thrill to be in Europe, something that she had never expected to happen to her. She had known that Ed Kurlnik would be the passport to a better life, and now – just a few short months after meeting him – things were moving at a pace almost too fast for her to keep up with. Occasionally she was bothered by the thought that her past might catch up with her. Some sly-faced man from the shadows might see her photo and step forward to announce, 'That girl is a hooker, nothing but a common little whore.' She was prepared if that ever happened. She would just smile sweetly and deny it. After all, who could *prove* her former life style?

Bobbie. The name stuck nervously in her throat. She had neither seen nor heard from her since the night at the pool. But Bobbie must have seen her picture in the paper, she must know what had happened to her. And it was not like Bobbie to miss a going opportunity. Dallas was quite prepared for the fact that she would eventually appear, and she was alert for when it did happen. She wasn't about to be black-mailed and have her whole new life hang on a thread. If Bobbie reappeared she was ready for her. And this time she wouldn't screw it up.

'Al King,' he announced coolly. *So you're the bitch that stood me up for lunch.*

'Dallas,' she replied, equally cool. *Conceited bastard. I have met your type before. Linda was right.*

'Did you have a good flight?' *If you play your cards right I'll take you back to my hotel and give you a glimpse of Al King cock.*

'Fine, thank you.' *He wants to get laid. They all want to get laid.*

'Good.' *Christ, but she's a knockout. Green eyes. Soft lips. Soft hair. A body that should be labelled instant hard-on.*

'The Atlantic crossing was a bit bumpy.' *If I was into men, I guess this is what they would look like. Dark and hard. Bastards.*

They had met at the scene of the location. The opening shot of the particular sequence they were to do together was of the two of them in an open sports car driving along. The camera crew were busy setting up.

Nicky had escorted her to the location, and Al had sauntered over and introduced himself.

'Dallas, dear,' announced the director, an effeminate gentleman in tomato red trousers with a bandana round his head, 'can we have you in the car, dear.'

'I'll have her in the car!' joked Al.

Dallas shot him a frosty look. I only do it for money. Ed Kurlnik's money.

'You too, Al,' continued the director. 'I want to start with a long shot of the car, nice scenery, hair blowing, everyone wishes they were there. Then we come in for close-ups. Dallas gazing

60

adoringly at you – you singing. Sound – put the machine on, let's get some atmosphere here.'

The sound mechanic switched on a portable machine, and Al singing 'Lady' came blaring into the afternoon sunshine. It was a funky soul song, with Al's incredibly sexy gravelly voice playing sensually with the lyrics.

Al leapt into the car and started miming –

'Lady you are pretty
Lady you are witty
Wanna be my Lady
Wanna drive me crazy
You got eyes like hot molasses
Hey baby
Hey maybe
Hey Lady
Lady Lady Lady
You are foxy Lady'

Dallas climbed into the car and openly yawned.

'Great!' exclaimed Al, 'a yawn I get.'

'Now, darling,' fussed the director, 'I want you to *gaze* at Al. Don't take your eyes off him. I want love, romance, a touch of sex.'

'I wouldn't mind a touch of that,' interrupted Al.

'I'm sure you'll never go short,' sniffed the director. 'Dallas, sweetie, you understand what I want? Every woman watching should be aching to change places with you.'

They rehearsed the shot several times until the director was satisfied, then they broke for lunch which was served from a mobile canteen. Nicky helped Dallas get a plate of cold meats and salads and hovered reassuringly by her side. They sat on the near-by bench. Al retired to a private caravan.

'How do you like our star?' asked Nicky.

'Silver, plastic, and tarnished.'

Nicky laughed. 'Don't let anyone hear you say that. Oh, here comes his brother.'

Paul had been delayed at the hotel on long distance calls, and as soon as he arrived Al said, 'She's here. Go find her and tell her to join me for a glass of wine and a quick fuck.'

'Are you serious?'

'About the wine. The other I'll ask her myself.'

'Terrific. I hope it will have all been worth it.'

'Got a feeling it just might be.'

Paul spotted her immediately. You could hardly miss her with that tangle of sun-streaked hair and incredible figure.

He approached briskly. 'Hello, I'm Paul King. Al would like you to join him for a drink.'

Dallas smiled. 'I bring love and kisses from Linda. She said to tell you New York misses you.'

'That's nice.' He shot a wary look at Nicky. It wasn't exactly *discreet* of Linda to send that kind of a message, suppose Melanie had been with him? 'How about the drink with Al?'

'Gee, thanks. But I think I'll just stay out here. The sun is *so* lovely, I'm really enjoying it.'

'Oh. You see Al thought it might be nice if the two of you got to know each other a little better.'

Dallas winked. 'I know.'

Paul felt suddenly awkward. The village pimp. 'Sure you won't change your mind?'

'Not unless it's part of my contract.'

'No, it's not,' Paul said stiffly, and he walked away.

Nicky shook his head in admiration, 'Wow! Mr King is not going to like this.'

'Mister King is not going to get this.'

'This is the second of his television shows I've been on and he gets *everything* he wants.'

'So he's just going to have to be deprived. I'm sure there are plenty of ladies around who wouldn't mind him jumping on their bones, but I am *not* one of them.'

Nicky grinned shyly. 'Would you come out with me tonight?'

'How *old* are you?'

'Twenty-two. We could go dancing. There's a good disco in Juan les Pins.'

'Sounds like fun, Nicky. And I know that you wouldn't even *think* of jumping on my bones.'

'Certainly not.' He smiled proudly. 'So it's a date then?'

'A date.' Even Ed couldn't get mad about her going out with a kid like Nicky, and she didn't want to sit in her hotel, she wanted to get out and see something of the Riviera.

'So what's the matter with the bitch?'

'I don't know, Jesus, Al, I don't even much care. You'll nail her – you always do.'

'I know *that*,' agreed Al coldly. He lit a cigarette, thought of his voice, stubbed it out, and swore softly. 'I felt like having her now.'

'So you'll have her tonight – big deal.'

'Yeah. I'll have her tonight. Arrange dinner – set something up.'

'Christ!' exclaimed Paul, 'I think the message is she wants you to ask her yourself.'

'You're right. That's the problem – she wants *me* to ask her. OK, boyo. Book me a table somewhere horny, order flowers, champagne. Jesus H, she had better be worth it.'

Paul frowned. Orders. Sometimes Al treated him just like another lackey. Linda was right. Maybe he should stop wetnursing Al and put a manager on the job. Then he could relax, enjoy his money, and organize everything from the air-conditioned comfort of his suite of offices in Park Lane. Maybe after the tour. He knew what Al was going through now, it wasn't the time to start making changes. Al didn't mean to issue orders, he didn't even realize he was doing it. Having everything done for him had just become a fact of life. It was all part and parcel of being a star.

'You could take her to dinner at the Colombe d'Or in St Paul de Vence. Romantic. Private.'

'Ask her, Paul.'

'I thought *you* were going to ask her.'

'You give it another try.'

'Oh shit – Al.'

'Arrange it. I'll romance her first and fuck her later!'

twelve

Edna King awoke to the sound of the phone ringing. It was eight o'clock, she was usually awake by that time, but lately she had been taking sleeping pills and they seemed to make it more difficult to get up in the mornings.

It was Melanie on the phone. 'Have you seen the papers?' she demanded shrilly.

'No,' replied Edna, already resigned to the bad news they would no doubt contain.

'I *warned* you, I *told* you we should have gone with them.'

'What is it?'

'I'll be right over.'

Edna climbed reluctantly out of bed. She knew what it would be, some item about Al and another woman. There were always items about Al and other women. Ignore them, he had continually told her. Never believe anything you read in the papers. Melanie appeared to take every word as gospel, and she never allowed an item to slip by Edna unnoticed.

The kitchen was already occupied by the maid and Nelson, who were enjoying a bacon and egg breakfast.

The maid, a strapping Italian, asked in her careful English, 'Something, Madam?'

'Coffee,' said Edna nervously, 'for two. In the lounge.' What she really wanted to say was, 'Get out of my kitchen, my house, my life.' What she really wanted to do was make herself a hot sweet cup of tea, and some thick fattening toast liberally spread with strawberry jam.

She had ordered coffee because it was what Melanie preferred. 'Tea is for peasants,' Melanie would sniff.

The newspapers were in a neat pile on the hall table, but Edna purposely left them untouched. Why spoil Melanie's fun?

She walked in the lounge and gazed out of the French windows into the garden. It was the start of another beautiful day, and the pool gleamed invitingly. Swimming was good exercise, maybe she should swim more. If only Nelson wasn't always lurking round the pool. When she put on her bathing suit he seemed to stare at her in a peculiar way, a penetrating way. She would have to ask Al to get rid of him. It really wasn't fair of Al to tell her not to be silly, it wasn't him he stared at.

Melanie came striding purposefully across the garden. She was wearing a purple track suit, and without make-up her prettiness faded, and was replaced with a petulant, pinched look.

Edna unlocked the French doors and let her in.

'Take a look at this!' Melanie thrust a paper at her.

On the front page there was a photograph of Al sitting in an open car smiling at a girl who gazed back at him with a faintly mocking smile. She was a very beautiful girl, with long legs propped on the dashboard, and a seductively unbuttoned shirt. The caption read 'Al King Meets His Queen', and underneath, in smaller print, it said, 'Al King enjoys a get-together with American beauty queen, Dallas. They will appear together on Al's forthcoming television spectacular.

'It's nothing,' Edna explained, placing the newspaper carefully down, 'just publicity.'

'Just publicity,' jeered Melanie, '*just publicity*. Are you blind? Look at the way he's looking at her.'

'It's publicity, Melanie. Al has to do these sort of things. *I* don't mind, so I don't see why *you* should.'

'Oh, charming! I'm trying to help you, Edna. If you're too naive to see what's going on, *I'm* not. Al is making a fool of you, and if I've told you once I've told you a thousand times, you should be by his side – otherwise one of these days you're going to *lose* him.'

The Italian maid came in with the coffee. 'Where, madam?' She smiled knowingly. Had she heard? Edna gestured to the table. Damn Melanie and her loud voice.

'I can't stay for coffee,' Melanie snapped, 'I have a masseur coming over. *Think* about what I've said. *Think* about the position you may find yourself in. It's not too late – yet.' She flounced out the same way she had come in, leaving Edna in a state of flux.

Lose Al. Impossible. Absolutely impossible. But was she being naive? *Was* Al making a fool of her? Edna shook her head in disbelief. She trusted him. She always had and she always would. Melanie was just trying to cause trouble for no reason.

Edna gulped down the hot coffee. If only her sister-in-law would leave her alone. If only everyone would leave her alone. If only she could go back to the days when it had just been her and Al . . . Just the two of them. No money, but what wonderful times they had enjoyed together.

Perhaps before he went off on the American tour they could go away somewhere. Maybe Brighton, where they had spent their honeymoon. What a week *that* had been. In the last few years Edna had noticed Al's gradual slackening of interest in sex. At first she had been relieved, in the early days he had wanted it constantly, she shuddered at the memory of his demands. Morning, noon, and night. Day after day. Even when she had been *pregnant*. Now he seemed content to just lie beside her. It had been months since he last made love to her. Of course she didn't mind, she knew that his work took a lot out of him. But a week in Brighton would do him good, even just a few days. She resolved to discuss this with him.

Satisfied with her decision she finished her coffee, and then drank Melanie's. It wouldn't do to *waste* it. Anyway, it went well with the packet of Bourbon Cream biscuits that the maid had thoughtfully provided.

Upstairs in his bed Evan stealthily inspected his collection of magazines. He found studying them a diverting pastime. He had his favourite girls and would quickly turn to the relevant pages and study the female of his choice. There was Bertha. Blond. Eighteen. Hobby – breeding horses. She liked big dominant men who knew what they were doing. She wore pearls, and see-through

65

nylon knickers, and appeared in a variety of poses with her legs apart.

Then there was Maralyn. A big girl, Maralyn, with enormous jutting breasts which she seemed to take a great deal of pleasure in playing with.

He really could fancy a night with Bertha or Maralyn. Oh yes. Actually he could fancy a night with anyone. Sixteen and still a virgin. It was ridiculous. None of the other boys at his school were in that position. They had all had 'experiences'. Evan had heard them discussing various aspects of what appeared to be highly exciting sex lives.

He brooded about his lack of female companionship, and anxiously perused his magazines, of which Nelson seemed to have a never-ending supply. He often thought of Nelson offering him the 'real thing'. How much would it cost? Would he know what to do? Where would it take place?

He had at last decided to ask Nelson to arrange it.

Meanwhile there remained Bertha and Maralyn. He just had time for one of them before school.

He chose Bertha with her nylon knickers, and clutching her firmly under his arm he made his way to the bathroom.

thirteen

He wanted her, and he was pushing. Gradually it dawned on Dallas that the only reason she was on the Al King television spectacular was because Al King himself had ordained it. It all fell into place. The offer of a drink on the night she had won the contest. The lunch she had never attended in New York. The request for her to join him in his caravan. And now a dinner invitation – which she had turned down.

'I wish you would change your mind,' Paul had said tightly at her refusal.

'I'm busy,' Dallas had replied. 'Anyway, I don't go out with married men.' Lies. Lies. Lies. What about Ed Kurlnik jetting in the very next day. Nobody was more married than Ed.

'Al is just extending his friendship,' Paul explained.

More like his cock, Dallas thought, and I am not for sale any more.

During the afternoon they taped the beginning of Al's song in the car. Dallas just had to sit there gazing at him. He was good-looking. *Too* good-looking. Arrogant, with an assurance that came from getting everything he wanted. Well, he wasn't going to get her. She wondered if his brother had told him yet.

Photographers buzzed around snapping numerous shots. She smiled at him, licked her lips, and threw her head back.

'You love it, don't you?' said Al.

'It's fun,' she replied carefully.

'I like your tits.'

'Good for you.'

'Why don't you want to have dinner?'

'I'm not in the mood for getting chased around a table.'

'What table? What are you talking about?'

'Oh come on. *You* know what I mean.'

'Don't flatter yourself, kid. Girls like you are fallin' off the trees to get me.'

'So go find a tree.'

The afternoon passed quickly, and shortly before they finished for the day, Nicky came over and in an embarrassed voice told her that he wouldn't be able to take her out after all. Poor kid, somebody had warned him off. Probably the brother. Well, screw all of them. So she wouldn't see the sights. She would go to bed.

'Dinner, darling?' the director inquired.

'I'm too tired,' she excused herself.

'See you in the morning then.'

'I don't believe it!' Al exclaimed, 'she's a dyke, must be.'

'Yes,' agreed Paul, although privately he thought nothing could be further from the truth.

'She's sharp too. Answers back. Maybe I could convert her.'

'Why not just forget her. She's a headache.'

'I'll fuck her, I'll forget her. It's that easy.'

'And if you don't fuck her?'

'Ah, boyo, that's the problem. You know me when I don't get what I want.'

Paul frowned. Indeed he did know.

'Violette Victor is in town. She's having dinner with us.' Violette Victor was a young French movie actress in current vogue.

Al's interest perked slightly. 'Have you met her?'

'I met her agent this afternoon. She's looking forward to meeting you.'

•

Later, on the Carlton terrace, they met with Violette and her agent. She was tall and skinny, with straggly brown hair and luminous almond-shaped grey eyes. Wide-mouthed, she smiled a warm greeting, and clutched Al firmly by the hand.

Paul breathed a sigh of relief. If *she* didn't take Al's mind off Dallas nobody would. She was a star, and her reputation as a nymphomaniac was well known.

The four of them had dinner up in the hills, and then Al and Violette vanished up to her suite at the Carlton, and neither was seen again until morning.

Al arrived an hour late at the location.

'You look like you haven't slept for a week,' stated Dallas.

'Are you a lesbian?'

'What a sweet old-fashioned question. If I was, it would be none of your goddamn business.'

'So you are.'

'No, I am not.' Why had she answered him? He had no right to know either way. She thought of her relationship with Bobbie and shuddered. Those were scenes better forgotten. No, she was definitely *not* a lesbian.

'Let's have dinner tonight.'

'I don't want dinner with you.'

'Why not?'

'You're too – I don't know – you're just too . . .'

'What?'

'*I don't know.*'

'If you don't know let's have dinner and find out.'

'You're too obvious.'

'Obvious?' He burst out laughing, 'Obvious! You can talk, with your tits hanging out from here to kingdom come!'

'You want to get laid.'

'I just got laid. Tonight I'd like dinner with you. We could talk, like get to know each other.'

'Why?'

'Why not?'

'Anyway I can't. My boyfriend—' she stammered over boyfriend, realizing she had picked the wrong word, 'is coming to town.'

'Who's your boyfriend?'

'Just a friend.'

'We could all have dinner.'

'No thanks.'

The director had lined up the shot and was calling for action. Al started to sing, and Dallas did the full adoring gaze. Idly she wondered who he had been with the night before, and then suddenly, for no reason, she felt a sexual excitement grip her, a feeling she had only ever experienced with Burt Keyes, and the beginning of her affair with Bobbie. She wanted to close her eyes and hang on, it was such a *good* feeling, and in spite of the life she had led, such an unusual feeling. She didn't understand it. What had caused it?

The sound machine boomed Al's voice over loud and clear. Oh Christ! Not feelings for this creep in tight trousers.

She could feel her nipples hardening, and she saw Al notice. Then the bulge in his trousers started to grow. He stared at her, casually slipping the clothes from her with his eyes. Bastard. He knew what was happening.

'Cut!' the director called, 'that was sensational, no retakes. Coming in for close-ups. Everything OK, Al?'

'Couldn't be better,' and he winked at her, 'could it?'

She turned away and let the make-up woman attend to her face. What had happened? And why? She couldn't think straight. Thank Christ Ed would be with her soon. If only she could manufacture that special feeling for Ed. If only . . .

'How was last night?' Paul asked.

'Not bad.'

'Not bad. I hear she's a killer.'

'Boney.'

'One of the biggest movie stars in France and all you can say is boney.'

'Do you love Linda, Paul?'

'That's a hell of a question.' They had never really discussed it before. 'Why?'

'Does it kick you in the gut when you see her? Like – pow. Know what I mean?'

'I know what you mean. Yes, I love her.'

'And Melanie?'

Paul shook his head. 'It's difficult. Melanie's my wife, mother of my kids. What's with the questions?'

'Just thinking.'

Violette Victor arrived for lunch and the photographers had a field day. She was not averse to publicity, and posed moodily in a faded denim jump suit.

Dallas was suddenly ignored, and she felt sharp pangs of jealousy at the switch of attention.

Al and Violette Victor. She imagined them in bed together.

Nicky came over to complain about being told he couldn't take her out the previous evening. She brushed him aside, and watched as Al and Violette disappeared inside his caravan. A lunchtime fuck. Charming.

Stupid, conceited, *star*.

In the afternoon they shot the second half of Al's song. They had to leave the car and run from the beach into the sea. Dallas had to throw off her dress, underneath which she was wearing a white bikini.

'You look absolutely marvellous, darling,' exclaimed the director, 'You remind me of Ursula Andress in that Bond film.'

'Who?' questioned Dallas.

The director raised an irate eyebrow. 'Are you kidding dear?'

Violette Victor had departed and Al seemed in good humour.

'You're happy,' remarked Dallas.

'I had a good lunch, know what I mean?'

She knew what he meant, and then before she could help herself she said, 'Get your cock sucked, did you?' She could have kicked herself as soon as she had said it.

Al started to laugh. 'Oh, boy! Little Miss America. What naughty words you come out with. Yes, as a matter of fact I did.'

Why had she said it? What did she care? It made it look like she *did* care. It made her sound like a really tough broad. Which of course she was, but that was supposed to be *her* secret. Oh shit, why had she said it?

'Good for you.' And for some inexplicable reason her eyes filled with tears.

'Changed your mind about dinner?'

'I told you, I'm busy.'

'Pity. I can see that you and I would get along really well.'

'Don't count on it.'

Al grinned. 'I'm counting on it. Anyway if you can't make dinner come to the Casino in Monte Carlo later, bring me some luck.'

'Doesn't Violette Victor bring you luck?'

'Violette Victor doesn't fill a bikini like you.'

'But she sucks good cock, right?'

'Right.'

Oh God, not again. What was she trying to do. She was carrying on like she was jealous or something ridiculous like that. Miss Toughie. Shut up, Dallas, you're behaving like a cunt.

'I think you and I could have one helluva good time together,' Al said seriously. 'Why don't you dump the boyfriend, whoever he is.'

Was he kidding? Dump Ed Kurlnik. Never.

'Not possible. Anyway I don't want to.' Her eyes dropped to his impossibly filled swim shorts, 'besides, he has more to offer me than you do.'

Now what a lie *that* was.

Ed arrived in a black chauffered Kurlnik Supreme, looking dapper in a dark blue suit.

He had ordered adjoining suites in the Hotel de Paris, and he kissed Dallas chastely on the cheek and booked an immediate phone call to Mrs Dee Dee Kurlnik on Fire Island.

So the immaculate Dee Dee was holding the fort at their holiday mansion. With or without the lovely twins? Dallas wondered viciously if she was screwing any of the local talent. Maybe she would dip her immaculate toes in the ocean and get eaten by a shark.

'How's it going?' Ed asked, as he waited for his phone call.

'Terrific,' replied Dallas, kneeling to unzip his trousers.

He turned away. 'Not while I'm on the phone.'

'Why not? I've missed you.'

Flattered, he turned back to her. 'Make it quick while I'm waiting for the call to come through.'

What other way was there but quick with Ed?

Al didn't fancy her. Movie star or not, she was just not his scene. Skinny body. Hairy armpits. Grating accent.

He had performed the night before, but that was it.

Lunchtime she had serviced him. Now she expected the compliment returned.

'We'll have dinner first,' he suggested, 'Paul's meeting us at The African Queen. You like Pizza?'

Disappointed, she slipped into a dress. 'Later, then,' she said, as if to reassure herself.

'Wouldn't miss it.'

He drove the Cadillac at his usual erratic pace. He wondered if Dallas would turn up at the Casino. God, she was beautiful. And that body. Quite unbelieveable. And he liked her style, she wasn't prepared to take the shit he dished out to everyone else. It was a pleasure to find a woman who answered back. He had known she would be different. He had sensed it. And he had to have her. Had to.

Dinner was a succession of autograph hunters. The tourist season was in full swing, and they went after Violette and Al endlessly.

Al couldn't wait to get to the Casino. The adrenalin was flowing. He needed some excitement.

He hit the roulette table, covering all his favourite numbers. 'Tonight's my lucky night,' he told Paul.

Zero came up.

Dallas and Ed dined at a small discreet restaurant overlooking the harbour. Conversation was sparse. It was so strange to be out in public together. Dallas drank most of the wine, and Ed told a long and boring story of a business transaction.

If they were married is this what their life would be like together? A succession of boring dinners. She had longed for the day when he would actually take her out, and the anticlimax was awful. Of course in New York it would probably be different. There everyone knew him, and it would be exciting to be seen together.

Mrs Ed Kurlnik. What respect *that* title would conjure up.

'Shall we go to the casino?' she asked casually after dinner.

'I don't gamble,' Ed replied.

I bet you don't, mustn't risk the precious millions. 'But *I'd* love to go. Can we?'

'Well . . .'

'*Please.*' She slipped her hand onto his thigh under the table, 'we'll do what *you* want later.'

'Just for a short visit then.'

He paid the cheque, undertipped as was his habit, and they climbed into the comfort of the Kurlnik Supreme, and were whisked over to the Casino by the chauffeur.

Dallas had chosen her outfit with care. A plain white dress. Long. One shoulder exposed. A thin silver choker, silver bangles on both arms, and gypsy hoop earings.

Ed, not known as a giver of compliments, had volunteered that she looked very nice. She knew she looked beautiful. She knew the dress emphasized every curve of her body.

She didn't know why she was in such a state of excitement

about seeing Al King. But she was. She wanted him to see her with Ed Kurlnik. She wanted him to realize that she wasn't just another dumb, pretty girl, available to any star who beckoned. Maybe then he would leave her alone.

'Sonofabitch!' muttered Al in disgust.

'We go now?' inquired Violette.

'Just another roll. Only one.'

'You'll lose again.'

'I like faith. Can't you try positive thinking?'

'I try. But your luck is *merde*.'

'Your enthusiasm kills me.'

Carefully he covered the table. Cheval twenty-six and twenty-nine. A wad of chips on red. Cover seven, eleven, seventeen, twenty, thirty-five. Musn't forget twenty-five and thirty-two.

The croupier spun the wheel. Al sucked in his breath. The ball rolled lazily round. Come on you bastard. He was down by ten thousand pounds. Enough by anyone's standards, three years' wages when he had been working on the roads.

Come on baby – roll into one of my numbers. The ball jumped into thirty-five, wavered, jumped out and landed firmly on twenty-six.

'Baby!!' screamed Al, and he looked up in time to see Dallas. For a moment he forgot about winning, and thought, Jesus Christ, I have to have her. Then he noticed the small elderly man with her, and his eyes swivelled back to the pile of chips being propelled towards him. With gambler's instinct he let the cheval on twenty-six ride, doubling it. It came up again. He had known it would. While Dallas was there he was a winner.

'Don't you gamble at all?' Dallas asked, her eyes scanning the room finding Al, and returning satisfied to Ed.

'It's a fools' game, for children.'

'But you love games,' she squeezed his hand, '*I* should know.'

He allowed himself a smile.

She nuzzled close to him. 'One drink and you can take me home to play, OK?'

'Yes.'

Paul had been trying his luck at blackjack. Gambling wasn't really his scene, but he didn't mind playing for fun, and anything was better than standing behind Al watching him go beserk. He saw Dallas come in, and recognized Ed Kurlnik at once. So here was the reason that she didn't want to know about Al. Sonofa-bitch. No wonder she played it cool. Ed Kurlnik. Who would have believed it.

He scooped up his minimal winnings and went right over to them.

Dallas was charm itself, carrying out introductions, and asking innocently, 'Is Al here?'

'He's playing roulette.'

'Why don't you all join us for a drink?'

'Great. I'll see if I can tear Al away.'

Ed was not pleased. As Paul departed he instructed, 'Tell them we just bumped into each other.'

Dallas widened tiger eyes. 'Of course, baby. I'm a friend of your wife's in New York. Or shall I be a friend of your daughter's?'

Ed pursed his lips. What kind of fool was he to be seen in public with this girl. He should have kept her shut away. He should *never* have arranged for her to win that beauty contest. She was changing from the lovely innocent girl he had first met in Los Angeles. She was becoming pushy.

Eventually Al came strolling over hand in hand with Violette. 'Why don't we go to Regines?' he suggested, 'it's just next door.'

Ed was quite pleased at meeting Violette Victor. He had seen a private screening of her new film where she had performed a most explicit sex act with another girl. He wondered if Dallas would consider ... Maybe later ...

The five of them went to Regines, an exclusive discotheque overlooking the sea, where they were given the best table in the room, and where the disc jockey immediately played Al's most famous record 'Random Love'.

'An oldie but a goodie,' Paul laughed. God, that record had been the beginning of it all.

Violette, realizing who Ed Kurlnik was, and being no slouch, engaged him in a lengthy conversation about a film she wanted to do, but for which nobody would put up the money as it was a very offbeat project.

Dallas let her have him. She wasn't jealous, she knew whose bed he would be in later

She sipped her Pernod on the rocks, and exchanged stares across the table with Al.

Women kept coming up to him, whispering little messages, giggling, slipping him notes.

'Doesn't it drive him mad?' Dallas asked Paul.

74

He shrugged. 'He's used to it, it's part of the game. Did anyone show you the papers today?'

'No . . . Why?'

'You and Al are all over them.'

'I'd love to see them.'

'I'll see you get copies.'

'Thanks.' Was he being nice to her now that he had discovered Ed Kurlnik was her man? No longer was she being treated as just another little ding-a-ling to lure to Al's caravan for a quick one.

Al removed a faded blonde from his left shoulder and stood up. 'Dance?' he questioned Dallas.

She glanced at Ed deep in conversation, and stood up also. 'I guess there's nothing better to do around here.'

The record was Ben E. King's 'Supernatural Thing' and Al started to gyrate his hips in the way he had made famous all over the world.

'You move like a stud waiting for some action,' laughed Dallas.

'That's just the way it is. Want some?'

'No thanks.'

'OK, big eyes. Just don't come begging later.'

'I promise I won't'

'Promises are made to be broken.'

They danced silently, enjoying the feeling of togetherness the beat gave them.

Bobbie had taught Dallas how to dance. 'You gotta let it all hang loose,' she had instructed, 'pretend you're balling a really *fantastic* guy – just let go – ya dig?'

Dallas had understood exactly what she meant, but had never put it into practice until now.

'Supernatural Thing' faded away, and Aretha came on at her best, singing 'You'll Never Get to Heaven'. Al pulled her close, very close, and they rocked silently together on the crowded dance floor. Like a roller coaster the feeling hit Dallas again. Great waves of sexual excitement.

She could feel him grow hard against her thigh, and she pressed towards him shutting her eyes.

'Let's get out of here,' he murmured.

'Let's not,' she whispered back, but her voice was shaky and she had to struggle for control.

'You mean to tell me you're really tight with the old guy?'

'That's right.'

'Bullshit.'

75

'Let's sit down.'

'Let's wait till I'm in suitable shape to sit down.'

She drew away from him. 'Can I get you a glass of cold water?'

'Only if you personally throw it over my cock!'

She couldn't help smiling. A man who gave her incredible sexual waves *and* made her smile. Impossible. If things had been different maybe she would have done something about it. But no. She was too smart. She had been around. Stars. They were all the same. Wham bam. Thank you M'am. Then on to the next little pushover.

Back at the table Ed was getting restless. 'I'll drop you at your hotel,' he told Dallas, fooling no one. 'Where are you staying?'

'The Hotel de Paris,' she replied demurely.

'See you tomorrow,' said Al, 'bright and early.'

'Goodnight,' said Ed, and to Violette, 'don't forget to write me the details.'

As they were leaving Dallas clung tightly onto Ed's arm. 'What was *that* all about?' she asked.

'She needs backers for her new film.'

'Ooh – backers, huh? And what would she give *you* in return?'

'Don't be stupid.'

'Stupid I'm not. You fancy her, don't you? Come on, tell me the truth, I don't mind. Come on, daddy . . .' Half laughing she threw her arms around him. And that was the precise moment when the camera flashed, and Ed Kurlnik and Dallas had their first photograph taken together.

fourteen

The scandal affected all three of them. The newspapers pounced on the situation with glee, and the photographs of Al and Dallas taken at the location were used in conjunction with the one of her and Ed leaving the nightclub so that it looked like she was conducting two different love affairs at the same time.

Denials came thick and fast.

After threatening to sue the photographer, Ed Kurlnik stated that Dallas was merely a casual acquaintance who had happened to be leaving the nightclub at the same time as him.

Wasn't it strange, replied the newspapers, that Mr Kurlnik happened to have been a judge on the 'Miss Coast to Coast' competition. And by further coincidence, was he aware of the fact that he and Dallas happened to have adjoining suites at the Hotel de Paris? They had been wanting to get something on Ed Kurlnik for years, and this was the perfect opportunity.

Al made a formal statement to the effect that he and Dallas were merely professional colleagues, and he couldn't understand the fuss, as everyone knew he had been happily married for sixteen years.

Dallas safely said 'No comment' as she had been advised to do in a sharp phone call from Beauty Incorporated.

Ed had flown immediately back to the safety of Dee Dee and Fire Island. 'We'll discuss it next week,' he had tersely told Dallas, 'just don't admit anything.'

She had finished the taping of the television special. There had only been half a day's work left, and an attentive Nicky had taken her to the airport. Al had been friendly but cool, he made no more mention of personal matters. End of the affair that never was.

Back in New York she received a lecture from Beauty Incorporated on the morals of being 'Miss Coast to Coast', and they hinted that if there were any further scandals they would have to think seriously of asking for her resignation.

Her phone never stopped ringing. Chat shows. Interviews. Playboys around town. She waited for the call from Bobbie, but it never came. That was *one* good thing.

She enjoyed all the attention she was receiving, so much so that she took no notice of the fact that there was no word from Ed. He would be scared to appear in her life again too soon. He would want a little time for things to simmer down. In the meantime she could enjoy her notoriety. Although she didn't feel she could go as far as accepting any dates. If she went out with anyone it was bound to be publicized, and Ed wouldn't like that. Or would he? It might be good to be seen out. She could always tell Ed it was to protect him.

She didn't quite know what to do until Ed solved the problem. He waited a week, and then a male secretary appeared at the apartment and packed up all his personal belongings. Dallas watched the secretary numbly. When he was finished he handed her a typed envelope and inside was the lease for the apartment in her name, and a cheque for ten thousand dollars. Bastard! Who did Ed Kurlnik think he was?

She could not believe that he would treat her in this way. She tried to contact him, but he had changed his private office number. For a while she was in a state of shock. Ed had been her passport to a whole new life. With him behind her she had felt completely protected. And now what did she have? Some ratty title, and a bit of half-assed fame. The thought had always hovered at the back of her mind that one day the immaculate Dee Dee would be divorced, and that she – Dallas – would become Mrs Ed Kurlnik.

Ten thousand dollars. What a paltry pay off *that* was from a man of his wealth. Why, goddamn it, he was treating her like some little hooker. The irony of that was not lost on her.

She went out on the town with anyone who asked, drank too much, and was photographed everywhere. Let Ed Kurlnik see how much he mattered to *her*. Let him eat his heart out – senile old fool.

Beauty Incorporated called her in for yet another lecture on morals. She had certain standards to keep up. The unseemly publicity would have to stop.

She made a half-hearted effort. Stayed home two nights in a row, stopped drinking. Then the contract with the wool firm fell through just when she was on the point of signing. Not quite the right public image, she was told. Screw that.

Beauty Incorporated wanted her to go on a field trip to entertain troops abroad with Manny Shorto, a randy old comedian. 'How much?' she asked.

'The publicity is enough,' was their answer.

Screw *that*. 'I want to make some money,' she told them, '*real* money.'

'You're very uncooperative,' they replied. 'Frankly, the best thing would be if you resigned.'

No way.

Days later Beauty Incorporated fired her, and Miss Miami Beach stepped simperingly into her shoes. The newspapers went to town on that one.

Dallas didn't care. She had a movie test to do, and a lucrative contract for a suntan commercial which she had arranged herself. She had also met Kip Rey, nineteen-year-old heir to the family shoe fortune. He was tall and blond, and the ex-fiancé of Ed's lovely daughter Dana. Somehow it seemed like poetic justice.

They had met at a party. She had gone to use the john, and Kip was already in occupation, throwing up.

'Hey – you all right?' she asked.

'If I was all right I wouldn't be spewing up the godawful food they served at dinner. You drive?'

'Yes.'

'Take me home.'

She had been at the party with a faceless man that she couldn't care less about. She didn't mind dumping him.

'Sure,' she agreed.

He had a Maserati parked in the street, and she had some trouble with the gear shift, but he instructed her, and she soon got it together.

They ended up driving down to Coney Island and paddling in the sea. They shared a few joints, and he made her laugh. He didn't want anything from her, so she started to see him every night.

He was a young man with a lot of problems. He hated his rich family, didn't want to work in the family bisuness, and used drugs like they were going out of style.

'Bad news,' Linda Cosmo informed her on one of their lunches.

'But I can relax with him,' protested Dallas, 'he doesn't hassle me.'

She and Linda met regularly. They got along exceptionally well, and Linda took incredible photos of her. They had already had five magazine covers.

'How did you and Al make out?' Linda had inquired upon her return from Europe.

'We didn't,' had been Dallas's somewhat terse reply.

'Good,' Linda had announced firmly – and that had been that.

Dallas did find herself thinking about him sometimes. His black eyes and hard body. Al King. SuperCock. Yes. She had made the right decision. Who needed to be just another one of the girls?

Kip took her to Puerto Rico for the weekend, and they stayed at a friend's house, and spent the entire three days bombed out of their minds on a variety of goodies that Kip supplied. They slept together for the first time.

Dallas felt nothing. His tall blond body did nothing for her. No waves. No jolts. Just plain professional fucking. No charge, kind sir, I am out of the business now. I don't even have to fake orgasms. I can be my good old-fashioned self.

'Don't you enjoy it?' he would mumble, too stoned to really care.

She would stare at him and not reply. What was there to enjoy when your body was anesthetized?

They played James Taylor and Dylan records, ate chocolate, went riding and swimming.

The night before they returned to New York he broke down

and cried. 'I'm no good,' he confided, 'I'm a weak sonofabitch. I don't even know how you can stand to be with me.'

Dallas shrugged. 'I like you, it's that simple.' But if she was truthful she would admit that the only reason she liked him was because he made no demands on her.

'I'm rich,' he told her, 'goddamn rich. When I'm twenty-one I get over three million dollars, then the bastards can't touch me. Let's get married, Dallas.'

She agreed. It seemed like a wonderful idea. Only she knew his family would never allow it, and it was two years before he was twenty-one.

They announced their engagement. Once more she made headlines.

Kip was whisked back to the family compound in New York to explain matters.

Dallas had to fly to Los Angeles to shoot the sun tan commercial, and do the screen test.

Kip assured her everything would be all right. They would meet again in a week's time in New York and discuss their plans.

Going back to Los Angeles made her nervous. So many bad memories. However, everyone connected with the commercial couldn't have been nicer. She worked hard all day, and collapsed exhausted into bed at night. Kip didn't call, but then she didn't expect him to.

She had a bungalow at the Beverly Hills Hotel and remembered the writer she had lived with there. Where was he now? Would he remember her? Out of curiosity she called the desk to inquire of his whereabouts, but they knew nothing of him.

When the commercial was finished she made her screen test. All the time she was there she half expected Bobbie to appear, but she never did. Maybe she had died – trashed out on one of her drug trips – what a relief *that* would be.

On the day that she was due to fly back to New York, Kip Rey was found dead of a drug overdose.

fifteen

Brighton was sunny, hot and crowded with day trippers. It was a mistake.

Al and Edna arrived at lunchtime, checked into the hotel, and by four o'clock they were on their way home.

'I don't know why I listen to you,' Al ranted. 'Paul said it was a ridiculous idea. Brighton for crissakes!'

'I thought it would be nice,' ventured Edna timidly.

'Nice!' roared Al, 'With me getting pawed by every little old lady in sight. I've bought you a beautiful home where we have absolute privacy. What's with the Brighton bit?'

'We spent our honeymoon there.'

'That's because I couldn't afford anywhere else. Grow up, Edna, don't go chasing the past.'

'Slow down, Al, you drive too fast.'

'Don't nag. You're becoming a prize nagger lately.'

Her eyes filled with tears. How could she nag him when she hardly ever saw him?

'I've been thinking,' she ventured.

He grunted.

'I've been thinking it would be a good idea for me to come with you on the tour. Not *all* the time, just when Evan is with you.'

'What the hell for?' he snapped. 'You don't even want *me* to go, you've made *that* clear. And anyway – you hate the whole bit – photos, questions. No, Edna, you stay at home, I'll feel happier that way.'

'But I *want* to come. We're never together any more.'

'No, Edna.' His tone of voice indicated that he no longer wished to discuss the subject, so Edna lapsed into a miserable silence.

He had returned from the South of France, furious

She had hardly dared mention the fact that the Engliss press were going to town on his so-called romance with Dallas. 'There's no truth in it, is there?' she had finally asked.

'Are you kidding? Don't tell me they've got you believing it now?'

'Of course not.' And she felt guilty for ever having listened to Melanie.

When Edna had suggested Brighton, to her surprise, Al had said yes. They had left the very next day, and now, only a few hours later they were on their way home.

'With this traffic we'll be lucky to make it by seven,' he grumbled, 'I should have brought the chauffeur. I don't know why I let you talk me out of it.' He zoomed out of lane to overtake, and shuddering, Edna hunched down in her seat.

'All set,' leered Nelson, pocketing the five pounds Evan had just handed him. 'She'll be here at six, back door. Let her in and take her up to your room.' He snickered. 'You'll find her a willing little partner. Don't be shy now.'

'I'm never shy,' said Evan aggressively. Although secretly he was shaking with fear at the very thought of it all.

'What's her name?'

'Her name? Oh – er, her name. Let me see now – Trudie, yes that's it – Trudie. Ever such a pretty bit. Better than the magazines – Oh yes, better than the magazines.' And he nudged Evan sharply in the ribs. 'Don't forget now, six o'clock.'

'Six o'clock,' repeated Evan numbly.

Nelson left, and Evan consulted his watch. Four o'clock. Two hours to wait. He didn't know how he would get through them. Thank goodness his parents were away for the weekend. To have the house to himself was a golden opportunity not to be missed.

He raided the bar and took a bottle of vodka and some glasses to his room. He drank a little of it, and felt his courage grow.

By six o'clock he was waiting anxiously by the back door. By six-thirty he was walking down the road looking for Trudie. By seven o'clock he was back in his bedroom with the realization that he had been conned. There was no Trudie, Nelson had been lying. And who could he complain to about his five pounds? Nelson knew that there was no one he dared tell. Sod rotten Nelson. He drank some more of the vodka, and never even heard his parents arrive home.

Al was in one of his moods. He screamed abuse at Edna. Stupid cow. 'I'm going out,' he announced, 'on the piss with the boys, so don't wait up.'

'But you haven't had a thing to eat, I'll make some . . .'.

He slammed the door in her face. Jesus, but he was uptight. He needed thawing out. He jumped into the Ferrari and roared next door.

Melanie answered the door. Brittle, horny, little Melanie. 'What happened to Brighton?'

'Piss on Brighton. Where's Paul?'

'He's at the office. Why don't you come in anyway?'

'I'm going to the pub, tell him to meet me there.'

'I could make you a drink.'

'Thanks but no thanks.'

She laid a hand lightly on his arm. 'Why not?'

He shook himself free. 'I'm not that much of a bastard.'

'And I am. Is that what you're saying?'

'One time was bad enough.'

'Oh, thanks a lot, you certainly know how to make a person feel good.'

'Melanie, sweetheart, I'm in no mood to mince words. You wanted a fuck one night – I gave it to you. I've felt pretty lousy about it ever since. Nothing personal but I don't ever want to repeat the exercise.'

She smiled tightly. 'I was offering you a drink, Al, that's all, a drink.'

'Terrific. But if you don't mind I'll get it at the pub.'

He jumped back into the Ferrari and roared off. He would always regret having given Melanie one. It had been a mistake, and one he hoped she would never be stupid enough to tell Paul.

At his office Paul checked the final arrangements for the tour. It was all looking good, tickets were selling briskly, Bernie Suntan was doing a marvellous publicity campaign. They would open up in Canada to iron out any kinks, then straight into the big one at Madison Square Garden, New York.

He placed a call to Linda. He seemed to be missing her more than ever. She was out, and he wondered where. Did she go out with other men when he wasn't there? He had never asked her, but suddenly he was feeling very possessive, and if she did, it would have to stop. Lately he was fantasizing how it would be if he was married to her and not to Melanie. Would it be great? Or would it be great for a couple of years and then turn into the state of war that existed between most married couples he knew?

It was only a dream anyway. He could never leave his kids.

Edna unpacked the suitcase that only earlier in the day she had so carefully packed for Brighton.

Al was so touchy lately. She knew he was worried about the tour, but why did he have to take it out on her?

She put her new nightdress on the bed. It was long and blue with discreet frills round the dipped neckline. She would wear it tonight. Al needed her. And when he got home she was prepared to forget the rantings and ravings. She would put him to bed and comfort him. She would do the things he had often urged her to do in the early days of their marriage, things that she had always considered slightly dirty and perverted. That would surprise him. That would please him.

That would at last make him *notice* her.

In the private bar of his local pub Al found plenty of hangers-on to sit with. They laughed at his jokes, allowed him to buy them drinks, and basked in his limelight.

He relaxed in their company. He forgot about Brighton and Edna and the whole aggravating day. He boozed it up on Scotch and Coke and became suitably drunk. He realized in the middle of it all how unhappy he was. He had everything. And yet he had nothing. Was that it? Was the fact that there was nothing left to reach for the reason for his unhappiness?

God, but he needed the tour. He needed to get away. He needed Dallas.

Needed Dallas? He almost laughed aloud. How had *she* crept into his train of thought? Some two bit broad with a rich boyfriend and a body. Who needed her?

But she was a challenge. She would give as good as she got. And how! Christ, he got horny just thinking about her, and that *was* unusual.

Now all that newspaper shit had petered out maybe he would see her again in New York. Not too long to wait. He would get Paul to arrange it . . . Yeah – good idea.

Paul arrived in time to drive him home. He was in no fit state to do so himself.

Edna met him at the front door and helped him up to bed. She laid him down and undressed him. He shut his eyes while the world weaved up and down.

Her hands stopped as they drew off his undershorts, and although he wasn't hard her head bent to kiss him.

He imagined himself in a shuttered hotel room with yet another fan and he pushed her away. 'Leave me alone,' he muttered. 'Why don't you all just leave me the fuck alone.'

Evan woke up with a splitting headache and a dreadful sour taste in his mouth. He lay in bed wondering what to say to Nelson. He wanted his money back, maybe he would threaten to tell his mother. Nelson would laugh and jeer and call his bluff.

Nelson wouldn't give him back his money. Evan knew that for sure.

Sun was streaming through the windows hurting his eyes. What are you supposed to do for a hangover?

He decided to take a shower in his father's bathroom, and was surprised upon reaching his parents' bedroom to find Al sprawled across the bed asleep. He had thought they were in Brighton. Wow – they must have come back early – perhaps it was just as well Trudie hadn't turned up. Evan blushed at the thought of his mother catching him with a girl. Crikey! She would have been furious.

Al suddenly stretched his arms and opened his eyes. 'Evan!' he exclaimed smiling, 'what's new, boyo?'

Evan clutched his pyjama trousers together, they gaped embarassingly. 'You're back,' he stated stupidly.

'No, we're still in Brighton,' Al laughed, and climbed out of bed. He was stark naked, and Evan's eyes rushed feverishly round the room searching for somewhere to focus other than his father's huge penis.

'Gotta take a piss,' Al said, 'don't go away, I've been wanting us to rap, but I never seem to *see* you. Where do you go all the time? Got yourself a girlfriend?'

'No,' muttered Evan, wishing he could tell his father about Nelson, but too ashamed to.

'Come on, a randy little sod like you.' The sound of Al peeing in the bathroom filled the room.

Evan edged towards the door. Perhaps his father wouldn't notice him go.

Al strolled cheerfully back in the bedroom. He was still naked, but to Evan's relief the size of his penis had subsided. Vaguely he wondered if his father was deformed. Or, crikey – maybe he – Evan – had an exceptionally small one. He would brood on *that* subject later.

Al was scratching his stomach. He studied his son. God, the kid was scrawny. He needed building up, he had no muscles. And that hair, shoulder-length grease.

'If you want to come on the tour you'll have to cut off some of that hair.'

'Why?'

'Because it doesn't suit you, that's why. It looks like shit, don't you ever wash it?'

'Sometimes.'

'I wash mine every two days, and I have it cut and styled every six weeks. I think I'll take you with me next time. You've got to be more aware of your personal appearance.'

'Why?' sneered Evan, 'I'm not a *pop* star.'

'No, and you never will be if you look like that.'

'Don't want to be.'

'OK. OK. Nobody is forcing you. What are you doing today? Want to come to rehearsal?'

'No thanks.'

'Want some money? Are you going out?'

'Can I have five pounds?'

'Sure, take it, only don't tell your mother, you know she doesn't like me giving you money.'

Evan grabbed five pounds from the dresser. Edna insisted he manage on three pounds a week pocket money, at least Al understood *that* side of things.

'I'll see you at dinner then,' said Al.

Evan nodded. 'I can come on the tour, can't I?' he blurted out, 'you promised I could. And *she's* not coming, is she?'

'Who's *she*?'

'Ma.'

'No she's not, and don't call your mother she. Maybe I'll take you.'

'You promised.'

'I didn't promise, I said maybe I'll take you. Don't hassle me. Get your hair cut and we'll see.'

Al threw himself into weeks of vigorous rehearsal schedule. He worked all day, and at night was exhausted and uncommunicative. Then he would come home, work out in his gym, eat a spartan meal, and collapse in bed.

Again he read about Dallas in the newspapers. It seemed you couldn't help reading about her, everything she did seemed to make news – from getting fired as 'Miss Coast to Coast' to getting engaged to some rich kid. It all seemed to happen so fast.

Al felt sorry for her – he had really liked her, and maybe without all the hysterical publicity they could have got something together. But he had a certain public image to maintain – and he wasn't stupid enough to blow it for an affair that would last how long? A week? Two weeks? Forget it.

Meanwhile the newspapers kept on dragging up the same old pictures of him with her from the television special, and hinting at a great romance still lingering on. He wanted to laugh. He hadn't even seen or spoken to her since the South of France. And he certainly had never given her one.

On the Saturday before Al went off to a health farm, Edna invited Melanie and Paul to dinner. Al decided he wanted one last blow out before starvation, so they went to Tiberio, a fashionable Italian restaurant in Mayfair.

Edna was uncomfortable. She was supposed to open up the conversation about joining the tour, then Melanie would back her up. Words stuck in her throat, and they were at the coffee stage before Melanie finally flashed: 'Only another week and you two will be off, how lucky can you get.'

Paul snorted. 'Lucky indeed. It's a circus.'

'Don't you think,' ventured Edna, 'It would be nice if Melanie and I joined you, maybe in California.'

'It's not *your* cup of tea, Edna. You would hate every minute of it. Crowds. Riots. *You* know what these things are like.' Paul paused, and waited for Al to join in, but Al was playing eyes across a crowded room with a young movie actress, and was not about to be interrupted. Paul plunged on. 'Of course I know Al would love to have you there, as I know I would love to see Melanie. But these trips are murder, and we wouldn't subject you to it.'

'I think,' said Melanie sharply, 'it would be fun. Don't you think so, Edna?'

'Yes, I'd like to be with Al, I'm sure I could put up with a little discomfort.'

'So!' stated Melanie brightly, 'let's arrange it. We can meet you in Los Angeles. Edna and I can do some shopping, and get some sun. It will be like a holiday for us.'

Paul frowned. The thought of Melanie and Linda face to face was too much to bear. 'Al,' he said sharply, 'what do you think?'

Al was dragged reluctantly into the conversation.

'Forget it,' he said, 'I've promised Evan the trip and you know what he's like, Edna, he'll think you're spying on him.'

'But, Al . . .'

'Stop nagging. I'll take you for a holiday when we get back.'

'If you've got the energy,' murmured Melanie, sourly.

'I'll have the energy,' Al replied sharply.

Melanie flushed. 'It looks to me like they don't *want* us along. Will we cramp your style?'

'Oh for Christ sake shut up,' interrupted Paul.

'Why? I've heard what goes on when you go on one of these

tours. Little groupie girls to cater to your every whim.'

'I said *shut up*, Melanie.'

'Don't get excited. Edna and I will stay at home like good wives, only don't be surprised if we turn up somewhere along the way to *surprise* you. A flying visit, now you couldn't object to that, could you?'

Paul signalled for the bill. The conversation was progressing in decidedly the wrong direction.

Edna brooded on Melanie's remarks, and when they were in bed she said to Al, 'Have you ever been unfaithful?'

He yawned. 'What kind of a crappy question is that? It's one o'clock in the morning, go to sleep.'

'I know you must be exposed to temptation. I know it can't be easy for you. What about that Dallas?'

'Edna, be a good girl. Stop listening to your cunty sister-in-law and go to sleep.'

'You know it's not easy for me to talk about things like this. You haven't made love to me for months. Is there someone else?'

'Jesus, Edna. Are you complaining? There are other things on my mind besides sex.'

'I've never refused you.'

He knew that. She lay on her back, parted her legs, and expected him to do all the work. Well, he just couldn't fancy that scene any more. 'I know, I'm just off sex, that's all.'

'I could,' she hesitated, 'well, you know, I could put you in my mouth like you always wanted me to.' She could feel the blush sting her face.

Al sighed. Oh no, Edna. It's too late, Edna. Oh Jesus! 'I'm tired. We'll talk tomorrow.' He turned his back. As far as he was concerned his marriage was over. The only problem was telling her.

Thank Christ for the tour. A chance to get away, think things out. He drifted into sleep, lurched into a nightmare. He was on stage. He was fat, and he was old, and when he opened his mouth to sing nothing came out. In his sleep he moved into the comfort and security of Edna.

book two The tour

sixteen

Bernie Suntan was sweating. What the fuck? Whoever sweated in London? Who knew it was a razzle dazzle heatwave for crissakes?

His blue and white striped cotton trousers stuck uncomfortably to his thighs. His red T-shirt emblazoned with AL IS KING was damp with perspiration. His feet flopped damply in his stars and stripes sneakers.

Paul King, beside him, was the picture of cool. Pale beige Yves Saint Laurent lightweight suit. Striped shirt. Dark shades.

They were at London Airport waiting for the star. Everyone else was aboard.

The plane, sleek and black, loaded with champagne, caviar, and liberal supplies of scotch and coke, waited patiently on the tarmac. AL IS KING decorated each side in bold gold lettering. From within, speakers roared out with the sound of Al's latest album.

An elite group of press waited on the tarmac, sipping iced Daiquiri cocktails, and nibbling small smoked salmon delicacies handed round by a bikini-clad hostess.

'What the fuck—' expanded Bernie, 'nothing but the best for the press.' And he winked at a lady interviewer of great power, and said, 'I never knew you had such insane legs!'

She blushed, taken aback for the first time in years.

Al's arrival was heralded by the white Rolls gliding over the tarmac and stopping nose to nose with the plane. The photographers jumped forward. On cue Al climbed out.

He was as thin and fit as possible. White trousers clung. A gold belt. White shirt open to the waist. Several gold medallions.

He grinned, strolled over, kissed the girls, posed for photos, answered questions.

'I must say you do look marvellous, Al,' enthused the lady reporter.

'Thank you, darling.' Bitch. Cunt. It was she that had written in her column only a few months previously that if Al King had anything else lifted the whole lot would collapse. He kissed her on the cheek for a photo, and nearly recoiled at the aroma of BO.

'Is this the start of a tax exile?' inquired one over-zealous reporter.

'No way,' replied Al, 'I'd miss my wife's cooking too much!'

'What about the former "Miss Coast to Coast". Will you be seeing her?' asked Bitch. 'I understand you two were quite cosy on that television special you did together.'

Al smiled calmly. 'My wife might see her. As I've said before they're old mates, perhaps if Edna joins me we will all get together.'

'What fun!' Bitch sneered unbelievingly. She needed a good seeing-to, that was her problem. 'And *will* Edna be joining you?'

'I hope so.' No way.

'How about having the girls out for a picture with Al?' suggested Bernie.

Everyone agreed it was a good idea, and 'The Promises' were called from the plane.

They were three stunning black girls. Rosa, at twenty-three, the eldest. Tall and reed-slim, with straight long hair and Chinese eyes. Sutch, twenty, curvy body and afro red hair. Nellie, small and slight, seventeen years old, delicately pretty. They wore identical outfits of white hot pants, thigh length white boots, and AL IS KING red T-shirts. They grouped round Al, and the cameras clicked.

Paul glanced at his watch. Time to go. He gave Bernie the word. Linda was meeting the plane in Canada, he didn't want to keep her waiting.

It took another half hour before everyone was safely aboard and the plane was finally taxi-ing down the runway.

Al went right back to his private bedroom, an elaborate room – featuring a circular bed, leopard print padded walls, and thick pile carpet. A small bathroom led off to one side reached through a concealed door. He stripped off his clothes, put on a towelling dressing gown and picked up the glass of iced champagne waiting for him. Forget the scotch and Coke for a while, too fattening. He smoked a cigar. This was it. This was the beginning, and he could feel a mounting excitement that nothing else compared with. Not even sex. And when had *that* last been exciting.

Maybe he should see a doctor. Hey doc, I've got this slight problem – too many beautiful girls, can't seem to be *bothered* any more. Can't seem to make the effort.

Paul came through. 'Everything all right?'

'Fine. Terrific.'

'Voice OK?'

'Never better.'

'Great, kid. You'll kill 'em!'

'Don't I always?'

Girls screamed when Al disembarked at Toronto. There was a healthy crowd. Banners proclaiming 'WE LOVE AL.' Policemen to protect him, hustle him to his limousine, ride him to his hotel.

His elation was building. Adrenalin flowing.

At the hotel there were flowers, fruit, booze, telegrams. A young girl smuggled her way in with room service and begged to suck his cock. When he declined she offered to suck Bernie's because he was 'close' to Al. Security removed her.

'Things ain't changed,' shrugged Al, 'Christ but it's good to be back!'

'What the fuck,' agreed Bernie, 'this is one scene that splits your head open more ways than one. We'll have a time, Al baby. Anything you want, just yell.'

Should he yell for Dallas, or should he put her out of his mind where she belonged? If he could forget about her that would be the best thing. Just another body, and he would be falling over them on this trip. He would not yell. He did not want her *that* badly. He would survey the available action and put Dallas away once and for all.

'You get some sleep,' suggested Bernie, 'Luke gonna put in time outside the door. He's a tight guy, be beside you all the way – but *nobody* gets past him. I tell you he's the bionic man. Anyway I'm goin' over to check out the Gardens. Pick you up for the television interview in a coupla hours.'

Bernie waddled off. Al opened the door and checked out Luke, who was to be his bodyguard on the trip. The bionic man was right. Luke was six feet four, black, and mean-looking. His muscles rippled before he even moved.

'Hey there, man,' greeted Al, 'want a beer or something?'

Luke shook his head.

Al went back in his room. Time to shower. Order a steak. More champagne. Gargle, So where was Paul?

Should he call Edna? He had promised he would. But he didn't feel like listening to her moans. He had promised Evan he could join the tour in Nashville, and Edna had wanted to come too. No way. No thank you. After sixteen years Edna was nagging her way right out of his life.

'I've missed you,' confessed Paul.

Linda hugged him, 'I've missed *you*, twice as much.'

'Only twice as much?'

'Well . . .' she laughed softly, 'maybe more. How was London?'

'The same. Work, work, and more work.'

'But you love it.'

'I wouldn't do it if I didn't love it.'

'Shall we stand here making small talk, or shall I slide you out of your lovely suit and have my way with you before big brother calls?'

'I wish you'd have your way with me. I don't think I can wait much longer.'

She grinned. 'You really have been missing me.'

'I really have.'

They started to undress each other, fumbling and pulling at belts and zippers.

'Oh my goodness, Paul, you've been saving up!'

'Just for you. I hope you appreciate what you're getting.'

They were silent for a while, delighting in each other, moving slowly, quietly. Then the phone rang. Paul groaned.

'Don't answer it,' begged Linda, 'at least not for a minute.'

The phone continued to jangle. 'I've lost my concentration,' Paul grumbled, reaching for the phone.

'That's not all you've lost.'

'Yeah, who is it?' he asked abruptly.

'Paul, boyo, where are you?'

'I'll be right there, Al. I was just coming.'

'Oh yes!' whispered Linda.

'Who are you with? Is Linda there?'

'Yes, she's here.'

'Bring her with you. Come on up, boyo. I'm fidgety, feel like a little company. Check out the lobby and see if there's anything worth giving one to.'

'What do you want, the groupie clap?'

'Shit. You're right. Who has numbers for Toronto? Find out and get me a piece, I need something before the show.'

'I'll try.' Paul shifted his body away from Linda.

'Do that.'

Linda sat up and reached for a cigarette. 'What did he want?' she asked tightly.

'To get laid.'

'Does he never stop?'

'I thought he had, but the urge is once again upon him. Pardon me while I make a few calls.'

'I didn't know you pimped for him too.'

'On tour I do everything for him. You had better get used to it.'

'Oh – that's great. Are we finished then? Shall I get dressed?'

Absently Paul replied, 'Yes.' He picked up the phone and called the desk.

Angrily Linda marched into the bathroom. One minute they had been making love – and now it seemed the furthest thing from Paul's mind. Well, he would have to beg for another chance. If this was a taste of Paul on tour he could shove it.

She dressed, brushed her hair, and touched up her make-up.

Paul came into the bathroom and nuzzled her from behind. 'All fixed,' he said cheerfully.

'Oh good.'

'What's the matter?'

'Nothing.' Her voice dripped sarcasm. 'Should there be?'

'Come on, Linda. You promised you would understand. We'll have plenty of time together later.'

She forced a smile. 'I understand.'

'Good girl. Come on, let's go, he's waiting.'

seventeen

Where had all the money gone?

Dallas shook herself awake from a massive hangover and surveyed the pile of bills that had just dropped through the mailbox.

She was spending faster than she was making. Ed Kurlnik's paltry pay-off she had blown on jewellery and furs. The money from the commercial she had frittered away. Clothes, clothes, clothes.

She squeezed orange juice, and sipped it slowly. What time had she arrived home? She could hardly remember, but she did remember with a smile fighting off Aarron Mack in his chauffeured limo. *The* Aarron Mack, Swedish czar of Mack Cosmetics. Friend of Ed Kurlnik. Old fart.

He could not believe that they were not going to end the evening in her bed. She had been giving him a strong come on all night. From the moment they had met at a party she had set him firmly in her sights. A friend of Ed Kurlnik's was far too good an opportunity to miss, even if he was somewhat older than Ed. He was in his early seventies, but well preserved, with a strong bullet head, and a fine set of white sparkly false teeth. Short though, barely five seven, and she towered over him in her Walter Steiger shoes. It didn't seem to put him off, he seemed to love it.

'Why not?' he had demanded when she wouldn't allow him to come up to her apartment.

'We've only just met,' she demurred.

'Are you an old-fashioned girl?' he had asked, grabbing for her breasts.

'No, but I like a little time to get to know a person.'

'You want money?'

'Please don't insult me.'

His hands were all over her. 'What *do* you want?'

She moved his hands. 'Time.'

'Dinner tomorrow?'

'I'm busy tomorrow.'

'The day after?'

'If you like.'

He squeezed her breast triumphantly, and she elbowed him sharply away. If she played her cards right Aarron Mack was a very viable proposition. His wife had recently died, and he was equally as rich as Ed Kurlnik.

Old rich men with hard-ons. It seemed to be her destiny. Kip Rey might have been her salvation; he had been fun to be with, but always so stoned, and sexually there had been the usual void. Absolutely no turn-on. She had cried at his death, but more at her loss than at his.

Since he had died she had slept with no one. There had been no reason to do so. She had thrown herself into the New York social scene. Getting fired had made her a celebrity, and she was invited to all the openings and parties. She enjoyed having her photo taken, and all the attention she received. She also enjoyed turning down countless sexual propositions. *That* was the real kick.

Men didn't understand her. She was young and beautiful, why wasn't she out fucking her brains out?

The doorbell rang. It was three dozen yellow roses and a box from Cartiers. She opened the box; it contained a diamond flower-shaped brooch. She tossed it to one side; might come in useful to sell one day.

Aarron Mack took her to dinner at The Four Seasons. She ordered caviar and Steak Diane, then left it all. She drank wine, and brandy, and Pernod on the rocks. Nowadays it took a lot of booze to get her where she wanted to be.

Later they went to Le Club, and they danced, his bullet head nuzzling discreetly against her bosom. She drank three Irish coffees, but obliteration seemed nowhere near. He suggested she visit his triplex penthouse for a nightcap. She agreed. Going up in the elevator he unzipped his fly and crammed her hand in. For an old man he was surprisingly erect. She snatched her hand away.

In the apartment they went out on the roof garden, and a butler appeared with champagne.

The city was spread out before them, a sea of lights.

'Get on your knees,' Aarron instructed.

One diamond brooch and she was supposed to get on her knees. Dallas laughed aloud.

'Please,' he added, and he was shaking himself free as if preparing to pee.

'No,' said Dallas slowly, 'you get on *your* knees.' And she opened the slit in her skirt provocatively.

'Later,' husked Aarron.

'Now,' insisted Dallas.

'I can give you wonderful presents,' Aarron promised, 'be a good girl and do as I ask.'

Dallas flicked her skirt briskly together. Her mind jumped back to a certain motel, an old man lying dead on the bed, Bobbie deftly pocketing his bankroll.

She turned to leave. 'I'm going home, Aarron. Find someone else to buy wonderful presents for.'

'You can't go,' he objected.

'Oh yes I can, I can do what the hell I like.'

She walked through the sumptuous apartment to the elevator. It could all have been hers if she had cared to get on her knees. But why should she? It didn't make her happy, nothing made her happy. For the thousandth time she wondered why her parents had never come looking for her. Life at the zoo with Phil sticking it in every night must have been better than this.

It occurred to her that if she went home and took an overdose of sleeping pills nobody would care. Not one single person. Maybe it wasn't such a bad idea after all.

She took a cab home. It was three o'clock in the morning. Idly she wondered if she had enough sleeping pills to do the job properly. How many did you need? The booze was finally hitting her, and by the time she arrived home she was weaving on her feet.

She nodded at the desk porter. He was asleep.

The apartment was on the fifth floor. The apartment that Ed Kurlnik had rented for her. The apartment where she had entertained him in so many different guises. He would be hard put to find a woman as versatile and imaginative as she was. Perhaps she should leave him a note. That would really put him away with Dee Dee. She couldn't understand why tears were rolling slowly down her cheeks, and yet she was smiling, giggling even.

She fumbled for her keys. Funny, the door seemed to be open, and there was a smell that she couldn't quite place.

She put her bag down on the hall table and groped for the light switch. Before she could reach it an arm enclosed her from behind. 'Don't scream,' a voice warned, 'I've got a knife and I'll split you from end to end. You hear me – bitch? You hear me?'

eighteen

Toronto was a sell-out. Fifteen thousand Al King fans waiting expectantly for the master.

Al was at tension pitch. Paul stayed solidly by his side. Whatever Al wanted, Al got.

It was hot. Before going on Al was sweating in the black satin jump suit that clung to him like a second skin. He swigged down a bottle of Perrier water, and watched from the side of the stage as 'The Promises' finished their set.

They rocked in unison – 'Easy baby – stay with me baby – give it to me baby – Easy baby.'

He could see the sweat rolling off their gleaming bodies and sticking to the suede skins swathed round their supple forms.

'Easy baby – make it baby – shake it baby – make me come . . . to you . . . OOOh baby . . . OOOh babee . . .'

The crowd roared its approval. 'The Promises' were just starting to hit it. Their latest record was zooming ahead in the charts.

Al had worked with them once before in Las Vegas, and they offset him perfectly.

They came running offstage, breathless, happy. 'The vibes are wailin' tonight, man,' said Rosa. 'Jeese – it is but *beeeautiful*!'

Al's musicians were starting up. The conga, the drums, the guitar, the tambourines.

He strode on stage.

'Who's gonna give it to you tonite
Who's got love that's outasite

I'm your lover
I'm your man
Hey momma – shake your can'

The crowd screamed. Al was one of the few white singers who sang soul the way it should be sung – the black way.

And yet that wasn't all. His amazing voice could turn from pure funk to sing the clearest ballad around and then double back to a horny throbbing rasp.

Out front Linda took photographs, and marvelled at the magic Al created on stage. It was almost as if he lifted the audience up and took them with him on his own private trip. She watched a girl shaken by her own tears. Another who simply could not look at him. Row upon row they were under his spell, wriggling, squirming, trying to keep the excitement under control but not succeeding. Then suddenly screaming, storming the stage, clawing at the security guards.

And Al, under the spotlight, singing, moving, thrusting, tempting them in his black satin, stretched tight over what appeared to be a giant cock.

'You wanna make it tonight
You wanna shake it tonight
We're gonna do it together
The way that we should
We're gonna love together,
Like I knew we would'

A thin, pale girl fainted, and was passed casually over people's heads and taken outside. By now everyone was standing, caught in his spell, rocking, swaying.

Al was caught up in his own spell. This was it. This was the ultimate. This was *the* orgasm. He could use his voice to far more effect than ever he did his cock. And his voice was ready, his whole body was ready.

He was making love to fifteen thousand people simultaneously and it was the absolute high. He never had got involved in the whole drug scene, and the reason was patently clear. Could a sniff of coke, a shot of H, a handful of mescalin, even begin to compared with this ? No way. No fuckin' way.

He was singing with his everything. His heart. His soul. His guts. And they knew it, and they loved him for it. And he was a part of them and vice versa.

When it was over he was drained, in a state of shock. Paul and

Luke bundled him under towels and raced him to a waiting car, and he was spirited away before the audience realized he was gone.

If the people had got hold of him they would have torn him to loving pieces.

He came out of it slowly. Back to reality, back to ground level. A shower. A massage. Gargle with the warm harshness of brandy.

'Incredible,' Paul told him, 'goddamn incredible.'

And he knew it was true. He never kidded himself on the quality of a performance. Relief flooded through him, and the tensions and insecurities of the previous few months were gradually exorcised. He had done it. He was better than ever. They had loved him. And *this* was only the first stop.

'Let's party,' he told Paul. 'Let's have us a time.'

Linda made her own way back to the hotel. She had no choice; by the time she got backstage Paul had vanished. Not that she expected him to be waiting for her, but he could have *told* her. She called his room, but there was no reply. She contemplated phoning him at Al's but decided against it.

She went downstairs to the lobby and bumped into Bernie. She had yet to prove her worth as a photographer and Bernie regarded her with a certain amount of suspicion. However, who wouldn't feel expansive after Al's performance. 'What the fuck,' said Bernie, 'you comin' to the party?'

'Wouldn't miss it. Where?'

'The Dragon suite. Go on down.'

She made her way to the lower level of the hotel and located the party.

Al and Paul were not there. It was full of newspaper reporters and Toronto personalities. 'The Promises' were flitting about being charming.

She took a glass of wine, and looked around for someone she knew. There were enough people connected with the tour, but no one she had really talked to. She sighed, wow – this was really going to be fun.

'Hello.'

She turned to confront the speaker.

He was a middle-aged man in a plaid suit with baggy eyes and a crew cut. 'Lonely?' he questioned.

'Not particularly,' she replied.

'I didn't think you *were*, I just thought you *might* be.'

'Thanks anyway, but I'm not.'

'The name's Hank Mason, newscasts are my game – Mason's the name.'

Linda looked desperately around for Paul.

'How's about us splitting from here, and I could take you to a nice cosy little place I know?'

'Thank you, but I'll pass.'

'Don't be like that. You looked lonely.' He belched discreetly. 'You're a pretty girl, don't get uppity with me for trying.'

'Look Mr er . . .'

'Mason.'

'Mason. I am not lonely. I appreciate your offer, now please leave me alone.'

He leered. 'I like 'em difficult.'

'Oh for Christ's sake – go away.'

'I bet you like 'em rough. A smack round the bottom – you like that, don't you?'

'Fuck off.'

'Or maybe you like girlies. Is that your kick?'

'Am I being too polite for your pin-sized brain? Go fuck yourself, buster.'

Before he could reply she saw Paul, and hurried over.

'Hi, sweetheart.' He kissed her absently. 'What are you doing down here?'

'Waiting for you.'

'You're in the wrong place.'

'How am I supposed to know that.'

'If you had waited in your room I would have told you. Wasn't Al sensational?'

She nodded. Maybe coming on the tour hadn't been such a good idea. Or maybe it had been a terrific idea. She was seeing a whole new Paul.

'Run upstairs and fetch your cameras, the party's in Al's suite.'

'Where are you going?'

'I've got to sort out some people here, I'll see you up there.'

So he hadn't even come looking for her. She frowned, but Paul was already drifting off. They were all shits, Dallas was right. They had become quite friendly in New York. Dallas was a toughie, but honest with it, and Linda had found that to be a surprisingly refreshing quality in a woman.

OK, Paul. I can be tough too. You want to play the casual bit, I can play too.

•

Al basked in it. He sat back and accepted the compliments. Christ, but he felt he deserved them. He had starved his ass off to be in prime physical shape, and rehearsed non stop for what seemed like months.

And it had all been worth it. God, the feeling he had now could not be beat. He was exhausted but elated. He felt like an athlete who has beaten every possible record.

The room was crowded with people anxious to join in his triumph. His musicians, a few select groupies, and a mixture of freaks who had talked their way in.

Three girls hovered nervously near him, ready for a wink, a nod, anything. They would slit each other's throats to get near him first should he give a signal.

He didn't bother. He felt perfectly satisfied. Anyway he had sent Paul off to look for some real local talent. Groupies gave him no charge. Beneath their bland young faces lay sharp little brains armed with tape measures and plaster casts.

He knew that he should call Edna. She would be waiting by the phone anxious to hear what had happened. But goddamn it, she had wanted him to fail, she had wanted him to stay home. She wouldn't be ecstatic about his success.

The Promises came flitting in. He had screwed Rosa that time they had been in Vegas. Once or twice between shows, it had been nice. But she had been involved with some gangster – and Al had decided the risk was not worth the prize. He wondered if he should renew old acquaintances. But getting involved with someone on the tour could turn out to be a drag. Whoever said never mix pleasure with business was a genius.

Rosa was coming over anyway. She kissed him. 'Babee, you were *the* best – you hear me – the best!'

He hugged her.

'We gonna have good times this trip, huh?'

'Yeah,' agreed Al. 'Oh yeah.'

nineteen

Dallas stood perfectly still. The arm that enclosed her from behind was steel-strong across her back. Fear shoved the alcohol out of her system, and she could feel the heavy, panic-stricken beating of her heart.

'Don't scream,' the voice warned again, 'and don't turn around.'

She recognized the smell. It was the strong aroma of pot hanging heavily in the air. Whoever it was in her apartment must have been there for some time. In the gloom she made out two suitcases stacked near the door, and her television set standing alongside them. She breathed a little easier. A robbery.

'Take the things and go,' she whispered. 'I won't do anything, I won't call the police.'

'Shut up.' The arm tightened round her neck, and the front door was kicked shut.

She could not see her assailant, but from the sound of his voice he was youngish. She could feel his body up against her. He was tall and skinny.

They stood silently in the darkness, then suddenly, inexplicably, he started to rub himself against her.

Oh God! She felt the vomit rise in her throat. He was going to rape her.

She was wearing a long silk jersey dress with nothing underneath, and his free hand roughly plunged into the top of it and released her breasts.

He giggled, a high-pitched maniacal laugh. 'Better than the grandma I had last week,' he boasted, 'she had tits on her like hangin' onions!'

She started to shake, shivers racking her body.

'I like 'em young,' the voice continued, rubbing the palm of his hand roughly across her breasts, 'young an' juicy with big tits. You like big cocks? I got a big one, m'am. You are gonna see a whopper.' He released his arm from around her neck, and both hands grabbed her breasts. 'Shall I give it to you up the ass?' he asked conversationally, 'I did that to a girl the other day, she screamed and hollered. You wouldn't do that, would you? I had to cut her a little to make her stop, real little cut across her throat.' He laughed again. 'Man, she sure was *screamin*'. I . . .'

Dallas spun suddenly round, arms crossed over her exposed breasts, eyes blazing with fury.

She was right. He couldn't have been more than eighteen. He had no knife, and he stepped back in surprise.

'Well?' blazed Dallas, 'where's your big cock then? I thought it would be ready for me. I like 'em big. Big and juicy. You got a juicy one, sonny? Want to show it to me?'

He looked alarmed.

'*Come on*,' insisted Dallas, 'don't tell me you're all talk?' she took her hands away from her breasts. 'Nice, huh? Big, huh? Just the way you like 'em.'

'What are you?' he muttered nervously, 'some kind of nut, some freak . . .' He was backing towards the door.

'Don't go,' said Dallas, 'thought we were going to have a little *rape* here. Come on, sonny, show me what you got. I *like* it up the ass, do you? Come one, sweetie. Or can you only get it up when you have some scared shitless woman on the floor? Well? Is that it?' Her voice became taunting, 'Only get it up *then*, sonny, is that right?'

'Jesus!' He opened the door. 'You're mad, you know that? You're some kind of freaky person. Jesus . . .'

He ran off towards the elevator, and she slammed the door, slid the chain on, and then started to shake. She sat on the floor, huddled her arms around her knees, and rocked back and forth. To hell with fear. To hell with standing there and just letting it happen. Fuck him, whoever he was. Because he was *stronger* than her, because he was a *man* she was supposed to stand there and let him do and say what he wanted. And after, when he left, when she was lying there, when the police came. What then? Did you *know* him? Were you a *virgin*? Oh well, how many men have you had then? Open your legs for the police gyno, and don't mind the policeman standing at the back of the room, he's used to it.

Fuck that.

But what if he had a knife? What if he hadn't been such a kid? Every day you read about murders. She shut her eyes. The shock started to hit her. She forced herself into the living room and swigged from a brandy bottle. The room was a wreck. He had shit on the carpet, thrown garbage round the room. In her bedroom and bathroom he had scribbled obscenities in lipstick all over the walls. Sick kid. He had probably copied it from some movie.

She knew she should call the police, but she also knew the publicity it would entail. Who needed that? After all he hadn't gotten away with anything. She had frightened him off empty-handed.

Meanwhile she couldn't stay there. No way. Never again.

Methodically she cleared up. By eight in the morning she had packed everything she wanted to keep. She called her only friend in New York, Linda Cosmo, and the telephone message service gave her an out of town number where she could be contacted.

She phoned, and a sleepy Linda instructed her to move into her apartment. 'I'll be back in a few days,' she explained, 'then we'll sort something out.'

Dallas called for a cab, picked up Linda's key from the janitor, and moved in.

She stocked up with food, double-locked all the doors, and stayed there until Linda got back.

twenty

The show at the Civic Centre Arena, Ottawa, was the same razzle dazzle smash hit as Toronto. Even better, perhaps, as Al gained full confidence.

Rave reviews filled the newspapers, and the tour's slogan – 'AL IS KING' was widely used. The concerts were a sell-out across America. A side rip-off industry sprang up amongst people lucky enough to have purchased blocks of seats. Soon tickets were going at five or six times the original price. A limit was set on people only being allowed two tickets per person, but the hustlers soon got round that.

Linda took an incredible photo of Al on stage. Like a God he stood before the masses. She had captured him in a moment of stillness above a sea of female hysteria. The picture was used world-wide to illustrate his triumph.

Bernie accepted her as an integral part of the tour from that moment on. Paul, however, didn't. He seemed offhand and disinterested. He was annoyed because she had apparently insulted a Toronto newscaster called Hank Mason, who had been the only person to knock Al in print.

'So what?' Linda had questioned, 'he was rude to me first.'

'Never insult the press,' Paul had warned, 'they can make or break us.'

Linda had considered the whole incident ridiculous. Al was an undeniable smash hit, how could one little newscaster affect that? Anyway *Al* hadn't insulted him, *she* had.

'He knows you're with the tour, that's why he knocked Al,' Paul had said, 'try and be nice to everyone.'

'Oh, sorry. Maybe I *should* have gone home with him and let him smack my bottom. Should I have?'

Paul had not bothered to reply.

Linda could not understand what had happened to them. They had waited and longed to be together, and now that they were it was an anti-climax. Paul seemed to spend his entire time finding girls for Al. One after the other they were paraded up to the

Master's suite for his inspection, but so far not one appeared to have passed muster.

Find 'em – fuck 'em – forget 'em – had once been Al's motto. Now it seemed to be find 'em – forget 'em. He couldn't even be bothered to try. They were boring, all of them. He wondered if age had finally caught up with him. But it wasn't that, he knew it. No problem getting it up, but it had to be for something better than a parade of dumbells looking to screw a star.

He tried it with Rosa, and it was good, but not good enough to try again.

He didn't need it anyway. The moments on stage were enough. The power orgasm. The joy of thousands of women having you at once. The mass fuck.

He looked forward to New York. That was the *real* start of the tour as far as he was concerned. His insecurities had swept away. His voice was better than ever. The fans were still there, still loved him, still wanted him. He felt like a weight had been lifted from his shoulders. Christ – to have failed, or only achieved moderate success. What would he have done then? Retired? He could never retire, singing was his life. But it couldn't go on forever, and if he did go it had to be at a peak.

He had finally phoned Edna.

'What's the weather like?' had been her first question.

What the fuck did the *weather* matter? He wanted her praise. He spoke to Evan.

'When can I come?' The boy had asked truculently.

What a family! Didn't they read the newspapers? Didn't they know that Al was King again?

He allowed a stoned blonde to give him a mediocre blow job before going to bed. She was delighted at the honour. He thought about Dallas, once, briefly, and wondered where she was and who she was with. Now there was a girl who would never do anything in a mediocre fashion.

He slept, and in his sleep he was surrounded by applause and warm bodies, and he slept well.

Linda said, 'I had a call from Dallas.'

Paul was reading *Variety*. 'Who?'

'Dallas. She had some kind of bad experience. I lent her my apartment.'

'Why did you do that?'

'Because she needed a place to go.'

'I didn't realize you were *that* friendly.'

Linda gazed out of the aeroplane window. 'What's the matter, Paul? What's happening with us?'

It was the first chance they seemed to have been alone together. Four days in Canada, and every night a party.

'Nothing's the matter. I *told* you what I'm like on tour.'

'Do you wish I wasn't along?'

He folded his *Variety* and stared at her. 'Do you?'

'I asked *you* first.'

'I don't know. I thought it was a good idea, it *seemed* like a good idea. But Al has to come first, and I know that bugs you.'

'OK, so he comes first. Understood. But I'm not even running a poor second. Since that first day you haven't even touched me ...'

'There hasn't been time. You know Al likes me to stay with him after a show. He can't sleep, he needs to talk, play cards, just relax. And when I do get to your room you're asleep and I'm bushed.'

'Wow! We sound like a couple of real swingers!'

'New York will be different. He'll probably find a girl he likes, then I can be with you.'

'What about Dallas? He likes her, doesn't he?'

'It's not mutual. She gave him a hard time. He doesn't need that whole bit.'

Doesn't he? mused Linda. We shall see. If she got Dallas and Al together. If they hit it off. Well – maybe her problems would be solved.

Dearest Al, I am offering you a swop. You may have Dallas, and I, thank you very much, will take back Paul.

Linda smiled. It wasn't a nice thing to do to a friend, but all is fair in love and war, and this was war.

New York was blisteringly hot. Crowds and photographers were at the airport to meet the plane. Al was whisked off to do a television interview and Paul, of course, went with him.

Linda took a cab into the city. She was hot, tired, and more than a little disappointed at the way things were going. She wanted a bath, and a think, and maybe a man – a transient stud purely for medicinal purposes.

Sometimes the only way to really relax was to lose yourself in a totally physical pastime. Linda had found that an occasional sexual scene was the only way she could turn off, and clear out her head. It did not mean that she loved Paul any the less, or that he wasn't a good lover, it was just that sometimes sex without emotional complications was a great therapy treatment.

She contemplated phoning Rik. She had seen him a few times over the last few months. He was a dumb actor with a beautiful body. They had met at their mutual supermarket.

She stopped the cab and made the call.

'You haven't called me for weeks,' Rik complained.

'I've been out of the city.'

'You could have let me know.'

'Sorry. I thought I might pop over.'

There was silence, then Rik said truculently: 'You really are a bitch, you *use* me.'

'Don't you want me to come over then?'

'Yes, of course I do.'

'I'll be there soon.'

She hung up and sighed. Rik was right, she did use him. But why should *he* complain, he had been using women for years.

She gave the driver his address and sat back. She felt no guilt. Why should she? Paul was still sleeping with his wife, and maybe an occasional groupie too – God knows, there were enough of them floating around.

She lit a cigarette and hoped that Rik was not going to start giving her a heavy about not calling before. She had never allowed him her phone number or address and it bugged him. If he started getting uptight he would just have to go.

He was easily replaceable.

Al smiled his way through the television interview. Stock questions. Stock answers. The interviewer was a well-known woman by the name of Marjorie Carter, who had her own news programme. She kept on giving him penetrating moody stares. She had formerly been a Washington journalist, and some said she had once had the ear of the President. Which one Al wasn't quite sure, probably Kennedy, as she was about forty, but strikingly attractive in that groomed, designer-label clothes way.

'That was fun,' she said, after the show. 'At least you can *talk*.'

'What do you mean by that?' Al asked.

'I keep on getting supposed superstars on the show who sit transfixed by their own image on the monitor. So out of it they can barely string their ums and ers together.'

'Sounds like a laugh.'

'I have tickets for your performance tomorrow. Is it worth seeing?'

Al smiled. Now they were off camera she wanted to put him in his place. 'Depends what you're looking for.'

'Excitement.' She had hot, frustrated eyes.

'I think I can help you there.'

'I'll come then.'

'Do that, and drop by the party later.' Maybe if she was lucky he would give her one.

Bernie came rushing over. 'Sensational! Al, you came over great – but right on. Jeeze . . .' He mopped at the sweat streaming down his face with a coloured handkerchief. 'Word's out you're here – we gotta make a quick side exit – like, cement yourself to Luke and move like you gotta crap.'

Bernie hustled Al up, and Luke – forever hovering – gripped onto his arm, and with Paul the other side they headed swiftly for the exit it was least expected they would emerge from.

Neither Bernie nor Paul revealed to Al that while he had been on the show they had received a death threat. A telephone call from some displaced head – 'I'm gonna kill that mothafukin' bastard son of a bitch . . .'

Nothing unusual about threats, but you always had to take them seriously. You never knew when some nutter would decide to do something about it. Once Al had been on tour, and a disgruntled husband had managed to smash his way into the dressing-room with an axe. It was only Paul's quick thinking that had saved Al. He had tripped the maniac up and sat on him until help had arrived.

They made the car in safety, sped to the hotel, entered through the underground garage.

'Set me up a poker game,' Al demanded of Paul, 'and a girl, lots of tit and ass and blond hair.'

Paul frowned. *Another* girl. Al seemed insatiable on this trip. He raised eyebrows at Bernie and Bernie winked in reply. 'I've got just the lady . . .' What the fuck – Al would never know she was a hooker.

twenty-one

Alone, holed up in Linda's apartment, Dallas did a lot of thinking. She was twenty years old. She was beautiful, and God knows she was at least as talented as half the girls who were making it in television and movies.

What was she *doing* with her life? She was bumming around New York going out with guys she didn't like, didn't want to lay, and only wanted to give a hard time to. Was this the revenge she was supposed to be getting for Ed Kurlnik splitting? Some revenge.

She was spending all her money at an alarming pace. And when that was gone – what then? Back to hustling? No thank you.

She was drinking too much. And if that freak hadn't broken into her apartment, God knows what she would have done. Perhaps she should thank him. OK, so she had no one – not one person who cared about her. But she had her health, her looks, her talent, and goddamn it she was going to make something of her life. Success was not such a distant dream. She was known, she had done a TV show and a commercial. She was always in the gossip columns. She wasn't some little unknown Miami hooker any more.

She formed a plan of action, and getting out of New York would be the first step. She would sell her jewellery and furs, and rent her apartment; that would give her capital. Then she would go to Los Angeles. She had received letters from a couple of agents who were anxious to meet her. She could go to an acting class there, she could study and learn. And if she was lucky enough to make it, she could have a baby. The thought delighted her. A human being. Flesh and blood that would belong to her. A little girl or a little boy, what difference, there would be someone she belonged to, someone who would eventually care.

Linda arrived back in the early evening.

'What happened?' she asked, disappearing into the shower. 'Make some coffee and we'll talk.'

Dallas made coffee, and without being dramatic told Linda exactly what had taken place.

'Jesus!' exclaimed Linda, 'it's unbelievable!' But she knew it happened fifty times a day. 'Why didn't you call the police? Don't answer, I know it's a dumb question. Anyway I'm glad you came here. I just can't believe you *talked* him out of it. Weren't you petrified?'

Dallas shrugged. 'I guess I just baulked at becoming another victim. I was so angry I forgot to be frightened.'

'The trouble is if they ever caught him all he'd probably get would be a telling off and a three-month suspended sentence. Girl at my school got raped, she was fifteen and so was the boy. They igr..red the fact that he held a knife to her throat – naughty, naughty, they said, and he was back in school the next week. The girl became a raving dyke and nobody cared.'

'I feel together now. It was rough at the time but I'm over it. Thanks for the loan of your apartment, it's so cosy here. I just crawled into bed and glued myself to the television. I can split now you're back.'

'You can stay if you like. I'm only here for a couple of days and I'll be sleeping over at the hotel.'

'Thanks, but I've got this urge to get out of New York. If you don't mind I might stay while I sort things out. Who do you know that will give me a good price on my jewellery?'

'Hey, if you need money I can come up with some, you don't . . .'

'No. I want to sell it. Thanks anyway. Really, Linda, you have been great, I don't know how to thank you. I mean I could have moved in and ripped you off – anything . . .'

'I knew you wouldn't do that. You needed help – I was able to. If *I* need help any time I'll be at your front door like fire!'

Dallas laughed. She had a friend, and it was a good feeling. Maybe Linda might have cared if she had taken the pills – maybe just a little.

'How was Canada?' she asked.

Linda made a face. 'Al was a sensation as I'm sure you've read everywhere. Paul was busy holding his hand. I took some good pictures.'

'I haven't seen any papers.' Dallas paused. 'How is Al?'

'He's screwed his way through Canada. America here he comes! I was going to ask you the ultimate favour and see if you would come out with us tonight, but I changed my mind – after what you've been through I certainly couldn't inflict Al on you.'

'I wouldn't mind . . .'

'You wouldn't? Hey, that would be great. Paul seemed to think that you and Al were deadly enemies. According to Paul you're the only female around who ever gave him a sharp no. As far as Paul is concerned Al has access to every woman in the world! I think Paul would be surprised if the Queen said no!'

'Listen, I'll come out, that doesn't mean I'll say yes.'

'Sure. Look, I'll give Paul a buzz and set it up.' Linda smiled to herself. This was going to work out just fine. Maybe Paul was right, maybe Al *was* irresistible to most women.

She shut herself in the bedroom and called the hotel.

'How did the television show go?' she asked.

'Didn't you watch it?' Paul sounded pissed off. Nothing unusual, lately Paul always seemed pissed off.

'I forgot.'

'That's great. Al will be delighted to hear that when he asks your opinion.'

Linda almost laughed aloud. 'Since when has Al wanted *my* opinion?'

'Are you coming over?'

'I thought we were going out.'

'Al's tired.'

'Maybe he'll revive when he hears who I've got him for a date.'

'Who?'

'Dallas. All set. Can we eat somewhere decent?'

Paul glanced over at his brother. He was immersed in a poker game with three men. The blonde hooker was draped over the back of his chair looking bored.

'It's a little late in the day for that lady to start changing her mind.' Paul lowered his voice, 'Al's well taken care of for tonight.'

'You mean he doesn't want a date with Dallas?'

'No way.'

'Did you ask him?'

'He's sitting right here.'

'Let me speak to him.'

'Linda, don't push it. Are you coming over or not?'

'Not.' She hung up the phone. Now why had she done *that*? A sudden show of independence, not such a bad thing. Let's play see if Paul will call me back.

Dallas was washing her hair. 'What shall I wear?' she asked.

'Forget it. Al's taken a pill and gone to sleep.'

'You're kidding. It's early . . .'

'He's got a big show at Madison Square Garden tomorrow. Tell you what, would you like to come and see it?'

Dallas shrugged. She felt suddenly let down. 'I don't know, can I see how I feel tomorrow?'

'Sure. But it's worth seeing. The master is at his peak, and it's some show.'

'I'm sure it is. But right now I feel like taking each day as it comes.'

'Of course. I'd feel the same way after what you've been through. What do you say? Shall we venture out to dinner on our own?'

'Why not?'

They went to a small Italian restaurant, ignored the stares of the men, gorged on salad niçoise and fettucini, and talked.

'Shouldn't you be with Paul tonight?' Dallas asked.

'He's holding big brother's hand.'

'Even while he sleeps?'

'Al demands full attention at all times.'

Dallas shook her head in amazement. 'I don't know how you can stand it.'

'I don't know myself. Listen, strictly between us Paul has become a pain in the ass. I think maybe my being on the tour is a bad idea, and this is only the beginning. Can you imagine how I'm going to feel about him in a few weeks?'

'It's probably a good thing. Get your head together on your real feelings for him.'

'Right now my real feelings are – ugh! *Never* get involved with a married one, kid.'

Dallas laughed. 'You're telling *me*. What the hell do you think Ed Kurlnik was? Married. Single. They are all shits.'

Linda sighed. 'Sometimes they can be nice shits.'

'Oh come on. You know better than that.'

'You're very bitter, Dallas. Don't let one guy who tried to rape you put you off the whole race. You're too young and too beautiful . . .'

Dallas laughed. 'Some day remind me to tell you about my past. That one guy was just one of many who formed my opinion on the entire male sex.'

When they got back to the apartment the phone was ringing. Linda picked it up quickly.

'Where the hell were you?' Paul sounded pissed off.

'Out getting laid.'

'Charming, really charming.'

'Dallas and I went to Piños and had some food.'

'Oh. Do you want to come over?'

'Just me?'

'No, bring ten or twelve of your neighbours if that's what gets you going.'

'Funny. I meant . . .'

'I know what you meant. Listen, sweetheart, I know she's your friend and all that, but for Al she is bad news. I can sense it, got a feeling. Know what I mean?'

'No, I don't know what you mean. But if you're offering me your fine English body I'll be right over.'

'I'm offering.'

'I'm there.' Linda put the phone down, turned to explain to Dallas, but she had gone into the bathroom. Linda knocked, but there was no reply. 'I'm going,' she called out, 'see you tomorrow.'

Dallas stared at her reflection in the mirror. Bye-bye Linda. He calls. You run. No wonder he treats you like shit. She waited until she heard the apartment door slam, then she emerged from the bathroom. It was twelve-thirty. She felt very alone. She bolted the apartment door, double locked it, checked that all the windows had safety catches fastened. There didn't seem much else to do.

Reluctantly she went to bed. But sleep was a long time coming, and when it did creep up on her it was full of bad dreams.

twenty-two

The bomb scare came five minutes before Al was due to go on.

Bernie happened to take the call, and his heart lurched into a series of sharp palpitations as he heard the quiet, nondescript voice explain to him that three bombs would go off at three-minute intervals during the course of Al's performance.

'Fuck you,' Bernie managed to scream down the phone before the line clicked dead in his hand.

'Another fan?' asked Al dryly.

Bernie nodded, his mind racing. How the fuck had they gotten through to Al in his dressing room anyway? And why call him? Why not the newspapers? The police? Anyone but him. Why should he have to be the one responsible for the fact that there may or may not be three bombs waiting to blow up hundreds of Al's fans? Jesus, wasn't it enough that he had the press to deal with? Wasn't that punishment enough?

Anyway, there was heavy security. It must be another hoax. Bernie frowned. Just pretend it never happened. Just sweat it out.

'See you, man.' Al was buoyant.

The gladiator off for the kill.

'What the fuck,' replied Bernie, 'give 'em your balls, baby.'

Al grinned. He was on top. Right on top. New York lay responsive and waiting like a particularly accommodating whore. He could do what he wanted. They had paid their money and they were ready to enjoy him, devour him, give him the greatest come of his life.

He strode on stage and was drowned in a mass sound-wave of screaming. He felt himself grow hard. The power hard-on. Boy, if he was fucking instead of singing he could go all night. He gave a boxer's salute, waved, grabbed the microphone and launched right into 'Blue Funk Rock'. The audience roared its approval.

Watching him, Dallas felt that she didn't know him at all. She didn't know him that well anyway. A few brief conversations, one dance, a strong attraction, that was just part of his whole charisma.

Watching him made her realize just how right she had been not to get involved.

This man rocking and weaving around the stage was public domain. He belonged to 'them', the people. He was, quite rightly, a superstar. She could see why. She could look at him objectively.

It all became clear. She had wanted him sexually because she was supposed to want him sexually. He was selling sex. So he had a great voice, but so did a lot of other singers. His appeal was the combination. The sexuality that radiated a message to every woman watching him.

Dallas smiled, it was a relief. She didn't need him, she didn't need anyone.

She glanced quickly at the fag hairdresser whom she had brought with her. He was entranced, his eyes bright, his body moving to the sound of Al.

She looked around her. Al seemed to have everyone mesmerized. She could recognize a few celebrities. Linda had given her exceptionally good tickets. Wasn't that Marjorie Carter? And God – Ed Kurlnik. What was *he* doing here? The cheap bastard. She wasn't sure, but it looked like he was with one of his daughters. Was it Dana? If it was they had both been engaged to Kip Rey, so they had much in common. Kip had told her stories Ed would *never* believe about his darling daughter.

She wasn't concentrating on Al. He had slipped away from her, a living, moving, phallic symbol, vocalizing obscene lyrics.

She forced herself to watch him, and gradually she too was caught up in the magic he weaved, the sheer magnetism of the man. But this time she knew, and by knowing the game she was safe, she could relax.

Al came hurtling off the stage, soaked to the skin.
Paul hugged him before he returned to his army of lovers.

Linda captured the shot. If Paul loved anyone it was Al. She wondered what an analyst would have to say of the situation. Latent fag? Brother envy?

Why was there Al? Wasn't the wife and kids enough?

Although she couldn't deny that Paul had been wonderful the previous evening. Kind, considerate, a caring lover. And they had talked long into the night and reconciled their differences.

They had both agreed that if her being on the tour screwed up their personal relationship then she would leave.

'I love you,' Paul had told her, 'and when the kids are older . . .'

He should package it and Al could sing it!

The party was so jammed that Dallas nearly turned around and left. Her hairdresser wouldn't let her. He pursed his lips and surveyed her coldly. 'Truman might be here, darling, you can't deny me *that*.'

The rumours abounded that simply everyone in town *was* there, and it seemed to be true. The photographers all but ignored Dallas and went in search of bigger game.

'I think I'll get drunk,' she told her hairdresser, as if he cared. He had spotted someone who looked remarkably like Jackie O. and was entranced.

Dallas lifted a glass of wine from a passing tray. She could see Ed Kurlnik across the room, and it seemed like too good an opportunity to miss. She made her way over to him, ready for some sort of confrontation, not sure what to expect.

'Hi, Ed,' she said softly.

He was startled, panic flashed across his face, but he recovered quickly remembering that Dee Dee was safely in Europe. 'Hello, Dallas, dear.'

The girl standing next to him was staring. It was his daughter Dana, a cool, classy-looking blonde. 'Daddy?' she questioned, moving protectively close to him.

'It's all right.' He gave her a short angry little shove. 'Why don't you go and get a drink, I'll join you in a minute.'

Dana glared at Dallas, a high flush suffusing her glacial features. 'If you're sure . . .'

'I'm sure,' Ed snapped, nervously cracking his knuckles, a gesture that made Dallas wince.

They waited in silence while Dana moved off, then Ed said, 'For Christ's sake if you see a camera pointing in our direction move away. You don't know what I've had to go through.'

'What *have* you had to go through?'

He scowled. 'Bloody murder. And I've missed you, goddamn it I've missed you. I don't think we should talk here. I'll come to the apartment later.'

'I'm not at the apartment any more.'

'Why not? I bought it for you, didn't I? You got my cheque, didn't you?'

'Yes, I got the kiss-off money.'

Ed frowned. 'It wasn't kiss-off money. Just a little something to tide you over until we could meet again.'

'You didn't *say* that. In fact you didn't say anything. Not even a phone call, Ed.'

'I had to be very, very careful. I shouldn't even be talking to you in public now.'

Dallas shrugged. 'I just thought I'd say hello.' She turned, as if to go.

Ed restrained her with his hand on her shoulder. 'Where can I see you later? We must talk.'

'Why, Ed? I thought everything was over.'

'Nothing's over,' he hissed, 'I can't do without you. God, people are staring. Where? Just tell me where and I'll be there.'

Dallas thought quickly. Why not string the old bastard along? What was there to lose?

She smiled suddenly, dazzlingly. 'Dress up time later? Is that what you want? Slave and master? Teacher and pupil?'

His voice was thick and heavy. 'Oh yes, oh yes.'

'The Essex House. Apartment eighty-nine, eighth floor. Come straight up.'

'What time?'

'In a couple of hours.'

'I'll be there.'

'I'll expect you.'

She watched him walk away. A small scared shitless billionaire with a hard-on. He rejoined his daughter. What a shock he would get when he showed up at The Essex House in the middle of the night and started hammering on the door of a strange apartment. She stifled a giggle. If only she could have been there to witness it.

Crowds of fans had gathered outside the club where the party for Al was being held.

Luke, Paul and Bernie formed a human guard and shoved Al through. He was immediately besieged by the photographers. They wanted photographs of him with this celebrity – that celebrity.

Smile, Al. Turn on the charm, Al. Turn on the bullshit.

He found himself being introduced to Ed Kurlnik, and he muttered, 'We've already met.' And Ed Kurlnik's daughter was holding too long onto his hand, and squeezing ever so slightly, and saying in dulcet Grace Kelly tones: 'You must come out to the house sometime. How about this weekend?'

After a while Marjorie Carter approached him. 'I've come to rescue you from the boring masses.'

'Who said I needed rescuing?'

'I did. How many times can you listen to people telling you how sensational you are?'

'All the time.'

Marjorie laughed. 'Modest, you're not. My car is parked out back for a painless getaway. My simple little apartment awaits your pleasure. Champagne, caviar, all your favourite things. Shall we go?'

Al surveyed her warily. He didn't like his women quite so dominant.

But she was a challenge, on the cover of two national magazines that very week, and supposedly the highest paid woman in television.

'Let's go,' he decided. It would make a change.

'Follow me,' said Marjorie, 'I've become an expert at escaping out back entrances.'

Al started after her. Luke fell into step behind him.

'Leave it tonight,' Al instructed, 'I'll see you back at the hotel.'

Luke shook his head. 'Got orders not to leave your side.'

'Fuck your orders. Who do you think you're working for anyway?'

Paul moved over. 'What's the problem?'

'Tell him to get lost.'

Paul sighed. 'This is New York, Al. It's just not feasible for you to be on your own. We've had a lot of threats . . .'

Marjorie joined in. 'My chauffeur is a karate expert, Al will be perfectly safe with me.'

Paul stared in surprise. 'Well . . .' he started to say. But they were gone.

On the way out Al thought he saw Dallas. Of course it wasn't her. He was always imagining he saw her. A girl in the street with the same kind of walk. A face in a car with the same wild abundance of hair. He shook his head. Why was it that she was the only girl he couldn't get out of his head?

116

He followed Marjorie Carter into the back of a black Lincoln Continental, parked, as she had promised, in the quiet of a back alley.

Marjorie Carter lived in some style in a penthouse apartment with spectacular views over New York.

'Are you married?' Al asked.

'Divorced,' Marjorie replied shortly, 'and not about to get trapped again. I enjoy my independence. Open the champagne, I'm going to change.'

Al felt like he was partaking in a scene from an early Hollywood movie. The ballsy career woman off to slip into a negligee. Shades of Joan Crawford. He remembered her movies from when he was a kid. Paul and he had always slipped into the local movies through an open window in the ladies toilet. In fact Marjorie Carter even reminded him of Joan Crawford.

Raven hair, strong features, a direct way of speaking. He didn't fancy her, couldn't fancy her. There had been a teacher at the grammar school he had attended who had also reminded him of Joan Crawford. She had caught him jerking off at the tender age of eleven, and reported him to the headmaster. Eight strokes of the cane. A very nasty memory.

Marjorie returned. It wasn't quite a negligee, it was a long fall of silk jersey, and she had quite obviously removed her underclothes.

Al coughed. Where was all his witty repartee, his sexy come-ons. Somehow, 'Want to fuck?' or 'Show us your tits' did not seem the right phraseology to throw at a Marjorie Carter.

She accepted a glass of champagne from him, dipped a minute cracker into the silver jar holding the caviar. Her breasts joggled through the thin material, dangerously close to drooping.

'Well,' she said, sitting on a leopard-covered sofa and clicking on a remote control television, 'shall we watch ourselves?'

'Huh?' asked Al nervously.

'A videotape of our interview.'

'Oh, yes.'

Their images flashed on to the television screen.

'You look beautiful, Al,' she purred.

Shouldn't *he* be saying that to *her*? But how could he?

On the television screen she was attractive in a stern, no-nonsense way. He could understand her success, she handled the interview in a masterly fashion. But of course she had done it so many times before.

'I think it would be nice,' she said, when the programme was half-way through, 'if we made love here. Or do you prefer the bedroom?'

There was no getting out of it. He hardly dared argue. And oh the magic of a little authority. His body was responding nicely.

'Here will do.'

'Good.' She stood up and slipped off the robe. 'My body is nice, don't you think?'

She had full, over-ripe breasts, that dominated a short body, stretch marks on her thighs, and a high mass of jet black pubic hair that seemed to trickle down her inner thighs.

'Very tasty.'

'You should have seen me when I was nineteen. Then I was really something.'

'How old are you now?'

'Does it matter?'

'No, just curious.'

'Five years older than you.'

'I'm thirty-six,' he said quickly.

'You're thirty-seven. I know every little detail about every guest I have on my show. Secret of my success.'

He put his arms around her waist and buried his head in her stomach, 'What else do you know about me?'

'That you're supposed to be very good, and I like a man who knows what he's doing.'

He reached up, squeezed her over-ripe breasts.

'Why don't you undress?' she asked.

Thank God he was hard. He stood up, slipped off his clothes.

'The great Al King, the legend lives!' Her tone was faintly mocking as she fondled him.

He started to push her head down.

'Don't!' she objected sharply, 'I like to fuck.'

She made him angry enough to straddle her immediately. Hammer it into her, the bitch, who did she think she was?

Her legs clasped him firmly behind the neck, her arms too. He noticed that she didn't shave under her arms, and for some strange reason that excited him further.

'Tight, aren't I?' she asked. 'I had the operation. Nice, isn't it. Some women have their faces lifted, I get right down to where it really matters.'

For the first time in months he found himself ready to come. Oh Jesus it was good. Ride along with it, wait for the moment.

She suddenly twisted free.

'Hey . . .' he objected, 'I was ready . . .'

'I wasn't. Are you out of practice or what?'

Him, out of practice. She had to be kidding.

He moved on top of her again.

'Don't forget,' she said sharply, 'ladies first.'

'I didn't know there were any around,' and he slammed it into her, and came with an explosion that nearly blew his ears off.

Marjorie was furious. 'I should have known it was all reputation.'

Al dressed quickly. He was sorry he had ever gone with her. There was more feeling in the abortive scenes he had with the groupies and hookers.

Marjorie turned the volume up on the television and lay back on the sofa. 'See yourself out,' she said, and from underneath the sofa she produced a black plastic vibrator.

Al didn't wait to hear the buzz.

twenty-three

Dallas saw Al at the party. She thought he saw her, but it was only a brief glance across a crowded room, and why should that make him stop?

After the fiasco in Monte Carlo he had probably never given her another thought, and indeed why should he? She was just another beautiful girl. His life was probably full of them.

She was hurt. She had thought there had been something between them. Well screw him – Mister Big Star.

Linda was edging towards her – 'You made it! What did you think?'

'Quite a show.'

'Horny little thing on stage, isn't he?'

'If you like that type.'

Linda laughed. 'I know, I know, *you* don't.'

Dallas just smiled.

The next morning she awoke early and took a cab over to her former apartment. No more hanging around New York. With the apartment rented at least she would have some sort of income.

Downstairs the janitor handed her a telegram. 'Came a coupla days ago,' he explained.

Dallas tore it open. It was from an agent she had met on her trip to the coast. Brief and to the point it read – 'Interesting proposition. Call collect. Cody Hills.' And there was a phone number.

She tucked it firmly in her purse, it would be something worth looking into, especially as she was on her way out there.

'Mr Mack's chauffeur bin trying to find you,' the janitor confided. 'Bin here every day. What shall I tell him?'

'Just tell him I've gone to Los Angeles.'

'Sure,' agreed the janitor. Maybe the chauffeur would be handing out another ten bucks for the information.

Dallas' next stop was the shop where he had left her jewellery to be appraised the previous day. The price they offered her seemed fair, so the deal was done.

Now she had income and capital. She felt excited about getting away. No ties. A new start. Why wait?

Three hours later she was on a plane. Linda had not been at the apartment, and the only place she could think of contacting her was at Paul's hotel, but she did not want to phone there, so she had left a note of thanks, and a present – an expensive Gucci hold-all Linda had admired. It was the first present she had ever bought for anyone and it was a good feeling.

The flight to Los Angeles was bumpy, but she managed to sleep in spite of the persistent attentions of a fat businessman in the adjoining seat.

'Call me,' he wheezed, as the plane came into land, 'if you ever get lonely.'

That was really funny. She was always lonely, but he would be the last person she would call.

Los Angeles was balmy and sunny. She took a cab to the Beverly Hills Hotel. The plan was to stay there only until she found a suitable apartment.

She called Cody Hills immediately. He suggested they meet for a drink, and she agreed.

The Polo Lounge was crowded as usual. Dallas looked around for Cody Hills, not even sure if she would remember him – their previous meeting at the studio had been very brief. She needn't have worried. He found her, authoritatively took her by the arm, settled her at a table.

'You look even better than I remember,' he remarked briskly. He was a pleasant-looking man in his late twenties, medium height and build, brown hair combed carefully forward to conceal the fact that he was going prematurely bald.

'Remember me?' he asked.

'Of course,' lied Dallas.

'Of course not. Redford I'm not. But I haven't been able to forget you, and when this thing came up I knew you were the right girl.'

'What thing?'

'First things first. What are you drinking?'

'Orange juice.'

'Fantastic. You take dope?'

'No. Hey – what is this?'

'It's just that the girl I'm looking for has to be a clean-living lady. Gotta think of the sponsors.'

'What sponsors?'

Cody glanced conspiratorially around. 'I am going to make you and me rich. Very, very rich. Does that grab you in all the right places?'

'I guess so, as long as I don't have to . . .'

He held up a hand. 'You don't have to do anything. Just trust me. Just keep looking the way you look, and trust me.'

'Can you please tell me what this is all about?'

'Certainly.' He waved at a passing friend. 'This is the situation. Saw your test – it stunk. Nothing new – all the beauty queen tests stink. They knock 'em off – just a formality. If you're lucky you end up in a Dean Martin movie stickin' out your whatsits and looking dumb. However – you are an incredible-looking young lady. I saw the television show with Al King. You looked spectacular. Racquel, Farrah, Sophie, you have a little bit of each of them – but something plus, something wild.'

'If the test stunk . . .'

'Don't go getting sensitive. Paradox Studios are launching a big new television series – "Man Made Woman" – sort of a late night "Bionic Woman" with sex. They have a girl signed – I happen to know they are not going to be able to use her.'

'Why?'

'Because she's a sex change. Looks sensational, but you cannot make a coast-to-coast star out of a girl who used to be a sailor! So, who better than "Miss Coast-to-Coast" herself?'

'But I've never even acted.'

'So they'll teach you. Honey, believe me, when they see you – you are in. I know it. I feel it. I was even prepared to pay your fare out here. And we will be able to negotiate a peach of a contract – a million dollar contract. They'll see you. Want you.

121

That's when we move. They'll be in a bind, they have to start shooting next week.'

'Don't they know about the sex change girl?'

'They will. Tomorrow. Authenticated evidence.'

'So what do you want me to do?'

'Just stay out of sight until I call you. No lounging round the pool, going to restaurants, shopping. Just fall in love with room service until I call you.'

'I was going to look for an apartment.'

'Honey, believe you me, after next week it will be houses you'll be looking at – big ones with pools and tennis courts.'

Dallas smiled, 'I guess I have nothing to lose . . .'

'And everything to gain. You *are* a bona fide female, I take it?'

The smile snapped off her face. 'Mr Hills. Is part of the deal me proving that to you?'

'Dallas. I would love to answer yes to that question, but I'll take your word on it. Besides, silicone doesn't move the way you move, and I'm late for dinner at my mother's house. I'm a second generation Portnoy.'

'A what?'

'A nice Jewish boy.'

Later in her hotel room, Dallas thought about Cody Hills. He was the first man who had ever offered her anything without expecting dividends in return. Of course it might all be pie in the sky, but he seemed so enthusiastic, so sure.

She wondered if she should confess to him the fact that she was an ex-hooker. But what good would that do? She decided against it. What was the use of lining up strokes against yourself before you had even begun?

Two days later Cody called her.

'Pack a bikini, things are in motion. I'll be up to fetch you in half an hour.'

He drove a dashing red Mustang. 'Climb in,' he instructed, 'I'm afraid I'm going to have to inflict my mother on you, but it's the only place I can think of where you can get a tan in private.'

'Why a tan?'

'To make you look even more delectable, delicious, and just a little bit savage.'

'I'll be savage if this all ends up as a pile of shit.'

'Shhs . . . Nice girls with sponsors don't talk like that.'

'Fu . . .'

'Dallas. Please. Not on the way to my mother's house!'

She couldn't help smiling. 'Where does your mother live?'

'The Valley. Nothing extravagant, but for God's sake don't touch anything unless you can put it back *exactly* where it came from! I'm afraid I'll have to leave you there for the day, and the minute my back is out of there she'll be after you like the CIA.'

'Now look . . .'

'Nothing about you. Just about me. How long have you known me? Where did we meet? When are we getting married? The usual Jewish mother questions.'

'Sounds like fun. What shall I say?'

'No comment. Act like a star, you may as well get some practice in.'

Cody's mother was a round, neat little woman. She settled Dallas in a sun lounger, settled herself close by, and revealed the family history.

'Cody is a good boy, a good son. But show business! The movie business! A *meshugenah* profession!'

Dallas found out that he had been an agent for five years. Before that he had worked around the studio doing anything he could. The industry was his life. Eventually he wanted to be a producer.

'He don't usually bring his girlfriends home,' Mrs Hills confessed. 'But you – well, it's good to see he has taste.'

'I'm not a girlfriend, I'm a client,' Dallas explained patiently for the third time.

'Of course you are' agreed Mrs Hills with no conviction, 'but my Cody will make some girl a wonderful husband, a Jewish girl of course. A Jewish actress if that's what makes him happy. Elizabeth Taylor he won't get – but a nice girl like Streisand – what a voice? I hear she's got a hairdresser for a boyfriend. At least she gets her hair done for free . . .'

Another two days passed before Cody imparted the news that they had an appointment. 'Lew Margolis himself. Head man at Paradox. One look at you . . . I know we got it made.'

They decided what Dallas would wear. A white safari suit in the softest cotton, and a white Stetson hat with her hair tucked under it.

They planned every move together. She would enter Lew Margolis' office with Cody and sit quietly whilst they talked. The first question that Lew directed at her she would slowly remove her tinted shades, and stare directly at him. The second question the hat would come off. After that, the jacket, under which she would be wearing a clinging T-shirt.

'It will work – by the fourth question we'll be in. Don't forget, right now they are *desperate* – and there just aren't any girls around with such perfect physical qualifications for the part.'

Cody's confidence was catching, and Dallas found herself almost sure of the fact that the part would be hers. What a wonderful start to a new life.

The night before the interview Cody took her to the 'Aware Inn' for an early dinner. They talked about general things, almost scared to trade the strong excitement they both felt. When he dropped her off at the hotel he kissed her chastely on the cheek.

'Tomorrow,' he said firmly, 'think positive.'

'I will,' she replied, grateful that he wasn't trying to rush her into the nearest bed, although she sensed that he wanted to.

'Pick you up at eleven.'

'I'll be ready.'

'Goodnight, star.'

'Goodnight, producer.'

'How did you know . . .'

'Your mother.'

'I guess you know all about my circumcision too.'

'Intimately.'

'See you tomorrow.'

'Tomorrow.' She leaned forward and kissed him softly on the lips before walking into the hotel.

The morning was bright with very little smog. Dallas breakfasted on figs and orange juice. Did her exercises in front of the open window. Made up and dressed with painstaking care.

Cody picked her up exactly on time. She noticed he had washed and plastered his hair down more carefully than ever. He wore a suit, Californian lightweight, but still a suit.

They drove in silence to the studios. A large sign proclaimed 'Paradox Television, The Greatest'.

Lew Margolis sat behind an Italian marble desk littered with various silver and gold awards. Framed photos of his family took pride of place on a marble side table. The floor was marble, the walls were marble.

Dallas didn't really notice any of this. She didn't notice because she was too busy remembering.

Lew Margolis had been the mystery client whose house Dallas had gone to with Bobbie on her last and final orgy.

Lew Margolis would know instantly and irrevocably that she was a paid whore.

twenty-four

Rave reviews on the Madison Square concert brought only a thin smile to Paul's lips. He was so furious at what he considered Al's irresponsible behaviour that it eclipsed all else.

Linda had never seen him so angry, and in a curious way the fact that he was ranting and raving about Al brought them closer together.

'Death threats here, mobbings there. Kidnapping and everything else, and he runs off with a woman *I* wouldn't even look twice at, and takes a *stroll* back to the hotel.'

'He's a big boy.' Linda pointed out.

'Let him be a big boy on his own time. This is business, and if anything happened to him. Jesus, Linda, you should see the crank mail he receives. There's a lot of husbands running wild who would be only too happy to take a slice off his balls.'

'I'm sure he can look after himself.'

'On the New York streets, at night, Muhammed Ali can't look after himself!'

'I should have offered to fix him up with Dallas. That would have kept him off the streets.'

'Do it. Tonight.'

'I don't know if she'll still want to.'

'Try.'

Al, for his part, awoke strangely refreshed. He blocked out the bad vibes of the previous evening and remembered only the fact that he had been able to screw and come. A rare achievement these days.

He lay in bed, ordered champagne, and read and re-read his rave reviews.

Dana Kurlnik phoned him at three o'clock. 'This weekend,' she said in imperious tones. 'What time shall the helicopter collect you?'

'I didn't say I'd come.'

'You didn't say you wouldn't. I'd like you to meet my twin. We're identical, you know. Don't you think that's fascinating?'

'Absolutely. Do you fuck together?'

'Absolutely. What time did you say you wanted the helicopter?'

'Twelve in the morning. Tomorrow. There'll be three of us.'

'Can't wait.'

'We'll only be staying the night.'

'Don't bet on it.'

American girls, they didn't half come across strong. Al yawned, got up, inspected himself in the mirror. He didn't like the bags that appeared to be forming yet again beneath his eyes. Something would have to be done about *them*.

He buzzed Paul, Linda answered.

'He's gone out,' she informed him, 'back in about an hour.'

'Why don't you come up. Want to talk to you.'

'Are you out of bed?'

'You're perfectly safe. I don't jump on my brother's girl. Not unless she asks me to.'

'Ha Ha. Can I bring my cameras?'

'If it's candid shots you're after I look like shit.'

'So what else is new?'

Al's suite was on the floor above, so Linda walked up, said hello to Luke stationed outside, and went in.

Al greeted her in a towelling bathrobe. 'Seen the reviews?' was his first question.

'Of course. Sensational, naturally.'

'Where's Paul?'

'He's not in a very good mood. He's gone to double check security for tonight's concert.'

'Is he pissed off at me?'

'It wasn't a terribly smart move was it? And why walk home? Anything could have happened.'

Al shrugged. 'I don't know, love. Felt like it. Listen – you, me, and Paul have been invited to the Kurlnik place for the weekend. I said we'd go, might be a giggle.'

'I wouldn't mind. When?'

'Tomorrow, we'll just stay the one night. Then on to Philadelphia for the show on Monday.'

'Sounds good to me, as long as Paul says yes.'

'He'll say yes. He always does what I want – you should know that by now.'

Linda sighed. 'Thanks a lot, you certainly know how to make a person feel good.'

'You want me to be honest, don't you?'

Linda lit a cigarette. Al always made her smoke more than usual. 'Not particularly, but if it makes you happy. By the way, nothing definite, but how would you feel about seeing Dallas after tonight's show?'

'Is she here?' Al asked, 'Jesus – that wasn't her at the party last night, was it?'

'The very same.'

'Why didn't anyone *tell* me? I'd like to see her, sure I would. Can you fix it?'

'I think so. She's staying with me. I've been trying to call her but she must have gone out.'

'Why don't you go on home, wait for her. Bring her to the concert. We'll go somewhere nice for dinner.'

'You're very anxious.'

'I like her. Is there anything strange about that?'

'Oh sweet! Our superstar has feelings too.'

'Jesus, Linda, you are some smart ass.'

Linda smiled. She felt she had scored a minor victory. 'I'll go home, then.'

'Do that. And call me. Better still have Dallas call me.'

'I'll try. She might be busy.'

'Fuck you, Linda. You enjoy every minute of me not getting what I want. You could have told me she was staying with you before this.'

So Paul hadn't told him. Bad Paul. 'I didn't know you cared.'

Al shrugged. 'I don't care. Like she's all right, we'll have some laughs. I don't *care*.'

'OK. OK. I'll call you later.'

If only he had been sure it was her at the party. He could have dumped Marjorie Carter easily enough. He had thought about Dallas so many times since the South of France. He had run and re-run the videotape of their television show on numerous occasions. He had read about her fiancé dying. He had seen the occasional photo of her in the gossip columns. She looked gorgeous. She always looked gorgeous.

He wasn't sure if she would still be talking to him. After the incident in the South of France he had frozen her out. Business relationship only. Screw the newspapers and all that publicity. It had petered out now. Even Edna had believed him when he swore there was nothing in it. And there *was* nothing in it. He had never touched the girl. Perhaps that's what was bugging him.

Anyway, that would all change soon. After the concert. Maybe before the concert if Linda got hold of her in time. He watched a bad quiz show on television, impatiently waiting to hear from Linda.

Finally she rang, terse and to the point. 'Our little bird has flown, jetted off to good old LA.'

'Oh shit!' said Al, and he was surprised at how disappointed he suddenly felt.

Fire Island was enveloped in a sea mist, but it didn't alter the sultry humidity. The Kurlnik estate jutted out towards the sea. It had its own private beach, indoor and outdoor swimming pools, tennis courts, and a mini golf course.

Dana Kurlnik was there to greet them. She was tall and bronzed, coolly groomed in tennis whites.

'My mother's away,' she informed them, 'and daddy is quite busy in the city. So it's just myself and Cara. Come, I'll show you the house.'

It was quite impressive. Picassos nestled next to Hockneys on the walls. Priceless antique furniture mixed unashamedly with ultra-modern.

'You must be hungry. We'll lunch on the terrace. Fifteen minutes all right with everyone?'

'Fine with me,' agreed Al, 'it doesn't take me fifteen minutes to take a piss.'

Paul and Linda exchanged looks. Dana appeared not to have heard.

'What a house!' exclaimed Linda.

'Yes,' said Paul wistfully, 'makes my place in England look like a shack.'

They were given a room with an old oak four-poster bed, and a sea view.

'This is lovely,' enthused Linda, 'veree romantic – you think so?'

'I think,' said Paul slowly, 'that we are the beards, and that Al knew all along old man Kurlnik wouldn't be here.'

'I did want to meet him. Dallas never mentions him. I think she was more upset than everyone supposes.'

Paul grinned. 'I think Al wants to get his own back through the daughters.'

Linda started to undress. 'Judging from the one we've seen I think she would welcome any getting his own back Al cares to give her.'

128

'Linda, why are you almost naked?'

'All the better to make love to you. After all, we have got fifteen minutes before lunch, why waste them?'

Cara Kurlnik appeared for lunch. Blonde, like her sister, and equally cool.

Linda couldn't help reflecting how old they both seemed to be. Not in looks, they were certainly good-looking enough. It was just their demeanour, sort of a weary, glacial, seen it all, done it all, attitude. And of course they probably had. Being the daughters of one of the richest men in America probably did not lead to a quiet and sheltered life. Their conversation was peppered with famous names and places.

Lunch was delicious. A mixture of seafoods and salads laid out invitingly on silver dishes.

Al gorged himself, swigging back the champagne the girls had thoughtfully provided. For dessert there were bowls of strawberries with thick cream ladled on top.

'Here goes my diet,' remarked Al.

'Do you have to diet?' questioned Cara. 'How boring.'

'Only when I'm working,' said Al quickly, 'I like to keep in shape, like a boxer.'

'Oh, you mean training. I would have thought it was only your voice you had to worry about.' Dana stared at him as she spoke. A cold, grey-eyed, stare.

'Al uses a great deal of physical energy,' Paul joined in. 'He's like a wet rag when he comes off that stage.'

'Does training include no sex?' inquired Cara.

'Are you kidding?' laughed Al.

Linda had been fiddling with her cameras. 'Anyone mind if I take some photographs?' she asked.

'Go right ahead,' replied Dana, 'would you like us to pose for you?'

'That won't be necessary – I don't work like that. Just carry on doing whatever you're doing.'

'I thought we might go ski-ing,' said Cara, 'the boat's all ready. You do ski don't you, Al?'

'Yeah, I ski.' He had learnt in the South of France, his first holiday after success had started to creep up on him. He had known it would come in useful one day. Edna had never learned. She had sat on the beach and complained that it was a dangerous, stupid sport. She had been quite surprised when after three abortive attempts he was up up and away. Perhaps if Edna had been the kind of woman who had learned to water ski their marriage might not be on the rocks today. And it was on the rocks. He knew there was no going home after this trip.

With all his success he had nothing, no one. Plenty of everything. But what did that mean when you were alone in bed at night. And whoever it was that shared his bed he still ended up alone.

He envied Paul. He had Linda. A strong, ballsy woman who obviously loved him very much. And what did Al get? He got the slags, didn't he? The star fucks and groupies. The ballbreakers like Marjorie Carter, and the nymphos like the Kurlnik twins. He could smell a nympho a mile off, however much money she had. And he would accommodate them, if he was able. And he would probably enjoy it, on a momentary basis. And they would say – 'Wow – what a stud Al King is'. And that was his life. Superstud. Superfuck. There must be something better somewhere.

'Are you going to change?' asked Dana.

'What for?' responded Al, 'it's private here, isn't it?'

'Yes, of course,' said Dana.

'In that case it's everyone in the raw.'

'I'd love to photograph the event, but I think Paul and I will sit this one out. Is it all right if we use the swimming pool?' Linda took Paul's hand and pulled him up, 'OK with you?'

'Yes, sure,' Paul replied, almost reluctantly. There had once been a time, in the early days, when identical twins would have meant a good time for both of them. Al had always been the puller, but Paul had never been averse to joining in. Until he grew up. Al never grew up.

'Well, girls,' announced Al expansively, 'lead me to your boat, and if you're good girls you can put on a ski each.'

'Don't you mono ski?' asked Cara, in patronizing tones.

'The hell with the fancy stuff. I like to keep it simple.'

'Naturally,' drawled Dana.

She would be the first to get it, Al decided. Stuck-up rich little snob.

Cara drove the Riva, whilst Dana and Al ski-ed. Both girls were wearing bikinis under their tennis whites. Al had ended up in his Y-fronts feeling slightly foolish. Dana, of course, only needed one ski, whilst Al, next to her, felt clumsy and inadequate on two.

Cara zoomed the speedboat expertly across the sea, until at last she cut the engine, and Al and Dana subsided into the water. Dana slipped easily out of her ski, and had swum to the boat long before Al came struggling aboard trailing his skis behind him.

As he climbed into the Riva he noticed both girls had discarded the tops of their bikinis. It didn't make much difference as they were both built like boys. Four indifferent, identical tits. He grinned, thought – what the hell – and slid out of his ridiculous wet Y-fronts.

Dana was busy rolling a joint. 'Hey – hey—' she exclaimed, 'the legend lives!'

Cara turned to stare, running a small pink tongue nervously across her lips.

The boat rocked gently in the waves. The sun had cut through the mist, and Cara started to lay out striped mattresses on the back of the boat.

'What have we got to drink?' Al asked.

'Champagne, of course,' replied Dana, 'isn't that your favourite? In the ice box at the front.'

He got out the champagne, popped the cork, found some glasses, and took it all to the back of the boat.

They lay out on the mattresses, with him in the middle. Cara produced a tape recorder, and the sound of Al singing joined them. Dana passed the joint around. He declined.

'I thought all musicians smoked,' said Dana in surprise.

'He's not a musician,' replied Cara dismissively, 'anyway most of the over thirty-fives prefer to drink.'

'Don't talk about me as if I'm not here,' interrupted Al. 'Grass doesn't do anything for me, why the hell should it?'

'Nobody's forcing you. How about some coke? Believe me, ski-ing when you're out of it on coke is a beautiful experience.' So saying Dana reached into a bag and produced a glass phial of white powder. She was wearing a small gold spoon on a chain around her neck, and she took off the chain, removed the spoon, filled it with white powder and snorted the stuff delicately and expertly into each nostril. 'Here,' she offered it to Al, 'it's the best.'

Al fingered some cocaine from the spoon, snorted just a little. Why not? He had been working hard, he deserved some relaxation.

Cara leaned across him to reach for the joint. He felt her nipples brush his chest. He looked down and watched himself harden. They all watched.

'Random Love' played loudly on the tape recorder.

Nobody seemed in any kind of hurry. Al snorted a little more coke, took a drag on the joint. He was starting to feel really good.

Cara took her glass and slowly tipped the champagne from it over his chest. He felt his nipples come erect, and Cara bent to lick the liquid off him. Dana joined in from the other side. He closed his eyes to the burning sun, sealing off the identical faces that were now administering to him from both sides.

'Jesus!' he muttered.

'Good, isn't it?'

Their heads were travelling down in perfect unison, licking, biting, kissing. Then they were attending to his balls with feathery, identical tongues. It was an incredible sensation, so incredible that he could hardly bear it. He needed to screw, to jam it in. But which one first? Lazily he rolled towards Dana, but she shoved him away.

They continued to work on him, slowly, methodically. It was sensational – but – 'I'm going to come,' he warned. He turned to reach Cara, but they held him down, and as he came, spurting all over himself, one of them snapped an amyl nitrate under his nose.

His orgasm seemed to go on for ever as he jerked and thrust up into nothingness. It was amazing, but it was frustrating. All the times he couldn't be bothered to screw, and now, when he wanted to, it was denied him. Still he couldn't complain. Although it was a strange sensation to come into nothingness.

Slowly he opened his eyes. Cara and Dana watched him expectantly. 'Good?' they chorused.

'Bloody good,' he agreed.

'Why don't you wash off in the sea?' Cara suggested.

'Yes.' He was covered in his own sperm. 'There's no sharks around here, are there?'

'Only the human ones – inland,' replied Dana coolly.

He slipped over the side. The water was invigoratingly cold. He swam away from the boat. It felt good swimming in the raw, it always had, even when he was a kid and stripped off to swim in the canals. He did a strong crawl, dived under the water, couldn't see much. Pity they didn't have diving gear aboard – although they probably did – they seemed to carry everything else.

He surfaced. The boat appeared to have drifted some distance away.

'Hey!' he yelled. But he couldn't see the twins. What if there *were* sharks? He felt a small stab of panic. Rapidly he started to swim towards the boat. He felt tired, a bit muddled. It was all the champagne, the joint, the coke, the ammi. Jesus, he could *collapse* out here. What the fuck were they doing?

He felt the sudden stab of cramp in his right side. It slowed him up. The boat was getting further away, the cramp was getting worse. Was it his imagination or was the sea getting rougher?

'Hey!' he screamed out. But nobody appeared to hear him.

twenty-five

Dallas stood in the doorway of Lew Margolis' office staring at the man who had the power to create a marvellous new career for her.

She pictured him not behind his marble desk, but at the door of his magnificent house in Bel Air, wearing nothing but a smile, and an orange-coloured bathrobe.

A year ago. Lew Margolis. She had known him only as 'Dukey'. Bobbie called all their clients 'Dukey'. 'Makes 'em feel wanted – kinda special,' Bobbie explained, 'cancels out the hooker dude relationship.'

Who was she kidding?

Dallas was nervous and edgy that evening. Things had already started with Ed Kurlnik, and if he ever found out what she really did . . . To protect herself, on professional engagements, she tried to look as different as possible.

Tonight she had tucked her long hair out of sight under a red afro wig. And she wore much more make-up than usual, and raunchy, hooker-type clothes.

'Come in, ladies,' Lew Margolis ushered them into a huge, white living room.

'She-e-et man, this is nice,' approved Bobbie, already stoned out of her head. 'Any other comers or is this just a cosy sweet stuff threesome?'

'Just the three of us,' replied Lew pleasantly. He was a man of about sixty with abundant dark hair and a prominent nose. He wore steel-rimmed glasses and walked with a limp.

Dallas took in her surroundings quickly. Nice house. The guy obviously had bread. He wasn't completely unattractive, so what did he need with them? She noticed two photo frames placed face down on a corner table. How many times had she seen that done. Mustn't let the family watch.

'So, Dukey, Babe,' trilled Bobbie, 'give me the action, and we're on.'

'*You two cunts get your clothes off*,' the pleasant tone had vanished from his voice.

Bobbie smiled. 'Money first, honey second. Three hundred for an hour. Fine with you Dukey, babe?'

He reached in his bathrobe pocket, extracted a stack of notes, counted off three hundred, and handed it to Bobbie.

She checked it through, stuffed it into her purse. 'Seems cool to little 'ole me. Clothes off, girl.'

Whilst Bobbie stripped provocatively and elaborately, Dallas peeled her clothes off quickly. Each time it became more difficult. She remained impassive and unsmiling, leaving the jokes and fun up to Bobbie.

When they were both naked his attention focussed on Dallas.

'Well? questioned Bobbie, hands on hips, legs astride, 'what we gonna play? You wanna little show? Or maybe a massage? What's it to be, man?'

'Upstairs,' he said thickly.

He led them up to a beautiful bedroom, dominated by a king-size bed. On the wall there was a portrait of the film actress Doris Andrews, noted for her portrayal of 'good girl' parts.

Lew flung open a closet of women's clothes. 'Dress yourselves,' he commanded, 'everything. Tights. Panties. Bras. An outfit. It doesn't matter if they fit or not.'

It was a peculiar request. But Dallas was used to peculiar requests. She sorted through the shelves, drew on some black tights, found a pair of black lace knickers. Whoever the clothes belonged to had expensive taste. She chose a black silk bra, and it fitted her perfectly. Over the top she slipped on an Yves Saint Laurent suit.

The clothes were much too big for Bobbie, and by the time she was dressed she looked ridiculous.

Lew Margolis watched silently until they were both finished. Then he handed them two identical wigs, and told them to put them on. The wigs matched the hairstyle of the woman in the portrait exactly.

'We're going to play pretend,' Lew said.

'Like – wow!' shrieked Bobbie, 'who you want me to pretend to be? Charlie Chaplin?' She imitated Chaplin's walk, then collapsed laughing on the floor.

134

Lew Margolis didn't smile. 'Downstairs. In my study..I will be a dentist.' He stared at Dallas. 'You will be the patient. Mrs M. And you—' he indicated Bobbie, 'just announce her.'

'Sounds like fun . . .'

They followed him downstairs. Bobbie making faces behind his back. He went into his study, closed the door.

'This dude is fuckin' nuts,' whispered Bobbie, 'a real head case. He wants us to look like his fuckin' wife! Why, I bet it's her clothes we got on. I bet . . .'

'Announce her,' shouted Lew, from behind the closed door.

Bobbie knocked, waited for his, 'Come in.'

'Mrs M. for her dental appointment, sir.'

'Show her in.'

Dallas walked into the study. On the desk the photographs were face down.

'Sit down, Mrs M.' said Lew plesantly, indicating a chair. 'Nurse help Mrs M. to get comfortable. Take her jacket.'

Bobbie helped Dallas off with her jacket. Lew had removed his orange bathrobe and was wearing a white dental coat and nothing else. 'Wait outside, nurse, I'll call if I need you.'

Bobbie went out, shut the door.

'Lean back, Mrs M. I'll just have a look at your teeth, see that everything's all right. Now, open your mouth wide.'

Dallas did as she was told. Then suddenly he leapt on a stool next to the chair, and jammed his penis into her mouth. It was unexpected. She gagged, nearly choking.

'Take it easy, Mrs M.' he said soothingly, 'It's what you come here for, isn't it? Everyone knows. Everyone. Even your husband. It's the talk of Beverly Hills how you're fucking around on your husband. You whore!'

They stayed three hours, collecting a total of nine hundred dollars. And they played doctor, hairdresser, dressmaker, head waiter, gynaecologist, gardener. And every game ended with his little speech about Mrs M. wanting it, getting it, and everyone knew, even her husband.

Driving them home Bobbie said, 'Now there is a dude with some problem. Do you think the wife is out fuckin' everything in sight?'

'I don't know and I don't care. I just hope I never have to see him again.'

Lew Margolis stood up from behind his marble desk. 'Come in, sit down. Cody has told me lots of good things about you.'

135

Slowly Dallas walked into the office. He hadn't recognized her – yet. But then of course she had the protection of her hat and shades. When she took those off ...

More than anything she felt bad about Cody finding out. He would feel so let down. She should have told him. But how did you casually reveal an item of information like that? Oh, by the way, Cody, forgot to mention it, it's probably not important anyway, but I used to be a hooker. Worked doubles with a stoned black kid, we must've laid half of Hollywood.

'Didn't I tell you?' Cody was saying excitedly, 'didn't I warn you she was sensational? And *who* could be more right for the part?'

'Yes,' agreed Lew, 'she is a lovely girl. How old are you, dear?'

'Twenty.' She took off her shades and stared at him, just as she had stared at the dentist, and the hairdresser, and the gynaecologist.

'Perfect age,' he looked her up and down, 'perfect everything.'

'Thank you.' With one gesture she removed the Stetson, and shook her mane of hair free.

'Has she done anything?' Lew asked Cody, 'Is there any film on her we could see?'

'An Al King television special and a commercial,' replied Cody quickly, 'I can arrange for you to see them within the hour.'

'Yes,' said Lew, 'but I imagine she photographs like she looks.'

'On camera she's even better.'

'I don't know about the name ...'

'It's unusual.'

'Yes, it's unusual. Ever acted, Dallas?'

She removed her jacket. Surely he would remember now? 'I've acted quite often. I've been told I'm very good.'

'We'll see about that. You certainly look the part. Why don't you run over to costume and make-up. We're all set to shoot a test on you. All right with you, Cody?'

'Fine, Mr Margolis.'

'You go with her. If the test hits the spot we're in business.'

Cody stood and extended his hand. 'I think we're going to be in business, Mr Margolis.'

The rest of the day seemed to pass in a dream. Dallas didn't think she would have got through it if it wasn't for Cody. He didn't leave her side, encouraging, admiring, boosting her confidence. And all the while she waited for Lew Margolis to suddenly remember.

He didn't. Anyway, if he did, it appeared to make no difference.

She tested, doing three different scenes which she had to learn there and then. Cody led her through every word. 'Unless you're the worst actress in the world the part is yours,' he confided, 'and when they see the test and realize how great you are, that's when I get called back to the big man's office. And that, sweetheart, is when schmucky little agent, yours truly, Cody Hills, shafts them right between the two big ones. We go for broke. A million dollar deal or nothing. That's when you have to hang in there and trust me. They'll kick, but in the end they'll pay. And they can afford to.'

'Whatever you say, Cody. By the way, is Lew Margolis married?'

'Where have *you* been? He's married to Doris Andrews. So you have no worries about bed being part of the deal. Why? He hand out any horny vibes?'

'No, not at all. I just wondered.'

'Wonder no more. Doris Andrews keeps a twenty-four hour eye on Lew, and him on her. No, you've got no problems with him – he's straight.'

Poor misinformed Cody. Lew never could tell him, because by revealing her he would reveal himself. Dallas sighed. Why couldn't things be nice and simple? .

Two days later, as Cody had predicted, they called him in to negotiate. He told them what he wanted. They told him to forget it.

Three days later Dallas signed a million dollar deal to star in 'Man Made Woman'.

It was an option deal, but if they picked up on all options, and there was no reason to suppose that the series wouldn't be a giant smash, then, as Cody comfortingly told her, she would not only be a huge star, but rich as well, with every opportunity to do the one movie a year her contract allowed.

It was an exciting time. Much more exciting than winning some stupid beauty contest.

Cody could not conceal his absolute delight, and went around the entire time grinning from ear to ear.

'I'm giving up the agency business,' he informed her. 'Going into production.'

'Production?' she questioned, 'production what?'

'*Our* production company. You concentrate on becoming a star. I'll concentrate on finding you the right property for your first movie.'

'Hey, mister, hang on there. I may be a big flop.'

' "Man Made Woman" will top the ratings. First season, you'll see.'

'Your confidence is very reassuring.'

He took her hand, held it tightly. 'Stick with me, it's catching. Even my mother thinks you're going to be a star.'

'I'm going to try, God knows I'm going to try. I've dreamed about a chance like this.'

'So has my mother!'

She couldn't help laughing. Cody, it seemed, could always make her laugh. She had started to lean on him, turning to him for advice on everything. He was looking at houses for her, something small to start off with, and then who knows? She had put herself entirely in his hands business wise. But she trusted him absolutely. After all, he had started the whole thing.

Cody Hills was the first man she had ever respected. Perhaps because from the very beginning he had always treated her nicely. No heavy come-on. No sexual hassle.

Maybe sex with Cody might mean something. There had been no one since Kip Rey, and that had not been a happy scene. She didn't crave sex, she didn't even think about it. But she did want to let Cody know she was grateful for everything he had done. And to her way of thinking sex was the only way to say thank you. So that evening, when they were enjoying a celebratory dinner, she suggested he came back to the hotel and spend the night.

'Who me?' protested Cody. 'Me and you? The princess and the frog?'

'Frog? Are you stupid. You're a very attractive man.'

'I am?'

'You am.'

'I'll probably kick myself black and blue in the night, but right now I don't think we should complicate our warm and business-like relationship with things that go grope in the night.'

'Are you saying no?'

'I am saying that you ask me again when things are not as bright as they are now. When you're tired, and fed up with being at the studio six a.m. five days a week, and pissed with your vacation time because it's not long enough, and sick of posing for publicity still, and . . .'

'Are you . . . ?'

'I am not a fag,' he interrupted, 'and if we slept together my mother would find out and expect us to get married or something sloppy like that. Let's put it this way – something special is worth waiting for. So please can you wait . . .'

138

'*Funny*!' She laughed until tears swelled her eyes. And she understood he wanted more than sex, and he wanted her to know that.

'Now that we're nearly rich,' he said, deftly changing the subject, 'how do you think I'd look with a hair transplant?'

'Horrible!' laughed Dallas, 'I like you just the way you are.'

A week after the contract was signed Lew Margolis summoned her into his office. He smiled warmly, asked her to sit down, offered her a drink. Then, from the floor behind his desk he picked up a bundle of women's clothes and flung them at her.

'Put these on, million dollar cunt,' he said, still smiling.

She should have known when she walked into his office. The photo frames on the marble table were all turned face down.

twenty-six

What would happen if he died out in the middle of the Atlantic ocean? Drowned, whilst two stoned little rich girls rocked and rolled on their private speedboat unconcerned about his fate.

What would Paul say when they arrived back without him? What would Edna say? And the newspapers of course would have a marvellous time.

Grimly he swam on, the pain in his side getting stronger and stronger. But fortunately the wind seemed to have dropped a bit, and he did appear to be making some progress towards the boat. He could hear his own voice echoing raunchily from the tape recorder. 'Random Love' again. His first big hit. How long ago that all seemed. Must be ten years. His first television appearance on a pop show to promote the record. A live audience of randy groupies. They had stormed the stage and tried to rip his clothes off.

Girls. Girls. Girls. From that moment on there had been a constant supply. What was it about fame that attracted women? He didn't flatter himself that it just happened to him. He had seen a wizened old comedian who could command the instant attention and availability of the most beautiful of girls. He had seen a very famous politician, fat and grotesque, who regularly bedded every female in his path.

It wasn't flattering to be aware of the fact that you could have any one you chose *only* because you were famous. If he was Al King, road digger, he would hardly be out here, drowning, with the fabulously rich Kurlnik twins. And he would not have been invited back to Marjorie Carter's body. Oh no. *That* type of woman wouldn't second glance him, however good-looking he was. And he was thirty-seven years old. According to all the books he had read on the subject he was past his sexual prime.

The hell he was.

He had reached the boat, and he hung onto the side, too exhausted to haul himself aboard. The cramp gradually subsided, and wearily he pushed himself up the ladder and into the boat.

The Kurlnik twins were on the mattresses at the back, their bodies entwined. Oblivious to all else they were making love to each other.

Al stared in disgust. He could have drowned, and all they cared about was each other.

Angrily he slid into the driver's seat, and gunned the Riva into action. It shot off, nearly dislodging the girls on the back.

Cara crawled to the front of the boat, her eyes blazing. 'You stupid bastard!' she yelled, 'you could have drowned us!'

They left Fire Island later that afternoon.

'I don't understand,' Linda complained, 'I thought we were staying the night. What's the problem?'

Paul shrugged. 'I've given up asking Al for reasons. Something must have happened while they were out ski-ing. He's burning, just leave him alone.'

'Don't I always?'

'You know what I mean. Stay out of his way. No photos.'

'*Yes, sir.*'

They returned to New York and Al closeted himself in his hotel suite. 'No calls, no birds, no games. I just want some peace.'

'I'll hang around,' Paul volunteered.

'No way, baby brother. I want to be alone.'

'What happened out there?' asked Paul, as curious as Linda.

'Nothing important,' stated Al blankly, 'that's the whole goddamn trouble – nothing important.'

'They seemed like nice girls . . .'

'Piss off, Paul. I don't need conversation.'

'I'll be around if you need me.'

'I don't. I'm going to sleep. Wake me an hour before we have to leave tomorrow.'

'If you're sure . . . Luke will be outside if you want anything.'

'I know that.'

Reluctantly Paul left. This was a mood of Al's he had never encountered before. Al wanting to spend a night by himself – unheard of. Especially at the peak of his success.

When Al was alone he phoned Edna. He hadn't spoken to her since Canada. Suddenly he missed his home, his son, even his wife.

'Hello,' she was anxious as always, 'is everything all right, Al?'

'Of course it's all right. Hasn't there been anything in the papers there?'

'Oh yes, the newspapers are full of you. Pictures, write-ups. I'm sticking them in the scrapbook.'

'That's nice. Evan around?'

'He's upstairs. I'm worried about him. He never wants to do anything or go anywhere. He spends all his time alone. And I found some magazines in his room...'

'Yeah? It's just a problem age. Tell you what, now that things seem to be moving so smoothly I thought I'd have him with me sooner. We go to Philadelphia, Monday – he can join us there.'

There was silence from Edna's end of the phone, then in a small voice she protested, 'But, Al, I'll be alone in the house. You know I get nervous when I'm alone.'

'That's crap, Edna. You've got a maid, a cook, Nelson. And goddamn Melanie right next door.'

'I know, but...'

'But nothing. He was joining us in Nashville anyway, so he'll come a week sooner – big deal. You said he's stuck in his room all day, this will give him a chance to see a bit of life.'

'Melanie says we should come too...'

'Melanie is a pain in the butt. Do I have to keep on reminding you how you hate these tours?'

'I know. You're right. Al, the shower is broken in our bathroom and...'

'What are you telling *me* for? Since when did *I* last mend showers? Tell Nelson, he'll fix it, what do you think I pay him for.'

'I still don't like Nelson.'

Al sighed. 'Jesus, Edna, I'm not asking you to jump into bed with him...'

'Al!'

'Have him mend the shower, and anything else that needs doing.'

'All right.'

'Call Evan, I'll tell him the news.'

There was a five minute wait until a surly Evan came on the line.

'You're joining us Monday,' Al enthused, 'so get yourself together.'

'I haven't got any decent clothes.' Evan complained.

'Don't worry, you can get it bigger and better here.'

'Yes.'

'Is that all you've got to say – yes? This will be the trip of your life, boyo, *I'll* see to *that*.'

Al hung up the phone.

As each day passed the thought of divorce grew stronger and stronger. For a moment he had thought he missed Edna, but speaking to her on the phone, listening to her whiney voice, well, he knew it was finally over.

It would be difficult to tell her. He could imagine the scenes and tears, but it had to be done.

He climbed into bed, took a couple of sleeping pills, and fell asleep watching Johnny Carson on television.

The show at the Spectrum, Philadelphia, was another smash.

As the tour progressed, so momentum picked up, and Al and 'The Promises' just got better and better.

'Beautiful show tonight, babee,' cooed Rosa, her dark skin agleam with sweat. She had said goodbye to her Mafiosa boyfriend in New York, and was once more available.

'Not bad,' agreed Al.

Bernie was throwing a small party in his suite at the hotel, just a private gathering for people connected with the tour.

'I hear you're bringing your boy out,' said Rosa, licking full red lips, 'your wife comin' too?'

Al shook his head, looked around for Paul.

'I left my man in New York. Won't see him until LA. Sure gets lonely at night.'

'*You*, lonely? Can't believe that.'

She pouted. 'Hey, Al. What's the matter? We had good times before, why not now?'

'I can't get involved, Rosa.'

'Hey man – *involvement* is the last thing in this little girl's head. Just a few good times, a few laughs. How about it, sport?'

'Not this trip.'

'I thought we were pretty good together.'

'So let's hang onto our memories.'

Rosa smiled. 'Sure. No hassle.' Her eyes drifted over to Luke stationed motionless by the door, 'You ever give that hunk time off?'

'You want him, he's yours.'

'He's a big mother! Real big and mean. Think I'll just hustle on over and hear the story of his life. By the way – you hear Magno Records all set to sign us to a *fantastic* contract? New billing – "Rosa and the Promises". Next year it will be *me* can use a body-guard!'

'I heard. It's great news. Congratulations.'

'Thanks to you having us with you on the tour. We were almost there, but this pushed the button.'

She undulated over to Luke, thin, black and beautiful. Al could remember the desire the first time he had seen her. He had been there, the desire was no longer present.

He finally caught Paul's eye and beckoned him over. 'I'm going to bed . . .'

'It's early,' protested Paul. 'I thought you might want a gin game.'

'No. I want to be at the airport in the morning, meet Evan myself.'

'You feel OK?'

'I feel great. Why?'

'No girls tonight. The blonde in the corner is hot at the sound of your name . . .'

'So why don't you fuck her? Why does it always have to be me?'

'Huh?' stuttered Paul, confused, 'I thought . . .'

'Goodnight, Paul.'

Bernie Suntan wiped the sweat from his brow with a large cotton handkerchief. He was too fat, that was the trouble, too goddamn fat. What the fuck was he doing running around airports in this unbelievable heat. He should be sitting in an air-conditioned office arranging deals – that was *his* forte in life. And with any luck, when this tour was over, that's just what he would be doing.

A ground hostess approached him, she was fresh and smiling. 'Your flight is just clearing customs, Mr Suntan. Our man will bring young Mr King right through.'

'Thanks, babe. You've been a big help.'

'Anything to help out Al King,' her eyes sparkled, 'I don't suppose there is any chance of getting tickets for tonight's concert?'

Bernie reached in his pocket. 'You just gotta mention it, babe, just gotta mention it.' He handed her two complimentary tickets, scribbling a number on the back. 'Give me a call later, there may be a party after. And bring a girlfriend – a pretty one.'

'I *will*! Is it possible that we might get to meet Mr King?'

Bernie regarded her through narrowed eyes. She *was* pretty. 'If you're lucky, babe, you may get to do more than meet him!'

She giggled and blushed.

'No shit,' continued Bernie, warming to his theme, 'Al's a wow with pretty little things like you.' He patted her reassuringly on the bottom 'wear something sexy. What's your name anyway?'

'Betty-Ann-Joe.'

'Well, Betty-Ann-Joe, tonight just might be your lucky night.'

She was positively glowing. 'Really? You think so?'

'Shit, babe, I *know* so.' He gave her a little hug, 'don't forget to call.'

'Oh, I won't.'

Outside the airport building, in a long Cadillac with black-tinted windows, Al waited impatiently.

Luke sat impassively in the front next to the chauffeur.

'Hey – here comes my boy.' Al jumped out of the car. 'Evan! You look great! How was the trip?'

'I feel sick,' complained Evan.

'Get in the car, you'll be all right. Hey, Bernie – they take good care of him?'

'The best. Al, say hello to Betty-Ann-Joe, she saw Evan got through customs with no hassle.'

Al hardly glanced at her.

'Mr King,' enthused Betty-Ann-Joe, 'I have all your records, every single one. It's been a real pleasure to help you out.'

'Sure,' agreed Al absently, climbing back in the car. 'Come on, Bernie, let's get this act together.'

Of course it was a mistake. Nothing Al said or did brought a smile to Evan's pinched and spotty face. He remained unimpressed. The truth of the matter was that being in his father's presence made him more insecure than ever.

He knew that people expected Al King's son to be something special, and when they were confronted with him it was all they could do to keep the surprise off their faces.

But anything was better than being stuck at home with his mother. And Nelson – slimy, horrible slob. He had expressed

144

great surprise at the fact that the girl he had arranged for Evan had never turned up. 'Little scruff, knew I shouldn't trust her.' But he had said nothing about returning Evan his five pounds, and when Evan had mentioned it days later he had assumed a hurt expression and said, 'I haven't got your money, I gave it to the girl.' The subject had not come up again. And Evan had been reduced to the cold comfort of his magazines. That was until his rotten mother found a stack of them and burned them in a ritual heap at the bottom of the garden.

'What's been happening?' asked Al, 'everything in good shape at the house?'

'There's a drought,' mumbled Evan, 'they've banned using hosepipes. Your grass has all burned up – looks like straw. Your apple tree's full of worms.'

'Any more good news?' asked Al ruefully. Evan knew how he loved his garden.

'Nothing much. Auntie Melanie scratched up her car. I think the swimming pool's cracking.'

'Terrific. Apart from that everything's fine though?'

'I think so.'

'He thinks so!' Al shook his head. 'We'd better get you some clothes. Tonight you'll watch the show, then after we'll have a party for you. How does that grab you?'

'All right.'

Later Al had a private conference with Paul. 'The kid needs to get laid,' he informed his brother. 'Those spots are signalling a desperate message. We've got to find him a girl for tonight. A young hooker who knows her job. He mustn't guess. Can you arrange it?'

'Al, for you we all pimp. But for Evan too? I think you're asking too much.'

'So have Bernie arrange it, I didn't mean you personally.'

'Why don't you ask him yourself? It's not like it's part of his job . . . he's already taken the kid shopping . . .'

'Fuck his job,' snapped Al suddenly, 'do I have to beg to get a favour done around here? Isn't it enough I sweat my guts out on stage every night so that everyone around me can get fat? Even you, Paul. Where would you be without me?'

'I never thought I'd hear you say that,' replied Paul with tight-lipped control, 'who the fuck do you think got you where you are today?'

'You helped, but I'd have made it anyway.'

'And so would I. I've got artists in London waiting for me to stop tagging along tucking you in nights and concentrate on their careers. And they'll be stars – the bloody lot of 'em, when I give them some time.'

'So why don't you go then? Fuck off. I can manage without you.'

Paul was white-faced. 'I think I will.'

Al stalked off into the bathroom and slammed the door. He felt incredibly tense and uptight. He needed a woman to vent his fury on.

Bernie had taken Evan out shopping, they wouldn't be back for a while. He picked up the phone and asked for The Promises' suite.

A soft voice answered.

'Rosa?' Al questioned.

'Rosa's out, this is Nellie.'

It flashed across Al's mind that she was only seventeen. But it was only a flash. 'Why don't you come up for a drink,' he suggested.

The hell with it. He needed a woman, anyone would do.

Paul nursed a large scotch. 'I have had it. Up to here. I'm not some frigging little gofer he can spit on when the mood takes him.'

'Calm down,' soothed Linda, 'I'm sure Al didn't mean it.'

'Ha!' snorted Paul, '*you're* sure Al didn't mean it. There's a twist. *You're* the one that's always telling me what a cunt I am to cater to him the way I do. And you're right. That's what I am. A grade A cunt.'

'Make it a prick and I'll be the first to agree with you!'

'Don't make jokes, Linda, please. If it wasn't for you, I'd be on the next plane out of here.' He handed her his glass for a refill. 'You think I need all this? I've got a young kid – writes all his own songs – sounds like Tom Jones ten years ago – could knock spots off Al. All he needs is a push. And I'm the one that can do it for him.'

'So what are you waiting for?'

'You know why I hung back. I thought Al needed me on this tour.'

'He probably did at the beginning. It could have been a disaster – then he *would* have needed you. As it is, he's a sensation. He needs no one.'

146

'You're right. You're always right.'

She nuzzled his neck. 'That's why you love me and that's why one of these days you'll marry me . . .'

Together they said: 'When the children are older!'

Paul couldn't help laughing.

'You see,' said Linda, pleased, 'I can even make you laugh when you're at your blackest. Now let's make love and forget about the whole thing. If you are going to make any moves at all I want you to have a clear head, so stop guzzling scotch and guzzle me instead.'

'How do you guzzle a person?'

'You've never heard of guzzle? What are you – a boy from a sheltered family? Come here and I'll show you!'

'What you done to Nellie, man?' Rosa's green eyes flashed dangerously.

'Screwed her. Is it a crime?' Al was still in a filthy mood as he sat in his dressing-room dabbing his face with pancake.

'You bastard!' spat Rosa. 'Motherfuckin' bastard! She's only a kid. Whyn't you pick on someone your size?'

'Is she complaining?' sighed Al patiently.

'No, she ain't complaining. She's all starry-eyed, thinks marriage is just around the corner.'

'So disillusion her.'

'Do your own dirty work,' stormed Rosa, 'I think you're a mean bastard pickin' on a kid like her. Ain't you got enough groupies and God knows what hangin' around you?'

'Leave it out, Rosa. I'm in no mood for lectures – especially from you.'

'*We* could have had some laughs, but that wasn't enough was it, you had to go shaggin' after little kids.'

'Get lost, Rosa.'

'You bet your ass, whitey.' She stamped out of the room.

Bernie, on the phone in the corner, pretended not to hear. But his stomach was already warning him that things were not going to progress as smoothly as he had hoped.

'Fix anything?' snapped Al.

'They got a girl of twenty. Redhead. Big knockers. Name's Susie. She'll be at the party.'

'Is she all cued in?'

'She will be. I'll see her myself when I pay her.'

'Good.'

The phone rang, and Bernie automatically reached for it. 'Yes?'

The voice, slow and distinct, was instantly recognizable. 'Tonight,' it whispered, 'the three bombs due to go off in New York, they'll be set tonight instead. Three-minute intervals.' The phone clicked dead before Bernie could say a word.

'Who was it?' asked Al.

'Wrong number,' sweated Bernie. His stomach had not been wrong. The thing that worried him was that this had sounded like a local call. Same thing in New York. OK, so nothing had happened in New York, but maybe this was the build-up. And where did the quiet, nothing voice obtain the private dressing-room numbers?

He would have to discuss it with Paul. Maybe it would be wise to contact the police.

Luke appeared at the door.

'"The Promises" just went on,' he informed Al.

Sitting near the front Evan felt nervous being amongst so many strangers. The girl next to him chewed gum and wore the AL IS KING T-shirt. She joggled around on her seat like a caged puppy. On his other side were two middle-aged women in flowered dresses. They chatted together in low, controlled voices. They reminded him of his mother.

He was glad when the lights dimmed and a red flash from the darkness of the stage produced 'The Promises'.

He fell in love instantly. She was the most beautiful girl he had ever seen. She stood to one side of the tall black girl in the middle. She was coffee-coloured, with long jet black hair, and a beautiful little face. She was dressed the same as the other two, but on her, somehow it looked different. The other two were stridently sexy. She was almost demure.

They swayed together –

'Come on sweet stuff
Sure can't get enough
Ohhh – you're sugar sweet
Ohhh – babee
Ohhh – babee
Love you like a bomb
Gotta love you long
Ohhh you're my desire
Ohhh – babee
Ohhh – babee'

148

Evan opened up his souvenir programme, found their picture. Her name was Nellie. She was seventeen. Only a year older than he was. And he would meet her, of course he would. They would be travelling across the country on the same plane.

'This is my son.' Proudly Al introduced Evan to everyone at the party. They all gave him the scarcely hidden look of amazement. At least Evan thought they did.

'Have some champagne, son.' Al thrust a glass at him. 'Go on, drink it up, get used to the good things in life early.'

'I've never . . .'

'Drink it down like a man, won't do you any harm.'

Evan gulped at the fizzy liquid. It had a revolting taste, much too bitter.

'You liked the show?' asked Al.

'It was all right,' mumbled Evan. He had liked 'The Promises', but when Al had come on, his toes had curled with embarrassment. Was that man on the stage posturing and gesturing really his father?

The girl sitting beside him had gone into a frenzy of madness. Even the two middle-aged women on his other side had appeared to go beserk.

The whole place was full of screaming women. They must be mad.

'It's a good job that I know all right from you means sensational!' laughed Al. 'You're Mr Cool. I don't think I've ever seen you crack a smile!'

Evan smiled weakly, and gulped at the champagne just to have something to do. He didn't see Nellie until she was right behind Al putting her hands over his eyes from behind.

'Peekaboo!' she trilled.

Al removed her hands. 'Oh, it's you,' he said, 'this is my son, Evan.'

'Hi there, Evan.' She had a very high sing-song voice. She was even prettier off stage, wearing red trousers and a peasant blouse. 'Lovely show, Al, really something,' she tucked her arm into Al's, her eyes shone with adoration.

Al deftly removed her arm. 'Nellie's one of "The Promises".' She'll look after you a minute, I've just got to see about something.' He strode off, leaving them together.

Evan was speechless. Frightened to open his mouth in case his voice let him down and cracked horribly – a circumstance that had been occurring of late.

'I didn't know Al had a big boy like *you*,' sighed Nellie in her funny little voice, 'how old are you?'

'Sixteen,' replied Evan, his voice staying at a nice deep level. 'I'll be seventeen soon.' Soon was about six months off.

'You don't look like him.' Nellie narrowed her eyes. 'Not at all.'

Evan was glad to note that he was taller than her. He drew himself up to his full height and thrust his glass at her. 'Have some champagne,' he suggested. Unfortunately his voice broke right in the middle of champagne.

Nellie giggled, but she took the glass anyway, sipped a little, sighed dreamily, and said, 'Your old man sure is something, *really* something.'

Al returned at that point with Bernie, and a hard-faced redhead.

'This is my son,' announced Al, 'Evan, say hello to Susie.'

Evan nodded quickly, and returned his attention to Nellie, who was taking sips of the champagne like a little bird.

Susie said in a loud voice, 'Hey now – what a looker! You told me he was nice – but what a *looker*!'

Evan stared at her in amazement. She was talking about *him*.

She placed her hands firmly on her waist and rocked back and forth, 'Hhmmm . . . If you're an import – then I'm in the import business!'

Nellie giggled. 'I think you all just got lucky,' she whispered at Evan.

He blushed. Susie reminded him of one of the girls from his magazines. She was wearing a green dress, low-cut and split up the side. She had jammy red lips, and flinty brown eyes. Her red hair straggled down her back. She winked at Al in an obvious fashion. 'Mind if Evan shows me around?'

'Around where?' croaked Evan anxiously.

'Go ahead,' said Al, 'show Susie the rest of the suite.'

'But there's only the bedrooms,' objected Evan.

'I *love* bedrooms,' enthused Susie, 'I love to see how other people decorate. That's what I am, y'know. A decorator.' She grabbed Evan by the arm. 'Come on, handsome. Show me the sights.'

Tensely Evan pulled away. Firmly Susie hung onto him again. 'Pretty, please,' she pouted, 'be a good boy, you won't regret it.'

Panic-stricken Evan turned to Al. 'Show her around,' said Al smoothly, 'We'll see you later.' And he turned away.

Susie dragged a reluctant Evan towards the bedroom.

'See no one goes in,' Al instructed Bernie.

'What was *that*?' asked Nellie, 'she looks like a hooker.'

'She is a hooker,' agreed Al. 'Little present for Evan.'

'Some present!' Nellie rolled her eyes. 'Poor kid was frightened to death.'

'He'll love it.'

'Oh yeah?' questioned Nellie, 'with a gorilla like that?'

'You should have seen *my* first fuck. Next to her that one's a princess!'

Nellie giggled. 'You are *bad*!' Then her voice softened, and her fingers touched his cheek. 'It was wonderful today, somethin' I bin dreamin' about since Vegas. You know I was fifteen then, just a little kid.'

'Listen, Nellie, don't go getting big ideas. This afternoon was nice but . . .'

'Mr King! Remember me? Betty-Ann-Joe. We met at the airport this morning and Mr Suntan got me tickets for your show and you were sensational but of course I knew you would be and I just had to come over and tell you how I felt because . . .' She droned on with a breathy enthusiasm whilst Al inspected her. Pretty, young, clean-looking. He had had it with celebrities and rich bitches. What he needed was a girl who wouldn't answer back. A girl who would be overwhelmed just by being in his company. He certainly didn't need Nellie, with fawn-like love shining out of her eyes. Best to discourage her right from the start. He regretted the fact that he had ever invited her to share his bed. Rosa was right – he *was* a shit.

He put his arm around Betty-Ann-Joe. 'So you liked the show. Come with me, young lady, and I'll show you something you'll like even better!'

Paul watched the scene from across the room, Linda by his side.

'I don't know how he does it,' she commented dryly. 'How come he's not a walking advertisement for the clap? I mean do you realize how many there have been in the last couple of weeks?'

'He's always been like that,' replied Paul. 'Now that he can have anything he wants I guess he feels he'll be losing out if he doesn't.'

'He can't *enjoy* it. Do you think he enjoys it?'

'Who knows? I don't discuss his sex life with him.'

'Oh come on – of course you do.'

'Of course I don't.'

'He's probably a lousy lay, always having to prove himself the way he does.'

'That he's not.'

'How do *you* know?'

'I just know.'

'Oh. Have you indulged at the same time then?'

'When we were young – yes.'

Linda laughed. 'Confessions of a raver. And I always thought you were so straight.'

'I was about eighteen at the time.'

She kissed him on the cheek. 'I wish I'd known you when you were eighteen.'

He looked around anxiously. 'I told you to be careful when Evan's around.'

'He's not around. He's locked in the bedroom with that dreadful hooker. I think it's an awful way to treat a young boy, it could put him off sex for life.'

Paul shrugged, 'My brother – he knows it all. Meanwhile little Nellie's in a state over there – apparently he found time to give her one this afternoon . . .'

'Oh, no.'

'Oh, yes. See if you can cheer her up before Rosa zeros in. I can see the shit hitting the fan any day now. Go on, I've got to have a talk with Bernie.'

'Take your clothes off,' commanded Susie for the fifth time.

Evan sat miserably on the corner of the bed. 'I don't want to.'

Susie sniffed. 'Jesus, kid! I'm trying to do a job of work around here, but you are not makin' it easy.'

'I haven't asked you to do anything,' snivelled Evan, wishing he was back in England, wishing he was anywhere except trapped in a hotel bedroom with this large red-haired monster.

'Listen, kid,' said Susie firmly, 'I got orders to fuck you. F-U-C-K. You understand what that means? I got paid already. I gotta reputation to consider, so at least unzip your fly, at least do that, goddammit!'

'I don't want you,' muttered Evan, scarlet with humiliation. 'I don't know who paid you and I don't care.'

'Your daddy paid me. Your daddy wants you taken care of.' Suddenly she took off the belt of her dress, and the whole thing seemed to disintegrate, falling to the floor, and leaving her stark naked, except for a laddered pair of tights. 'OK, sonny. Here's the goods. *Now* can you flip it out?'

'Go away,' mumbled Evan, 'go away and leave me alone, I think I'm going to throw up.'

'Sheeit!' Susie scooped up her dress and threw it back on. 'Why couldn't I have had the daddy? Listen, kid, I ain't givin' nobody back no money. You want me to go, say somethin' happened. All right?'

'Yes.'

'Oh, and say it was great, outasite, mind-blowing! OK? I've got me a reputation to consider.'

'Yes.'

'Right on, kid. We're a team.' She inspected herself in the mirror, smiled secretly and added, 'You don't know what you're missing . . . Tell your daddy to give me a try – no charge.' She winked and left.

Evan remained huddled on the bed. He was so confused. He had wanted a girl. But not like this. Not paid for and arranged by his father. And what about Nellie? Did she know? If she knew he wanted to die, simply and quietly die.

Damn his father. Damn his bloody famous father. He wished something terrible would happen to him, something really terrible . . .

twenty-seven

'I think,' said Dallas slowly, 'that you have made a mistake.'

Lew Margolis chuckled. 'A mistake! Don't talk crap. I recognized you the moment you walked into my office. No one could possibly forget *that* body.'

'Am I supposed to be flattered by that remark?'

Lew leaned back in his chair, enjoying every minute of the confrontation. 'You can be what you like, suit yourself – *Mrs* Margolis.'

Dallas shook her head in amazement. 'You're sick, you know that? You're really sick.'

'Why?' he snapped, suddenly angry.

'Because if I *was* the girl you thought I was . . .'

'Which you are . . .'

Dallas ignored the interruption. 'If I *was* that girl, what makes you think that in a million years I'd go back to doing what I was doing?'

'Everyone has a price,' said Lew flatly, 'and all women are whores anyway. Take my wife,' he picked up a photo frame and stared at a glossy smiling photo of Doris Andrews. She had a scrubbed fresh look familiar to moviegoers the world over. 'She'd screw a snake if it had the bad sense to venture onto our estate. I know all about her, so I take my revenge. Can you blame me?'

'Divorce would seem like a better idea.'

'Why should I divorce her? I love her. Take your clothes off, Dallas, put on those things, I only have fifteen minutes. I want to be a real estate agent, this is my office and you've come to discuss selling your house and buying a bigger property.'

'Forget it.'

'Don't be a silly girl.'

'What are you threatening me with if I don't, Mr Margolis?'

He raised his eyebrows in a gesture of surprise. 'I am the man who is going to make you into a star.'

'I know. I signed the contract already.'

'Contracts can be broken.'

'People can sue.'

'In this town power rules. Surely you know that by now?'

She shrugged, trying to conceal her sudden nervousness, trying to maintain an outward calm. 'People can also tell true life stories.'

Lew laughed loudly. 'Who would believe *you*? A girl who got fired because she wasn't a good enough actress for the part. Besides, you're forgetting, I'm married to Doris Andrews – her reputation is public domain and pure, pure white. Anyone trying to throw mud would end up covered in it.'

'Why did you hire me? Why did you agree to pay me all that money? Why would you even *think* of making me a star?'

'Because your agent was correct – you *are* the right girl for the part, and as you know, we need someone immediately. But no one is irreplaceable, there are other girls, maybe not as good as you – but available – and accommodating.'

She brushed her hair back with her hands, and fought to keep the tears of frustration from appearing. 'Let me get things straight,' she said slowly. 'I want to be absolutely sure I understand you. The contract is only good if I do what you want, is that it?'

He nodded.

'And if I don't, I'm out. Right?'

'Right, I'm afraid. Does Cody Hills know of your former occupation?'

'Keep him out of it,' snapped Dallas quickly.

'He'll have to know,' stated Lew blandly, 'if I drop your contract he'll have to know.'

'Why?'

'He seems like a smart young man. I'm sure the moral implications will put him off sueing.'

'You've worked it all out, haven't you? Either way I get screwed.'

She wanted to scream and shout and hurl abuse at him. She wanted to claw his filthy little eyes out, kick him where it hurt, smash his mouth in. Instead she managed to smile coolly while she gathered up the clothes he had thrown at her and placed them in a neat pile on his desk. Then she leaned over the desk, selected a cigarette from his silver Dunhill box, lit it, leaned back, and said, 'OK, Mr Margolis. You win, and why shouldn't you – you're holding all the cards. But not now, not while you only have fifteen minutes.'

'But . . .'

'No buts. It's my turn to take control. You want me to be in control, don't you? We can have more fun that way, lots and lots of fun . . .' How easily the hooker dialogue returned. The stern bantering that most men loved. 'Now you be a good boy and do things my way. I promise you a trip, sugar, that will blow your little mind.'

'When?' he asked eagerly.

'Tomorrow. Not here, but at my house.'

'I can't be seen going to your house.'

'Who will see you? The virgin queen doesn't have you followed, does she?'

'No . . . but . . .'

'We can play swimming instructors, wouldn't that be wild? Do you swim?'

'I used to . . .'

'And you will again.' She smiled, blew him a kiss with her fingers. 'I'll be Mrs Margolis – you can be Mark Spitz if you like. She would like him, wouldn't she? Young, strong . . . Can you play the part?'

He nodded, a pleased expression covering his features. 'You know what I want don't you? You're a smart girl. I knew you'd see things my way. There's no reason we can't both enjoy it.'

The smile was stuck on her face like a mask. 'No reason at all.'

She left the studio in a controlled state of fury. She drove her rented car to her rented house in the Hills.

She walked around, stripping her clothes off as she went, then naked, she dived into the kidney-shaped pool, only letting her tears come when the water hit her.

She swam up and down the pool, powerful strokes cutting through the bland blue water. And she cried herself out. Exhausted herself, until at last she clambered out of the pool, flopped down on the grass, and lay spreadeagled to the sun, thinking.

Blackmail. Pure and simple blackmail.

You pull my schlong, and I'll pull the strings for you to be a big and beautiful star.

But what if she was a star already? What could Lew do then? 'Man Made Woman' would make her a star. It wouldn't take that long. How many visits from Lew Margolis would she have to endure? The thought of even one made her flesh creep. Once a hooker always a hooker was bullshit. She would sooner wait tables than go back to that life.

There had to be an answer.

At first, staring at Lew as he sat smugly behind his fine marble desk spelling out the way it was, she had wanted to kill him. That's why she had suggested the swimming bit. But of course it hadn't worked with Bobbie, so why should it with him? But oh the satisfaction of dragging him under, feeling him squirm, seeing his fear when she let him up.

It was just a dream. She was incapable of murder – indeed the thought disgusted her – just as Lew Margolis disgusted her.

She was often haunted in dreams by the corpse of the old man so long ago in that Miami hotel. She would wake sweating, her legs shaking, her heart pounding.

If only she could turn to Cody for help. But he would be so disappointed in her, and even more disappointed as he saw their million-dollar deal go flying out the window. She wondered if he would be shocked. Were people shocked by things any more? He would be hurt, that was worse. She would have let him down, and no way did she want to do that.

She rolled onto her front. What to do? Lew Margolis was blackmailing her, there must be a way she could turn the tables on him.

It came to her in a series of thought waves, piece by piece.

Photographs. Everyone believed photographs.

Lew and she. One time. Repugnant thought. But if she could get photographs.

How?

She had never held a camera in her life. But if she could hire someone . . . Silly thought, it would only lead to more blackmail . . .

But it was the answer. The living room and bedroom overlooked the pool. Huge glass windows, an unimpaired view. How did she find a photographer? How did she trust anyone? Linda.

The name sprung into her mind. Linda would help her if she told her the truth. If she agreed, it was the perfect solution. Perfect.

Dallas relaxed at last, giving herself to the sun, and deciding the best way to ask Linda. She certainly couldn't tell her over the phone, maybe there would just be time to find out where she was, get on a plane, and if Linda cooperated they could fly back together and get everything organized for Lew Margolis' visit the next evening.

She was about to get up when she heard footsteps approaching, then Cody's voice, 'Hey, lady, your slip is showing, but don't panic, my eyes are covered and I can only see what I let myself.'

She rolled over, stood up, and wrapped a towel around herself sarong style. 'You can look now.'

'God, you're a tease!' He uncovered his eyes and grinned. 'You promised to call me the second you got back. What did he want?'

She shook her head, playing for time, wondering what the hell to tell him. 'I don't really know,' she said at last, 'sort of a pep talk about morals, I guess.'

Cody nodded. 'I thought it would be something like that. He's running scared after his he/she shock. Are you all right? Your eyes are red. Have you been . . . ?'

'Cody, I got a call from my aunt. Remember I told you I had this aunt back East that I lived with until I was sixteen?'

'You told me she was bad news . . .'

'I know I told you that, but she still brought me up. If it hadn't been for her, after my parents were killed, well . . .' She shrugged helplessly. 'She needs me. A personal problem. I'm going to see her.'

'You can't go. Are you mad? You start shooting in three days. You're supposed to be resting, getting a tan, studying your lines.'

'I can study my lines on the plane. Look – I've got it all arranged, flight booked, everything. I'll be back day after tomorrow, I promise you. Back in time to get twelve hours' sleep before the big day.'

Cody frowned. 'The studio will never allow it.'

'The studio doesn't have to know.'

'It's a stupid move.'

'It's one I have to make.' She clasped his hand, squeezed it. 'I wouldn't let you down, surely you know that much about me?'

He nodded in resignation. 'Yeah, I suppose so.' Then more vigorously, 'So get packed and dressed and I'll drive you to the airport for my sins.'

'Your sins you can keep. I'll take my own car to the airport, leave it there, it will be simpler that way.'

'I could meet you tomorrow.'

'Cody, I want a producer not a chauffeur.'

'I could come with you . . .'

She feigned annoyance. 'I don't think you trust me.'

'Of course I trust you.'

'Then please, be a sweetheart and haul your ass out of here so I can get ready. I'll call you the moment I arrive. I promise.'

He was reluctant to leave, but she finally got rid of him.

Poor Cody. What a pack of lies she had fed him. But it couldn't be helped, it was all in a good cause.

Some good cause, saving her own ass.

She located Linda in Miami. It *would* have to be Miami.

She was on a plane there within the hour.

twenty-eight

The push-ups were tiring Al out. 'Forty-seven, forty-eight, forty-nine, fifty.' He collapsed on the floor gasping for breath. 'Your turn, Evan, boyo.'

Evan watched his father through narrowed eyes. No way was he going to compete with him. 'I don't feel like it, dad.'

'Give it a try,' commanded Al, 'you want to stay scrawny *all* your life?'

Reluctantly Evan squatted down on the floor, but fortunately the phone rang before he was forced to humiliate himself.

Al picked it up. 'Yes?' he questioned. Pause. Then – 'Oh, Edna, it's you again.' Pause. Then – 'I told you yesterday he was fine, there's no need for you to keep phoning.'

When he hung up he was in a filthy mood. Edna hadn't bothered to call him once, but now that her precious little Evan was around she was on the phone every day. He had been right to get the boy away from her. Evan was a mummy's boy, frightened if anyone so much as farted. And his spots were as bad as ever. He still looked skinny and a misfit in spite of all the new gear.

Al would have liked to have discussed the boy with Paul, but since their argument there had been a certain coolness between them. A coolness that Al now regretted.

Being a star meant never having to say you were sorry. But he *was* sorry, although he didn't know how to say so.

The tour was taking on a certain sameness. Philadelphia a smash. New Jersey the same. Kansas City ditto. And now Miami – gateway to the retired sun-seekers of the world.

Installed in a suite at the Fontainebleau, Al could not even venture out. To do so meant instant mobbing from droves of beehive-hairstyled ladies in town on a hairdressing convention.

He had discovered that Evan was not the ideal travelling companion. The boy was a permanent fixture, not allowing Al the freedom he needed. Somehow he had thought that underneath all the whiney crap Evan would be just like him. Misguidedly he had thought that if he stuck a cigar in his mouth, plied him with champagne, and turned him on to pussy, the boy would miraculously change.

No such luck. Evan remained his usual surly self. Refusing champagne, choking on cigars, and backing away in a panic if a member of the female sex hovered anywhere near.

Al walked over and stared out of the window at the crowded swimming pool many storeys below.

'Bullsheeet!' he said slowly, 'Bullsheet you fuckers!' He was bored. Horribly, restlessly bored.

'What are we going to do this afternoon?' ventured Evan.

Al throttled back a vicious reply. He had become a fucking entertainments director!

What he would like to do, what he needed to do, was spend the afternoon in bed with a dumb blonde. A really dumb blonde who wouldn't bother him with any talking.

'I don't know,' he said, 'maybe Bernie can take you somewhere. I'm tired, thought I might go back to kip.'

'Oh,' the boy's voice was disappointed. 'But you promised we could go scuba diving.'

'How can we do that?' asked Al, exasperated, 'when you can't even swim?'

'I can watch from the boat.'

'Tell you what,' Al had a sudden idea, 'you can have a swimming lesson, I'll call down and arrange it.' That would give him at least an hour free.

'I'll never learn,' complained Evan, 'I've had lessons for years.'

'Can't give up on it,' insisted Al, 'it's only a matter of time, then pow – it's like fuc . . . dancing – you never forget.'

'I can't dance.'

What can you do? Al felt like asking. I've lavished everything that money can buy on you, and you still can't do a fucking thing. Thank you, Edna. Before my very eyes you have raised a pain in the ass.

Ignoring Evan he picked up the phone and called the desk. A swimming lesson was arranged instantly. As soon as he got rid of the boy he hoped that a blonde could be arranged equally instantly.

Actually all he had to do was saunter out of his room and take his pick, but who needed that trip?

He called Paul, but someone at the desk informed him that Mr Paul King had gone out on a yacht for the day with Miss Cosmo.

What the fuck did they think this was – a vacation? He hoped in a moment of malice that Melanie called and got the same message.

Evan had changed into swimming shorts.

'Take you socks off, for Christ's sake!' snapped Al. 'You look like a walking advertisement for the English abroad.'

Grimly Evan peeled off his socks. What a rotten trip this was turning out to be. His father either completely ignored him, or went out of his way to embarrass him. Al King's son. What a cross *that* was to bear.

He allowed his mind to linger fleetingly on Nellie. She was so pretty, and sweet and nice. He could admire her from afar, it was better that way. If only it had been *she* that his father had arranged for him. That would have been wonderful, instead of that monstrous big Susie girl. And the embarrassment of facing Nellie after that evening. But she had been sweet about it. Hadn't mentioned it. In fact there had been no chance for him to talk to her since then. She seemed to go out of her way to avoid Al. Maybe she didn't like him, and Evan could understand *that*. However, Evan enjoyed the fact that sometimes he felt her eyes in his direction, but he was too shy to stare back.

He wished he could be more like his father towards women.

He wished he looked like his father.

He wished he was famous and rich and everyone jumped when he spoke.

He wished his father was dead.

Finally rid of Evan, Al decided to take off for the afternoon. He was sick and tired of playing nursemaid. Fuck it. He was a star.

A superstar. *He* should be the one out for the day on a yacht, not Paul.

He rifled through the piles of invitations littered around the suite. Parties. Receptions. Mostly from people he didn't know and didn't even want to know.

What to do? He had to get out. To stay meant the imminent return of Evan, and even if he was locked safely in the bedroom with a blonde it wouldn't be the same.

He picked up an invitation to attend a luncheon party for the English Ambassador, got dressed quickly, had Luke summon his limousine, and they were away.

'This is nice,' Linda murmured. She lay in a sun chair, sipping a Banana Daiquiri, and observing the frenetic activities of the other guests on the yacht as they scurried from group to group frightened of missing something or someone.

'Not bad,' agreed Paul. But he was frowning, and he couldn't help wondering if Al was all right. Since the argument they had maintained a cool business relationship, or at least Paul had. Al, in his way, would have been quite happy to pretend the whole incident had never happened. But Paul was deeply hurt, and childish though it was, he wanted an apology, and he was determined to hold out until he got one.

Linda was delighted that she suddenly had Paul all to herself. He attended to business, saw that the shows went smoothly, and then he was all hers. No hanging around to see what Al wanted to do. No hand holding, ass kissing, pimping. It was a refreshing change.

When Paul seemed to weaken she reminded him that Al had Evan with him anyway, and Bernie and Luke were in constant attendance to see to his every need.

That was fine, reasoned Paul, but he could see Al becoming more and more restless as the tour progressed, and he thought to himself – fuck you – stubborn bastard – apologize for Chrissake and I'll be there to smooth things over – look after Evan – find you prime pussy – whatever you want.

'I *like* the rich life,' Linda remarked. 'Why don't *we* buy a yacht and just take off where no one can find us. You've got enough money, haven't you?'

Paul grimaced mockingly. 'So! It's my money you're after.'

'Never! It's your body, it's always been your body . . . Come here, you sex machine. Come here, you big . . .'

'Stop it! Hands off, someone will see.'

'Don't be so English.'

'Don't be so American, and get your hands off my . . .'

'All right. All right!' Linda stretched languorously and laughed. 'Am I getting brown?'

'Not bad. You like lazing around in the sun, don't you?'

'Yes. I could see myself living this kind of life. You know, I don't see why we can't . . .' she began, then stopped abruptly, her mood changing mid-sentence. She knew why they couldn't buy a yacht and take off. She knew why they couldn't be together. She reached into her purse, produced a cigarette, lit it, drew deeply, stared at Paul. 'I hate the fact that you're married,' she stated flatly, 'I really hate it.'

'Why are you bringing that up. I never tried to hide it,' he defended.

'Nope,' Linda laughed in a brittle fashion, 'I guess you never did.' She thought of the unknown enemy, the wife, and for the thousandth time wondered what she was like – even more important, what Paul was like when he was with her. Did they make love? Well of course they must do. Was it good? Linda bit deeply into her lip. She wasn't going to ask. She wasn't going to behave like the other woman. She was just going to cool it, like she always had. And in the end – where the hell did it get her? Nowhere fast, that's where it got her. If she was smart she would cast her eyes around for someone new, someone free.

She sighed, shivered slightly, drained her drink and said: 'Let's circulate, Paul, let's see who else is on this floating piece of ostentation.'

Maybe she should start to play games. Maybe *that* was the way to get through to him. But oh Christ who needed all that game-playing crap, not at her age, that was stuff for teenagers.

'Do we have to?' Paul groaned.

'Yes,' insisted Linda. 'I thought I saw Ramo Kaliffe a minute ago, and I'd love to meet him.'

'Lead the way,' said Paul resignedly. And he wondered what Al was doing.

twenty-nine

Arriving at Miami Airport hit Dallas like a giant shock wave. It brought back every bad memory. Was it really only two years ago that she and Bobbie had fled the city like a couple of thieves?

She remembered the night in detail . . . The old man dying on them. Bobbie pocketing his bankroll. The mad dash to their crummy apartment where they packed up in record time. And then the airport where Dallas had felt that at any moment a hand would descend on her shoulder and she would be arrested . . .

She jumped as a voice growled, 'Wanna cab?'

'Yes, please.' She climbed in and directed the driver to the Fontainebleau.

More memories. She had practically started her career at the Fontainebleau. She shuddered when she realized how many men ago *that* had been.

'Al King concert at the Sportatorium tonight,' the driver remarked, 'it's a madhouse over there, big hassle with forged tickets. You here on vacation?'

'No.'

'You look familiar, like I know you. You on TV?'

'No.'

'Had a girl in the cab last week. An actress – English. She . . .'

Dallas tuned out as the cab driver droned on. She found herself wondering if her parents were still at the zoo. If her husband was with them. If any of them had ever given her a second thought.

If she had more time she could drive out there. Not of course to go in, but just to see if the zoo was still there . . .

Bastards. She had been seventeen years old and they had just let her walk out in to the world on her own. A girl so innocent that she had thought the first guy that screwed her was doing *her* a favour.

The cab pulled up at the Fontainebleau.

'You sure do look familiar . . .' the driver mused.

She ignored the remark, paid him, and walked up the steps into the hotel.

Linda was not there. Paul was not there. But the desk clerk pointed out Bernie Suntan waddling across the lobby on his way out.

Dallas hurried over to him. 'Mr Suntan,' she said quickly, 'I . . .'

He continued walking. 'Sorry. No free tickets, kid. Kaput. All gone. Follow us to Chicago and I'll see what I can do.'

'I don't want tickets,' she said. 'My name is Dallas, I'm a friend of Linda Cosmo, and I have to get hold of her immediately. It's most urgent. Can you help me?'

Bernie stopped, stared, let out a whistle. 'Jeeze, you are one beautiful lady! Saw the TV thing you did with Al, excuse me for not recognizing you at once but this tour is ageing my facilities! For you I gotta ticket.'

'I don't want a ticket,' Dallas explained patiently, 'I just want to see Linda.'

'Of course you do,' agreed Bernie, rubbing sweaty palms together, 'and we shall share a car to the Sportatorium and we shall find her for you.'

'Thank you.'

The cab driver had been right about it being a madhouse at the Sportatorium. Huge crowds roamed around outside surging angrily in different directions. Mass blocks of tickets had been forged, and many genuine ticket holders had been unable to gain entry.

'If we could catch the rip-off merchants life would be a lot easier,' Bernie complained, as their car edged its way through the crowds. 'Gonna take you to Al's dressing room while I find Linda, she's a good kid – takes a bitch of a picture. You should see the show.'

'I did. I saw it in New York.'

'You did? Wish I'd known, could have done a nice little thing with you and Al. Pictures . . . old friends. Could have been a nice plug for you.'

'I don't think that's such a good idea. I think Al's nervous of his wife.'

Bernie burst into raucous laughter. 'Al? Nervous of his wife? Craperooney, baby – pure craperooney. Al's screwed everything that moves on this tour. No offence . . . I mean what the fuck . . . *everyone* knows about Al.'

Dallas agreed. 'Sure. So if you were a girl would *you* want to be photographed with him?'

Bernie laughed some more. 'If I was a girl I'd piss my way out of his sight in record time. He treats 'em all like shit.'

'Him and who else?' stated Dallas dryly.

'You're something,' guffawed Bernie, 'I like you. When I'm a producer gonna keep you in mind.'

'How kind of you.'

'What the fuck . . . If you can't help friends in this life who can you help?'

'Quite right,' agreed Dallas briskly, 'do you think we can find Linda now?'

'The Promises' were on stage belting out 'Love Power', shimmering in black sequin boiler suits.

Al was in his dressing room, drinking hard. He had already demolished a bottle and a half of scotch, and did not feel like doing the show. Fuck the show. Fuck the people. What was he, a puppet?

Evan, in one corner of the dressing room, puffed uneasily on a cigarette.

Luke had rushed off to summon Paul.

Bernie, unaware of any dramas, waddled in with Dallas behind him.

Al didn't see her. He scowled at Bernie in the mirror and said, 'Where you been, Bernie? Out water ski-ing? Or maybe Disneyland took your fancy? Don't know why you took the trouble to come here at all. Why do any of you bother? I do the work, the rest of you should stay away, just pick up the money. You shitass. Here's a nice little item for you. Al King will not appear tonight. Al King is all fucked out and just wants to sleep. You like it? Does it grab you by the balls?'

'Al!' protested Bernie. 'Baby! what's the matter? I just got off the phone to Chicago setting everything up. I would have been here sooner if . . .'

Dallas backed quietly out of the room as Bernie spoke. She did not need this whole bit. Al King was obviously every bit as impossible as she had thought he would be.

Paul was striding towards her. 'What's going on?' he snapped in an irritable fashion. 'What are *you* doing here?'

'Question one – I don't know. Question two – looking for Linda. Is she here?'

'She's photographing "The Promises".'

'Thanks, I'll find her.'

'Did you see Al?'

'Some other time, I think.'

Paul nodded, and went into the dressing-room.

Dallas located Linda at the side of the stage. She watched as Linda went about her business, not disturbing her until she stopped to change film. Then she stepped forward and Linda nearly dropped her camera in surprise.

'I have to talk to you. Can we go somewhere?' Dallas asked.

'Sure, I'm about finished. Why are you here?'

'It's a long story, and I need your help. That's why I'm here.'

'We'll take one of the cars back to the hotel,' Linda decided. 'I don't think tonight's the night I'm going to miss the shot of the century. Hey, Larry,' she called to one of the roadies, 'tell Paul I had to go – catch him later.'

Dallas had thought long and carefully about how much she should tell Linda, and in the end she had decided that only the truth would help. Of course, certain things she would leave out – such as the old man dying, and her attempt to drown Bobbie. But apart from that she had planned to be quite open about everything. Linda was too smart to fall for any phoney story. To acquire her help she had to be honest, and that meant the whole messy story. If Linda was the friend she hoped she was, she would help out.

They sat in Linda's hotel room, ordered drinks from room service, and Dallas began her story. She talked for two hours, with only occasional nods from Linda to encourage her. And when she was finished she was surprised to find that she was crying.

Linda handed her a Kleenex, and Dallas said, embarrassed, 'I haven't cried since I was a kid.'

'It's a sad story,' commented Linda, 'God, Dallas, I never knew any of this. I mean I never thought you were the virgin type, I knew you'd been around – haven't we all. But this . . . Jesus!'

'It's funny, y'know talking about it and all, it seems so remote. Like half the things happened to someone else. I can't really believe I did all those things, screwed all those men. I can't believe it was me. And now this sonofabitch wants me to go through it all again. He'll make me a star but I'll be his paid whore.'

'I'll help you,' said Linda quickly. 'I'll take the pictures. But you haven't thought it out clearly. If you're in the pictures with him he can turn the whole thing around. *You* can't be in the photos, we'll have to hire a professional.'

'He won't go for that.'

Linda lit a cigarette. 'He will if you're in it too. We'll get hold of a black girl – someone that will remind him of Bobbie. You'll be there – involved, but I'll make sure the only photos I get are with him and the other girl.'

'It's a marvellous idea. But I am not exactly in a position to come up with a black hooker between now and tomorrow night.'

Linda frowned. 'LA must be crawling with them. Bernie might be able to help out there – he knows everyone.'

'But you promised not to tell anyone.'

'Of course not. Is asking him for a girl telling him anything? I'll make up some story, I'll have to for Paul anyway – he is not going to be thrilled to discover I'm off to LA for the day.'

'Listen,' said Dallas seriously, 'anytime, anything. One of these days I hope I can pay you back.'

Linda laughed. 'Wait until the job is done before you thank me. It won't be *that* easy – but with a little luck we'll make it. Now come on, let's take ourselves over to Paul's suite – they should be back soon, and I'll give him the news of my impending absence. Probably do him good – maybe he'll miss me. Only maybe mind you – but it's a chance!'

Paul persuaded Al to do the show. He finished the bottle of Scotch, reeled on stage, and the audience screamed. He did a lousy show but the only person who knew about it was him. The screaming never let up for a minute, so who could possibly hear that his voice was slurred and not up to par. He even inserted the word fuck in place of love on several occasions, and no one was any the wiser.

'Morons!' he mumbled as he was bundled into his car and sped back to his hotel. He wanted to party, but passed out instead, and Paul left him on his bed with Luke watching over him and strict instructions to contact him when he awoke.

It was time to forget about their fight, Paul decided. He had not realized that Al was heading into one of his states, he had thought he was flying high. Thank God he hadn't left the tour in a fit of ego. Al really needed him, and he would be there.

When Linda told him that she had to go to Los Angeles for a couple of days with Dallas he didn't mind a bit. It was a relief in fact, giving him absolute free time with Al – a fact that Linda would have bitched about.

Linda noticed his attitude, and she smiled coldly saying, 'It might even be longer than a couple of days.'

'Take as long as you need,' Paul replied absently.

Sonofabitch. What did he care? If only she could summon the strength she wouldn't come back at all.

They arrived in Los Angeles early the next morning and drove straight to the house. Linda prowled around inspecting the facilities she would have for her photography.

Bernie had come up with the phone number of a black call girl. As Linda had thought, he had a special little book with a listing for every preference. His eyes had bugged out as to *why* Linda wanted the number of a black hooker in LA. But she had just smiled and said, 'Everyone to their own, Bernie sweetheart,' and left it at that.

The girl – exotically entitled Diamond, answered the phone on the second ring in a lazy Southern drawl. Linda said they had a proposition, and could they talk. Diamond agreed, noted the address, and said she would be with them in an hour.

She turned up two hours later, a dazzlingly pretty girl in her early twenties with an abundance of long black hair and a Diana Ross smile. Her only problem appeared to be short legs and a dropped ass. Apart from that she was a knockout.

Linda fed her some story about a married man whose wife needed pictures of him in action.

Just as Diamond was objecting, Linda mentioned a fee of five hundred dollars, and the deal was clinched.

Diamond left in a cloud of Hermes perfume promising to return later.

'We're all set,' Linda announced, 'do you think you had better call old Lew and make sure he'll be here?'

'He'll be here,' said Dallas bitterly, 'I just hope I can go through with it.'

'Come on!' chided Linda, 'just think of the outcome . . . Think of the time when *you* can screw him.'

'Yes,' agreed Dallas, 'I can just imagine his face when I show him the photos. It would never occur to him that I'd have the brains to work this out. He thinks I fucked my brains out when I was a working girl.'

'Listen, kid, I hate to say it, but they all credit women with minimal thinking capacity. Hey – you know what I think? I think a few drinks around here would not go amiss. And how about a little grass – you got any?'

'In a red box under the fridge. Linda, isn't it ridiculous – I'm nervous.'

Linda smiled. 'Aren't we all? But forget about it, relax. Tonight we're going to win for a change, I just know it.'

thirty

Al awoke with one of the worst hangovers he could remember. His head pounded in a series of drumbeats, his eyes hurt, even his teeth ached.

He tried to remember . . . Jesus, the show. What had happened with the show? Had he appeared? He honestly couldn't remember.

He lay very still, trying to ignore the fact that he had to piss, trying to concentrate.

He remembered going to some lousy afternoon party. Some gathering full of snobbish English exiles. Miami-based chinless wonders. Tinkly-voiced, horse-faced girls who regarded him as some kind of freak. It had somehow brought back every bad memory of the days before the fame.

He had left the party abruptly and gone to a whore-house. The man least likely to have to pay for it had selected a jolly little Cuban girl, and spent three hours getting boozed in her pathetic little room.

He hadn't screwed her, merely humiliated her. And after, he felt like a real shit, and had continued on his drinking jag all the way to the concert.

He remembered vaguely Evan joining him somewhere along the way. And Bernie, and Paul arguing with him. But had he gone on? He truly couldn't remember.

The desire to piss was too strong to resist, and by the time he came out of the bathroom Paul was sitting on his bed. They regarded each other warily. Neither quite sure what terms they were on.

'Fuck the push-ups this morning,' mumbled Al, 'What I really need is a couple of gallons of orange juice and a new head.'

Paul picked up the phone and requested a jug of fresh orange juice from room service. 'Food?' he questioned.

Al made a face.

'So,' said Paul, hanging up, 'what's the problem?'

'No problem. Just felt like cutting loose.'

Luke had filled Paul in on Al's activities of the previous day. 'What made you go to that party?'

'What did you want me to do? Sit here and play footsie with Evan? You'd all pissed off – I couldn't even find Bernie.' He hesitated. 'How did the show go?'

'You staggered around a lot. Insulted the crowd. Fortunately there was so much screaming you could have stripped off and sung Bollocks and no one would have noticed. At least we got you on.'

'Where's Evan?'

'I sent him down to the coffee shop.'

Al held his head. 'The kid is driving me nuts, gotta get him off my back. Gotta send him home. *You'll* have to tell him, *I* can't.'

'Thanks a lot. The boy idolizes you. If you send him home it's going to be an A one rejection – he'll become even worse. I think you should give him another chance.'

'Another chance at what? He won't drink, smoke, or screw. Watches me like a hawk – I can't take it, makes me nervous.'

Paul opened the door for room service, and poured Al a hefty glass of orange juice. 'Just leave him alone. Stop worrying about him. First of all it's wrong to have him in your suite – we'll get him his own room in future. Don't have him follow you everywhere – let him make his own friends.'

'I wish he would.'

'Leave him alone and he will. I'll have Linda take a friendly interest in him when she gets back.'

'Where's she gone?'

'To Los Angeles with Dallas – she has some problem – Linda's helping out.'

Al's interest perked. 'What problem?'

Paul shrugged. 'Don't know. Dallas flew in, grabbed a hold of Linda, and they flew off this morning. I think that . . .'

'Dallas was here?'

'Last night.'

'Why didn't you tell me?'

'I just did.'

'That's great, isn't it. He tells me when she's gone.'

' *You* were gone last night. You were lucky to do the show. You were . . .'

'Do me a favour, Paul. Piss off. Your voice is pounding into my head and I can't take any more.'

'Sure. Plane leaves in two hours. Press reception and television interview arranged to take place at O'Hara Airport upon arrival. Kup show to be recorded this afternoon. Party in your honour tonight at the Macho Mansion.'

Al groaned. 'If I'm not dead by that time . . .'

Paul smiled thinly. There had been two calls that there was a bomb secreted on Al's plane, and at this very moment the plane was being thoroughly searched. 'You'll make it.'

Al grinned. 'Sure I will. Sauna. Massage. Stomach pump. By the way – you got a phone number for Linda?'

'I didn't know you cared.'

'I do. She's lovely but taken. Do you mind if I phone Dallas?'

Paul wrote a number on a piece of paper. 'Be my guest.'

After Paul left, Al felt relief. Things were back to normal between them. It made him feel a lot better. God almighty, if Paul couldn't understand his moods by now . . .

He poured himself some more orange juice, gulped down several Bufferin. Forced himself to take a cold shower, then decided he couldn't miss doing his push-ups and got through half of them before collapsing.

Only then did he pick up the telephone and ask for the number Paul had given him. He didn't know what he was going to say if Dallas answered, but he wanted to talk to her, just say hello again. Of course she would have to fly into Miami the night he was pissed out of his mind. It seemed to be fate that they kept on missing each other.

The operator told him to hold on. He waited impatiently and was surprised at how disappointed he was when he was informed that the number did not answer.

Shit! What *was* it about Dallas?

He folded the piece of paper with the number on it and put it carefully into his pocket. Later, he would call again later.

Edna King peered at herself in the bathroom mirror. Melanie had persuaded her to have her hair cut. She had dragged her to a place called Mr Capones, and a tall, thin, leering Italian had chopped off her shoulder-length mouse, and she had emerged with short blond curls.

Reluctantly she did have to admit it looked better. Although what Al would say she didn't know. He would probably be furious. He was always telling her he liked her just the way she was – well, that was what he used to tell her. He hadn't told her much of anything in the more recent times they had spent together.

She stood up and admired her new svelte figure. Thanks to Melanie watching her like a hawk she had lost ten pounds. And her make-up was much better since Melanie had taken her to that place where they had taught her to apply things in a more subtle fashion. But what would Al say when he found out how much she had spent on a whole new wardrobe of clothes? He would be furious. 'Don't be silly,' Melanie had argued, 'he spends more on clothes in a month than you have in your entire married life.' That *was* true, but still, *he* was the star of the family.

Edna smiled at herself tentatively in the mirror. Melanie has persuaded her to go to the dentist and have her crooked front tooth capped. It still surprised her to smile and see the difference.

She sighed. She just hoped that Al wouldn't be too angry.

Melanie had laughed at her fears. 'You look wonderful. Younger, prettier, smarter. Al will be knocked out, just you wait and see.'

And it wouldn't be that long to wait. Melanie had booked the tickets already which would fly them both to America on a surprise visit.

Edna rubbed nervously at her subtle brown eye-shadow, blending it in even more. At least Melanie was right about one thing, she did look much better, whether Al approved or not.

Macho was the giant success men's magazine of the seventies. What *Playboy* had been to the sixties, and *Penthouse* to the early seventies, *Macho* was now. Its enormous sales left all its rivals trailing in its wake. The appeal of the magazine was that it had something for everyone. Month after month it featured beautiful, nearly naked, very famous ladies. Nude men with vibrant hardons. Unknown Nymphets indulging in near porn. Incredibly elegant fashion lay-outs. A very comprehensive Arts section. Political writers of great esteem. In fact it was the cream of all the top magazines combined into one.

Van Valda, owner, founder, and editor supreme, had set himself up in a Chicago mansion bigger even than Hefner's former palace. He lived there in splendid isolation surrounded by an ever-changing procession of Nymphets.

To be a Nymphet you had to be between fifteen and seventeen, very pretty, and quite dumb. Any job which phased you out at eighteen did not appeal to intelligent girls.

At the Macho mansion a huge party was being prepared for Al King, and his reputation had preceded him. Nymphets fluttered back and forth squealing with joy. It wasn't often that a true life superstud honoured them with his presence. Usually they had to make do with Van – who couldn't get it up. Or visiting important men who could only just get it up.

'I wonder if he's as sexy as he sounds,' breathed one pink and white fifteen-year-old.

'Better!' assured a more sophisticated sixteen-year-old. 'I know

172

a girl who knows a girl whose sister has had him! She says . . .'

Hot little rumours flitted back and forth all day. And six baby Nymphets crowded onto Van's giant bed to watch Al's arrival on Van's giant-sized television screen.

Van smiled paternally. He was a thin, undistinguished-looking man of forty, whose one desire in life had been to make a lot of money, and surround himself with beautiful and sexy females. The money part had gone without a hitch, but somewhere along the way his hard-on had vanished, and for two years he had been painfully impotent. Painfully, because the desire was still there, but the implement was not.

He fondled a gorgeous little thing's right breast, always hopeful. She smiled and encouraged him. He put his hand down the pants of another girl, and she wriggled around.

He stopped both activities. He would sooner watch one of his famous porno home movies. Maybe Al would be interested in seeing one later. He could run the Ramo Kaliffe, always good for a laugh.

'What time will he be here, daddy?' burbled a sweet little redhead. 'Will he fuck us? Will he fuck all of us? Wouldn't that be fun, girls, wouldn't that be really boss?'

They all squealed their agreement.

Van climbed off the bed. Better get his equipment together, this was one movie he didn't want to miss.

Mob scenes at the airport heralded Al's arrival. He stepped from his plane, impeccable and sexual in an all-black outfit. He made a boxer's salute at his fans, smiled for the cameras. Behind him Paul marvelled at his tenacity. A few hours before he had been a complete wreck, now he was like a new man.

He handled his press conference beautifully. He combined just the right amount of aggressiveness with a humorous charm, and the ladies and gentlemen of the press loved it, especially the ladies.

Bernie hovered protectively, ready to combat any difficult questions. But they didn't come, and everything went off smoothly.

Paul noticed Evan scowling in a corner, and he went over to him. 'How's it going? Enjoying yourself?'

Evan shrugged and mumbled, 'S' all right.'

Paul felt guilty that he had paid hardly any attention to his nephew. But he didn't want him finding out about his relationship with Linda. Evan would tell Edna. Edna would tell Melanie. Melanie would go raving mad.

'Spoken to your mum?' Paul inquired.

'Yes,' muttered Evan.

'Everything OK at home?'

'Yes.'

A great conversationalist Evan was not.

'I suppose you miss home.'

'No, I don't miss it. Don't miss anything.'

'Yes . . . Well . . .' Paul was lost for words. No wonder Evan was driving Al mad. Maybe the best idea was to pack him off home.

Evan watched his uncle walk away. He must think he was stupid or something. Ignoring him all the time, and now suddenly finding the time to speak to him only because that woman had gone away. Through the glass windows he could see 'The Promises' being ushered into a limousine. A trail of photographers had followed them; he was glad they hadn't *all* stayed with his stupid father. Tonight he would talk to Nellie. He would say something, anything, he had made up his mind. He would wear his new jeans suit, wash his hair, use some of his father's make-up to cover his spots. He would do it. Definitely. She had looked at him on the plane today, really stared. He had been surprised that Al hadn't noticed, he had been sitting right next to him. But of course his father never noticed anything about him. Why should he? The only important thing in *his* life was himself.

The press conference was over and everyone was walking out to the cars. Evan trailed behind. If he stayed far enough behind he would be put in the car *after* Al. He had learned *that* little trick in Miami. Who wanted to travel with the star? People peering in the car and making remarks. Ugh!

Paul was beckoning to him but he pretended not to see. It was easy when you knew how. Head down, shuffle a lot, play deaf.

When he looked up, the car with Al in had gone.

At the hotel there was a long handwritten letter waiting for Al from Van Valda. It welcomed him to the city, wished him every success on his tour, gave him an enthusiastic run-down of the party in his honour, and insisted most profusely that Al check out of his hotel immediately and move into the Macho Mansion. In a childish scrawl Van had written:

There is plenty of room for you and whoever you care to bring. We are at your service – I have a cook on duty twenty-four hours – a choice of over a thousand movies to run at any time – and any other kind of entertainment you desire. We do hope to welcome you as more than just a party guest.

Sincere regards,

Van

'Sounds good,' commented Al. 'Why aren't we staying there?'

'If you remember,' replied Paul, 'Bernie checked it out with you in New York and you said no way. You agreed to the party but that was it.'

'Yeah – I think it's coming back to me. Wants me to do a naughty picture for his rag.'

'Right on. They were willing to pay whatever you wanted.'

Al laughed, 'Sure! Me, a hard-on, a suntan and a caption saying King Cock!'

Paul joined him in his laughter. 'They have been after you or Warren Beatty since the magazine started.'

'So let them get Warren.'

'You're kidding. If they are lucky they'll end up with Woody Allen. I hear rumours that his price is a million and a false nose!'

They both fell about laughing.

Later Al was driven over to the television studios and recorded the Irv Kupcinet show. He had done the show before on a previous American trip, and Irv was the perfect host. It all went very well.

By the time it was over Al was tired and half contemplated cancelling going to the party. But as it was in his honour he could hardly do that. So he went back to the hotel, changed, killed half a bottle of champagne, and set off with Paul, Bernie, Evan, and 'The Promises' for the Macho Mansion.

Another evening of fun.

He could have done without it.

thirty-one

Nervous as she was, Dallas managed to greet Lew Margolis with a dazzling smile. She looked incredible in a black halter top and long silky trousers.

Linda and Diamond were safely out of sight. Stevie Wonder played softly on the stereo. The champagne was open and waiting.

Lew seemed delighted by the entire set-up.

'Nice little place,' he murmured, 'private. Cosy, nice. No – I don't want any champagne – get me a Perrier water.'

'Don't you drink?' asked Dallas.

'Bad for me.'

'Oh come on, one glass won't hurt you.' She thrust a glass at him, and was relieved to see him sip at it.

He consulted his watch. 'I can only stay an hour,' he warned.

'I've got a surprise for you.'

He narrowed his eyes. 'I don't like surprises.'

She smiled, 'You'll like this one.'

'I don't like *any* surprises. Get your clothes off.'

'My clothes off? I thought you wanted to play games, I thought we were going to play swimming instructors.'

Lew scratched his head. 'I don't know. I don't think I need to.'

'Don't need to what?'

'Play games.' He laughed, pleased with himself. 'This could be game enough, just having you and knowing what I know.'

Dallas forced the smile to stay on her face. What a pig!

'Let's go out to the pool,' she suggested, 'it's such a beautiful night. I have such beautiful plans.'

'I've been looking for a cunt like you,' Lew sneered harshly. 'Good-looking, ambitious, ready to do anything. You will do anything for me, won't you? Christ! I can get it up just talking to you. You know what that means?'

She took him gently by the arm and guided him out to the pool.

Reclining on the diving board totally naked, apart from silver sequins decorating her nipples, was Diamond.

Dallas thought how gorgeous the girl looked. When she was lying down you didn't even notice the short legs or dropped ass. And she had big rounded breasts which were emphasized by the decorative sequins.

Diamond propped herself up on one elbow. 'Mr M,' she trilled, 'how good to see you again. How really exciting. Why don't you just come on over here and play with my hot little pussy while your lady wife goes and prepares herself for her swimming lesson.'

Lew turned to Dallas. 'Surprise!' she said, giving him a little push in Diamond's direction. 'Go and have fun, I'll be with you in a minute.'

Lew didn't argue. The sight of Diamond was too appealing, and anyway he probably thought that Diamond was Bobbie, and that they were reliving old times. Even if he realized that they were different girls he would just think that Dallas had tried to recreate a scene that he had obviously enjoyed.

With a sigh of relief Dallas watched him limp off towards Diamond. Then she hurried into the house and alerted Linda. She drew the drapes halfway across the huge glass windows, turned the lights off.

Linda knelt down with her cameras. 'If he looks straight through the window he'll see me,' she warned.

'I know, I know. Don't worry, we'll keep him much too busy to notice.' As Dallas spoke she slid out of her trousers and top. Underneath she wore the briefest of bikinis. She gulped quickly from the champagne glass. Oh God! This was the moment she had been dreading. Taking a deep breath and holding her head high, she went back outside.

Dinner at his mother's house was the usual bringdown. She was a nice old lady but she nagged the shit out of him.

When was he going to get married? Buy a new car? A house? Have children? Go to the dentist? *Stop* going to the analyst?

Cody pulled his car up at a stop light, glanced at a girl in the neighbouring Pontiac. He thought she smiled at him, but she had driven off before he could definitely decide. He felt depressed, although for the life of him he couldn't understand why. He was on the threshold of having everything go the way he had planned it would. He was on the brink of recognition and success. People who had formerly ignored him on the street would now start accepting his phone calls.

Hollywood. What a town. You could live and work there all your life as he had done, and unless you made waves nobody knew that you even existed.

He was about to make waves. Big ones.

He was the man that had discovered Dallas.

He was the man who had negotiated her a million dollar contract. And soon the whole town would know about it, and schmucky little nothing agent Cody Hills would suddenly be a big man. An in-demand man. The personal manager and agent they would all want.

In short, he would be hot.

Of course he had planned the way things would be. And when Dallas had first arrived in Hollywood to do the screen test he had known that somehow she was going to be his big chance. He saw in the wild-haired, sensuous girl more than just a great body. He sensed the smell of stardom. Sure the test stunk. Why not? The cameraman should have been retired, the director was someone in authority's brother, and the actor they tested her with was a fag. Testing beauty queens was a routine job that talented people wouldn't touch.

Cody always made it his business to be around when they were shooting those tests. You never knew when someone would come along. Someone special. Someone like Dallas.

He had watched her, and waited patiently for an opportunity to use her. 'Man Made Woman' turned out to be just such an opportunity. The girl they had originally signed had been big, blonde and beautiful. Too big, too blonde, and with a deep husky voice that didn't quite match.

Cody had done some private investigation, and come up with facts that surprised even him. He knew that when the truth was revealed no way could the studio use her.

But he took his time. First he wired Dallas, and when she called him and was already in Los Angeles he was delighted. He quit his job at the agency – they had never appreciated him but they soon would. And he concentrated all his efforts on getting Dallas the job. He never wavered. He named the terms he wanted for her, and would not budge. Sharp instinct told him the terms would be met. They were.

Everything had gone according to plan. Well almost everything.

He pulled into a gas station and stared morosely out of the window. What he hadn't planned on. What had come as a complete shock – was the fact that he had fallen – corny as it was – yes, fallen straight in the deep end love with his client. How unsmart could you get? Cody Hills caught in a trap he had so deftly always managed to avoid.

Living in Hollywood, being an agent – successful or not, being a male, meant there was *never* a shortage of female company.

He had had girls. Oh, had he had girls!

Irene, short and dark, who used to knit him socks and try out the Kama Sutra with him.

Evelyn, who shared a mutual difficult relationship with her mother.

Connie, who shared his analyst.

None of them beauties, true. But they were warm and female and loving.

'You are not Paul Newman,' his mother had announced to him recently, a slight note of surprise in her voice as if secretly she had half expected he was. 'You'll soon be thirty. What about marriage?' She made it sound like an offer! Marriage did not feature in his future plans. Irene, Evelyn, Connie, they would all make wonderful wives for someone. But not him, no way him.

So where did that leave Dallas? Right up front, that's where. But God! A woman like her. It would be an insult to even approach her in the way he wanted to. And of course she was the gateway to the main chance, and he couldn't even think of jeopardizing their business relationship.

But it was not going to be easy. Oh God, no.

She had gone away for one day and he was a seething mass of nerves. Where was she? Who was she with?

She had phoned him from New York she said, but when he checked with the operator he had found the call had come from Miami. Why was she lying to him? Well, why not, she probably had a boyfriend that she didn't want him to know about.

Miserably Cody paid for the gas, consulted his watch. It was only nine o'clock, too early to go home, too late to call Irene, Evelyn, or Connie.

What he would do, he decided, was drive up to Dallas' house, check it out, see everything was all right.

Good idea. He switched on the car radio and set off down Sunset.

Linda glanced at her watch. It was exactly nine o'clock. She was dying for a cigarette, but there was no time for such luxuries. Quickly she changed the film in her camera. It was difficult in the dark but she managed it without too much trouble.

Training her telephoto lens to the window once more she was able to immediately catch another revealing shot of Diamond and Lew Margolis. He was enjoying himself now, clad only in his sports shirt and socks.

..Dallas stood back from the couple, still wearing her bikini. Ingeniously she had thought of a ruse which had been successful in making her a non-participant. Allowing Diamond and Lew time alone together at the beginning had sharpened his interest in the black girl. When Dallas had emerged in her bikini she had become very businesslike.

'My swimming lesson,' she told Lew firmly, 'and keep your hands to yourself.'

That had surprised him, and when his hands had started to try and remove her bikini she had immediately rebuked him.

'I'm Mrs M.,' she told him witheringly, 'The Mrs M. And I don't like strange men trying to touch me. Only my husband can touch me. Understand?'

Diamond had been right there to comfort him. 'Poor baby,

poor little swimming instructor. Don't want to mess with those *married* bitches, they only mean trouble. Come teach me how to crawl, babe!'

Lew loved the game. He loved doing things to Diamond whilst Dallas watched. It was almost as good as if the *real* Mrs Margolis was there. Miss Prissy Lips. Miss No Fuck Your Husband but screw everything else in sight.

He smiled as he reached his finale in Diamond's mouth. Linda captured it all.

As Cody approached the house he was surprised to see several cars parked outside. He was even more surprised when he realized that one of them was Dallas'. For a moment he couldn't quite collect his thoughts. She had gone away, taken her car to the airport, phoned him to inform him that she would not be back until the following morning. Well, she was back all right.

He didn't turn into the drive. He parked his car on the roadway and walked by foot towards the house.

He didn't mean to spy on her. He had no intention of sneaking around. But why hadn't she let him know she was coming back sooner than expected? And who the hell did the other two cars belong to?

His better judgement told him to get in his car and go on home. Dallas was a free agent, she could do what she wanted. She didn't have to check with him every time she sneezed.

But he couldn't do that. He was burning with curiosity about who she was entertaining.

He contemplated marching straight up to the front door, ringing the bell, and, when she answered, saying: 'Surprise, surprise – just happened to be passing and saw the lights.' But then he realized that there were no lights on, and anyhow he couldn't possibly be just passing when she lived at the top of a hill.

He could hear music coming from around the back, the swimming pool area. Slowly he edged through the bushes, hating himself, but determined to see who she was entertaining.

The tableau that greeted his eyes was not what he had expected. Dallas standing, arms akimbo, clad in the briefest bikini, watching a couple on the diving board making the most intimate form of love.

Slowly Cody backed away. His head was churning with mixed emotions. Was that how the love of his life got her kicks? Watching other people? Or maybe things were just beginning. Maybe later she would become a participant ...

He felt more depressed than ever. Christ! This was the girl he was risking his future on. A deviate. A voyeur.

Jesus! What if the studio ever found out?

Coldly Dallas watched Lew Margolis struggle back into his clothes. He was hurrying, obviously late for some event.

Diamond had discreetly vanished.

'Not bad,' Lew remarked expansively, 'but you missed out. Next time I'll spend more time, service both of you, wouldn't want you going to bed with a twitchy cunt!' He laughed happily at his own humour. 'Next week. I'll let you know what night.'

'Yes,' murmured Dallas. She just wanted him out of her house as quickly as possible.

'I think . . .' he began. But the ringing of the telephone cut him off.

Dallas stared at the phone. She couldn't answer it. It might be Cody, and she had told him that she wouldn't be back until the following morning.

Lew waited expectantly.

The phone rang insistently.

'Aren't you going to answer it?' growled Lew.

Dallas shook her head.

'Why not?' he wanted to know. 'Boyfriend checking up on you?'

She shrugged.

'Answer it,' Lew commanded. 'Answer it and talk dirty to your boyfriend. I got a few minutes.'

She snatched the phone off its cradle, 'Yes?'

From far away in Chicago, Al King said, 'Hey, beautiful, this is Al. How come you and I are always just missing each other?'

'I can't talk now,' Dallas snapped, and she slammed the phone down.

Lew belched. 'You've got to learn to do what I say.'

'Next time,' she replied tightly.

Lew withdrew a stack of notes from his jacket, looked at them reflectively and then stuffed them back in his pocket. 'I almost forgot. Don't have to pay for the services any more.' He laughed again, squeezed her right breast harder than was necessary, and finally left.

She listened to his car draw away. Bastard! What a bastard! He thought he had her good and tied up. Well, she would show him.

Linda was in the kitchen.

'What do you think? Dallas asked breathlessly.

'I think he's a dirty old man,' commented Linda. 'I'm shocked! I didn't know such things went on outside of magazines and movies.'

'Did you get what we wanted?'

'He got what *he* wanted. And that girl – wow – that's what I call a professional. She handled him like a fish!'

'Linda...'

'Yes, I think we got exactly what we wanted. Of course can't really tell until I develop them, but I think we are in business.'

Diamond appeared, fully dressed and groomed. She smiled. 'Everything cool?'

'You were wonderful, and thank you,' said Dallas.

'Old guys are so pliable,' remarked Diamond, still smiling, 'you wouldn't think they've been screwing all their lives, they're just like little children. I got two regular clients – I think one must be eighty – why he's like a naughty *schoolboy*.'

'Do you enjoy your work?' ventured Linda.

Diamond shrugged. 'What's not to enjoy. I don't work myself too hard. I got my own apartment, car, plenty of clothes. And a stud whose looks would blow your brains!'

'Doesn't he mind?' asked Linda, unable to understand how such a great-looking girl could sell her body for money.

'Mind?' laughed Diamond. 'Honey, he is in the same business. And if ever either of you two ladies are in the market for a great big beautiful screw – well, I can recommend my guy. He is the *best*!'

'Oh,' said Linda, suddenly embarrassed, 'well I don't think that...'

'Don't knock it,' interrupted Diamond, 'the long cold night may come when you had a fight with your husband, fella, whatever. Well y'all might feel a little horny. Now you don't want to go cruisin' for some stud who'll just as soon as give you a social disease. What you'll need is a few hours of my man. He is pure funk. You can't go wrong.'

'Don't you get jealous?' inquired Linda, intrigued about the whole situation.

'What's jealous?' laughed Diamond, 'I still get my piece of the action.'

Dallas finished counting out the five hundred dollars and handed it to Diamond. She wished that she had looked on the hooking profession in the same easy-going fashion that Diamond appeared to. But every memory she had of it was bad. Being used, like a commodity. Ugh! She shuddered.

Diamond left, and Linda got down to work. She converted the kitchen into a dark-room and got right into developing the rolls of film.

It wasn't until the images of Lew Margolis and the black girl started to take shape that Dallas suddenly remembered about Al King phoning. Linda was busy pinning the pictures up to dry when Dallas told her about it. 'What do you think he wanted?'

Linda stood back to survey her work. 'Your body, I expect, he's always had a yen for you. Wow – I think I could get a job with *Macho* any day – just look at these shots!'

'Just what I needed. Linda, you're a genius!'

'Tell it to Paul, if he doesn't get our act together soon I might just be tempted by the thought of Diamond's big beautiful boyfriend!'

'I'll tell him, I'll tell him.'

Linda inspected another picture fresh from the solution. 'Dallas, babe, I think you and I are in the blackmail business!'

thirty-two

Van Valda had assembled a cast of stars. Anyone who was a half-assed personality and who happened to be in Chicago was invited to the party to honour Al King.

There was a brilliant but drunken writer who weaved about insulting everyone. There was an elfin-faced movie star recently featured naked between the pages of *Macho*. There was a socialite lady of chiselled beauty who trailed an outrageous fag gossip columnist. There was Marjorie Carter, in town to do a taped interview with Van Valda, and she froze Al with a look. There was a male movie star with bedroom eyes and a pocketful of cocaine that he was being more than generous with.

And amongst this group of luminaries frisked at least twenty special hand-picked Nymphets.

They all wore the same uniform, which consisted of crotch-hugging hip shorts and miniscule fluffy sweaters, short enough to show off plenty of tummy, and if the arms were stretched up, the underside of bouncy baby bosoms.

Some of the ground rules for being a Nymphet contained the riveting information that no panties or bras were to be worn at any time, and that a Nymphet's bust measurement must be no less than 34 (C cup) or more than 36 (B cup).

Van Valda had laid down the rules himself.

Nymphet of the month was a freckle-faced redhead named Laurie-Poo, who because of her position was allowed first crack at Al. She sprang to his side the moment he arrived, announcing coyly, 'I am your Nymphet for the night, my name is Laurie-Poo, and anything you want you just have to ask me. Any thing,' she added, in case he was too thick to get her point. 'Now what can I get you to drink, Mr King, sir?'

'Rustle up some champagne, sweetheart.' He looked around and made a face at Paul.

Then Van Valda came strolling over clad in a silken Kung-Fu jacket and velvet trousers. Van extended a firm masculine handshake, nodded at Paul, and confided, 'I can have any woman in this room, so can you, Al, so can you. I don't expect there are many men who can say that.' He puffed proudly on a phallic-looking pipe.

'Henry Kissinger,' suggested Al drily.

Van chose to ignore that remark. 'Glad you could make it,' he said, 'the Macho Mansion is at your disposal. Anything you want is yours,' he paused, then added meaningfully, 'anything.'

'I'm getting the message,' replied Al pleasantly, 'but right now all I want is a drink.'

Van looked outraged. 'You don't have a drink yet?' He hooked his fingers into the shorts of a passing Nymphet, 'Mr King doesn't have a drink yet,' he said sternly.

'Oh dear!' she cooed.

'We only just got here,' remarked Paul.

At that moment Laurie-Poo returned balancing a tray professionally on one hand. It was loaded with full glasses of champagne, and little dishes filled with Polynesian titbits. She placed the tray on a table, a glass of champagne into Al's hand, and a fried shrimp into his mouth.

Van nodded his approval. Al nearly choked.

Across the room, marooned by the door, Evan stared around in amazement. He had never seen anything like it. Is this how people really lived? The Macho Mansion was an incredible place, and Evan felt awed that he had been allowed in. Perhaps there *were* some good points to being Al King's son after all.

He stood at the door to a huge luxurious living-room. A Macho fantasy room filled with chocolate leather couches, chrome and marble tables, marvellous quadrophonic sound equipment issuing forth the voice of Al King, giant television screens on every wall with headphones for any guest who did not wish to miss their favourite programme.

In the middle of all this luxury was a sunken bar, set firmly in the centre of a miniature lake. Nymphets tripped lightly back and forth across a small bamboo bridge, holding aloft loaded trays.

Evan could recognize at least two movie stars. His mouth dropped open at the daring outfit of the female one. Why, her breasts were completely visible through some type of gauzy top. He stared, completely mesmerized.

'Hey – close your mouth – somethin's gonna fly right in!' It was Nellie by his side. She giggled. 'Some set-up huh?'

'Yes,' croaked Evan, overwhelmed at her sudden attention.

'So how ya doin'? Havin' all sorts of fun?'

He looked around quickly to make sure she was talking to him. She was.

'It's not bad,' he managed.

'Yeah,' she agreed, 'know what you mean. I guess you must feel the strain too. I mean being with Al all the time – I guess he's not that easy to be with – kinda tied up in knots, tense, never sure of what he wants.'

Evan was not quite sure how they had arrived at discussing Al, but anything was all right as long as she stayed next to him.

She looked particularly pretty in a yellow boiler suit which emphasized her delicious dark skin.

'Have you been here before?' he ventured.

'Where? Chicago?'

He nodded.

'Oh sure, bin through every crummy joint in the town. Never rated an invite *here* before. It's kinda unreal, like one of those men's magazine lay-outs.' She tossed her long black hair back. 'Believe me, *I* understand the pressures Al has to go through. You can tell him that from me, tell him Nellie says she understands. Right?'

Evan sensed that she was about to move off. He gripped her by the arm and blurted out quickly, 'You're the prettiest girl here.'

She giggled, surprised. 'Why thank you – I never knew you cared!' Then seriously she added, 'Don't forget to give Al my message.' And she was gone, plunging into the centre of the room, immediately surrounded by an admiring group of men.

•

Al found the whole scene oppressive. He did not care for Van Valda, a boring man who puffed smugly on his pipe and groped every female who came within range. He did not care for the other guests, mostly hangers-on who grouped around the celebrities and told them how wonderful their last book/film/record/concert was. Their conversations were interchangeable.

The whole party was bullshit.

He couldn't even fancy the plastic baby Nymphets. Especially not the one who had attached herself to him like glue.

Looking around he suddenly thought of Dallas, and of how she would stand out in this crowd. A real woman. The best-looking woman he had ever seen.

And why hadn't he had her by now? Where was the King magic? A little persuasion and she could be his.

He reached in his pocket, found the bit of paper with her number on, and instructed Laurie-Poo to take him to a private phone.

She led him into an office of which one entire wall was an aquarium. She waited expectantly.

'Get lost,' he told her, 'I don't need my hand held for a phone call.'

'I'll wait outside,' she stated primly.

He gave the operator the number he required in Los Angeles, and leaned back in the plush leather swivel chair. He smiled as he listened to the phone ringing, planning what he would say. Nothing heavy. Just some light conversation, and then casually he would suggest she catch the show, he could send the plane for her.

She picked up the phone, her voice brusque.

'Hey, beautiful,' began Al easily, 'this is Al. How come you and I are always just missing each other?'

'I can't talk now,' she snapped, and bang, his connection went dead.

For a moment he was stunned, hurt. Then anger took over. She had hung up on him. The bitch had put the phone down! He couldn't believe it! It had never happened to him before. Who the hell did she think she was? So she was beautiful, big fuckin' deal. Hundreds of girls were beautiful. Bitch! Bitch! She was under his skin. She was getting to him. Women were not supposed to get to you. Women were supposed to be ready, available and accommodating.

Angrily he got up, marched out of the room, brushed past

Laurie-Poo. He found the movie star with the cocaine indulged himself generously. Then he noticed Evan, still huddled ignored by the door. He turned, located Laurie-Poo right behind him, and whispered in her ear.

She listened, disappointment suffusing her chubby features. Then she set off in Evan's direction.

Van Valda was at his elbow. 'Everything all right, Al? Feel like a private party?'

Al followed Van and a select group out of the living-room and into a private elevator. Apart from himself there were the two movie stars, male and female, and the drunken writer. The female movie star trailed her fingers lightly over his fly. Her elfin face glowed. She attended to Van in the same way.

The elevator took them directly into Van's bedroom. The room appeared to be all bed and mirrors and video screens. The carpet was thick fur.

The female movie star flung off her clothes, such as they were, and collapsed, spread-eagled, on the fur carpet.

Male movie star immediately started to service her with his tongue.

Discreetly Van set his hidden cameras in motion. This would certainly be a good one for the library. He then sprung a switch, and photographs of six different girls leaped onto the screens.

'Choose whichever you want,' he suggested blandly.

'Give me the little Chicano,' moaned the female movie star, 'is she as talented as she looks?'

'More so,' replied Van smugly.

Al studied the photos. Two busty blonds, a black girl, the Chicano, an ugly redhead with giant knockers, and a delicate Chinese.

'I'll take the redhead,' Al said. 'Are they real?'

'Of course they are,' replied Van, offended.

The writer rubbed himself reflectively. 'Bring them all in,' he mumbled, 'I can't choose.'

Van smiled. This was going better than he had expected. He pressed a series of buttons, and within seconds the girls came filing in.

The redhead went straight to Al. She was very tall, perhaps six foot in the black ankle strap shoes she wore with black stockings and an old-fashioned suspender belt. Van had found from experience that men over thirty-five were distinctly turned on by stockings and suspenders. And as most of his famous guests were in that age group he always made sure that at least two of the available girls wore them. Tonight it was the redhead and the Chicano.

The redhead was quite thin. A fact which accentuated the enormous boobs which sprung forth from her body like two particularly lethal weapons. Apart from the shoes, stockings, and suspenders, she wore an open-nipple bra of black fur.

At the sight of her Al started to laugh. She was like a walking dirty picture.

Van, although he did not indulge himself, had allowed a small pouty Nymphet in, carrying a tray of drugs. Cocaine, grass, even methadrine for the really dedicated.

Al smiled. How the Kurlnik twins would love it here! He helped himself to a joint. Dragged deeply. Sat on the edge of the giant bed.

The girls who had filed in stood in a silent line waiting to be summoned.

The writer staggered over, pawed at one of the blonds, 'C'mon baby, get'em off.'

She was wearing a purple jump suit zippered down the front. 'Help me out of it, daddy!' she purred.

The writer lurched against her. He was so drunk he could scarcely stand up.

Al glanced over at Van. He did not seem about to participate. 'Which one is yours?' inquired Al in a friendly fashion.

'Don't worry about me,' replied Van blandly, 'Rita!' He gestured to the redhead. 'Take your bra off. I think Mr King would like to see what you're hiding.'

Rita obeyed, slipping and sliding out of the bra like a seasoned stripper. She did indeed have the most enormous boobs Al had ever seen.

Van smiled in a paternal fashion. 'I heard they were your weakness,' he confided, 'and Rita's are all her own, she's not just another Los Angeles silicone job, y'know.'

Female movie star sat up to take a look, select a joint, then she vanished down on the floor.

By this time everyone except Van and Al had taken time out to remove their clothes. The Chicano and Chinese had joined the movie stars on the floor. Rita, stripped and ready, and the black girl, in a see-through Andy Warhol T-shirt, stood around waiting.

Van sat one side of the big bed. Al the other.

'Please do go ahead,' Van offered, watching the writhings

around him with all the excitement of a dead fish. 'Rita, help Mr King with his clothes.'

Rita and her outsize protuberances bore down on Al. He held her off with a hand. 'Van? Which one is yours?'

Van puffed quickly on his pipe. 'Don't worry about me, go right on and enjoy yourself.'

'While you watch?'

Van looked offended. 'If it bothers you . . .'

'You bet it bothers me.' Al stood up, his mouth tightening into a disgusted line. He indicated Van's other guests. 'What are we all supposed to be – the cabaret?'

'Now Al – please. I arranged all this for you. I thought you would enjoy . . .'

'No shit?' interrupted Al coldly, 'and I'd like to bet my ass that you're photographing the whole event.' He moved threateningly close to Van, 'Am I right, buddy boy?'

Van squirmed uncomfortably. 'Any pictures or film taken of my guests is never used other than for my personal library.'

'Horseshit,' said Al tensely, 'get'em stoned, get'em fucking. Your personal library must be worth a fucking fortune.'

'If you like,' suggested Van, quickly, 'I could show you some films . . .'

'Jesus!' Al laughed in disbelief, 'you don't let up, do you.'

The redhead, still standing, shifted uneasily and raised her eyebrows at the black girl. The black girl, stoned and bored, ignored her.

'You're a slimy sonofobitch,' Al said, heading for the elevator. 'I didn't like you on sight, and now I like you even less.'

'But, Al. The party, I did it for you . . .'

'You don't even *know* me. I'm not the asshole you seemed to think I would be. Porno photos yet!' He indicated the movie stars writhing about on the fur carpet oblivious to the fight going on above them, 'and when do you break the news to those poor schmucks? Hey – listen – have I got some photos of *you*! And hey presto – they're in your pocket from that day on. Right?'

'You've got the whole thing wrong,' argued Van woodenly.

'Bullsheeeeet! Who are you kidding – you prick.'

He stepped in the elevator and as the doors closed he saw the female movie star surfacing yet again, and inquiring in a sweet girlish voice, 'Anyone for head?'

Later, back at the hotel, Al and Paul had a good laugh about it. 'You just wouldn't have believed it,' Al explained, 'Uptight,

189

sitting on his bed getting ready for the action like an old queen.'

'Maybe he is. Maybe that's his scene.'

'Who, him? Surrounded by eight million girls. Come on.'

Paul rustled up a poker game and they played late into the night.

It wasn't until he was alone in his bed that Al allowed Dallas to intrude into his thoughts.

He had to have her. And one way or the other he was going to see that he did.

thirty-three

Dallas awoke in a fog. She was awake, but she could not manage to open her eyes. She lay very still whilst the fog cleared, and she could collect her thoughts.

Briefly she remembered the previous evening. It had all gone so smoothly. And thank God it was over.

She opened her eyes. There were still things to do. It was time to get up. She glanced at the bedside clock. Ten o'clock. Naked, she jumped out of bed, shook her hair loose, flung on a thin silk robe.

Linda was in the kitchen making coffee.

'Where are the photos?' Dallas asked anxiously.

'Don't worry. The negatives are in an envelope ready for you to take to the bank. And two separate sets of prints are in here.' Linda indicated a kitchen drawer. 'Phew! I've got to tell you I'm glad it's over.'

'*You're* glad it's over.'

'It was an education though. To think that funny little gimpy guy runs a studio, is married to Doris Andrews, *and* plays games with hookers on the side. Wow – how many hats of different colours can a person wear?'

Dallas shrugged. 'If I told you some of the things I know . . .'

Linda gulped her coffee. 'Don't! Enough is enough. I don't think I can take any more right now. I've spent the entire evening dreaming about Diamond's boyfriend. I didn't even know there were such things as *male* hookers. I'm a sophisticated New York girl of thirty-two, and I *didn't even know about male hookers*. I think I want one!'

Dallas couldn't help smiling. 'What on earth for?'

'For what do you think? I mean the thought of going to bed

with a guy who is there purely for your pleasure. Terrific! Don't get me wrong – Paul is marvellous in bed, but sometimes I think to myself wouldn't it be sensational to be absolutely selfish. Just lie back and give the orders, and don't worry about whether it's good for him or not. Bliss! It comes to me in a sudden flash why female hookers have always been so popular! Imagine telling a husband or lover to give you head for four hours – he'd laugh you out of bed. But a male hooker – the pursuit of personal pleasure would be limitless!'

'You could always buy one of those vibrating tongues they advertise in *Movie World*.'

'Dallas! Where's your sense of togetherness. I don't want a vibrating tongue. I want the whole man! Hey – how much do you think they charge?'

'You're not serious, are you?'

'Why not? When I was in analysis my shrink always used to tell me not to hold back. "Experience the fruits of life," he would say.'

'Why did you stop?'

'He wanted me to experience his penis. Right in the middle of a fifty dollar session! He was about eighty and totally bald. I'm sure you can understand why I declined.'

Dallas toyed with her coffee. 'I . . . I really don't understand.'

'Huh?'

'I mean I don't understand people's – er – hang-up with sex. And believe me, Linda, I've had so many men. Bald, eighty, young, rich. You name it, I've had it. And you know, it all means nothing. I couldn't care less if I never went to bed with another man. Sex turns me off – not on.'

Linda nodded. 'I can understand your attitude. Christ, you've told me enough about your life for me to realize the problems you must have.' She looked thoughtful, 'Analysis would be really good for you, help you sort things into perspective. And then you need a really terrific guy to get you together in bed. You need a *loving* relationship.'

'I was thinking of Cody . . .'

'The agent guy you told me about?'

'Yes. He's been so kind. He's really nice, and I know that he wants to go to bed with me.'

'Do you love him?'

Dallas laughed bitterly. 'What's love, Linda? That's one scene that will never come my way.'

'Don't be so sure . . .'

'Of that I'm sure. I like Cody. I guess I respect him . . .'

'And you would grit your teeth and sleep with him. Right?'

'Right.'

'Forget it. You need a little passion in your life if it's ever going to work for you.' Linda drained her coffee, refilled her cup. 'I'm going to make a really bizarre suggestion, you'll think I'm nuts, but think about it before you say no. You've spent most of your life operating as a hooker, servicing guys, seeing that they get their rocks off in just the way *they* want it. Any perversion goes, right?'

Dallas nodded.

'Well,' Linda continued, 'who more than you could use the ministrations of a male hooker? For me it would be a luxury. For you it could be a necessity.'

'Oh no, I don't think . . .'

'Wait. Give it some thought. What's to lose? Right now you hate sex. Well, you're an intelligent girl, *you know* that is not a normal attitude. Not the gateway to a balanced and happy life. Cure yourself. Find out what *you* like. Find out with a guy who is there *just* to give *you* pleasure.'

They were both silent for a moment, digesting what Linda had said.

'Do you know,' Linda continued, 'that in sex therapy they pay partners to give you pleasure. It works. Thousands of men and women have been cured. Frigid women. Impotent men. Premature ejaculation. All kinds of things. I'm not saying that's *your* problem – but whatever your hang-up I'm sure it can be cured with the right treatment. I have to confess to you that I find sex one of the joys of life – and you're my friend – I don't want you to miss out. You are so young and beautiful. Sort yourself out now. Put the past behind you. Jesus, I'm talking too much. Give me a cigarette and shut me up.'

Silently Dallas handed her a cigarette, and shook one from the pack for herself, although she didn't normally smoke.

'It's not such a bad idea, Linda,' she finally said, 'I guess it does make sense. There have been times – far and few between – when I've realized sex can be a kick . . .'

'Terrific. At least you know what I'm talking about. Touching, feeling, giving way to pure sensual delight. Nothing like it, kid.'

'Maybe a sex therapy clinic . . .'

'Maybe not. You want the world to know your secrets? Soon you'll be famous, television makes you a star overnight. A male hooker – maybe Diamond's guy. Much more discreet. He doesn't

192

have to know your secrets, he's just there to give you a good time. A clinic will investigate you like the CIA!'

Suddenly Dallas began to laugh. 'Honestly, Linda! Can you imagine *me* paying for it! What a switch!'

'Stranger things have happened . . . Hey, I think you should get dressed and get those negatives over to the bank. I think I'll feel better when they're locked up.'

Dallas stubbed out her hardly-used cigarette, 'Yes, boss.' She got up, glanced out of the window at the California sunshine.

'Linda? You don't *have* to leave today, do you?'

Linda drained her coffee, thought briefly of Paul. Realized that he hadn't even bothered to call her yet.

'No, I guess I don't.'

'That's great. I'll call Cody, let him know I'm back, then he can take us out to lunch – I do want you to meet him.'

'Can't wait.'

'You'll like him, I know you will.'

Watching Dallas, Linda was surprised at the gradual change in her. When they had first met, Dallas had been a very withdrawn, cold person. Of course she understood the reasons why now, but it was wonderful to observe the emergence of a much freer, warmer personality.

'I've got a fitting at the studio at two-thirty,' Dallas was saying, 'maybe after, we could drive down to the beach. If I didn't start work tomorrow I would really show you around. Perhaps when the tour finishes you could come back, spend a couple of weeks – a month – as long as you like. That's if sleeping on the couch isn't too awful.'

'It's very comfortable. I might take you up on that. Somehow I don't think I see Paul whisking me back to London with him. Did I remember to tell you *never* to get involved with a married man?'

'Hang on there – I'm all booked out to a male hooker!'

Dialling Cody's number Dallas felt bad about the line she would have to feed him. Lies. God how she wished that she didn't have to lie to Cody. But it was for his own protection – for their mutual protection.

He answered on the fourth ring. 'Cody Hills.'

'Dallas,' she replied, copying his businesslike tone.

'Oh, you're back,' his voice was flat.

'Such enthusiasm! This is your star, don't I get more than an "Oh, you're back"?'

He hesitated then, 'Sorry, been on business calls all morning. Was everything all right?'

'Perfection. I sorted it all out. Hey – do I merit a lunch at least? My girlfriend, Linda, is with me and I want you to meet her.'

'I'm supposed to be viewing office premises . . .'

'Terrific. We'll come with you. Where shall we meet?'

Aggravated he gave her the address. He hung up the phone, went in the bathroom, took a handful of stomach pills. An incipient ulcer had been lurking for years.

He was mad at himself for not being able to conceal his annoyance with her. But annoyance wasn't even the right word. Jealousy would be more like it. And Christ, you really had to be a schmuck to be jealous of a client.

If he wasn't careful he would give himself away. 'What was that orgy at your house last night?' 'That was no orgy, that was my idea of fun.' Shit! Her personal life was none of his business. If he was smart he would keep it that way.

He had a sudden idea, and glancing at his watch he quickly picked up the phone.

After securing the negatives in a safe deposit box, there was time to do a little shopping. They wandered down Rodeo Drive peering in shop windows. Linda bought an Indian ivory choker and matching bangle.

'Looks amazing with your hair,' Dallas assured her. 'If only we had time we could drive down to Palm Springs and go to the Indian reservation, they have a shop right at the top of a mountain where they sell all silver and turquoise stuff they make themselves. Cody told me about it. I'd love to go.'

'So would I. I really don't know why I cheated myself out of a trip here before. I'm an American who has never seen America!'

'You're seeing it now with the tour.'

'Hotel suites. Limousines. Concert halls. Sports stadiums. Boring parties where everyone hangs around Al. Oh, and did I tell you his son has joined us now?'

Dallas looked surprised. 'His son?'

'Poor kid, I feel sorry for him. A spotty teenager who is obviously petrified of his father – and Al in his stylish way keeps on throwing grotesque whores in his direction.'

'What about his wife?'

'What about her? I don't think she's allowed out. Who knows if she even exists. Al is the supreme chauvinist. An egotistical son of a bitch.'

'You really like him, don't you?'

'I see right through him.'

'A man like that must have tremendous problems.'

'The only thing tremendous about Al is his dick! And boy – is he spreading the news – as well as the legs of every female who crosses his path.'

'He hasn't changed then?'

Linda laughed. 'Al, changed? You must be kidding!'

Dallas launched into another subject of conversation, but her thoughts lingered with Al. His timing on the phone call had been bad. What else could she have said to him with Lew Margolis standing right there. Anyway what was there to say? Hello. How are you. Goodbye.

She remembered his arms around her the night they had danced together in Regines in Monte Carlo.

She remembered the sudden warm excitement when he looked at her. When his black eyes travelled down her body.

She remembered the way they had joked together. The conversations loaded with sexual innuendo.

As she thought about him her body responded, and suddenly, walking down Rodeo Drive, she was seized with a strong sexual longing. A feeling so powerful she could hardly believe it. It was a feeling she had experienced so little in life. One time with Burt at the zoo. A couple of times with Bobbie. And now.

Maybe Linda was right. Maybe a man who would think only of her pleasure was what she needed. Or Cody, if only she could will this feeling in Cody's direction.

They had reached the car. Thankfully Dallas slid behind the wheel. She banished Al from her thoughts and tried to concentrate on what Linda was saying. Al King was bad news. Even *she* knew that.

Cody saw the car Dallas was driving approach, he managed a wave, indicated the parking lot attached to the building, and then turned to Irene who stood demurely beside him. Irene had been his brilliant idea – well, actually Evelyn, not Irene – but Evelyn had been in the midst of mother problems and unable to make lunch. Irene was second best, and she looked it. He had not seen her for several weeks and she appeared to have gained ten pounds. And why had he never noticed how hairy she was? Throughout their two-year intimate relationship he had never before noticed the fact that she had the suspicions of a moustache. She did have great legs though – short but great.

'It's nice to see you again, Cody,' Irene said, 'I couldn't imagine why I hadn't heard from you.'

'I told you what with leaving the agency and everything I've just been so busy. But I'm really glad you could manage lunch today.'

She squeezed his arm. 'I have missed you. When am I going to see you—' she paused meaningfully, 'properly?'

He wondered briefly if a moustache and an extra ten pounds would effect their previously quite erotic sex life. He decided it probably would.

'I don't know. Work, work, work – you know how it is.'

'Oh I know, I know. You don't have to tell me. Why this week my boss . . .'

'Here they come,' interrupted Cody, and as usual he was knocked out by Dallas. She really was the most unbelievably beautiful girl. She strode towards him like a graceful leopard, her long hair blowing around her face. Her body emphasized by the thin silk shirt tucked into white jeans. He hardly noticed the girl with her, every female seemed to be non-existent next to Dallas.

'Hi there,' she said, presenting him with a hug and a kiss, 'told you I'd only be away a minute. This is Linda, she's going to be spending a few days with me.'

He smiled at Linda, blackly wondering if she had been involved in the previous night's orgy.

Irene stepped forward. 'My name is Irene Newman,' she announced formally, pumping Dallas by the hand, 'no relation to Paul!' giggle, giggle. 'I'm so pleased to meet you, Cody has told me all about the wonderful contract he's gotten you.' She paused, squeezed Cody's arm in an intimate fashion. 'If there is anything I can do for you, please say. Cody tells me you're new in town. I know he's rented a house for you, but y'know – any girl things I can help out on – beauty parlour, gym – oh and I have a marvie place where I get a discount on sports clothes. If you like I can . . .'

Cody listened in amazement. Irene the talker. Was there no end to the surprises she had in store for him?

They viewed the office space, Irene chattering throughout.

'What do you think?' Cody asked Dallas.

'Wonderful!' replied Irene. 'You could move in tomorrow, all you need is a desk, and a nice chair. I know a place on Fairfax . . .'

Dallas shrugged helplessly.

On the way down in the elevator she pulled Cody to one side. 'I think we'll pass on the lunch. I didn't realize you had a date, why didn't you say?'

'It doesn't matter, she's just an – er – old friend. Come on – you must have lunch.'

Dallas glanced at her watch. 'No, really I have to be at the studio by two, I won't have time. Linda and I will grab a hamburger somewhere.'

He nodded miserably. What a bad idea Irene had been. 'I'll call you later, then.'

'Fine,' she dazzled him with a smile, 'maybe we can have an early dinner.'

'I don't know, I might be tied up.' He could kick himself for being so petty and stupid, but he couldn't help it.

She looked disappointed.

'But I'll try,' he added lamely.

'Do that,' she replied with an understanding smile.

thirty-four

Bernie had noticed the two girls in every city they had visited. He had seen them only as part of huge crowds of girls who hung around the hotel entrances and concert venues. They had not really registered properly until Chicago, when he had suddenly realized that they were following Al across the country. They were both quite young, but neither of them was very pretty.

He ambled over to them, and found out their names. I mean – what the fuck – these two were true fans. A little publicity wouldn't go amiss. He could throw a few free tickets their way, some souvenir programmes, a T-shirt or two.

Plum was nineteen and fat, a little larger than Bernie himself.

Glory, on the other hand, was extremely skinny. Sixteen, with freaked-out hair and a funny pointed face.

They were ecstatic that they had finally been noticed. Plum informed Bernie that they had pooled their savings, given up their jobs, just to be close to Al. Sometimes they hitched across country, sometimes took a train. From Miami to Chicago they had invested in plane fares to get them there in time.

'Well, girlies, today you just got lucky,' Bernie announced, 'be back here around six and I'm gonna take you in and let you meet the big man himself. How does that grab you?'

'I'll faint,' quavered Glory. 'Man, I'll just faint right away!'

'Can you give us tickets for tonight?' asked Plum shrewdly.

'Sure,' agreed Bernie. 'You mean you came all this way and you don't have tickets?'

'Yean we *got* tickets. But like we need the bread – so we'll make a little green stuff on ours – *use* yours.'

Bernie shrugged. 'Whatever turns you on.'

Glory giggled. 'Al turns me on. Like he turns my legs to jelly, man. Like when I'm not even stoned, he *turns me inside out*. Ain't no one can do that to me less I'm out of it.' She gripped Bernie's arm tightly. 'You know him, you're tight with him – tell him if he wants a trip will blow his head off . . .' she paused, scratching desperately at her frizzy hair, her eyes glazed over, she almost fell.

'She's just hungry,' said Plum stoically. 'We haven't eaten since the plane yesterday, and the crap they expect you to eat. I wouldn't give that crap to a cat.'

Bernie fished in his pocket, counted out five dollars, handed it to Plum. 'Get some food, and a wash or something. Fix yourselves up, I'll have photographers here.'

'On five bucks we're gonna eat, wash, and fix ourselves up? Who you kiddin'?'

'So don't eat. You want to meet Al be back here at six.'

Plum scowled. 'Cheap.'

Glory, revived, muttered, 'I could blow the brains off a monkey!' and lapsed back into a daze.

Bernie peeled off another five dollars. 'Buy her a steak, make her human.' He started to walk away.

'Don't forget our tickets,' Plum shouted after him.

Al had slept most of the day away. Then at five he had woken, decided he needed a woman, and Paul had tracked down Rita of the pneumatic boobs for him.

'Don't tell Van I'm here,' she had pleaded, 'he wouldn't allow it. I'm supposed to work exclusively for him.'

'Are you a pro?' Al asked.

'Of course not. I'm a model. Van pays me – very generously, so sometimes I do him little favours.'

'Open your legs,' Al said crudely, 'I want to see if you've got a camera hidden up there!'

She did not appreciate the joke. But she did service him expertly, and left him with a strong feeling of disgust.

He did not take kindly to Bernie's suggestion of a photo session with two fans who were trailing him across the country. But Bernie insisted. It was a story bound to make all the newspapers, and a nice human interest story for either *Time* or *People*.

Glory and Plum turned up promptly at six in full battledress.

Bernie would have bet that Plum had used the money to get Glory a shot of whatever she was hooked on. From a quiet little zombie she had turned into Miss Personality.

Plum looked even fatter in blue jeans and a satin jacket. Glory even thinner in red stockings on stick legs, and a voluminous sweater.

They pawed at Al like a couple of agitated puppies whilst the cameras clicked away. He smiled, joked, put his arms around them, presented them with signed photos.

The cameras kept flashing.

Glory whispered in his ear, 'I'd like to swallow your cock all down in one piece, right into my stomach.'

Al pushed her pleasantly away, extracted himself from Plum. 'Enough, boys,' he said to the photographers.

'Dynamite!' wheezed Bernie. 'World-wide coverage tomorrow.'

'Get 'em out of here,' hissed Al, 'I've got a show to think about.'

When he strode on stage nothing else mattered. The disgust, the problems with Evan, the boredom, Edna, Dallas. Everything was obliterated as his music came crashing protectively round him.

He opened up with 'Blue Funk Rock', followed it with 'Keep It' – both his own compositions. Then he launched into a medley of songs made famous by some of his favourte artists. Al Green's 'Let's Stay Together', Bobby Womack's 'I Can Understand It', Wilson Pickett's 'Midnight Mover', Stevie Wonder's 'You Are the Sunshine of My Life'. And to finish, Isaac Hayes' 'Never Can Say Goodbye'.

The audience loved it. They would love it if he stood on his head and whistled Dixie!

He was halfway through 'Random Love' when it happened. An explosion so muffled that only the people in the immediate vicinity were affected. But as some of those people were blown to bits, the panic and chaos spread within seconds.

One moment Al was on stage singing his guts out to an ecstatic screaming audience of thousands. The next he was being dragged off stage by Luke and Paul, whilst pandemonium raged below.

The bomb, a small one, had been placed beneath a seat. It killed two people, mutilated seven, injured fifteen. By the time police and security guards were able to gain control of the panicking crowds five people had been trampled to death in the rush to leave the stadium. Fifty-eight people had been injured, and hundreds were in shock.

It was an Al King concert many would never forget.

Why? was the question everyone asked. How could anyone be so twisted and deranged as to want to kill innocent people?

If a man with a gun had got up and shot Al it would have been understandable. After all any public figure from a politician to a rock star knew he lived under constant threat of assassination. That was one of the hazards of making it in the envy-ridden sixties and seventies.

But to maim and injure like this . . .

Two seventeen-years-old girls killed. A boy with his leg blown off. A woman without a foot . . . The list of horrors was endless.

Bernie thought of the voice on the phone and shuddered.

Fortunately he had reported the threats to the police. But there had been no telephoned threats in Chicago. No sick and twisted voice telling him what was going to happen . . .

The police questioned him at length. They took charge of the hate mail Al received. They questioned everyone connected with the tour. They even questioned Al.

By the time they were finished it was 4 a.m. and Bernie felt drained and exhausted. He collapsed into his bed at the hotel, not even bothering to remove his clothes. Fuck it. He needed sleep. The next morning he would have the world press to deal with. He had already spoken to the overseas news agencies. This kind of publicity . . . Who needed it? It would either make or break the tour. People were funny, if they got scared . . . Jesus -- what the fuck. He swigged from a bedside bottle of scotch and then let his bulk sag onto the bed. His eyes closed, only for a minute it seemed because immediately the phone was ringing. He snatched it up – 'Bernie Suntan,' he said quickly.

'I told you,' the voice whispered, 'I warned you. I gave you a chance to stop him from performing his vile obscenities. God will punish sinners. This is just the first of many.'

The line went dead.

Wearily Bernie struggled awake and called the police. Why did this maniac, whoever he was, have to pick on *him* to confide in?

Lying in bed Al could not sleep at all. If it was not for him none of this would have happened. If he had not been appearing at the concert the crowds would not have been there – the bomb would not have been placed – the people would not have been killed and maimed.

Once before, early in his career, something dreadful had happened. As he was escaping from a theatre one night a girl had somehow or other got enmeshed under the wheels of his car. She had not been killed, but crippled for life. He had not been driving, it was not his responsibility. But he had never forgotten that girl, and over the years he had sent her a continual stream of money and gifts.

Guilt money.

In a way he did feel guilty that he had so much. But Christ knows he worked hard enough for it. Each show he did seven pounds of sweat rolled off him. Hard physical work. It was harder than digging ditches.

He thought of phoning Edna to let her know that he was OK. A news flash had probably reached England by now. But would she care? It was Evan *she* cared about.

Evan was asleep in his own room somewhere in the hotel. Thank God he had not wanted to attend the concert that night. It had been a good idea of Paul's to suggest that he didn't keep him in the suite. They had been too much on top of each other, that's why the boy had been getting on his nerves. Now things seemed much better. He gave Evan money and told him to go out and enjoy himself. Evan had not objected.

Evan, in fact, was quite enjoying it. He had amassed one hundred and sixty dollars from the money his father threw his way. And he was free to buy girlie magazines, and candy, and sit in his room and enjoy them.

He put on the colour television and hardly budged from his room. Nobody bugged him. Occasionally Al would call him on the house phone and ask him if he wanted to come up to the suite. He always had an excuse.

He had been watching a repeat of 'Kojak' when the news came through about the bomb at Al's show. For one icy, hopeful, moment he thought that maybe his father had been killed. But no such luck. He listened with fascination to the reports of the bomb. Then anxious to see for himself, he left the hotel and took a cab over to the stadium.

He couldn't get anywhere near because of ambulances and fire trucks. He tried to push through suddenly thinking of Nellie, but he got shoved back along with the rest of the ghouls who had come to watch.

Surprisingly there appeared to be an air of cheerfulness amongst the crowds. Smiling, happy faces, hoping to get a glimpse of someone else's misery.

A television crew roamed around, sticking microphones in front of people's faces to get their comments.

'Why did you come here?' A girl reporter asked a woman carrying a baby.

'Better than television,' the woman laughed, 'like it's real drama – y'know. Wouldn't wanna miss it.'

'Were you at the concert?'

'Naw – jest came over when I saw the news.'

Evan realized there was nothing to see. He had missed all the good bits. He looked around for a cab, but there was none about. He had no idea how to get back to the hotel, but he started to walk anyway, hunching his shoulders into his denim jacket, cursing the fact that he had not chosen to attend the one concert where something decent had happened.

He did not notice the group of boys following him, boys about his own age.

He did not notice them closing in on him, surrounding him, jeering.

He stopped, unable to proceed anyway. Fright made him go cold.

'Hey, asshole!' screamed the tallest boy, 'you got any money, honey?' They all laughed, circling him.

'W-w-what?' stammered Evan.

'Green sticky stuff, asshole. Give it – now!'

Terrified, Evan groped into his pockets, found some change, handed it over.

'Wowee – fifty fuckin' cents! We found ourselves a real rich little motha!'

Evan thought quickly of the one hundred and sixty dollars in twenties stuck in the back pocket of his jeans. They wouldn't get that.

'I haven't got any more money,' he said quickly, his voice breaking.

'What's with that accent, asshole?' questioned the leader, 'You foreign or sumpin'? Jeeze! Now listen, prick . . .'

'Pigfuckers!' yelled one of the boys, and they melted away into the night as if they had never existed in the first place.

Relieved, Evan ran over to the patrol car cruising by. He informed them who he was, where he was staying, and what had happened.

They told him off for walking around alone at night, shoved him in the car, and took him back to the hotel.

In exchange he had to promise to produce Al for them to meet with their wives next morning. He had no idea now on eartn he'd fix *that*.

Safe in bed, his hundred and sixty dollars in a neat pile on the bedside table, he relived the scene. All of a sudden he was the hero of the piece. He had told *them*. Oh boy – he couldn't wait to tell Nellie all about it. Maybe now she would like him. Maybe now he could ask her out.

He fell asleep and dreamed that *he* was Al King. A far brighter star than the original.

When Al found out about Evan's adventure the next day he was pissed off to say the least. He posed with the policemen and their wives because he could hardly do anything else. But it was the last thing he needed. There was so much else going on. A trip to the hospital to visit the victims. Interviews to keep the world press happy. Television appearances.

Marjorie Carter came to the hotel with her camera crew. She was a professional to her fingertips. The interview was real human interest stuff. How did he *feel*? What would he *do*? Did this tragedy change his plans for the future?

Neither of them mentioned the night they had spent together. They were both excruciatingly polite.

The concert that evening was cancelled in deference to the victims, but Al promised that he would return to do another show sometime in the future.

He had no intention of ever setting foot in Chicago again.

He balled Evan out. Why had he come running over to the stadium? Why was he so fucking stupid that he walked the city's streets alone at night? Didn't he know people could get *killed* that way?

Evan was contrite. He had only come because he was worried about Al. He had only hurried over to see if he was all right.

Al felt a sudden rush of warmth and love towards the boy. He wasn't such a bad kid after all.

Van Valda sent a long and tearful letter of regret that such a thing could have happened in Chicago. He seemed to have forgotten all about Al's insults on the night of the party. 'Please come back and stay with us at Macho Mansion,' he begged.

Al threw the letter away.

Edna phoned, absolutely hysterical. Al calmed her down. Assured her that he and Evan were okay. Assured her there was no further danger, and wished he could be sure of that fact himself.

By six o'clock the entire Al King entourage was aboard his

private plane, and without a backward glance they took off into the cloudy skies.

None of them was sorry to leave.

thirty-five

Dallas had been working on 'Man Made Woman' for a week, and it couldn't be going better.

The crew were friendly. The director, Chuck, was interesting and sharp. His wife, a striking black girl called Kiki, was designing the clothes, and some of the outfits were incredible.

Cody arrived every day to have lunch with her. He seemed to have gotten over his recent strange mood. Dallas had put it down to the fact that maybe he had been having problems with his girlfriend. She had been surprised when he had turned up that day with Irene. Funny, but she had never really thought about him having another life away from her. He had spent so much time with her. He had always been available. The fact that he suddenly produced a girlfriend had been something of a jolt. She had complained to Linda.

'Hey,' Linda had pointed out, 'the guy's normal. What did you think? That he jerked off in a closet?'

'Just didn't think about it.'

'Well, you should have. He's a sweet guy, he's probably got lots of girlfriends.'

'But I . . . Oh shit, forget it.'

She didn't want to talk about Cody's love life. She didn't want to admit that she was secretly annoyed that he wasn't waiting patiently in the wings for her. After all she had offered herself to him. And what was it he had said – in the nicest possible way of course – he had said that they shouldn't complicate their business relationship. Terrific. The one guy she would sleep with didn't want to.

More and more her mind flicked over the possibility of calling Diamond and asking for the services of her boyfriend. What was there to lose? Maybe she would enjoy it. Maybe she should at least give it a chance . . .

Linda had left. Dashed off at the first news of the bomb in Chicago. As Paul's girlfriend she was anxious to be by his side.

As a photographer she was desolate that she had missed the event.

Dallas couldn't help wondering how Al must feel. She had even tried to call him in Chicago to offer a few words of sympathy, but he had already checked out of the hotel.

Every time she thought about Al, she got that feeling. It swept over her leaving her in a state of agitation. It didn't please her. She, who had always been so much in control.

She knew that she needed a man. Her skin was breaking out, and she was becoming irritable for no reason. Several guys at the studio would be happy to oblige, but they were all your usual macho merchants, horny studs looking to screw anything that crossed their paths.

Lew Margolis had not intruded on her personal life since the one night with Diamond. She had seen him once when he turned up to view the week's taping. He had barely nodded in her direction.

She was prepared for him. The negatives locked securely in her safety deposit box at the bank. The photos hidden beneath her bed.

She dreaded a confrontation, but it had to come, and the longer it took, the better.

Meanwhile she was working hard, doing her best, and enjoying every minute of it.

Cody kept a firm eye on things. The series was going to be as sensational as his every expectation. Dallas was positively glowing, and on camera she looked like a dream.

He had decided to swallow his feelings, and devote himself entirely to looking after her again. She seemed to have no more secrets. She was open and warm with him. Perhaps that one night had been an exception. Everyone went a little wild on one occasion. He could remember the time when an early girlfriend had insisted that he tied her to a bed and beat her. He had done it, felt guilty but done it anyway, and the girl had been delighted in spite of her screams. Every time he had stopped she had screamed, 'More! More! More! Harder! Harder! Harder!'

Now if anyone had witnessed *that* little scene . . . He shuddered to think about it.

After the lunch Irene had phoned him constantly. *He* knew it was over. Why didn't she?

She sent him a pair of hand-knitted red socks, and when they had no effect she sent him a blue pair with his initials on.

He sent her back a potted plant with a please forgive me note.

She visited his apartment and scrawled 'Bastard' all over his front door in lipstick. He knew it was her because who else wore 'Crimson Pirate' lipstick.

The new office was nice. He bought an odd antique desk, a leather swivel chair, and hired a buck-toothed sixty-year-old secretary. They both sat back staring at each other, waiting for the phone to ring. It didn't.

Becoming a hot agent and personal manager was not instant. It was obviously going to take a little hustling on his part. He had to let people know he was available, ready for new clients. They probably all thought he was too big time now.

In the meantime he read scripts, and novels. He was looking for Dallas' first film. It would have to be a big one. 'Man Made Woman' was just a beginning.

Saturday, Dallas was on location all day. Everyone was working overtime to get the first show out on schedule.

They were shooting at the beach, and it was a glorious day. Hot, sunny, no smog.

Kiki had designed her the most incredible swimsuit. White strips of leather winding round her body.

'I'm going to get the most peculiar suntan!' she joked to Cody when he appeared in the afternoon.

'You look great,' he enthused, 'it's a shame you're so ugly!'

She stuck out her tongue and wiggled it at him.

'Talented as well as ugly!'

'Why don't you shut up, Mr Hills. I *was* thinking of inviting you to dinner and watching you barbecue some delicious steaks I am planning to buy – or maybe *you* could buy them. What do you think? An evening at my house?'

'The thing I love about your invitations is that they always involve *me* paying out money.'

'Oh, I'll *pay* for the steaks. I just don't know when I'll have time to *get* them.'

He kissed her lightly on the cheek. 'I can't, beautiful client. My mother has got a sister in town from Cleveland who can't get through the evening without her very successful Hollywood agent nephew coming by to tell her inside stories of John Wayne and Doris Day.'

'*John Wayne and Doris Day!*'

'I told you she's from Cleveland. They've never heard of any other movie stars there. Unless you count Lassie and Rin Tin Tin.'

'Rin Tin who?'

'Don't make me feel old, I'm only twenty-eight.'

'And sexy with it.'

The assistant called Dallas over for the next shot.

Cody watched her. He couldn't take his eyes off her. None of the men could.

Two takes and she was back beside him.

'So no dinner tonight then? Stood up for an old lady from Cleveland.'

He sighed. 'I told you earlier this week that I would be tied up tonight. I'd ask you to come but they'd marry us off before the end of the dinner! Tell you what – I'll drop by after.'

'Nope. I wouldn't mind an early night. I *am* kind of exhausted.'

'We could barbecue tomorrow. Maybe ask Kiki and Chuck.'

'Terrific.' She smiled brightly. But she didn't feel bright. She felt disappointed and lonely. However, she didn't want Cody to know she felt that way. If he knew, he would cancel out on his mother and cause family problems. She knew what a difficult relationship he had there. Talk about love/hate. So she smiled and said she didn't mind and joked and laughed with him.

Maybe an early night *would* do her good. She had been working like a dog. Up at all hours, falling into bed at night completely flaked out.

But it wasn't going to work out. She was too keyed up and restless. She needed someone . . . something.

She knew that tonight was the night she would try out Diamond's boyfriend.

thirty-six

The crowds were larger than ever. It had been the same way in Nashville and Memphis. And now at the Coliseum in Houston, Texas, they were out in force.

If Al King had been a superstar before, he had now become almost a cult figure.

'Al is King! Al is King! Al is King!' chanted the mobs who did not have tickets and were stuck outside.

The bomb in Chicago had triggered off the most amazing reaction. Both Paul and Bernie had been worried that it would affect attendances, and that there would be a lot of returned tickets. But quite the reverse had happened. A ticket for an Al King concert was like gold dust. On the side the rip-off merchants were selling them at astronomical prices.

Gratifying as he found it, it also made Al nervous. So many people expecting so much. He sensed an attitude of expectation from the hordes that he couldn't quite fulfil. He knew what it was. They wanted blood. They wanted excitement. They wanted another bomb.

Every crank in America wrote threatening letters. Three lunatics confessed to having planted the bomb. Security was rigid everywhere he appeared. Concert halls, theatres, stadiums were searched before anyone was allowed in. Then began the painstaking task of frisking the audiences as they filed slowly towards their seats. To attend an Al King concert you had to arrive at least two hours early.

The Promises' manager wanted them to quit the tour. Paul was furious, and wouldn't allow it. They had an iron-clad contract, and no way could they slip out of it.

Paul knew *why* they wanted to quit. All the stuff the manager was handing him about the girls being frightened was so much crap. The truth was they had an amazing new record contract, and had been offered their own television series.

Rosa's Mafiosa boyfriend arrived from New York, and caused nothing but trouble. He hated Al, in spite of the fact that Rosa insisted nothing had ever gone on. He lurked around wearing three-piece black suits with an obvious shoulder holster, and patent leather shoes. He watched Rosa like a hawk, and even she started to get a little jumpy.

Nellie was getting sick. She had lost a lot of weight, and looked like a skeleton. She kept bursting into tears for no reason. Everyone knew about her enormous crush on Al. Everyone, that is, except Evan.

Evan was enjoying himself. He had managed to save another forty dollars, making a grand total of two hundred. He was delighted, and counted it lovingly every night.

He was left to his own devices. No one bothered him. As long as he showed his face occasionally things were cool. His hair grew very long. His skin even more spotty as he consumed nothing but candy. He had found magazines on sale that surpassed anything he had ever seen before. People actually *doing it*. Girls showing everything. Animals. He was sickened and excited. God, if Nelson ever saw *this* collection *he* would have to pay. Evan snickered at the thought, and packed his magazines neatly at the bottom of his suitcase.

Linda had returned to the tour to find Paul preoccupied with business. Twice during the week he had had to fly back to New York for meetings, and not once had he offered to take her with him.

She took her pictures, and brooded, and decided maybe when they reached Los Angeles she would stay there. Christ! A year was long enough to screw up your life for any man. Yes – in Los Angeles she would give Paul an ultimatum. If he went running back to his wife and kids – which she knew he would – then at least she could get over him in the sun surrounded by lots of horny would-be actors. Good therapy.

Al was invited to a lot of parties in Houston. The city seemed to be full of oil millionaires with randy wives all waiting to throw their palatial mansions open for Al's inspection – not to mention their legs.

He did the party bit. He even screwed a couple of the wives and one daughter. Nothing memorable.

When they flew out of Houston he was glad. He could never understand why all those rich people fell over backwards to entertain him. And the husbands didn't even seem to mind him having it off with their wives. On the contrary – they seemed positively *proud*.

The next stop was Oklahoma.

Al lolled on the big double bed in his private bedroom on his private plane. He wasn't tired, but he didn't feel like socializing with the others. He was bored with the endless games of backgammon and gin rummy. He was bored with listening to his musicians discuss their last lay. He was bored with Rosa's flinty-eyed boyfriend staring at him, and Nellie giving him tearful looks, and Sutch *always* playing Stevie Wonder tapes on the cassette player that never left her side.

He was bored with Luke.

And he was extra-bored with Evan, who looked like shit, and complained every time you talked to him.

Bernie bored him with his endless talk of this publicity break and that. Didn't Bernie realize that his job was a piece of cake? Didn't he realize that Al King would fill the newspapers with or without the help of Bernie Suntan?

And Jesus, what was with bringing those freaks aboard for the ride – those two clap-ridden groupies. Whose plan was this, for Christ's sake?

Angrily Al buzzed for Paul.

'What's up?' asked Paul, coming in cheerfully. 'Thought you wanted to sleep.'

Al scowled. 'I'm sick and tired of my plane being used as a travelling knocking shop.'

'Huh?'

'I want Rosa's boyfriend off. He wants to follow her across the country let him do it on his own money.'

'Hey – Al . . .'

'Hey Al nothing. The creep gets up my ass. And tell Bernie I don't ever want to see him bring those two freaks aboard again.'

'They ran out of money. Bernie thought . . .'

'Tell Bernie to shove his thoughts right where it will do them most good.'

'OK, Al.' A sudden air pocket nearly jolted Paul off his feet.

'What the fuck is the pilot doing?' demanded Al.

Paul did not dare tell him that the pilot was showing Evan how to fly the plane. Al was not the only one who was bored, the tour was getting to all of them. Personally, in spite of the gigantic success it was, Paul could not wait for it to finish. He had so much to do. The offers Al was receiving were incredible. Above all expectations. There was a new record contract to negotiate. Two films. A tour of Australia that promised enough money for instant retirement. He would have to sit down with Al and find out what he wanted to do. Just a formality really, because Paul made all the career decisions. He had already decided that Al should do one of the films. There had been many offers in the past – indeed, early on in his career Al had appeared in a bad British comedy as a horny milkman – but nothing that had been just right. Now both these films he was being offered seemed tailor-made. Of course the main thing was that neither part would tax Al's acting abilities. And quite frankly who knew if he had any to tax?

Lost in thought, Paul didn't notice Glory squeeze quietly into the room behind him. It wasn't until Al roared, 'What the fuck is *she* doing in here?' that Paul saw her edging along the side towards the bed. He grabbed her quickly by the arm. God, but her arm was so thin he thought it might snap off!

'I had to put my eyes on your room, man,' she mumbled, 'like

210

where does the master sleep, y'dig man? Like give my eyes your body and I'll die happy.' She rolled wild eyes in her pointed face, licked dry lips. 'You are . . .'

Before she could finish, a red-faced Plum came bursting in, followed by an even redder-faced Bernie.

For one horrible moment Al thought the two freaks had come to rape him. The fat one and the thin one throwing themselves on his body, ravishing him. He shuddered.

Everyone was speaking at once. Plum was screaming complaints at Glory. Glory was mumbling inanely. Bernie was blustering 'What the fucks' all over the place, and Paul was coldly shoving them all out.

When they were gone, with the door shut firmly behind them, Al said, 'I think that proves my point, Paul. No more strangers on this plane. Do you realize if that little freak had had a gun she could have blown my head off? So much for all my fucking protection *then*.'

'You're right,' agreed Paul, more shaken than Al could see. The skinny girl had been totally out of it, stoned shitless. 'I'll talk to Bernie.'

'Don't *talk* to him. Blast his fuckin' bollocks off!'

'Right.' Paul left the room hurriedly.

Linda tried to stop him as he rushed past. 'What's happening?'

He could see Bernie and the fat girl arguing and gesticulating near the front of the plane. 'In a minute,' he told Linda, and strode down to Bernie. 'I want them off,' he said sharply, 'as soon as we land.'

'Yes,' agreed Bernie, embarrassed.

Plum turned to Paul, fat red cheeks blazing. She indicated Bernie. '*He* said we could see where Al slept. He *said* so. He promised. We both gave him blow jobs an' he *promised*.' She glared balefully at Bernie, who was gazing out of the window. 'He's a fat slob,' she continued, 'I wouldn't have sucked his fat cock if it hadn't of meant gettin' near Al. Nor would she.' She indicated Glory, spread out on a seat, staring disinterestedly into space.

Paul's anger dissolved. He wanted to laugh. Naughty old Bernie getting it off with these two outlandish little girls.

Bernie was scarlet-faced at having been caught.

'Well,' said Paul, 'what can I say? I guess you thought you had a deal.'

'Yes,' replied Plum, still annoyed.

'Al doesn't like to be disturbed. Bernie shouldn't have made promises he couldn't keep. And you shouldn't do things you don't want unless you have a contract. At least you've had a free ride.' He smiled, after all they were Al's fans and he didn't want them leaving the plane pissed off and ready to sell their stories to the nearest newspaper. 'Have you got tickets for the show in Oklahoma?'

'Can we have six? asked Plum quickly.

'Six?'

'We've got friends there.'

Paul kept smiling. 'Fine. Six tickets. You want a couple of T-shirts and some pictures?'

Plum nodded. 'You're nice – you know that. Nice.' She leaned down and prodded Glory who had fallen asleep with her mouth open. 'Say thank you to this one, he's nice.'

Glory opened red-rimmed eyes. 'You want me to suck his . . .'

'No!' said Paul quickly.

Plum grinned, revealing a missing front tooth, 'We wouldn't mind. We both wouldn't mind. I mean you're nice. Besides, you're his brother, and that's family.'

Paul backed away. 'I'll get you the tickets, hang about.'

'We wouldn't move,' leered Plum.

Evan didn't know what was going on. He didn't much care either. After an interesting half hour with the pilot he had manoeuvred himself into a seat next to Nellie, and they had been making idle, wonderful conversation.

'I don't understand these girls who follow stars,' said Nellie crossly, 'it's so dumb. Don't you think it's dumb?'

'Yes,' agreed Evan. He would agree with whatever she said. He would agree if she told him to throw himself off the plane.

'*I* could never do a thing like that, *I* could never throw myself at anyone.' She placed a small, delicate hand softly on his knee. 'Did you give Al my message?'

Message. What message? He couldn't remember any message. 'Yes.'

'What did he say?'

'He er um, he was er. He said – um, he was pleased.'

'Pleased!' Her pretty face lit up. 'Pleased. Oh I knew he would be. I knew it!'

'Yes.' Evan paused, then plunged on with – 'I've saved two hundred dollars. I mean I've got two hundred dollars. I wanted to – um – buy you a present.'

'How lovely,' she giggled, 'I think I'll go and see Al.'

'What?'

'I think I should. I mean if he's pleased . . . Well I think I should just – you know – tell him personally.'

'Tell him what?' Evan was confused.

'My message, silly.' She leaned over and kissed him lightly on the cheek, 'You've been such a help to me.' And then she was clicking off her seat belt, and heading for Al's private room.

Evan watched in amazement. What had he said? Why had she gone?

Rosa stopped her as she passed. 'Where *you* goin', girl?'

'I just got a message,' Nellie replied, eyes shining.

Rosa shook her head in disgust. 'Do yourself a favour and forget him. He's just a user.'

Nellie smoothed down her long black hair. 'I don't need advice.'

Rosa shrugged. 'Don't come cryin' to me again. He's only gonna give you another glimpse of the magic horn – then it's onto the next. I *know* it, girl. Don't forget – I *bin* there.'

'Oh Rosa, don't be jealous!' said Nellie, kindly, 'it's not *my* fault he likes *me*.'

Rosa sent her eyes heavenwards. 'Jesus, save the children, or what's left of them.'

Nellie reached Al's door. Knocked. He didn't answer so she opened it tentatively, saw he was asleep, and crept in.

She silently approached the bed, stared down at him. She remembered how good it had been that one time in Miami. So very good. Spoiled by the fact that he hadn't wanted to speak to her since. But now that she knew her message had pleased him. Well, that made things different. He wasn't mad at her after all.

On impulse she peeled off the dress she was wearing, wriggled out of her panties, then quietly she snuggled into the big bed with him.

He was in the foetal position. She curled her slight body into his back, following the curves of his body.

He turned lazily, still asleep, but hard. She opened her legs and he entered her. She breathed his name softly, moving to accommodate him.

He came very quickly, eyes still closed. Then he mumbled, 'Go to sleep, Edna,' and turned his back on her.

Edna! Nellie lay there unfulfilled and trembling.

How could a man make love to a woman and still remain asleep? Unless of course he thought that woman was his wife.

Oh God! She was so humiliated.

She crept out of bed, frightened lest he wake. She dressed. It was her own fault, she should have wakened him.

How *could* she have done it?

She slipped out of the room, bumping straight into Paul.

'Oh!' she jumped nervously.

Paul gave her a suspicious look.

'I just wanted to talk to Al about something,' she stammered, 'but he's asleep.'

'Do me a favour, Nellie,' said Paul pleasantly, 'don't go into Al's private room unless he invites you. He does not like being disturbed. Any problems, come to me. OK?'

'Sure, sure Paul. I just er – I just, y'know, wanted to ask him something. Nothing important.'

He watched her walk away. Poor kid. Everyone knew how she felt about Al.

'She was in there for ten minutes,' remarked Linda, whose seat was nearest to Al's door. 'Perhaps she's murdered him.'

Paul glared at her, but walked into Al's room anyway. His brother slept peacefully.

What he would have to do, Paul decided, was station Luke outside the door. Al's private bedroom was becoming more like Grand Central station every day.

Edna King felt uncomfortable in the masculine striped suit.

'Latest fashion,' Melanie had assured her, 'suits you very well.'

Melanie herself was wearing an Yves Saint Laurent dress in a flattering blue colour. The sort of colour that looked good on Edna.

They sat together side by side on the huge jumbo jet. Edna had never liked flying, and her palms were wet with nerves as she waited for the take-off. Melanie was calm and collected, smiling at a man across the centre aisle, arranging her *Vogue* and *Harpers* and daily newspapers in a neat little pile.

Edna wondered wildly what would happen if they crashed. Al would be furious with her. And what would happen to Evan? Why oh why had she ever let Melanie talk her into this trip? It was sheer madness. 'The boys will love it,' Melanie had assured her. 'Once we're there, they'll love it!'

Of course the deciding factor had been Al's birthday. He was to be thirty-eight years old in two days' time, and Edna had spent every birthday with him since the day they were married.

'You'll be his present,' Melanie had enthused, 'just think how thrilled he'll be!'

Melanie had gone ahead and arranged everything. Even the bomb in Chicago had not put her off her plans. They were to fly directly to New York, stay there two days, and then fly to New Orleans, arriving on the evening of Al's birthday.

Melanie had called Paul before they left, and told him that she and Edna were off to a health farm for a few days and would be incommunicado. Paul had said what a good idea, and asked to talk to the children.

Melanie knew that Paul would be furious when they arrived. But so what? She was his wife, Al's sister-in-law, she was entitled to *some* of the glamour. Things had been quiet with Paul and Al away. Thank goodness Mr Capone was around to while away several boring evenings. He might only be a hairdresser, but he did give an incredible blow dry!

Melanie smiled, patted Edna reassuringly on the knee. 'I never thought I'd get you this far,' she said brightly.

'Nor did I,' replied Edna, and she shuddered as the huge jet roared into life.

thirty-seven

Dallas hurried home from the location and immediately phoned Diamond before she changed her mind.

'Julio will be delighted to visit you around eight o'clock,' Diamond said, the perfect secretary.

Julio! Dallas realized that she didn't even know what he looked like. He could be five foot tall and seventy-three. And she was going to pay him for a service that at one time men had paid *her* for.

She drew a long, warm, bubble bath, tried to relax in it, couldn't. She brushed her hair, creamed off her make-up, wrapped herself in a towelling bathrobe. After all it wasn't like this was a date. It was a business appointment. A therapeutic trip.

She smoked a little grass, not too much, just enough.

This whole scene was Linda's idea. Why wasn't she here to hold her hand?

At exactly ten to eight the doorbell rang, and Dallas nearly jumped out of her skin. She peeked at herself in the mirror. Wrapping her robe tightly around her she opened the door.

Cody stood there, smiling, and holding a brown paper carton.

'I ate dinner at a record pace. Listened to ten boring stories about Cleveland, and decided you *were* business, so I did have a legitimate excuse to get the hell out. My mother wasn't pleased, but the only thing that would please her would be me marrying Golda Meir's daughter – and I don't even know if she's got a daughter!' He handed Dallas the carton, 'it ain't barbecue – but it's Jumbo Jims from Dolores', and chocolate malts, and banana cream pie. I thought we could live a little.'

Silently Dallas took the carton.

Cody walked inside. 'You look like you were just going to bed. I bet you didn't even bother to eat.'

Dallas shook her head. Food had been the last thing on her mind.

'So we'll eat, then I'll let you get some sleep.'

'I thought you already ate,' Dallas ventured.

'You call my mother's cooking eating? You must be kidding!'

Dallas didn't know what to do. She didn't want to hurt his feelings, but at the same time she wanted him out of there fast. She cringed at the thought of him bumping into Julio. And oh God – if he found out what Julio was doing there . . .

Why had she ever arranged it? Goddamn Linda and her stupid ideas!

Cody sat himself down on the couch. 'It's been a great week,' he said enthusiastically, 'you're even better than *I* thought. I didn't know you were going to turn out to be an actress on top of everything else. Is there no end to the surprises you have for me?'

'Cody. The hamburgers were a lovely idea, but you *did* tell me you were busy tonight.'

He stood up. 'You want me to go.'

'No, don't be silly. It's just that I did sort of arrange a date, and he'll be here any minute.'

Cody hit his forehead with the palm of his hand. 'Stupid me! I should have called. No problem, I'll just take my hamburgers and go.'

'It's not that I wouldn't have sooner spent the evening with you . . .'

He laughed, but she could tell that she had hurt his feelings.

'I understand, sweetheart. Don't worry about it.' His eyes flicked quickly over her bathrobe and unmade-up face. 'I could leave you the food. I'm not really hungry. It will just get wasted.'

'*I know*,' said Dallas, suddenly, 'you sit down. I'll get rid of my date. How's that? He was second choice to you anyway.'

'Wouldn't dream of it.'

'Well I would. Just sit down and shut up. I don't want him to see you.'

'Look, Dallas, I really think . . .'

At that moment the doorbell rang. Dallas made a gesture for Cody to be quiet. She shut him in the living room and went to the front door.

Julio was six foot two, black, and the best-looking man Dallas had ever set eyes on. He was about twenty-nine, beautifully dressed in a white silk shirt and French-cut black slacks. He smiled, displaying perfect white teeth. Parked behind him in the driveway was a gleaming white Ferrari. Business must be good.

'Hi,' he said easily, 'I'm Julio.'

'Oh,' replied Dallas blankly. She was not sure what she had expected, but it certainly wasn't Mr Perfect. What's a nice boy like you doing in a business like this? She was tempted to ask. But instead she said, 'Julio. There's been a slight problem. I'm afraid it's not possible for me to keep our er appointment tonight. I'm sorry you've been troubled, but of course I'll pay for your time. How much do I owe you?'

His smile remained. He took her hand, kissed it, 'I have not been troubled. Perhaps you would care to make another appointment.'

She shook her head, kept her voice low, 'I can't right now.'

'But you'll call when you can?'

'Yes.'

'In that case – no charge.'

'But I've wasted your time.'

'My time is never wasted.'

'If you're sure . . .'

'Of course.'

She shrugged. 'OK then, another time.'

'Another time.' Still smiling, he turned, got into the Ferrari, and roared off, saluting her with a friendly wave.

She leaned against the door. Oh if Linda had been here to witness *this* scene. She wanted to laugh, it all suddenly seemed so funny. If Cody hadn't turned up she would have invited Mr Perfect in to make love to her. And she was sure he would have been excellent. But no way could she have gone through with it, no way at all.

She thought of Cody sitting in her living room waiting for her. Dear, sweet, Cody, with his thinning hair and sense of humour.

Why was she looking elsewhere? He wanted her, she was sure of that. So why not?

He didn't mean to sneak a look, but he couldn't help himself. He was sorry when he saw a really great-looking black guy climbing into a white Ferrari.

A black guy. Let's digest *that* little bit of information. Oh sure, he was as liberal as the rest. He had supported civil rights, equal education, job opportunities. He had watched 'Roots' along with everyone else.

But shit. Sexually. Well, everyone knew that sexually they were hung like the Taj Mahal! Once a girl went to bed with a black man she didn't want to know about a white man. Direct quote from his mother. Like *she* would know.

Why the hell had he pushed his luck and come running over like a schoolboy. Of *course* she wouldn't be sitting around on her own just because he wasn't free. Why hadn't he learned his lesson the other night? Call first, schmuck.

Dallas came back in the room, 'All taken care of.'

Cody stood up. 'I think I'd better go.'

'Hey—' she pushed him playfully, 'I just cancelled my date for you.'

'But I still think . . .'

She wound her arms around his neck, moving her body close to his. 'That means I want *you* to stay.'

They were the same height. If she wore high heels she would be taller than him. He wished he had had a chance to clean his teeth after eating his mother's cooking. All these thoughts rushed through his mind as they kissed. He felt rooted to the spot. With Irene or Evelyn he would know what to do next, but with Dallas . . . She could feel his instant hard-on through her bathrobe. Christ, she would be able to feel it if she was wearing armour plating! He could not remember being this excited since high school when Janet Dell had jerked him off in the back of her father's car!

Dallas was undressing him. 'Hey,' he objected weakly.

'Hey—' she agreed, manipulating him out of his trousers. 'Oh yes,' she added, when she noticed his bulging jockey shorts.

He was embarrassed. He didn't want to touch her. He knew if he touched her it would be all over.

She was fiddling with the belt on her bathrobe.

'Let's go in the bedroom,' he suggested weakly.

'Let's,' she agreed.

218

It was dark in the bedroom, and when she switched the light on he turned it off.

She took off her bathrobe and lay down on the bed.

He had never seen a body like it. Legs like it. Breasts like it. Skin like it.

'Come here,' she said, holding out her arms.

As if he needed an invitation. But it was a mistake. He knew it was a mistake.

Ten seconds later his fears were realized. Instant come. He didn't even get it inside.

She laughed it off. 'Such enthusiasm!'

But he felt destroyed, like a young boy. And he couldn't get it up again, in spite of her kindly administrations.

'I'm sorry . . .'

'Don't worry about it.'

'It's never done that before.'

'It's a naughty boy.'

Shit! She had it in one.

He closed his eyes and wished for death or something along those lines. With Evelyn he could go all night. With Irene he was Mr Playboy personified.

'Why don't you sleep here?' Dallas suggested.

'I think I'll go home. Expecting a call.'

'If that's what you want.'

She didn't even argue, and who could blame her? If she got rid of him early enough she could call up Superspade and really get it on. But he knew he was being unfair, it was she that had suggested he stay.

Miserably he dressed.

She didn't seem too put out. Any other girl would have been screaming for equal orgasm by this time.

She stayed in bed, modestly covering herself with a sheet, and when he was dressed she said, 'What about the hamburgers?' And he brought the carton into the bedroom, and she munched a cold hamburger with great relish whilst he watched.

'See you tomorrow, then,' she told him cheerfully when he was ready to leave. She didn't seem upset by his performance – or rather lack of it.

He kissed her chastely on the cheek and made his escape.

Dallas watched him go, sorry that he had not wanted to stay the night. She had been right about Cody. He was a genuinely nice guy, and she was touched by his obvious lack of experience in sex. He wasn't a groper, a jumper, a lecher, pulling at her body

219

in a lustful frenzy the way most men did. He was a little bit shy, a little bit reticent. She sat up and hugged her knees. He was the kind of man she could live with.

OK, so he didn't make any bells ring. But she hadn't expected he would. Sex had never been a turn-on, just a way to make some money. Linda was wrong about it all being so wonderful.

Yes, Cody was the guy for her, of that she was sure.

But in the back of her mind was a feeling of disappointment. No sexual waves. No incredible flooding of the body and emotions. No hot and cold thrills. For a second her thoughts lingered fleetingly on Al King, then sternly she shut him out. Cody Hills was the man for her. Cody Hills was the man she wanted to marry.

thirty-eight

Evan didn't know how it happened – well, not exactly. One moment he had been enjoying a more than friendly conversation with Nellie, and ten minutes later, when she had come back from a visit to Al, she seemed distant and upset. She didn't even sit down next to him, she went and huddled alone in a seat at the front.

He didn't have the courage to follow her. What if she snubbed him?

Probably his bloody father had hurt her feelings. He was good at doing that. As long as *he* was all right he didn't care what he said. It amazed Evan why people were still so anxious to jump at his every command. He treated them all like dirt.

When the plane landed, Evan hung back as usual. There was always such a fuss at every airport. Photographers, crowds, two-faced smiling officials. Evan hated it all.

He was concentrating on staying out of the way, when the fat girl spoke.

'Hi,' she said, bringing her face and bad breath very close to him 'whachasay we all ride inta town together.' She wasn't asking him, she was telling him.

'I don't think . . .'he began.

'You got a ride, dontcha? Glory an' I don't take up no room. Like we got no bread left. Like not even bus fare.'

'Yeah,' agreed Glory blankly, hitching up a laddered red stocking.

'OK,' muttered Evan. He knew who they were. They followed Al everywhere.

He got in the last of the fleet of black Cadillacs sent to meet Al and his entourage. The girls squeezed in with him. A couple of the musicians were already in the car.

'Get lucky, Evan?' one of them laughed, nudging his colleague.

'Aw shut y'face,' snapped Plum, 'after what we done f'you guys on this tour y'd think *one* of you would see we got a ride.'

'Anyone riding you needs insurance!' laughed the musician.

'Don't come to me next time you want it,' spat Plum. 'Y' all stink anyway.' She turned to Evan. 'Friggin' animals. Don't 'preciate nothin'.'

'Nothin',' echoed Glory, scratching at her frizzy mop of hair.

The car drove straight to the hotel. The two girls followed Evan into the lobby, and waited while he collected his key.

He pretended not to see them as he headed for the elevator. But they fell into step, one on each side of him.

'Y'don't mind if we use y'room for a few minutes,' stated Plum. 'Gotta wash, pee. You're real nice. Know that?'

No. He didn't know that. But it was nice to hear. In fact he had never been told that before. He warmed slightly towards the big fat girl.

They crowded into his room. 'Jeeze, I'm hungry!' exclaimed Plum. 'D'you think we could have room service? Jeeze – what I could do with a coupla cokes and a 'burger.'

Why not? He didn't have to pay for it. 'Order what you like,' he said magnanimously. After all if they thought he was nice he didn't want to spoil their opinion of him.

After scanning the room service menu, and choosing a mammoth meal, the two girls vanished into the bathroom. They stayed locked away until a knock at the door announced the arrival of the food. Then they emerged, wearing different outfits, although how they managed it Evan didn't know, for they possessed one scruffy-looking carry-all between the two of them.

Glory seemed to have perked up considerably. 'Nice room!' she exclaimed as if seeing it for the first time.

'Big! Too big for one guy all on his own. Food! You sure are one wonderful person. Cute too.' She winked at him. 'Wish we had some booze. Got any booze?'

Evan shook his head.

'Booze makes me do veree dirty things!' Glory added, rolling her slightly protruding eyes, 'how 'bout you?'

'Don't drink,' muttered Evan.

'Never?'

'Champagne.'

Glory fell about laughing, 'Shit man! Champagne. 'Scuse me for bein' in the same room!'

'Leave him alone,' interrupted Plum quickly.

'I ain't hassling him. Honest I'm not. He's the man. Like look at this food – got me droolin'.' Glory picked up some french fries with her fingers and stuffed them in her mouth. 'Yum! Good stuff.' She narrowed her eyes at Evan. 'Ain't you all eatin'?'

'I might have to eat later with my father.'

'Oooh! With my father!' Glory mimicked his accent, whilst Plum mouthed 'shut up' at her. 'French fries no good for your spots anyway,' yawned Glory.

Evan reddened.

'Don't go gettin' uptight 'bout your spots. *I* got spots too. All over my bum. Wanna see?' She started to unzip her jeans.

'Not *now*,' objected Plum, 'I'm eating.'

'Tell you what,' laughed Glory, 'you can squeeze my spots if I can squeeze yours! A deal?' She stuck out a skinny hand with nails bitten down to the quick. Evan took it. They shook solemnly. 'You're a real nice person,' Glory smiled, 'I think we're all gonna get along just fine.'

'How do you like our city?' the girl interviewer asked.

'The best!' replied Al firmly. He knew what they would all ask, and he gave them all the same answers. 'Saw a great show when I was a kid – *Oklahoma*. Howard Keel singing his whatsits off.'

'Howard Keel?' she questioned, smiling politely.

'Yeah – Howard Keel – you remember . . .'He trailed off. How could she remember? She was only about twenty something. The young, smart ones. They always sent the college ladies to interview him. Why didn't he ever get an old bag? Someone who knew what the fuck he was talking about.

I will be thirty-eight in two days' time, he thought. Two years after that I will be forty. And I don't want to be poncing around the world dodging randy females when I'm forty. I don't want to be married to Edna either.

'I beg your pardon?' said the interviewer.

'I beg your pardon what?'

'I – I thought you said something.'

'Just your ears playing tricks on you.' He took a swig of champagne and surveyed the girl. She was pretty in a *Cosmopolitan* way. He leaned forward, fixing her with his deep black eyes.

She moved uncomfortably on her chair. 'I wanted to ask you,' she began.

'Let's forget about the boring questions,' he said, 'let's just get it all off and fuck.'

'Oh!' She blushed.

'Come on,' insisted Al, 'this is your chance for an exclusive. Isn't that what all little girl reporters want?'

She opened her mouth to reply. Didn't know what to say.

'Clothes off,' suggested Al. He leaned back and waited. Wouldn't it be nice if she said no. But no such luck. She was soon unzipping, unbuttoning, and unhooking.

He yawned. What could you expect from a girl who had never even heard of Howard Keel?

Bernie Suntan conferred with the security heads at the Fairgrounds Arena. Everything seemed tight.

Goddamn weather. The goddamn heat never seemed to let up. He had to carry a supply of T-shirts because he sweated his way through six of them a day.

Goddamn tour. He wished they were in LA already. His town. A civilized place where you could walk by the pool at the Beverly Hills Hotel and see *other human beings*.

He was sick of being nice to morons and bums and nothings. Little people with small minds and little jobs on hick newspapers. Douche bags all of them.

He swigged from a can of beer. He was still smarting with embarrassment at the scene on the plane. Those two pigs that should never have been allowed out without a leash. Jeezus! That they should tell Paul about what they had done to him. Jeezus! Ugly would be an overestimation of their condition!

Had he not been stoned and extremely horny he would not have put his tool in their direction in a million years. But Jeeze – he had been working his balls off, and where was the thanks? Major coverage in every city. Magazine pieces that you would sell your mother for. Every television show. What the fuck – he was doing a GREAT JOB!

Of course if he had had the time he could have found himself a sweet piece. But who had time? And those two gorillas had been available and grinding their teeth for a thrust of what he had to offer.

Fat he may be. But he could cream chicks with the best of them.

He finished his beer, crumpled the can. What the fuck. They were out of his life now. He had told them in no uncertain terms to quit hanging around him.

Roll on LA.

After half an hour Al was bored. He sent Miss Girl Reporter packing and lay morosely on his bed studying the ceiling. Hotel rooms. He hated them.

Paul called to say they would be leaving for the Arena in an hour.

Al hauled himself into the shower, soaped his body, rinsed away the previous half hour.

He shaved. Studied his face. Plucked out a few eyebrow hairs that were daring to cross the bridge of his nose. He brushed his teeth, played with some dental floss.

He didn't look like a person who was nearly thirty-eight. Squinting at himself in the mirror he decided he looked no more than twenty-nine – well, thirty at the most.

Satisfied with his appearance he decided to phone Evan. He felt a bit guilty about the fact that he hardly saw him any more. But it was a relief – having Evan in his pocket had started to drive him crazy.

Evan answered the phone in his room with a surly, mumbled 'Yes?'

'Coming to the show tonight?' Al asked cheerfully.

'Yes,' answered Evan.

'Good. Why don't you come to the suite and we'll drive over together.'

There was a short, muffled silence, then Evan said, 'Think I'll see you there. Can I have some extra tickets? I've got some friends I want to bring.'

He had friends! At last! 'Sure, sure. How many do you want? I'll have Bernie arrange it.'

' 'Bout six.'

Six friends! When he worked, he worked quickly! 'They'll be at the box office. You and your friends want to come to the party after?'

'I dunno. We might.'

'Try to make it. You need any money?'

'Yes.'

'Come over and I'll give you a fifty.'

'Can't. I've got someone here.'

'A girl?' Al was delighted.

'Yes,' muttered Evan. 'So can you leave the money at the desk for me?'

'It will be my pleasure, son.' Al hung up the phone well pleased. So Evan had finally got himself connected. What a relief! Not that he had been worried. He knew the kid was normal – after all he was Al King's son, wasn't he?

'I got you the tickets,' Evan said.

'Clever!' sighed Glory.

'Why did you want six?'

'To sell of course. Gotta make bread every way y'can. Know what I mean?'

Evan nodded. Why hadn't *he* thought of that.

Plum was smearing lipstick on. 'We'd better get moving. We've got – let me see – yeah we got twelve tickets to sell now. Reckon we'll make at least two hundred.'

Glory whistled. 'Like – rich, man.'

Plum nodded. 'It'll keep us goin'.'

'My father is leaving me fifty dollars at the desk,' Evan announced proudly.

'So we're all rich!' laughed Glory, latching her thin arm through Evan's equally thin arm. 'We can buy us some real good poppers and come back here and like – y'know – have a real *mean* time. Wanna do that, Evvaan?'

'Yes,' he said quickly, 'let's do that.'

Plum threw her arm around him. 'You're one of us now, man,' she said kindly.

He positively glowed. He was one of them.

Bernie spotted them first, Al's kid and the two barracudas.

He complained to Paul, who didn't believe him. 'Evan, with those two? You must be mistaken.'

'You want me to tell them to leave the kid alone?' Bernie blustered. 'Mistaken I ain't. The three of 'em bouncing around out front as tight as thieves.'

'Let me ask Al,' Paul decided. It was up to Al to decide the company Evan should keep.

Al said 'Jesus!', shook his head and laughed. 'I guess it can't do any harm. Leave him alone if that's what he wants.'

Paul passed the word to Bernie, who snorted with disgust. If it was his kid . . . Aw – what the fuck . . . Fortunately it wasn't.

*

They counted out the money.

'Two hundred and sixteen bucks!' exclaimed Plum in delight.

Glory slid her arm tightly around Evan's waist, 'Wanna add your fifty?' she asked slyly, 'wanna be our partner?'

'Yeah,' agreed Plum, 'if you go with us y'gotta pool your bread too. S'only fair.'

'OK,' squeaked Evan. He reached into his jeans' pocket for the money, pleased he hadn't told them about his two hundred dollars.

Plum took the fifty, added it to their money, and then placed the wad of notes firmly in her bra. First she extracted a twenty which she handed to Glory. 'She'll score for us,' Plum explained to Evan, 'now you're our partner you can join in *all* the fun.'

He shivered in anticipation. They weren't Nellie, but they liked him, accepted him, and if he couldn't have Nellie . . . Well . . .

Glory vanished off into the crowds who had not managed to get into the concert.

'She won't be long,' Plum informed him confidently, 'she's gotta nose f' the best score. Few quacks be just right.' She nudged him knowingly. 'You're not into the heavy stuff are you?'

He wanted to ask what heavy stuff? He wanted to ask what quacks were? He wanted to know score what?

He stood silently. Maintain an aura of being one of them. Mustn't ask questions. Mustn't act like a fool.

Once, at school, one of the seniors had been caught smoking grass. He knew what grass was. His father had offered him some once, stuffed a vile-smelling cigarette in his mouth and said: 'Drag on that and if you ever want it again come to me; I don't want to catch you doing it behind my back.'

Glory returned, skipping and laughing. Both girls seemed to have forgotten about the concert, indeed they had sold all the tickets, including their own.

'Let's go back to the hotel,' Plum suggested, 'an' have a good time.'

Glory giggled shrilly. 'Can you give us a good time, Evan? Can you? Can you give *both* of us a good time?'

He smiled bravely. Why not? If his father could do it why couldn't he?

'Yeah,' he croaked, 'let's go.'

thirty-nine

Dallas waited for their relationship to develop. She waited for Cody to tell her something corny like he loved her. She waited for him to make love to her again.

He did none of those things.

He phoned her on the Sunday to tell her his mother was sick and he couldn't come over.

He turned up at the studio on Monday for lunch as usual. And it was as usual. No mention of what had taken place between them. No words of love. No physical contact. He was exactly the same as he always was. Sweet, charming, funny. He had a script he wanted her to read. He had two important magazine interviews he had arranged for her. He had a franchise on 'Man Made Woman' T-shirts he wanted to discuss with her. He had a top photographer coming in from New York specially to photograph her.

What with working and doing all the things Cody had arranged she did not have much time free.

At first she was hurt by his attitude. But the hurt soon turned to a cold anger, and she felt used and debased.

How dare he treat her like this. Cody Hills. Short, balding, not even rich – yet. And she had gone to bed with him, given herself to him – and he didn't want to know.

When the call from Lew Margolis finally came she was in just the right mood for it.

'I'll come to your house,' he informed her, no doubt hoping she would arrange a second session with the luscious Diamond.

'No. I'll come to your office,' she insisted, 'I have a surprise for you.'

The date was made, and she went home, selected sòme of the best photos, and slid them into the cellophane pages of a leather-bound album. It was a touch she was sure Linda would have appreciated.

Cody was destroyed. Dallas was everything he had ever dreamed about in a relationship. But Christ! What did she want with him? She could have anyone.

He loved her. He loved everything about her. But he knew it was a love that would destroy their relationship. And God Almighty – ultimately theirs was a business tryst. And that's the way he had to keep it.

Regarding things clearly and logically he could see where it was all at. She was looking for something – someone, and he just happened to be there. Yes – it could be great, until she found what she was *really* searching for. And then what? Wasn't he better off being her agent, manager and friend? That way he would always be around.

Mr Cody Hills regrets that although he would give his left leg to keep on trucking, his head rules his heart (fortunately), and he is too smart to screw up a golden opportunity.

He hated himself. He knew she was hurt. But one of these days she would thank him. This is where analysis got you. Made you so smart you cut off your own balls!

On the Sunday, after being with Dallas the previous day, he had steeled himself into action. He had phoned Connie.

'My God! I figured you died! she exclaimed, 'where have you been?'

'Working,' he explained, 'can I come over?'

'I was just washing my . . .'

'I'll be there in time to dry it!'

'Haven't changed, have you?'

He hoped not. He rushed over to her apartment on Fountain, and within fifteen minutes had talked her into bed – wet hair and all.

She did not have a body like Dallas. No one had a body like Dallas.

He did not come all over her in one schoolboyish spurt. He indulged in twenty minutes polite foreplay and seventeen minutes of polite fucking. He then spent a further half hour being affectionate and considerate. Fell asleep for an acceptable hour, and then went home.

Things weren't what they used to be.

Lew Margolis looked through the book of photographs once, then a second time. He didn't speak.

Dallas, sitting across from him, lit a cigarette and tried to appear as calm as possible.

Lew studied the photos yet again.

'Like them?' Dallas inquired. She couldn't stand the silence. Let's get this show on the road and over and done with.

'Is this the surprise you had for me?' he asked at last.

'I thought I'd show them to you first. Thought it might make rather a nice anniversary present for your wife. I understand you've been married nine years next week.'

'Once a cunt always a cunt,' he said wearily. 'How much?'

'How much for what?'

'The pictures.'

'No charge, Mister.' She glared at him. 'Just no more private meetings between us. Get your rocks off on somebody else's time.'

His lips tightened. 'We had an arrangement, you agreed.'

'I agreed shit. You blackmailed me, and now I'm throwing the ball back into *your* court.'

'I can make or break you.'

'Likewise.'

They stared at each other, then finally he said, 'You don't want to fuck me means you're a silly girl. You got the pictures means you're smart. But it's all a game – remember that – just a game. And I am an *ace* player – *an ace*. What are you? Some down-and-out hooker I gave a break to.'

'Thank you, Mr Margolis,' her voice was thick with sarcasm, 'may I please go now?'

He flicked through the photos again. 'Yeah. Go. You've won this round – but if Doris ever sees these pictures you'll find yourself washed up on the beach one morning along with the rest of the garbage. Remember that, it's not an idle threat.'

'I'll remember. But *you* remember there's a letter with my lawyer should anything happen to me. And the negatives will become very public property.'

'You've been seeing too many movies. Get your ass back to work. If I can't hump you I may as well make money out of you.'

She stood up. Christ! Was it worth it? She felt more dirty than if she'd slept with him a hundred times.

'Get lost, cunt,' he added. And it was the last she saw of him until Cody received an invitation for the two of them to attend a dinner party at the Margolis residence two days later.

'I don't want to go,' she told Cody.

'Are you kidding?' he argued. 'An invitation to one of their dinners is like the seal of approval in this town. He must really like you.'

She had no alternative but to accept the invitation. To refuse would certainly make Cody suspicious. Besides she was curious to see what Lew had in mind.

The dinner party was on a Saturday. Dallas spent the day doing pictures with the photographer from New York who was an outrageous, amusing fag. He was full of gossip about the so-called Beautiful People, and told the most scandalous stories. He also took magnificent photos, and she continued her love affair with the camera. It was the only love affair she had.

When Cody picked her up she was tired, irritable, and not at all looking forward to dinner at the Margolis'.

'You look wonderful,' Cody told her.

'Wonderful enough to make love to?' she questioned. It was the first time either of them had mentioned it.

Cody was prepared. He knew that eventually she would have to say something. He pulled the car over to the side and turned to her. 'You want to hear a really corny speech?'

'Try me. I'd like to hear *something*. It's our anniversary, you know. Exactly one week ago we made fast abortive love – or rather we *nearly* did. And I'd like to know why you've been trying to forget it ever happened.'

'I . . .'

'How do you think I *feel*?' she continued, her emotions rushing to the surface, 'I don't enter into relationships easily, you know. You have no idea what it took for me to sleep with you.'

He was temporarily speechless. He hadn't expected *this*. What about the night he had sneaked up to her house and seen her taking part in an orgy? What about her big black boyfriend?

'Well?' she demanded. 'What's the problem, Cody? Don't I turn you on?'

Another laugh. She turned him on so goddamn fast it was over before it had even happened.

He took her hand. 'You know I adore you . . .'

'But?' she interrupted.

'But I think if you and I indulge in any sort of a thing you're going to regret it.'

'Oh, come on!'

'I mean it, Dallas. Don't you understand this is just the beginning for you. Once a week you're going to be on millions of TV sets all over the country. Your face – you – will be public property. You'll have all the pressures of being a star, plus all the advantages. *I* don't want to get in the way of all your advantages.'

'What are you talking about?'

'You know what I'm talking about. You'll be able to have any guy you want, and I don't want to be shoved in the background like some schmuck. It may surprise you but I've got an enormous ego.'

'Terrific,' said Dallas coldly, 'really terrific!'

'What?'

'Your opinion of me.'

'It's not my opinion of you. I love you – and because I love you I don't want to put you in a position of feeling guilty.'

'Ha! We haven't even made it properly and already I've discarded you for ten other men!'

He sighed. 'Basically I'm being selfish. I don't want to get kicked in the teeth.'

'But I wouldn't . . .'

'But the chances are you would.'

'Chances? What chances? I think you're full of shit.'

'So does my mother – that's why she wants me to get married to a nice kosher lady who'll stuff me full of Ex-Lax hidden in the chicken soup!'

Dallas couldn't help laughing. She felt better after their talk, and in a way she understood how he felt, but that was only because he didn't know her very well. 'Take me to the party, Cody. Maybe I can get drunk and rape you when you're not so busy protecting your *enormous* ego. *I* think we have a future together – let me see if I can convince *you.*'

The first person she saw at the party was Ed Kurlnik.

The second person she spotted was Aarron Mack. The two of them were engaged in an animated conversation – well, about as animated as two elderly billionaires could be.

Two of the richest men in America, and they had both wanted her. Not bad for a girl who had had to make it on her own.

Lew Margolis was bearing down on her, a fatherly smile suffusing his false teeth. 'Glad you two kids could make it,' he said warmly.

Tonight she was kid. What had happened to cunt?

'Mr Margolis,' eagerly Cody shook hands, 'so nice of you to think of us.'

'My pleasure. Got to look after my little star!' He winked at her. 'Right, Dallas?'

'Right, Mr Margolis.'

'Call me Lew, no need to be formal. Come, I want you to meet my wife.'

Dallas had seen Doris Andrews in so many movies that meeting her was like coming face to face with an old friend. The same wispy brown hair, cornflower-blue eyes, kindly smile, a little girl voice. 'So pleased to meet you, Dallas dear. Lew has told me all about the wonderful series you're doing for him. It sounds such fun.'

Dallas could hardly imagine the ordinary-looking Doris Andrews seducing every man she came in contact with. Lew's games were probably a figment of his very vivid imagination.

'Let me introduce you around,' said Doris, adjusting the Peter Pan starched white collar of her dress. She certainly lived up to her screen image.

Both Ed and Aarron had spotted her at the same time, and their conversation was abruptly terminated, whilst they both tried to wander over in an unobtrusive way.

Aarron reached her first, as Ed was waylaid by a woman who Dallas realized with a shock was Dee Dee Kurlnik.

'Dallas!' exclaimed Aarron, clutching both her hands, 'you leave New York just like that. No word, no address. I am hurt.'

She stared down at his bullet head. God, all the money in the world couldn't make you tall.

Doris smiled. 'Aarron, I didn't realize you knew our little star.'

There were a lot of things Doris didn't realize.

'Yes, we are old friends.'

'Of course you are,' Doris grinned, 'you know every beautiful girl in America! He's such a naughty boy, Dallas, you'll have to watch him!'

Naughty boy! The man was seventy-three years old!

Dallas smiled weakly and looked around for Cody. He was in deep conversation with Ed and Dee Dee. Oh Christ! This was a nightmare. Lew Margolis must have planned the whole thing.

A waiter hovered with a silver tray. She snatched a glass of champagne and gulped it down.

'Now that I have found you again,' Aarron said smugly, 'escape will not be so easy.' He leered at her breasts. 'I have thought about you many times.'

She remembered their last dismal date. Such fun that she had contemplated suicide. She remembered him exposing his withered penis to her, expecting her to immediately get on her knees.

'I think I had better circulate,' she said.

'Why?' he wanted to know.

'Because I think I should.'

He shook his head in admiration. 'I like your spirit. I liked it in New York. You don't care about my money, do you?'

'Not particularly.'

'I like that. Most women will do anything for money.'

'Really?' Her sarcasm was lost on him.

'You'd be surprised,' he brooded darkly, 'but you are so different. I knew that at once.'

'Good for you.'

232

'I am in California for only three days. I want you to keep those days free. We shall be together.'

'I'm working.'

'Tomorrow is Sunday. We'll take my plane to Palm Springs.'

'I don't want to go to Palm Springs.'

'We'll go where you want. I like your fiery spirit. You remind me of my dear departed wife. She was Swedish, you know. We were married for forty-six years. She was an independent woman – like you.' He coughed, bending over and choking vigorously.

Dallas took the opportunity to escape. She walked out beside the Olympic pool and hoped that Aarron wouldn't follow her.

So this was a chic Hollywood dinner party. Not quite what she had imagined. Apart from Cody and herself everyone was so old.

She sipped her champagne and marvelled at the mosaic initials embedded on the bottom of the pool. Inside she could see Cody still talking to Ed and Dee Dee. Aarron was looking around wondering what had happened to her.

She recalled the last time she had visited this house. As a hooker. Who would have thought that she would come back in such a different position. Oh come on, Cody – what the hell are you talking to those two old farts about?

Beautifully laid out tables were in position on the huge patio. Six tables, ten places per table. Sixty people. Some small dinner party.

She circled round the tables glancing at the delicate engraved place cards set in their exquisite silver holders. The names read like a Who's Who of Hollywood. She found her own name positioned between two men she had never heard of. Now if she could only find Cody's place – a quick switch and no one would be any the wiser. Dallas was still innocent of Hollywood party procedure. Doris Andrews had spent hours sweating over who should sit next to whom.

'You want some help?' A waiter who had been hovering on the sidelines approached her.

'No, it doesn't matter, thank you.' She headed back for the house.

Doris Andrews was just emerging. 'Ah, Dallas, dear. What are you doing out here? Aarron's looking for you. I think you made quite a hit there. I didn't even know you two knew each other. He's such a sweet, sweet man, and so lonely.'

'And so rich,' Dallas added drily.

'But of course. Isn't everyone?' Doris touched her lightly on

233

the arm, then hesitating slightly she asked, 'You do like men, don't you?'

'What do you mean?'

Doris's fingers drummed a light pattern on her arm. 'Sexually.'

'Sexually?' Dallas questioned, suddenly at a loss for words.

Doris laughed throatily. 'Men are such brutes. Big and hairy. Rough. Unthinking. A woman's touch is so much softer . . . kinder . . . Do you know what I mean now?'

'I think I'm getting the message.'

Christ! Doris Andrews dykesville! Public image – Miss Clean – Husband's image – Miss Randy. Lew – you are playing the wrong game!

'Well, dear. Perhaps you and I will take lunch together one day. I can give you the benefit of my experience. Twenty years in this shitty business – you have to know how to handle yourself. I can see you're going to be someone special . . .' She trailed off. 'Must get dinner organized. You run along and enjoy yourself.'

'Yes,' agreed Dallas, still in a state of shock. Doris Andrews. The only screen virgin left in Hollywood!

She wandered back into the house to be pounced on immediately by Aarron demanding to know where she had been.

'I went for a walk,' she replied, annoyed at being questioned. Then she saw Cody free from the Kurlniks at last, and beckoned him over.

He came on the trot, eager and delighted by the entire party. Before she could introduce him he was pumping Aarron by the hand and saying, 'Mr Mack. It's a real pleasure to meet you. My name is Cody Hills. I am Dallas' agent and manager.'

'Good,' wheezed Aarron, 'then you can instruct her to come to Palm Springs with me.'

Cody laughed with just the right amount of deference. 'Mr Mack, unfortunately I can't instruct Dallas to do anything. A very headstrong young lady is Dallas.'

They both regarded her with patronizing smiles.

She was furious. Headstrong indeed!

'Mr Mack, I know why you are in Los Angeles,' Cody continued. 'It's the big search, isn't it? You are looking for the new Mack girl. Well, has it ever occured to you that Dallas is just the girl you're looking for'

'Is she not signed for a television series?'

'Yes, she is. And that could be just the tie-in to make the new Mack girl *really* exciting. 'Man Made Woman' as *your* Mack girl – wearing *your* cosmetics – *your* perfumes. Think of the excitement *that* would generate. Of course . . . she doesn't come cheap.'

Aarron was impressed with the idea. His small eyes gleamed.

'What do you think, Mr Mack. Is this a great idea or is it a great idea?'

Dallas walked away. Neither man noticed her go. Cody would have made a great Coca Cola salesman. She had never seen anyone so turned on by his own ideas. Maybe he was right. Maybe he wasn't the man for her. She was seeing a side of him that she wasn't sure she could stomach. Mr Kiss-your-ass. She had kissed too many asses in her life to go through that scene again.

'Dallas!' Ed Kurlnik had stationed himself behind a potted palm and was hissing her name.

She marched over to him. 'How dare you stand me up in New York!' she said loudly.

'Sshh!' he mumbled.

'Don't sshh me. I waited at Essex House all night. You never came.'

'I did,' he whispered.

'Your wife's coming over. Are you going to introduce us?'

'What?' he jumped. 'Dallas, I . . .'

She strolled away feeling good.

Two of the richest men in the world grovelling for her favours. Wow – if this was a taste of being a star – she liked it.

forty

'Look out the window,' said Paul.

Al, emerging from the bathroom, went to the window, and saw, eighteen storeys below, crowds of girls blocking the street outside. They held a giant banner aloft – 'Happy Birthday, Al – You are King.'

'I think you should make an appearance,' Paul said, 'they've been there all day.'

'How's the security?' snapped Al. He was starting to get slightly paranoiac about his personal safety.

'There are cops all round the hotel. The management suggested you give 'em a wave from a first-storey balcony. Then we can smuggle you out to City Park through a back entrance.'

'OK. Fine with me. That flight knocked me out this morning. I guess I've slept the day away.'

'It's your birthday – do what you want.'

'I thought I always did anyway.'

'Yeah – every day's a birthday for you Al.'

'Right on, baby brother – right on!'

'You get yourself together then, I'll let them know you'll be out on the balcony in an hour. Does that give you enough time?'

'Yeah.'

Paul left. Al switched on the television. It would take him five minutes to dress. Idly he switched channels until he found a Western. Christ! Paul Newman looked young. An unlined, un-lived-in face. Must be a really old movie. Of course Newman still looked terrific – but you knew he was just another old guy that looked terrific. What was it that aged a person?

Al rushed to the mirror and studied his own image. A thirty-eight-year-old superstar. Thirty-eight. Wasn't that nearing middle age? Al King middle-aged – never. The thought filled him with dread. His life was speeding along and leaving him behind. Dreary days – only the nights – lit up with champagne, and cigars, and women, offered any diversions. And was it worth the hang-overs?

Of course the hours on stage were still magic. A level of communication he could reach nowhere else in his life. But suddenly it wasn't enough. He wanted more. More what? He didn't really know, if he did he would buy it.

He lit a cigar, too soon after waking for a smoke, but what the hell. Maybe cancer would save him from ever being senile. He smiled grimly. As it happened he didn't feel too good, nothing specific, just a sort of draggy feeling that he couldn't put a name to.

He slouched in front of the television, not really watching it at all. He was worried about Evan, worried at the company he was keeping.

At first it had been a joke – Evan and the two freaks. Al had thought it would have been a five-minute relationship. But Evan let them attach themselves to him with a vengeance. He even asked if he could bring them with him on the plane from Houston. Reluctantly Al had said yes. Against his better judgement, but Christ Almighty it was the first time the kid had made friends, and he didn't want to come the heavy father bit. He had tried to discuss the girls with his son, but Evan refused to carry on conversations – he just mumbled inaudible yes's and no's.

What they had, Al finally realized, was a communication problem. And sod it – it wasn't *his* fault – he had given the boy everything that money could buy. Evan just didn't appreciate things.

The whole problem was Edna's fault. Christ! She would have a blue fit if she saw him now.

Al sighed. He would let it go. Let Evan get them out of his system. After all, he too had banged a few slags in his time.

Linda bumped into Paul in the lobby.

'I got some great shots!' she enthused.

'I think he's depressed.'

'Who?'

'Who! Only you would ask who.'

'So-rrry.'

'Did you manage to wrap everything yet?'

Linda mock saluted. 'Naturally, I have not forgotten it is Big White Master's Birthday.'

Paul glanced at his watch. 'Listen, I've got to move. Be sure to get everything organized.'

'You betcha ass, black eyes. See you later.'

He kissed her cheek. 'Later.'

Linda watched him walk across the lobby. Sentimental bum. He was making as much fuss about Al's birthday as if it were for a child. Rather sweet really. But then that's what had hooked her on Paul in the first place – his inherent niceness.

She observed Evan enter the lobby, his two bizarre companions flanking him as usual. She wished that Paul had not put the block on her photographing them – because wow – what a picture *that* trio would make.

'Hello,' she said, as they passed on by.

Evan's glazed eyes flicked briefly in her direction. She wondered if Al knew that these two freaky girls had got his son flying on some drug or other. Probably not.

She wondered if she should be the one to tell him. Probably not. She sighed. Some birthday present.

As the lights dimmed, the audience roared its approval. Their patience was stretched to the limit, even 'The Promises' had had trouble holding them. They wanted Al. They didn't want to wait.

As the total darkness swept over the audience the sound of

drums started slowly, to be joined by tambourines, then the guitar and congas.

The opening bars of 'Random Love'.

Suddenly Al standing centre stage bathed in brilliant spotlights.

The audience was on its feet as one, screaming their appreciation.

The waves flooded over him. He assaulted them rhythmically – swaying, moving, bending, leaning – until they were almost a part of him. Total fucking.

The spotlights tracked his every move, following him like relentless slaves. He swigged from the champagne bottle waiting on top of one of the amplifiers, and the mob screamed 'Happy Birthday Al' and surged dangerously near to crushing the mass of security guards in front of the stage.

He decided against doing his usual set, and switched into a rasping parody of Jagger's 'Satisfaction' – then Stewart's 'Maggie May' and his own 'All Night Stand'. The crowd went mad.

'S'good to be in New Orleans,' he told them. They screamed. He did some very funky, very beautiful Bobby Bland hits. Then he rasped into a medley from his new album which was to be released any day. And then 'Bad Black Alice', his current single, which was racing up the charts.

He was halfway through that when the crowds broke through security and came clambering up on stage like small mad locusts. He felt panic and terror as he saw the mob descending. He was paralysed with fear. He just couldn't move.

A girl grabbed him round the neck before he even realized what was happening. She was thrown bodily off him by Luke who appeared miraculously quickly. Another girl gripped him round the legs, her hands clawing and strange little grunts emitting from her throat as she too was pulled off him.

It was like a bad dream. One moment music and harmony – the next the dark eruption of violence as Luke and Marvin half dragged him from the stage kicking and shoving the locusts out of their way. His feet hardly touched the ground. That's how fast they got him out to the car.

'Holy shit!' He exclaimed as the car raced off, 'What the fuck happened?'

'I told 'em they didn't have enough guys out front,' Luke said stoically. 'I told Bernie they'd break through.'

'What did he say?' asked Al, sudden anger coursing through him.

'You know Bernie, but I told him.'

Sure. Al could just imagine. Fat Bernie had probably shrugged and said 'What the fuck.' After all it was no skin off his nose if Al got torn to pieces by his fans. Think of the publicity . . .

Evan, Plum and Glory were near the front when it happened.

'Jest fall with the crowd, man,' Plum yelled with excitement, 'and hold on!'

Panic swept over Evan as pressure from the crowds behind propelled him forward. Hold on to what?

Glory was laughing and scrambling towards the stage. Plum grinned solidly. Neither girl seemed in the least put out by the sudden chaos.

Evan saw people swarming over the fallen security guards using them as footrests to get a hoist up towards the stage. It didn't seem to matter that Al was no longer on the stage.

'Hang on in there, man,' trilled Glory, 'just keep on a movin'.'

He could hardly do anything else. And then from behind he could hear pain-filled screams as more security guards moved in wielding heavy truncheons in all directions.

He wanted to get out of there. But there was nowhere to go, nowhere to turn. Then suddenly he felt himself falling, knees buckling. And he knew if the mob behind him didn't stop he would be trampled to death.

Edna didn't like New York. And – momentous decision – after all those years she finally admitted to herself that she didn't like Melanie. She had always known in the back of her mind that her sister-in-law was a pain – but suddenly she found that she could come right out and think it – maybe even say it – only to Al of course, she wouldn't want to be disloyal to the family. The thing was that Paul was so nice. She had always been fond of him. Like her, he only had Al's best interests at heart. Together they had supported Al on his climb to fame, and together they were still the only two people really close to him.

To see Melanie at work was a shock. Edna had always suspected that she played around, but to see her blatantly flirt with every man who crossed her path was disgusting.

Melanie had arrived in New York armed with a book of telephone numbers. People she had met, friends and business acquaintances of Al and Paul's. She didn't care who she called. 'I'm not sitting in a hotel room for two days,' she had told Edna when she objected, 'I'm going out to have fun!'

239

Edna sat in the hotel room by herself whilst Melanie did just that. The first night she didn't arrive home until 4 a.m. The second she didn't bother to appear at all and breezed in with room service delivering breakfast. 'Do you honestly think that Al and Paul aren't out having themselves a good time?' she demanded of Edna.

'I'm sure they're working very hard,' Edna insisted.

'Oh sure! And the rest. Don't you know these tours have girls following them across the country? Girls who will do anything. A man would have to be the Pope to resist *that* kind of temptation. Paul and I have an understanding.'

Edna tightened her lips and didn't pursue the conversation. Melanie was just not a nice person. It was quite obvious she had used and manipulated her to get her to agree to the trip. Now that they were almost there she didn't care any more. Edna was no longer useful.

The flight to New Orleans from Kennedy Airport was delayed by three hours. Melanie was furious, and bounced around the airport trying to cause a fuss. She finally caught the attention of an airline official who settled them in a private lounge, and plied Melanie with vodka.

Edna leafed through magazines and willed the plane to be ready to take off soon. She didn't want to miss Al's birthday. After all, that was the whole point of the trip.

'Thank Christ you weren't there.' Paul took Linda's face in his hands and kissed her.

She wriggled free. 'I miss all the good things. When I think of the pictures I could have gotten . . .'

'You could have been crushed to death. I've never seen anything like it, it was frightening. Christ knows how many injuries we're going to have with this one.'

'Is Al all right?'

'A little frantic. We're still trying to locate Evan. No one seems to know whether he was there or not. Since he's been hanging around with those weirdos he does his own thing.'

I saw him earlier with them in the lobby, but that was long before the concert.'

'Bernie's at the theatre, I'm going to take a ride over to the hospital. Now what I want you to do is to put a time stop on all the party arrangements – just a postponement – I hope we can go ahead later. Meanwhile do me a favour and go and sit with Al – and if Evan turns up, contact Bernie.' He kissed her. 'I'll be back soon, sweetheart.'

Linda did as she was told. What a wonderful secretary I would have made some lucky executive, she thought, as she darted around the hotel issuing instructions.

Wife – no. Secretary – yes.

Everything done she made her way up to Al's suite. He slouched morosely on the couch watching a late newscast of the event on television.

'Some birthday!' he said bitterly.

'It's not over yet,' she replied briskly. 'Any word on Evan?'

'Nothing. I should never have let him go wandering off all over the place with those two freaks.'

'You didn't know this was going to happen.'

Al made a face. 'This, that. I should know where the fuck he is. I was just so goddamn relieved he had found some friends that I let him do what he wanted.'

'Can I fix you a drink?' Linda asked, going over to the bar and sorting through the bottles.

'Bourbon and coke. Heavy on the bourbon.'

'Coming right up.' As she was mixing his drink the phone rang. 'Shall I get it?' she inquired.

'Yeah. I don't want to talk to anyone unless it's about Evan.'

She picked up the phone.

'Got him!' announced Paul triumphantly, 'a little worse for wear, but still in the land of the living.'

'Wonderful!' exclaimed Linda. She handed the phone to Al. 'Paul's found Evan, he's all right.'

'Thank Christ for that,' Al replied, relief sweeping on him.

The girl was totally naked apart from gold paint all over her voluptuous body. She emerged from the giant cake holding aloft another smaller cake with thirty-eight candles burning brightly. 'Watch out you don't singe your tits!' somebody shouted, and there was much raucous laughter.

Al accepted the smaller cake from her, weaving unsteadily on his feet. 'Gotta thank everyone,' he slurred, 'for makin' this a great evening. 'Specially Paul.' He patted the naked girl on her bottom. 'You another present darlin'?'

'Yeah – go on give 'er one!' A musician shouted. 'An' if you don't want her send her over here!'

Al sat at the head of a long table. On one side of him was Evan, surly and bruised, with his arm in a sling. On the other side sat Paul, and all along the table were the other members of the tour.

The birthday dinner party had turned out to be a big success, with everyone getting good and drunk to relieve the tension of what had happened earlier.

Al had loved his presents. A solid gold digital watch from Paul. Cufflinks shaped like a nude woman from Bernie. A leather-bound book of the best photos of the tour from Linda, and numerous sweaters, shirts and novelty gifts from everyone else.

Evan had not given him anything; and Nellie had embarrassed him with a thick chunky gold identity bracelet inscribed 'Love from Nellie always'.

'Cut the cake,' Linda enthused, 'it looks delicious.'

'Sure,' agreed Al, 'you want to get off the table, darlin'?'

The naked Golden Lady allowed herself to be helped down to an accompaniment of lewd remarks.

'Get her a chair,' demanded Al, 'sit down next to me, darlin' – have some champagne.' He offered her a glass, but moved it out of reach when she went to take it. He did this three times, and she went along with the joke. Then – wham – he threw the glass of champagne all over her, and the rivulets of liquid mixed in psychedelic patterns with her gold body make-up.

She laughed along with the rest of them, and sat down.

'Want some cake?' Al asked, warming to his audience.

'Oh no . . .' she began, but too late. Al had picked up the cake and aimed it directly at her chest. Chocolate sponge, soft cream, and icing squelched its way across her bosoms.

'Anyone for dessert?' Al laughed.

Further down the table Nellie got up and hurried from the room.

Evan watched her go and wished that he could follow her. His arm hurt, his body ached, and he wished he knew where Glory and Plum had vanished to.

'Hey, Evan, boyo,' Al was nudging him, handing him a spoon. 'Have some cake, help yourself. Go on, son, have yourself a time!'

forty-one

'If a day in Palm Springs will turn you into the Mack girl, why won't you go?' Cody persisted.

'I don't understand you,' raged Dallas, 'are you dumb or something? The guy wants to get laid – LAID. Is that what you want me to do to become the Mack girl? Because if it is just tell me and then we'll both know where we stand.'

'You can handle him.'

'Ha! I can handle him. Sweet. Lovely. But I *don't want* to handle him. Are you with me? I *don't want to*.'

'Not physically, stupid.'

'Don't you call *me* stupid. I have had a tough life – and if I was stupid I wouldn't be here today.'

'What sort of a tough life have you had? A girl with your looks.'

Dallas laughed bitterly. 'Oh boy! You're not even interested in my background. What do you care? Here I am – all ready for you to promote. What does my *past* matter. *You* don't give a shit.' She paused, stared at him wearily, 'Why don't you just go on home, Cody?'

They stood outside her house arguing. She was tired and angry. She had hated the party. Hated the bullshit. And hated Cody for even suggesting she go along with it.

'Aarron Mack is calling me first thing,' Cody said, 'I promised him I'd talk to you.'

'Why don't *you* go to Palm Springs with him?' Dallas suggested sweetly. 'He liked you, he's old, almost senile – I'm sure he won't notice whether it's you or me pulling on his rocks.'

'You really can be disgusting.'

'Almost as disgusting as you and your suggestions.'

'I am not suggesting anything,' argued Cody desperately, 'I'm just saying that if you went to Palm Springs with him the Mack girl contract would be ours. You could fly back the same day. He just wants to be seen with you – that's all. I'll come too if you like.'

'God, you're naive! How can anybody live in this city, work in the film business, and *still* be naive!'

'Trust me, Dallas. I got you "Man Made Woman", didn't I? I got you an unbelievable deal didn't I? Well, I'll get you a million dollar contract to be the Mack girl. You want it? Come to Palm Springs and I will not leave your side – I promise.'

'You promise?' She was starting to weaken.

'Naive agent's honour!'

'Oh God! You really are a hustler!'

'I know. Will you come?'

She sighed, smiled. 'I guess a million dollars *is* tempting. But you must not . . .'

'Leave your side,' he finished for her, 'I'll call you first thing and give you the schedule.'

*

Palm Springs was gloriously hot. Aarron kept a small house there. Six bedrooms with bathrooms en suite, a gigantic living area, Olympic-size pool, and modest golf course.

'Nice little place,' Dallas observed drily.

'I don't use it much,' Aarron explained, 'two or three times a year. If you would ever care to avail yourself of the facilities please feel free to be my guest. Do you play golf, Cody?'

'Sorry, no.'

'Don't be sorry. I don't play myself. I just have it for my guests.'

'I'd like to sunbathe,' Dallas decided.

'Of course,' Aarron agreed, 'and then I have arranged a small luncheon party for you.'

'For me?'

'As it was such short notice I was not able to contact many people. But twenty-five should suffice.'

'Oh yes,' nodded Dallas, winking at Cody. 'Small but nice!'

She changed into a white crochet bikini, and lay out on a yellow striped chaise lounge.

Aarron sat on a chair, clad in a bathrobe, and sheltered by an umbrella. He never took his small beady eyes off her.

Cody reluctantly climbed into his swimming shorts. He wasn't athletic, never had the patience for exercise and keep fit. He was decidedly flabby around the middle – and embarrassingly white for a person who had lived all his life in California. He was ashamed for Dallas to see him, but with the clever use of a towel he managed to negotiate a spot somewhere between her and Aarron without revealing too much of himself.

After regarding Dallas intently for some length of time Aarron finally said, 'You've changed.'

She shielded her eyes from the sun and glanced up at him. 'I have?'

'Very much so. In New York you were different.'

'I was?'

'I felt there that you were a girl who would go out with a man simply for his money.'

She yawned. 'It didn't get you anywhere though, did it?'

'I apologize if I insulted you in any way. I see now that you are not that sort of a girl at all.'

'Thanks,' she replied sarcastically.

Cody tried to get up unobtrusively, tripped, and fell in the pool. He wasn't fond of the fact that Aarron Mack was conducting a conversation over his head as if he didn't exist. If it wasn't for me, Aarron, old sport, she wouldn't even be here today.

He decided to swim the length of the pool ten times. Get rid of some of his flab and give them a chance to talk.

'Would you *like* to be the Mack girl?' Aarron asked.

'Would you expect any personal favours in return?' Dallas replied coolly.

Aarron shrugged. 'I am an old man. I am not demanding.'

'That's not an answer.'

'I could offer you more than you've ever dreamed of . . .'

'And wonderful presents.'

'What?'

She laughed softly, 'Just remembering, Aarron.'

'Will you think about it?'

'Nope.'

'Why not?'

'Because my body is not for sale – whatever the price.'

'I could marry you . . .'

She sat up. 'Could you really?' Her voice dripped sarcasm.

'Isn't that what you want?' He was puzzled and hurt.

What she wanted was to laugh in his face. Screw Cody for forcing her into a position like this. A proposal of marriage! Shit! From *the* Aarron Mack. Double shit! A few months ago this would have been it. The Golden Opportunity. Just lie back, open your legs – your mouth – whatever – and revel in the money. But things were different now. She was a person. An individual. And no one – but no one – could buy her.

'I'm sorry, Aarron,' she said in a kindly fashion, 'I'm very flattered, but I just don't want to get married.'

'You don't want to get married,' he repeated blankly. 'Then what do you want?'

She opened her arms to the sun, lay back. 'To enjoy life. To do the things *I* want to do.'

'Do you *want* to be the Mack girl?'

'We just had that conversation.'

He hesitated. 'No strings.'

'No strings?'

'You have my word. But we shall be friends, and maybe in time . . . who knows . . .'

She sat up again, her eyes shining. 'Of course I would adore to be the Mack girl. And I thought you were just another dirty old man!'

He smiled tightly, his perfect false teeth gleaming brightly in the sun. 'I'll talk to your manager after lunch. There are a lot of things to be worked out.'

'Thank you, Aarron.' She stood up and kissed him lightly on the cheek, 'You're really a very nice man.'

Cody was elated. Persuading Dallas to spend the day in Palm Springs had been a master stroke on his part. He had personally seen to it that she never had to spend one minute alone in old man Mack's company – and it had been easy really. All those interesting and influential people turning up for lunch, staying all afternoon, and then, when they left, Cody had reminded Aarron that Dallas had to get back to LA, and Aarron had put his plane at their disposal.

It was only when they were leaving the house and saying their goodbyes that Aarron took him to one side and told him that he wanted him to fly to New York to discuss a contract. 'You'll fly in with me on Tuesday,' Aarron said, 'that suit you?'

Yes, it suited him.

Negotiations took place. Cody made his points – business-wise he was sharp as a razor. Dallas ended up with a contract that would pay her more money than either Lauren Hutton and her famous Revlon deal, or Margeaux Hemingway and Faberge.

Once again Dallas was news. Every newspaper carried her photograph. Every magazine wanted to do a cover story on her.

Cody's phone did not stop ringing. The deal he had made for his client was world-wide news, and whereas the 'Man Made Woman' contract might have been a fluke, the Mack girl contract really clinched the fact that he was hot stuff. Suddenly clients were lining up to avail themselves of his services.

He didn't plan to handle just anyone. He wanted a small stable of three or four clients who were the tops. Maybe his thinking was old-fashioned, but what he wanted to provide was a very personal service. He wanted to mould and guide and direct, and not push his artists into the hands of lackeys and hangers-on. If you were lucky enough to get taken on by Cody Hills – by God, you wouldn't get lost in the shuffle.

In exchange he demanded a straight twenty-five per cent of all earnings. Considering some stars were paying their agent ten per cent, and another twenty per cent to their manager, this wasn't a bad deal.

Within days he had signed a top rock star, an English comedy actor, and a young stud who had just finished his first movie.

Cody's stable was complete.

*

The smile was set on Dallas' face, so much so that her facial muscles ached.

'Last one!' promised the photographer, 'you *look beautiful*.'

The camera clicked, her smile collapsed. 'Terrific!' she exclaimed, glancing at her watch. 'I think I have a fast five minutes left for lunch.'

Kiki, the clothes designer, smiled. 'These photos will be worth missing lunch for.'

'Tell that to your husband when I faint in the middle of this afternoon's shooting. I'm starving! Is Cody around?'

'He called, said to tell you he'll be over later. Come on, let's get you out of the dress and I arranged for a salad tray to be left in your dressing-room.'

'Thanks, Kiki. Do you and Chuck work as a team? I never seem to be out of sight of either of you.'

'Yeah,' replied Kiki laconically, 'I get you to be photographed in my clothes on condition I have you back on the set in time. It seems to work.'

'For everyone except me! I don't want a salad. I want a fat juicy steak with french fries, and a couple of thick chocolate malts. I don't even get time to go to the bathroom any more!' But Dallas smiled as she complained. She felt marvellous. On top of everything, before the first 'Man Made Woman' had even been shown she was a star. Before the first Mack girl photos were on every billboard, in every magazine, she was a star.

Everyone was clamouring for her services. Cody was inundated with scripts and books. The representatives of commercial products were knocking at his door, anxious to use Dallas. All the television game and chat shows desired her presence. Every magazine thought a cover story on her was a great idea. All the Hollywood eligibles wanted to date her. Party invitations abounded.

Cody said, 'We shall proceed slowly. It would be easy to grab at everything, but it would also be a mistake.'

She agreed with him. He had made it happen for her, and she was prepared to accept his decisions.

Since the party she had neither seen or heard from Lew Margolis, and she took this as a good sign. Perhaps now he would leave her alone.

Aarron Mack had of course returned to New York, and he made a daily solicitous phone call to her. She didn't mind that, in fact she was rather flattered that his original lechery had turned into an almost fatherly concern.

She was not interested in dating the Hollywood rota of known studs – a rather boring group of pseudo-sophisticated macho-hams who liked to notch up every new famous female on an imaginary fuckbelt.

Parties she had never enjoyed. Perhaps the word party was too synonymous with orgy in her mind.

She enjoyed working, and posing for pictures and becoming a somebody. She enjoyed bumming around with Cody, Kiki and Chuck in the evenings. No chic restaurants, or discotheques. Just little places where you could get a great meal, and not get involved in all that table-hopping shit.

Watching television, barbecuing, and staying home were favourite. Or dropping by Tower Records on the way home and picking up some great new albums and playing them on the in-credible stereo equipment she had invested in.

The question of sex did not arise. Cody seemed determined never to mention the subject again, and she didn't want to push him into anything. If he wanted to wait – well, let him wait. She would just have to prove to him that she wasn't about to rush into bed with every superstar who asked – and they were all ask-ing. With a little patience on her part Cody would eventually come around, of that she was sure. He was a man, wasn't he? And he was just the sort of man she wanted as a husband. He would make a great father, she could see him with dozens of kids . . .

'What are you grinning about?' Kiki inquired, 'can we share the joke?'

'It's not shareable – not yet. But I promise that you and Chuck will be the first to know.'

'Come and eat your salad, starvation is making you too mysterious.'

Later that evening Dallas came face to face with Al King, and for one short moment she forgot about Cody, and her plans, and the waves of excitement came flooding back.

She stood very still, breathed deeply, and surveyed the huge display of Al King albums in Tower Records. He seemed to be staring at her from every angle. Not only was there a full-colour photo of him on the cover of the album, but the sleeve opened up to present a double-space pin-up. A three-quarter shot of Al bar-ing his chest, his teeth. Brooding with his eyes. His black hair curled in an almost gypsy fashion. An ivory horn hung phallically on a thick gold charm around his neck. The album was called 'AL IS KING'. Dallas decided not to buy it.

She wandered around bumping into piles of Al King albums

stacked up on the end of every aisle. There was no avoiding him. A huge poster leered down from the wall.

She chose a new Temptations album, a Marvin Gaye Greatest Hits, and a Linda Ronstadt for Cody. On the way to the check-out she picked up a copy of 'AL IS KING'. What the heck – may as well buy it, he did have a great voice.

She drove quickly home, guilty and excited. Why guilty? Nothing had ever happened.

She ran in the house, kicked off her shoes, and extracted the record from the sleeve.

It wasn't until she had put it on the turntable that she realized she was not alone.

Sitting in the corner, huddled in a chair, was Bobbie.

forty-two

The plane finally took off. Melanie, slightly sloshed, fell into an open-mouthed sleep immediately.

Edna sat tensely by her side, unable even to close her eyes. She stared out of the window and wondered for the hundredth time what Al's reaction would be at seeing her. He wouldn't be pleased. You were not married to a man for sixteen years without knowing how he would react in certain situations. He hated her coming on tours because he knew *she* hated it. But this time *was* different. This time Evan was there, and he at least would be pleased to see her. And she wouldn't stay long – whatever Melanie said. If Al wanted to send her home she would go. The last thing in the world she wanted to do was upset Al. Maybe Evan would come home with her. Maybe he had had enough. She comforted herself with that thought, and at last fell into a fitful sleep.

'You got beautiful pair tits,' slurred Al, rolling across the bed with the naked Golden Lady.

She laughed. She could afford to laugh. She was one of the highest-paid call girls in New Orleans – and sleeping with Al King was no hardship.

'You want I should shower?' she asked, in a high nasal twang. Remnants of birthday cake mixed with the gold paint still on her body.

'I want two of you,' he demanded, 'got a friend?'

She pursed golden lips, 'Won't *I* do, honey? Just lil' ole me all on my ownsome?'

'Want two,' mumbled Al, 's'my birthday, y'know. Want two.' He reached for her silicone boobs and kneaded them roughly.

She jerked away. 'I guess I could call Lynn . . .'

'Yeah – call Lynn.'

'Yeah, I'll call Lynn. Only whose gonna pay . . .' She stopped speaking abruptly. Paul King had given her strict instructions about not admitting to Al that she had been paid.

Al was gulping scotch from a bedside bottle. He hadn't heard her.

She climbed off the bed. 'I'll go in the other room an' call Lynn,' she announced. 'Whyn't you take a shower, honey? Be nice an' sober for the two of us.'

'Who's drunk?' roared Al. 'Who – my dear girl – is drunk?'

She stifled a rude laugh and muttered, 'Bombed outa his skull,' to herself, and she wasn't surprised, for she had witnessed some of his drinking downstairs, and oh boy could he pack it away. Any other man would be laid out cold by now. She was a little zingy herself. Not too much – a professional girl always made sure it was never too much – but just enough to have a real good time.

She left him on the bed and went into the other room. First she called Paul to ask him if it was all right to bring in another girl. Paul said to get six girls if that was what Al wanted, and the money would be left at the desk.

She then called Lynn, who was asleep after a heavy evening at an advertising reunion, and said no way was she doing any more work that night.

'It's Al King,' whispered Golden Lady.

'Shit! Whyn't you say?' complained Lynn, 'I'll be right there.'

'Who was that?' demanded Linda, as Paul hung up the phone.

'The girl from the cake. Al's calling for more troops.'

Linda stretched. 'I don't know how he does it. Did you *see* what booze he got through?'

Paul reached for her. 'It runs in the family, cast-iron stomachs.'

'Yeah, and the rest!'

Evan lay on top of his bed wondering what he should do. His arm hurt, his body ached, and he still bristled with the humiliation of his father's birthday party.

The whole evening was a daze, from the moment he had been knocked flying at the concert. People had trampled over him, and then more bodies had fallen on top of him, and that was the last he remembered until waking up to the sound of an ambulance horn blaring – and he had been in the ambulance along with others – and they had all been taken to a hospital – and fleets of nurses and doctors had descended on them prodding and pushing and stitching and bandaging.

'You got a sprained arm,' a doctor informed him. 'The rest is just bruises and shock. Guess we'll keep you in overnight just in case. Give your details to the nurse and we'll contact your parents.'

They had shoved some sort of injection into him, and an elderly nurse had appeared with a sheaf of forms and asked him his name. 'Evan King,' he mumbled, 'I'm Al King's son.'

'I think this one's delirious,' she told the doctor.

Fortunately, shortly after, Paul arrived. He signed some papers and said, 'Thank Christ you're OK. Your father's going mad. Get dressed, we're getting out of here.'

Evan felt distinctly groggy. The injection had been a sedative, and he wouldn't have minded at all spending the night at the hospital and sleeping it off. But Paul had other plans. The party must go on. Nothing must spoil Al King's birthday.

Evan sat through the party half asleep. He picked at his food, gagged at the champagne, and blushed with embarrassment when the naked girl came climbing out of the cake. Not that he hadn't seen a naked girl before. He had. Both Glory and Plum had initiated him into the disgusting joys of manhood. But that was different, they were his friends, he was one of them.

Now, lying on his bed, inspecting his watch and discovering it was two-thirty in the morning, he wondered for the hundredth time where they were. The last time he had seen them was at the concert. They had run forward with the crowd, smiling and laughing, not trying to hang back like he had, getting knocked down and trampled on. They hadn't even tried to help him, although he was being unrealistic even thinking that they could. But where were they? Ever since they had become friends the three of them had been inseparable. They all slept in his room, taking it in turns to use the bed. Why – all their possessions were in the one shabby carry-all standing in the corner. That at least gave him some security. They couldn't take off anywhere without their things.

He wished he had one of the pills that Glory called quacks. They really made you feel good, sort of full of confidence and ready to talk to anyone. Glory took them by the handful, but he stuck with Plum and used them sparingly.

'She needs them more than us,' Plum explained sagely, 'like

she's trying t' get over the heavy stuff – she was in a real bad scene for a while. She's fine now – had a gig in hospital – that's some straightener.' Evan had nodded wisely as if he understood what on earth she was talking about.

Now they were both missing, and he felt lost without them. Maybe they had got hurt after all. Maybe they had been taken to another hospital . . . Just as he was beginning to panic there was a muffled knock at the door. He hurried to open it, and there they were, Glory hanging limply onto Plum.

'Where have you been?' Evan demanded, for once his voice not breaking.

'Sshh, man,' whispered Plum, 'she's not feelin' so good. Let's get her on the bed.'

Glory was indeed extremely pale, her eyes glazed and popping out of the sockets alarmingly. Evan helped Plum to drag her onto the bed, and she immediately curled into a tight ball and began to snore.

Plum yawned. 'I guess that's her for the night,' and she started to remove the patchwork smock top she was wearing.

'*Where have you both been*?' hissed Evan, '*I* was in the hospital. My arm – look at my arm.'

Plum regarded him wearily. 'S'your own fault. We told you t'move with the crowd. You gotta flow, man, or y'get the shit kicked outa you.'

He sat on the end of the bed, defeated, and watched as Plum unzipped her jeans, and lumbered out of them. She wore no pants, and now she was clad only in a dirty bra which might once have been pink. Her body, although fat, was surprisingly smooth. Acres of smooth white flesh. Evan felt himself stirring. She noticed. He ripped off his clothes clumsily with his one good arm. He wasn't at all embarrassed. She had seen him naked before, they both had. They had admired his skinny body. They had stroked it, and fondled him. They had taken his private parts into their mouths and they had told him he was all right. They had opened their legs for him and allowed him to do whatever he wanted. He had looked and marvelled, and finally he had put it in. Now he wanted to do it again, and although he preferred Glory, Plum would do.

'I'm wiped out, man,' Plum complained, 'just split from a wild party. Anyway we can't use the bed – she's out.'

'The floor,' Evan mumbled, 'we can use the floor.'

'Shit!' complained Plum. But she lay down anyway and parted her massive thighs.

Evan leapt upon her like a randy dog. Plum farted delicately. It didn't put him off. Perhaps at last he was his father's son.

Arthur Sorenson sat at the reception desk and consulted his new stainless steel watch with the fluorescent dial. It was an eighteenth birthday present, an event he had celebrated two weeks previously. The dial read two forty-five exactly. He had been on duty for one and three-quarter hours and soon it would be time for coffee.

He glanced around the deserted lobby, proud of the fact that he was in charge all on his own. Mr Ridley usually shared the evening shift with him, but tonight Mr Ridley had called in to say his daughter was sick – caught up in the riot at the Al King concert. Mr Ridley had said it would be all right for him to do the evening shift on his own, as long as he didn't leave the desk, not for *any* reason. Mr Ridley had worked for the hotel for twenty-two years. Arthur Sorenson had worked there for two weeks. He felt pleased that Mr Ridley had chosen to trust him after such a short time.

He whistled tunelessly, and watched as a cab pulled up outside, and let off a lone male passenger. By his foot was an emergency button which connected straight through to the police station. These days you couldn't be too careful. His foot hovered near it as the man approached the desk.

'Good evening, sir,' he said politely, wondering if maybe he should amend that to, 'good morning', in view of the time.

'Two twenty – key,' the man growled. He was fat and sweating and outlandishly dressed.

'Yes, sir.' Arthur's eyes glanced quickly at his book, ascertained the party's name, reached for the key, and said, 'Thank you, Mr Suntan, sir.'

The fat man grabbed the key and vanished into the elevator.

Arthur glanced at his book again. Bernie Suntan. What a name! Of course he was part of the Al King party, that would account for it. They were a rowdy group. One of the maids had told him about the party earlier. What a wow that must have been! And only five minutes earlier a woman had arrived at the hotel. A strange woman wearing dark glasses and a belted mink coat. Strange, as it was the middle of summer, and hardly the weather to be wearing a mink coat. She had asked for Al King's room, and while he telephoned to check if it was okay to send her up she had examined a run in her tights, examined it all the way up to the top of her thigh. It was quite obvious that her entire outfit consisted of only tights and a mink coat.

If he let himself Arthur could get quite excited at the thought. He tried not to let himself. He watched her into the elevator and wondered at the stamina of Al King. A riot. A wild party. And now this.

Arthur wondered if perhaps he should think of following a singing career rather than that of a hotel clerk. Everyone said that he had a nice voice. But then of course show business was an erratic profession – and being a desk clerk could lead to all sorts of things. Mind you – it didn't seem to have got Mr Ridley far.

Arthur sighed, glanced at his watch again, and wondered if taking a coffee break would count as leaving the desk. After all it would only take him a few minutes to fix a cup of coffee, and anyway who would know?

Melanie complained from the moment the plane landed. They couldn't get a cab. There were no porters to carry their luggage.

'I just don't know!' Melanie exclaimed in disgust, 'you stay with the cases, Edna, I'll soon get something organized.'

Edna stood forlornly by the luggage trying to ignore the attentions of a drunken businessman who had arrived on the same plane and was also having trouble getting transport.

She wanted to cry. She was tired, fed up, and she had missed Al's birthday by hours. By the time they got to the hotel it would be nearly three in the morning. Al would be asleep, and probably not at all pleased at having his rest interrupted.

Damn Melanie and her stupid plans. The whole point of this trip had been to arrive on Al's birthday.

A lone tear of anger and frustration rolled down her cheek. The drunk was at her side in a flash, 'Mustn't cry,' he mumbled. 'We'll all have a party. Want a party, little lady?' His lewd wink was the last straw, she turned her back and the flood of tears started in earnest.

'What's the matter with you?' Melanie asked scornfully upon her return. She brought with her a good-looking airline official, who piled their luggage onto a trolley, and in no time at all was driving them into the city himself.

By the time they reached the hotel he and Melanie were exchanging addresses and long meaningful looks.

A slow worker Melanie was not.

'Ha Ha! Gotcha!' Lynn shrieked. She had discarded the mink coat and the tights, and was joining in a game of spray the shaving foam with Al and Golden Lady.

Spurts of white foam were all over the place. Golden Lady was giggling hysterically as Al massaged some foam into her pneumatic breasts.

'Not so *hard*,' she hiccoughed.

'Frightened they'll drop off,' jeered Al.

'If they do she can always buy another pair!' laughed Lynn, who was rather proud of her own small but natural boobs.

'Bitch!' shrieked Golden Lady. 'Jealous bitch!'

They launched into a mock struggle, an act that had obviously been staged before for many a satisfied customer.

Al watched, his interest waning, his head pounding. Why didn't he just give them some money and send them both home. He knew they were hookers. So what? At least with a hooker you knew where you were, at least they didn't come running at you with an autograph book between their legs.

His interest revived as slowly their struggle turned into something else. Golden Lady was sliding her hands up the inside of Lynn's thighs, her thumbs were spreading the forest of black hair, and she was kneeling in front of the dark girl. She bent her head. So that's why they called it head. Sweet old American expression. In England it was going down. In America the only going down you did was in elevators!

'Yeah!' Al encouraged. He felt himself hardening, the first time that night. Golden Lady with all her efforts had not managed to get it up.

She glanced slyly over at him, relieved that at last something was working. For a moment there she was worried that she might have lost her touch.

Lynn was arching her body back, moaning and sighing. The girls worked well together, complimenting each other by their very different colouring.

Lynn's screams, whether simulated or the real thing, indicated the end of that particular episode, and Golden Lady rose triumphant. She headed towards Al, her body a mixture of gold paint, remnants of cream cake, and shaving foam. She had a hard but pretty face which would age into craftiness. She bent to his toes, licking them, prostrating herself on the floor, her tongue travelling quickly up his legs, her mouth dying to enclose him.

Lynn, making a fast recovery, came over and started to knead his nipples. It was the Kurlnik twins all over again, but these two hadn't quite got their act together. Whereas the twins had merged into one woman with four hands and two tongues, these two were stimulating him in a distracting way. He wanted to come quickly and get rid of them both. But as soon as he tried he knew it was going to be an effort. All the booze he had put away was slowing him down, and no amount of tongues or mouths was going to make him come in a hurry. He would just have to sweat it out. And try to enjoy it.

'Wouldn't you know it!' exclaimed Melanie sharply, 'nobody at the desk. What kind of a place is this?'

Her attentive escort smiled. 'One of the best hotels in town.'

'You could have fooled me,' complained Melanie, and she stamped her foot childishly.

'It *is* three o'clock in the morning,' Edna pointed out.

'Don't I know it,' whined Melanie, 'I'm exhausted,' she raised her shrill voice, 'is anyone around?'

Her escort shrugged helplessly, 'I hate to leave you lovely ladies like this, but I have to get back to the airport. I'm supposed to be on duty, I should never have left.'

Melanie fixed him with her cornflower-blue calculating eyes 'You've been marvellous,' she said, sotto voce, 'just one more. little favour . . .'

'Name it.'

'Hop over the other side of the desk and tell me the room numbers for Al and Paul King. I'm certainly not going to wait here all night.'

'Is that all?' He smiled, and vaulted in true macho man fashion over the desk.

Melanie nodded her approval.

'Let me see now . . .' He rummaged around, found the current reservation book and read out, 'Al King – penthouse suite, twenty-ninth floor. Paul King, suite 120, twelfth floor.' He checked a panel beneath the desk and came up with two keys. 'They're doing a wonderful job of looking after their guests in this hotel – anyone could just saunter in here and take their pick of who to rob. All set ladies?'

Melanie leaned forward and kissed him lightly on the cheek, 'You're a doll.'

Returning to the desk a few minutes later Arthur Sorenson was most disconcerted to find a pile of luggage sitting in the middle of the lobby. No people, just luggage.

Goddammit, he had only gone for a cup of coffee. Why had whoever it was chosen that particular time to arrive? And where the heck were they?

His eyes slid automatically to the two elevators. When he had left on his coffee break they had both registered lobby, now one of the indicators showed that the elevator had travelled all the way up to the twenty-ninth floor.

Goddammit, if Mr Ridley found out he had left the desk . . . This was his first job, and he liked it. He enjoyed working the early morning hours, it left him plenty of free time during the day.

He eyed the luggage suspiciously. Those suitcases belonged to someone, and that someone had just dumped them in his lobby and calm as you like gone on up to the twenty-ninth floor. He realized with a sudden sinking feeling that Al King was ensconced in the Penthouse suite on the twenty-ninth floor, and nobody but nobody was supposed to go up there without clearance. Al King was some sort of security risk.

Arthur frowned. What to do?

If Mr Ridley was around he would know what to do. But Mr Ridley wasn't around, and Arthur Sorenson didn't know what the heck to do. So he did what he considered was the safest bet, and that was exactly nothing.

When he was fired early the next morning he wondered why.

Al shoved the golden head, 'Suck it!' he commanded.

The lady obliged, until he pulled her away by the hair and gave the dark-haired girl her turn.

He stood naked in the middle of the living room, both women kneeling on the floor in front of him. All the lights were on, the television spewed forth a decrepit Western. The room was a wreck, furniture overturned, shaving foam everywhere, clothes littered about.

He pushed down on the dark-haired girl's head, forcing her to take him deeper into her mouth.

'Come on, baby,' he crooned, 'take it all, swallow it down.'

The dark-haired girl did her best.

None of them heard the key in the door. None of them noticed the door tentatively open. They were all fully absorbed.

'Suck, suck . . . Shit!' Al started to reach orgasm, the dark-haired girl hanging on in there, Golden Lady twisting herself round his legs, determined to get in on the act.

Edna stood in the doorway transfixed with shock. At first she had thought it must be the wrong room, but as she tried to back quickly out she realized it must be the right room because that was Al standing there, *her* Al, with those two filthy women doing things to him, disgusting things, degrading things. And the funny thing was he was *letting* them. He was just standing there allowing them to molest him. Allowing them to suck on his private parts like vultures.

Edna felt the vomit rise in her throat, she couldn't control it.

Golden Lady saw her first. 'Who the frig are you?' she demanded, unwinding herself from around Al's legs and standing up.

Al saw her next, but didn't recognize her for a moment. The clothes, the hair, everything was so different. Realization dawned like a nagging stomach ache.

Melanie let herself quietly into Paul's suite. She switched on the lights in the living room and looked around. It was really quite nice, although she was sure that Al's was probably better.

She checked herself in the mirror. Yes, she looked good, a little tired, but certainly a restful night's sleep would take care of *that*.

She was pleased with the way things had been going. One smile and they came running after her in droves. If she hadn't had Edna trailing along behind her she *really* could have had a good time. As it was she had had fun.

She smiled secretly to herself. Paul didn't realize how lucky he was having a wife like her.

She peered round the bedroom door and saw a huddled shape in bed. Carrying her toilet case she went quietly into the bathroom. A nice refreshing shower and she would surprise her husband in bed.

forty-three

It was a tremendous shock, but at the same time it was no surprise at all. For all along Dallas had known that eventually Bobbie would turn up. The only question in her mind had been when.

Bobbie didn't say a word. She just huddled in the chair staring at Dallas, her afro wig curled to ridiculous heights, her eyes red-rimmed and watery.

Calmly Dallas switched off the stereo. 'How did you get in?' she asked.

'Hey, sugar sweets, aintcha never heard of pickin' a lock? Sweetstuff, I was *born* on the street – ain't never come across a lock to defeat me yet.'

'You chose the wrong profession – you should have been a burglar,' said Dallas drily. She refused to be intimidated by this person. 'What do you want?' she added coldly.

'Some greetin'!' complained Bobbie, 'some shit ass greeting from such an *old* friend.'

Dallas glared at her steadily, 'Cut the crap, friend. Tell me what you want and get out.'

Bobbie seemed to have developed a nervous facial tick. It looked like some kind of obscene wink. She stood up, and Dallas noticed how painfully thin she had become. She wore white shorts and scuffed boots and her thighs had an unattractive hollow appearance. Her face was thick with make-up. She seemed to have aged years.

With a shudder Dallas remembered her relationship with this girl. Personal and business. It all seemed like another world away.

'How about a drink?' Bobbie asked, attempting a camaraderie that had ceased to exist long ago, 'you all are doin' pretty fine – guess you can afford a shot of somethin' for good ole Bobbie.'

'Do you need money? Have you come here to blackmail me?'

'*Blackmail*! Shit, girl. I taught you everything you know. If it wasn't for me you'd still be peddlin' it for twenty bucks a night. I got you out of that scene. Blackmail – shit! You were some green little kid with a foxy pair of tits and a hot box. Blackmail! Ain't that a bitch!'

Dallas picked up her purse, 'I can give you two hundred dollars, it's all I have in cash. But get this straight – don't come back for more. I'm not giving you this money because I have to. I'm giving it to you because I'm sorry for you.'

Bobbie laughed uneasily, 'Sorry for me! You paranoid or something'? Ain't *nobody* gotta be sorry for me. I'm together, like really in tune. You wanna give me two hundred bucks – sure I'll take it. I don't need it, but shit I deserve it.' She snatched the money and stuffed it in the waistband of her shorts. She seemed uncertain as to whether to continue the conversation or not, but Dallas made up her mind for her by walking to the door and flinging it open.

'Goodbye, Bobbie, don't come back.'

'Some welcome!' Her facial tick seemed to get worse, but her mind seemed to be on the money tucked into her waistband. She headed for the door, and as she passed, Dallas noticed that her whole body was shaking. On a sudden impulse Dallas grabbed the black girl's arm and pushed up the sleeve of her sweat shirt. The whole arm was a mass of angry red tracks. 'You really did it,

259

didn't you,' Dallas said in a rush of sympathy.

Bobbie pulled her arm sharply away, 'Go fuck yourself,' she growled, 'you fuckin' big time motha! Don't you go givin' me your shit ass "what a *bad* girl Bobbie is" crap.'

'You need help . . .'

'Fuck help. I ain't *never* had any.' She laughed in a cavalier fashion, 'dontcha know? I was born with a pair of cement balls – they'll keep me going.' She walked in a jaunty way out of the door. 'You'll need a friend one day. Don't come a runnin' to my door, sweet stuff.'

Then she was gone, walking off down the hill in her scuffed boots and ridiculous wig.

With a heavy feeling Dallas knew that she would be back. The two hundred dollars was only a beginning. A girl with a habit like that to support was going to run out of money real fast.

'I think you should handle me,' the girl said. She was incredibly pretty, with an abundance of blond curls, and a devastating smile. Her tongue flicked out and licked full glossy lips. 'I don't know why you're fighting it, you know we'd be good for each other, I'd be a very cooperative client.' She emphasized cooperative, leaving Cody in no doubt about what the cooperative would encompass.

He cleared his throat, glad that his desk stood protectively between them. 'Well, Carol . . .' he began, continuing with a quick line of bullshit that he was getting quite proficient at. He called it his 'don't call me I'll call you' line.

It was amazing the people who had wanted to become clients. If he was just after a quick buck he would have signed all of them.

Carol Cameron was not an unknown little starlet. She had starred in two very successful sex horror movies – not hard core either. The trouble was she couldn't act, and she had screwed half – if not all – of Hollywood to get where she was today.

Cody did not fancy her, and even if he did it would not make any difference to his decision. Sex would not get in the way of business. He had proved that with Dallas.

Carol knew a turndown when she saw one. She stood up, smoothed down the revealing jersey dress she was wearing. Her nipples strained to escape the confines of the material. 'Think about it, Cody. Why don't you drop by my house later and have a drink?'

'I'm having dinner with my mother,' he replied quickly. Sometimes his mother came in very useful.

'So later,' Carol purred, 'you're not going to sleep with your mother, are you?'

He laughed at what he supposed was a joke. Very bad taste, like the lady who had made it.

'I don't think I can . . .' Why was he making excuses? Why didn't he just tell her no. 'No,' he said.

'No?' she questioned.

'No, I er can't.'

She pouted, 'Shame! Perhaps another night. I'll call you.'

Mental note. Tell secretary he was always out to any calls from Miss Carol Cameron.

'Wonderful! I'll look forward to it.'

She blew him a kiss and undulated out of his office. It was horribly old-fashioned to undulate. Dallas strode – long purposeful, sexy strides, like a beautiful leopard.

Thinking of Dallas reminded him it was late, and she would be home from the studio by now. Kiki and Chuck were coming over, and they were going to barbecue. He had promised to pick up the steaks, and agreeing to see Carol Cameron had made him late. He swore softly, gathered up some papers he wanted to go over later, and left the office.

Dallas was drinking too much. She had dived into the Vodka before dinner, heavily indulged in the wine during dinner, and now was into her third Cointreau on the rocks.

'I thought this was going to be a quiet evening at home,' Cody said, following her into the kitchen whilst she stacked the plates in the dishwasher.

'So it is,' she replied brightly, 'everyone's having a good time, the steaks were great.'

Gently he extracted the glass from her hand. 'You're working tomorrow.'

She snatched it back, 'I'm working every day,' there was a hard edge to her voice, 'I'm a working girl, always have been.'

'What's the matter?' Cody asked patiently.

'Matter?' Her eyes filled with sudden tears. 'Why should anything be the matter?'

Kiki breezed into the kitchen, 'I'm taking my man home,' she announced, 'sorry about eating and running, but if I don't get him home now he's going to be a permanent fixture in front of your TV!'

'Take him home and give him one for me,' Dallas shot a baleful look at Cody. 'That's about all I'll get tonight!'

'Oh boy!' exclaimed Kiki. 'We'll get out before the dishes fly!' he winked at Cody. 'See you all tomorrow.'

She thought it was all a big joke. A lovers' quarrel. Everyone thought that Dallas and Cody were lovers.

'I hate you,' Dallas said spitefully when Cody returned from seeing their guests off, 'I really hate you, and what's more I think you're a fag. You hear me – a FAG.'

Her anger at finding Bobbie in her house was finally erupting. And Cody was the nearest target.

'You're drunk,' he said quietly, 'why don't you go to bed.'

'Fag!' she jeered, 'closet queen!'

His mouth tightened. 'I'm going home. We'll talk tomorrow.'

'Yeah, go on home – or better still why don't you run on over to mommy's?' She tore off her shirt and faced him menacingly, her naked breasts perfect in their splendour. 'I'm offering you for free something that other men have had to pay for. But it's too much for you, isn't it? You'd sooner sink it into some nice tight ass . . . You'd sooner . . .'

He approached her swiftly, gripped her by the shoulders. 'What do you mean – other men have had to pay for it?'

She was suddenly sullen, 'Nothing.'

He shook her, 'What do you mean?' He was now as angry as she was.

She tried to shrug him off, but he had her in a tight grip. 'I said nothing . . .' she muttered.

His anger collapsed. 'I don't know you, do I? I worship you and I know nothing about you.' He let go of her and turned to go.

She ran after him, pulled him round to face her, 'I was a hooker,' she screamed, 'a cheap twenty dollar hooker! Does that satisfy you? Does that make you feel better? No wonder you don't want to fuck me . . .'The tears came on top of the anger and she fell on to the couch sobbing.

He was shocked, genuinely shocked. But then he knew that he had never investigated her past because he was frightened of what he would find out.

He went to her, held her in his arms, comforted her while she poured out her life.

She left out Lew Margolis and the pictures. She left out Bobbie and their relationship. She left out her marriage at sixteen.

She told him what it suited her to tell him. She told him what she thought he could accept and still keep loving her.

In the early hours of the morning they chartered a jet, flew to Las Vegas, and got married.

Cody knew when he was needed.

262

forty-four

When Melanie slid confidently into bed alongside her husband, she was aghast to find herself embracing feminine curves. Linda had been similarly aghast, and Paul had been hopeful that perhaps a freak earthquake might hit New Orleans.

Meanwhile Edna was in a state of shock, seeing her beloved husband indulging in the sort of activities that she had thought only existed in perverted people's minds. As she threw up she could think only of the fact that she was ruining somebody's carpet, but somehow, for once in her life, it didn't seem to matter, and she stood there vomiting, oblivious to the hostile state of the Golden Lady who Al had kicked half way across the room.

'Jeeesus Chriiist!' exclaimed Lynn, as Al wrenched her head off him, 'what *is* this?'

'It's my wife,' explained Al, sobriety hitting him like a hammer. 'Get the hell *out* of here!'

It wasn't the first time that Lynn had been caught in a similar situation. Wordlessly, she grabbed her mink coat, flinging it over her nakedness. 'Come on!' she said to Golden Lady, who was grovelling around on the floor looking for her clothes.

Al said, 'Edna?' As if not quite sure it was really her.

She looked at him with pain-filled eyes. 'I'm sorry . . .' she began.

'*She*'s sorry!' huffed Lynn, pushing past with Golden Lady who was in a most bedraggled state. 'If I was you, dear, I'd get a new lynx coat at least!'

Al waited until they were gone, then he walked over to Edna, took her arm, and led her to a chair. He slumped on the sofa next to her and muttered, 'Why didn't you tell me you were coming?'

'Put some clothes on, you'll catch cold,' she said in the normal voice of a mother scolding a child. Her eyes refused to meet his, they darted nervously round the room. She got up, 'Where's the bathroom? I want to clear up that mess.'

'Leave it,' he commanded.

'I can't leave it,' her voice was all choked up, 'I can't leave it, Al. And I'm sorry I came, and I'm sorry I upset you. I knew it wasn't a good idea. I told Melanie . . .' Her voice began to quaver. 'How could you? How *could* you?' She broke into tears. 'I only wanted to be with you on your birthday . . . That's all. Oh, Al, why did you do it?'

Why did I do it? Because I've been doing it for years one way or another. Because when I get off that stage I'm about ready to explode. Because you've never been around when I've really needed you. Because you think sex should take place in a bedroom, in the dark, once a week, using one position only. And whenever I've suggested anything else you've backed away in horror.

'You can divorce me,' he stated blankly, and was amazed at the relief that came flooding over him as soon as he said it.

'I don't want to do that,' she interrupted quickly, 'we're very happy. I love you. I think that in time I can forgive you. After all if it was only this once . . .'She trailed off, waiting for him to assure her that it was only this once.

He said nothing.

'Where is Evan?' she ventured.

It hadn't taken her long to ask about her precious son.

'He's all right,' Al replied brusquely, 'you can see him in the morning.'

'Yes,' she agreed, 'we'll all feel better in the morning. This will seem like a bad dream in the morning.' She sighed deeply, and summoned a tenacious whisper of a smile. 'I'm going to try and forget it ever happened, Al. I'm going to forgive you.'

'You sonofabitch!' Melanie shrilled. 'I could understand you having it off with some little tart – but *sleeping* with the bitch, spending the *night* with her. Who is she?'

Paul shrugged, 'It doesn't matter who she is.'

'It doesn't matter who she is!' mimicked Melanie. 'You can bet your boots it doesn't matter who she is – because *you're* not seeing her again! That is if you ever want to see your *children* again.' She paused triumphantly, knowing she had gotten to him with *that* threat.

They had been bickering ever since Linda had left. God, Linda handled it well, Paul thought. After the initial scene of French farce she had leapt from the bed, coolly shut herself in the bathroom, dressed, and left without a word to either of them – in spite of the temptation of Melanie's spiteful verbal attack. Paul had wanted to applaud her dignity.

'I should have thought,' sniffed Melanie, determined to get as much mileage as possible out of the event, 'you could have done better than that. I should have thought that while you were picking it might have been a nineteen-year-old nympho. Or are you losing your touch? Are all the best ones going in Al's direction? Was this hag one of Al's rejects?'

Paul wanted to slap her right across her pretty pointed face. But he knew it was important to stay calm, appear cool. If Melanie so much as suspected that Linda was anything serious . . .

'She was some girl I picked up in the bar,' he admitted, 'some nothing girl.' Christ! If Linda could hear him she would never talk to him again.

'Absolutely charming! And I suppose if you had got syphilis or something from her *I* would have been the one you would come running home to with it.'

'Don't be silly.'

'Oh – don't be silly,' Melanie narrowed her eyes and glared at him, 'what are you? A fool? You *could* have got infected, she looked like a tramp. I want you to go to a doctor tomorrow.'

'All right, I'll go to a doctor if it will make you happy,' Paul muttered.

'Thank you. I think it's the least you can do.' She yawned, ready to forget the incident for the time being. Actually it had been rather exciting catching dull old Paul like that. He *had* become exceedingly dull in the last few years, only interested in business and making money. Well, she couldn't complain about that – but it certainly was a change from the man she had married. A man whose sole interest in life had been getting her into bed.

She felt a tingle of excitement, and she thought of the good-looking airline official who had driven her to the hotel, and the tingle became an itch. She thought of the naked woman climbing out of bed with Paul. She had not been an old bag. She had been a very attractive female, a fact that Melanie would never admit.

She moved closer to her husband. 'Did she have nice boobs?' she asked, her voice becoming babyish.

He knew what to answer. He was not a fool. 'Not as nice as yours.'

'As mine?' She feigned surprise, 'but mine are only little. Do you like them little?'

He was relieved that forgiveness had been so quick, and he reached for his wife and massaged her small breasts the way she liked him to. She moaned immediately, and lifted the slip she was wearing. He pulled off her panties, all the time thinking about Linda. He bent his head to her breasts, and she moaned even louder. One thing he enjoyed about Linda was her delicious silence. He did not have an erection, but fortunately Melanie did not bother to notice. She had other ideas. She was pushing his head down and opening her legs.

'I can't let you make love to me properly,' she gasped, as he attacked her with his tongue, 'not until you've had a doctor look at your thing. I don't want to catch anything, do I?'

In her room Linda was busy packing. She was numb with fury, number with disgust – and both emotions were directed at Paul. Her lover, her big brave man. He had practically shit himself with fear.

She relived the evening in her mind. The party, everyone had had a good time, everyone had still been recovering from the events of earlier, so a lot of drinking had gone on, and when she and Paul had returned to bed they were both slightly out of it. They hadn't even made love. They had kissed goodnight, cuddled up, and gone to sleep. Just like an old married couple.

The next thing that Linda could remember was hands on her, hands that snatched themselves off her in double quick time, and a high pitched voice screaming, 'Who the hell are *you*?'

Paul had woken, switched on the light, and recoiled in horror at the woman who appeared to have joined them in bed. He said one startled word – 'Melanie!' That had been enough for Linda. Wordlessly she had left the bed, found her clothes, and gone into the bathroom to dress.

She didn't know what else to do. Paul was struck speechless, and the skinny blonde – his wife – was screeching insults at him.

He was still speechless when she came out of the bathroom. The blonde stared at her, started to say something. But Linda didn't wait to hear, she got out of there – fast. And when she was out of there, and in her own room, she suddenly saw the whole scene in a much clearer light.

Bloody hell – she wasn't a hooker, for Christ's sake. She was Paul's long-standing girlfriend, he professed to love her. And yet he had not uttered *one* single word. He had not tried to protect her in any way, shape or form. He had been scared shitless.

Yes, she could understand that it was unexpected. But it *had* happened. It *was* a confrontation, and he *could* have dealt with it like a man.

Grimly she finished packing. She had no intention of hanging around to listen to his excuses. First plane out in the morning to New York – and fuck Paul King.

•

Evan awoke to the sound of the phone ringing. He had not slept properly anyway. How could you sleep properly three in a bed? Glory was in the middle, lying on top of the covers with all her clothes on, still fast asleep. Plum was squashed on one side, her vast nude body covered only partly by the sheet. She lay on her back and emitted harsh snores. Evan had about three inches of space on the other side. He felt worse than ever, his arm throbbed violently, and his body ached all over.

He licked dry lips and picked up the phone. On the other end was his father who didn't waste any words.

'Get those two slags out of your room if they're with you. Clean yourself up and get yourself up to my suite.' There was a short pause, a heavy sigh, then, 'your mother is here.'

Holy crap! His mother!

Evan glanced guiltily at the two sleeping girls. *His mother*! If she should ever find out . . .

He didn't know what to do first. Dress. Wake them. Hide.

He ran in the bathroom, peered at his spotty face, ran back to the bedroom, shook Plum, who merely groaned and turned over.

Frantically he grabbed Glory by the shoulders, and she sat bolt upright, startling him. 'Wassashitsamatter?' she mumbled.

'My mother,' he explained, his panic-stricken voice uncontrollable, 'she's *here*. She's with my father, *she's here*.'

'So what?' Glory questioned, her thin mouth set in a mean line.

Evan was speechless. He had expected Glory to react in the same way that he had. He had expected her to leap up, dress, wake Plum, and get the hell *out* of his hotel room.

Glory was lying down. Glory was preparing to go back to sleep.

'You've got to go,' Evan said quickly, 'you and Plum. If my mother comes down here, sees you . . .'

'So what?' repeated Glory, even more meanly than the first time. She was not pleased at being woken.

'She'll go mad,' stammered Evan.

'Take away your train set, will she?' mocked Glory, 'smacka naughty little boy's ass?'

Evan reddened, his spots standing out lividly.

'Shit!' exclaimed Glory in disgust, 'You're just like all the rest. Had your good time – now we can just piss on off.' She gave Plum a vicious kick, 'Wake up, fatso, we're gettin' the push again.' She climbed off the bed and gave Evan a bitter stare before going in the bathroom, 'And t'think *I* thought you were one of us. What a laugh!' She slammed the bathroom door, leaving him with Plum who had sat up and was looking at him suspiciously.

267

'Why have you upset Glory?' she asked.

'I didn't,' he protested.

'You must have.'

'I woke her up because my mother is here and . . .'

'You want us to go,' finished Plum.

'I don't *want* you to go. But my mother . . . Well . . .' He shrugged helplessly.

'You're frightened of her?'

'Not frightened . . .'

'I know, I know. You've got some shitty mother hang-up. Think she knows best and all that guff. *I* had hassles with my mom – old bitch. One day I walked, no more hassles. It was that simple.'

There was a crash from the bathroom.

'You *have* upset Glory, 'accused Plum. 'Why'd you have to do that? It will take me all day to get her together.'

'I didn't mean to . . .' said Evan miserably. 'I wouldn't upset either of you. You've both been . . .' His eyes filled with tears which he tried unsuccessfully to blink away.

'Aw, c'mon,' comforted Plum, 'don't *you* go gettin' upset. Anyway, I think I got an idea. Whyn't you go an' see your Ma – try an' grab some bread from Al, and I'll talk to Glory, try and get her to go along with my idea.'

'What idea?' Evan asked hopefully.

'You'll know. I'll tell you when y'come back. But it's a trip – a real head trip f' us all. Now don't forget – get some money – steal it if you can – he'll never notice.'

More cheerful now that Plum had taken control, Evan nodded. He was still one of them. Nothing had changed.

Al did not sleep well at all. It had been some birthday. First the riot, then the drama with Evan. The party, and following orgiastic goings on with Golden Lady, and her friend, and then the sudden appearance of Edna.

It had all been too much.

He had terminated further discussions on his sexual goings on by telling Edna of the riot. She had been suitably sympathetic – in fact in no time at all she was acting as if nothing had happened, but when he mentioned that Evan had been slightly hurt she had gone mad, and he had to forcibly restrain her from dashing down to his room. Somehow, Al thought, she would not take too kindly to the sight of her son and the two queens of freaksville! If indeep they were still with Evan. Certainly a double discovery in one night would not be to anyone's advantage. Al had persuaded her into bed – purely for sleeping purposes. And he had spent a restless night lying by her side wondering how he could tell her that their marriage was over.

He got up early, while Edna still slept, and crept into the living room to phone Evan.

He then phoned Paul, wondering how *he* had fared.

'Paul,' stated Al tersely, when his brother answered the phone. 'Two questions. Where was Luke – who according to you never leaves the outside of my door. And how did Edna get my key?'

'What can I say . . .' began Paul, his voice destroyed.

'Nothing,' flashed Al. 'Call me back with some answers.'

'I *have* the answers. Do you think I've slept? Luke got the shit kicked out of him spiriting you off stage yesterday – he went off duty outside your room after he saw you safely inside from the party. *I* told him it was all right. Did *I* know?'

Al snorted, 'Some fucking security!'

'The key is another matter. I think we can sue the hotel. The manager has already dumped the night clerk. Have you seen the papers?'

'The papers? Is the fact that my wife caught me with a couple of hookers in the papers?'

'No. But it's not too good. Some joker got a picture of you at the party feeling up that blonde from the cake – the bastards ran it on the front page next to a kid all bashed up from the riot.'

'Oh, that's fucking marvellous isn't it?'

'I've been on to Bernie. He's working on killing it already. It's the kind of spread can go world wide.'

'Just what I need.'

'On the good side "Bad Black Alice" made number one today.'

Al felt the depression lift for a moment. He was number one again. Top single selling record in America.

They had all thought he was past it. They had all labelled him a has-been. But he had shown them – Christ! Had he shown them! The tour was a smash. Now the single was at number one. What the hell had he been worried about anyway?

'I think,' Paul was saying, 'before we leave today you should visit some of the kids in the hospital with Edna. We'll have photographers there, get it out on the news agencies. Fortunately there were no serious injuries – the worst is a broken arm. The rest seem to be bruises and shock and the aftermath of hysteria.'

269

'Arrange it.'

'I think it's a good idea.'

'Don't give me speeches. I said arrange it.'

'I thought you'd say yes. Bernie's already got it in hand.' Paul paused. 'Was everything all right with Edna?'

'Sure,' answered Al sarcastically, 'there I was with my cock in some slag's mouth. Edna was delighted. I said – "Hello, darlin', come in and join the orgy." She was thrilled.'

'As bad as that, huh?'

'Worse. She's forgiven me. And what about you?'

'I'll tell you later.'

It didn't take Paul long to discover that Linda had packed up and checked out. He could hardly claim to be surprised. In fact he was relieved. It would have been an impossible situation if she had stayed, and Melanie had discovered who she was . . . Christ! What a situation. If he hadn't been caught in a compromising position he would have given Melanie the bollocking of her life. How dare she take it upon herself to come and surprise them. It certainly can't have been Edna's idea – Melanie must have been jollying her up for weeks.

Paul wasn't worried about Linda's sudden departure. She knew the way things were. She understood. She was just being discreet. God, but she was a wonderful woman, as soon as he had time he would call her. She was probably a little mad, well, disappointed really. But he would find a way to make it up to her. As soon as he could pack Melanie off, Linda would be back by his side.

It was *his* turn to work on Edna now to get her the hell out of America and back home safely to England.

With Al's support – which he had no doubt would be forthcoming – it shouldn't be too difficult.

Edna was shocked when she saw Evan. In a way it was worse than seeing Al with those two terrible women.

Evan was thinner than ever, battered and bruised, tired-looking, and *filthy*. His hair hung in lank, greasy strands. His acne formed a pattern of angry relief against his dull pallor. His clothes – certainly not an outfit *she* had bought him – looked like he had slept in them for a week.

She stepped forward to hug him. He pushed her away, mumbling about his arm.

For the first time since leaving England she was glad that she had come. God, in his infinite wisdom, had sent her to fetch her son. Rescue him might be a better word.

Al obviously noted nothing amiss. 'How's it going, Evan?' he asked in an amiable fashion. 'Arm OK?'

Anger formed in Edna's breast. An anger she had never known existed before.

'When did he last eat?' she snapped at Al.

He shrugged, 'I don't follow him around with a tray.'

'I can see that. He looks half starved. Evan! When did you last eat?'

Evan scratched at a spot, 'I dunno . . . I'm not hungry.'

Edna shook her head bitterly, 'What does he look like?' She turned to Al, her voice unnaturally sharp. 'I thought you were going to look after him. I thought I could trust you. Why, he's not even in the same room as you,' her voice rose, 'and thank goodness for that. Has he seen a doctor?'

'He was at the hospital yesterday.'

'Did *you* speak to the doctor?'

'No, I . . .'

'I want a doctor for him *now*. I want him properly examined. I want his arm X-rayed. I want him to get the sort of treatment you expect for yourself.'

Al was amazed. Edna had never spoken to him like that in her life. She was positively bristling with anger. She even looked different.

He wanted a divorce. All Edna cared about was Evan, she had now made that painfully obvious.

'I'll get him a doctor,' he said dully. 'I'll get him what the fuck you want.'

Evan wiped his nose with the back of his hand and regarded his parents blankly. All he wanted to do was to get out of there and back to his friends.

'Don't swear in front of him,' hissed Edna. 'I don't want him to learn your gutter language.'

'Can I go?' mumbled Evan. 'I feel like lying down.'

'You can lie down here,' replied Edna. 'You can also have a bath and put on some clean clothes. Give me your key and I'll fetch your things.'

'Oh no,' squeaked Evan, flushing, 'I'll get them.'

As Edna started to object, Al interrupted, 'Let him go. We have to ride over to the hospital for the photographs now, then the airport. Go get packed, Evan. You'll come to the airport with Paul.'

271

'But . . .' began Edna.

Al silenced her again. 'He's all yours in Tucson. You can bathe him and feed him and get him all the doctors you want. Right now turn a little of your attention in *my* direction.'

Edna, appeased with promises, was meek again. 'Yes, Al,' she said, 'but after Tucson I think it would be best if I took Evan home.'

'I think you're right,' agreed Al, relief flooding through him.

And neither of them noticed the look of panic that swept across Evan's face.

Bleary-eyed Bernie jostled amongst the photographers and reporters at the hospital. He winked and joked and laughed while they all marked time waiting for the star.

He personally felt like shit. What the fuck . . . Why was it always him that got all the flak? Was the riot *his* fault? Was security *his* bag? How about brother Paul stepping forward for a little of the blame. It was Paul who put the ceiling on what they were going to pay for security – and if he hadn't been so busy with foxy Linda he would have realized that as the tour gained momentum so the crowds got wilder. Jesus Christ – if he – Bernie – was in charge, things would be different. He could go nuts just thinking of the way it would be.

He had a monster hangover. After Al's party he had taken himself off to a very famous New Orleans cat house. A place that hadn't changed a thing – except the girls – in fifty years! The madam was seventy-three years old. A character of gigantic proportions in a curly red wig and New Frontier dress.

Bernie had chosen himself a genuine French girl who had known all the tricks of the trade and used them in an expert fashion. It had been a pleasing experience, far different from the grubby little groupies he had used on the trip.

What the fuck . . . In Los Angeles girls queued up to be seen in his company. Beautiful girls.

Bernie Suntan. In Los Angeles he was a celebrity himself.

Al arrived at the hospital. There was a buzz amongst the photographers. Bernie noted how good he looked. Nothing seemed to phase Al.

'Put your arm around Edna,' Bernie reminded.

Al obliged, smiling, turning on the famous King charm.

Bernie handed him a stack of record albums, and watched as he walked around the ward talking to the kids in their beds and signing records for them.

The cameras flashed, recording every moment. With any luck these pictures would be syndicated, wiping out the nasty taste of the riot and Al with the naked Golden Lady.

The public would love it. He was leading a life they all envied. The wife. The hospital visit. That was the good image. On the other hand everyone suspected he was a great lover and had a wild side.

Perfect combination. The good and the bad.

Al had it down to a fine art.

Linda was back in New York by lunchtime.

She took a cab straight to her apartment, where she shut herself in the tiny kitchen, and smashed every dish she possessed.

It was a very satisfactory relief of tensions. One that a psychiatrist had taught her in her early days of analysis.

Afterwards she swept up the mess, dumped it in the hallway garbage shute, and made herself a strong cup of black coffee.

The tiny apartment did not please her. It had a musty smell, the furniture looked tacky. Originally she had furnished it from junk shops, and at the time it had been fun, not to mention cheap. Now, eight years later, it was an unsatisfactory dump. She had known that for a while, but somehow she had imagined Paul *would* leave his wife, and then would be the time for changes.

'Dumb schmuck!' she muttered to herself. Taken in by the oldest line in the world. He loved her – but . . . And the but was bigger than both of them.

Enough was enough. And she had definitely had enough.

She called her agency to let them know she was back. Her Al King pictures were selling all over the world, and she was gratified to learn how much money she was making.

She was tired, but after a shower she picked up the phone and called her actor friend, Rik. He was distinctly unfriendly because she had not contacted him as promised.

'I *tried*,' she lied, 'but your number is always busy. Can I come over ?'

'You always do this,' he complained.

'I've been working,' she explained. 'You're the first person I've called since I got back, which is approximately one hour ago.'

'Am I supposed to be flattered ?' he ask petulantly.

'Aren't you ?' she cajoled.

'Hmmmn,' he was ready to forgive her, 'Did you miss me ?'

'Of *course* I missed you. I thought about you lots.'

'I think I might have a job,' his voice perked up. 'Only off Broadway, but . . .'

273

'That's great!' she interrupted, 'I'm on my way over – OK?'

'I suppose so,' he relented.

She hung up. God Almighty – what you had to go through to get a good fuck these days!

The hospital visit was a success. Al was in good spirits again. On the way to the airport he formed some plans in his head. Edna sat silently by his side forming plans of her own. She was shocked at the condition of Evan, and she wanted to get him home as soon as possible. Never mind about what Melanie wanted to do – *she* was going home.

Al was thinking that it wasn't such a bad thing Edna turning up the way she had. In fact it was a good thing. She had caught him in action, and that could be his lever for a divorce. Edna, I'm just not good enough for you. You've seen the truth at last. I can't go on doing this to you. I refuse to hurt you any more. The perfect solution. How could she argue with him? He was doing it for her.

And he could handle the whole thing long distance. Too ashamed to face her and all that shit. Of course he would see she had everything she wanted. The house in England, plenty of money. In fact in a way he *was* doing it for her. She had been a loyal wife. He did treat her badly. She deserved some nice unfamous schmuck – which with all the money she would have would be no problem. He would have to make sure no con men came sniffing around. He would work something out with his lawyer to take care of everything.

It was a very satisfactory decision. He would put it into motion as soon as she left.

Another bonus was the fact that she would also be taking Evan off his hands. The responsibility of having the boy along was too much. In the meantime he would go out of his way to give them both a good time in Tucson. A last family fling.

More photographers waited at the airport, and Al waved and laughed, one arm around Edna, as he boarded his plane. Fuck it. He was a superstar. He was number one. How could he have ever doubted himself?

Paul was waiting on board with Melanie. He looked uptight about something. Probably she had been giving him a hard time.

Al grinned, thumped him on the shoulder. 'Hey – baby brother. We should be celebrating – what's the long face for? Let's get the champagne in action, let's . . .'

'We can't find Evan,' Paul said tightly. 'He's gone. Vanished.'

'Huh?' Al could not believe what he was hearing.

'He's done a split with those two freaks. Here's the note that was left for you.' Paul handed Al a grubby bit of paper.

It was written in Plum's untidy scrawl – TAKIN' EVAN ON TRIP. DON'T WORRY. SEE YOU IN L.A.

Al read it through twice, unwilling to digest the information.

Edna would go ape shit.

There went his plans.

'Jesus!' he said at last, 'Jesus H. Christ! The kid's a worse fuckin' moron than I thought he was!'

Paul nodded. 'I hope that's all it is. I just hope. But don't blow out the possibility that they may have kidnapped him.'

forty-five

Cody impressed upon Dallas the importance of keeping their marriage a secret.

It would be bad for her career.

Lew Margolis wouldn't like it.

Her future fans would feel cheated.

Aarron Mack wouldn't like it.

The main reason, he kept quiet about. His mother. Bad enough that Dallas wasn't Jewish – but an actress too! He would have to break it to his mother gently.

It was no hardship keeping the event a secret. They had flown to Las Vegas late at night, instructing the pilot to be ready to fly back to LA within the hour. They had taken a cab along the neon-lit gaudy strip, and finally chosen a 'Little Chapel of the West' advertised in flashing lights as a twenty-four-hour wedding parlour.

The preacher had slipped a creased suit over his pyjamas. His wife, with rollers in her hair and a cigarette dangling from jammy lips, had served lukewarm white wine in glasses advertising a nearby gambling salon.

Two witnesses were pulled in off the street for a few dollars each. The wedding ring was a cheap cigar band. The whole ceremony took no more than ten minutes.

'We'll do it properly later,' Cody promised her in the cab on the way back to the airport.

'Yes,' agreed Dallas, wondering why she didn't feel suddenly secure and happy.

They were back in LA in time to get a few hours' sleep before Dallas was due at the studio.

'Shall I stay?' Cody asked.

'Of course,' replied Dallas. What the hell did he think they had got married for if not to be together?

She showered, brushed her teeth, and went to him naked.

He stroked her body, muttered words of love, made love to her in a perfectly adequate way – a vast improvement on the time before.

She hated every minute of it. She hated the feel of his hands, his tongue, his male organ. There was no joy, no waves. He could have been a customer – another trick. He did the same things, went through the same motions.

'Did you come?' he asked anxiously when they were finished.

A man who needed to ask would never know.

'Mmmn,' Dallas mumbled, turning her back to him so that he wouldn't see the tears.

She had made a mistake. It wasn't his fault. He was blameless – only wanting to do what made her happy. But he had been right, they should have waited.

'Goodnight, Mrs Hills,' Cody murmured. 'Did I remember to tell you that I love you?'

A week later Bobbie was back.

This time she appeared at the studio, thin and jumpy in studded suede hot pants and a see-through shirt. She was hanging around outside Dallas' dressing room, and pounced on her during the lunch break.

'Hey, sugar sweets,' she greeted cheerfully, as if they were the best of friends. 'What's happenin'?'

Dallas hustled her quickly into the dressing room. 'How did you get here?' she questioned, her voice weary. She had expected Bobbie back, but not this soon.

'I got influence,' Bobbie's facial tick went into sudden uncontrollable action, and she started to rub her red-rimmed eyes. 'I need some more bread,' she mumbled, 'just a fuckin' loan 'til I get myself back in action.'

'No more money,' Dallas replied. 'I told you that before.'

'Dontcha get tight-assed with me,' suddenly Bobbie was screaming, 'you owe me plenty – *plenty*.'

'I owe you nothing.'

Bobbie rolled her eyes, 'Sweetshit! You got no memory on you, girl. I dragged you out of that pisshole you was givin' it away in. *I* discovered *you*. We go back a long way together. We got memories – mutual memories . . .'

Anger was starting to bubble up inside Dallas. Anger and frustration. The unfairness of it all.

'Go away, Bobbie,' she said tightly. 'Go away and don't come back if you know what's good for you.'

'Just another coupla hundred,' cajoled Bobbie, her mood becoming pleading. 'Just two hundred and I'll leave you alone. I know you don't want me around. I know I'm an embarrassment – but shit, girl, try and see it my way.'

'I do see it your way. I see you've got your eyes on what you think is a bank.'

'You're doin' pretty good . . .' whined Bobbie. 'What's a coupla hundred to you? I got a need . . . I gotta pay the man . . .'

Dallas stared at the black girl. She was pathetic. But pathetic or not she had to get her off her back. Lew Margolis was enough to have hanging over her, she didn't need this too. She dug into her purse, came up with sixty dollars. 'It's all I've got,' she said flatly.

Bobbie snatched the money from her. 'It'll do,' she sneered, 'for now. I'll be back next week. Get a bundle together for me and I'll leave you alone. It's only fair y'know. You gotta see things my way, sweet stuff – I am responsible for you gettin' this all together – without me you'd be nowhere.' She shoved the money up the leg of her hot pants and sighed, 'We girls gotta stick together. You and me had some good times.' She ran her hand lightly over Dallas' arm. 'Remember, honey? Remember?'

Dallas pulled her arm away. 'You try remembering the swimming pool, Bobbie. No more money – get it? *No more money*.'

Bobbie giggled, 'Yeah – I remember that little scene. But you had nothin' to lose then. Now you're riding high. By the way, sugar sweets, how's Mr M? Still the same sweet old-fashioned guy? He remember you? He remember that hot juicy box? He remember the *good times*? Maybe I should pay him a visit, give him a little reminder. What do you say?' Her eyes glazed over whilst she was talking, and she patted the money reassuringly. 'Think about it, kid. I'll pay you a visit in a coupla days and we'll talk some more, gotta go now – gotta get my head together.' She teetered off on ridiculous high-heeled wedgies.

Dallas slumped into a chair. Oh God! What was she to do? Lew Margolis hadn't stumped her, why should a stupid stoned hooker be a problem.

She pressed her fingers into her temples, massaging, thinking. Her mind remained a blank. Nothing. No solution. Somehow she would have to figure something out. In the meantime she would just have to keep on paying.

Cody patted his stomach, 'Delicious!' he exclaimed, 'the best spaghetti I've had all day!'

Dallas smiled, 'It will get better.'

Cody held out his hand, 'Come and sit down, I'll do the dishes.'

'You mean you'll load the machine.'

'I mean I'll scrub the pans.'

'You're so good to me.'

'Gotta treat a star like a star. I want you to read that script tonight.'

'I can't tonight, Cody, I'm really wiped out.'

He was immediately sympathetic. 'Tough day?'

'It's just tiring.'

'Only four more weeks and they'll have the first six in the can. We'll have a honeymoon – go anywhere you like.'

'I can't wait. It's some schedule.'

'They have to work this way. A segment every six days – that's the way to make money. When you figure it out over a year it's not bad at all. You make twenty-four shows a year – that's only five months' work and the rest of the time is yours.'

'Thanks a lot. With the Mack thing – personal appearances – and hopefully a movie – I'll have no time left at all.'

'What do you want time for?'

'I want to have a baby.'

Cody sat bolt upright, 'You want to *what*?'

'A baby. I want a baby.'

He laughed. 'Married a week and she wants a baby! We've got all the time in the world – next year we'll cut 'Man Made Woman' down to twelve shows a year. Think you can wait?' She glared at him. He thought she was joking. Well, to hell with him – she didn't need his permission – she only needed his cooperation – and she wasn't short of that. Now that they were married he expected to make love all the time, and each experience made her more withdrawn physically. It was as if he was making up for lost time. Not that he didn't try to please her. He tried too goddamn hard, forcing his tongue in every possible crevice in his vain attempts at giving her pleasure. 'Don't do that,' had become her battlecry, and although she tried to make her tone pleasant she

278

wanted to scream 'Leave me alone – don't touch me.' And of course he knew he was doing something wrong, and because of that tried all the harder.

'I think I'll go to bed,' she said.

'I think I'll join you.'

'You don't have to, it's early.'

'I want to.' Christ, did he want to! And yet what was going wrong between them?

His original instincts had been right. He should have stuck to his guns, given her time. Now they were married – married for crissakes! And she didn't even want him. He knew it. He sensed it. And his gut reaction was never wrong. He should have taken his own advice and left her alone. He had known it wouldn't work. But to turn out this bad so soon? Without even another man edging him into obscurity. He just couldn't figure it.

She had wanted *him*. There had been no gun at her head. And now with the baby talk . . .

She lay in bed totally wiped out. Bobbie. Fucking Bobbie. What was she to do?

For a moment she contemplated telling Cody – handing the whole bag over to him. But the things Bobbie would probably tell him . . . She couldn't face *that*. No – the best thing was to just keep paying – and paying and paying.

Her eyes filled with tears, and she turned her back as Cody climbed into bed beside her. His hand tentatively caressed her shoulder and she lay rigidly still. The hell with him – he could whistle for it tonight.

Doris Andrews – Mrs Lew Margolis – turned up at the studio the next day. She behaved like a queen visiting her subjects, and they all bowed and scraped in her direction. She smiled graciously, accepting compliments as she picked her way carefully across the set of 'Man Made Woman', finally stationing herself beside the camera operator.

'Hello, dear,' she waved at Dallas, who was just about to do a third take on a difficult scene. 'I've come to take you off for lunch.'

Dallas smiled weakly. Just what she needed. Lew Margolis' dykey movie-star wife.

She did the scene, Chuck called cut, and there was nothing else to do but be enveloped in clouds of *Joy* as Doris kissed her firmly on both cheeks.

'I've been meaning to visit you for days,' Doris said in her girlish voice. 'I wanted to congratulate you on becoming the Mack girl. Wonderful news. So good for your career. But didn't I tell you at my party that I knew you were destined to be someone special?' She chuckled intimately. 'Some of us have it – some of us don't. You've got it, darling girl. I could tell as soon as I set eyes on you. And I should know – Lord, should I know. Twenty years in this business . . . God – that sets you up . . .' She trailed off, her cornflower-blue eyes misting over momentarily. 'I've arranged lunch in Lew's private dining room. Just the two of us – Lew's not here today, he's at home, a slight chest cold, but I always insist he stays home if there's the tiniest thing wrong with him. He loves me to baby him.' Her lips tremored slightly. 'All men like to be treated as children. Remember that, my dear, and you'll never have any problem keeping a man. Not that you would of course – with that fine figure, those lovely breasts . . . Tell me, do you exercise to keep them so firm?'

Dallas said quickly, 'I never eat lunch, Mrs Margolis.'

'Doris, my dear, call me Doris. All my friends do.' She linked her arm through Dallas'. 'And I'm sure we're going to be friends. I feel a very warm closeness towards you, as if we had known each other for many years. Today you *shall* eat lunch. A little salad, a few slivers of smoked salmon. Some fresh pineapple. I ordered it specially for you.'

There was no getting out of it. Dallas made a face behind her back as she followed Doris out to a powder blue Corniche which whisked them over to Lew's office. First the husband, now the wife. Why the hell didn't they both leave her alone?

Lunch was laid out and waiting. A bottle of white wine to go with it. 'I don't drink when I'm working,' Dallas objected.

'Of course,' agreed Doris, but she poured her a glass anyway. 'Now, Dallas dear, tell me all about yourself. Were you born out here?'

Picking at the food Dallas fabricated a suitable background for herself. Doris nodded over every word, her blue eyes misting over at references to parents killed in a car crash and – the truth at last – a fiancé dying of a drug overdose.

'I've never taken any kind of drugs,' Doris admitted in a breathy whisper. 'I suppose when I was growing up drugs just weren't an issue, and of course Lew would never want me to experiment now.' She gave a self-conscious laugh. 'Lew's a very straight-laced man you know.'

'Really?' questioned Dallas, cramming smoked salmon into

her mouth and spooning some pineapple onto her plate. The sooner this lunch was over the better.

'Oh yes,' continued Doris, giggling like a naughty child, 'he has ruled over my career with an iron hand. Love scenes confined to an occasional kiss. No naughty words. All my films have appealed to a wide family audience.' She hesitated, then – 'He even censors our private life together.'

Dallas really didn't want to hear about it. She studied her pine-apple and wished that Doris would shut up.

'He's a very jealous man. Has me followed, watched. I'm never allowed to be alone with another man – never. But I don't mind.' She leaned forward intently. 'You see, Dallas dear, my interest has never been in other men . . . Do you understand me?'

'I've always enjoyed your movies,' Dallas replied brightly, 'I think I must have seen them all on television. Why even . . .'

Doris patted her gently on the arm. 'Am I embarrassing you, dear? I wouldn't want to do that. But somehow I sense in you a kindred spirit. You see I feel that you too have been used by men. Before I married Lew . . . Well, I came to Hollywood when I was seventeen – a young innocent farm girl – and between seventeen and Lew Margolis I sucked more hot cocks to get work than I care to remember. Enough to last me a lifetime.' She patted at her lips delicately with a lace handkerchief. 'Perhaps I sound crude to you, but sometimes it is such a relief to find someone with whom you can be totally honest. I feel so close to you, Dallas. You see my husband has never been able to get an erection, and I don't mind, I don't mind at all. We have a marriage of the minds. Sex is not important to me. But when I see a girl like you. A beautiful sensual girl with breasts I want to touch . . .'

'Mrs Margolis – Doris,' Dallas interrupted quickly, 'please don't go on. I'm not into that scene, really I'm not.'

Doris smiled softly. 'Don't be frightened to admit it.'

'I'm not frightened.'

Doris's blue eyes bore into her. 'I can sense these things, dear, you can't deceive me. Perhaps you're not ready for a relationship just yet, but you will be – you will be. Just a little time in this town. The men are vultures, they'll eat you up and spit you out. I just want you to know that we can be friends and perhaps lovers. I hope lovers.'

Dallas nodded. She wanted to say – don't call me, I'll call you – but somehow she didn't want to make fun of this woman – this world-wide star of family entertainment whose husband could only get it up for hookers.

'I understand, Doris,' she said softly, suddenly enormously sorry for her.

Doris smiled, 'Good.' She glanced at her neat gold watch. 'My goodness – I must get you back to the set. I'm glad we've had this little lunch.'

'Yes,' agreed Dallas.

They drove back to the set in Doris' powder-blue car, and lounging around outside, carelessly chatting to an electrician, was Bobbie. She was becoming a permanent fixture.

'Hey, babe!' She teetered over to Dallas, balancing precariously on outrageously high-heeled boots worn with the perennial hot pants. ''Bin lookin' for you all over.'

'You're not wasting any time,' muttered Dallas bitterly, at the same moment waving and smiling at Doris as she drove off.

'Yeah, man. Well, like how long sixty bucks gonna last me? You're rollin' in it, sugar sweets – let's not get tight-fisted when y'all got soooo much to lose. Lay a thousand on me and I'll flit outta your life like a fast shit!'

'I don't have any money on me. I gave you every last cent yesterday.'

'So get it.'

'I can't get over to the bank. I'll give you a cheque.'

'No cheque, sugar sweets. Cash. Today.'

Dallas thought quickly. If a thousand dollars would keep Bobbie off her back for a while it would be worth it. She could always send someone over to her bank to cash a cheque. At least it would give her some thinking space. She needed time to figure out what to do about Bobbie.

'I'll get it for you.'

Bobbie blinked nervously. 'Good girl.'

'Where shall I send it?'

'Bring it yourself. No messengers.' She scribbled down an address. 'I'll be waitin'. Oh – an' chicken – none of your smart-ass ideas 'bout hittin' on me. I gotta friend with a letter. Anything happens to me you got yourself up shit creek.'

Dallas nodded grimly. They must have been watching the same television programmes.

Bobbie wobbled happily off.

Kiki, on her way to the set, linked arms with Dallas. 'Who was *that*?' she asked.

Dallas shrugged. 'Some freak chasing autographs.'

'I wonder how these people get on the set,' Kiki complained.

'Tell me about your lunch – Chuck says you were last seen being spirited off by Doris Andrews. What's she like?'

Cody spent two hours on the phone locating the best house he could in Acapulco for their honeymoon. He wanted to surprise Dallas. Wanted her to have something nice to look forward to.

When it was all arranged he got nervous in case she wouldn't want to go to Acapulco. He had sent off a heavy deposit, but the hell with it . . . If she didn't want to go there he would sacrifice his deposit. True love indeed.

He had been thinking about what she had said. A baby. At first an unthinkable idea. But on second thoughts, if that was what would make her happy. After all she was a girl with no family. She had had a rotten life. If she wanted a baby . . .

It could be worked out. If only she would be prepared to wait a few months. Long enough to get twenty-four of the shows in the can, and all the Mack girl photos for the initial six months. It wasn't such an impossible idea after all. And his mother – maybe it would soften the blow. A baby to look forward to.

He would have to think about it seriously. If that was what would make Dallas happy – well, it *was* a possibility. It *could* be planned. He remembered with horror the one and only time he had knocked a girl up. She had been a secretary at one of the studios. It had been *she* who had insisted on an abortion. In fact she had planned the weekend together in Tijuana, and treated the whole thing as one long jaunt. Shocked at her callous attitude, he had dutifully spent the weekend with her, paid all the bills, and never seen her again. At least it proved he was potent.

Dallas left the studio at six. She consulted the scrap of paper Bobbie had scribbled her address on. It was on Santa Monica Boulevard – the massage parlour and porno shop end.

Christ! Dallas wasn't pleased, but she had the money stacked neatly in her shoulder bag. And she had a little speech planned to lay on Bobbie. No more blackmail. If she wanted it Dallas had decided she would pay for her to take a cure. If she didn't want it – too bad. This thousand dollars was the last payment.

The traffic on Santa Monica was heavy. It was going home time – and everyone seemed to have decided to go home via Santa Monica.

Dallas scanned the numbers looking out for Bobbie's address. She hadn't bothered to call Cody to tell him she might be late, as she hadn't realized Bobbie lived so far away.

At last she found it. A seedy walk-up apartment house sandwiched between a used army clothes shop and an 'ORAL SEX – The Only Way' neon-lit parlour. She hadn't expected Bobbie to be living in the lap of luxury – but this – what a dump.

She parked the car a half block away and walked back. A drunk sat by the shabby open door. A sign read 'Rooms by the hour'. Dallas shuddered. Suddenly she didn't want to go in. Didn't want to climb the narrow staircase and search for Apartment 4B which was probably only a room anyway.

The drunk reached for her leg and she stepped smartly past him and up the stairs. Rock music blared from behind a door marked 1A, a baby crying from 1B. Both rooms on the second floor seemed silent. She continued up to the third floor, and jumped when the door of 3A opened and a hollow-eyed youth emerged, stared at her, and clattered off down the stairs.

She paused to catch her breath, anger creeping over her that she had allowed herself to get in this position. If only she could wipe out her past, just erase the whole lousy memory. Lew Margolis, Bobbie . . . Why did these people have to keep on reminding her . . . And who else was waiting out there to reveal her?

Wearily she reached the fourth floor. A door stood uninvitingly open, she checked the number, it was 4B.

'Anyone around?' she called, unwilling to enter the small darkened room.

'Fuck off!' screeched a woman's voice from behind the closed door of 4A. This was followed by a man's laughter.

Bobbie lay on the floor naked and shivering. She had been badly beaten up. Her face looked unnatural; swollen and cracked lips, trickles of blood coming from her nose, and one eye so puffed up that you could hardly see it.

She rolled towards Dallas with a groan and an attempted smile. 'Hey, sugar sweets,' she mumbled, 'y'all bring the money? I need it man, like I *really* need it. They're comin' back, and next time they're *really* gonna work me over!'

forty-six

Al issued instructions that complete secrecy must prevail concerning Evan's disappearance.

But too many people knew, and items of gossip leaked out and were exaggerated.

Edna was completely hysterical and had to have a doctor in constant attendance to keep her sedated and quiet.

Upon arrival in Tucson a private detective was hired. 'He'll pick him up in no time,' Paul assured Al.

'If you had been watching out for him this would never have fucking happened,' spat Al, his anger hissing out in the direction of anyone who came his way. 'Why wasn't someone watching him? Goddammit, I'm supposed to be the singer on this tour. Am I supposed to do everything else too?'

Paul shrugged. What could he say? He returned to his suite, and Melanie, and recounted the conversation with his brother.

'He's right,' agreed Melanie, peering in the mirror and applying powder blusher with a brush. 'Poor Al, you *should* have been keeping an eye on Evan.'

Jesus! Paul was speechless. Linda would have comforted him, told him that of course it wasn't his fault – which it wasn't.

'You always side with Al,' he complained. 'Maybe you should have married *him*.'

'Maybe I should,' agreed Melanie crisply. 'I would have been much better for him than that whining hag he's stuck with.' She finished applying the blusher. 'There! How do I look?'

'Like the bitch that you are.' He stormed out of the room. What did he need it for? A stupid, vain, nagging little bitch! Linda was right. He should face up to it and leave her. He would still be able to see his children. He would have visiting rights. But, God, they were still so young . . . Maybe if he could just stick it out for another couple of years.

They were in a park on the outskirts of town.

'Move up,' Glory giggled. 'Shift that skinny ass an' give me some space, man!'

Evan shifted around awkwardly in the sleeping bag. Glory shifted with him. They were both so thin that their bones crunched together.

Plum, huddled in her own sleeping bag next to them, mumbled, 'Shut y' face. Gotta get some sleep.'

They had bought the sleeping bags as an investment against staying in hotels. As it was summer they provided adequate warmth and comfort, and during the day folded neatly into back packs which were quite easy to carry.

Upon leaving the hotel in New Orleans they had taken a bus

out of town, then left it after an hour and hitch-hiked back the way they had come. 'Throw any snoopers off our tracks,' Plum explained. 'Daddy is sure to try an' grab you back.'

Evan had no desire to be grabbed back. For the first time in his life he felt like a free person with his own identity. It didn't occur to him that his mother would be worried sick. He knew he could look after himself, and it was about time *she* realized it.

'You gotta hard-on?' Glory was asking. 'Little me feelin' horny. You feelin' horny Evvvan?' She was wriggling her hands down between them, feeling through his Y-fronts, pulling his very erect member out.

'How can we do it in here?' Evan asked, excitement flooding through him so strongly that he almost came at her touch.

'Keep still,' she commanded, manoeuvring him between her legs. She giggled. 'Easy does it. Push. C'mon, man, *push* for shit's sake.'

He felt himself slide inside the familiar contours of her body. She was different from Plum, more slippery and slidey.

'Put your mouth to mine, man,' she whispered. She had a pill in her mouth which she transferred skilfully to his. 'Swallow it,' she encouraged, 'swallow it down an' keep on fuckin'!'

The little sod had ruined everything. Screwed every one of Al's plans, and now he was stuck with a hysterical Edna who seemed to think that he was entirely to blame for Evan running off.

'He split because of you,' Al said at last. 'You've always molly-coddled the crap out of him. He probably couldn't face it any more.'

Edna shook her head in pain. 'I trusted you with our son. I trusted you . . .' She started to cry.

Al left the room. This was all he needed. Stuck with Edna. How could he be expected to work under these conditions? He needed space . . . He needed to drink without her complaining every time he took a swig. He needed to get laid. It was essential to have a dumb and busty blonde ready and available.

He stormed down to Paul's suite, but there was sister-in-law Melanie in a low-cut yellow dress thrusting tits (too small) and sympathy (too close to home) at him. He didn't need *that*.

In the elevator on the way back to his suite he bumped into Nellie. Sweet dark-haired Nellie, who touched his arm and said, 'I understand, Al. I understand.'

There was the afternoon to get through, so he said, 'You want to buy me a drink?'

Her face lit up. 'Oh, yes.'

'What are we waiting for? Let's go to your room.'

He vaguely remembered another afternoon he had spent with her. But it was only a hazy memory.

He went to her room, lay on the bed whilst she fussed around drawing the shades, pouring him a drink, loosening his clothes.

'I knew you'd come back,' she whispered. 'I was sure you'd come back to me.'

He wasn't really listening. His mind was going in a dozen different directions.

'Do you want to make love?' she was asking.

Make love. Is that what they called it?

She had taken off her dress to reveal black silken skin and small breasts with hard extended nipples. He liked more voluptuous women, but she would do.

'You knew it was me on the plane. You did, didn't you?' she asked.

He didn't know what the hell she was talking about. 'Yeah,' he agreed, ' 'course.' Her long black hair fell in a sweeping curtain as he pushed her head down on him. He wanted no more than a blow job. He didn't want to become involved with her face or body. He just wanted release.

After fifteen minutes he shoved her away. He couldn't come.

Goddamit, Evan, you have even ruined my sex life.

'What's the matter?' Nellie asked softly, 'Am I doing something wrong?'

He rolled onto his stomach ignoring her. He would have been better off with Sutch, big-titted Sutch whom he had never had. Or even fiery Rosa. Or better still, all three.

'What room is Sutch in?' he questioned.

'Why?' asked Nellie, blinking nervously.

'Don't bug me,' snapped Al.

'She . . . she's in the room opposite.'

He climbed off the bed, zipped up his trousers.

'Later,' he said, and walked out.

Nellie ran to the door, watched him through the spyhole. He walked to the room across the hall, knocked. Sutch opened the door clad in a pink silk kimono. Al said something, Sutch grinned, and he walked in and closed the door.

Nellie stuffed her fist in her mouth to stop herself crying out.

All this time she had thought . . . imagined . . . but she meant nothing to him, absolutely nothing.

She walked into the bathroom and slid a razor blade out of the wall dispenser.

287

She sat on the side of the bath and stared at the sharp glint of fresh steel. Slowly she brought it to her wrist, and slowly she cut deeply into the taut flesh until the blood ran in a heavy river down her naked body.

'I wondered when you'd get around to me,' laughed Sutch. 'Honey – I ain't bin countin' the days, but I *sure* knew the day would come!'

She poured him a hefty Scotch and wrapped her kimono firmly round her, emphasizing her large unfettered breasts.

She had what he was looking for, and he reached for them.

She slapped his hand away. 'Say please!' she chided, tossing her afro mane of orange hair.

'Please,' he said, ripping her kimono down the front, allowing her ripe and juicy body to be exposed.

She shook her boobs at him provocatively, as he had seen her shake them many times on stage – although on stage they had always been covered by flimsy strips of material.

'Nice,' he said.

'Nice,' she agreed, 'nice 'n yummy. Want a taste thrill, baby? Suck on a tit, I'll roll us a joint.'

Why hadn't he discovered Sutch before? She was more than enough to while away a boring afternoon with her plump sexy body and laid back humour.

He followed her to the bed. Stevie Wonder was belting away on a portable tape machine. Sutch propped herself against the bed back and proceeded to roll a joint from the equipment she had on the bedside table. Al threw off his clothes and joined her.

'My, my,' she exclaimed. 'Bless my little cotton socks! It's *all* true – every goddamn spunky inch of it!'

'Turn over,' he commanded, 'get on all fours. We'll have the joint later.'

'Yeeees sireeee!'

Melanie wandered around the suite picking up things and inspecting them. Invitations, magazines, gifts from fans.

Edna sat in a chair wrapped in a dressing gown, her face white and drawn.

'I don't know,' Melanie was saying, 'I'm sure he's all right. You know what boys are like. If he's with those two girls . . . Well, they'll look after him. He's probably having a wonderful time.' She spotted a mirror, and leaned forward to study herself intently.

'I look so tired!' she wailed, 'Fine trip *this* has turned out to be. All I've seen is the inside of an aeroplane and lousy hotel rooms.' She adjusted a curl, coaxing it into place with some spit, then turned once more to Edna. 'Why don't we go out tonight?' she suggested. 'After the show. It would do you good. You could put on some make-up, and one of your new dresses. I can get Paul to book a table at the best place in town.'

'No,' said Edna flatly.

'Why not?' persisted Melanie. 'Aren't you bored? We've been stuck in this hotel for two days. I'm going out of my head, and fat chance *I've* got of getting taken anywhere without you and Al.'

'Too bad.'

Melanie wasn't sure she had heard Edna correctly. 'Huh?'

'I said too bad,' snapped Edna. 'I don't care if you are bored. *I don't care, Melanie.* You're a selfish bitch. Yes – I said it – a bitch.'

'Edna!'

'Don't Edna me. I wish I'd never let you talk me into this trip. If I hadn't come here none of this would have happened. I blame you, I really do, so don't come whining to me because you're bored.'

'Thank you very much. I love you too.'

'Just go away and leave me alone.'

'A pleasure!' Melanie flounced from the room, turning at the door to give a parting shot. 'Fine thanks I get for making you look halfway decent instead of the frump you usually are.'

Edna ignored her. She didn't care what she looked like. She just wanted Evan back.

The press were on to something. More of them than usual were at the Community Centre, milling around getting in everyone's way. With 'Bad Black Alice' being number one with a bullet, interest in Al was at its peak. The Rock papers had all sent representatives in the hope of getting an exclusive interview.

Bernie had organized an informal party after the show just to keep the press happy. He hoped to persuade Al to give a mass interview – with maybe a promise of some exclusives for the more important papers the next day.

A thin girl from *Rolling Stone* kept on cornering him. 'Word's out Al's son been abducted. True or false?' she asked.

"False,' sweated Bernie. 'Where did you hear that?'

'Word's around.'

Yeah. Fucking word would be around. All they needed was the rumour to make the papers put the idea into those two freaks' heads that they could get *money* for returning little Evan safe and sound.

The crowds were packing in. Al arrived in the company of Sutch. The photographers leapt forward.

What the fuck was he doing with *that* one? Bernie groaned. Out of the three Promises she was the wild one. Her husband was in jail on a drug bust, and she never set foot on stage unless she was out of her head on coke. The other two were angels in comparison to Sutch. Rosa, the lead singer, stuck with her Mafiosa boyfriend and kept to herself. Nellie was just a sweet little girl whom everyone loved.

Al strode into his dressing-room, swigged from the bottle of Jack Daniels set out and waiting for him.

'Any news?' he asked Bernie.

'Paul's on the phone now.'

'Security good?'

'The best.'

'It better be. One more fuckup and I walk.'

Bernie scratched absently under an armpit. 'If you could make a press conference tonight – after the show. I set up a party. Booze. Food. I think you should do it.'

'If I feel like it,' allowed Al.

If he felt like it. Who the fuck did he think he was all of a sudden? You never played superstar with the press if you wanted to stay up there. You kissed ass and sucked cock – metaphorically speaking of course – although certain stars were not averse to doing the real thing if it kept their name in lights.

Rosa appeared at the door of the dressing-room. She ignored Al as she always did except when on stage.

'Where's Nellie?' she directed at Bernie.

'I don't know. Where is she?'

'*I'm* asking *you.* Didn't a car go to fetch her?' Rosa had taken to staying at different hotels on the tour, and making her own travel arrangements. Her 'boyfriend' preferred it that way.

'Yeah, of course. Didn't she arrive with Sutch . . .?' Bernie trailed off, remembering that Sutch had arrived with Al.

Rosa twitched her head angrily. 'Find her, Bernie, we go on in twenty minutes. She's probably sittin' in the hotel waitin' for Sutch.'

'I'll call the hotel. No panic.'

'Sure, man, no panic. Only we don't go on unless there's three of us.' She swept off.

Al had started to apply his make-up. Dark pancake base. Slight kohl emphasis on the eyes. He swigged continually from the liquor bottle.

Suddenly Bernie got that feeling. It slipped in under his gut, a nagging ache that warned him of trouble. Sweet shit . . . What the fuck . . . They'd soon be in LA. Couldn't be soon enough for him.

Two days on the road and already Evan was feeling tired. Of course he was enjoying it, having a wonderful time. But didn't either Plum or Glory ever think of taking a bath? And greasy hot dogs washed down with Coca Cola did not seem to be a very *balanced* diet. And when they were hitching, the two girls seemed prepared to climb into anything that stopped. What if a maniac stopped? A maniac all set to rape and murder all three of them. He had read dreadful things about what happened to hitch-hikers.

His arm still hurt. His bruises still hurt. And the novelty of being squashed in a sleeping bag alongside Glory was wearing off. She snored, and she never washed, and she was always stoned.

Also he noticed in panic in the mirror in a men's room that his spots were getting *worse*. Soon his face would be one large red patch.

'Why don't we stay in a hotel tonight?' he suggested.

'*Come on*,' laughed Plum. 'Are you *serious*, man?'

'Why not?' he persisted. 'We can afford it.'

'We can?' questioned Plum. 'I'm holdin' the bankroll, man, and we are almost busted.'

'But what about my two hundred dollars and the other money we had?'

'S'nearly gone.' Plum was unconcerned by this fact.

'How can it have?'

Plum fixed him with a mean look. 'You want a written account? We *spent* it, man – like *used* it, y'know. Sleeping bags, food, an' how do you think Glory's bin payin' f'all the goodies she's scored?'

He didn't argue further. But he thought with a certain longing of a warm bed, a juicy steak, and a hot bath.

They were riding in the back of a truck and Glory, asleep in a huddle, suddenly awoke. 'Where are we?' she asked, yawning and rubbing her eyes.

'Who knows?' snapped Plum. 'I'm gettin' a big heavy question session 'bout where all the bread's gone.'

'Yeah?' Glory was not really interested. She was reaching in her jeans' pocket and digging out some pills. She stuffed several in her own mouth and then offered the remaining few to her friends. Plum shook her head. Evan took two, swallowed them. Without water they stuck in his throat, but he knew they would eventually dissolve and then he would feel better – much better.

'You mothafucker!' screamed Rosa at Al. 'You stinkin' mothafucking sonofabitch!'

Bernie had called the hotel to locate Nellie. The car was still out front waiting for her. There was no answer from her room. An assistant manager at the hotel had been dispatched to her room with a pass key. He had found her on the bathroom floor in a pool of her own blood. She was still alive, but barely. At the same time that Bernie was being informed on the phone an ambulance was rushing to the hotel.

Within five minutes Nellie was receiving emergency treatment on her way to the hospital.

Bernie had broken the news to Rosa who had gone mad with fury. She had stormed into Al's dressing room and started screaming at him.

Assorted news media gathered in a fascinated group outside the door.

'Pig!' screamed Rosa. 'If it wasn't for you . . . You white piece of *shit*! You hear me, prick – *you hear me!*'

'The whole of Tucson hears you!' intervened Bernie. 'Please, Rosa, it's not Al's fault.'

She shook free. 'Don't give me *that* shit. Ever since the day that mothafucker crept into her bed she ain't been the same girl. She *loves* him – this piece of white crap – she *loves* him. The kid lived for a look – a smile. I could *kill* him.' She sprang suddenly, like a pouncing tiger, all red sequin dress and clawing fingers.

Bernie dragged her off Al, who just sat there staring at himself in the mirror.

'Enough,' said Bernie, holding her against his massive bulk.

She went limp in his arms. 'Get me a car to the hospital,' she muttered, 'and get me out of the sight of that mothafucking prick.'

Bernie half carried her from the room and back to her dressing-room.

Sutch had her head cradled on the dressing table and was sobbing. Make-up ran in colourful rivers down her face.

'I'll arrange a car,' said Bernie. He didn't feel too good himself.

Nellie had been everyone's favourite. 'What about the show?'

'Fuck the show!' spat Rosa. 'Let superprick do it on his own. I ain't *never* sharing a stage with him again as long as I live!'

A little more scotch. Gargle. Spit out. Got to do the show alone. So what? Why not? He was the star for Crissakes. He was the one they had all piled in to see. Al King. Number one with a bullet. Number fucking one.

'Are you all right?' asked Paul.

'Sure,' laughed Al. Why shouldn't he laugh?

It wasn't *his* fault some silly little girl had slit her wrists. It *wasn't* his fault – no matter what anyone said. So he had given her one. So what? If all the girls he had ever given one to slit their wrists . . . He laughed. Jesus! What a sight. There wouldn't be room for them in all the hospitals!

He went to swig from the scotch bottle again but it was empty. Empty! Would you believe that? A star with an empty bottle.

'Hey Paul – bring another bottle.'

'You've had enough, you're going on in five minutes.'

'Don't tell me I've had enough.'

'You've drunk *the whole bottle* yourself, goddammit.'

And another half bottle with Sutch. And two fine joints. And a touch of coke to keep him in peak condition. And some pretty good fucking. Just like old times. Why hadn't he discovered Sutch earlier?

'More, Paul,' he demanded, and he stood up and the room swayed. But that was OK. The room had rhythm – just like him. He laughed aloud. Paul's worried face swam before him.

'Point me to the stage,' he demanded. 'Wait a minute – gotta piss.' He unzipped his fly and let out a stream of urine in the general direction of the wall.

'Al!' Paul turned to Bernie. 'He'll never make it. We'll have to cancel the show.'

'Cancel and we got ourselves a riot,' pointed out Bernie.

'The show muss go on . . .' slurred Al.

'Let's get him on and let's get it over with,' said Paul quickly.

Bernie shrugged. What the fuck . . . It wasn't *his* funeral.

Evan awoke stiff and uncomfortable. He wriggled out of the sleeping bag and surveyed his surroundings.

The girls had got them all invited to a party in an empty house. When the party had finished they had stayed on utilizing the bare floorboards as a home for the night. Some party. A lot of drugged people swopping partners. Evan had huddled miserably in a corner. He did *not* want to join in. He did *not* feel like one of them.

Glory had jeered at him – 'Poor little baby mommy's boy,' she had taunted. 'Frightened to show his pee pee!'

Perhaps it had not been such a good idea to have decided to travel to Los Angeles with them. His parents never taunted him – never. They were a pain – but from what he had heard all parents were the same.

He prowled around the empty, depressing house, and his thoughts turned to bacon and eggs, sizzling sausages, and hot coffee. His stomach grumbled with hunger. He had eleven dollars. If he didn't wake the girls that would be enough to buy himself a decent breakfast. He glanced at his watch. It was only 8 a.m. and the girls never stirred until ten at the earliest – wherever they were sleeping.

He pulled on his jeans and crept from the house. He didn't even know what town he was in, but he set resolutely off, and within two blocks spotted a drug store.

He took a stool at the counter, and was just about to study the menu when the headline of the newspaper on the rack caught his eye. 'AL KING SENSATION' it screamed in heavy black newsprint.

The show was a near-miss disaster. Somehow Al managed to stagger his way through it. A performance punctuated with raging expletives, half-forgotten lyrics, and general sloppiness.

The screaming fans prevented themselves from seeing the real truth. But the press were there with their pencils sharpened.

The worst point was when Al fell. Sprawled happily in front of thousands of people, gave them the V sign, and staggered back on to his feet. There was almost a moment when Paul thought Al might repeat his bizarre performance in the dressing-room, and pee all over the audience with the famous King Cock. But he restrained himself, albeit reluctantly.

Once off stage he was wrapped in towels and rushed to the hotel where Paul had a doctor waiting to see him. The doctor examined him and pronounced him on the verge of a complete breakdown.

'Bullshit!' screamed Al. 'Bring on the girls!'

The doctor injected him with a sedative and warned Paul that he should have complete rest for at least a month. 'Impossible,' Paul muttered under his breath. He knew Al was as strong as a horse. But there had been a lot of additional strain. The bomb. The riot. Edna's arrival. Evan's disappearance. Nellie's suicide attempt. He wished that Linda was around to discuss things with. She had a habit of always coming up with the right decision.

Maybe he *should* cancel a few of the concerts. Give Al a rest. After all, going on like he had tonight was going to do him no good at all. And they did have to replace 'The Promises' – even if Nellie recovered – and it was touch and go at the moment – she wouldn't be able to work again for months. Besides, Rosa had threatened never to appear with Al again.

Maybe if he cancelled all the gigs before Los Angeles – that would give Al a break – enough to get himself together. He could always do the cancelled gigs later – something could be worked out. Yeah – that might be the answer. With the single at number one it wouldn't do Al any harm – and Jesus – the state he was in it could only do him good.

'I'll order you some food,' he said, 'then you should get some sleep. Edna wasn't feeling well – she's sleeping in another room.'

'Fuck Edna!' slurred Al truculently. 'Frigid bag! Get me 'nother bottle of Jack the Lad.'

'Listen, Al . . .'

'Listen, brother,' mimicked Al, weaving round the room, 'I did the show, didn't I? I did the fucking show. That's all anyone cares about, isn't it? Now piss off an' leave me alone.'

Reluctantly Paul left. He knew better than to argue with Al when he was in that mood. Luke was stationed outside the door. 'Don't let him out,' Paul warned. 'I'll be in my room if you need me.'

In the middle of the night they needed him. A terrible crashing noise was coming from behind the locked door of the suite. By the time the manager was called, the pass key found, and they managed to get in, the crashing had stopped. Al had completely wrecked the entire suite. Slinging what he could out of the window, breaking and smashing whatever else was in his way.

He lay in the middle of the wreckage fast asleep, snoring and smiling.

In the morning he remembered nothing about it.

'I've often wanted to do what you did myself!' sighed the manager, as they tried to work out the cost of the damages.

'Double whatever the bill is,' Al said magnanimously. 'Wreck a room on me!'

The next morning the papers screamed news of Al's bizarre

concert performance, and Nellie's attempted suicide, and without actually saying so they managed to give the impression that Al was responsible.

Paul kept the newspapers away from both Al and Edna, and after a conference with Bernie he issued a joint statement from Mr and Mrs King expressing their deepest sympathy about Nellie who was a dear and close friend of both of them.

Evan never spent his eleven dollars on breakfast. In fact he never had breakfast at all. He read with a sweeping horror about Nellie. *His* Nellie. And his heart lurched at the filthy allegations about her and his father.

He had to get to Tucson. He had to get to the hospital.

He spent his eleven dollars on phoning Tucson and tracking down Uncle Paul. He didn't care if they were angry with him. He didn't care about anything except getting to the hospital and seeing Nellie.

Paul seemed relieved to hear from him, and gave him instructions on what to do.

Whilst Evan hung on the phone Paul looked up a car hire firm in the area – which fortunately was only about a hundred miles away – and arranged for a car to pick Evan up. 'Don't get lost on the way,' he warned.

Get lost! No way! Nothing would stop him getting back to Nellie.

He had forgotten about Glory and Plum safely tucked up in their sleeping bags. Even if he remembered, it wouldn't have worried him. They could look after themselves. Nellie couldn't.

Paul broke the good news to Edna. She was perfectly composed. 'Book us on the next flight to London,' she said calmly.

'Are you sure?' ventured Paul.

Al was still under sedation in the bedroom.

'Yes, I'm sure,' said Edna quietly. 'Very sure.'

This was a different Edna to the one Paul had known for so many years. The other Edna wouldn't have dared make such a decision without consulting Al.

'Melanie will go with you,' said Paul.

'I'd prefer she didn't.'

'Why?'

'Because I don't like her. I'm sorry, I know she's your wife, but I have to be truthful.'

Paul stared at her with a sudden admiration. He didn't like Melanie either – but he would never have the nerve to say so. What had happened to Edna? Had she suddenly sprouted balls?

'That's fine, Edna. I'll just book seats for you and Evan.'

'Thank you. I'm going to pack.'

He watched her leave the room and felt good for her. She was walking tall for the first time since he had known her.

The car ride to Tucson took three hours. Evan sat stiff-backed and anxious all the way. He told the driver to go straight to the hospital where Nellie was.

'I'm supposed to take you to the hotel,' the driver complained. 'Deliver you personally, not let you out of my sight.'

'I *have* to go to the hospital first,' Evan insisted.

Reluctantly the driver agreed. The kid looked desperate.

They stopped him at reception at the hospital. He knew he must look a scruffy sight.

'I'm Al King's son,' he told the receptionist, 'I have to see Nellie – she's expecting me.'

The receptionist eyed him suspiciously. She didn't believe him. She had been bugged by press and fans all morning. 'She's dead,' she said coldly, 'died this morning at eight o'clock.'

forty-seven

The first reaction Dallas had was to turn and run – get the hell *out* of there.

But how could she go? How could she leave Bobbie in the state she was in?

One part of her warned, 'Don't get involved.' On the other hand you wouldn't leave a dog like this. After all, at one time Bobbie had befriended her – abortive as that friendship had turned out to be.

Decision made, Dallas slammed the door behind her shutting out the muffled sounds of love-making coming from the other apartment.

She didn't know what to do. Should she try and move Bobbie? What if something was broken?

An Indian bedspread was draped across the window secured

only by string. Dallas removed it and covered the shivering black girl's body. She couldn't help noticing the gnarled tracks of heroin addiction covering both of Bobbie's arms. The veins were bruised and discoloured, covering old scars where she had injected herself over and over again. Unable to find more space on her arms she had started on her legs. Dallas shuddered.

Bobbie was rolling her eyes around and around. Dallas placed a dirty pillow under her head. 'What happened?' she asked. 'Who did this to you?'

'Hey,' mumbled Bobbie, focusing at last. 'The man, baby. Who else? I tole him I was gettin' the bread – I tole him.' Her head rolled to the side. 'Get me a shot of scotch – s' over there – kitchen.'

Dallas took quick stock of her surroundings. A small, dark room. Couch that doubled as a bed. Table littered with make-up, magazines, clothes. A jagged piece of glass propped up in the middle to do duty as a mirror.

The kitchen consisted of a cracked formica unit in the corner.

Amongst crowds of empty bottles littering the top, Dallas located one a quarter full of Scotch.

She handed it to Bobbie, who sucked greedily from it.

'Is there a phone here?' Dallas asked.

'You don' wanna phone, sugar,' mumbled Bobbie. Her voice was very weak.

'But you need a doctor.'

'Yeah. But I don' need the shit goes with it. I'll be fine. You just hand me the bread and get out before they come back.'

'Before *who* comes back?'

'Whadda you care? I'm leanin' on you for bread – that's all. So be wise – like I taught you.' She tried to sit up, but couldn't make it. 'I need some stuff . . . I got a beeeg need . . . Be a nice girl – reach outside the window – there's a ledge – pass it to me. Those cocksuckers don' know it all . . .' She wiped blood from her mouth and looked at it with surprise. 'One shot and those bastards can take a flyer up their own assholes . . . I'm gonna own the world . . . the world, man. Like I'll have myself a house. Best fuckin' house in LA. Best fuckin' girls . . .' Her eyes were rolling again. 'You wanna come an work for me, sugar . . . Wanna be my star . . . Wanna be my lover . . .' Her mumbling was becoming incoherent. 'Nevah was given a fuckin' thing in my life . . . Worked ass . . . Hey – get me the stuff – get me the magic . . .' Her eyes closed. She had passed out. The bottle fell from her hands gurgling the remains of its contents out on to the threadbare rug.

Dallas picked it up. This was it. This was the bottom line. Bobbie had sunk pretty low – but whose fault was it? She had started off with none of the breaks. Hooking at thirteen. And now hooked in another direction. Heroin. The land of peace and glory for those that had nowhere else to go.

Dallas cradled her head and tried to remove some of the blood. 'It'll be OK, Bobbie,' she crooned, 'I'll look after you. I'm going to get you into a hospital, get you cured.'

Bobbie's eyelids fluttered. But she did'nt open her eyes. She seemed to be breathing in a very laboured way.

'I've got to get help,' Dallas muttered. She ran from the apartment and hammered on the next door.

'Get lost!' shrieked a woman's voice.

'I need help!' pleaded Dallas.

'Honey, don't we all!' replied the voice.

'Please! The girl next door is very sick.'

'That little junkie! She can drown in her own piss for all I care.'

Nice place. Was it worth trying the other apartments, or should she go down to the street and try to find a phone? She decided to try the street, and started off down the stairs. On the second floor her way was blocked by two men coming up.

'You know where's the nearest phone?' she asked.

They made no move to let her pass. One was a heavy-set black, the other a tall skinny white man with yellow hair and jumpy eyes.

'Whatcha' all needin' to telephone for?' asked the black.

'I need some help . . . with a sick friend.' As she spoke she knew with a feeling of dread that these two men were the 'they' that Bobbie had been mumbling about.

'Move on up,' stated the black firmly. 'Y'all must be the friend Bobbie said was bringin' her a present. Gotta admit we di'nt believe her.'

'I'm going to call a doctor,' Dallas said, trying to keep her voice controlled.

'Y'all goin' to pay us her little debt first.'

'How much does she owe you?'

'How much you got, foxy? And how come I ain't nevah seen you around?' His hand moved like lightning, brushing over her breasts, removing her shoulder bag. He opened it, found the stack of bills, whistled admiringly. 'Must be over a thou here . . . Business pretty good, baby?'

'Does she owe you all that?' Dallas asked coldly.

'Don' worry that foxy little head 'bout it,' he smirked. 'She gotta habit to support she gotta learn how to support it. Who you

299

work for? Might just pay you a visit – a *free* visit. Wouldn't wanna see you all messed up like your friend.'

'You did that to her? Why?'

He laughed. 'Why? She wants to know why.' He cackled some more, ' 'Cos I'm *mean*, bitch, real fuckin' *mean*.' He reached forward and squeezed her breasts.

'Let's get outa here,' said the other man, 'we got what we came for.'

'*You* may have got what you came for. I wouldn't say no to fucking this sweet piece – fucking her good.'

'Another time. We got work to do.'

'Another time. I'll get your address from Bobbie,' his hand slid down her body, pushed between her legs, 'remember it'll be for free.'

She shoved him away, thankful that she was wearing jeans.

Cackling he started off down the stairs. 'Keep it hot for me, foxy. Y'all are in f' a thrill.'

She bit her lip to stay silent. She knew what men like that were capable of doing. She had seen what they had done to Bobbie. And Bobbie was her prime concern.

There was a telephone in a bar half a block away. She called emergency and told them to send an ambulance.

If you were smart – she told herself – you would get the hell out of here and go on home. But how could she leave until she saw that Bobbie was properly looked after? Besides, she wanted to let them know that she would be willing to pay for Bobbie's treatment, and then a cure. A private nursing home where she would be well looked after.

She ran back to the seedy apartment house, hurried up the four flights of stairs, pushed open the door.

Bobbie had dragged herself over to the window, managed to get her heroin, managed to inject herself with the help of an old belt pulled tight to locate a welcoming vein, and a plastic syringe.

She was slumped on the floor by the window. The belt hung loosely round her arm. The syringe was on the floor beside her.

She managed to smile at Dallas. 'Hey – glad you're here.' She was groggy and rubbing her eyes. 'Feel kinda funny – kinda bad. Pills. Booze. Little shot of H. Guess I mighta overdid it, sugar. Like we had some laughs once . . .' Her voice turned into a rasping choking gurgle, and her eyes rolled back for the final time.

She was dead.

From the next apartment a woman could be heard screaming

in the throes of orgasm. A man laughed, a harsh unkind sound. Rock music drifted up from the second floor. In the distance came the blare of the ambulance.

Dallas hurried from the room. There was nothing she could do now.

Cody paced angrily around the house, glancing at his watch for the twentieth time. She was late. Very, very late. And he had checked that she had left the studio on time. He had checked with Kiki and Chuck, and she hadn't gone home with them.

So where was she?

She was with another man, that's where she was. Maybe the black stud with the white Ferrari. Or maybe the little group he had spied her orgying with that night. Or maybe the guy she had flown off to see when she had lied to him she was visiting an aunt.

He felt sick with jealousy. An emotion he had never felt in his life.

It was all so wrong – he should never have gotten involved. *Never*. She was playing him for a sucker . . . She was his *wife*. His *wife*. And she was out screwing another man.

It was to have been such a great evening. A celebration. He had completed a terrific deal that afternoon for his English comedy actor to star in a top movie. It proved to him that his magic touch wasn't confined to Dallas.

He had booked a table at the Bistro to celebrate. And he had planned to tell Dallas about the house he had rented in Acapulco, and also that he was delighted with the fact that she wanted to have a baby, and having thought about it decided that they could definitely slot it into their schedule.

So where was she?

She was impulsive. Maybe she had just moved out. They hadn't argued, but he was only too painfully aware that she wasn't happy.

Maybe she had had an accident. But she was a good driver.

He was getting dumped sooner than he had thought.

He heard her car in the drive, and sat down trying to compose himself. Stay cool. Stay calm. See what she had to say.

She entered the house, flopped down in a chair and stared into space. She seemed almost unaware of his existence.

'You're home,' he stated, rather unnecessarily in the circumstances.

She looked dishevelled. Her long hair mussed, her face tired and drawn. Some fuck, he thought, some good fuck. He didn't want to think it, but the thought was there and refused to go.

'Where have you been?' he asked, although if he knew her at all he knew he should leave her alone.

She glanced at him with indifference. 'Out,' she replied.

'Where?' he asked pointedly.

'Driving.'

'Driving where?'

'Why don't you leave me alone?'

'Why don't you tell me where you were?'

'Why don't you fuck off?'

He stood up. 'I guess it's no use my asking who he is.'

She didn't reply, just looked at him coldly.

He shrugged, trying to conceal the hurt he felt. 'You wouldn't listen to me. I told you this would happen. I knew it . . .'

She sighed. 'You're wrong.'

'I'll do whatever you want. But let's get out of it now – with dignity – without the screaming and accusations. Without the shit I want to throw at you.'

'Whatever you want, Cody.'

'I don't want to call you names . . .'

'So don't.'

Her apparent indifference infuriated him. He walked slowly, stiffly, to the door. 'I'll stay at a hotel tonight.'

She didn't stop him. She sat in the chair and stared into space, and he left before the tears slid silently down her face.

Once in his car Cody immediately regretted leaving. Hasty – much too hasty. So anxious to get out before she said things he didn't want to hear. Anxious to preserve his dignity – sanity.

So she had been with another man – so big deal. It was him she had come back to. But he didn't want to be in that position. The jealous husband, the schmuck waiting at home for the crumbs of her company.

He would get out now. Immediately. A quickie divorce. And then things could go back to the way they were. Friendship. Business. So he wouldn't have her body, but he wouldn't get torn to shreds every time someone else did. Or would he?

He drove furiously along the strip. Maybe he should have listened to what she had to say. Who was he kidding? She had had nothing to say. She acted as if he didn't exist, didn't matter. He had tried to forget about her past – what little she had told him of it. So she had been a whore – but that was a long time ago. And she had stopped being a whore. Whore – what a beautiful old-fashioned word – probably one of his mother's favourites. But could he ever forget?

Why the hell had she ever told him? He slammed his foot down hard on the accelerator.

He had nowhere to go. He had given up his apartment. Going to his mother's was out. A hotel was too depressing a thought.

Feeling sorry for himself he headed in the direction of Connie's apartment. A little sympathy was the order of the day.

Dallas remembered the good times.

The beginning of her relationship with Bobbie. The fun. The laughs. Of course hooking wasn't everyone's idea of having a terrific time – but in Miami with Bobbie it hadn't been *bad*. Just another way to make some bread. And they had had each other. The first *real* relationship Dallas had ever experienced. The first person who gave a shit.

Bobbie had taught her to cook, dance, fuck, laugh. Bobbie had taught her how to look after herself, protect herself, get herself through the day.

And then had come the old man in the motel, the trip to LA, and the sudden disintegration of everything that was fun.

And the drugs. Bobbie had been fairly straight until LA. Tinsel city had scored again. Shit! It could have been *her* that had gotten hooked on drugs. There but for the grace of Ed Kurlnik . . .

Dallas shuddered, hugged her knees to her chest.

She thought of Bobbie's skinny pathetic body lying on the floor of the shabby room. The two animals who had beaten her up. They should be in jail . . . But there was no one to put the finger on them – only her – and she knew enough not to get involved. Forget *that* scene.

It was funny – she should be glad that Bobbie was dead. She should be out celebrating – after all, it was the perfect solution. And yet she could only feel sorrow. A sense of loss. Ridiculous really – but that's the way it was.

Vaguely she remembered Cody walking out. Poor Cody – he thought she had been with another man. If only he knew . . . If only she could have confided in him . . .

But it was better this way. Much better.

She was a loner, she didn't need anyone. Better that Cody should realize this. Besides, his opinion of her was the lowest. He had immediately assumed she had been with another man . . .

Screw him . . . Tomorrow she would give him the good news that they weren't really married anyway. She had pretended to forget, but she had known all along that she still had a husband in Miami.

'What in heck do you think you *want*?' questioned Connie, keeping Cody firmly in place by way of a chain lock on the door.

'Let me in and I'll tell you,' he replied, feeling like an unwelcome door-to-door salesman.

Connie stood her ground. 'Our mutual shrink tells me that you treat me like dirt. He says that you are a user and that I should throw you out of my life. Period.'

'Did you tell him my name?' asked Cody, alarmed at losing face with his analyst.

'Certainly not. You – better than anyone – should know we deal only with initials. And by the way, why haven't you been to see him for three weeks?'

'How do you know that?'

'I just know . . . You should go see him, you've got problems. Any man who treats women as sexual objects needs help.'

'*Me*?'

'Yes, you. How do you think you've treated me?'

A woman emerged from the apartment opposite and stared.

'Let me in, Connie,' whispered Cody urgently.

'No. I'm sorry – but I'm a person. A human being. I am not here for your sexual convenience.' She started to close the door.

'*But I don't want sex!*'

Connie gave him a superior smile. 'Of course you don't,' she said understandingly, and slammed the door shut.

The woman opposite cackled, and darted back into her apartment before Cody could think of a suitable remark to throw in her direction.

He had been seeing Connie on and off for two years. Why the sudden cold shoulder? Didn't she know he was going to be rich and powerful? Didn't she care?

He knew who would care. Her name sprung to mind immediately. Carol Cameron would not close any doors in his face. She would throw everything open – everything.

He drove to the nearest bar – looked her up in the phone book – somehow he had known she would be listed – and drove right over to her address.

She answered the door of her small house after a long pause. Clad in shorts and a T-shirt over very obviously nothing, she looked younger than she had in his office. She was not wearing make-up, that was why. And her hair was more tousled and natural-looking, not teased into lacquered curls.

'Cody!' she exclaimed. 'Why didn't you call? I look a mess.'

'You look lovely.'

'Gee, thanks.'

'I'm accepting your offer of a drink.'

'That's marvellous. Just come in, settle yourself down – I've just got to take care of a few things.' She led him into a pink living room strewn with fluffy toy animals. 'What can I fix you?'

'Vodka.' He glanced around. Pictures of Carol lined the walls. A nude portrait had place of honour.

'I won't be a minute,' she said, 'just make yourself comfortable.'

'I'm not interrupting anything?'

She giggled. 'Nothing I can't finish at another time.'

She left the room and he could hear a whispered conversation, then a few minutes later a door slammed. Goodbye boyfriend. Don't kid yourself it's on account of your irresistible sex appeal, Cody, my boy. The fact is most girls are career girls – and career comes first.

He flipped through some magazines. They were full of pictures of Carol in various forms of undress.

She was taking a long time. He glanced at his watch.

Why had he come here anyway?

A little company, a little warmth. Who was he kidding? He wanted to get laid. He wanted to feed his bruised ego.

'Hello,' said a childish voice. Carol stood in the doorway, posing. Her face was a mask of make-up. Her hair (or was it a wig?) carefully curled.

She wore very high-heeled furry pink mules, pink frilly panties with a strategic open heart on the front revealing bleached pubic hair. And a frilled pink bra with an open heart dead centre both sides allowing amazing nipples to point threateningly at him.

'You are going to handle me, aren't you?' she lisped. 'Baby *wants* to be handled by you.'

Yes. He was going to handle her. But not in the way *she* expected.

Oh God, if his mother could see him now!

He stood up. Decadent Hollywood here I come!!

forty-eight

The rest did Al more good than Paul could have hoped for. They went to ground in an Arizona ranch house that did not even have television. There was just Al, himself, Luke, and a Mexican couple who looked after the house.

Al spent his days soaking up the sun by the swimming pool, and occasionally going riding. There was tennis and squash, billiards and table tennis. The house was completely cut off with only one telephone for emergencies. Paul had borrowed it from a millionaire who occasionally liked to get back to the simple life. It wasn't that simple, but it *was* completely isolated.

Edna had flown back to England along with a reluctant Evan.

Melanie had been a problem, but Paul had solved that by allowing her a two-week vacation in New York by herself before flying home. 'It will be too boring for you to stay here,' he had explained. She hadn't argued.

Bernie had flown on to Los Angeles to set everything up. Al would now do two concerts there – then a special charity event in Las Vegas – and then they would take the plane on to South America where Al was getting a million dollars for just two concerts. It had been an offer that Paul could not refuse. And it would more than compensate for the lost revenue of the cancelled shows.

So Al was drying out. No booze. No drugs. No women.

Sun. Exercise. Healthy food. Rest.

He had lost weight, gained a suntan, and looked and felt good.

Meanwhile 'Bad Black Alice' remained at number one with a bullet. And the album – 'Al is King' – was fighting it out for the number one spot with Rod Stewart.

A new group had been hired to replace 'The Promises'. Three black girls who called themselves 'Hot Fudge'. Paul had flown to Los Angeles to see them, and signed them on the spot. They were sisters, and their mother travelled with them, so Paul foresaw no big problem there. They were also sensational on stage – dynamic, fresh and sexy.

Everyone had been upset by Nellie's death. Al more than anyone. He had told Paul about that fateful afternoon. 'I never knew she *cared*,' he explained, 'if I had known I'd never have gone near her. I thought she just wanted some laughs.'

'Sure,' Paul agreed. But privately he thought how anyone with half an eye could see that Nellie was besotted. The fact was that Al never noticed anyone's feelings except his own.

Paul had called Linda the very moment that Melanie was on a plane. But she never seemed to answer her phone. All he could get was the answering service, and after five calls where he left his name and number it occurred to him that she had no intention of calling him back. At first he was angry—What right did she have to do this to him? But gradually he realized that she had every right. There were no ties between them. She was a free agent.

He suffered in silence. Brooding about what she was doing, who she was seeing, who she was sleeping with . . .

Al didn't even bother to ask where she was. But then Al didn't even begin to understand what a real relationship was all about.

After three weeks they were ready to move on. Paul had never seen his brother look so good – which was just as well because Bernie had lined up a gruelling schedule of television appearances, press interviews, and parties.

It was back to the grind. The glare of the spotlight.

Was Al ready?

He was as ready as he'd ever be.

'Got a cigarette?' asked Linda.

She was in Rik's depressing small apartment, in Rik's lumpy bed, having just eaten Rik's over-active and engorged penis.

'No smoking, honey, you promised.' He lay on his back, arms propped behind his head, a pleased smile on his face.

'I want a cigarette!' she snapped.

'All right, all right.' He leaned over her and reached under the bed producing a packet of filter tips. It was *his* idea that she give up smoking, certainly not hers.

He lit the cigarette for her, placed it in her mouth. 'Bad for you,' he admonished.

She drew deeply, inhaling the delicious poison into her lungs. She glanced at Rik. He was back in his supine position, still smiling.

He was beautiful – but God he was boring! She had been seeing him for three weeks on a regular basis, and he was driving her nuts!

She had thought that a good steady screwing would take her mind off Paul. But she had been wrong.

She got out of bed and started to dress.

'Where are you going?' asked Rik, the smile vanishing from his face.

'I feel like a walk.'

'I'll get dressed.'

'Alone.'

'You promised you'd stay the whole night.'

'I can't.'

'But you promised.'

'Listen Rik, I don't think that we had better see each other again.'

'Whaaat?'

'For a while anyway.'

He leaped off the bed and held her firmly by the shoulders. 'Why?' he pleaded. 'What have I done?'

She shook free. 'It's nothing you've done, it's just that,' she shrugged, 'I don't know, I'm beginning to feel hemmed in, like trapped.'

His lips tightened. 'That's ridiculous.'

'It may seem ridiculous to you, but it's the way I feel.'

He turned his back on her. 'Why didn't you tell me earlier?'

'Earlier when?'

'Before we made love.'

'What difference does *that* make?'

'It makes a lot of difference.'

She tried to make light of it. 'Hey listen, kid, I never turn a great lay down!'

His hurt face made her realize she hadn't said the right thing.

'I'll call you, Rik,' she said, 'in a day or two.'

He stared at her. How come she was using all his lines?

'You never call when you say you will,' he muttered.

She smiled brightly. 'This time will be different, you'll see.' And before he could object she was out of his apartment, on the street, hailing a cab, and making some decisions.

Back in England, back at her house, a cowed and silent Evan by her side, Edna did something she had been wanting to do for years. She fired the cook, the maid, and with the most pleasure of all – Nelson.

He was not easy to get rid of. He leered at her and said, 'I'll be seeing Mr King about it when he gets back.'

'No,' replied Edna, 'you're seeing me now, and I'm telling you that I'd like you to leave – today.'

Nelson narrowed mean eyes. 'So that's the way it is, then. Pushed out without so much as a by your leave.'

'I'll pay you two weeks' money,' said Edna firmly.

'That's not enough,' Nelson grumbled, 'rich people pushing us poor around. You think with money you can do what you want.'

'Is four weeks' wages enough?' questioned Edna.

'Make it six, missus. That's only fair.'

'All right.' She would have agreed to anything to get him off the premises.

She counted out the money and Nelson snatched it greedily. 'You'll be alone, then, all alone 'til the master gets back.'

'Thank you, Nelson,' she said brusquely, dismissing him.

Insolently he picked at his nose. 'I'll have to pack up me things,' he said, 'you don't mind that, do you?'

She turned away, filled with relief that she had been able to fire him. 'That will be all right,' she replied curtly, 'but please make it fast.'

He sniggered. 'Yes, *m'am*,' and ambled off down the garden muttering to himself.

She had done it! Soon she would be alone in the house. *Her* house. She could cook meals without feeling like an intruder. She could clean her own furniture, dust her own shelves. She could swim in the pool without that horrible man leering at her. She could tend to the garden, grow her own vegetables. And if Al didn't like it when he came back . . . Well, he would just have to lump it. She was going to do what made *her* happy for a change.

Upstairs Evan lay on his bed, his eyes open and unseeing. If he hadn't run off . . . If he had been there when she needed him . . . *He* was to blame for Nellie's death. It was *his* fault.

Tears trickled down his face, weaving their way through his acned skin.

He didn't know what to do. He just didn't know . . .

Jetting into Los Angeles was a trip unto itself. The California faction of the Al King fan club were out in force. The police held the crowds back whilst he was transferred to the obligatory long black limousine.

'Welcome Welcome Welcome!' screamed the fans, holding their banners of undying love aloft.

A female journalist of much clout was waiting in his limo for a taped radio interview. The programme was syndicated all over America.

Bernie Suntan was on hand looking fat and sleek and happy. This was *his* town. Here, he was in control. He handed Al a typed list of top Hollywood hostesses who all wished to give parties in his honour. In the Hollywood social circles giving parties for visiting celebrities was *the* thing to do – whether you knew them or not. They were all vying to do the honours for Al.

*

Al ticked off Doris Andrews – because he had always loved her movies; and Karmen Rush – because she was *the* female superstar of the moment, and while not exactly beautiful, she had a charisma matched only by her sensationally powerful voice. He didn't fancy either of them, but more important he was a fan of them both.

Bernie was well pleased with Al's choice – national coverage on both events would be guaranteed. Karmen Rush and her entourage had already requested tickets for both of Al's concerts.

The stars were turning out in legion to see Al, and Bernie was delighted to see how well he looked. In Tucson he had been puffy-faced, tired, and drawn-looking. The transformation was remarkable.

Linda arrived in Los Angeles on the same day, although she wasn't aware of that fact until later when she saw all the press and television coverage. She had not planned it this way. In fact she had not planned anything. She had just decided that she had to get out of New York for a while – so she had packed a few clothes, her cameras, and here she was. Free. She wanted to stay that way. Just because Paul was in the same town didn't mean she had to see him.

She called Dallas at the studio, who insisted that she come and stay with her.

'My plan is to get a little apartment,' Linda told her. 'But while I'm looking, your place would be just wonderful.'

'Come by the studio and pick up the key,' Dallas said, 'I'll leave it at the main gate.'

As soon as he was settled in his bungalow at the Beverly Hills Hotel Al handed Paul a slip of paper. 'Call her,' he said.

Paul looked at the number blankly, 'Call who?'

'Dallas.'

'Dallas?'

'You going deaf?'

'I thought . . .'

'You thought what?'

'Goddammit, Al, you know what. She always gives you a hard time. You need all that crap?'

'I'll decide what I need.'

'Anyway, she's a heavy number now. You can't pick up a magazine or paper without finding her picture or a story.'

'So?'

'Well . . .' Paul hesitated, then plunged ahead. 'She didn't want to know about you before. What makes you think . . . ?'

'Just call her. Your opinions I can do without. I pay you to do – not think.'

'You *pay* me?'

'Don't split hairs,' snapped Al in an irritable fashion. 'Call her, tell her I'd like her to be my guest at the concert tomorrow.'

'Sure, boss,' drawled Paul sarcastically. They had had three weeks of peace and rest. Al had actually started to behave like a human being. Now he was back to his old self. Christ almighty! To say that he *paid* him – it was an insult. Maybe Al thought that he could stroll onto the street and just hire anyone who could do the job that he did. Why, without him, Al would have drowned in his own juices long ago.

When this tour was finished they were going to have to get some things straight. Either his brother treated him with some respect or it was *over*.

Paul left the bungalow, screwed the piece of paper up with the phone number on and threw it into the bushes. It was pointless to call anyway. She would only turn Al down. She always did.

Besides, Bernie had two thick black books that were going to keep Al more than busy.

forty-nine

Dallas had slept badly with the help of two seconal – which *hadn't* helped.

She got up an hour before she was due at the studio and packed up all of Cody's things. Two suitcases. Most of his personal stuff he kept at his mother's. Thank God he hadn't *told* his mother.

She was so relieved it was over almost before it had begun. If Cody was agreeable they could just continue the way they were before. It had been *her* mistake. She didn't love him – whatever love was. And she certainly couldn't put up with the sex – no way.

She swam, fixed orange juice and toast, and tried to blank the whole Bobbie business out of her mind.

She couldn't. She kept on seeing the dingy little room, Bobbie lying on the floor . . .

If only she could arrange a decent funeral, at least send flowers. But to get involved was hopeless, and she knew it.

The phone rang just as she was leaving. It was Cody.

'I'm sorry, I'm sorry, I'm sorry,' he said, 'I was suspicious, jealous, I didn't wait for you to explain, I ...'

She cut in. 'You were right, Cody, you called the shots, I lived up to your non-expectations. I guess it's the way I am.'

'But I didn't ...'

'Look – we have to talk. Can you come by the studio for lunch?'

He agreed to meet her. She sighed, it wasn't going to be exactly easy telling him that they were never married, that it was all a put-on. Maybe he would be relieved ... She was.

Carol Cameron slept nude, wearing only a black sleep mask and massive ear plugs. If a rapist broke in she would probably never even know he was there!

Cody slid from her king-size bed early in the morning, and fixed himself coffee in her chintzy kitchen. He was exhausted. He had never known making love could be so *energetic*. If they ever gave out an Oscar for energy and initiative in the sexual stakes Carol Cameron would be sure to win!

He wondered what she thought of him. Good? Bad? Indifferent? Excellent?

He remembered the first girl he had ever slept with. A secretary (he had a history of secretaries!) several years older than himself – he had been twenty – a late starter due to his mother monitoring his every move. Anyway, after the big bad deed he had waited patiently for her verdict, but she hadn't said anything, until finally he was forced to ask. 'How was I?' 'Adequate,' she had replied with a yawn.

Adequate! The word had stayed with him all his life.

Did Carol Cameron think of him as 'adequate'? He thought not, remembering the compliments she had showered upon him. 'Enormous!' (untrue) 'Never seen anything like it!' (unlikely) 'You're the best!' (could be true, but with her track record probably not).

Hmmm ...

In the clear light of morning he was sorry that he had come here. He was a married man, and whatever Dallas had done did not give him the right to rush out and do it too.

Now Carol Cameron would put the word around that he was an easy lay – especially when he told her he wasn't going to handle her. Maybe she would put the word around that he was enormous and he could spend the rest of his life disproving it ...

What was he thinking of? He had a wife. Dallas had never

commented on his sexual prowess at all. She was always very silent and undemonstrative. She seemed to have enjoyed it more the very first time when he had been unable to get it up for more than a few seconds.

Of course with her previous record, sex was probably not the ultimate turn-on. But he had hoped to change all that. Maybe other guys were changing it every day. Maybe she could only get it on with big black studs . . . Group scenes . . .

He mustn't think like that.

He picked up the phone and called her.

'Cut!' shouted Chuck. 'Okay – print it. Let's break for lunch.'

'You want to have lunch with us?' Kiki asked Dallas.

'No thanks. Cody should be here – oh, there he is.' She strode over to him. 'Hi.'

He kissed her chastely on the cheek. 'Hi.'

They walked in silence to her dressing-room. He sat on a chair while she unzipped herself out of the silver track suit she had been wearing for the scene.

He marvelled at her body as he always did. The long legs, finely-muscled stomach, magnificent breasts. She shrugged her way into a loose kimono and lit a cigarette.

'I've got a confession,' she said, 'I think as my almost husband you should know.'

He was confused. 'What are you talking about?'

'Us. We were the marriage that never was.'

'Huh?'

'We were never married. I wasn't quite straight with you – you see I already have a husband.'

'Is this some kind of joke? If it is I don't think it's very funny.'

'It's no joke, Cody. I was married at seventeen to a guy in Miami. We never got divorced. So you see . . .'

He stood up knowing that his skin was turning a dull red with anger. 'I see.'

She stood up too. 'It's best this way. No hassles. You were right, I should have listened to you.'

He stared at her. God, she was beautiful. But God she was a bitch. Didn't she realize she had just cut off his balls?

'It can all be like it was before,' she was saying, 'business and friends.'

Now she was handing them back to him neatly packaged, the way *she* wanted it.

'I packed up all your things – maybe you could collect them

this afternoon before I get back. I don't think we should string things out.'

'No, of course not,' he said tightly. He wanted to hit her, strike out. But he had never hit a woman in his life, and besides – she was still Dallas – and he still loved her.

She kissed him lightly on the cheek. 'I'm sorry I lied to you. I don't why I did – but I guess you understand.'

Oh sure. He was a schmuck, wasn't he? Schmucks always understood.

'Do you want any lunch?' she was asking him casually.

Don't tell me she was going to eat at a time like this? He could throw up all over her.

'No,' he said quickly, 'there's things at the office needing my attention.'

'Well . . .' she stretched. 'Shall I call you tomorrow?'

'Yes, of course.' He just wanted to get *out* of there.

She moved very close to him. 'You're *sure* you understand.'

He forced a laugh. 'What's to understand?'

He drove around in a daze for two hours afterwards, finally stopping at a drive-in for a coffee. He still couldn't face eating.

The coffee rumbled uncomfortably around in his stomach. He felt sick. He had to find a hotel – it was either that or back to the comforting Miss Cameron. He couldn't face the office.

He drove up to the house to collect his suitcases which Dallas had so thoughtfully packed for him. Boy – when she wanted somebody out there was no hanging about. But he couldn't hate her. He had known this would happen – not quite so soon perhaps – but eventually.

Why would a girl like Dallas want to be married to a guy like him? He couldn't think of one good reason, and he realized it was time to go back to his analyst for a fast course of self-esteem.

Linda picked up the key and drove her rented Mercury up to Dallas' house. The sun was shining. The Californian disc jockey blathered on about nothing on the radio. The attendant in the supermarket she had stopped at had given her a ripe juicy cantaloupe as a gift along with the big bag of groceries she had bought.

Los Angeles was a nice city. Warm and friendly. Fun. She wanted to have fun, she had been working much too hard. She was planning to relax, take it easy, photograph a few movie stars.

A man was putting suitcases in a car outside the house, and she recognized him as Cody Hills. God, she hoped he wasn't moving out on *her* account.

314

She honked the horn. 'Hello there,' she shouted.

He turned to look at her. Blank, No recognition.

'Linda Cosmo, Dallas' friend,' she said, jumping out of the car.

'Oh, hi.' He looked glum.

'I'm coming to stay for a few days – just 'til I find an apartment.'

'Good.' He was about as interested as a frog.

'Gorgeous weather,' Linda remarked. She had always had a compulsion to make inane conversation.

He was busy slamming the boot down on his car. He was quite attractive really, a little more hair, lose a few pounds . . . She tried to remember what Dallas had said about him – something about him being nice . . . too nice . . . Was there such a thing as a man who was too nice?

As she was thinking, she was carrying the groceries from the car, trying to manage her large Gucci hold-all, and all of her camera equipment. It didn't work. She tripped and dropped everything. Oranges and apples were rolling about wherewhere. A yoghurt lost its top and spilled out. A carton of eggs smashed.

'Shit!' she exclaimed.

Cody got out of his car. He had been just about to drive off.

'You want me to help you,' he stated.

'I want you to help me,' she agreed.

He looked at her properly for the first time. She had the most direct, deep, interesting eyes. She looked like the sort of woman you could *talk* to.

She smiled. He smiled back.

'You chase the oranges,' she said, 'and I'll get the eggs before they turn into an omelette!'

Suddenly he was very, very hungry.

Doris Andrews' well modulated nasal twang said, 'I want you to come to a party I am having on Saturday night. A very *special* party.'

Dallas held the phone away from her ear and made a face. She had just walked into the house and been caught by the phone ringing. She was grimacing at Linda who was waiting to greet her.

'Hey – listen – I really *hate* parties,' Dallas said.

Doris chuckled. 'I know just how you feel, dear. But there are certain parties you have to be seen at, and I'm sure you'll agree that mine is one of them.'

'I don't know . . .'

'You're not turning me down are you?' chided Doris softly.

'It's just that . . .'

'I won't take no for an answer, dear. Nor will Lew. There will be many important people here, people you should meet.'

'OK,' Dallas agreed reluctantly, 'but I have a houseguest. Is it all right if I bring her?'

'Is she pretty?'

'Not *your* kind of pretty!'

'Dallas! What we discussed was between us.'

'I know, I know, I was only kidding. Can I bring her?'

'Of course. What's her name?'

'Linda Cosmo.'

'Fine. Placement, you know. If she's pretty I'll seat her next to Aarron, with you on the other side. Oh, by the way, the party is for Al King. Lew is trying to get him for a picture. See you Saturday, my dear, between seven and seven thirty. No later.'

Dallas put the phone down.

Linda rushed over, hugged her. 'Good to *see* you. Am I a surprise?'

'Tonight is full of surprises,' said Dallas. 'That was Doris Andrews . . .'

'The movie star?'

'Who else? I only get calls from stars now, you know. *Anyway* – party on Saturday night for – guess who?'

'Al King.'

'How did you know?'

Linda shrugged. 'Girlish intuition or some such crap.'

'Are you and Paul . . .'

'Split. Yes. Weeks ago. His wife caught us in bed together. How do you like *that* little scenario?'

'Sounds cosy.'

'*Not* a trip to be recommended.'

Dallas smiled. 'Tell me a trip that is? Are we going to the party?'

Linda shrugged. 'Whatever . . . I don't care . . .'

'We'll go, then,' Dallas decided. She couldn't resist the opportunity of seeing Al King again. Not that he meant anything in her life . . . But what was there to lose?

fifty

Two days of interviews, photographs, television, and work. Rehearsing with 'Hot Fudge'. Ordering some amazing new outfits from Nudies – the renowned Beverly Hills tailor shop. Catching up on all the latest albums – sent over to him with a magnificent stereo music-centre by his record company. Meetings with a producer he wanted to use on his new album.

'I spoke to Dallas and her answer is still no,' Paul lied, 'but has Bernie got some numbers for you! I . . .'

'Forget it,' snapped Al. 'I'm not in the mood.'

Paul had never known a time when Al was 'not in the mood'. Especially after three sexless weeks in Arizona. Especially with a big concert coming up. Why wasn't he demanding a big-breasted dumb blonde? Some rock stars sniffed coke, got high, shot speed, to get it on just before a show. Al's vice had always been a woman. A faceless, big-breasted blonde. Now – in Los Angeles – city of the quintessential ding-a-ling – he didn't want to know. Paul couldn't understand it.

Al had spoken to Edna once a week since her return to England. Short, flat conversations, dealing with the trivia of domesticity. Had the garage sent a man to wax his cars? Did she forward all the tax forms on to the accountant? How was Evan?

Evan was in bad shape. He was in a state of extreme nervous tension, although Edna thought he was his normal surly self, and as part of her new policy left him alone.

His arm was better. His bruises had faded. But he had a new, more pressing problem. Something terrible had happened to him. Something so horrible that he was at his wits end about what to do.

He had a venereal disease.

Oh, he knew what it was all right. He could remember in vivid detail the films they had shown at school during a sex education class. The frightening pictures of a diseased penis – withered, dripping, covered in sores. And of course he remembered the teacher's warning words about impotency and pain and sometimes even death!

God! He had it. He knew he had it. He would probably *die* from it!

He couldn't possibly tell anyone. The shame and embarrassment would be too much to bear. Perhaps dying would be the best thing.

He sat in his room and brooded over his symptoms which seemed to get worse. If he did die his mother would surely find out. If only his father was home . . . He would understand. He might even be sympathetic. He would certainly help him.

Three and a half weeks of pain culminated in the fact that he couldn't even pee any more without going through the most excruciating agony. That decided him. He forged his mother's signature on a cheque, cashed it – there was no problem as they knew him at the bank. He then told Edna a friend had invited him to stay in Scotland for a few days, hiked out to London Airport, and got on the first available flight to Los Angeles. It was the first time in his life he had gone to his father for help.

The concert at the famous Hollywood Bowl was a sell-out.

'Every fuckin' celebrity in town 'bin fighting for tickets,' exclaimed Bernie happily, 'don't know how I'm squeezing 'em all in. You think I'm gonna turn away Streisand and Beatty? Best fuckin' turn-out this city's seen for a long time. Is Al in good shape?'

'He's sober, straight – don't know what's the matter with him,' Paul replied. 'I've never seen him put on such a low profile.'

'Don't knock it,' urged Bernie. 'We don't need another Tucson scene. I got a truckload of photographers grabbing my balls for a piece of the action tomorrow. You think Al would mind if *Newsweek* came in the helicopter?'

'Ask him.'

'Come on, Paul, *you* ask him. *I* can't talk to him – nobody can talk to him any more except you.'

Paul hadn't realized it before, but what Bernie said was true. Al had retreated into a non-communicative state with everyone. Maybe it had been a whole better scene when he was drinking – maybe not.

'I'll ask him,' said Paul. 'If there's room I'm sure he'll say yes.'

'There'll be room,' wheezed Bernie. 'Now about tonight, I've arranged for the car to pick you up six forty-five. I think as guest of honour Al should arrive early. Doris Andrews won't have any photographers in the house – except *Women's Wear Daily* – but she's laying on facilities for the press outside – and if her guests don't mind having their picture taken that's straight with her. She's not a bad broad – the old man's a pain in the ass . . .'

'I know,' interrupted Paul, 'I had a meeting with him yesterday.'

'Anything exciting?'

'He's got a property he wants Al to do.'

'Shall I leak it?'

'Hold back, Bernie. I don't know – Al's not in the mood for making decisions. He's going to read the script – I'll let you know the strength in a day or two.'

'Right on. Karmen Rush's boyfriend bin buggin the shit outta me 'bout *their* party for Al tomorrow. Should be some wild gig.'

Paul nodded. 'As long as they know it's got to be after the concert.'

'Sure they know. They're all gonna *be* at the show.' Bernie smirked with pleasure. Had he done a job on Al. His city – *his* fuckin' town – and he had made Al a hero. Tonight the Doris Andrews/Lew Margolis bash would have the crême de la crême of Hollywood society. The older group. A mixture of the A and B groups – the elite Beverly Hills moneyed talent. The respectable movie stars and their suitable partners. The moguls and their wives, with a beautiful girl or two thrown in for added flavour.

The Karmen Rush party after the show tomorrow would be pure freaksville. The young side of Hollywood. The new Hollywood. Millionaire rock stars and their old ladies. Groupies. Druggies. Models. Designers. Promoters. Hustlers. Porno magazine chiefs. And Girls Girls Girls.

Bernie was looking forward to it. Karmen Rush had made her home in a fantasy mansion on the beach at Malibu. She had started off owning one smallish house, and over the course of five years and much fame had gradually purchased six neighbouring houses and joined them all together making one wide strange incredible mansion. Karmen's house was almost as famous as she was.

Bernie had only ever attended one party there – but it would remain in his mind forever. He had gotten stoned out of his head – the drugs were flowing – and had woken up in a rubber dingy in the *ocean* with a spaced-out starlet!! Fortunately they had not been too far from shore, but he could still summon a shudder at the memory. The ocean for crissakes! What the fuck – that's what living was all about.

'Why are you wearing that?' asked Linda.

Dallas turned in front of the mirror. 'Don't you like it?'

'For a snack at a drive-in it's perfect. But for the party tonight?'

Dallas frowned. 'Why should I get all dressed up? A room full of dirty old men leering all over me – ugh!' She was clad in a huge black mohair sweater over trousers. She had pulled her hair back in a ponytail and scrubbed her face of make-up. 'Do you think I look awful?' she questioned. 'Maybe if I look awful they'll all leave me alone.'

'Kid – *you* could never look awful. If that's your kick for the night do it. I should care. But – and please take this in the way it's meant – isn't being the Mack girl more than your photos all over the magazines? Isn't it creating some sort of image? I mean Aarron Mack might take one look at you tonight – clap himself on the head – and say "holy shit! I made a mistake!" And then you'll be out how many zillions of dollars?'

Dallas couldn't help laughing. 'Very funny. Do you mind hanging around getting drunk or something while I change. It means we'll be late – probably ruin Doris' "placement" – but I guess you're right.'

She inspected her clothes. If she was going to change she may as well do it in style. There was a little white jersey number – a Halston – understated and clinging. She slipped into it – it was no longer understated.

She untied the rubber band holding her hair back, and bending forward brushed it vigorously. Then she sat at the dressing table and smudged kohl round her eyes, gold on her cheeks and eyelids, shiny lip gloss on her mouth. She added emerald earrings – the one gift of Ed Kurlnik's that she had kept – and she was ready.

'Why did I tell you to change?' sighed Linda. 'I looked pretty good before. Now I feel like the poor relation!'

'Nonsense. You look great. I wish *I* had your kind of looks.'

Linda laughed. 'You're such a flatterer.' As it happened she did feel pretty good about the way she looked. Two days in the sun had taken away her New York pallor, and she had gained a few pounds in places where it flattered her. Most women had to diet, but Linda was a natural-born skinny. It didn't bother her – clothes always hung better on thin women – but sometimes she yearned for the kind of curvy body that most men lusted after.

Screw it – men had never been a problem to get. It was marrying them that was the trick. She thought of Paul, tried to blank him out, couldn't, wondered if he would be there tonight. Hoped he would, wished he wouldn't.

'Are we ready?' asked Dallas.

'We're ready. Whose car?'

'You can drive if you don't mind – they'll have parking service.'

They set off. Both beautiful in their individual ways. Dallas, tawny and sunstreaked – all teeth, hair, and body. Linda, slim and chic, darkly arresting.

They were good friends – *close* friends. In the last few days they had both done a lot of talking. Dallas had confided to Linda about Cody – unaware of the fact that Cody had already told Linda – but she didn't give him away. In fact she didn't tell Dallas she had seen him. He had asked her not to, and she had respected his wishes. She could understand and sympathize with both of them.

Who was right?

They had both made a mistake. Cody was a really nice guy. He deserved more than Dallas was prepared to offer him.

And Dallas – well, she was very special. She needed a strong macho man who would control and look after her – and at the same time be father, brother, lover to her. All the men she had missed out on.

Linda wondered if such a man existed. If he did she wouldn't mind grabbing him for herself!

'Al King!' Doris Andrews clutched him by the hand, and memories of a dozen movies flitted through his head. He had grown up with Doris Andrews, along with Tony Curtis, Rock Hudson, Janet Leigh . . . He felt like he knew them all. It was just like meeting an old friend.

'Hello, Doris,' he said, kissing her warmly on both cheeks. He had never wanted to fuck Doris Andrews – Janet Leigh yes – but Doris had always been the big sister type. 'I've wanted to meet you for years,' he continued, treading carefully because he knew how pissed off *he* got when a well-meaning fan said, 'I love you, I've always loved you – ever since I was a little girl.' And it was usually some middle-aged hag who looked ten years older than him. Of course Doris probably wasn't *that* much older than him – seven or eight years top wack – which would make her forty-six or seven. She looked in very good nick.

'It's *my* pleasure, Mr King. I'm so glad you're letting us have this little party for you tonight. I only hope I've managed to include everyone you would enjoy meeting.'

Janet Leigh? What a kick to meet *her*. He looked around, recognizing several world-famous faces. And they had come out to honour *him*. Dressed up in their best glad rags to see *him*.

He nudged Paul. 'Not bad, huh?'

'Where? asked Paul, immediately assuming that Al had seen a girl he fancied. Al's abstinence was beginning to worry him.

'The turn-out, schmuck! Just look around.'

Doris was summoning a waiter. 'What will you have to drink, Mr King?'

'Call me Al, and I'll call you Doris.'

She gave him the famous twinkling perennial virgin smile. 'Lovely! Now – who would you like to meet?'

The boy who took the car said, 'You're late, ladies.' He was about nineteen, with a Ryan O'Neal face and a Burt Reynolds body.

Dallas ignored him. Linda smiled. He smiled back.

'Hey . . . How about . . .'

Dallas dragged Linda inside before he could finish.

'Not bad!' Linda exclaimed.

'They're hanging off the trees in this town,' Dallas drawled laconically. 'Every good-looking stud in America gravitates to LA all ready to become a movie star. Didn't you ever listen to the words of "San Jose"?'

'I knew there was a reason I came here!' Linda said. 'Prime Californian cock!'

'Linda! You're really disgusting.'

'What's disgusting about it? Why shouldn't I be honest? I'm not out to murder anyone – I just want to get nicely laid – by young randy studs. Ain't nothing wrong with *that*.'

Dallas laughed. 'You're incorrigible! It's lucky you never saw Julio.'

'Who's Julio?'

'Diamond's boyfriend. Remember? The male hooker.'

'You *saw* him?'

'Nothing happened. I made an appointment and backed out.'

'*You* would. What was he like?'

'I don't think I'd better tell you.'

Linda licked her lips. 'That good?'

'That good. Even *I* thought so. Hey – come on – we'd better go in – we can't stand in the hall all night – Doris is going to be furious as it is.'

The entire pool area was tented, pink and white candy-striped awnings with fairy lights hanging in little clusters.

Tables surrounded the pool covered in plain pink cloths. Silver and fine glassware glinted at each place setting. There were ten tables seating twelve people per table.

Al was at a table with Doris Andrews on one side of him and Mrs Harmon Lewis on the other. Mrs Harmon Lewis was extremely rich, extremely ugly, and extremely powerful. She was head of one of the largest talent agencies on the coast. She had been married to Harmon Lewis – the famous four foot ten-inch cowboy star of the forties. Since his early demise at the age of thirty – falling off a box while making cinematograph love to a five foot eleven-inch Swedish star – Mrs Lewis had been ena-moured by very short men. She herself was a healthy five foot four inches – but she seemed to get her kicks from wearing the highest possible heels and the shortest possible men. She had managed to propel to fame a five foot one-inch matinée idol, and a five foot nothing comedian. 'There'll never be another Harmon!' was her constant lament. But it did not stop her from looking.

Al, of course, was much too tall to ignite even the smallest flicker of her interest. But he was the star guest, and everyone knew Mrs Harmon Lewis insisted on being seated next to the star guest.

Al, trapped between the two women, decided the time had come to break his boycott on liquor. Fuck it. He felt great, looked great, what harm would it do to go back on the booze? Nellie's death had hit much harder than anyone cared to see. The whole Tucson scene had frightened the shit out of him. Losing control was not his bag. So he had stopped drinking just to prove that he could – and he could – any time he wanted.

He reached for the wine.

Doris – the perfect hostess – immediately gestured for a waiter. 'Changing your mind?' she inquired.

He laughed. Earlier he had told her he didn't drink. 'Why not? That's what minds are for, isn't it?'

Dallas stood at the top of the steps leading to the patio, and gazed down at the beautifully laid-out tables, and the people eating and chatting.

Linda, a step behind her, muttered, 'Talk about making a late entrance...'

'The only kind,' Dallas murmured.

And she was right, because one by one every pair of eyes stopped to look at them, until a hush hung over the gathering – only a momentary hush – but it was enough to make an impact.

Doris came trotting up the stairs. 'You naughty girl!' she hissed. 'You're *so* late. I had nearly given up on you!'

'I'm sorry. Car broke down. Doris, I'd like you to meet my friend, Linda.'

'Hmmm,' absently Doris shook her by the hand. She was more

concerned about her placement. 'I've had to move you around. I couldn't leave Aarron with two empty seats beside him. I've put your friend at Lew's table.'

'That's all right,' Dallas said.

Doris replied somewhat huffily, 'I should hope so. Come, let's sit down.'

Seeing Dallas was like getting an electric charge. Al had forgotten quite how beautiful she actually was. The sensual face framed by the streaked mass of hair. The body in the clinging white dress, with quite obviously nothing underneath. Every man in the place was staring at her.

Al went to stand up as she passed, but stopped himself in time. Let her come to him.

But she didn't. She glided past and sat down at the next table. She did not appear to even notice him.

As luck would have it they were seated almost back to back.

He swivelled round and tapped her on the shoulder. 'Don't you say hello any more?'

She turned and stared at him with her incredible green eyes. 'Hello.'

Doris came back to the table, squeezing between them. Dallas turned her attention back to Aarron Mack, who was toasting her with champagne.

Her thoughts were not on Aarron. They were on Al. It was like chemistry. She was drawn to him like a magnet. As soon as she saw him strange things happened. Things that she could hardly control. Her head felt light, her skin flushed, her stomach knotted into a sort of sick feeling. What the hell *was* it about him?

Aarron said, 'You look beautiful, beautiful. I toast your beauty.'

She lifted her glass and clinked it together with his before swallowing the champagne down.

Behind her she was only too aware of the fact that Al was only inches away.

Lew Margolis was talking business. He did not acknowledge his wife's introduction of Linda as she sat her down at his table.

Linda didn't mind. But she wondered if *he* would mind if he knew it was *she* who had taken the pictures Dallas had shown him. How different he seemed from the man beside Dallas' pool that night. How tempting it would be to say, 'Excuse me, Mr Margolis, but I have seen you in action. Uncensored action!'

The fact that he was talking business with Paul – who hadn't even seen her – did not help matters. She looked around the table. Strangers. Famous strangers. No one was taking the least bit of notice of her.

On one side she recognized a television star of a cop series. On the other a fag screenwriter. They were both engaged in conversations on *their* other sides. Charming! How to be really, really popular! Was there something her best friends had failed to tell her?

She tapped the TV star firmly on the shoulder. She couldn't let Paul see her just sitting there. 'Hi, I'm Linda Cosmo. I was wondering if I might do a photo lay-out on you? I'm out here from New York sort of scouting interesting stories. You may have seen my Al King cover on *People* a few weeks back.'

The TV star had been about to give her a brush. After all, at a party like this who was she? But the words 'photo lay-out' and '*People* cover' changed all that.

'Yeah—' he said enthusiastically, 'I was wondering why they hadn't gotten around to me yet. Yeah – I'd like that. When do you want to do it?'

Linda smiled. Mention publicity to an actor and you were away and running. Pity his reputation as a closet queen went before him.

Dallas could not force one morsel of food down her throat.

Aarron said, 'Are you not feeling good?'

'I'm feeling fine, I'm just not very hungry.'

Aarron summoned the waiter. 'More champagne at this table.'

Dallas drained her glass. Goddamn it – the presence of Al King right behind her was turning her into a nervous drunk!

Aarron patted her on the leg. 'It's good to see you relax.' His hand lingered just that moment too long.

She could not summon the strength to remove it.

'When you come to New York for the launching I have something very serious I wish to discuss with you,' Aarron said, 'you must promise me you will give it your full consideration.'

She nodded. Why the hell had she come to this party anyway?

Turkish coffee was served, with wafer-thin imported peppermints for the ladies, and the best illegal Havana cigars for the men.

A small group of musicians started playing romantic Italian sounds. Room was cleared to make a dance floor.

Mrs Harmon Lewis eyed the short bass player and said, 'Doris gives the best parties in town!'

Al was busy receiving a stream of celebrities who were playing musical chairs – dodging back and forth between tables. He had made a discovery. The worst star fucks of all were the stars themselves! They were positively fighting for a few minutes at his table. *Him*! Al King. Ex-road digger. Ex-Janet Leigh-inspired wanker!

He should be flattered. But he found it funny. And all he really wanted to do was to grab hold of Dallas and get out of there.

'When did you get here?' asked Paul, in a tone of voice which clearly said, 'What the hell are *you* doing here?'

'Few days ago,' smiled Linda. 'Why?'

They were talking across the table which didn't make things easy.

'I tried to call you,' Paul said. 'You never called back.'

'Shall we dance?' the TV star suggested to her.

'Love to,' replied Linda. She shrugged slightly in Paul's direction as if to dismiss his question.

He glared at her.

'Excuse me,' said Dallas, getting up from the table. She was dying to go to the bathroom. She made her way inside the house. The guest powder room was occupied.

She made her way upstairs. Mr and Mrs Margolis' boudoir. Memories! Memories!

She walked into their bathroom. More memories!

The champagne was beginning to make itself felt. She was very lightheaded. She went to the john, brushed her hair, applied more lipgloss.

She didn't hear the door open behind her, she didn't realize anyone was in the room until the smell of *Joy* enveloped her, and Doris had her enclosed in a strong embrace – one hand cupping her left breast.

'I love you, Dallas,' she whispered, her little girl voice strained, 'I love you.'

Dallas only felt revulsion. She tried to push her away, but Doris was strong ,and held on.

'I'm not *into* women,' protested Dallas.

'Oh yes you are!' insisted Doris, 'I'm never wrong – never. Open your legs for me and you'll never want another man.'

'Leave me *alone*!' snapped Dallas. 'Just *leave me alone*.' She shoved Doris off and rushed from the room.

Why didn't anyone ever believe her?

*

'If you can spare the time perhaps *we* can dance,' said Paul coldly.

Linda was just sitting down after dancing with the TV star for the third time.

'If you like,' she said.

He got up and came round to her side of the table. 'Having fun?' he hissed.

She smiled coldly. 'About as much fun as you and your wife have had for the past four weeks.'

'My wife left shortly after you did.'

'How shortly?'

'A matter of days. Haven't you read about what's been going on?'

'I was sorry to hear about Nellie.'

'We all were.'

'Including Al?'

'It wasn't his fault.'

'Sure.'

'There's no need to use that sarcastic tone.'

'Oh sorry. I wasn't aware that I had to check with you about what tone I could use.'

'Don't let's argue. I've missed you. Come on, let's dance.'

Al watched Dallas walking back to her table. Mrs Harmon Lewis was regaling an intimate item of scandal. He wasn't listening. He couldn't give a toss. He gripped Dallas' wrist as she passed.

'You and I are going to dance,' he stated.

'But . . .'

He stood up, 'No buts.' He guided her to the dance floor and, at last, held her. He was immediately hard.

'You remind me of an Arab I once knew . . .' she murmured demurely.

'*An Arab?*'

'Yes. Didn't you know they consider it a great compliment to get a hard-on as soon as they dance with a woman.'

'Who told you that crap?'

'This Arab I knew – Charles something or other. It's like burping after a meal if you enjoy the food.'

'Horse crap!'

'That you have to fart for!'

'Nice. Very nice.' He pulled her even closer. 'Why haven't you returned my calls?'

She looked surprised. 'What calls?'

'Don't give me that . . .'

'Don't give *me* that. You haven't called.'

'No, but Paul has.'

'He hasn't.'

'He hasn't?'

'He hasn't.'

'Sonofabitch! I'll kill him. I've been thinking about this since the South of France. Remember?'

How could she ever forget? 'Nope.'

'Regines. Dancing together.' God she felt marvellous.

'Oh yes – wasn't that shortly before I got the icy treatment?' She tried to edge away from his persistently hard body.

'Who's talking about icy treatment? What about the time I called you from Chicago?' He pulled her firmly towards him.

'You're holding me too tight. I can't breathe.'

He released her slightly. 'Why don't we split from this boring party?'

'And do what?'

'What do you think?'

'Oh, no!'

'Oh no why not?'

'Because I do not want to.' Liar! Liar! For the first time in her life she did.

He shrugged. 'We can do what you want. Drive to the beach, grab a hot dog, take in a strip show, buy some new sounds at an all-night record shop.'

'OK.'

'OK what?'

'OK to everything. It sounds like fun.'

He laughed. 'You'd really sooner do all that than ...'

'Yes!'

'What are we waiting for then?'

'You can't leave.'

'Why not?'

'You know why not. You're the guest of honour.'

'So what? I don't know any of these people, and what's more I don't think I want to.'

Out of the corner of her eye Dallas saw Doris emerge from the house. She seemed completely recovered from the incident in her bathroom. She was smiling and nodding. Lew was sitting at a table with his cronies. Dallas was thankful not to have had to have talked to him.

'I can't leave Linda,' Dallas said.

328

'Linda's all right.' Al indicated that she was dancing with Paul. 'Why don't we ask them to come with us ?'

'Whatever you want.'

'You're being very nice tonight. Whatever *I* want. I thought it was always a question of what *you* want.'

'If it was a question of what *I* wanted we'd be in a bed somewhere screwing our . . .'

'No way.'

He smiled, enjoying her company, enjoying the thought of what he knew would happen later. He threw up his hands in mock despair. 'I'm not arguing!'

She laughed, happy for the first time in weeks. 'You'd better not!'

Giggling and laughing they collapsed in the back of Al's limousine.

'What did she *say* ?' Dallas asked again.

'She said, "Mr King – you are the rudest man I have ever met." Her eyes filled with tears – and I said, "Darlin' I've got a headache, what can I do ?" And *she* said, "You can stay, you prick !" I nearly fell over. Doris Andrews using language like that. Disgusting!'

Dallas giggled. 'I could tell you worse things about Miss Andrews than that.'

'You could ? Go on – tell.'

'I can't.' She indicated Luke, who was driving the car. 'It's secret.' She felt extremely lightheaded, almost carefree for once in her life.

'Where to first ?' asked Al.

'You promised the beach.'

'You heard the lady, Luke. The beach it is.'

'What about Paul and Linda ?'

'I said we'd meet them in an hour at Pips. He wanted to square things away with old man Margolis. You know Paul – business first.'

'I didn't get a chance to talk to Linda. I was so busy sneaking out before Aarron grabbed me – was everything back to normal with her and Paul ?'

'Didn't ask.'

'You're so concerned.'

'I'm concerned with being alone with you. Anyway – Paul lied to me. He told me he'd called you. Who the fuck does he think he's playing games with ?'

'Maybe he thought he was doing you a favour.'

'I'll pick my own favours.' He took her hand and held it. When was the last time he had held a girl's *hand*? When was the last time he had bothered to *talk* to a girl? He was enjoying every goddamn minute of it.

The car sped silently down the winding curves of Sunset.

'What about some music?' Al asked. 'Who would you like to hear?'

'Bobby Womack,' Dallas replied.

'*Bobby Womack*! How about Al King?'

'Bobby Womack please. Or Rod Stewart. Or David Ruffin. Or . . .'

He silenced her with a kiss. Burying his hands in her mane of hair. Holding her head so that she couldn't move.

He could not remember the last time he had kissed a girl. He was Al King. He did not need the preliminaries. It was either fuck or out.

Kissing Dallas was more exciting than any of the dumb bimbos he had screwed.

He was exploring her mouth with his tongue. Wow – he had forgotten what fun kissing could be. He was so horny he could have come there and then.

At the beginning she had returned the kiss, but now she was pushing him away.

'I want you,' he muttered. 'I want you . . .'

She leaned back in the seat, gazed out of the window. 'No,' she said.

He reached for her magnificent breasts. He could see her nipples were hard through the thin material of her dress.

She slapped his hand away. 'Forget it!' she snapped.

'What's the matter?' he asked in a puzzled voice.

'Do I have to have a reason for not wanting you? Or is it part of the ride to have sex with the great Al King if he takes you in his car?'

'I thought you felt the same way I did.'

'You thought wrong.'

They sat in silence for a few minutes, then Al said, 'Luke, we got any Womack tapes?'

Silently Luke slotted the 'Home Is Where The Heart Is' tape into the machine, and the sexy voice of Bobby Womack serenaded them with 'How Long'.

'OK?' demanded Al.

'Terrific' replied Dallas.

He took her hand again, and they listened quietly to the music which was assaulting them from all four speakers.

Nearing the coastal road Al spotted a drive-in. 'Hot dog time?'

Dallas replied, 'It's on our list, isn't it? Plenty of relish.'

'Luke – two hot dogs – one ketchup – one relish.'

Luke swerved the big car into a parking bay, and got out.

'What do you want to do at the beach?' Al asked.

'Can we take a walk along the seashore?'

'We can do whatever you want.'

Luke returned with the hot dogs and they munched them hungrily.

'Been reading about you,' Al said. 'It's all happening, huh? Long way from that old guy you were with in the South of France.'

'That old guy is one of the richest men in America.'

'Is that why you were with him?'

'How's your wife?'

'What's my wife got to do with this conversation?'

'The same as my old guy – exactly nothing.'

Al laughed. What a change to find a woman who answered him back. She hadn't even said yes the first time. Of course she would the second time – but that was only to be expected.

Dallas breathed deeply. She was with him. It was nice. It was fun. But it was all a crock of shit. He was just another superstar on the make. All he wanted was her body. All he wanted was to add her to his list. He was a married man – at the most it would be a few nights of good times. Who needed that? She certainly didn't. So what was she doing with him? She couldn't explain it.

They walked along the beach hand in hand. Dallas had taken off her shoes, and Al had rolled up his trousers. They talked about inconsequential things. A television show they both liked. A book Dallas thought he might be interested in reading.

'Hey – why don't we swim?' Al suggested.

'You're kidding – I'd feel like that girl in *Jaws!*'

'Come on, it would be great. Look at those waves.'

'*You* swim.'

'Is that a challenge?'

'Go ahead.'

'Hold this,' he handed her his jacket, stripped off his shirt, took off his trousers. The hell with it – he stepped out of his Y-fronts. Let her see the treat he had in store for her.

She didn't bother to look, just said, 'Be careful, I'm not very good at mouth to mouth resuscitation!'

He ran into the dark sea, ducked under a huge wave, and was swimming strongly out to the calmer waters. He trod water and looked to shore. She was standing there holding his clothes. 'Come in,' he shouted. 'It's like a warm bath.'

She waved. She couldn't hear him.

Dallas sat down on the sand. Why – when he kissed her – had she not shoved him away immediately? Why had she dissolved into soft mushy pieces? Why had she wanted him with a passion she had never felt in her life before? It had taken every bit of will power she possessed to push him away. How come he was invading her feelings?

In the distance she watched him swimming back to the beach, and come staggering out of the sea. He ran towards her. 'It's freezing when you get out,' he laughed. 'Real brass monkey time! Hey – can you run up to the car and see if Luke's got a towel or blanket or something I can dry myself with.'

She did as he asked, and the impassive Luke gave her a large rug which she carried back to Al. He wrapped himself in it. 'You missed a treat.'

'Yeah. Why are you shivering then?'

'Smart ass.'

'Get dressed, we'll be late for Paul and Linda.'

He tried to put his arms around her.

'You're all wet!' she complained.

'So help me get dry.'

Laughingly she pushed him away. 'I'll see you in the car. Hurry up!' She didn't trust herself with him.

Waiting at 'Pips' the Beverly Hills discotheque they found a disconsolate Paul. 'Your friend,' he complained to Dallas, 'what does she want from me? I said I was sorry. Does she want it written in my blood? Why is you hair wet, Al?'

'Went swimming.'

Paul shook his head in amazement.

'Where's Linda?' inquired Dallas.

Paul said, 'You may well ask. I tried to talk to her but she doesn't want to know. Maybe you could talk to her for me.'

'Yes – you talk to her for him,' interrupted Al, 'just like he called you for me.'

Paul glared. 'I was only doing what I thought was . . .'

'Shut up,' said Al amiably. 'Order champagne, Dallas and I are going to dance.'

They pressed together on the crowded dance floor, and once again Dallas could feel his insistent hardness.

'Having a good time?' he asked.

'Not bad.'

'That's what I like – enthusiasm!' He hugged her tightly, unaware of the fact they were getting a lot of attention and stares. 'You're going to come to my concert tomorrow. Then after, Karmen Rush is giving a big party for me. Yes?'

'I don't know...'

'Stop giving me a hard time. I've got the message you're not an easy lay. I'm asking you to a concert and a party, not a twenty-handed orgy. Right?'

'Right.'

'I still want you...' he whispered in her ear. 'Don't tell me you aren't feeling the same way...'

She was saved from answering by Cody Hills. Cody in a suit and tie, dancing with the definitive dumb blonde.

'Cody!' she exclaimed, surprised to see him. 'What are *you* doing here?'

It was obvious to Cody that to get through the whole traumatic experience with Dallas he was going to need outside help.

Carol Cameron was ready, willing, and available. She was also very pretty. And if you had an ego that needed repairing – well, she was the best sexual mechanic around – and where better a place to starting restoring a shattered ego than in bed?

Of course after a few days her conversation did begin to pall. It was always about herself. Her new photos. Her acting classes. Her clothes. Her hair. Her face. Her *career*.

Because he felt it was only fair to do a trade – she wasn't giving him her body for *nothing* – he took her on his books and got her the small but interesting part of a hooker in a double part 'Kojak'. She was delighted, and dragged him to 'Pips' to celebrate. Whereupon who was the first person he bumped into? Dallas of course. Dallas nuzzled on the dance floor with Al (goddamn English sex maniac) King. And why did she stare at him in a state of surprise and say, 'What are *you* doing here?' As if he was some kind of freak who should only be seen during business hours.

He managed to give her a cool smile and mumble something about he came here often.

Meanwhile Carol was freaking out over Al King, and digging Cody in the ribs muttering, 'Introduce me! Introduce me!'

Cody did as she asked, and Al dismissed her with hardly a glance, and who could blame him when he was dancing with Dallas.

When they were out of earshot Cody said, 'Let's go home.'

'Let's stay,' enthused Carol, jiggling about in her tighter than tight gold pants and lurex sweater.

'We're going,' Cody insisted. At least with this one he was going to be the boss.

'If you're going to *force* me . . .' she pouted.

'Yes,' he said. She didn't argue further.

Dallas and Al left 'Pips' at two in the morning, Paul tagging along with them.

News had leaked out that they were there, and several photographers sprung into action. Paul tried to shield his brother.

'Forget it,' said Al. 'I'm not bothered.'

He might not be bothered now, mused Paul, but he would not be too thrilled in the morning when his picture was flashed all over the newspapers. Especially when the news services flashed it all the way to England, and Edna got a load of it.

They all got in the car. 'Where to now?' asked Al.

'Drop me at the hotel,' said Paul.

'You'd better take me home first,' suggested Dallas.

'We haven't finished our list,' objected Al. He sneezed.

'You've caught a cold,' Paul accused. 'You should get some sleep before tomorrow. All we need is for you to lose your voice.'

'I can sleep all day.'

'You're taping the Johny Carson show in the afternoon.'

'Anyway, I'm beat,' interrupted Dallas. 'Whacked out. So if you want me to come tomorrow . . .'

'If I take you home now is that a promise?'

'I suppose so.'

'OK, we'll drop Paul . . .'

'We won't drop Paul. You're both at the Beverly Hills, aren't you? So drop me first.' She gave Luke the address.

'I thought . . .' began Al.

'I know what you thought, and you thought wrong.'

He grinned. It was good to be in on the chase once more – gave the whole game a little excitement. The big E had been missing from his life for far too long.

They dropped Dallas at her house. 'See you tomorrow,' Al said.

'Probably,' she replied.

'Don't give me that – its a definitely.'

'Well . . .'

'Tomorrow,' he said firmly.

'If you say so . . .' She walked in the house and they drove off.

Al felt marvellous. Paul was glum.

'Put on one of my tapes,' Al instructed Luke. 'No – don't. Put on the Womack tape we were playing before.' He sang along with it. 'Isn't she great?' he asked Paul. 'She's the kind of girl I could really like – you know, she's different, kind of ballsy. She's there. Know what I mean? She's not just standing around waiting to get humped. Makes a nice change.'

For how long? Paul wanted to ask. None of them lasted more than five minutes. He only liked this one because she was giving him a hard time.

At the hotel the red light was flashing on Al's phone indicating there were messages. A memo pushed under his door read, 'Contact the front desk – urgent.'

Perhaps Dallas was calling him to tell him she had changed her mind.

He picked up the phone. 'Al King here,' he snapped. 'What's the message?'

'One moment please, Mr King, I'll put you through to the front desk.'

There was a pause, then a man's voice came on the line. 'Mr King. Sorry to bother you – but we have a young man here claiming to be your son. An Evan King. He has a passport from England verifying the fact. Shall we send him over? I didn't want to do anything until I'd checked with you.'

'Send him over,' said Al dully.

What the fuck was Evan doing here?

fifty-one

Linda saw no reason why she should hang around and watch Paul discuss business with revolting Lew Margolis.

Paul had apologized to her. 'I'm sorry my wife caught us in bed together but what was *I* supposed to do?' If he didn't know, she wasn't going to be the one to tell him. Now he was saying Al wanted them to join him at 'Pips'.

Did he honestly expect one little apology to make everything all right? If he did he was more of a fool than she had thought. And to add insult he was already saying, 'Al wants us to . . .'

Well, screw what Al wanted. *She* didn't have to trip ass over elbow to do what Al wanted. Let them all run – Dallas too, if that was her scene. But she was free, white, and twenty-one . . . Well maybe not exactly twenty-one – but free and white for sure.

She slipped quietly away from the party, and she hadn't given the parking boy a second thought until he gunned her rented Chevrolet up the drive for her, hopped out and said, 'I'm getting off now. Could you drop me on the Strip?'

She looked him up and down. Surveyed him as she would a prime leg of lamb in the supermarket. He was young, but certainly experienced. That cocky grin – she tried not to laugh at her choice of adjectives – bulging jeans, muscle-bound T-shirt.

'Sure,' she said casually, 'jump in.'

He slouched in the passenger seat, chewing gum. 'Where's your friend?' he asked.

As if you don't know – she thought. You saw her leave and planned your exit with me because I'm the only woman on my own and you probably do this all the time, you randy little stud. 'She had to leave.'

'Yeah?' He blew a bubble with the gum.

Bubble gum yet! She really was baby snatching!

'You connected with the movie business?' he asked.

'I'm a photographer.'

'Neat!' he sat up very straight. 'I'm an actor, you know.'

'Oh really?'

'Yeah – I'm just parking cars for a friend – like helpin' him out. I've been in a "Marcus Welby" and "Bionic Woman".'

'That's exciting. How old are you?' If he was over eighteen she would allow him to have her. She would even pay for the motel room. Younger, and he was on his own.

'Nineteen, nearly twenty,' he said.

She smiled.

Two hours later they lay on their backs, smoking pot that he had thoughtfully produced, in a Westwood motel.

'Again?' he asked.

'Why not?'

He rolled her onto her stomach, forcing her on all fours, entering her from behind. He performed like well-oiled machinery. In. Out. In. Out. All pistons working. He was bringing her to her fourth climax. She groaned. He mumbled what she took to be a few obscenities. 'I'm gonna come,' he announced.

It was his first time. 'Go ahead,' she murmured, 'you deserve it!'

He exploded inside her – wiping out all thoughts of Paul. He didn't collapse. He was still rock hard. She came a little after him. She had to force him off her. 'Enough!' she gasped, 'I can't take any more!'

Why was it would-be actors were such amazing lays? And how come when their star rose their cocks diminished?

She giggled softly. It was a problem she would probably never find the answer to.

Dallas was asleep when Linda finally got back to the house at 4 a.m.

She took her clothes off and swam in the invitingly warm pool. She had dropped her parking boy off on the Strip as she had promised him hours before.

'I'll call you,' she had said.

'I'm not on the phone, I'll call you,' he had countered.

'Impossible,' she had said. 'You must have a number where I can reach you.'

Reluctantly he had produced a number where she could leave a message for him. 'Why can't I have *your* number?' he had complained.

She hadn't answered. She had blown him a kiss and driven off.

The danger was in trying to make a relationship out of one night of lust. Men had learned that lesson long ago. Women were only just beginning to learn.

In the morning the doorbell rang waking them both up at the same time.

'Linda – you there – can you get it?' yawned Dallas from the bedroom.

'Got it,' retorted Linda, inspecting an amazing array of flowers through the spyhole in the door.

She signed for them, baskets and baskets of red roses. The card was addressed to Dallas. Paul wouldn't know about displaying such unbridled generosity.

'Here.' She wandered in the bedroom handing Dallas the card. 'There's a flower shop outside.'

Dallas opened up the card. 'Al' was typed neatly in the centre. Nothing else, just 'Al'. She handed Linda the card to look at.

'He really likes to commit himself, doesn't he?' mused Linda. 'But you're one up on everyone else, I've never heard of him sending any of his girls flowers.'

'I'm not one of his girls,' snapped Dallas irritably.

'Don't tell me the great A.K. struck out?'

'I'm telling you.'

Linda clapped her hands together. 'Hurrah! The Master has finally failed.'

Dallas stretched and yawned. 'But I must admit I *was* tempted. If it hadn't of been for what I *knew* about him . . .'

'The original fuck and run merchant,' interrupted Linda.

'I know. But, Linda, you know me. I am *never* tempted. I don't even like sex.'

'So what makes you think things would be different with Al?'

'It's just a sort of feeling – more a sensation. He held my hand, it was so goddamn exciting I wanted to faint!'

'Oh Christ!' exclaimed Linda. 'You sound like you're in love.'

'In love! Are you kidding? I've *never* been in love. I wouldn't even know what it felt like.'

'Exactly. Did you get stomach cramps? Couldn't eat? Sweaty armpits? A feeling of euphoria?'

'Well, now that you mention it . . .'

'Shit!' Linda clapped herself on the forehead. 'Why did you have to pick on a creep like Al? Couldn't you propel those feelings in a nice guy like Cody's direction?'

'We bumped into Cody last night. He seems to have taken the whole thing very well. He was with a blonde who resembled that dragon he turned up at lunch with in no way whatsoever.'

'What do you want him to do – sit at home and cry?'

Dallas climbed out of bed. 'I'm going to look at my flowers. By the way, what happened to you?'

'San José.'

'Huh?'

'The song – remember? Would-be actor pumping gas and parking cars. He was pumping all right!'

'You didn't?'

'I did, and it was a truly beautiful experience – apart from which he's a great lay!'

Dallas screwed up her face in disgust. 'I don't know how you could do it.'

'*You* did it for long enough.'

'That was for money.'

'Well this is for like. I *like* screwing.'

'But what about Paul?'

'He's different. I love him – correction, I loved him – I'm not sure how I feel any more. But while I'm finding out I'm certainly not going to give up my sex life. Coffee?'

'If you're making.'

Dallas arranged her flowers around the house. They looked beautiful. She showered, dressed, and washed her hair. She couldn't stop thinking about Al. Aarron phoned.

'Why did you leave so early?' he wanted to know.

'I didn't feel good,' she lied.

'Why don't you come to Palm Springs with me today? I'll fly you back in time for the studio tomorrow morning.'

'No, Aarron. It's my only day off and I want to do a lot of things around the house.'

'I'm going to New York tomorrow. Perhaps next weekend.'

'Perhaps.'

'I'll telephone you on Wednesday.'

She hung up. He had behaved like the perfect gentleman with her apart from hands that lingered too long on her knee. She knew if she wanted to she could get him to marry her. She could be Mrs Aarron Mack. He was old. How many years did he have left? But the days of wanting to be married to a rich man were far behind her. She wasn't sure what she wanted now – but it wasn't that.

Al phoned at four o'clock. He sounded different – edgy and cold. 'I'll send a car for you,' he said, 'there's no room in the helicopter.'

'Hey – listen,' she replied, 'maybe I shouldn't go.'

'I *want* you to be there.'

'Well I'm not traipsing out there all alone in a car.'

'Christ! Don't *you* be difficult, I've got problems enough.'

'I don't want to add to your problems,' she snapped icily, and hung up on him.

He phoned back immediately. 'What's with you?' he demanded.

'What's with *me*? What's with *you*?'

'Aw – shit. My son arrived out of the blue, just flew in and dumped himself on me.'

'Why don't you send him back?'

'It's not as simple as that – he's got problems.'

'What problems?'

'If you're really interested he's got a dose of the clap.'

'Oh!' She was silent. There wasn't really much to say to that.

'Did you get the flowers?'

'They're fantastic. Thank you.'

He sighed. 'Look, how about if you bring Linda to the show?'

'I don't think so . . .'

'Why not?'

'She's busy.'

'Have you got any other friends could come with you? We could take them with us to the Rush party after.'

She thought of Kiki and Chuck. They would probably love to go. 'I'll make a phone call. Can you call me back?'

'Please understand if *I* can't call you back – I'm right in the middle of an interview. Bernie or Paul will call you. Tell them how many tickets you want. The plan is we'll meet back at my hotel after the show, we'll go to the party from there. Does that suit you?'

'If you say so.'

He hesitated. 'I wish I was with you now. Did you sleep?'

'Yes. Did you?'

'No. I lay awake thinking of what you and I *should* have been doing.'

She laughed softly: that was exactly what *she* had been doing.

'Listen, I'll see you later,' he said. 'Don't let me down.'

'I'll be there.'

'I'll be singing just for you.'

Sentimental bullshit! She hung up the phone and wondered how the hell she had got into this state. She had been determined not to be affected by him, and for some stupid reason she was walking on air at the sound of his voice.

Linda was crosslegged in front of the television watching a rerun of 'Starsky and Hutch'. 'He's a horny little devil!' she remarked.

'Who is?' asked Dallas.

'Little Dave Starsky. Who else?'

'I thought perhaps you were talking about your boyfriend from last night.'

'You're kidding – I've forgotten about him already.'

'I don't suppose you fancy coming to Al's concert at the Hollywood Bowl tonight, and after, a party for Al at Karmen Rush's?'

Linda lit a cigarette from the butt of one she was just finishing. 'I honestly don't think I could sit through one more Al King concert. Besides it would mean seeing Paul, and I really don't want to.'

Dallas nodded. 'I knew you'd say that, although I can't understand why you don't want to see him. He was in a terrible state last night – really miserable.'

'Good. Let *him* be the unhappy one for a change. I've had it with his weak excuses – *other* people get divorced when they have young kids. What's so different about Paul?'

'Maybe he's frightened about the money she would take him for.'

'He's too smart to get taken financially – she would get exactly what he wanted her to get. Did you know he's tight to the point of being mean? He's never even bought me so much as a flower!'

Dallas glanced at her watch. 'I've got to call Kiki – maybe she and Chuck will want to make it tonight.'

'While we're on the subject of phone calls . . .'

'Yes?'

'If you don't mind . . .'

'What?'

Linda grinned. 'Would it bother you if during your absence I made an appointment with your male hooker?'

'*My* male hooker?'

'Well – Diamond's. I'm really in the mood for an expert.'

Dallas started to laugh. 'I don't believe *you*!'

'Do you mind?'

'Why should I mind? Be my guest. He's black, you know.'

'I couldn't care less if he's orange!'

Dallas sighed. 'You really want to pay for it?'

'Why not? It's all part of life's rich field of experience. Besides – I never screwed around when I was with Paul – well, not much anyway. Now I want to make up for lost time before I hook myself up with another married schmuck.'

'I'll find you the number.'

Bernie had lined up two sycophantic, siliconed, typical Hollywood blondes for Al's use.

'Forget it,' snapped Paul, who was not in the best of moods. 'He's not asking so I'm not pushing.'

'I'll keep them around anyway.'

'Do what you want with them.'

Bernie had already done *that*. He had auditioned them personally and was ready to pass them on.

Al glided through interviews, taping the Johnny Carson show, and the helicopter ride to the Hollywood Bowl in perfect humour. The only sour note was created by Evan, who had sprung himself on Al in the early hours of the morning. In the longest conversation he had ever had with his father he had confessed to a 'problem' that he had been unable to confide to his mother. With patient questioning Al discovered what the 'problem' was – and in no time at all had summoned a doctor who had examined an embarrassed Evan, given him a shot, and said it was nothing more serious than a mild dose of the clap.

Al did not know what to do. He should be mad at the boy – but what the hell – it took balls to climb on a plane to America just like that. And it was good to know that Evan – for the first time in his life – had come to him with a problem instead of running to his mother.

Of course Edna would freak out. And once again he was stuck with Evan. But he didn't have the heart to send the kid on the next plane home. At least not until he got him cured.

Meanwhile – how to tell Edna. And not just about Evan. But about the fact that he had made up his mind that he wasn't going back to her. He wanted a divorce. He had made his decision, and he wasn't about to change his mind.

The crowds congregating at the Hollywood Bowl stretched for miles. A steady stream of cars searched for parking spaces. The stars rode by in their chauffeur-driven limousines with the special window stickers allowing them the closest drop-off points.

'There goes Karmen Rush!' the fans screamed, banging on the tinted glass windows of her black Rolls Royce. She acknowledged them with a queenly wave, only her sphynx-like eyes betraying the fact that she was stoned out of her head.

'Ramo Kaliffe, Ramo Kaliffe!' The fans chanted as the Arabian matinée idol zoomed past, flanked on either side by two girls who looked exactly like the two blondes Bernie had on standby for Al.

Bernie, in the press enclosure, was sweating more than usual. Jeeze! What a turnout. The photographers were having a field day as the stars rolled up. Rock stars. Movie stars. Sports stars. Television stars. It seemed they had all decided to make the pilgrimage to watch Al perform.

Waiting to stride out into the spotlight Al felt remarkably calm. A can of beer was the only alcohol beverage he was imbibing.

'Is she here yet?' he asked Paul for the fourth time.

'Yes,' said Paul, although he really didn't know and didn't particularly care. He wasn't sure if he liked the fact that Al was obviously struck on Dallas.

'I told you she'd come,' smiled Al.

'Hot Fudge' were swaying and weaving their way onto the stage. They wore black satin cat suits with no sides, and the longest tightest boots imaginable.

Their sound was stronger, more funky than 'The Promises'. They were more raunchy altogether.

Al had decided he preferred them. He listened to the applause. He noted their mother – a fat black lady jiggling about and mouthing each word at the side of the stage. She caught him studying her and winked broadly. He winked back.

'Hot Fudge' were on their closing number. The applause was enthusiastic. They ran off the stage into the excited arms of their mother.

Al tensed himself for his entrance. The MC was cracking a couple of jokes. The audience were shifting around impatiently. Come on, man, we've sat through 'Hot Fudge' – we've made the right noises – so what are we waiting for?

'And now—' the MC was shouting, 'the man you all want to see – the man you've been waiting for – the man himself – *Al King*!!!'

book three

fifty-two

The sun was shining in Rio de Janeiro. It was a perfect, cloudless day.

'Fetch your mama her robe,' Jorge Maraco requested of his daughter.

'Sure, poppa,' replied Cristina, leaping up from her position by the family swimming pool and running into the house.

Jorge turned to his blonde wife, 'You see,' he said, 'I don't know why you worry about her. She is polite, considerate, obliging.'

'To you,' replied his wife pointedly. 'She'll do anything for you.'

Jorge puffed on his cigar. 'She is a good girl. A credit to her family.'

'You only see the side she *wants* you to see. I tell you, Jorge, I am worried about her. Some of the company she keeps . . . It's not right. After all she is only seventeen, still a child.'

'She has a woman's body.'

'What difference does *that* make? You should be *more* concerned because of that fact.'

Jorge reached lazily for his wife, and patted her affectionately on her bare thigh. Evita Maraco was wearing a one-piece white swimsuit which showed her voluptuous body off to full advantage. She drew away from her husband. 'You are not taking me seriously,' she accused.

'I am,' he protested, 'I always listen to everything you say.'

'Yes, and I am always right. Hasn't eighteen years of marriage taught you that?'

'It has taught me never to argue with a beautiful woman.'

'In that case you must talk to Cristina – today. Her thoughts and actions should be taking her in a more serious direction. Why, when I was her age, you and I were engaged to be married.'

'I paid your mother for the privilege.' Jorge chuckled at the memory. 'You were my poor little carioca washing clothes to take home the money for mama.'

'Lucky for you I washed *your* clothes,' snapped Evita. 'An old man like you not married – you were a disgrace to your family!'

344

'I was only forty,' protested Jorge.

'Forty! A spoilt rich child. *I* saved you.'

'Yes,' agreed Jorge, 'you saved me from a life of wine, women, and . . .'

'Boredom!' snapped Evita.

He reached for her thigh again.

'Stop it!' she chided. 'Are you never satisfied?'

He sighed, 'Never. Eighteen years wanting the same woman. I would not have believed it possible.'

Evita could not help smiling. She *had* tamed him. When they had married his reputation as a womanizer had been legendary. Jorge Maraco – the slippery millionaire industrialist – still single at forty. A world-wide dallier with some of the world's most beautiful women. What a catch he was. And who had caught him? A penniless working girl from the slums.

She had been seventeen, the same age as her own daughter was now. But what a different kind of life she had led. A life filled with poverty, despair, and work. It was only her beauty that had saved her. Her long white-blond hair which was so unusual, her cinammon elongated eyes, chiselled features, and full ripe body.

Jorge had come across her in the kitchens of his house one day, and fallen irrevocably in lust. Love, of course, had followed – helped by the fact that Evita refused to go to bed with him until they were married. Her virginity was the only possession she had to bargain with, and she used it wisely.

Cristina had been born a year after they were married, and until recently she had given them no problems. She was a bright scholar, and had always mixed with the right friends. But now – Evita felt uneasy. Cristina remained her usual polite and charming self to her father – but when he was not at home she became mean, moody and extremely rude. It was only a recent occurrence, a matter of months really. Before that Evita had been hoping that Cristina would become engaged to a boy she had grown up with. Up until a few months previously they had been steady companions – but then suddenly the change. And Cristina had become secretive and mysterious about where she was going and who she was seeing.

It could not go on. Evita had made up her mind that Jorge should talk to his daughter, find out exactly what *was* going on.

Cristina Maraco stared at her reflection in her mother's dressing room mirror. She was not thrilled with what she saw. How unfair that she should be the image of her father – dark and squat – why couldn't she have inherited her mother's classy blondness?

Jet black hair hung in a tangle of thick frizzy curls around her olive-skinned face. She had a boyish body, wide shoulders, small breasts, sturdy legs, wide ass.

She *hated* the way she looked! Boys didn't. Boys said she was sexy. Boys were always trying to grab her tits or ass. Or kiss her sulky pursed lips.

Boys were a pain.

Nino wasn't. Nino was different.

Nino didn't grab. Nino said, 'I want to sleep with you, Cristina.' Nino was only nineteen. But he wasn't a boy – he was a man.

Not like Louis – the boy her mother liked. The boy her mother wanted her to *marry*. Louis was draggy. Full of himself and his family's money. Just because his father was unbelievably rich.

Money was bad. Money was corrupting. Nino had taught her that.

She grabbed her mother's robe from the closet and held it up against herself. Ugh! Silk, in some yucky print. It had probably cost a few hundred dollars. Enough to clothe some poor family for a year.

Her mother spent a fortune on clothes. And her jewels! She had diamonds and emeralds as big as marbles!

Cristina wandered over to her mother's dressing table and idly sorted through the many bottles and jars. Evita was beautiful. What did she need all this junk for? If she was ugly it would be understandable. But she was exquisite, and young, and *it wasn't fair* . . .

Cristina grabbed up the robe from the floor where she had thrown it, and ran downstairs.

'You were a long time,' remarked Jorge, withdrawing his hand from Evita's thigh, but not quick enough for Cristina not to notice. They were always at it – her dear parents.

'Couldn't find it.'

Evita stood up and slipped the robe over her swimsuit. 'I'm going to rest,' she announced. She stared meaningfully at her husband. He gave an imperceptible nod.

Cristina dived into the pool. She was a very fast swimmer, churning her way up and down the pool at a record pace. She did fifteen lengths, then climbed out, shaking her head like a wet puppy.

'You swim well,' Jorge remarked.

Cristina flopped down beside him. 'Poppa, I've swum well since I was three years old. Why are you telling me now?'

'I remember when you learned to swim,' he said. 'Your instructor threw you in and out of the water like a sack of potatoes. I thought your mother would have a fit.'

Cristina smiled politely, and wondered how long it would be before her father followed Evita into the house. It was their Sunday ritual. Out by the pool after lunch. Into the house before five o'clock. It was the only day Cristina saw Jorge. The rest of the time he was at the office or visiting his factories, and when he returned home he usually preferred a private dinner with Evita.

Nino had said it was wise to present herself to her father in a good light. She had told him what a bitch Evita could be, always questioning and prodding for information about what she was doing.

'I don't see Louis at the house any more,' Jorge remarked. 'Is he sick?'

Cristina shrugged. 'It depends what you call sick, poppa.'

'What do you mean?'

She made a face, 'Oh – *you* know.'

'I know *what*?'

'Boys. They're always . . . Well – *you* know what I mean.'

Jorge sat up. 'Do you mean to tell me that Louis . . .'

'Yes.'

'He didn't . . .'

'No.'

'Thank God for that!' Jorge chuckled. 'You're a sensible girl. I never doubted that. Perhaps you could explain to your mother . . . She would understand. You see, we give you so much freedom, Cristina, and I think it worries her. Other girls have chaperones, strict parents. I have never believed that is the way. But I know you would never let us down . . .'

'*Never*, poppa.'

Jorge smiled. He had talked with his daughter. She was a good girl. *He* had never doubted the fact.

'Well, Cristina, I think I shall go inside now. Are you going out?'

'Yes, poppa.'

He kissed her absently, anxious to get inside to Evita. She would have showered by now. The sheets would be scented. The shades drawn down. They would make love passionately. They always did on Sundays.

'See you, poppa.' Cristina kissed him lightly on the cheek, and jumped back into the pool.

'Yes, yes.' He hurried into the house.

Cristina watched him go. He was fifty-eight but he looked much younger really. He had the same sturdy body as she did, all his own teeth, and his eyes were strong and clear, not bloodshot and runny like some of the old men who were his friends.

She snorted. His friends! What a bunch they were. At parties and barbecues they could hardly keep their rheumy old eyes off her! They thought she was the sweet little virgin daughter. Good little Cristina. Sweet little Cristina.

Oh how sweet to see the surprise on their faces if they were to learn the truth.

She, Cristina, was not a virgin.

She was a woman of the world. A woman of experience.

She had been sleeping with Nino for six whole weeks!

She turned on her back in the pool and let her thoughts take over.

Nino. Even his name created a warm dark excitement.

The first time she had seen him she had known that here was someone different. She had been with a large party enjoying the carnival ball at the Municipal Theatre. She had been wearing a spangled outfit – her mother's choice, but nice all the same. And her hair had been threaded through with silver streamers, and her make-up had been a fantasy of silver patches and dots.

He, of course, typical Nino, had taken no trouble with his appearance at all. With his looks he didn't need to. He was nicely thin, with hidden muscles, and a stomach so hard it was like wood. His hair was black – even darker than hers, and he wore it just as it grew – a tangled mass of jet curls. She had since copied the style, nagging and cajoling her hairdresser to get it exactly right.

His eyes were the most amazing thing about him. Black, fringed with the longest lashes. But it was the way he used them. His gaze was so penetrating, so intimate. His eyes seemed to bore right through you.

Louis, on the other hand, was the sort of boy parents liked on sight – and of course they liked him even more when they realized who his father was.

Before Nino she had quite liked Louis. But after Nino, she had realized he was just another nothing little rich boy with no point of view towards life.

'He has no fire,' Nino had explained simply. 'I do not want you to see him any more.' So she hadn't.

Her first meeting with Nino had been a disappointment. He had ignored her. He was with a rich American girl who was vacationing in Rio, and she had known some people in Cristina's party, so they had all joined up. Cristina had been immediately struck, but he had dismissed her with a cursory glance.

'Who is he?' she had asked Louis, 'and why is he so rude?'

Louis had grinned. 'He wouldn't be so rude if he knew who you were. He only goes out with girls who have money. He's a trouble-maker.'

'How do you know?'

'School. He had a scholarship there. Nobody liked him. He is not one of us. His family are nothing.'

She had tried to ask Louis more, but he changed the subject, and took her off to dance, and she had watched Nino with the American girl, whispering to her, and nuzzling into her neck.

Cristina had not been sorry when she heard three days later that the American girl and her parents had been robbed of thousands of dollars worth of jewellery and travellers cheques.

She had not seen Nino again for two months, until one day she was out shopping with her friend, Marie Therese, when she saw him striding down the street. 'Hello,' she had said, and he had stared at her with those black intense eyes, and said, 'Who are you?'

She had started to stammer. 'Cristina Maraco, don't you remember, we met at the carnival ball – I was with Louis Baptista. You were with an American girl. You must remember?'

His eyes had strayed to Marie Therese who was extraordinarily pretty. 'I remember,' he said, staring straight at Marie Therese. 'You girls coming to the beach this afternoon?'

'Yes,' Cristina replied quickly, 'where will you be?'

He shrugged. 'Ipanema.'

'Whereabouts?'

'You'll find me,' one last penetrating stare in Marie Therese's direction, 'if you want to.' He strode off.

'Who was *that*?' Marie Therese asked, her cheeks flushed pink. 'My parents would *never* let me go to Ipanema beach on my own. Who is he, Cristina?'

'Not a very nice type,' Cristina said dismissively; and as soon as she could get rid of Marie Therese she had rushed home and changed into her briefest Tanga, and rushed off to Ipanema, where it took her two hours to find him.

'Where is your friend?' he had asked.

'She had work to do,' Cristina explained. 'She is studying French with her fiancé.'

Later, when they knew each other better, they had laughed about Cristina making up a fiancé for Marie Therese. 'But it was always you I wanted,' Nino would say mildly. 'Always you.'

He was with friends at the beach. A different class of people than Cristina was used to. One girl paid particularly close attention to Nino. She kept on grabbing his leg and trying to pull him down on the sand beside her. He resisted her advances, and indulged in polite conversation with Cristina. What did she do? Where did she live? When she told him who her father was he said, '*The* Jorge Maraco?' After that he took her swimming, and spoke sharply to the girl who touched his leg, and they walked along the beach and he held her hand.

Later, when she said she had to go, he had asked when he could see her again. They had made a date for the following Friday, and she had rushed home on winged feet, spent a boring evening with Louis, and lived only for Friday.

From that day on her life had changed. Nino had taught her so much. He had explained about poverty, about how the rich had everything, leaving nothing for the poor. He had taken her on his motor scooter for a tour around the Favellas – a shanty town of rotten shacks on a hill overlooking the affluence of the more fortunate. She had seen filthy babies playing in the mud, old people so thin that their bones stuck through their ragged clothes. Mothers with ten children struggling to see they got one decent meal a week.

She had been horrified.

'One day,' Nino assured her, 'we will change all this. My life is dedicated to seeing equality amongst our people.'

He took her to visit his grandmother, a wizened old woman who was his only living relative. She, too, lived in a shack. She had no teeth, hardly any hair, a skin disease. She looked a hundred years old.

'You would not believe she is only fifty,' Nino said. 'That is what a life of poverty has done for her. My mother died giving birth to me in that same shack. Now perhaps you will begin to understand my bitterness.'

That night Cristina cried herself to sleep.

Two days later Nino asked her if she would be willing to help.

'What can I do?' she had asked, 'I have some old clothes . . .'

'We don't want your charity,' Nino had spat with a venomous anger.

'Well . . . what?'

'Your parents have friends. People with a lot of money. Do you think they would feel it if they were relieved of some of their possessions?'

Cristina was startled. 'What do you mean?'

'You know their houses. You could find out their movements . . .'

'No! I couldn't. I know what you are asking me to do and it wouldn't be right.'

'All right.' He had taken her in his arms and kissed her. 'I respect your feelings. I won't ask you again.'

He lived in a small one-roomed apartment. They had spent many hours there together. She allowed him certain privileges – privileges she would never have allowed Louis. They would kiss and caress, and sometimes she would allow him to remove her sweater and bra. She never permitted him to go further than that.

'I want to sleep with you, Cristina,' he had told her that evening. 'We are not children playing silly little games. I need a real woman.'

'It's impossible,' she had replied, 'I couldn't . . . It would be shameful. My father would never forgive me.'

'Your father need not know. And as for being shameful – God – I thought I had changed your mind – opened up your head – but if you can still harbour petty bourgeois ideas like that . . .' He trailed off in disgust.

'I have to wait,' Cristina said hesitantly.

'Until when?' snapped Nino.

She was blushing. 'Until I marry.'

To her surprise Nino burst out laughing. He leapt off the bed and said, 'Time to go home.'

She was relieved. She thought he had dropped the subject. But the next day when he did not turn up at the time they had arranged to meet she was worried. She waited three days for some word from him. He did not contact her. In desperation she went to his apartment. He opened up the door wearing only jeans which he was busy doing up. He looked surprised to see her, and blocked the door.

'Where have you *been*?' she asked accusingly.

He shrugged. 'Around.' From behind him there came a woman's laugh, and then the woman herself. She was half wrapped in a sheet. She hugged Nino from behind, and said in a teasing voice, 'Come back to bed, sugar plum, Pussy's lonely . . .'

Cristina's face blazed red. Nino shrugged. 'I am a man . . .'

Cristina had left. And after two days of crying and thinking things over she had made up her own mind.

She dropped Nino a note asking him to meet her.

He had turned up at the appointed time looking better than ever. He was casual and friendly, as if nothing had happened. They talked. She told him of her decision, and hand in hand they strolled back to his apartment.

She didn't smoke, but he made her puff on a special cigarette which he said would relax her. She was so nervous. But he was calm and in charge.

He undressed her slowly, mouthing compliments about her body. Then he made her lie on the bed and watch while he stripped off. She could hardly breathe with excitement. She had seen him nearly naked on the beach so many times, naked except for the tiny bikini shorts he wore. Now he was throwing off his shirt, unzipping his jeans, and walking towards her.

She gasped. She had seen men with no clothes on before. Her father in the shower once, pictures in a magazine.

But never like this, never so turgid and swollen. It was like a weapon.

He lay beside her and started to kiss her. She was used to that part, even the part when he brought his head down to her breasts. But she wasn't used to the feel of his penis so hard and insistent on her leg.

'Hold it,' he instructed her.

She did so, ridden with guilt at the thought that what she was doing was wrong.

'Stroke it, here – I'll show you how.'

She rubbed it in the way he told her to, and he started to groan – low animal noises that both disgusted and excited her. Then he pushed her quickly away, and pulled open her thighs, and thrust his head down between them. She froze, unable to move, not wanting to move. His tongue began to open her up, probing, investigating. Until at last she too started to make her own animal noises.

'Are you ready to try?'

'Yes,' she whispered. 'Yes, yes, yes . . .'

He moved his head up, and reached for a package beside the bed. 'I'm going to wear protection,' he told her matter of factly, 'but I don't usually like to. It spoils it for me. Next week I'll send you to a doctor I know and he'll fix you up.'

It crossed her mind that he was very experienced, but then he was a man – why shouldn't he be?

He rolled the thin tube of rubber over his penis. 'Bring your knees up, try to relax,' he told her. 'It may hurt a little, but only the first time, only this once.'

She looked into his eyes. His deep, brooding intense eyes. 'I'm frightened . . .' she began. But he wasn't listening, he was on top of her and forcing his way between her legs. Thrusting, pushing . . . It hurt in a pleasureable way.

'Relax,' he kept on saying, 'just relax.'

She began to make more animal noises, and a feeling of tenseness built up inside her. A tenseness that wanted to burst right out.

'I love you, Nino, I love you,' she cried out.

He was silent. Sweat beading his forehead. He balanced his weight on his arms, and churned in and out of her.

She was gasping now, reaching for the climax. Reaching . . . Reaching . . .

Then she was caught up in something so pleasurable that she could not control herself. Her legs twisted themselves around his back, her nails raked into his skin. 'Nino, Nino, Nino . . .' she yelled, 'Niiiinnno . . .'

It was over for her. The strength flooded from her body. She felt positively euphoric.

Nino was pumping into her harder and harder. His eyes were closed. His mouth set in a thin line. Then he too reached his orgasm. 'Rich bitch!' he screamed. 'Rich capitalist bitch!' He collapsed on top of her, groaned, rolled off, turned his back.

She lay very still. She felt so *good*.

She turned and studied the outline of her lover's ass. So tight and firm. So much nicer than hers. Gently she put her hand on it. He rolled to face her.

'That was wonderful,' she sighed, 'why didn't you tell me it would be like that?'

'It usually isn't,' he replied. 'Are you sure this is your first time?'

She giggled. 'Of course, silly. When can we do it again?'

That had all taken place six weeks previously. Six glorious weeks of what it was like to be a woman.

Cristina lay spreadeagled in the warm water of the swimming pool. Nino had never said he loved her, but she was sure he did. He would tell her in his own good time. She had *proved* that she loved him beyond doubt. She had told him about her parents' friends, the Von Cougats. She had drawn him a map of their house, and pinpointed the safe and alarm system control. She had also told him of a ball they would be attending, and Nino and his friends had acted without hesitation. The Von Cougats had been

353

relieved of over a hundred thousand dollars' worth of jewellery.

Cristina had understood. Nino was right, the Von Cougats wouldn't even miss it.

'We need as much money as we can get,' Nino told her. 'With money we can buy power – we can buy the instruments of terror – we can *force* the rich to listen to us.'

'Yes,' agreed Cristina, although she really didn't understand what he was talking about.

Nino was a member of some mysterious organization. He attended secret meetings, and talked about his 'leaders' with an air of reverence.

When Cristina asked about it he silenced her with the words, 'Not yet. When you are ready I'll take you to a meeting.'

When would that be? He wouldn't tell her.

'Soon,' he would tell her, 'we will have enough money to start our campaign. Then you will see some changes in this city – then you will see the capitalist pigs brought to their knees.'

Cristina had nodded. All that mattered to her was Nino. As long as she had him she didn't care what happened.

Enough thinking. She leapt out of the pool and ran into the house. The door to her parents' bedroom was firmly closed.

If they only knew what she had been up to . . . She shuddered at the thought. They would lock her in the house and never let her out again!

Evita stretched and sighed. There was no getting away from it, her husband was a selfish lover. She could hear him singing happily in the shower. Jorge Maraco.

How surprised everyone had been when he had chosen her as his bride. It had taken years before his friends had accepted her. Now her early days of poverty seemed like a bad dream. It was almost as if her life had begun the day she had set eyes on Jorge.

She had not been a disappointment to him. She had come to his bed a virgin, and he had been the only man she had ever slept with. Although it was not for want of other men trying – she had often received secret notes and phone calls from Jorge's so-called friends. She had turned them all down. She had been absolutely faithful. Except . . . She blushed at the memory. One lapse in eighteen years of marriage. Her blush deepened. One lapse . . .

Three years earlier Jorge had taken her to Acapulco. There was a film festival in progress, and the town had been filled with movie stars, directors, and producers. Jorge appeared to be on nodding terms with everyone. He loved the gaiety and excitement. Evita was somewhat intimidated by it all. She encouraged Jorge to go out and about, attending receptions and screenings, whilst she stayed mostly at the hotel, lying under a large umbrella beside the swimming pool.

It was during this time she had struck up a friendship with the American film star, Doris Andrews. Doris' husband was in the entertainment business and he too seemed to be out all day. Doris and Evita became close friends, sharing gossip, ordering long cool Planters Punch together, exploring the tourist shops.

Evita had never suspected that Doris was anything but completely normal. Until one day, returning from a shopping trip, they had both collapsed exhausted from the heat in Doris' suite. They had lain side by side on the large bed, giggling, laughing. Doris had slipped off the pink mu-mu she was wearing. It had seemed perfectly natural, after all it *was* hot, so Evita had slipped out of her beach dress also.

They lolled on the bed clad only in panties.

'What lovely breasts you have,' Doris had said, and she had leaned over and touched them and murmured, 'so full, so firm.'

Evita had smiled. Her breasts were lovely. She was proud of them.

'I wish mine were better,' Doris had complained, cupping her own small boobs. 'What do you think of them?'

Evita hadn't really thought about them at all. But she looked, and noted the erect nipples, and noted that her nipples were also extended. And it had seemed perfectly natural when Doris had started to stroke and caress her.

One lapse . . .

And she had not repeated it. She had insisted to Jorge that they flew home that very evening. He had been surprised, but hadn't argued. He never argued with her.

Jorge emerged from the bathroom, a towel tied round his middle. 'I spoke to Cristina,' he said. 'I told you we have nothing to worry about. She is a good girl. It is Louis we have to worry about. He tried to take liberties with her. She refused him. That is why she sees different friends now.'

'But who are her new friends? She never brings them home, we know nothing about them . . .'

'If it will make you happy I'll tell her we must meet them.'

'Yes. I think we must.'

'Of course.' He dropped the towel and approached his wife. His penis was erect and ready.

Just once Evita wished he would use his tongue instead. Doris Andrews had used her tongue . . .

'Evita!' Jorge sighed, positioning himself above her. 'My darling Evita!'

fifty-three

Melanie King was still in New York. If Paul knew he would be furious. She had taken elaborate precautions to make sure that he didn't find out. His only concern was the children, she didn't kid herself on *that* count.

She phoned nanny and made up a mass of lies as to why nanny should say she was back in London if Mr King phoned.

Nanny sniffed her disapproval. 'About my time off . . .' she began.

'You can have two weeks to visit your mother when I get back,' Melanie promised rashly.

'Very well, Mrs King.'

Melanie had hung up relieved. That took care of *that* end of things. She had herself to take care of. She was twenty-eight years old, and she wasn't getting any younger. Paul was dull and boring. She had thought when they married that being Al King's sister-in-law would bring a lot of excitement into her life. It had brought nothing of the sort. It had brought a boring life stuck in a house next to boring Edna – and it *just wasn't good enough*.

She had come to New York determined to have a good time before returning home. She hadn't counted on running into Manny Shorto again. Now that she had . . .

She had first met Manny eleven years ago. She had been seventeen, pretty, innocent, and stupid.

Manny Shorto, the famous American comedian.

Eleven years ago he had seduced her, used her, tricked her, trapped her.

She had been one of the dancers on the television spectacular he had come to England to star in. He had promised her the earth, delivered her three mediocre screws, and flown back to America leaving her confused and pregnant.

She had been forced to sleep with two film extras and a camera operator to get enough money together for an abortion. Then, a few months later she had met Paul King. Without hesitation –

when he asked – she had married him. She had never loved him. She had always expected something better to be just around the corner.

Now Manny Shorto was back in her life. And he didn't even remember her! The bastard.

But he wanted her – oh how he wanted her. His wife had died of cancer, and he lived alone in a large hotel suite surrounded by hangers-on. He was more than a star – he was an American legend.

They had met again at a party. He asked her out – she said no – he sent her some presents – she said yes – he tried to screw her – she said no – he sent her some more presents – she still said no.

She was his type. There was no denying that. 'What do you want?' he asked. 'Name it – you got it.'

She wanted to be Mrs Manny Shorto. *She* wanted to be the star's wife.

Now if she played her cards right . . . If she could only stay in New York long enough . . . This time *she* was going to screw *him*. This time *she* would win.

The Hollywood Bowl concert was a smash. Even Bernie had to admit that he had never heard Al in better voice. He grabbed the audience in his fist, and held them there in a dazzling performance. They screamed their approval – stars and fans alike. At the end of his 'tribute to other singers' he dedicated Bobby Womack's version of 'We've Only Just Begun' to a 'wild-haired, green-eyed lady out front'.

Dallas, sitting with Kiki and Chuck, smiled slightly. No one knew it was for her. It was their secret.

He over-ran by half an hour, and everyone stamped and clapped and cheered for him to stay longer – but it was time to go – and he gave them his boxer's salute and vanished.

'Wow!' exclaimed Kiki, 'he is *too* much – but the best. I never realized what impact he has. Jeeze – I'm weak at the knees. That is one horny man!'

Chuck laughed. 'I'd look horny if my pants were cut to within an inch of my life!'

Kiki giggled. 'You're horny anyway, baby.' She hugged him, 'In fact – you are the horniest! I can vouch for that!'

They got caught in a huge traffic snarl-up, and it seemed like hours before they reached the Beverly Hills Hotel. There was a hassle to get directed to Al's bungalow, and Chuck nearly got involved in a fight.

There was a mob of people at the bungalow. Dallas found Paul and asked what was happening. 'Go through to the bedroom,' he said. 'He's waiting for you.'

She edged through the crowd, and Luke ushered her into the bedroom.

Al was lying on the bed in a towelling dressing gown. He sat up when he saw her and said, '*Where have you been?*'

'The traffic . . .'

He reached around her waist and pulled her onto the bed with him. 'Let's fuck,' he said urgently, 'I was thinking about you all the time . . .'

She shoved him away. 'What is it with *you?*'

He leapt on top of her, pinning her arms down. 'What is it with *me?* I haven't had a woman for weeks. I can have my pick, but I've been waiting for you . . . Do you know what it means for me to wait?' He lowered his mouth onto hers. She flicked out her tongue to meet him. He relaxed his hold on her arms and pushed his own tongue into her mouth.

She bit his tongue sharply, at the same time springing free and rolling off the bed. 'I don't want to screw you. Get it? I'm not another one-night lay. Another silly little star fucker.'

He started to laugh. 'Is my tongue bleeding?'

'I don't believe you,' she huffed, picking herself up from the floor. 'I walk in the room – you *attack* me. There's a million and one people right outside. Honestly . . .'

'I love you,' he laughed. 'I really love you.'

'Good,' she replied. 'Now get dressed and we'll go to the party.'

He saluted, still smiling. 'Yes m'am.'

She couldn't help smiling too. 'And don't get smart, or we won't go.'

Karmen Rush wanted him.

She was a lady who always got what she wanted, or all hell was let loose.

She was a not too attractive female who had styled herself into a devastating cult beauty. Her aquiline features she emphasized with deliberate shading. Her too-close-together myopic eyes she hid behind black contact lenses, and emphasized the outer eye and lid in a dramatic Egyptian fashion. Over her thin mouth she drew a shape of a more inviting nature, which she filled in with a dark brown lipstick. She dieted fanatically to keep her thinner than thin figure. And her hair she had dyed a jet black, and wore it very long with the help of various hair pieces.

Her magic voice was all her own.

She was one of the very few bankable female stars in the world.

At the age of thirty-two, she had devoured three husbands, and was currently sharing her sumptuous house with a young dress designer by the name of Kealey Nova. His friends sometimes called him Keelin' Over, on account of the fact that he was always stoned out of his head, and had a habit of falling down flat at the most inopportune moments. Karmen never seemed to notice. She sailed through everything like a queen, her face an impenetrable mask. As long as she was never disturbed during the three hours it took for her to get herself together every day – then she seemed unruffled by anything.

When Al arrived at her house she took him by the hand and husked, 'Beautiful . . . Beautiful . . .' in his ear.

He had always wanted to meet her. She did not leave go of his hand, and she had a grip of steel.

The house was alive with freaks – music issued forth from every corner – an old Shirley Temple movie played soundlessly on a giant screen.

Karmen fixed him with her deadly eyes. 'Come with me,' she whispered, 'I want to tape record our first conversation.'

Dallas gave him a little shove from behind. 'Go on,' she urged, 'I'll be fine.'

'But . . .' Al began.

'Go on!' insisted Dallas. 'I don't mind – really.'

'I'll be back in a minute then.'

Karmen dragged him away.

'I can't get over this house,' Kiki was saying, 'Dallas, have you looked around – it's insane!'

The house was indeed weird. Not furnished in the conventional sense – but littered with exotic cushions and rugs, and only lit by long black candles that were stuck in holders ranging from exquisite silver to wine bottles.

On the walls priceless Picassos jostled next to old movie posters. The back of the house was sheets of glass which led out to the beach and the ocean. Various huge dogs wandered about apparently harmlessly. Word had it that at a gesture from Karmen they would attack and kill.

'Kinda cosy!' joked Kiki. 'What do you think, Chuck baby, shall we take it?'

'Christ! Be careful what you drink!' Chuck replied. 'There's not one normal person here. They'll slip you acid before you can say hello!'

Dallas wandered onto the beach. She didn't mind the fact that

Karmen had spirited Al off. In fact in a way she was pleased. If he was so anxious to get laid let Karmen do him the honours. At least it would give her an excuse to stop seeing him. And she wanted to stop seeing him – she wanted it to be over before it had begun. That was the only way she would be safe.

Paul arrived at the party a little later. He had stayed behind to get rid of the people at the bungalow. He couldn't spot either Al or Dallas, and assumed that they had finally got it together and were hidden away somewhere consummating the relationship. Good. That would mean the end of Dallas. It didn't seem right for Al to be so hung up. Paul preferred him the way he knew him – this whole Dallas trip was unusual.

He looked around. It was pure freaksville. What was he doing here? Why wasn't he out trying to get Linda back?

A stoned redhead swayed over to him. 'What star sign are you, lover?' she asked. 'If you're a Scorpio we're in luck. My horoscope promised me a Scorpio today and you look like a beautiful human being.'

'No, no,' he backed away. He couldn't turn on to women the way Al did. He couldn't produce an instant hard-on with a complete stranger. It just wasn't his scene. He needed more. He needed a certain mental communication before anything physical could happen.

He wanted to leave. This wasn't his kind of party. Quietly he headed for the door.

Karmen said, 'Your vibes are reaching me, Al. I knew you and I were tuned into the same thought waves.'

They were in her bedroom. A room painted black with no ceiling. The ceiling was the sky littered with stars.

'Like it?' she asked. 'I designed the whole house myself.'

'Nice.'

'Nice! It cost me a goddamn fortune! Listen, Al. We can lock ourselves away from the party. We can party on our own – just the two of us. You want to snort a little coke? I've got the best stuff – or is grass your treat? Whatever. Name it.'

'Hey,' he objected, 'thanks for the offer, but I came here with someone.'

'So? Who is she? Some nothing chick you can hump any day of the week. I'm offering you *me* – Karmen Rush.' With a gesture she undid a clip, and the black halter neck dress she was wearing slid to the floor.

Her body was so thin that her ribs were visible, and her hip bones jutted out, emphasizing the fact that she had shaved off every inch of pubic hair. Her nipples were black flowers – painstakingly designed. A black heart was tattooed on her waist.

She stared at him. 'Don't tell me you're not king. Don't tell me all I saw up there on that stage was a pair of old socks.' She turned her back on him and walked contemptuously over to the black fur bed. She flopped onto it, opening her legs.

He could see everything. There was no black bush impairing his vision. He had not had a woman for over four weeks. Besides which, this was Karmen Rush – *the* superstar lady – asking him – begging him . . .

He wanted to get back to Dallas. He wanted to . . .

He unzipped his trousers. One quick fuck wasn't going to make any difference.

Twice Linda nearly dialled the number. Twice she copped out at the last minute. What was it about California? She felt *so* horny. Was it something they put in the water? Or was it just her way of getting Paul out of her system?

The parking boy had been fun, a laugh, a one-night stand. But a hooker – wasn't that taking things a bit too far?

Men had been using hookers forever. Yeah – but probably men who couldn't get it on for free elsewhere. Either that or they wanted to do things they didn't want to do with their wives.

But what the hell. She wanted something different. She wanted a man who was dedicated to pleasing her. Dedicated. Not some dude who expected as good as he gave.

Determined, she picked up the phone again. But just as she was dialling, the doorbell rang.

She slammed the phone down and went to the door. It was Cody Hills. He looked distraught. 'Where is Dallas?' he demanded.

'She went to the Al King concert at the Bowl. You want to come in? You look like you could do with a drink.'

Morosely he followed her inside. She fixed him a vodka on the rocks and he gulped it down.

'So what's up?' she asked, 'you look in a state.'

'Yes,' he agreed, 'I have to get hold of Dallas. I've got bad news – really bad news.'

Dallas sat on the beach for a while, and the while grew into a long time. So she went back inside, and found Kiki and Chuck.

There was no sign of Al. No sign of Karmen. 'I'll be back in a minute' indeed. What bullshit!

'I'm going to leave,' she said, trying to keep the hurt out of her voice.

'But what about Al?' Kiki asked.

'He's a free agent. There's nothing between us, you know.'

'Sure,' agreed Kiki, 'just an electric charge you could cut with a knife.'

'Yeah – so electric he's run off to screw rent-a-witch.'

'Who?'

'Do I have to draw you a picture? Our lovely hostess. Listen Kiki – I don't give a shit, I'm splitting.'

'Wait until we finish eating and we'll come with you,' Chuck joined in. 'After all – it's up early again tomorrow – back to the grind.'

Dallas nodded. She was tired. She only had to hear the words 'up early' and it was instant yawn time. She would go home, get into bed, and forget about Al King.

If she had been smart she would have forgotten about him in the first place.

Edna rose at seven. There was so much to do, and with Evan away visiting friends she planned to spring-clean his room.

The house was looking wonderful, sparkling clean, the way it had never looked before. She had been horrified at the filth she had found. You pay people to look after your home, and what did you get? You got dust swept under couches, cobwebs in the hall light fixtures, thick grease in the oven, a permanent rim around the bath, unpolished silver, unmoved furniture.

Edna had soon taken care of all that. She had personally scrubbed the house from top to bottom. Now all she had to do was maintain it.

She made herself a cup of tea. Oh, the luxury of an empty kitchen! Then she strolled round the front of the house and picked up the newspapers from the mail box. On the front page of one of them, there was a large picture of Al and Dallas. They were laughing, looking at each other. Al's expression was of rapt interest.

Calmly Edna read the blurb.

'Al King Meets his Queen Again'. That was on top. Underneath the story read: *Los Angeles, Saturday, Superstar Al King (38) and Ex 'Miss Coast to Coast' Dallas (20) seemed to find plenty*

*to laugh about at a party in his honour given by Doris Andrews (43).
Earlier in the year Al's name was romantically linked with Dallas.
The claim then was 'just good friends'. Isn't it wonderful how friend-
ships last?'*

Edna folded the paper carefully and returned to the house.

She couldn't make up her mind what to do first. Wax the kitchen floor, or start on Evan's room. She decided on the kitchen
floor. Humming softly to herself she switched on the radio.

How nice to no longer have Melanie coming around to try and
rub her nose in it. Because, quite frankly, she couldn't care less.

'I'm sorry,' said Karmen blankly, 'I must have given you too
much.'

Al, struggling his way to consciousness through a throbbing
headache muttered, 'Too much what?'

'Ether,' replied Karmen matter of factly. 'I put a pad over your
face when you were coming – it usually produces the most hallu-
cinatory effects. I guess you must have breathed too deeply or
something. You've been asleep for hours, the doctor was quite
worried.'

Al did not believe what he was hearing. Ether! She could have
killed him. The woman was totally insane.

He wanted to throw up. He felt terrible. 'You stupid bitch!' he
slurred. 'You're mad, fucking mad.'

She pinched the bridge of her nose with dangerously taloned
black-painted nails. 'I tried to wake you. I did everything to wake
you.'

Al focused on her boyfriend standing behind her. He looked
very spaced-out and very nervous.

Al tried to stand. 'I want to get out of here,' he said, 'I don't
need fucking maniacs in my life. Where is the doctor anyway?'

'When he saw you were coming to he left. He doesn't like to get
involved.'

'Jesus!' Al spat in disgust. 'Get me my driver – Luke. I want
out.'

'Sure, man,' Keeley said, 'I'll arrange everything. Don't you
worry about a thing.' He unlocked the bedroom door and exited.

Al staggered to his feet. He noticed he was fully dressed. The
last thing he could remember was giving this ugly bitch a good
hammering. Then – pow – nothing until now. Ether! Christ
Almighty!

'Who dressed me?' he demanded.

'Keeley.' replied Karmen. 'You could have just slipped quietly away. I didn't think you would want to go with your pants off.'

Al glared at her. What could you say to a psycho screwball? She was nuts.

She stared impassively at him, unruffled by the whole event.

Keeley came bouncing back in the room followed by a concerned Luke.

'Where the fuck were *you*?' Al demanded, not waiting for a reply. 'Get me to the car.'

Karmen fluttered her hands vaguely in the air. 'It could've been a beautiful experience,' she murmured. 'You could've *thanked* me.'

'Sod off, you dumb bitch.' He followed Luke through a side door and out to the car. He still felt weak. 'How long was I in there?'

'Nearly three hours,' replied Luke. He didn't dare to ask what had happened.

'Where's Paul?'

'He came and left.'

'Dallas?'

'She left hours ago.'

'Figures,' said Al glumly. Nobody had been concerned. Nobody had been worried. They had all thought he was having the hump of a lifetime – why disturb him?

Fuck it. He deserved it. He had been so hung up with Dallas . . . Then the first superstar that had exposed her skinny body had pulled him. Terrific. What will-power. What strength of character. What a pile of shit.

He was disgusted with himself.

'Stop off at the first liquor store we pass and buy a couple of bottles of Jack Daniels,' he instructed Luke.

What the hell . . . Dallas wouldn't want to know about him now. She wouldn't believe him whatever story he told her. He had blown her out in front of her friends, humiliated her. He didn't even have the courage to call her. For one lousy star fuck he had crapped on the first relationship he might have had in years.

The concert had been such a triumph. He had been riding on a natural high. Was his ego so insecure that he'd felt obligated to screw Karmen Rush? Or was it just that he was plain horny after being without a woman for so long, and when she had taken off her clothes . . . When she had opened those white thin superstar legs . . .

Luke stopped the car at a liquor mart, and ran inside.

Al slumped back in the car. A few shots of Jack Daniels would soon get him together again.

Kiki and Chuck were very kind. Too kind. They chatted about all sorts of unimportant subjects as they drove back to Beverly Hills.

Dallas wanted to scream, 'I don't care! I don't mind! Al can have who he wants, it doesn't bother me!' But she knew they were only trying to pretend they hadn't noticed the fact that Mr King had done the fastest walk-out on her on record.

'That Rush woman is really creepy-looking,' Kiki gushed. 'Did you *see* the make-up? *Three* inches of white base.'

'To cover her famous spots,' Chuck joined in.

'Yeah,' Kiki continued, 'do you know she never even appears at the studio without her make-up – I swear to God – 6 a.m. she marches in *fully made-up* – then she throws out the make-up guy – locks herself in his room – takes off all her "going to the studio" make-up – and does a whole new job on herself! Martha Scott told me – she did her hair on her last picture. Now the hair is another story . . .'

Dallas tuned out whilst Kiki droned on. She couldn't care less about Karmen Rush. It could have been anyone. She had known about Al's reputation up front – that's why she had held back. And thank God she had. At least this way she could walk away from it feeling no pain. If she had slept with him . . . If she had liked it . . .

Well she hadn't. It had taken extreme self-control, but she hadn't.

What a laugh that a man like Al King could turn her on where all others had failed. A superstud. A type of sexist pig that she should really loathe. Maybe he would have struck out too. Maybe if she *had* gone to bed with him it would have been as distasteful as it was with everyone else.

Oh well . . . No use wondering about *that*. Forget him. Concentrate on work. Concentrate on becoming a star. Concentrate on *herself*.

'Isn't that Cody's car?' Kiki was saying.

Dallas glanced out of the window. It was indeed Cody's Mustang parked neatly beside Linda's rented Mercury. What was he doing there? Fortunately she couldn't spot a white Ferrari, so Linda must have changed her mind about Julio. 'Coming in for a drink?'

'Sure...' began Chuck.

'No,' interrupted Kiki hurriedly. 'I'm beat, I really am. We'll see you tomorrow.'

Dallas knew what *she* wanted. She wanted to see her back together with Cody.

They said their goodbyes and Dallas walked into the house.

Cody jumped up when he saw her. His face was white.

'What happened between you and Lew Margolis?' he snapped. 'Because whatever it was Lew wants you *out* – off the series. What was it, Dallas? For Christ's sake what was it?'

fifty-four

'I can't,' insisted Cristina.

'Why not?' replied Nino, lazily.

They lay on the beach, hands entwined.

'I keep on explaining to you why not.'

'Because it's *your* house. Because it's *your* mother's jewels. If you really think about it – then you would say – yes, Nino – I'll tell you when it is a good time, Nino – I'll tell you where the safe is ... how to open it.'

Cristina pulled her hand away and sighed. 'You ask me too much. First the Von Cougats, then the Bogatos – now you want to rob *my* house – my parents' house.'

Teasingly Nino threw sand over her stomach. 'So. It is fine to rob *other* people's houses. But when it comes to you ...'

Cristina blushed. 'It's not just that. You stole from the Von Cougats – the money your organization gets for the jewellery goes to help the poor. No one was hurt. They are insured. As you said, no one will even miss it.'

'Yes,' his hand massaged the sand lightly into her stomach.

'So I told you about the Bogatos. *I* made it possible for you to rob them.'

'You were very helpful.'

'Yes, Nino,' her eyes filled with tears, 'but you didn't tell me that you and your friends would have to kill the dog ...'

'It attacked us ...'

'And wreck the house. Cover the walls with slogans, rip up priceless paintings.' She started to cry. 'I wasn't going to mention it – I felt too sick to mention it. But now – what you are asking me . . . it's impossible.'

His hand moved slowly down her stomach, his fingers hooked into the thin knot of cord holding the bottom half of her Tanga together. 'I think we should go home,' he whispered.

She stopped crying and shivered slightly. He had her under some kind of unbreakable spell. 'It's early,' she protested weakly. 'I thought we were going to surf.'

He laughed. 'Who wants to surf when we have better things to do?' He stood up and offered his hands to pull her off the sand.

They walked slowly back to his apartment. Her body was tingling with the anticipation of what he would do to her.

'Ah, Cristina, Cristina,' he sighed when they were in his room, 'what a baby you are, what a little innocent.' He was undressing her as he spoke.

'Do you love me?' she blurted out, unable to hold back any longer.

'I love you as I love the stars, the sky, the beach, the ocean.'

It was no real answer, but she was satisfied. It was more than he had said before.

'I love *you*' she crooned, 'oh how I love you, Nino.'

He did not reply. He silenced her with his mouth.

Later, when Cristina had left, he lay on his bed and stared at the ceiling. The paint was cracking and peeling, sometimes little flakes would fall down onto him whilst he slept. He never slept well. He was always restless. His dreams were always full of nightmares. He craved for some action. He craved for his organization to start its reign of terror. The preparatory work was boring – at least the work he was stuck with was. 'You're the good-looking one, Nino,' his leaders had told him. 'You're the one who will be able to captivate the ladies – the *rich* ladies.'

Fund-raising was his job – whilst the others were out buying arms, making stockpiles of bombs – and compiling lists of victims for Operation Kidnap – *he* was satisfying women in bed. It was not a job he enjoyed. He had a girlfriend – Talia – a tough, intelligent twenty-three-year-old, who worked in the smuggling side of the operation. For the last few months he had hardly seen her at all. It was a most unsatisfactory situation. When he made love to Cristina he shut his eyes and tried to pretend it was Talia. It never worked. Talia was a woman of fire, whilst Cristina was just a silly little rich girl.

Cristina Maraco. Just how useful could she be? Her father was a very rich man . . . Blackmail or kidnap had been discussed, unless she could be used in some other way. Her mother's jewellery would be a help. Perhaps she would be able to supply more information on families such as the Von Cougats and the Bogatos. 'String her along some more,' were Nino's instructions. At least she was better than the Americans. He shuddered at the thought of the American women he had serviced. Big women with big demands. 'Do this, Nino, baby.' 'Do that, Nino, sweetheart.' 'Just there, don't stop.' 'One more time, Nino.' Ugh! How he hated them. Capitalist pigs from the worst capitalistic country of all.

His eyes were closing. Sleep was coming. The nightmares were coming. No use fighting it. He succumbed.

'Where have you been all day, Cristina?'

Wide-eyed and innocent. 'Just to the beach, mama. I *told* you I was going to the beach.'

'You look so . . . flushed.'

'I have a headache, mama, I think I will go and lie down.'

Evita nodded. She didn't know what it was, but she just had a feeling that Cristina was up to something. When Jorge returned home late in the evening she tried to explain her feelings to him.

'Up to *what*?' He laughed.

'I don't know. I can't explain.' She paused thoughtfully. 'I think she has a boyfriend.'

Jorge grimaced. 'According to her she has a lot of new friends. And after what Louis tried on I don't blame her.'

'I think,' Evita said hesitantly, 'that she is sleeping with someone.'

'Impossible!' Jorge shouted, his complexion turning a dull red. 'How can you say such a thing?'

Evita shrugged. 'It's just a feeling I have.'

'You're wrong. She's a good girl, that much I know about my own daughter.'

'We've allowed her too much freedom. How do we know what sort of people her new friends are? At least with Louis we knew his family. Do you know that she never even has time to see Maria Therese – her best friend.'

Jorge frowned. 'On Sunday I will tell her to bring some of her new friends to lunch. We will meet them and make our own judgement.'

Evita nodded. 'Yes, I think that would be a good idea. *You* ask her, she will only find some excuse for me.'

Jorge kissed his beautiful wife lightly on the lips. 'Problems, problems, as if I don't have enough all day! But you are wrong, my darling, I know you are wrong. Cristina is a good girl. I would bet my life on that!'

Evita took one look at Nino and saw immediately the Favellos in his eyes. She knew without doubt that here was a boy who came from exactly the same background as she did.

He was good-looking, marvellous-looking in fact, with his wild curly hair, and intense jet eyes. Evita could certainly see what attracted her daughter physically. But he was obviously a boy who lived on his wits. His clothes were the standard dress of the young – a uniform almost. The tight faded jeans, a collarless shirt, old tennis shoes. But round his neck hung an expensive gold chain with some sort of religious medallion, and Evita couldn't help thinking it was a present from a rich female. His kind always had rich women – she had seen so many boys like him who would sell their bodies to the tourists for whatever they could get out of it.

All these thoughts were churning quickly through her head as Cristina introduced him. Jorge had requested that Cristina bring her new friends home – but she had turned up with only one – this boy – and Evita could understand why. Her daughter was in love. It was quite obvious as she gazed at Nino with naked admiration shining from her eyes.

Jorge shook Nino firmly by the hand. 'Do you two youngsters want to swim before lunch?' he asked.

Cristina looked quickly at Nino, questioning him with her eyes.

Nino nodded, glancing around at his luxurious surroundings with a mixture of contempt and envy.

'Go ahead,' offered Jorge. 'Cristina, show your friend to the changing room.'

'Not necessary,' said Nino, unzipping his jeans and fixing Evita with a sudden moody stare.

'Don't do that here,' Cristina said quickly. 'Poppa doesn't like a mess of clothes round the pool – Come on, I'll show you where to change.'

Nino zipped his jeans up again. 'Sure,' he said, still staring at Evita.

She returned his stare with a polite smile. She hated him on sight. He represented a certain type of male she loathed. Arrogant. Mean. Conceited. A sexual aggressor. Young as he was, his character was quite clear to her.

Cristina grabbed Nino by the hand and led him off down the gardens towards the changing rooms.

Jorge turned to his wife, a complacent smile suffusing his face. 'You see,' he said triumphantly, 'he seems like a nice enough boy.'

'Don't be a fool,' snapped Evita in reply. 'You haven't said two words to him. Who is he? Where does he come from? What does he do?'

Jorge frowned. 'Give me time. I can't start questioning him the moment he walks in our house.'

'He's from the Favellos.'

'How do you know?'

'It's in his eyes, it's in his smell.'

'Evita. Don't condemn him before we even know him. He's Cristina's friend, she likes him.'

'She more than likes him.'

'What do you mean?'

'Your daughter is a woman – she likes this boy as a woman would like him. Did you see the way she looks at him?'

'No I didn't,' replied Jorge irritably. 'I wish you wouldn't always jump to conclusions and make hasty decisions about people.'

'I have an instinct for knowing things. This boy is no good.'

Jorge turned away from his wife. Sometimes she could be very annoying with her 'instincts'. A year previously he had been forced to terminate a lucrative business deal because Evita didn't like the man he was dealing with.

'You will be fair,' Jorge insisted, 'you will not judge this boy on two minutes – you will judge him after we have spent the day in his company. I am sure if he is a friend of Cristina's he will turn out to be nice, polite and respectful.'

'Hold this,' urged Nino.

'I can't, not here!'

'Hold it. Stroke it.'

'Nino. My parents are just down the garden. They'll wonder what we are doing in here.'

'Put it in your mouth.'

'Nino!'

'Do it. I command you. Get down on your knees and put it in your mouth.'

'No!'

'If you love me you will.'

Her eyes were filling with tears. They stood in the changing room close together. She in her tanga. He with his jeans around his ankles, his brief swim suit around his knees, and his penis swollen and distended.

'If you loved me you wouldn't ask,' said Cristina miserably.

'I *have* to ask. I can't go out like this. It's *your* fault I'm like this.' Reluctantly she sunk to her knees. 'But if they come looking for us . . .'

He grabbed her head and guided himself into her mouth. 'Ah!' he sighed, 'that's good, that's very good.' Slowly he rocked back and forth. It was the first time she had allowed him into her mouth, although she wasn't averse to the feel of *his* tongue.

He was excited because of the woman. The beautiful woman with the glacial features and white blond hair. *She* was the kind of woman he had always dreamed of having. A madonna in a white bathing suit, with the body of a lush peasant girl. The combination was irresistable.

The joke was that she was Cristina's mother. A woman Cristina had called a bitch and a hag, and God knows what he had expected – some sort of old, jewel-ridden bag! The joke was on him. Cristina's mother was cool, ladylike, and so young.

'Aaach!' He climaxed quickly, pushing himself deep into Cristina's mouth. She gagged and tried to push away. He wouldn't allow her to until he was finished. Then he withdrew, satisfied – doubly satisfied because of where the event had taken place.

Evita watched the young couple emerge from the changing rooms, and turn towards the pool. She had known he would wear the smallest of swimsuits. She had known his body would be deeply suntanned, finely muscled and hard. After all he probably lived by his body, therefore it had to be in perfect condition.

What did he want with Cristina? Did he want to marry her? Was he foolish enough to believe that they would allow it?

Cristina was no great beauty. Oh, she was pretty enough, attractive, but she was not the sort of girl that would have a boy like that running around after her unless there was something in it for him – something more than just sleeping with her, because as she watched them cavorting in the pool, she was sure that he was indeed sleeping with Cristina. When you started life living in a shack amidst a sea of other shacks you developed an antenna for sexual knowledge. Evita knew at a glance.

She sipped slowly the glass of chilled white wine Jorge had poured for her. How lucky she had been to meet him. What a miraculous escape it had been for her. If not for Jorge . . .

'So this is how my little rich girl lives,' breathed Nino, surfacing behind Cristina and grabbing her round the waist, 'your own swimming pool, all the luxuries. I never even knew what a *bath* looked like until I was fourteen years old.'

'That's not *my* fault,' objected Cristina, wriggling free and striking off down the pool.

He swam after her, keeping his voice low so that her parents couldn't hear him.

'Do *you* think it's fair? Do you?'

'You know I don't, but there's nothing *I* can do about it.'

'But there is.'

'Please don't let's discuss it here.'

He placed his leg between hers under the water.

'Don't!'

'Why not?'

'You *know* why not. *Please* behave yourself, Nino.'

'And if I do, will you promise to do something for me?'

'I thought I just did!'

'Not that. Something important. Something that will help the organization.'

'If I can . . . You know I'll help if I can . . .'

Jorge was clapping his hands together beside the pool to attract their attention.

'Have you two had enough yet? Lunch is ready and I am hungry.' He glanced quickly at his watch. He had a schedule to adhere to. He didn't want to miss his afternoon siesta with his wife. It was all very well Evita wanting to meet Cristina's friends, but if it was going to interfere with his schedule . . .

Cristina swam to the edge of the pool, and hauled herself out. 'I'll have to change, poppa, I'll be as quick as I can.' She threw Nino a towel, 'You can use the changing room, I'm just going into the house.'

Nino caught the towel, smiled politely at Jorge, and glanced covertly at Evita. She wasn't kidding *him* with that glacial expression, she had noticed his body, she had noticed how great it was. Young, hard, virile. He strolled with deliberate slowness to the changing room.

Cristina ran into the house and up to her room. She had not wanted to tell Nino, but the thing he had made her do to him before they swam had made her feel sick. She rushed into her bathroom and rinsed her mouth out with strong mouthwash, then she cleaned her teeth. It had been mean of him to force her to do

372

that. Especially in the changing room, within earshot of her parents. He had known she would not dare to object too strongly. He was so wonderful, and yet at times he could be so mean. He teased her a lot. He said her legs were too short – her breasts too flat – her ass too low. Then, just when she would be near to tears, he would kiss her, and laugh, and insist that he wouldn't want her any other way.

There were times when she wished that she had never set eyes on him. There were also times when she did not know how she had ever managed to exist without him.

If he asked her to marry him she would. Whatever her parents said.

She was amazed that he had agreed to come and meet them. 'If it will help you out,' he had shrugged. 'We don't want them locking you away 'cos they think you are mixing with undesirables. We'll show them what a fine upstanding guy I am.'

'What do you do, Nino?' asked Evita.

She and Jorge sat at the luncheon table with him, waiting for Cristina.

'I study,' replied Nino, trying to engage her in a moody stare, but not succeeding.

'Oh yes, and what do you study?' Her tone was ever so faintly mocking.

'Politics.'

'Very good,' boomed Jorge, 'excellent. Hoping to be President one day, eh?'

'Not exactly.'

'Where do you study?' inquired Evita.

'What is that girl doing?' complained Jorge, glancing impatiently at his watch.

'Shall I go and find her for you, sir?' volunteered Nino.

'No, no, I'll send Maria.' He summoned the maid, a fat, surly girl. 'Go and tell Miss Maraco we are waiting, and to come at once.'

She bobbed a nervous curtsey. 'Si, señor. I tell her.' She rushed off.

Jorge indicated the plate piled high with delicious chunks of melon in the middle of the table, 'Let's start. Help yourself, Nino. Make yourself at home.'

'Thank you,' replied Nino politely, and he shot another look in Evita's direction, but she seemed to have decided to ignore him.

Bitch! She thought she was too good for him. He helped himself to some melon.

'Where is your home?' inquired Evita.

Questions, all she could ask was questions.

'My family were killed in an automobile accident when I was very young,' he replied smoothly. 'I live with an aunt who has always taken care of me.'

What lies! 'Oh. Where is that?'

He was saved from answering by the appearance of Cristina. She had changed into jeans and a shirt similar to his. Somehow it really annoyed him that she tried so hard to look exactly like him.

'All that time to end up looking like a ragbag,' complained Jorge. 'You have such pretty dresses. On a Sunday it would be nice if you could wear them.'

'Oh, poppa! Sometimes you are so old-fashioned.'

'Old-fashioned,' sniffed Jorge, 'old-fashioned because I would like to see my daughter wear something that makes her look like a girl. What do you think, Nino?'

Cristina looked to him for support. He said, 'I must agree with you, Mr Maraco. I like a girl to look like a girl.'

You weasel, Evita thought. You nasty little weasel.

Cristina blushed a dull red. 'I don't care,' she said defiantly. 'Anyway, Nino, it was *you* that said it was wrong to waste money on clothes.'

'Really?' said Evita, 'did you say that, Nino?'

Now it was his turn to be embarrassed.

'I didn't mean not to buy any clothes at all.'

'What *did* you mean?' Evita had him on a spot.

'Well – you know,' he looked around helplessly at Jorge in his hand-made silk shirt and immaculate French trousers, Evita in her three hundred dollar towelling beach robe. 'I just meant that to own an excess of clothes when there are people starving on the outskirts of the city is wrong.'

'Starving?' questioned Evita, 'I hardly think they are starving.'

'You wouldn't know,' flashed Nino.

'And *you* would?'

She had caught him. He had been determined not to get involved in any arguments or discussions with them. He knew these kind of people. One threat – even a minor one like him – and they would order him out of their daughter's life. It wouldn't do to have their luxury rocked by a would-be revolutionary hanging around.

He shrugged. 'No, I don't know.'

Evita laughed coolly. 'And I thought you were going to be a young man with a cause.'

He shovelled some melon in his mouth. 'No cause.' Bitch! Bitch! Bitch!

The rest of the lunch passed without incident, and at exactly three o'clock Jorge rose from the table and said, 'I know you young ones will excuse us,' and helping Evita from the table, added, 'It's been nice meeting you, Nino.'

As soon as they were out of sight Cristina giggled. 'No cause,' she mimicked.

Nino turned on her angrily. 'What did you *want* me to say? That I think the way they live is disgusting? That their outlook is selfish and bourgeois? That they should do something useful with their money instead of sticking it on their backs and fingers and wrists?'

'Poppa supports many charities.'

'Charity!' spat Nino. 'The people shouldn't have to accept charity. By right, if all the money was divided, *everyone* would have enough. There would be no need for *charity*! Come on, let's get out of here, the stink of useless money is making me sick.'

Jorge stripped, preparing for his shower. 'Quite a nice young man,' he commented.

'A trouble-maker,' replied Evita. 'I know his kind, I grew up with his kind.'

Jorge held her by the shoulders, helping her off with her robe. 'You can be a hard woman.'

'We must stop Cristina from seeing him.'

'And how do you propose we should do that?' He began to peel down the straps of her white swimsuit.

She shrugged, the gesture freeing her breasts. 'I don't know, it's something we must talk about. Maybe a trip – a long trip.'

Jorge fingered his wife's breasts. 'Whatever you want,' he said. 'You know you always get what you want.'

'I want you to start seeing Louis Baptista again,' Nino said.

He and Cristina lay naked on his bed having recently finished making love.

She sat up. 'What?'

'Now don't get excited. I have my reasons.'

He pulled a pile of newspapers from under the bed and laid them out. He picked up one and read an item that had been circled in red.

'Rock/soul superstar Al King has accepted millionaire impresario Carlos Baptista's offer to do two concerts in Brazil. His fee will be an astounding one million dollars.'

'Why are you reading me this?' Cristina asked.

'One million dollars is a great deal of money.'

'Of course it is.'

'Can you imagine what the organization could do with a million dollars?'

'I don't under . . .'

'Stop saying you don't understand and listen to me. I am trying to explain to you. If the great Al King was kidnapped – what a simple matter for them to pay one million dollars to get him back. The money is already available – instead of paying him, they pay us. Get it?'

'Don't be silly, Nino. It would be impossible – people like Al King are guarded all the time – and anyway – kidnap is a bad crime. If you were caught . . .'

Nino jumped off the bed irritably. 'We just talk about it and already I am caught! What faith you must have in me.'

'I do have faith in you. I know you can do anything you want to. But how could you possibly kidnap Al King?'

'With *your* help.'

She was startled. '*My* help?'

'You and your friend Louis – Carlos Baptista's son. You told me he was mad about you.'

'I stopped seeing him when you and I started to see each other.'

'That doesn't mean he will not be thrilled when you telephone him and resume your relationship.'

'But I don't want to.'

He sat down on the bed again, reached under her shirt and started to caress her. 'But for me you will. If you love me you will.'

'Why?'

Was she being deliberately dense? 'We have three weeks. Right now Al King is resting in Arizona, then he goes to Los Angeles and then he comes here. Three weeks will give you more than enough time to grab young Louis with your charm and newfound talents. From him you will be able to get all the information we need about Al King. We will be able to plan the best form of action.'

'But . . .' He silenced her by pressing his mouth down on hers. She would cooperate. Of that he was sure.

fifty-five

Las Vegas. A razzle dazzle city in the middle of nowhere, filled with lovers and gamblers, con men and hookers, entertainers and mafiosa, winners and losers.

Las Vegas. If Los Angeles was the City of Angels, Las Vegas was the City of Devils. Blackjack. Craps. Roulette. Poker. And many other harmless little games to part a man and his money. Or a woman. Although their Las Vegas role was slightly more servile. Women worked according to their looks and their age. The beautiful, tall, spectacular show girls, baring it all. Their more energetic, but equally pretty sisters were the dancers. The attractive girls with dipped necklines dealing you in blackjack. The not quite so attractive girls donning black tights and cute shortie costumes to serve you free cocktails. The over-thirty ladies, with the same shorty costumes, baring ass and tit, patrolling the lobbies and restaurants, trying to sell you tickets for Keno, or some such fun games; And then the motherly waitresses in sensible white uniforms serving you Corned Beef Hash and Frank Sinatra sandwiches in the various delicatessens that no decent hotel would be without.

Al flew into the city in a suitably drunken haze. A haze that he had existed in since the fateful Rush party.

At first Paul had been delighted to see big brother back to normal. But three days and ten blondes later he wasn't so sure.

Al was back to normal with a vengeance.

A series of events had taken place.

Item one. Al had phoned Edna to explain to her about Evan. Not the whole truth, just the fact that he was with him, and safe, and that he would keep him there a while longer.

Edna, to Al's surprise, had received the news calmly. Then, just as he had been about to end the conversation, she had requested a divorce. Edna had asked *him* for a divorce! No hysterics, no crying. Just a matter of fact statement that they would both be better off without one another. Of course the thought had been in his mind for some time. But for Edna to suggest it! Jesus Christ! It was an outrage! How dare she!

He had mumbled something about they would talk about it later, and hung up. The next day Edna had announced it to the newspapers. The newspapers yet! Edna who baulked at having her photo taken with him! She had given an intimate interview to a hard-nosed bitch who made him out to be a combination between Casanova and Dracula!

Item two concerned Dallas. The fact was she lived up to his expectations, refused to speak to him, sent back his flowers, and in a face-to-face confrontation outside her house told him to go fuck himself. He had given up after that. Battles he didn't need.

Item three was the film Paul wanted him to do. The script was right, the money and percentages were right, the contracts were being drawn up. Paul had negotiated the deal with Lew Margolis. Somehow Al had doubts. He was a singer. What gave everyone the impression he could turn into an actor overnight? As far as he was concerned he hadn't made up his mind yet, whatever Paul thought.

Meanwhile, in Las Vegas, he concentrated his energies on going straight to the tables. A path was created through the tourists whilst whispers of 'Al King, Al King, Al King' reverberated through the place. An admiring crowd gathered around the roulette table he picked, and oohed and aahed as he proceeded to lose thirty thousand dollars.

He shrugged, grinned, moved over to the crap tables. The crowd followed him.

A florid-faced dress manufacturer was just about to roll the dice. His face broke into a huge smile when he spotted Al, and he handed him the dice. 'Here you go, Al, you take 'em – maybe it'll change my luck.'

He took the dice, squeezed them hard – 'Five thou on the line,' he told the houseman. The houseman turned to the pit boss for confirmation. The pit boss gave an imperceptible nod.

Al rolled. The crowd were silent. He threw a five and a two. The crowd cheered its approval.

'Let it ride,' he told the houseman. The man added five thousand dollars' worth of chips to the stack already there.

He blew on the dice, rolled again. This time a four and a three. Lucky total of seven again.

'I knew it!' The florid-faced man exclaimed, scooping up the chips he had won betting on Al's throws, 'I knew you were a lucky devil.'

Several females were edging as near to Al as they could. A particularly large-bosomed redhead was making the most headway.

'Let it ride,' instructed Al. He hurtled the dice down the table. Five and a two again. He was up twenty thousand dollars. Not bad. But of course he was down thirty thousand on roulette. If he let the twenty ride and he won he would be up ten thousand. What the hell, it was only money.

'Again,' he said.

The crowd held its breath, then, just as he was about to roll, the big-bosomed redhead grabbed his hand holding the dice, and gave it a wet and sloppy kiss. 'For luck, baby,' she breathed, nudging him with her bosom.

It was too late for him to stop. But he knew he would crap out. Knew the redhead had blown his luck.

He was right. Two miserable ones showed up on the dice. The crowd groaned.

'I could offer you a consolation prize,' the redhead suggested.

He ignored her, signing the chit the pit boss handed him. So he was down fifty thousand dollars. So what?

'Could I have your autograph?' a very fat lady was asking, 'for my little niece. Charlene. C H A . . .' She spelled the name as he scribbled an almost illegible Al King on the book matches she had given him.

He walked away. The redhead followed him. 'Buy me a drink?' she suggested. She had nothing much to offer except the boobs and the hair.

'Are you a hustler?' he asked.

'Of course not!' She appeared deeply offended.

'Shame. I thought you and I could work something out.'

She bit her lip, then coyly said, 'What did you have in mind?'

'A good fuck.'

Paul was on the phone. Lately he seemed to spend half his life on the phone. It was a bad line and he could hardly hear. 'I'll call you back, Melanie,' he said. He had been trying to reach her for days, but she always seemed to be out. Finally he had left a message for her to telephone him. He wanted to talk to her before they flew off to South America. Who knew what the phone connections were like there?

'You can't phone me back, I'm not at home,' Melanie's voice seesawed down the phone.

'I can hardly hear you,' complained Paul.

She said something that he couldn't hear at all, then, '. . . can't see there is any point.'

'What?'

'I can get it in Mexico,' she screamed.

'Get what?'

'A divorce.'

He thought she was talking about Edna. 'Why does she want to go there?'

There was a series of electronic noises, then the operator interrupting, saying: 'You've been cut off. I'll try to reconnect you on a clearer line.'

He banged the phone down. It rang again immediately. It was the manager just wanting to inform him that Al King had signed chits totalling fifty thousand dollars. Terrific. Now he would have to haul Al away from the tables before he did any more damage. He had only been down there half an hour.

There was a knock at the door, Bernie stood there sweating.

'Have you seen Al?' Paul questioned.

'Yeah. He just boarded the elevator with a real water buffalo. Jeeze – you've got to have a grudge against your tool to go near a barracuda like that.' Bernie wheezed his way over to the table with the booze on, and poured himself a shot. 'With his money he should buy himself a new wife!'

'At least he's away from the tables.'

The phone rang and Paul snatched it up.

Melanie's voice came through clearly. 'I'm glad you agree,' she said, 'I've even decided to let you have the children.'

'What?'

'You want them, don't you? They'll be better off with you. Manny and I will be leading an erratic life – not the sort of life children will fit into.'

'What the hell are you talking about?'

'Aren't you listening to me?' Melanie shrilled. 'Do I have to go through it all again?'

'You want to go to Mexico with Edna. Is that it? Well, I can tell you now . . .'

'You fool!' snapped Melanie, '*I'm* divorcing *you* in Mexico. I'm marrying Manny Shorto and we want to do it as soon as possible.'

Paul did not believe what he was hearing.

'You can keep the children,' Melanie shrilled on, 'as I said before they'll be better off with you. Of course the Mexican divorce will be a temporary step until we can arrange a proper English divorce. Manny wants everything to be done properly, he . . .'

She talked, whilst Paul sat down and listened unbelievingly. She had never gone home. She had stayed in New York. She had run into Manny, an old flame. Jesus – old was the operative word – he must be at least seventy. They had rekindled the flame. This time it had been too big for both of them . . .

Paul replaced the receiver, cutting off her voice. First Edna, now Melanie. What was going on? He slumped into the couch.

'Everything cool?' inquired Bernie, scratching under a sweaty armpit.

'You're going to love it,' replied Paul, still in a state of shock, 'Melanie's divorcing me. She's getting married to Manny Shorto.'

Bernie laughed, 'Come on, man . . .' He trailed off when he realized Paul was serious. He didn't know what to say, Paul was slumped out like a man in an accident – yet he had been balling that Linda Cosmo most of the trip – so the wife couldn't mean *that* much. But who knew with married couples . . . What the fuck . . . For the first time in his life Bernie was at a loss for words.

Al sat fully dressed in the living room of his luxury suite whilst the redhead danced for him. She had discarded every stitch of clothing except for her shoes. The huge knockers were a silicone job, with sad inverted nipples. Her frizzy red pubic hair grew down the inside of her thighs. She was not the most tempting sight he had ever seen as she weaved and swayed somewhat clumsily in front of him.

He could make them do anything. What were they, dumb zombies? A half hour ago this woman had been a total stranger, now she was prepared to do anything for him. If he asked her to lie down and open her legs so he could take a few photos she would do it. She would do it for Marlon Brando, Robert Redford, Al Pacino . . . Any famous man. The list was endless. She would probably even do it for Richard Nixon – and definitely for Jimmy Carter.

Al was just deciding how he could get rid of her when Paul came bursting in.

The redhead stopped dancing abruptly, and looked for something to cover herself with.

Paul ignored her. 'We made a winning double,' he announced, 'Melanie's divorcing me – wants to marry Manny Shorto. Are you ready for that?'

Al started to laugh.

Paul said, 'What the hell are you laughing at?'

Al was doubled up with laughter – 'She got herself a star. For Christ sake – surely you can see the funny side of it?' He beckoned the redhead over who had decorously covered herself with a cushion, favouring her lower half.

'What would you do, darlin', if Manny Shorto wanted to marry you?'

'Huh?'

He reached for a siliconed tit and bounced it playfully. 'Would you say yes? Come on – truth now – would you say yes?'

'I'm married,' she replied, not quite comprehending the question.

'Married!' he exclaimed. 'What the fuck are you doing here then?'

'Separated,' she added quickly.

'The bitch never even went back to England,' Paul said morosely. 'She shacked up in New York with that old prick – leaving the kids all alone.'

Al gave the redhead a little shove in Paul's direction. 'Want to give her one?' he offered, 'wham bam it out of your system?'

'No thank you,' said Paul, at the same time as the redhead objected with – 'Hey – what is this?'

'Oh sorry,' Al apologized, 'you only fuck stars, is that it?'

'I think I'll get dressed . . .'

'Do that,' Al agreed, 'pack the silicone away – oh and next time your husband's home borrow his razor and shave your thighs – right now you remind me of King Kong's mate.'

'My husband could beat the shit out of you,' she hissed, 'who do you think you are?'

'Just a superstar,' he sang.

'I can't get over it. After all I've given her.' Paul sat down, shaking his head.

The redhead picked up her clothes and put them on as fast as possible. Two bright spots of anger burned into her cheeks.

'Faggot!' she spat at Al as she was leaving.

'For you – any day,' he minced in reply. 'Never could get it up for a gorilla!'

She slammed the door with a resounding bang.

'Did I interrupt something?' asked Paul, startled by the noise of the door.

'Absolutely nothing. Why don't you fix us a couple of belts and tell me the whole story.'

Dallas lay in bed, shivering slightly, unable to sleep.

Who the hell did Lew Margolis think he was playing games with? Some out-of-town hick? Some dumb little girl?

She would soon show *him*.

She relived the latter part of the evening in her mind. The part where Cody was waiting for her to get home, his face drained of colour and worried.

What had she done to upset Lew Margolis, he wanted to know. What *had* she done? Because Lew Margolis had summoned him to his house on Sunday and informed him 'Man Made Woman' was being cancelled. 'Dallas just doesn't come across, just doesn't make it,' Lew had said – his face as impassive as a snake's. 'I'm opting out now, no good throwing more money into it.'

'Now?' Cody had stammered.

'As of today,' Lew agreed, 'tell your client not to bother turning up tomorrow. She won't be needed.'

Cody knew that something was desperately wrong. He had seen the daily rushes himself. Dallas came across like a million dollars. She looked magnificent, and her acting abilities were more than adequate for the part.

'What about her contract?' Cody had asked.

'It will be honoured up to the first option date,' Lew replied. 'That's only fair.'

Cody had been speechless. The whole thing was ridiculous. Lew Margolis must be some kind of nut. Then it came to him. This had to be a personality clash. Something had happened between Dallas and Lew. Something big enough to cause this lunacy. For it was lunacy – Lew's studio stood to lose if they opted out on 'Man Made Woman' before it even reached the television screens. Everyone stood to lose.

'So what happened?' Cody insistently questioned Dallas.

She shrugged. 'Nothing.'

'It can't have been nothing,' he snapped. 'You were at his party last night. It must have been something that happened there . . . something you did or said. Did he ever try to come on with you?'

Dallas didn't dare to glance in Linda's direction. She wanted to tell Cody not to worry. Everything would be fine in the morning. Everything would be fine when she reminded Lew Margolis of a certain set of photographs. 'No, he never did. The only approach I've ever had from that family has been strictly female.'

'Female?' echoed Cody, puzzled.

'Doris.'

Cody made a disbelieving face.

'She's a dyke,' Dallas insisted. 'She tried to grab me – I turned her down.'

'Come on, Dallas,' he said patiently, 'this is *the* town for gossip, and not a word of Doris Andrews being a lesbian has *ever* got around. If she was, the world would know.'

'Well, she is,' insisted Dallas stubbornly.

'Hmmm . . .' Cody was still sceptical. 'We'll have to work out a press release – we'll have to tread very carefully. I just don't know . . .'

'Let's all sleep on it. Tomorrow might change everything. Besides, I am bushed, I can't even think straight . . . Hold any statements until we speak tomorrow.'

He nodded. God, she was taking it well. Any other actress would be hysterical by now. He wondered if she fully realized what she was losing. Not just the money, but the shot at instant fame, the shot at becoming a household name in a matter of weeks. Without that cherry the other offers might dry up. After all, who was she? And the big question would be why had she been dropped? Acting was like gambling in a way. One minute you were hot – the next cold. It could happen to anyone. But when you were cold – oh boy – nobody wanted to know.

Thank God she had the Mack contract. Although he would have felt a lot more secure if her face was on every billboard. Aarron Mack was no fool. He would want to know why Lew Margolis was firing her. And what was Lew Margolis going to say? Cody didn't even want to think about it.

'Another drink?' Linda offered.

He declined. He had to find a hotel to spend the night in. The thought of another evening with Carol Cameron was too much to take.

Dallas was up at six. She drank endless cups of coffee, and at nine o'clock she called Lew Margolis at the studio and got his secretary who said that he wasn't in yet. Of course she could phone him at home, but Doris would be there, and that just wouldn't be wise.

She waited until ten, and called the studio again. 'Mr Margolis is in a meeting,' the secretary said.

'Tell Mr Margolis to call me back as soon as he can. It's urgent.'

Linda was just waking. 'What's the plan of action?' she asked.

'I'll make that bastard sorry,' Dallas replied, her eyes steely. 'Who the fuck does he think he's messing with?'

Linda said, 'You need any help, I'm here.'

Dallas nodded. 'Thanks. But this creep I can manage all on my own. He seems to have forgotten about the photos.'

'I know that now is probably not quite the time to ask – but I'm busting to know. What happened with you and the great white master last night?'

'He's a prick,' replied Dallas dismissively. 'I guess you were right.'

Linda didn't probe. She could see that Dallas' mind was elsewhere.

Lew Margolis did not call back.

At eleven o'clock Dallas drove to the studio. She drove past the studio gates with a wave, and parked near Lew's office. His secretary looked flustered to see her.

'It's all right,' Dallas said, 'I'm sure he's expecting me.'

Unsure, the secretary buzzed her boss.

'Send her in,' he commanded.

Dallas strode scornfully into his office and perched on the side of his marble desk.

'Hi, Lew. What seems to be the problem?'

His small eyes flicked over her body. He chomped steadily on a thick cigar. 'No problem.'

'I think there is.'

'Yes?'

'Yes. I think you've made a couple of hasty moves. I think you're forgetting a few things.'

His nostrils twitched, a nervous habit he had acquired twenty years previously. 'Cunt,' he said evenly, 'stupid cunt. I took a lot from you, but when it comes to messing with my wife . . . You filthy whore.'

'What are you talking about?'

'You know goddamn right well what I'm talking about,' he sneered. 'Pervert! Degenerate! I took a lot of flak from you – but when you try to put your stinking hands on my wife . . .'

Gradually it dawned on Dallas that Doris had been making up stories. She got off the desk. Stood facing him, shaking with fury.

'You're screwing your facts up. *I* never tried to touch your wife – she came after me.'

'Lying cunt,' stated Lew, not believing a thing she said. 'You go near my wife again and I'll have you fixed permanently. I'll have your legs broken – you face smashed up. Please believe me, these things can be arranged.'

Dallas attempted to keep her voice even. 'I don't know what Doris has told you, but . . .'

Lew ground the remains of his cigar into an ashtray. 'Don't even mention her name,' he warned.

'I'll mention what I like,' she flashed back .'I'll mention certain photos I have of you that Doris might be interested in seeing.

Keep this shit up, and they'll be in her hands today.'

Lew laughed. It wasn't a pleasant laugh. 'What photos?' he jeered.

'You know what photos.'

He laughed again. 'Do you think I'm a fool? Do you think I have got where I am today by letting cunts like you get the better of me? Those photos don't exist any more – they ceased to exist weeks ago. The set hidden in your house – gone. The set you gave me – destroyed.'

'You're forgetting the negatives.'

'I'm forgetting nothing. Go to your bank – check out your safety deposit box.' He chuckled. 'Sometimes it helps to have power in this town.'

'You're bluffing.'

'Don't count on it. I was going to keep you on in the series – you were good – you could have been a big star. But when you tried to lay your filthy whore's hands on my wife you went too far . . . So get out.' His eyes gleamed with malice. 'You never honestly believed you'd got the better of *me*, did you?'

She left the studio in a hurry, drove straight to her bank. He had to be bluffing – how the hell could anyone open another person's private safety deposit box. Banks were places of trust, it was impossible.

She requested her box, went in a private cubicle to open it, stared in dismay. It was empty.

She wanted to scream. It was so unfair.

'Who has been to my box?' she asked the clerk.

He looked at her in surprise. 'No one m'am.'

What did he know? Nothing. She could complain, make a fuss, it would all be to no avail.

Tears of frustration filled her eyes. Men. They had been screwing her all her life – if not physically then metaphorically.

She wanted revenge. Lew Margolis was not going to get the better of her. No way.

A plan was already forming in her mind. A plan that would need a certain amount of working out.

She strode out of the bank to her car. Thoughtfully she drove home.

Al King was sitting in his chauffeured limo outside her house. He leapt out when he saw her and started mouthing apologies. She brushed past him. 'Go fuck yourself, Al,' she muttered, and slammed the door in his face.

•

Doris Andrews said, 'This is a very sweet house, dear.'

'Thank you,' replied Dallas demurely. 'Can I fix you something to drink?'

Doris laughed softly in her breathy fashion. 'Much too early for me. But maybe an orange juice if it's freshly squeezed.'

'Sure,' said Dallas brightly, 'it will only take me a sec. Why don't you sit out by the pool?'

Doris said, 'What a sweet pool,' and took herself outside, and settled on a lounger.

Dallas rushed into the kitchen, grabbed some oranges, cut them in half, and squeezed the juice out.

She reached for a half-smoked joint she had left in an ashtray, and dragged deeply. It was her third one that day. She knew the only way she would be able to go through with her plan was if she was well stoned.

It had been easy to persuade Doris to come to her house. One phone call. A hint of promise.

The difficult part had been getting Linda to go along with the plan. 'Not again!' she had complained. 'I think you're playing it too close. Lew Margolis is obviously a man with connections – it could be *dangerous*.'

Dallas had been her most persuasive, and a reluctant Linda was ready to do her part.

The orange juice was squeezed. Dallas poured it into a glass crushing a speed pill in with it. Wouldn't do any harm in case Doris suddenly developed inhibitions. She carried the juice outside. 'I should be very cross with you,' she said, 'you've been telling your husband things about us that aren't strictly true.'

Doris widened blue eyes – a famous screen gesture that had saved her from countless villians. 'I only hinted. Just the teensiest little hint. You see I was jealous,' she giggled self-consciously, 'when I saw you leaving my party with that – that – monster!'

Dallas said, 'Your teeniest little hint got me fired – you know that? Booted out of the series. Is that what you wanted?'

Doris looked immediately contrite. 'Oh no! My dear, I'm so sorry. I had no idea . . .'

Not much – thought Dallas – you conniving jealous bitch. You saw me leave with Al after turning *you* down, and your ego couldn't take that. So you screwed me – but good.

'I didn't think you did,' she said, 'but all the same . . .' she shrugged, 'I'm out, and I just don't know what to do.'

Doris quickly said, 'I'll talk to Lew, I'll tell him I made a mistake.'

'You know it won't do any good. You told me yourself how jealous of you he is.'

Doris nodded sadly. 'That's true. Oh dear, what have I done?'

You've used *your* power – just like your husband used his. And you both think you've fixed me. But I am no shrinking out-of-town hick. You'll both see how smart I am.

Dallas patted her gently on the hand. 'Don't worry about it, drink your orange juice. Do you mind if I swim?'

'I feel so badly . . .' Doris started to say. But the words stuck in her throat as Dallas stepped out of the shorts and halter top she was wearing, revealing her totally beautiful naked body.

Doris stared.

Dallas ran her hands casually over her own body, lingering for a second on her erect nipples. 'You going to swim?' she asked Doris. 'It's quite secluded here, au natural is the order of the day.' She reached out and started to unbutton Doris's silk shirt. 'Here, let me help you.'

Doris didn't move. Dallas finished unbuttoning the shirt, took it off her. Then she unhooked the white bra Doris was wearing. It was padded, giving Doris curves she didn't possess.

Slowly Doris lifted her hands and cupped Dallas' full breasts. She said, her voice no more than a breathy whisper, 'I knew you would be beautiful,' and she pulled the younger woman close to her so that she could take her breast in her mouth.

Dallas closed her eyes tightly. Just pretend you're not even here. Just hope that Linda is already in action capturing photos that Lew Margolis will *really* find interesting.

Cody went along with Dallas' request that he release no statement to the press. 'It would be better coming from us than from the studio,' he suggested.

She was adamant. It was almost as if she expected some miracle to happen and that she would be reinstated as 'Man Made Woman'. Unbeknown to her, the studio had not cancelled the series at all. They had merely replaced Dallas with another girl. Chuck had told Cody. 'It's ridiculous!' he had exploded on the phone. 'How can you change the star of a television series halfway through? Anyway Dallas was marvellous in it – they've replaced her with a girl who has nothing – the public will never buy it. Everyone here thinks Lew Margolis has blown his stack.'

Cody agreed. He remembered the outcry when the 'Bionic Woman' had guested on a couple of 'Six Million Dollar Men' segments and been killed off. The public just wouldn't accept it, and to its cost the studio who owned the series had had to bring her back to life.

Cody knew that when the series was shown the public would want Dallas. As far as he was concerned Lew Margolis had gone stark raving mad. The man was a fool, and eventually he would have to pay for it – Cody would personally see to that.

Meanwhile he had Aarron Mack to worry about. He was anxious to meet with Dallas and have a private discussion.

'I have heard certain disturbing rumours,' he had told Cody on the phone, 'and I wish to see the young lady and discuss them. I will send my plane for her to meet me in Palm Springs tomorrow.'

'I'll come with her,' Cody said.

'I'd sooner meet with her alone.'

Cody had a bad feeling. His gut reaction was not in good shape. Either that or he was developing an ulcer.

Linda lit a cigarette. Her hand was shaking.

God! Miss Sophistication. One lesbian scene and she was a mass of nerves.

How could Dallas do it? It was difficult to understand. This whole blackmail thing was going too far. Once – to help a friend out. Twice – Linda was disgusted with herself. It was sickening. And to have had to have watched Dallas and Doris Andrews together. Ugh! She was certainly no prude. But two women together . . . It was not that they had done much of anything – a man and a woman doing the same things would have been fairly tame stuff – but two women doing it. Linda couldn't reconcile herself to *that*. Lesbian tendencies she had never had, and this had put her off forever.

She went into the bathroom and lifted the photos out of the solution. They were good. Clear. Revolting.

Dallas had shut herself in the bedroom and Linda was glad. In a way she was almost embarrassed to face her. It made things somehow different between them.

As soon as she had finished the pictures she wanted to get away. Dallas had asked too much in return for sleeping on her couch. The very next day she would find herself an apartment.

Dallas lay on her bed staring blankly into space.

What had happened to her Californian dream? A nice home, a steady career, a baby. What did she want now?

389

She had her house, that was okay. But the desire to have a baby was gone. Who needed to bring children into a world like this? Career was important too. The desire to be someone. And she enjoyed working. When she was before the cameras she could really forget everything and become the character she was playing. So why couldn't they all leave her alone? Why did she always have to be on her guard, scheming, planning, plotting a way to come out on top?

Bobbie had known how to escape the pressures of just existing. Heroin. It had killed her. Maybe she was better off.

Dallas turned over and lay on her stomach. She had showered when Doris left, scrubbed her body thoroughly. Sex became more and more of a hassle. She hated it. She went through the motions with a complete lack of feeling. The scene with Doris had been particularly difficult.

Why did they want her? The face. The body. Is that all they saw?

She shut her eyes, squeezing them tightly so that the tears that had suddenly formed couldn't escape.

Cody had phoned earlier to tell her that Aarron Mack requested her presence in Palm Springs the next day. What did he want?

She reached on her bedside table for the bottle of seconal pills – took one – two – three.

Soon she was asleep.

The insistent ringing of the telephone woke her the next morning. She could hear the ringing, hoped that Linda would pick it up. Goddamn it. The phone kept ringing. She reached for it, mumbled hello.

It was Cody, cheerful and bright, reminding her that he would pick her up in an hour to take her to the airport.

'*Why* do I have to go?' she complained.

'Because we don't want to blow *this* deal – he needs jollying up.'

'Terrific. Play with his balls and lick his ass.'

'I'll ignore that. You know how to handle him.'

'Sure.' Sourly she hung up.

She got out of bed, stretched, yawned. She felt terrible – heavy and hungover. She reached for a joint, lit up. Soon she felt better.

There was an envelope and a note from Linda in the kitchen. The envelope contained a set of photos complete with negatives. The note read, 'Here you go – guess they are what you wanted. Got great deal on apartment – so am moving. Will call you. Thanks for everything – Linda.' Dallas crumpled the note in her hand. She didn't blame her.

Critically she examined the photos. They were better than she had hoped. Doris revealed as Lew had never seen her before, and obviously not a reluctant participant. Good.

She carefully chose two, sealed them in an envelope, and addressed it to Lew marked 'Personal and Private.' Then she sealed the negatives in another envelope, which she planned to deposit at a bank near the airport under a false name. Let Lew find them there. The remainder of the photographs she hid around the house. As long as the negatives were safe it didn't matter if Lew found these.

She dressed. Smoked another joint. Packed a small bag in case she stayed overnight in Palm Springs.

Cody picked her up on time, chatted inanely all the way to the airport. He thought he was cheering her up. Before boarding Aarron's plane she squeezed his hand, 'Don't worry, kid, everything's cool.'

'I know, I know,' he agreed, 'let me know what time you'll be back and I'll meet you.'

She giggled. She suddenly felt great.

Cody realized she was stoned, but it was too late to stop her from going.

'Don't call me, I'll call you,' she chuckled. 'Be a good fella.'

He didn't like to see her in that kind of state. He wished he was still around to look after her. 'Watch it,' he said sternly. 'Don't do anything you don't want to. Remember we have a contract, he has to honour it.'

'Course I'll remember.' She winked lewdly. 'I won't even fuck him unless he asks me!'

She slept on the short flight to Palm Springs. Slept in the car on the way to Aarron's estate.

He sat beside the swimming pool, a gnarled, nut-brown figure in snappy red-striped bathing shorts.

He kissed her hand, offered a choice of champagne or mineral water. 'Are you hungry?' he asked solicitously 'Shall we eat lunch now or later?'

She opted for later, changed into a bikini, and flopped out beside him, immediately falling asleep.

He watched her sleep. How could he believe what he had heard about her? She breathed deeply, her magnificent breasts almost escaping from the brief bikini top. He wanted to reach over and touch her. He didn't care what he had heard. He was determined to possess her.

She slept for almost three hours, then she woke, stretched,

rolled into the swimming pool, splashed around, emerged, and said, 'I'm sorry Aarron. Did I sleep for long?'

He nodded, 'You must have been tired, it's past four. I'll tell them to serve lunch.'

'Great! I'm famished.' She excused herself, went into the house, got a joint from her purse and smoked it in the john.

Lobster, caviar, and smoked salmon with an array of salads waited. She ate heartily, and then polished off half a delicious chocolate cake.

'That was good!' she exclaimed.

'You were hungry,' Aarron stated.

'Yeah. I guess I've been working too hard. It's really nice to have a few days off.'

'A few days off?' He paused, obviously puzzled, 'but I thought—'

'Oh, don't tell me you've heard the rumour about me being off the series too.'

'Yes.'

'Don't believe it. I'm having a week off.'

'But Lew Margolis telephoned me himself.'

Dallas laughed. 'Poor old Lew. I think he's getting senile. It's all a mistake. I told him I needed a rest, he seems to think I want more money. Everything's a bit confused, but I can promise you I'll be back on the set next Monday. By the way, what was it you wanted to discuss with me?'

She had Aarron completely puzzled. He had prepared a speech, but it didn't seem to fit now. Finally he said, 'I am really most perplexed.'

'Why?' she asked, pouring herself some more champagne.

Aarron shook his head sadly. 'I have known Lew Margolis for many years. We are not close friends but we are old acquaintances. I should warn you that he is saying some very strong things about you.'

Dallas widened her eyes in surprise. 'About me?'

'Of course I do not believe what he is saying,' Aarron hastened to add, 'but all the same, they are disturbing things, and I think we should discuss them. You see, being the Mack girl will identify you very closely with all the Mack products, and should there be even the slightest grain of truth in what Lew is saying . . .' He paused to have a short coughing fit. 'I can be quite frank with you, Dallas. Mack cosmetics is my company, but I am getting on in years, I have had to make certain tax provisions for my family.

I have a son and a daughter, they are both married. I have five grandchildren.'

'So?' questioned Dallas impatiently. She didn't want his life history, she wanted him to get to the point.

'I make the final decisions, but there is a family board of directors at Mack cosmetics. They are happy that you are to be the Mack girl, but any scandal . . .'

Dallas laughed. 'I thought we had a contract?' she questioned mockingly.

'Oh yes,' agreed Aarron, 'with options of course.'

'Of course.'

'If anything Lew Margolis is saying about you is true . . . Then you would be paid up to the first option . . .'

'And not used.' She finished for him.

'Exactly.'

She sipped her champagne, her green eyes glinting dangerously. 'So tell me, Aarron, what exactly is Lew saying about me?'

He looked uncomfortable. 'I don't believe it. I know it can't possibly be true.'

'But you felt you had to ask me anyway, just in case.' Suddenly she hated him, sitting in his Palm Springs mansion so rich and secure.

'Yes.' He was relieved she was so understanding.

'Spit it out, Aarron, I can't wait to hear.'

'He said that you were a prostitute. That you and a coloured girl used to work together. Also that you were a lesbian and the two of you used to give shows.'

Dallas threw back her head and roared with laughter. 'He said *that* – about *me*. It's unbelievable! And anyway, even if there was the slightest bit of truth in it, how the hell would *he* know? The whole thing is utterly ridiculous – I mean it's absolutely laughable!'

'I knew it couldn't possibly be true,' said Aarron quickly. 'I just wanted to hear you deny it.'

'Deny it? It's hardly worth denying, it's so ludicrous. Who could possibly believe it? I told you the man is getting senile.'

'If you wish I can have my lawyer draft a letter on your behalf to restrain him from repeating such a vicious story. It would be best to stop him now.'

'Yes. I think we should.'

Aarron leaned across the table and patted her fondly on the shoulder. 'I knew there was no truth in it. I remember in New

York when we first met how you wouldn't even let me touch you.'

She lowered her eyes. 'I'm like that, Aarron. A man must be prepared to wait with me.'

He sighed happily. 'Yes, yes. I understand. In spite of your looks, at heart you are really just an old-fashioned girl.'

She hid a smile that threatened to break into uncontrollable laughter.

'Yes, Aarron, you are so right. At heart I'm really just an old-fashioned girl.'

At Aarron's request she decided to spend the night. Why go rushing back to LA. For what? Anyway she wanted to wait until Lew received the photos. Let him stew a little before she contacted him. Let him call Cody and beg to have her back on the series. Let him suffer when he saw the intimate pictures of his wife.

Aarron wanted to take her out to dinner, but she pleaded a headache, and retired to the guest suite, where she sat in bed watching TV and smoking another joint.

There was an interview with Al King arriving in Las Vegas. He was there for a big charity concert the next day. She stared at his image on the screen, dragging on the joint, and beginning to get the feeling that seemed reserved only for him. He was a bastard. He had stood her up for a skinny bag. Screw him.

Why not? He was available. Why not get him out of her system once and for all?

Yeah – why not? She had nothing better to do.

She grinned. She could just imagine his surprise when she turned up in Las Vegas.

fifty-six

Cristina telephone Louis Baptista. He was delighted to hear from her, even though she had given him a most abrupt and hurtful brush several months previously.

'Can we see each other again, Louis?' she asked sweetly.

He was hesitant, he had started to date other girls, started to forget the hurt. 'What did you have in mind?' he questioned falteringly.

'I don't know. I've been thinking about you a lot. Maybe we could go riding in Tijuca forest like we used to.'

'Yes, all right.'

'If you *want* to, that is.'

'You know I want to.' His voice was gruff.

'Tomorrow?'

'I'll collect you from your house at noon.'

'That would be fine.' She banged the phone down, and stuck her tongue out at Nino, who stood by her side. 'Satisfied?'

'Excellent. I bet he was thrilled.'

'Of course.'

'Is he still mad for your childish body?'

'I expect so.'

'I told you it would be easy.'

'I *knew* it would be easy. I just didn't want to do it.' She threw her arms around Nino. 'Do I *have* to see him?'

'Only for a few weeks. It won't be so bad. Then when it's all over, if you still want to, we can go to your parents and tell them we want to get married. And if they don't approve, we'll do it anyway.'

She hugged him. 'I wish we could do it now.'

He removed her arms. 'You know that's impossible. Listen, I have a meeting this afternoon. You had better run on home.'

'Can't I come with you?'

'No.'

'Why not? If I'm going to be a part of it why can't I come?'

'Because they wouldn't like it.'

She pouted. 'Who are *they*? And why wouldn't *they* like it?'

'How many times do I have to explain things to you? Before you can become a member of the organization you have to have *proved* yourself. After all you are not one of us.'

'I should think setting up these two burglaries would have proved whose side I was on.'

'*I* know whose side you are on, and after the kidnapping – if all goes well – you'll be accepted. But not now – not yet. Don't push.'

'All right. But when I'm your wife they'll *have* to accept me. *Then* I'll be one of you.'

He laughed bitterly. 'Yes. Poor.'

'I'll go home now. Shall I come over after seeing Louis tomorrow?'

Nino hurriedly said, 'No. Certainly not. Concentrate on Louis. I don't want to see you for a week.'

'A week! Nino, that's impossible. I couldn't live that long without seeing you.'

'In three weeks, if this is successful, you won't have to live two minutes without me. Isn't that worth giving up something for?'

She sighed. 'I suppose so . . .'

He cupped her face and kissed her gently. 'A little something to be getting on with. Well – child, I'll see you in a week.'

'If I live, and don't call me child.'

'I'll call you woman when you have proved that you are.'

'I thought I had done *that*.'

'Maybe – we'll see how you get on with Louis.'

She stuck out her tongue again. 'Pig!'

'Child!' He guided her to the door.

'I'll phone you every day,' she said.

'No. Not even that. I want *all* your energies to go in *his* direction.'

'But, Nino . . .'

He placed a finger on her lips and moved her gently out the door. 'Goodbye, my love, do a good job.'

When she was finally gone he let out a groan of relief. A whole week! It was too wonderful to contemplate. He would be free to see Talia, spend some time with her, sleep with her. A solid diet of Cristina was so boring. Now if it had been her mother . . .

Louis was essential to the plan. As Carlos Baptista's son he would obviously have access to places Al King would be – and access was the most important part. Unbeknown to Cristina the kidnap had been planned. Why should he tell her? Who was she but a stupid little rich girl whose mind could be manipulated by his body. And his body was going to become famous and powerful as a result of the Al King kidnap.

He smiled. When this plan proceeded to its triumphant conclusion he would no longer have to tout his body. He would automatically become one of the leaders. He knew it would be so. Besides, his fortune had been told, and it was in the cards.

Nino was confident that the cards never lied.

The week dragged by as far as Cristina was concerned. Louis, thrilled to be reinstated in her life, was happy to spend every day with her.

They went riding in Tijuca forest twice. They took the cable car to Sugar Loaf Mountain, which was a really tourist thing to do, but which Louis said would be fun. They went to the Botanical Gardens, the Museum of Modern Art, the Jockey Club, the Yacht Club.

Cristina found herself mixing once more with all her old friends.

How childish they all seemed to her. How unaware of what was happening in the world. All they seemed concerned with was parties, new cars, and having fun.

The girls would group together and giggle about the boys. '*He* tried to put his hand up my shirt.' 'Santiago is a *great* kisser.' Such silly things. Cristina could hardly believe that only months before *she* had been a part of this juvenile group. Oh, the things she could tell them now! How she could shock them!

One afternoon she was cornered by Marella Bogatos who insisted on telling her the gory details of the robbery her family had experienced. 'It was so dreadful, Cristina, you just can't imagine. They cut off the poor dog's head – *cut it off.* Then they wrote terrible things all over the walls *in his blood.*'

Cristina shuddered. She was sure Marella must be exaggerating. Nino and his partners in crime couldn't possibly be that cruel. Thank God she had never allowed them to rob *her* house.

'These people must be sick,' Marella continued. 'They must be animals. Mama has had a complete breakdown, and we are selling the house. It's not what they took, Cristina, it's just the horrible feeling that their senseless violence has left.'

For a moment Cristina felt sorry for what she had done. Then she thought of Nino – of his impassioned appeals for equality – his sincereness about his cause. He was right. To redistribute some of the wealth was a good thing.

She ached to be with him. Louis was sweet, he had always been sweet. But he was a baby. A rich, spoiled baby.

On the day before she was due to see Nino, Louis took her to an open-air concert outside the Opera House. After, he said he wanted to surprise her, and he drove his red sports car up into the mountains to a small country house his parents kept there. He had obviously been there earlier in the day because the table was laid for two, with candles waiting to be lit, and a cold supper in the fridge.

'Surprise!' he said. 'I wanted tonight to be special.'

'But I thought we were going dancing.'

'We can go later if you want. I just thought it would be nice if we were alone together. We always seem to be surrounded by people.'

Suddenly he was all over her. 'I like you, Cristina. You know how much I like you. I thought for a while that we were finished – you became so cold. Now we're together again I want to ask your father's permission for us to be married next year.' He reached into his jacket pocket and produced a small box. 'Here, I've brought you a ring. I love you, Cristina, I always have. We were meant to be married.' He plunged his mouth down on hers, kissing her frantically.

Nino had not instructed her how to deal with *this* situation. She had another two weeks to go. If she shoved Louis away and told him her answer was no, that might spoil everything. Instinct told her she had to play him along. So although she didn't feel like it, she kissed him back, and let his hands linger for a moment on her breasts before pushing him away.

'Don't, Louis.' she reprimanded him sharply.

'I'm sorry. I don't mean to take liberties with you. It's just that I want you so much, I always have.'

Idly she glanced at the ring he had presented her with. It was a heart-shaped sapphire surrounded with diamonds. It must have cost a fortune. It *was* beautiful. She took it from the box and slipped it on her finger. It fitted perfectly. She could wear it for two weeks . . . Give it back to him when she told him that they couldn't marry.

'Do you like it?' Louis asked anxiously. 'If you don't we could change it.'

'It's very pretty.'

'*You're* very pretty.' And he was grabbing her again, exploring her mouth with his tongue, allowing his hands to slip from her shoulders to her breasts.

In spite of herself she felt excited. He wanted her so much that she couldn't help feeling a surge of power. She was a woman and he didn't even know it. How surprised he would be if he knew how experienced she was.

She had noticed the bulge in his trousers, and that gave her a feeling of power too.

Louis was a good catch. Marie Therese had been mad about him for years, and Marie Therese was much prettier than she was, but it was *she* he wanted.

'Have you ever been with a woman?' she gasped, pushing him off once more, and watching him to gauge his reaction.

'No,' he said, flushing.

'But you must have,' she insisted. 'All boys of your age must have had *some* sort of experience.'

He turned away from her. 'I don't think I should tell you.'

'Of course you must tell me. If we are to be engaged, I must know everything. There can be no secrets.'

'When I was seventeen my father took me to a whore house.'

'How exciting!'

'Cristina! It wasn't exciting. It was disgusting. Old women with floppy bellies. I did what I had to do and never went back. My father thought that made me a man.'

'And did it?'

'It made me sick. I swore I would wait until I found the girl I loved.'

'And here I am,' Cristina teased.

Louis was very serious. 'Yes. Here you are. And I am glad that I have waited, because we will be able to start out together. It's the way it should be.'

She wanted to laugh in his face. How young and naive and romantic his words were. Poor Louis. He was such a baby.

Evita could not understand it. One moment her daughter was starry-eyed about the boy called Nino – the next – Louis was back in her life.

Jorge was triumphant. 'I told you not to worry about her,' he crowed. 'She probably quarrelled with Louis because he tried to take liberties with her. Now he realizes he cannot get away with that kind of behaviour. Our daughter is a good girl.'

'Perhaps,' mused Evita. But she wasn't satisfied. Something wasn't quite right, and she decided to go ahead with plans to take Cristina off for a long trip somewhere.

Her plans were shattered when Cristina flashed an engagement ring under her nose.

'Louis wishes to meet with poppa,' her daughter said. 'Some old-fashioned idea about getting his permission.'

'It's wonderful. I'm so thrilled for you, my darling,' Evita said. But still she had a feeling of disquiet. Cristina did not appear to be particularly excited at the prospect of being engaged to one of the richest young men in Brazil.

'We'll throw an engagement party,' Evita said. 'We'll make it a marvellous occasion. Would you like that?'

'Oh, mama, I don't want a fuss. Can we wait a few weeks?'

'Certainly, dear.' But Evita couldn't imagine why she would want to wait. 'Whatever happened to that young man you brought home? What was his name? Nino?'

'How should I know?' replied Cristina crossly. 'He was just a friend.'

Evita was quick to catch the evasive quality of her daughter's voice. Somehow, in spite of the engagement, she felt that they had not heard the last of Nino.

He lay on his crumpled bed and grinned and said, 'You didn't waste any time then?'

Cristina grinned back as she stood beside the bed. '*Some* people find me irresistible.'

He patted a space beside him. 'Come join me and collect your reward.'

'I can't. I have to get home, Louis is picking me up. We're spending the day at his house.'

'How nice. No time for me any more. I can see you did manage to live the week through without me.'

'Nino! I'm doing it for us. *You* were the one who said I have to concentrate on Louis absolutely.'

Nino raised his eyebrows. Yes he had said it, but he hadn't expected her to take him quite so literally. He had imagined she would come running to him, unable to wait to leap into his bed. He hadn't wanted to sleep with her, but he had steeled himself to the fact that he must. Now she obviously didn't want to. Was he losing his touch?

He rolled off the bed and held her loosely round the waist. 'Time for a kiss at least?'

She giggled. 'Please! I'm engaged to another man. We can have none of this.'

Suddenly he was angry. 'Are you sure you are not taking this game too seriously?'

She was contrite, showering his face with kisses. 'I'm sorry – sorry – sorry. I'm only doing what you *wanted* me to do.' Secretly she was thrilled, because Nino seemed almost jealous.

'Yes, of course,' he said. 'So what information do you have for me?'

'Plenty. I've found out everything I can. Louis thinks that I am Al King's greatest fan! I can't even stand him – my mother buys all his records.'

'Well?' questioned Nino, impatiently.

'Let me see now.' She paused provocatively, enjoying her small moment of power. 'He's arriving in Rio the day before the concert . . .'

'What time?'

'I don't know.'

'Find out. It's important.'

'He's travelling in his own plane.'

'Who with?'

'I don't know yet, but apparently Louis' father will be getting a list. Mr Baptista will be meeting him at the airport with television, photographers – a whole big deal. Then in the evening there's to be a big party for him, to which I am naturally invited.'

'Good. Be sure to meet him. Be sure he will remember you.'

'How do I do that?'

'We'll think of something, but it's important that he knows you.'

'Why?'

'I'm supposed to be asking the questions. I have a lot to work out.'

'Anyway – I don't know what he'll do the next day – but in the evening there is the concert, and apparently he'll be leaving for the airport immediately after. Something about he's nervous of crowds and wants to get out before the people leave the stadium. I think Louis said a helicopter will be waiting to take him to the airport.'

'You've done very well.'

'I try to please. When do you think you will take him?'

'I don't know.'

'If you manage it before the concert I guess they'll pay you the money quickly. How many hours will you hold him? You won't hurt him, will you?'

Nino shook his head. How stupid she was. 'Everything will be fine. Nobody will get hurt.'

'I've got to rush. Can I see you again this week?'

'Phone me as soon as you find anything else out.'

She kissed him. 'I love you so much, Nino. I'll be glad when this is all over and we can be together.' She left quickly.

Nino sat thoughtfully on the side of his bed. She was playing games. She didn't realize this was for real. She didn't even realize the major part she was going to have to play in it.

Oh well – she would learn. If she wanted him she was going to have to pay for the privilege. And she would. He would make sure of that.

fifty-seven

Dallas hailed a cab at Las Vegas airport. 'Take me to your leader!' she giggled at the driver.

'Hey, lady – you wanna go somewhere – tell me – I'll be happy to oblige. You wanna play games find another cab, I gotta livin' to make.'

She mock saluted. 'Yes, officer.'

'So – where to?'

It suddenly occurred to her that she had no idea where Al was appearing. 'Big charity telethon show,' she mumbled – Christ but she was stoned. 'Al King.'

He gunned the cab into action. Fortunately he seemed to know what she was talking about. She was delightfully out of it – spaced halfway to the moon.

She giggled quietly to herself. Wouldn't do to annoy the driver. 'Mustn't annoy the driver . . .' she found herself mumbling out loud.

He clacked his lips in disgust and ignored her. Dumb hooker. Any woman arriving unescorted in Vegas was automatically a dumb hooker. And this one was worse than most – with her messy clothes and tangled hair. Pretty enough – but who the hell did she hope to pick up in the state she was in?

'I've been here before,' Dallas announced. 'Came here with a friend called Bobbie coupla years back. She died, y'know.'

'I didn't know that,' the driver replied, his sarcasm lost on her.

She shook her head. 'It doesn't matter.' She tried to recollect her day. It seemed she had just woken up and here she was. No. Somewhere along the way it had been a long day, and now it was night. She giggled quietly, and reached for the remains of a joint stuffed in her jeans pocket. She lit up.

'Put that out,' snapped the driver, 'you think I wanna get busted?'

'Think I wanna get busted!' mimicked Dallas.

'Watch it, sister.'

She started to sing, 'I ain't your sister whacha say to that mister?' Then she laughed so hard she couldn't continue singing. Wasn't life fun? Why had she never realized it before? 'I was in Palm Springs this morning. Woke up there – beautiful day, so I swam, lay around in the sun.'

'Why didn't you stay there?' asked the cab driver sourly.

'You know something – I nearly did. But hey – how would *you* like to fuck an old guy of seventy?'

He swerved the cab over to the side of the road with a great mashing of brakes. 'Out!' he commanded. 'I don't havta listen to your foul language in my cab. I gotta daughter your age.'

'Oh Christ!' muttered Dallas.

'*Out*!' he screamed.

'Shit! Don't go gettin' your balls in a sweat, sugar! Hey – I sound just like Bobbie. You know Bobbie?'

He was red in the face.

Dallas climbed out of the cab, and he threw her bag out after her.

'Scum!' he muttered.

'Bum!' she replied, still laughing, unperturbed at being dumped at the side of the road.

Yes. She could remember Palm Springs. She had left there sometime in the afternoon, been flown to Los Angeles in Aarron's private jet. At LA airport she had booked herself out on the next flight to Vegas. Didn't want to see anyone. Didn't want anyone to know where she was.

Let them all sweat. She would return when *she* was ready.

On the plane she had met a lovely lady with freaked-out hair and granny glasses, who had sold her a fine supply of Qualudes and some good grass. Fortunate, because she was starting to run out.

Why had it taken her so long to find out what a good time you could have when you were stoned? She had smoked joints on and off for years without much effect. But suddenly – jeeze – use enough – mix in a few amphetamines, a little speed, and you could be flying in no time at all. It was a *wonderful* feeling. Pure. Clear. Mind-expanding. For the first time she could understand Kip Rey's hang-up. And to think she had been the one to criticize him, put him down, when all he had been doing was escaping to wonderland. Of course, he had died. Accident. Unfortunate.

A truck was pulling over to the side of the road, the driver whistling at her. 'Need wheels, baby?'

She smiled. Nice, kind guy. 'Sure.'

'Climb aboard.'

She threw her bag into his cab, jumped in.

'You got a great pair,' he said. 'They for real?'

''Bout as real as your balls.'

He laughed, jamming the big truck into motion. 'Where to, big eyes?'

'Caesars Palace,' she said mentioning the first place that came to mind.

'I'll give you door-to-door service, 'cos I like you. What you gonna give *me* in exchange?'

'Whatever turns you on, sugar sweets.' Pure Bobbie dialogue. It amused her to use it.

He opened his legs slightly, patted his crotch. 'I could use a hand job.'

Wasn't this where she had come in?

She waited until the truck stopped at a traffic light, jumped out.

'What the f . . .' began the driver.

'You're too late,' shouted Dallas, 'I gave it up. Give *yourself* a hand job, sport. You might enjoy it!'

She looked around. Where the hell was she? Shit. What a lousy idea *this* trip had been.

Three numbers, but they were screaming for more. Al looked to the side of the stage and shrugged. The sooner he was off the sooner he could get back to the tables. Fifty thousand down was a bummer – a loser's trip. He was a winner – and he was going to win it back – every goddamn dollar.

The redhead had been the catalyst, if she hadn't huffed and puffed all over his dice he would have won. She was a definite loser – thank Christ he hadn't touched *her*. She probably would have given him a dose.

One more chorus of 'Bad Black Alice'. These charity telethons were a pain in the ass. But he had agreed to do it. Every goddamn star in Califirnia had agreed to do it. The money was being raised for invalid children and as far as Al was concerned that was one charity you did anything for. Top priority.

Karmen Rush was waiting at the side of the stage to follow him on. He ignored her.

Christ it was hot – he was sweating like Bernie. Jeeze!

Luke was waiting with towels. Paul was waiting with a choked expression – he was more pissed off about Melanie giving him the boot than Al was about Edna. Poor sod. He should be dancing in the streets with joy – after all *he* had the children – his prime concern.

Al knew what he was going to do. He had made up his mind. After South America he was going to return to Los Angeles. He was going to buy himself the best goddam house around – and he was going to do the movie – give it a try. Then he was going to take six months off to write some new songs – stuff he really wanted to do.

Beyond that he didn't know. By that time his divorce should be through. He would be free.

Free to what? Fuck America?

He was sober again. Cold stone sober. The telethon hadn't given him much of a high. After playing such large venues a small audience was a bit of a come-down – millions had been watching him on television – but that wasn't the kick. The real thrill was having them out there before you. Feeling them. Smelling them. Peaking with them. The ultimate orgasm. He was looking forward to Rio. Two hundred thousand in one fell swoop. What an experience *that* should be.

The patrol car cruised to a stop beside Dallas, and one of the policemen leaned out. 'What are you doing out here?' he asked.

'Some creep gave me a lift and tried to rape me. I jumped out and here I am!'

'Hop in,' the cop said, 'where you headed?'

Thankfully she climbed in the back of the car.

'I want to get to the big charity telethon that's going on here tonight.'

'You got a ticket?'

'No, but I got a friend.' Stay straight, she warned herself, don't let them see you are out of your head.

'You hitch all the way here?'

Did she look *that* bad? Come to think of it she hadn't looked in a mirror all day. She had just thrown a T-shirt and jeans over her bikini when she left Palm Springs – all right in a hot little asshole of a town during the day – but not quite right for now. 'Yeah,' she said. Who needed conversations?

'You looking for a job here?'

'Not really.'

'It's tough city if you don't have a job. My cousin can always use pretty waitresses – Joe Vondello's on the strip – tell him Mac sent you.'

'Thank you, Mac.'

He laughed self-consciously. 'Any time.'

They dropped her outside the hotel where the telethon was taking place.

'I'll stop by Joe's in a coupla days - see how you're doing,' the cop said.

'Thanks,' she waved. Wow! Close! They could have taken her in for being out of control of her own body! She giggled at that, and wandered in a side entrance of the hotel and found a ladies' room.

Her appearance in the mirror sent her into gales of laughter. She did look a wreck. No make-up, uncombed hair, staring wild eyes. She fished some dark shades out of her bag and covered her tell-tale eyes. Then she popped a couple of pills, and realized that she hadn't eaten all day, and the nagging pain she had suddenly acquired was hunger.

She drifted out amongst the slot machines and roulette wheels. 'Where can I find Al King?' she asked a security guard.

He looked at her blankly. 'Who?'

'Forget it. Where's the telethon?'

'In the Princess room – it's all full – booked weeks ago.'

'Yeah?' She weaved slightly, moved away from him, and on impulse sat down at a roulette table. She fished in her bag, found a fifty and slid it over to the house man. He handed her a stack of dollar chips in exchange. She piled half of it on twenty-nine. The other half on thirty-five. Twenty-nine came up. She had won just under nine hundred dollars. 'Let it ride,' she said.

The houseman gave her an imperceptible wink from beneath his green-tinted head shade, and spun the wheel. Twenty-nine showed again.

A buzz went around the table. The houseman paid her thirty thousand six hundred and twenty-five dollars in placques. She tipped him the odd six hundred and twenty-five. The pit boss stepped forward to see what was going on.

'My lucky night,' laughed Dallas. Wow! Even money was easy to make when you were stoned!

'Dallas?' a voice questioned, 'Dallas babe. What the fucker-ooney *you* doin' in town?'

She turned to see Bernie Suntan. Big, fat, sweaty Bernie.

'I came to see Al,' she smiled, 'is he around?'

'For you he'll be around. You feel all right? You look a little shaky.'

'Terrific, just terrific.' She pushed her stool away from the table, went to stand up, felt sick. Then the room was spinning . . . spinning . . . spinning . . . And she blacked out.

As she fell the last words she heard were – 'Thirty thousand bucks . . . who wouldn't faint at winning that.'

*

'You want to make the party?' Paul asked. 'Everyone's going to be there.'

Al stepped out of the shower. He felt refreshed.

'I'm going to give the tables my undivided attention,' he said. 'You want to join me?'

'Your undivided attention lost you fifty thousand dollars earlier. That's a lot of money.'

'You're telling the man who is just about to make one million dollars for two days' work that fifty thousand dollars is a lot of money?'

Paul frowned. 'Stop jerking off, Al. You owe a fortune in taxes in England, and I suppose Edna is going to squeeze you 'til your balls drop off.'

'Edna might have changed, but not that much. I will take a bet with you she asks for nothing.'

Paul laughed disbelievingly.

'As for my English tax situation – it's all in hand, isn't it? And now that I'm a tax exile . . .'

'You are?'

'I told you I'm not going back.'

'Then you should have left before April.'

'Now he tells me.'

'I've been telling you for years. You never wanted to leave before.'

'I had Edna to think of.'

'Since when did you ever think of Edna?'

Al began to dress. 'You know your problem?'

'Please tell me.'

'You need to get laid. You're becoming like an uptight old lady.'

'We can't all solve everything with a stiff prick.'

'We can't all get stiff pricks either. You got a problem there too, Paul?'

'I'm going to the party. Go lose all your money, you stupid fuck.' Paul stalked out.

Al felt sorry when his brother had gone. He knew he was going through a bad time what with Melanie giving him the push and Linda pulling a number about not wanting to resume their relationship. But Jesus! What was *he* having – a picnic?

The trouble with Paul was he thought he was perfect. Nobody was perfect. What Paul needed was to go out, get good and bombed, and jam it into some randy blonde. He thought he was too good to do that. That's what really pissed Al off – why was it okay for him and not good enough for Paul? Al could remember the days when they had gone at it together. Share and share alike. But his brother had changed through the years. He had gotten uptight.

The hell with it – what was he worrying about Paul for – he could look after himself. Let him go to the party and mix with the stars – personally he couldn't give a shit. What he had in mind was a good hot poker game. Should be easy enough to find *that* in Las Vegas.

He finished dressing and was just about to leave the suite when the phone rang. He indicated to Luke, who was reading a magazine in the living room, to pick it up. 'I'm not here,' he mouthed.

Luke picked up the phone, listened for a moment, turned to Al. 'I think you'll want to be here for this. It's Bernie Suntan – says he has that lady downstairs – the one you like.'

It was the longest sentence Al had ever heard Luke utter. 'What lady?'

'Dallas.'

'He says . . .'

Al grabbed the phone. 'Bernie? What's happening?'

'Like – your friend Dallas is here. She seems kinda out of it. I just hadda pick her up off the floor by the roulette table.'

Al couldn't imagine Dallas being any other way except in complete control. 'Is she ill?' he asked urgently.

'Well . . .' Bernie scratched his head and stared at Dallas – who was lolled out giggling on a chair in the manager's office. Who was he to tell Al she was stoned out of her head? 'I think she'd like to see you.'

'Bring her up – what are you calling me for, schmuck? You *know* I want to see her.'

'Sure,' agreed Bernie, banging down the phone. You could never do anything right for Al. If he had taken Dallas up to Al's suite without asking he would have gotten a right bollocking. 'Come on, sweetheart.' He took Dallas by the arm. 'The big man is waiting.'

She giggled. 'Mustn't keep him waiting, huh Bernie? Mustn't keep the great white master waiting.'

Bernie was disappointed. He had thought this one was different. The few times he had seen her she had appeared to have conducted herself with a certain amount of class. But now she was just like all the rest. He could imagine what would happen when Al got a load of her in this state. One bang and out. Anyway, they were off to South America in the morning . . . What the fuck . . . Al would have been much better off taking advantage of some of the numbers in his little black book. Did he have some hot numbers! After all – Los Angeles was *his* town, and he could have imported anything Al wanted to Vegas – anything!

He thanked the manager, and guided Dallas out of the office. If she was what Al wanted then she was what Al was going to get.

They made an incongruous couple. The fat man in the lewd 'I choked Linda Lovelace' T-shirt teamed with white bermudas and tennis shoes, and the giggling girl with a mass of tangled hair and dark glasses.

'You got your cheque somewhere safe?' Bernie asked. The manager had exchanged her chips for a more secure way of carrying her money.

She patted her jeans pocket. 'Yeah.'

They boarded the elevator, attracting curious stares. Dallas started to sing in an out-of-tune voice. She smiled at two middle west matrons and their gaping husbands. 'I'm a gonna get laid,' she announced, 'I'm a gonna make it with Mister Superstar himself. Isn't that exciting?'

The two women turned away, clicking their mouths in disgust. The men glanced at each other, grinning with embarrassment.

Bernie nudged her to shut up.

She nudged him back. 'For a man who choked Linda Lovelace you sure are shy.' She winked at the two men. 'Right, fellas?'

The elevator stopped and emptied out.

'What's the matter with you?' Bernie muttered, pressing the button for them to ascend even higher. 'You turned into some kind of exhibitionist?'

'My, my. What long words you know,' she drawled. 'Al teach them to you?'

He pressed his mouth into a tight line. Fresh broads he didn't need. The sooner Al was shot of this one the better.

After stalking from his brother's room, Paul got to thinking that perhaps what Al had said was true. Perhaps he *did* need a woman. How long was it? Long enough. He had been choked and mortified to have suffered from a wet dream two evenings ago. A horrible experience, and something that had not happened to him since he was sixteen years old. Phydically he needed a woman. For once in his life he would just have to do it without the mental stimuli.

He wondered for the fiftieth time what Linda was doing. She

wasn't the type of woman to just sit around. She enjoyed sex – she wouldn't go this long without finding another partner. He hadn't had much success at winning her back. He knew it was because he was just offering her the same old deal. Now things were different. Now Melanie had forced his hand. *She* had left him. And he had what he wanted, he had his two children. How would Linda feel about becoming an instant mother? He wasn't too sure she would know how to handle it. He wasn't even sure any more if she would *want* to handle it. All that talk about how much she loved him . . . Of course if he phoned her, told her that *he* had left Melanie . . .

In the meantime he was going to follow big brother's advice and get laid.

'Where is she?' Cody's voice on the phone was desperate.

'I don't know,' Linda replied. 'I moved out yesterday morning. How did you track me down?'

'I called your agency in New York. Are you sure you don't know where Dallas is?'

'Of course I don't know. If I did I would tell you. Anyway, I thought she was going to Palm Springs.'

'She did. Stayed there last night, and was flown back to LA on Aarron's plane this afternoon. She never arrived back at her house.'

Linda glanced at her watch. It was eleven in the evening. 'Maybe she's visiting some friends.'

'I know all her friends. I've checked them all out.'

'Maybe there are a few you don't know.'

He was defeated. There were probably legions he didn't know. 'Yes,' he agreed miserably. 'I do have to talk to her, it's really urgent. You have no idea where I could find her?'

'No idea. What's the panic anyway? Is she back on the series?'

He was surprised. 'How did you know?'

'Just a feeling . . .' Lew Margolis certainly hadn't wasted any time. One glimpse of his wife's picture . . .

'They want her at the studio first thing tomorrow – got to re-shoot this week's segment – they're already out three days.'

'She'll turn up, I wouldn't worry about Dallas, she can look after herself.'

He was irritable. 'I know *that*. The whole situation is so strange, it's almost like she knew Margolis would change his mind. You know she didn't want me to release a press statement, and she was right.'

Linda yawned. 'Sixth sense, I guess. Listen, Cody, I was just going to sleep, so if there's nothing else . . .'

'I'm sorry,' he was immediately contrite, 'I hope I didn't wake you. I just thought you would know where she was. Can I give you my number in case she contacts you?'

'She won't contact me. She has no idea where I am.'

'Did you two have a fight?'

'No. I just felt the time had come to move on. You know, being with Dallas the whole time can sometimes become stifling.'

She was telling *him*. Ruefully he said, 'Yes I do know that. What do you have now – an apartment?'

'One room on Larrabee. Very pretty, communal pool – you must come by sometime.'

'I'd like that.' He hesitated, then, 'If you're not busy for dinner tomorrow . . . Do you like the Aware Inn?'

'Lovely.'

He was pleased. 'I'll pick you up around eight then, and in the meantime if you hear anything . . .'

'I won't hesitate to call you.' She put the phone down and wondered why she had accepted a dinner date with him. He was nice – that's why. He was attractive and kind and thoughtful, and why the hell couldn't Paul be like him?

Cody hung up and wondered yet again what kind of game Lew Margolis was playing. He couldn't figure it out. What was the point of it all? And where was Dallas? Didn't she realize he would be worried about her? Didn't she care? He was finally facing the fact that she didn't. There was only one person in Dallas' life, and that was herself.

'You're looking terrific,' Dallas giggled, 'horny and virile. Doesn't he look *great*, Bernie? A real sexy hunk of man! Hey Al – did you ever think of posing for one of those women's magazines – like *Playgirl* or *Viva*? I mean you *should* – you've got the body. Hasn't he got the body, Bernie? Great pectorals, I bet!'

Bernie backed out the door. 'I'll see you at the party, Al. Gotta rush now. Gotta change.'

'Oh – no more Linda Lovelace,' lamented Dallas. 'Shame! I bet she would have enjoyed being choked by you!' She kissed an amazed Al lightly on the cheek and wandered into the suite flopping down on the couch.

'She's out of it,' Bernie hissed. 'You want Luke should get rid of her?'

'Is she drunk?' Al asked.

'Stoned, baby – son-of-a-bitch stoned.'

'I'll handle it,' Al said shortly. 'Luke – you can take off, I won't be going out.'

Luke edged past Bernie. 'I'll get something to eat, then I'll be outside if you need me.'

Bernie said, 'Aw, Al, you should show your face at the party.'

'Forget it. Those things are a pain in the ass.'

'But . . .'

'Goodnight, Bernie.' He slammed the door in his face. Then he turned and walked slowly into the living room. Dallas was still on the couch. She had lit a joint and was dragging happily. She smiled at him, offered him a drag.

He shook his head.

'Well,' she said, 'wanna fuck now or later?'

He stared at her. This was the one woman he had desired and been unable to have. This was the one woman that was going to be different. She was different all right. She was full of surprises. *She* was speaking to him like *he* usually spoke to them.

So – here was the opportunity. Why wasn't he stripping off his clothes, going at it, and sending her out of his life? What was he waiting for?

He had wanted her desperately – he still did. But not like this, not while she was obviously spaced out and unaware of what was going on.

'What are you doing in Vegas?' he asked quietly.

'Came to see you, sugar sweets. Came to consummate our meeting of the minds.' She giggled uncontrollably. 'Came to get *fucked*. By the *King*. Al is King, isn't that what I'm always hearing? So prove it, man, show me. I'm ready, willing and able.' She broke into song, 'Ready, willing and able! Hey, sugar, come and kiss me, huh? Come and see if you're gonna be the one lights this baby's fire!'

'What happened? What got you into this state?'

'*State*! like *what* state?'

'Come on, you know what I mean.'

She rolled off the couch, bumped onto the floor, giggled, dropped the joint, attempted to stand, swayed against him. 'Shall I take my clothes off?' she slurred. 'Want to see what I'm offering you? I thought you *wanted* me. That's why I'm here babe, service with a smile – and no charge. You like that – no charge.'

He held her firmly by the shoulders. 'Where are you staying? I'm taking you home.'

She grinned. 'I am not staying anywhere. I am with you. Hey –
you got any coke? May as well make this a big trip. Whatcha say?'

He guided her into the bedroom and eased her on to the bed.
'Why don't you rest a minute, you look tired. I'll get you some
goodies . . .'

She threw her arms wide. 'Wow – whole room is spinning – like
it's a whole roundabout trip.' She closed her eyes. 'Gotta make
sure . . .' she mumbled, 'goddamn dyke . . . nice to be here . . .'
She lapsed into sleep. He had known she would. Whatever she
had been taking apart from the shit had finally knocked her out.
Anyone could see she was exhausted. She looked terrible, un-
kempt and dirty.

He sat on the side of the bed and watched her. In the morning
she probably wouldn't be talking to him again. If he had done
what she wanted he *knew* she wouldn't have been talking to him.

Al King. Gentleman. When had *that* transformation taken
place?

He gently removed her shoes, and pulled a cover over her. She
was still muttering in her sleep, but nothing intelligible. He went
in the other room and emptied out the contents of her bag.
Amongst the jumble of clothes and make-up he found two bottles
of pills and a tin with about eight rolled joints in. He confiscated
them all. Then he called her house in Los Angeles hoping to reach
Linda. There was no reply.

What to do? He wasn't about to just fly off and leave her in the
morning. Then it occured to him that she could come too. His
plane had to stop off in Los Angeles to pick up Evan, and he
would surely reach Linda by then, so maybe she could come to
the airport and collect Dallas.

Three days in South America and he would be back. And when
he returned that was the time to work something out with Dallas.
She wasn't just another dumb piece of ass – she was the woman
he wanted – and she was just going to have to realize that. Maybe
tonight would prove it to her. He could have done anything he
wanted – but he hadn't. When it happened, he wanted them *both*
to know about it.

No way was it going to be a one-way fuck.

No way.

fifty-eight

Cristina was kept so busy that she hardly had time to think. Louis took care of that. After asking her father's permission to marry her, and receiving it, he plunged them both headlong into a series of engagements.

In spite of her protests everyone wanted to give parties for them, and she could hardly refuse.

Louis showered her with gifts. He was sweet, and fun. In spite of herself she was having a good time. She had never felt so important before, suddenly she was the centre of attention. Her girlfriends were consumed with envy. 'Cristina, you are so lucky,' Marie Therese sighed. 'Louis is so nice, everyone adores him. I've had my eye on him for ages – especially when the two of you broke up. He always wanted you though – can't imagine why!'

'Cat!'

'I'm just jealous, that's all. I'm sure I won't find anyone to marry me for years – probably not until I'm ancient – twenty or something. And you'll have such a wonderful life together. Oh, you are so lucky!'

For a moment she agreed with Marie Therese. She *was* lucky. Then she remembered the truth of the situation. Her marriage plans were merely a smokescreen. Nino was to be the man in her life. She shivered at the thought of his hard, dark body, so different from blond Louis'. Different in every way. Louis was rich. Nino was poor. Louis came from an excellent family. Nino's family consisted of an aged crone who lived in the slums. Louis adored her. Nino – well, she wasn't sure *how* Nino felt. He *said* he loved her, but only when she asked him outright. Louis would give her everything – a beautiful home, clothes, jewels. Nino scorned material possessions, they would probably have to live in his small one-roomed apartment.

It crossed her mind that she might be making a terrible mistake, and there was no one she could discuss it with. No one she could turn to for advice.

At the end of the week she didn't telephone Nino at the appointed time. She had meant to, but somehow it slipped her mind.

He phoned her the next morning and insisted that she came over to his apartment at once.

'I'm going sailing . . .' she objected.

He was furious, 'You are coming here,' he insisted.

Sulkily she had cancelled her meeting with Louis, making up some excuse about having to go to the dentist.

Nino greeted her with a kiss which surprised her. She had expected him to still be angry, as he had been on the phone.

'I've missed you, carioca,' he whispered, 'my body has been screaming for your touch.' His hands started to caress her. 'Have you missed me? Have you wanted me as I have been wanting you?'

For the first time in their relationship she felt that what he was doing was wrong. She attempted to move away from him, but he was all over her, his hands under her sweater, up her skirt.

'You still love me?' he whispered. 'You still want me to touch you?' His hands were busy, and her objections soon turned to moans of acquiescence. She clung to him, emotions rushing to the surface. 'I do love you, Nino, I do, I do.'

He laughed softly. 'You sound like you've been having second thoughts.'

'Don't be silly, as if I could.'

He started to undress her, but suddenly he stopped. 'I don't know,' he muttered.

'What is it?' she asked anxiously. He had tuned her body to a fine pitch, and she was more than ready for him.

'Maybe it would be better if I didn't touch you.'

'Why?'

'I don't know – you just seem – different.'

'But I'm not, I'm not. Please, Nino, please. Make love to me and everything will be like it was.'

He spread her legs, lowered himself on top of her.

She arched her back, twisted her legs behind his neck.

As he plunged inside her she suddenly thought of Louis and was ashamed. What would he think of his fiancée if he could see her now?

When they had finished making love, Nino produced a pad and pencil and started to question her about Al King. Details. Details. She told him what she could.

'We only have a week,' Nino reminded her.

Only a week? She shuddered at the thought.

'You must telephone me every day,' Nino said, 'report on every little thing.'

'But what *is* the plan?'

'I can't tell you yet. Be patient, you will know soon enough.'

She was suddenly frightened. 'Nino, I won't be involved, will I?'

'Of course not.'

'But you said before, you mentioned something about Al King must be sure to know me. Why?'

'Purely for access. No one will know you have anything to do with it.'

Nervously she bit on her nails. 'And us? Don't you think it would be better if we waited a few weeks before running off together. It might be suspicious if I drop Louis immediately.'

He shrugged. 'Whatever you say.'

'It's not that I don't want to be with you as soon as possible . . .'

'I understand.'

How he controlled his fury he didn't know. He waited for her to dress and leave and then he let rip. 'Rich, capitalist, bourgeois bitch!' he screamed, punching the mattress in anger. 'I'm good enough to service, madame, but not good enough for her to run off with!' He could read her stupid little mind. She *liked* being engaged to Louis Baptista. She was enjoying it. Well, she would be sorry – very, very sorry indeed. They would *both* be sorry by the time *he* had finished with them.

Cristina rushed home feeling relieved that she had settled things with Nino. She would help him as much as she could with information – she had promised that much. But after – well, she just wasn't sure any more. She wanted time to think things out. Maybe she wasn't as much in love with Nino as she had thought. Maybe it was just a sex thing. She had heard stories about people becoming trapped sexually. She shuddered at the thought. It couldn't happen to her – could it?

Perhaps she should try a few things out with Louis. Experiment sexually. *He* wouldn't be averse to trying. If she enjoyed it just as much with him . . . Well . . . After all, Louis had so much more to offer . . .

Evita read the letter through a second time. It was written in neat girlish script on lilac notepaper. Anyone else reading it would find it to be an innocuous exchange of greetings between two friends. Evita found it a frightening reminder of her one lapse.

'How are you?' Doris Andrews wrote, 'I have often thought of you and Jorge in the past year.' Words leapt out at Evita – 'short vacation . . . Must get away . . . Would love to see you . . . arriving next week . . . will phone you . . .'

Jorge, sitting across the breakfast table from Evita, said, 'Who is the letter from?'

'Doris Andrews,' Evita managed to reply calmly. 'You remember, don't you? The American film star we met in Mexico last year ...'

Jorge reached for the letter. 'Yes, yes, of course.' He scanned it quickly. 'How nice. You liked her, didn't you? Why don't we invite her to stay with us?'

'Oh no,' Evita replied quickly, 'not now, not with all the bother with Cristina ...'

'Your daughter is engaged to a wonderful boy and you call it bother.' He shook his head in bewilderment. 'A couple of weeks ago you were complaining because you didn't know who she was seeing ... What *would* satisfy you?'

'I will be satisfied when she and Louis are safely married.'

Jorge's eyebrows rose. '*Safely* married?'

'I just don't feel right about her engagement. Why won't she allow us to have a party for her?'

'We'll have a party for Doris Andrews if it's a party you want. I think it would be a nice gesture, don't you?'

'I don't know ...' Evita fluttered her hands vaguely.

'Well, I do,' Jorge said decisively. 'You love giving parties. All that plotting and planning that you are so good at. Yes. We shall definitely have a big party. Go ahead and organize it, my dear.'

Later, when Jorge had left for his office, Evita read the letter through once more. She had never expected to hear from Doris again, never expected to have a rude reminder of her one indiscretion. A letter was bad enough. But the fact that Doris was coming to Rio ... If only she could go away somewhere, hide. But that was impossible, already Jorge was planning a party. He had known that she and Doris had become close friends; if she wanted to leave as soon as Doris arrived it would look strange. Jorge was no fool. Eventually he would work things out.

Evita sighed deeply. If Jorge ever found out ... She would sooner die. She would be so ashamed.

And yet ... If she was honest she would have to admit that she had enjoyed every minute of her sexual interlude with Doris. Jorge thought he was a wonderful lover, but his hands were hard and strong, whereas Doris' had been soft and demanding in a completely different sort of way. And her tongue, so intuitive, finding every secret place of excitement within seconds. Evita thrilled at the memory. What if it happened again? She wasn't sure if she would be able to stop Doris. She wasn't even sure if she would want to ...

Quietly she went to her desk and sat down in preparation to compose a reply.

417

'My dear Doris, how nice to hear from you after all this time. Yes, I too remember what a delightful time we spent together in Acapulco. Jorge and myself are so pleased you will be visiting our city. Perhaps you would allow us to give a party in your honour . . .'

Louis was breathing heavily.

'Kiss me again,' Cristina whispered. 'Kiss me properly.'

They were clutched in each other's embrace in the front seat of Louis' sports car.

Louis groaned. 'Do you know what you are doing to me, Cristina? Every night I have a terrible stomach ache . . . I go home and I cannot sleep. We will have to be married as soon as possible, I just can't go on like this. I can't control myself for much longer. We must arrange a date, we must talk to our parents.'

'I said kiss me again.' She was glowing with power. Louis was under her spell, he would do anything for her. She captured his mouth once more, pushing her tongue out to meet his. His hands slid to her breasts. For once she didn't push them away. After a few minutes he snatched them away of his own accord. 'I can't go on like this,' he muttered in a strangled voice.

'We don't have to,' Cristina whispered. 'We're engaged. Anything we do together would not be wrong.'

He wasn't sure that he had heard her correctly. 'Are you saying . . .'

'I'm saying let's go to your house in the hills. Is it empty?'

'Yes. But, Cristina, are you sure?'

She felt that she was such a woman of the world. 'Yes, Louis,' she replied softly, 'I am sure.'

Wordlessly he started the car. Cristina smiled to herself. He was so anxious.

The small sports car sped up into the mountains. Cristina felt quite calm at what she was about to do. It was an experiment. If Louis could satisfy her in the same way that Nino could . . . Well then, why *shouldn't* she marry Louis? After all, Nino with his theories and ideas would be so demanding. Besides she *liked* having money, a fact she would never dare confess to Nino.

Louis had to break a window to gain access to his parents' weekend house as he did not have a key with him. 'I never thought you would ever allow me to do this,' he said, as he let her in the front door. 'Are you sure? Are you really sure?'

'Of course I am, silly. I don't want you going home every night with stomach ache, you could do yourself harm.' She looked around. 'Where shall we go?'

He took her by the hand. 'Upstairs.'

Halfway up the stairs they heard voices. Louis froze.

'Who is it?' Cristina whispered, alarmed.

'I don't know,' Louis whispered back. 'You go out to the car, I'll investigate. Hurry.'

She rushed back to the car which was parked around the back. Suddenly she was nervous.

Louis joined her within minutes. His mouth was set in a grim line. He jumped in the car, took off the handbrake and allowed the car to coast silently away from the house.

'What is it?' Cristina hissed.

'My dear father,' Louis replied, obviously upset, 'in the bedroom with a woman.'

'Oh! You mean we caught him?'

'You could say that. Only he didn't see me. I looked through the keyhole. Tonight he's supposed to be in Sao Paulo.'

'What a lucky escape! Can you imagine if we had burst in on him?'

'You would think he wouldn't take a woman to a bed he shares with my mother,' Louis complained.

Cristina tut-tutted in agreement. But secretly she was intrigued at the thought of portly Mr Baptista in bed with a woman. She wondered if her own father did such things . . . The thought excited her. 'Stop the car, Louis,' she whispered urgently, 'I want to do it with you. I want to do it with you now!'

When they met, five days later, Nino sensed the change in Cristina immediately. He was furious. After all, she did not know that he had not been completely serious about his intentions. As far as *she* was concerned he loved her and was preparing to marry her.

A lot she cared. He had misjudged her. She wasn't the pliable, stupid, little girl he had thought. She was stupid all right – but devious stupid.

'I'm so tired,' she complained to Nino. 'Parties, parties, parties.'

He managed to smile sympathetically. Only a few more days . . . keep her sweet for a few more days. 'You look well on it, carioca,' he assured her.

'Do I?' she asked, knowing full well that she was positively glowing. The experiment with Louis had turned out to be an unqualified success.

'Do you have a copy of the list of everyone travelling with Al King for me?'

She fished in the straw bag she carried, and produced it. 'I took it from Mr Baptista's desk. Honestly, I felt like a private detective in one of those American television serials!'

'Clever girl.' He took the list and studied it.

'I can't stay,' she said quickly. 'Today Louis is taking me to Paqueta Island. He wants to know where I am every minute. You know, I've been thinking – I don't know if we should see each other for a while. It might not be wise.'

Carefully Nino placed the piece of paper on a table. He held Cristina playfully around the waist. 'Do you mean we will not have time to make love today?'

She attempted to squirm free. He held her extremely tight. 'Well, carioca? Not today, huh?'

'No, not today, Nino.'

He held her even tighter. 'You still love me though?'

'You're *hurting* me . . .'

'Not as much as I could.' Suddenly he let go of her and she lost her balance and fell back on the bed.

He stood over her, slowly unzipping his jeans.

She lay back, frightened at the menace in his eyes.

'You know what I want you to do,' he said.

'I told you . . .' she began.

'I thought you loved me,' he mocked. 'If you love me you'll do anything for me.'

'Next time.'

'And when will that be?'

'Soon. I promise you.'

'And this is the girl who was not sure if she could live three weeks without me. What happened, carioca? Does Louis have a bigger one than me? Or is it just the fact that his is coated in money and mine is merely coated with the slime of the Favellos?'

She reddened. 'Don't be silly, Nino.'

'Don't be silly,' he mocked. 'Do you think I am a fool? Do you think I don't know what is going on?'

She lowered her eyes. 'I'm sorry.'

'You're sorry!' he exploded, 'just like that – you're sorry. And what about me? What about my plans?'

'I'll still help you,' she said quickly. 'I promised I would and I haven't let you down. I got you the list, didn't I? And if I find out anything else I'll let you know . . .'

'Thanks,' sarcasm dripped bitterly from his lips, 'how kind of you.'

She attempted to sit up. He pushed her back with one hand.

'I'll tell you the plan,' he said coldly. 'Listen carefully.'

She was frightened, his eyes were alive with a hatred and contempt that she had never seen before.

'Al King arrives on Thursday – in two days time. Naturally you will be at the party Louis' father is throwing for him. Be sure to meet him, talk with him and the people close to him. Be sure they know you are to marry Carlos Baptista's son. Friday is the day of the concert – you attend – but early on you and Louis slip away and go straight to the airport. You make sure that you reach there before Al King does. I will meet you there. That is all you have to know for now.'

'What are you talking about?' Cristina gasped. 'I can't do that. What are you thinking of?'

'I'm thinking of the Von Cougats and the Bogatos. I'm wondering what they would say if they found out it was sweet little Cristina Maraco who had provided the plans to their houses – in her own sweet handwriting – plans that enabled them to be robbed. I'm also thinking of your father. Would it interest him to know about his daughter and me? Would he like to know what you and I do together? Would your mother be pleased to hear from the doctor who fitted you for a diaphram? The doctor I arranged for you to see?'

Cristina's face drained of colour. 'You wouldn't . . .' she whispered in horror.

'Try me,' Nino replied arrogantly. 'Or maybe I could compare notes with Louis on your performance.'

'You pig!'

Nino shrugged. 'Of course if you help me out with Al King then I will have no need to tell anyone anything – ever.'

'But how could I explain going to the airport, leaving in the middle of the concert, to Louis?'

'I'm sure you could think of something.'

'But why do you need us?'

'For access. To board his plane. Don't worry – you will be in the clear. I promise you no one will know we are connected. Once I'm on the plane you can go – we need never see each other again.'

She covered her eyes with her arm. What a mess she had got herself in.

'Do we have an agreement?' Nino persisted.

She took her arm away and stared at his handsome arrogant, hateful face. 'All right,' she muttered. What choice did she have?

'Good. I will contact you by phone to give you further details – times and places, and I want a report from you twice a day in case any plans get changed.' His mouth twisted into a thin smile. 'Well, my little carioca, shall we make love before you go? Or are you still in a hurry?'

fifty-nine

Dallas woke up slowly, stretched, spread her arms out, opened her eyes, and wondered where the hell she was.

She felt hot, and kind of sweaty, and realized that she still had her jeans and T-shirt on.

She tried to remember, but everything seemed to be a vague blur, the clearest memory being Palm Springs.

She sat up, looked around the ornate hotel bedroom, located the bathroom, and locked herself in there. She stripped off her clothes and stepped under an icy shower. The cold water refreshed her. She grabbed some soap and washed herself thoroughly, including her hair. Then she wrapped herself in a towelling bathrobe which was hanging behind the door, and turbaned her hair in a towel. There was a tube of toothpast lying on the side, and she squeezed some onto her fingers and rubbed it over her teeth, rinsing her mouth out with water.

Things were becoming clearer. She could remember getting on a plane to Las Vegas and meeting a frizzy-haired girl who had fixed her up with a lot of good things. Wow – that was it. She had gotten good and stoned, and come to think of it a joint and some pills wouldn't be such a bad idea now. She felt depressed and down. Al King . . . Al King . . . Hadn't she been following up some wild idea of visiting him? Christ! She *must* have been stoned!

She walked out of the bathroom looking for her bag. Then she noticed that there were men's clothes around the room, and a suitcase that wasn't hers.

She tied the bathrobe tightly around herself and walked into the living room.

Al King was sitting at a room service table drinking orange juice and reading a newspaper. He looked up when she came in. 'Good morning. How did you sleep?'

She stared at him, waiting for recollection of the previous evening to come flooding back. Nothing. She bit her lip. Now her goddamn head was beginning to throb.

Al smiled pleasantly at her. 'Want some breakfast?'

She shook her head. Breakfast wasn't what she wanted. 'You seen my bag?' she muttered, disgusted with herself for what obviously must have happened.

'It's over there.'

She picked up the bag and headed back to the bedroom, emptying the contents out onto the bed. A bikini. A T-shirt, denim shirt, some shorts. Bottles of make-up, a hairbrush, small hair dryer, several packs of chewing gum, a hand mirror, box of Kleenex, tube of sun tan cream, and a make-up bag. That was it. The entire contents.

She turned the bag upside down and shook it. A few hairpins fell out. Where the hell were her pills? Her joints? Shit. She *couldn't* have demolished them *all*.

She went in the bathroom and picked her jeans up off the floor, rifling through the pockets. She pulled out a cheque and squinted at it in amazement. Thirty thousand dollars. Made out to her. She went back in the living room waving it in the air. 'Where did I get this?' she demanded.

'Don't you remember?' Al asked innocently.

'If I remembered I wouldn't be asking, would I?' she snapped.

'What *do* you remember?'

She glared at him. 'Nothing.'

'I'm not surprised. You were flying without wings. Maybe you can tell me what happened to set you off.'

She slumped into the chair opposite him and picked at a bread roll. 'I feel like Doris Day,' she said miserably. 'Every old movie I ever see of hers she wakes up with some guy and doesn't know whether they made it or not. You know – like she was drunk or something. So come on Rock Hudson – fill me in.'

'You won the money at roulette. We didn't make it – oh, you wanted to – but I figured it might be more fun to wait until you knew who you were screwing. Old-fashioned of me, I know, but I'm like that.'

She laughed suddenly, clutched her head and said, 'Ouch! That hurts. You mean I *won* thirty thousand bucks? Wowee!!'

'I thought you were going to say "you mean you didn't screw me? Thank you Al, I always knew you were a first class gentleman"!'

She laughed again. 'Doesn't really matter one way or another,

423

does it ? I'm not a virgin like Doris Day – or didn't you realize ?'

'I realized.'

'Never mind. For one me, there's always hundreds of others. What am I doing here anyway ?'

'*You* tell *me*.'

She shrugged. 'Don't know. Guess I had this stupid idea of you and me finally getting together. I'll be honest with you, Al. I find sex no great turn-on – I thought maybe with you . . .' She trailed off.

'I could have had you doing cartwheels last night. In LA you didn't want to know about me. Why the sudden change of mind ?'

'Can I have some orange juice and coffee ? And maybe some eggs. I feel like I haven't eaten for six years. Hey – I had some joints in my bag – you seen them ?'

He shook his head. 'I'll order you breakfast. How do you want your eggs ?'

'Scrambled. Oh and some toast and jelly – and some crispy bacon.'

He phoned room service, glanced at his watch. Time was running tight.

'I should call Cody,' she mused, 'he's probably going out of his head.'

'I thought you were working.'

'I have taken a week off, courtesy of Mr Margolis. Do you know him ? Such a charming man. He and his lovely wife.'

'I think I might do a movie for him.'

'Lots of luck !'

'You still haven't told me how you managed to appear in Las Vegas stoned out of your head.'

She made a face. 'It wasn't easy.'

'I'm glad you're here though. I wanted to explain about Karmen . . .'

She held up a hand. 'Nothing to explain. *I* don't care.'

'But that's it. I *want* you to care . . .'

'Oh, Al, please. Don't get corny with me. I understand. I'm a very understanding lady. You can screw who you want.'

'Then why wouldn't you talk to me in LA ?'

'I could *really* appreciate some grass. With your influence couldn't we summon some up ?'

'You're changing the subject.'

'What subject ?'

'Look I have to be on my plane in an hour. We're stopping in

LA to pick up my son . . . Then I have a couple of gigs in South America, and I'll be back in a few days. Why don't we plan on getting together when I get back?'

'Just like that, you're flying to South America today?'

'I can drop you in LA.'

'Terrific. What makes you think I want to go back there?'

'Don't you?'

She reached over and drained his orange juice. 'Where's the food? I'm getting desperate.'

An idea was forming in his head. 'I said don't you?'

'As a matter of fact I don't.'

'So why not come to Rio with me? No strings – I won't touch you – or I'll touch you. Whichever you want.'

'Why do you want me to come?' she asked suspiciously.

'Because I like you. I think we understand each other. I think we could have some laughs.'

'I have to be back in LA next week.'

'We will be.'

She smiled, dazzling him. 'Why not?'

Paul nudged the girl who was asleep beside him. He had been nudging her on and off since 6 a.m. in the hope that she would wake up and leave. It wasn't that he didn't like her. She was an attractive girl of twenty-nine, intelligent, articulate, good in bed. She was one of the producers on the telethon, not some little nothing groupie. They had made love once, quite satisfactorily as far as he was concerned. But he had been unable to rise to the occasion a second time, and far from being put out, she had produced a life-sized penis substitute from her purse, and requested most politely that he use it on her. He had done as she asked, albeit reluctantly, and he had been somewhat put out by the amount of orgasms she had proceeded to achieve. With his cock – one. With a plastic substitute – multiple. It didn't seem right somehow.

She obviously had no intention of ever waking up, so he got out of bed and stamped his way around the room a lot before going in to shower and shave.

He was halfway through shaving when she strolled into the bathroom, squatted on the john and peed noisily.

'How are you this morning?' she asked amiably.

'Rushed.'

'Shame. I thought we might . . .'

'No time.'

'That's cool. I have a lot to do myself. If you want to reach me in LA you can call me at the network.'

'I will.' He knew he wouldn't.

'You're better-looking than your brother,' she remarked, getting off the toilet and running the shower. 'Not that I'm into looks – but you are.'

He wasn't flattered. He didn't enjoy being compared to his brother in any way.

He finished shaving, hurried in the bedroom and dressed. He wanted to call Linda. He wanted to tell her that he loved her. He wanted her to tell *him*.

Instead he booked a call to London. He was worried about his children being all alone in the house with just the nanny. He wanted to assure them that he would be home soon.

The girl producer strolled nakedly into the room and started to dress. He watched her, willing her to hurry. She retrieved panty hose from the floor, sat on the bed and slid them on. Then a skirt from a chair, high-heeled shoes, and lastly a shirt which showed off her perky nipples.

She collected her purse, picked up the penis substitute which sat lewdly on the bedside table.

He wondered why she carried it. In case nothing better came along?

'I'll see you around, Paul,' she said casually, 'give me a buzz when you get back.'

'Yes,' he said. No – he thought.

He waited until she closed the door, then he placed a call to Linda.

He paced the room, expecting both calls to come through at once. They didn't. The operator informed him that there was no answer at the number he had given her for Linda. And he had to wait half an hour before he got a line to England.

Nanny was most huffy. 'This isn't good enough, Mr King,' she informed him, 'I haven't had my day off for weeks.'

'I'll pay you double,' he promised her. 'Just wait another week and I'll be back.'

'I think it's disgusting,' she sniffed, 'absolutely disgusting!'

'Yes,' agreed Paul. 'We'll discuss it when I get back, nanny.'

'We certainly will!'

He checked his watch. Better call Al to make sure he was awake. It was a long trip, he could always sleep on the plane if he had been up all night. He wondered how much money he had managed to lose at the tables. The sooner he got Al away from Vegas, the better.

Evan waited impatiently at the airport in Los Angeles for his father's plane to pick him up. He felt a lot better, the few days in a private clinic had not been too bad. Everyone had been very nice to him, one young Puerto Rican nurse in particular – of course she had known he was Al King's son, which was probably why.

He had watched a lot of television, and the time had passed quite quickly. They had treated him with a course of injections, and apparently all he needed now was some follow-up shots and everything would be fine. No sex until after your check-up, the doctor had warned him sternly. Chance would be a fine thing. Now that Glory and Plum were out of his life who would look at him? He missed them, in spite of the fact that they had given him the dreaded disease. After all, they hadn't known. He kept on wondering what they had done when they realized that he had just walked out on them. Did they miss him? He had no way of contacting them. His only friends. He had thought that maybe he would run into them in Los Angeles. After all that's where they had been heading. But no such luck. His father had dumped him straight into the clinic – to get him out of the way no doubt. There was no reason for him to stay in a clinic, he could have received the treatment as an out patient. But no – the famous Al King didn't want his horrible spotty son around – so he had hidden him away.

At least he was going to Brazil. That was *something*. And to be fair to his father at least he hadn't been sent home.

He flicked through the bunch of magazines he had purchased. *Playboy, Penthouse, Macho.* Idly he wondered if the doctor's no sex instructions had included masturbation. After all – you couldn't give a magazine centrefold a dose of the clap, could you?

On the plane Dallas said, 'I must call Cody. Really – otherwise he'll be contacting missing persons.'

'I'll have Bernie get in touch with him when we land at LA. Does that suit you?' Al replied.

'Yeah, that's fine. Have him say I'll be reporting back for work on Monday. Oh, and Al – I know I keep on asking you – but can't we have Bernie score a few joints for us? I'm in the mood to get stoned.'

'Where is he going to score at the airport?'

'He can make a call, can't he?'

'By the time they get out to the airport we'll be long gone.'

She made a face. 'Big fuckin' star and I can't even get high.'

He laughed. 'You need to be high to travel with me?'

'I must have been high to agree to come. What am I doing here? I don't even have any clothes. Maybe I should get off in LA.'

He took her hand. 'I want you to stay. You can pick up some clothes in Rio, anything you need.'

'I *need* some grass. *Someone* on this plane must have a joint.'

'You're really that desperate?'

She shrugged, smiling. 'Not desperate. But if I don't get one I'm going.'

He wondered how angry she would be if she knew that it had been he who had confiscated her supply.

'Stay where you are,' he warned. 'Don't move – I'll see what I can do.'

'Oh yeah?'

'Oh yeah.' He set off down the plane to where Bernie was playing gin rummy with some of the musicians. He sat down ostensibly to watch, but once out of Dallas' sight he pulled her tin box out of his jacket pocket and extracted a joint.

'Gonna join us for a game?' Bernie wanted to know.

'Not today,' Al replied. 'Got other things on my mind.'

'I'm down three hundred bucks,' Bernie complained. 'If this goes on, by the time we make Rio I'll be busted out.'

'So learn to play,' chided Al. He glanced over at Paul, sitting alone on an aisle seat studying some papers. 'How'd the party go?'

Paul nodded. 'It was nice.'

'You take my advice?'

'What advice was that?' Paul replied tightly.

'To get laid, schmuck!'

'We can't all ...'

'I know, I know,' Al interrupted. 'We can't all go through life with a stiff prick. But it beats the hell out of wanking!' He laughed at his own humour, and made his way back to where Dallas was sitting. He could have suggested that they sat in the bedroom – but he didn't want to rush things. She was with him of her own accord, let things happen nice and naturally. One joint wasn't going to turn her into the stoned zombie she had been the previous day.

He gave her the cigarette. She lit up, inhaling deeply, leaning her head back, finally allowing the smoke to drift lazily out of her nostrils. 'Better!' she sighed.

'You like that?'

'Why not? Don't you?'

'I can take it or leave it. Give me a healthy slug of scotch any day. Something that hits you in the gut with a punch you can feel all the way down to your balls!'

'I don't have balls.'

'Oh no? You could have fooled me.'

Playfully she punched him.

'I *like* a ballsy woman,' he objected. 'I can't get anything going with most of the doormats that come my way. I could shit all over some of 'em and they wouldn't object.'

'From what I hear you usually do,' she remarked dryly.

'So what do you hear?'

'That you are Mister Super Prick – in both senses of the word.'

He groaned. 'What a reputation! Is that why you wouldn't go out with me?'

She dragged on her cigarette. 'Maybe.' She studied him through slitted eyes. 'Maybe not.'

'You and I together . . .' he began.

She quietened him with a finger to his lips. 'Let's take it minute by minute. No promises. No crap. No commitments. I don't want you to change for me.'

'But you make me feel different.'

'So be different – until the next Karmen Rush comes along . . .'

'I didn't . . .'

'Goddamit, Al. *I don't care.* Be Mister Super Prick, I really don't care. We'll have a few laughs – I won't give you any heavies. We'll have a good time, no strings on either side.'

It wasn't good enough. His stomach churned at the thought of her with another man. He hadn't even had her yet, and he knew that she was all he would ever want. In the past, with other women – he had never given a monkeys about what they did when they weren't with him. They could have laid the entire team of the Harlem Globetrotters for all he cared. Even Edna. Of course Edna never would have . . . But if she had been that way inclined . . . Well, so what? Now here he sat next to a woman he hardly knew and he felt he could kill for her. He wondered how *she* felt. Surely she must feel something. Surely she must notice the electric current which surged between them? An invisible magnetic force that drew him closer and closer. He had never felt like this in his life.

'Mr King. Please can you fasten your seat belt.' The stewardess interrupted his thoughts. 'And extinguish all cigarettes. We are coming into land at Los Angeles.'

'Sure, Cathy,' he smiled at the girl, then he took the joint from Dallas and stubbed it out.

'Careful,' she admonished. 'Or is there more where that came from?'

'How many do you use a day?'

'Whatever I feel like. Why – does it bother you?'

'Only when you fall down.'

'I promise not to fall down. Only in the direction of your bed – does that suit you?'

No, it didn't suit him. He didn't want her to speak like that.

With a sudden surge of dread he realized that Evan would be boarding the plane shortly. Evan, who had to be told about the divorce Edna wanted – unless he had already read it in the newspapers. Christ! Why did *he* have to be the one to tell him? Couldn't Paul do it?

He glanced at Dallas. She had shut her eyes. Mussed and untidy she was still the most beautiful girl he had ever seen.

Linda was all set to photograph the television star she had met at the Margolis' party. She was looking forward to it – it marked the start of her career in California. She had definitely decided to live there for a while, maybe permanently. Who needed the hassle of New York when you could make a living in Lotus Land? Deep down she knew it was just a temporary move, a time to get herself together. She *needed* the excitement and energy of New York – she *needed* the hassle. But this would do – for the time being.

Just as she was leaving the apartment the phone rang. She knew it was Cody.

'I haven't heard from her,' she said into the receiver.

'You haven't heard from whom?' It was Paul's voice.

'Who is this?' she asked falsely.

'It's Paul. Don't play games – you *know* it's me. Look, I'm at the airport, I've only got a minute. I tried to call you last night – it would be nice if you told people when you changed your number.'

'I didn't know *people* would be calling me.'

'Well, I am.'

'I noticed.' She placed the hold-all with her camera equipment on the floor. 'How did you get my number?'

'Dallas told me you had moved, so I called your agency. She's travelling with us.'

Linda nearly dropped the phone. '*Dallas* is travelling with you? Cody is doing his nut looking for her – he's really going mad. Does he *know*?'

'Yes, I think Bernie's contacting him now. Listen – I don't want to talk about Dallas, I want to talk about us.'

'Go ahead.' Yeah – go ahead, you bastard – tell me all about how your wife doesn't understand you and now that she's safely out of the way I can come back.

'I've decided to leave Melanie.'

There was silence.

'Did you hear me?' Paul continued. 'I'm going to divorce her. I mean it, Linda. We can be together. We can get married. Anything you want.'

'Ohmigod!' she gasped, she could hardly believe what she was hearing. 'Are you kidding me?'

'I'm not kidding you. I mean it, and I've told her – and does this prove to you that I love you?'

'I'm in shock, Paul. Honest to God I'm in shock.'

He laughed. 'Look – I can't really talk now – the plane is waiting. I'll try to call you tonight. I'll be back in four days, then I want to fly straight to England. I thought you could come with me.'

'I don't know what to say . . .'

'Say yes. It's what you wanted, isn't it?'

'Of *course* it is. Oh darling, it's wonderful. Did you tell her about us?'

He hesitated for a fraction of a second, then, 'Yes. I certainly did.'

'You told her it was me at the hotel in Tucson?'

'Does it matter?'

'Sure it matters. What do you think we've been fighting about?'

'I told her.'

'You told her you loved me?'

'Yes. Yes. Yes. I have to go now. I'll try to call you later. Start packing.'

'Paul?'

'Yes?'

'I love you.'

'You too.'

She put the phone down, and shakily reached for a cigarette.

Mrs Paul King. Linda King. Should she change her name on photo credits, or should she just add to it and become Linda Cosmo King – sort of like Farrah Fawcett Majors. She giggled. It was all so unexpected. Jesus! She would be a married lady! He had done it, he had finally done it. He had left his wife for her.

Where would they marry? What should she wear? Could she have one last fling with Julio – male hooker supreme – before giving up all other men forever? Would she really have to give up all other men? *That* was a sobering thought for a start. Not any? Ever? Not even birthdays and Christmas?

Mrs Paul King. She would see England, meet his family, his children.

Children. How did she feel about them? Frankly she had never had anything to do with children. Weren't they all supposed to be nasty little monsters, especially other people's. And Paul's children were half Melanie's. Would they have straggly yellow hair and shrill voices?

Maybe they shouldn't marry at once. Now that they could, maybe they should wait. Perhaps living together would be fun, just for a while, just so she could get used to the idea.

She noticed the time. Running late for the television star. Just time to try and call Cody, make sure he knew where Dallas was. The line was busy. She didn't have time to try again. Picking up her camera hold-all she rushed out the door. Soon to be married or not she still had a living to make.

Al greeted Evan warmly. 'Everything all right? They treated you good? You look fine.' The sight of Evan's acne – worse than ever – made him wince 'How about something to eat?'

'No thanks.'

'Well find a seat, get settled.'

'Where are you sitting?'

'I'm at the back – got an – er – friend with me. Why don't you sit with Paul. I know he wants to talk to you. Cathy – put Evan next to Paul.'

The stewardess took Evan's arm and steered him to a seat.

Al returned to Dallas. She was still asleep, her head balanced at an awkward angle. He got her a cushion and inched it under her head. She grunted. He smiled to himself. This must be love – since when did he ever bother about a girl's neck?

Linda took a series of marvellous photos. The television star seemed to be prepared to do anything for a camera, and by the end of the session she had him reclining across the bonnet of his imported Rolls Royce wearing an orange caftan and holding a can of beer. Let his fans work *that* one out!

'You must have lunch,' he insisted when they were finished, and led her out by the pool where a neatly dressed Mexican had laid out twin lobster salads on a poolside table.

His butchness was dropping rapidly and his closet queen tendencies were coming out full force. 'That woman I work with is a bitch!' he confided. 'Everyone thinks she is such a dear. But I know, believe me I know. I had to kiss the bitch the other day.' His voice rose in disgust. 'Kiss her! And do you know what she did? The bitch ate onions for lunch. Can you imagine?'

Linda smiled in sympathy.

'You don't know what it's like working on a series,' he further confided, 'stuck with the same people day in and day out. Only the guest stars change – and who do we get?' His voice filled with contempt. 'Out-of-work movie actors who look down their nose at me. I'm a star, baby, a *star*. But do they appreciate that fact? Oh no. You can bet your sweet ass they don't. What a drag to be stuck in a television series, they say – when most of them would give their left tit to be in my position.' He picked disconsolately at his lobster. 'That bitch, my co-star, thinks *she's* the star of the series. *She really thinks so*. If I left, the whole thing would fall to pieces. Who do you think gets the ratings?'

'I'm sure it's you,' said Linda kindly.

'You bet your sweet ass it's me. Do you think anyone would switch on their set to see that bitch?'

The Mexican appeared silently and respectfully and informed the television star that he was wanted on the phone. 'I won't be long,' he said. 'Help yourself to anything you want.' He vanished into the house.

Linda smiled. The sun was shining, everything was working out, she felt marvellous.

She picked up a newspaper to glance at. The gossip column was a who's who of what was going on in Hollywood that week. Al King was mentioned – an obtuse item that tied him together with Karmen Rush. She read on, suddenly transfixed, and could hardly believe what she was reading. '*Paul King, younger brother and manager of the great Al, was as surprised as everyone else to find his young and extremely pretty wife Melanie announcing her engagement to the one and only Manny Shorto. Slight snag is the*

433

*fact that she will have to divorce Paul first. Better hurry, Melanie –
Manny celebrates his seventieth birthday next week.'*

Linda slapped the paper back on to the table. 'Bastard!' she
said out loud. 'Rotten lying stinking bastard!' And to think she
had fallen for his lies. 'I've left her, Linda. I love you, Linda. I've
told her all about us, Linda.' The hell he had. Wifey had given
him the boot, and he was settling for second best.

Well, screw him. He could stick his marriage proposal right up
his lying ass. Second best she was not!

Dallas was only half asleep, but she kept her eyes closed anyway.
She didn't feel like making conversation. The joint had taken the
edge off her nerves and she felt nicely relaxed.

She was trying to figure out why she had agreed to come. Was
Al King really what she needed in her life right now? He was a
selfish, bossy, womanizing chauvinist. Why was he the only person who created a spark of excitement? Why did she want to be
with him?

She had to find out. If it was a sexual thing she had to know.
Three days in South America should be long enough to get him
out of her system once and for all. She had made up her mind what
she was going to do. She was tired of the struggle. Tired of fighting the Lew Margolis' and Doris Andrews' of the world. When
she got back to Los Angeles she was going to marry Aarron Mack.
Marrying him would protect her from all the hassles – and if there
was one thing she felt she needed it was some protection in life.
As Mrs Aarron Mack she would automatically be treated with the
respect that all his money deserved. So she didn't love him. So
what? The time had come to put herself first – and she intended to.

sixty

The excitement at the airport in Rio was tense. The usual assortment of crowds, fans, police, photographers and television crews
waited impatiently for the Al King jet to land.

Cristina found herself boxed into a private enclosure with
Louis, his father, Carlos and several of his assistants. It had been
Louis' idea. 'Would you like to come to the airport to see Al King
arrive?' he had asked. 'Yes,' she had nodded. He thought she was

the singer's greatest fan. And why shouldn't he? She had done nothing but ask questions about the man.

Oh God! How she wished she had never heard his name. How she wished she had never agreed to help Nino.

But it was too late to back out now. Nino had trapped her with his insidious form of blackmail. Her most fervent wish of all was that she had never set eyes on him. How ashamed she was of that relationship – if it wasn't for her shame she might have confessed everything to Louis. But what would he think of her? How could he possibly still want to marry her after her confession?

No, the only solution was to go along with what Nino wanted her to do. If she helped him this last time she would be free of him.

Al pushed Dallas gently. 'Seat belt on,' he commanded.

She opened her eyes. She really had fallen asleep. 'Are we there?'

'Coming in to land.' He had changed into skin-tight black trousers, a black silk shirt, and a positive gold mine of chains.

'Ready to face your public?' she asked.

'But of course. You like the gear?'

'You look terrific, Mister Superstar,' her tone was faintly mocking.

'You don't look too bad yourself.'

'I look horrible. I want a bath, some decent clothes, and a make-up job.'

'I like you just the way you are.'

'I bet you've been using the same old lines for years – they're *so* corny. How do I get off this plane without being seen?'

'What's with the not being seen bit? You're with me.'

'No thank you. *You* look prettier than me right now. I want privacy.'

'Funny.'

'I mean it.' She put on her tinted shades. 'I'll see you at the hotel later.'

He nodded. 'If that's what you want. You can go with Paul and Evan – I think you should meet him anyway.'

'Why?'

'Why what?'

'Why do you want me to meet Evan?'

Al frowned. 'He is my son, you know.'

'So?'

'So . . .' Al faltered. Why *did* he want her to meet him? He had never introduced any of his girlfriends to Evan before. Why start

435

now? 'I don't know . . . We're all travelling together . . . Jesus! Do I have to have a *reason*?'

She laughed. 'Be a good superstar and bring me some grass to the hotel.'

He was annoyed. 'Don't keep calling me that.'

She laughed some more. 'Aren't we the touchy one!'

The plane was swooping in to land. Al could see the crowds from the window.

'You stay on board until Paul fetches you,' he instructed. Maybe having Dallas on this trip hadn't been such a brilliant idea after all. She could be some smart ass.

'Yes, sir!' She saluted. 'Anything you say, sir! Oh – and don't forget the joints, Al, I'm depending on you.'

Evan sat sullenly in his seat. The plane had landed, the star had disembarked. Now all that was left were the remnants. Everyone had gone except the woman at the back of the plane. His father's woman.

Evan hadn't really been able to get a good look at her. But now she had moved into an aisle seat, and he could see masses of hair, dark sunglasses, and jeans and a shirt.

He hated her, whoever she was. It was women like her who had broken up his parents' marriage. Paul had told him about the impending divorce. 'It's for the best,' he had said. For whose best? Evan wondered. Certainly not *his*.

Where would he live? Which one of them would want him?

He wished that he'd never come back. He wished that he was still travelling across America with Glory and Plum, having good times, having fun. If it hadn't been for Nellie . . . Poor beautiful Nellie. And her death was his father's fault too.

Evan scowled. Why was he unlucky enough to be born with a father like Al King?

Paul reappeared. 'All clear,' he shouted. 'Let's go.'

Evan gathered together his magazines and set off towards the exit.

Dallas followed him. Paul took her arm. 'Tremendous reception Al got,' he said.

Dallas smiled. 'Paul, you're a man of connections. You think you could get me some grass?'

Paul frowned. First Al. Now Dallas. Why were people always asking him to do things for them?

*

Nino was in the lobby of Al's hotel when he arrived, heralded by a rush of photographers. He leaned unobtrusively behind a pillar and watched the star.

Al King was older than he had expected, and taller than he appeared in photos. But he was good-looking all right.

Nino picked at his teeth with the side of some book matches, and watched Al all the way into the elevator. He took note of everyone around him. The tall black man who hovered watchfully in the background was obviously Al's bodyguard. The others appeared to be the usual hangers-on that stars collected around them. Nino watched the indicator light on the elevator ascend to the tenth floor. It paused there, and within minutes returned to the lobby. The fat man who had accompanied Al up got out and waddled towards a cluster of photographers standing in the lobby.

Slowly Nino strolled towards the busy reception desk. He smiled at a girl working there. 'Time for your coffee break, Didi?' he asked casually.

Her face lit up, 'Nino! You are early.'

'Only ten minutes. Can't you get away now?'

She looked quickly at her watch. 'I don't see why not.' She called to one of the boys behind the desk, 'Drago, I'm taking my break now.'

He nodded.

'One minute,' she instructed Nino. 'I'll get my purse.' She vanished into a room marked 'Employees Only'.

Nino strolled over to the magazine stand. Didi had been so easy. They were all so easy. A little sweet talk. A few false declarations of love and passion, and they were yours.

He had manoeuvred a meeting with Didi nine days previously, as soon as Cristina had told him what hotel Al King would be staying at. Within two days he had slept with the girl. Within five she had agreed to give him the information he required. He had fed her some story about a thesis he was working on. The life and times of the very rich.

Didi came hurrying over. She clutched his arm, and kissed him warmly. 'I've missed you,' she declared.

'We only saw each other last night,' he replied.

'I know. But I have still missed you.'

They walked from the hotel, arms linked, Didi chattering on about the injustices of working in a hotel. If Nino had more time he might have considered recruiting her for the organization. She was perfect material, and she would be able to furnish invaluable information about the guests who booked into the hotel. However, she would need working on, and Nino didn't have time for that now. He had much more important things on his mind.

'Did you get me what I asked for?' he questioned.

'Yes,' she replied smugly, 'I have a duplicate list of the Al King party and what rooms they are in. I copied it out first thing this morning when the reservations were confirmed.'

'Good girl.'

Didi smiled. 'I have an hour's break. Will that give us time to go to your room?'

Nino hid a grimace of disgust.

'Of course,' he replied, 'isn't that the reason I came to see you?'

'Shall I open the shutters, señorita?' the bellboy asked. Only he wasn't such a boy. He was tall and muscled, dark-haired, with knowing eyes.

Linda would adore him, Dallas thought, Linda would probably ravish his fine young body. 'Hey,' she said, 'you look like a guy knows his way around. Can you get me some grass?'

'I beg your pardon, señorita?' the boy replied carefully.

'Grass. Shit. Hash.'

The boy continued to look wary.

'Something to *smoke*—' Dallas pantomimed dragging on a joint, then she rolled her eyes and indicated joy. 'You get me?'

'Ah!' the boy said at last. 'It is expensive . . .'

'But you can get it! I knew you would be able to help me. And some pills,' she pantomimed popping pills into her mouth, 'something good. Qualudes if you can – anything, it doesn't matter. Something to get high – you with me?'

He nodded. 'It is expensive . . .' he began.

'Sure it is,' agreed Dallas, fishing in her purse, and producing two fifty dollar bills, 'and I need it *fast*,' she came up with another fifty, 'like in an hour.'

He grabbed the money hungrily.

'*I'll* open the shutters. *You* get going.'

He hurried from her room.

She giggled. That would fix Al – because she knew *he* wasn't about to come up with anything. And now that she had discovered how much fun life could be – with a little help – well, she wasn't about to give it up.

If only she had realized before. All that misery she had gone through. The shame of hustling guys – no wonder Bobbie had felt no pain. Being high was a whole new way of life. A way of living where nothing much mattered – everything was cool.

Marrying Aarron Mack would be a wonderful experience. No longer was he a dirty old man trying to grab a thigh. He was a beautiful human being. He would give her money, and protection, and respect, and money, and a position in the rat race, and money. She laughed out loud. Maybe she wouldn't even bother going back to work on Monday. Who needed all that fame shit? Who needed getting up at 5 a.m. and spending hours being beautiful?

She thought briefly of Cody. Bernie had told her he had called him for her. 'He's kinda uptight,' Bernie had understated. 'He says they were waiting for you all week to show up at the studio. I told him you'd make it first thing Monday. Maybe you should call him yourself.'

She didn't want to call him. He would only tell her off for disappearing. Who needed that trip?

So she would finish the series. Yes – for Cody she would finish it. Then they could all go to hell. She was *through* catering to other people. What had other people done for her except screw her rotten?

She threw open the shutters and was suitably impressed by the view. A magnificent stretch of white beach, bright blue ocean, and in the distance fantastic mountains. The beach was crowded with bikini-clad people. Cars lined the periphery. Transistor radios wafted out the sound of samba.

Dallas was glad that she had come here. It looked like the kind of place you could have a good time in. A place where you could forget your problems and just be happy.

She caught sight of herself in a mirror, and it reminded her that she was supposed to purchase something to wear for the party that evening. Al had thrust a thousand dollars in her purse and told her to get whatever she liked.

She had accepted the money. Why not? Once a whore always a whore. Wasn't that how the saying went?

In the jewellery store Al tried to decide between a small diamond heart to hang around her neck, or a lavish aquamarine and diamond ring. The heart won. If he started giving out rings someone might get the wrong impression.

'Send the bill to my hotel,' he instructed, and for good measure picked out a chunky gold identity bracelet for himself. Then, feeling generous, he purchased a slim digital gold watch for Paul, and a rough gold lion pendant for Bernie. He thought of Evan, but couldn't decide what he would like, maybe money would be best. But then he noticed a rough gold penknife, and that seemed suitable, so he got him that.

'Anything else, Señor King?' the wide-eyed manageress asked. She was a redhead, voluptuously squeezed into a green dress. Under normal circumstances Al would have considered giving her one. The thought didn't even occur to him.

'That's it,' he said, then he remembered Luke waiting outside the shop. He walked to the door, put his head out, asked Luke his birth sign, then came back in and chose a thick gold chain with the appropriate medallion hanging from it. That took care of everyone. Paul would organize minor presents for all the others on the tour.

Al walked out to his limousine. He felt really good. The concert the next day was a real challenge, and he was looking forward to it. Two hundred thousand people in one go, and according to Carlos Baptista it was a sell-out.

Dallas would be there to watch him. If things worked out she would be watching him for weeks – maybe even months.

He hoped she would hold his interest. He hoped this affair was going to be different. Tonight he would have her. No – they would have each other. He felt himself harden at the thought. Christ! He had wanted her long enough, it was about time.

Evita entered Cristina's room. She was wearing a dramatic black dress which bared one shoulder, and was held in place by a massive diamond clip. Her white-blond hair was piled high in a severe chignon. 'Darling, are you ready?'

Cristina scowled at her own reflection. 'I look fat!'

'You do not.'

'Beside you I do.'

Evita sighed, 'It's because I am wearing black.'

'I wish I could wear black. I hate this dress.' She twirled in front of the mirror, and the red dress she was wearing twirled with her. 'I look like a little girl!'

Evita laughed. 'How could you?'

Cristina made a face at herself in the mirror. 'I wish I could wear jeans,' she muttered, 'I knew this dress was a mistake.'

'You look perfectly delightful,' Evita assured her daughter, 'Louis will be quite bewitched.'

'He already is,' replied Cristina sourly. She was becoming more and more tense. All she could think of was stupid Nino, and the stupid things he wanted her to do. How on earth was she supposed to get Al King to notice her? She had been introduced to him at the airport and his stupid glazed smile had not even focused in her direction.

How on earth was she to get Louis to take her to the airport in the middle of the concert? The whole thing was ridiculous. Nino was asking too much.

With a shudder she remembered what Nino had threatened to do if she did not cooperate. Oh God! The shame! Louis would never speak to her again.

'I think you should take a wrap,' Evita was saying. 'You're shivering. Do you fell unwell?'

'I'm fine,' replied Cristina, wishing her mother would go away and leave her alone, 'perfectly fine.'

Al wore a dinner jacket of black brocade with matching vest, and pale blue evening shirt, and the tighter than tight trousers which were his trademark. He didn't feel tired, in spite of a day that had included the plane trip from Los Angeles to Rio. Television interviews. Photo calls. Press reception. And now a large party in his honour.

Paul said, 'Do you want me to fetch Dallas?'

Al shook his head. 'You take care of Evan and go in the car with Bernie. Here – a little something.' He handed his brother the package with the watch in.

Paul opened it. He was amazed. It was the fifth watch Al had presented him with in the last two years. Didn't he realize? 'Great – thank you,' he said, taking off his Cartier and replacing it with the new watch.

'Solid gold,' Al pointed out unnecessarily.

'I can see,' replied Paul.

'Cost a bomb,' added Al.

Yes. No doubt. Paul knew he would have to settle the bill in the morning. Al never dealt with the money side of things. He just spent. Sometimes indiscriminately. Frankly Paul thought he should never have shelled out a thousand dollars to Dallas. She had just won thirty thousand, let her spend her own money.

'I'll see you there then,' said Paul.

'We'll be right behind you,' assured Al.

He waited until Paul had left, and then he checked himself out in the mirror one more time. He looked good. Couldn't argue with facts.

He wondered if he should have a drink – maybe a fast blast of Jack Daniels. Six bottles stood unopened on a table, compliments of Carlos Baptista. He decided against it. Tonight he wanted to have all his wits about him. He wanted to remain razor sharp. Maybe later he and Dallas would share a bottle of champagne. But only if she wanted to.

He picked up the box with the diamond heart in, and dropped it into his jacket pocket, then he set off to fetch her.

The bell boy had not let her down. Six joints and two bottles of pills, and no change. But she hadn't minded that. The hell with it, it was only money.

She smoked three of the joints, and swallowed a few pills. She didn't know what they were, but the bell boy assured her they would have the desired effect. They certainly did. This time she was *really* flying.

When Al called to say he would be picking her up in twenty minutes she had not even started to dress. In fact the six hundred dollar gown she had purchased was still in its box. She had been lying out on the balcony admiring the view. The twinkling lights fascinated her. The parade of cars driving along the promenade that separated the hotel from the beach. The samba music which never seemed to stop.

She threw off her jeans and shirt and stood under a warm shower. It was so pleasant that she stayed there for ten minutes. Wet and naked she danced around the room drying off. Who needed towels?

She opened the box and extracted the dress, a gorgeous funnel of white silk jersey. She slipped into it, unaware that it was back to front and that her breasts were totally exposed.

She applied some make-up in a smudgy fashion, and shook her hair which was in a wild tangled mass.

Al's knock at the door coincided with her lighting another joint, and she stubbed it out hurriedly. He wouldn't be pleased. She must appear absolutely normal. Mustn't disappoint him.

She flung the door open. 'Hi, Al.' And she started to giggle. 'Good to see ya!'

The smile vanished from his face. 'Where did you get it?' he asked coldly. He had told all of them. Bernie. Paul. Luke. They all knew if she asked to say no.

She weaved back into the room. 'I'm ready,' she slurred, 'ready t'go t' the party.'

His eyes travelled down her body, fixing on her breasts, and suddenly he wanted her so badly that nothing else mattered.

He walked towards her, took her in his arms, kissed her.

Her mouth was slack.

He moved his hands over her incredible breasts.

She slumped in his arms.

'I want you,' he said, his voice fierce, 'can you understand that? I want you.'

She fell back on the couch, still giggling. Her legs parted. The folds of white jersey parted. She was wearing nothing underneath.

'G' ahead,' she giggled, 'be my guest, man.'

He turned away, smashing his fist into the palm of his hand. 'Why?' he screamed, 'Why? Why? Why?'

'You all gonna wake the neighbours, sugar sweets,' she slurred. 'Come on over here and I'll give you a blow job – calm you down. A *professional* blow job. Did I ever tell you I was a *professional*? Fucked my way from here to Kingdom Come! Hey Kingdom Come. That's funny – get it? Get it? Al Kingdom come . . .' She dissolved into peals of laughter.

He threw off his jacket, dragged her from the couch, ripped the back to front dress off her. Lifted her like a sack of coal over his shoulders and carried her into the bathroom where he dumped her unceremoniously in the bath.

'Hey,' she grumbled, 'you're rough.'

He turned the shower attachment on, and icy water cascaded over her.

She tried to struggle up, gasping. He shoved her back.

He soaked a towel and wiped it over her face. She spat a string of obscenities at him. He ignored her.

He went in the other room, tipped out the contents of her purse and found the remaining joints and the pills. He marched back in the bathroom. She was climbing out of the bath. He held the bottle of pills up to her face, 'What are they?' he demanded.

'How the fuck do I know,' she snapped.

'Throw up,' he said sternly, 'stick your finger down your throat and throw up. You don't know what this junk is.'

'The hell I will.'

'The hell you won't.' He grabbed her by the hair and forced her head back. 'You going to do it or shall I?'

'Get lost,' she hissed.

'OK,' he said, 'OK.' He prised her mouth open, jamming two fingers in.

She bit down sharply, drawing blood. He didn't withdraw his fingers, and she felt the vomit rising, could do nothing to stop it.

She threw up half over him, half over the floor.

He let her go. She slid to the floor. He threw a towel over her and marched back into the other room wrapping Kleenex round his bleeding fingers.

He called room service, ordering a pot of black coffee. Then he stripped off his ruined vest and shirt.

She was sobbing on the bathroom floor, still stoned, but manageably so. He scooped her up, dumped her back in the bath, this time he let the water run warm, and she didn't struggle.

'Goddamn it,' he said. 'You know how to be difficult.'

She hunched her knees up, covering herself. He took this as a sign that she knew what she was doing. 'Don't go away,' he said, 'I'll be back.'

He set off down the corridor to his suite, startling the maids who lapsed into torrents of excitement.

Luke, waiting outside, did not bat an eyelid at the state Al was in. If Al had something to tell him he would do so, if not, well, he was the boss man, that was his prerogative.

Al collected two bathrobes – he always travelled with at least six – and went back to Dallas' suite.

She was in the same position, her head slumped on her knees.

'Out,' he said, gently but firmly.

She stood up docilely, and he tried to ignore the body, but Christ! Even under these conditions he was getting a hard-on.

He helped her into a bathrobe, and she accepted his help silently.

'We're going to talk,' he said.

She nodded.

He took her into the living room, sat her on the couch.

'Wait,' he commanded.

Again she nodded, slumping back and closing her eyes.

He went in the bathroom, took off his trousers and put on the bathrobe. Then he cleared up as best he could.

Al King, superstar, clearing vomit off a bathroom floor?

Who would believe it?

Even he didn't believe it.

The Kleenex wrapped round his fingers was soaked with blood, and the two fingers hurt like hell. He held them under the cold tap and wrapped them in fresh tissue.

He could hear the phone ringing, but he didn't rush to answer it. He knew who it would be – either Paul or Bernie wanting to know where the hell he was.

Dallas appeared to have fallen asleep. This was getting to be a habit. Only tonight was supposed to be special. He snatched the phone up in a fit of temper. 'Yes?'

Paul's voice. 'Where are you, for Crissake?'

'I am at the hotel,' replied Al, evenly, 'I should have thought that was obvious due to the fact that you just telephoned me here.'

'Cut it out, Al. Half of Rio has turned out to meet you. Carlos Baptista is getting jumpy.'

'Am I getting paid to do a show tomorrow? Or am I getting paid to attend Carlos Baptista's party?' Al's voice was icy.

Paul knew the danger signals. Best to placate him. 'Will you be long?' he asked pleasantly.

'As long as I fucking please!' snapped Al, banging the phone down.

Screw Paul for bothering him. But at the same time he knew he was being unfair to his brother.

He walked to the door, whistled for Luke. 'Call Paul at the party,' he instructed, 'tell him I can't make it – he can give them any excuse he likes. And inform the front desk *no* calls – either my suite or Dallas'.'

Nervously Cristina skirted the room. She had danced twice with Louis, once with her father, and where was the famous guest of honour that she was supposed to get to know? Everyone was asking the same question. Where was Al King?

His brother was there. His son was there. His publicity man was there. But where was the star himself?

Cristina spotted her future father-in-law deep in conversation with Paul King. She took a deep breath and walked over.

'Hello,' she said gaily, 'have you seen Louis?'

'What?' snapped Carlos, not at all in a good mood.

'Er – Louis,' stammered Cristina, 'I seem to have lost him.' She turned to Paul King. 'Hello again, we met at the airport earlier today. Cristina Maraco, Louis Baptista's fiancée.'

'Run along, dear,' interrupted Carlos brusquely, 'we're in the middle of a business conversation.'

'Oh – sorry.' She felt herself blushing ,and was furious with Nino for having put her in such an undignified position. Paul King completely ignored her. The two men resumed their conversation as if she had never interrupted. So much for getting to know the people surrounding Al King. Then she noticed the son, at least someone had *said* it was the son, although she could hardly believe that the spotty, insignificant boy standing in the corner was actually the great Al King's son. She could not remember seeing him at the airport.

Resolutely she walked over to him.

'Hello, I'm Cristina Maraco, Louis Baptista's fiancée. I don't think we have met,' politely she extended her hand to him.

He seemed to back away, hiding his hands behind him.

Cristina dropped her hand. Stupid boy, no manners, and what a horrible skin. 'Louis is Carlos Baptista's son,' she continued by way of further explanation of her position, 'I'm looking forward to meeting your father. Where is he?'

'Don't know,' mumbled Evan, highly embarrassed by this strange girl picking *him* out for conversation.

'Oh,' said Cristina, momentarily at a loss for words, then, 'what's your name?'

'Evan,' he replied.

She smiled, 'Nice. Want to dance, Evan? You do samba, don't you?'

'Where is the star?' Evita asked Carlos.

'My dear Evita, if I knew – he would be here. His brother tells me he is tired and is sleeping. I arrange this party for him. Two hundred of the most interesting people in Rio to honour his arrival in our city,' Carlos made a gesture of despair, 'and he is tired. He is sleeping. What can I do?'

Evita smiled sympathetically. 'You can get me another glass of your delicious champagne.'

Momentarily distracted, Carlos said, 'You are looking as beautiful as ever, Evita. My God you are a wonderful-looking woman. Couldn't we . . .'

'Here comes Jorge,' Evita interrupted lightly. She was used to Carlos' vaguely erotic suggestions. She laughed them off as she laughed off all the propositions she received. Jorge would never believe how unloyal most of his friends could be when it came to his wife.

Jorge approached, smiling 'Where is . . .' he began.

'Please!' interrupted Carlos, 'do not ask. My one prayer now is that he turns up for the concert tomorrow. Two hundred people I can explain to. Two hundred thousand might present me with a problem!'

*

Al allowed Dallas to sleep for a couple of hours. He paced the room and wondered what the hell he was doing there. He couldn't find an answer. He had started off wanting a girl, a body – and now here he was – *concerned*, for Chrissake.

He drank the coffee which arrived, then stood on the balcony gazing out at the breathtaking array of twinkling lights.

The smell of the sea drifted up, and he thought about the evening he and Dallas had walked along the beach at Malibu, and he had swum and she had sat waiting for him. God – she had seemed like a different girl then. Together, sure of herself, in control. He wondered what had happened to get her going on this destructive drug trip. And it was a destructive trip, any fool could see that. Okay – a couple of joints never did anyone any harm if that was your scene – but once you started indiscriminately popping pills at the same time – then you were headed in the wrong direction. She seemed to be striving for total oblivion. Where was *that* going to get her?

Christ – *he* knew about total oblivion. He was an expert. But he had always had people around to look after him. Dallas seemed to have no one who really cared.

When he woke her she was subdued like a small child who has done something naughty and been found out. She huddled in his large bathrobe, legs tucked underneath, and regarded him with watchful green eyes.

'Hungry?' he questioned.

'Starving,' she replied.

He called room service and ordered her some scrambled eggs and himself a steak sandwich.

'We missed the party,' she said solemnly.

'We sure did.'

'Is it too late? Couldn't you still go?'

'I don't want to go,' he replied.

'But it was in your honour . . .'

'I know.'

She shrugged helplessly. 'I don't know why you stayed with me.'

'I can't quite figure it out myself. But I intend to find out. You and I are going to talk – I mean really *talk*. No bullshit. I want to know what's happening with you. I started out wanting to get into your body – now it's your head I'm interested in.'

'Settle for the body, Al. I think I owe it to you.'

'With no charge?'

She flushed. 'What?'

'When you're stoned all you can talk about is giving it away for free.'

447

She turned her head away from him. 'Take no notice of what I say when I'm stoned.'

He leaned forward, put his hand under her chin, and forcibly turned her face to look at him. 'I want to know about you, Dallas. I want to know it all. Everything.'

She laughed bitterly. 'Why not? Why don't I tell you the whole pretty story.'

'Yes, why don't you.'

She shifted uncomfortably. Her head was beginning to ache. Christ – why was he bugging her? What did he want from her? 'You really want to know?'

'I wouldn't be here if I didn't.'

Fuck it. She would tell him. Get rid of him once and for all. 'You asked for it,' she said roughly, then adopting a sing-song voice she began.

'I was born twenty fun-filled years ago in the house back of a crummy private zoo my dear parents owned in a backwater off the main highway leaving Miami. I was a real event in their lives – something else to study – like the chimps or bears. Only I wasn't kept in a cage – not a visible one, that is. I had no schooling, no playmates except the animals, no toys, no books.' Her eyes filled with angry tears. 'I had fuck all if you want the truth. I wasn't even allowed to talk to the paying visitors in case they would corrupt me with stories of the outside world where *real* people lived. When I was sweet sixteen my father took me into town to pick up the monthly supplies – the first time I was allowed out. Can you believe that? Some guy rode back in the truck with us – kept on giving me fishy looks. It wasn't until later I found out he'd been picked as a husband for me . . .'

Talking about it was like a catharsis. She had never told anyone the truth before. Even with Cody she had tailored the story to suit herself. Now it all came pouring out – everything. Bobbie. The old man in the motel. Her months of degradation in Los Angeles. Meeting Ed Kurlnik. Trying to kill Bobbie. Fixing the judges on 'Miss Coast to Coast'. She didn't try to hide a thing. If Al wanted the truth that was exactly what he was going to get.

The food arrived and they both ignored it. He poured her some coffee, and she gulped that as her voice wavered and shook and neared tears as she told her story.

When she reached the part about Lew Margolis and his black-mail attempt, Al stood up and walked to the balcony. She told him about Diamond and Linda helping out with the photographs.

Then about Bobbie coming back, Doris Andrews, her short marriage to Cody, Bobbie's death. She didn't leave out a detail. Finally she told him about Lew's latest attempt at blackmail, and the steps she had taken to resolve it.

'That's it,' she said at last, her voice blank. 'You wanted it – you got it. Can you blame me for wanting to get stoned? Can you blame me for not wanting to know myself? Jesus Christ, my parents knew a long time ago I was worth nothing. They never came looking for me – never gave a shit. I've been in every newspaper – on the cover of nearly every magazine in the country. They still don't want to know. They have never attempted to reach me. I'm telling you – they knew right from the beginning. They must have been delighted when I took off. They didn't lose a daughter – they lost a maid. I guess they hired a replacement the very next day.'

Al hadn't uttered a word. He stood by the balcony, his face impassive.

'Why don't you go?' asked Dallas brusquely. 'Piss on off while you've still got the chance. You know all about me now. A hooker. A dyke. A murderer. A blackmailer.' She laughed grimly. 'Some record!'

He turned slowly. 'Do you *want* me to go?'

'Sure. Go. I'm a big girl. I can take care of myself. I've got a cheque for thirty thousand dollars somewhere – I'll make it back to LA and I'll see you around. You know, Al, you and I would never have made it – we're just too different.'

'Different!' he snorted. 'Different! You've got to be kidding! So you were a hooker – you slept with guys for money. Well I slept with women for free – hundreds, thousands probably. I didn't like them any more than you liked the guys you went with. *But we both had our reasons for doing it.*' He paused to light a cigarette. 'You're not a murderer. You didn't kill Bobbie. And the old guy in Miami had a heart attack. It was an accident. How do you think I feel about the bomb killing two girls at my concert in Chicago? I feel like shit about it – but it was not my fault – I don't think of myself as a murderer. *It was an accident.*' He walked over to her, held her roughly by the shoulders. 'Blackmail. I blackmail people every day of my life. You do this for me and I'll do that for you. Only I call it by another name – business. And you want to call yourself a dyke – go ahead. Only a couple of homosexual experiences do not make you into a dyke. We all experiment with sex – when I was a kid I tried it with everything

449

except sheep! What I'm trying to say, Dallas, is don't pin labels onto yourself. Don't put yourself down. So you had a rough past – so *forget* it.'

'How can I forget it when I'm still forced to do things I hate myself for?'

'Who's forcing you?'

'I have to protect myself . . .' she began hesitantly.

'Tear up the photos of you and Doris – destroy the negatives.'

'But . . .'

'It will be all right. I can promise you that. You'll still be "Man Made Whatever" if that's what you really want. Forget about yesterday – start living for today. Hey – are you as hungry as I am?'

Softly she said, 'Yes.'

He phoned room service, but as it was now four in the morning they had closed down.

'Well—' suggested Al, 'how do you feel about a cold steak sandwich?'

sixty-one

The Maracana soccer stadium had been transformed into a vast theatre in the round. In the centre of the pitch a platform had been erected, littered with microphones, amplifiers, and musical equipment.

Two hundred thousand people chanted and sang patiently. Police guards were stationed all around the inner circle of the stadium a foot apart. Some of them had dogs with them.

Carlos Baptista was justifiably proud of his security arrangements. No star in his care had ever been involved in any kind of riot – he made sure there was always more than adequate protection. That was one of the reasons he was always able to get the biggest stars. That, and the fact that he was always ready to pay top dollar. He was paying Al King one million dollars for two concerts – but he still expected to make money on the deal – what with the entrance fee and the various concessions he had arranged. Television rights alone had fetched in a princely sum. What a stroke of genius it had been on his part to have thought of hiring the fabulous Maracana Stadium as a venue for Al King. Perfect.

The star himself had been charm personified at a meeting that very morning. He had apologized profusely for not turning up at his party, and when Carlos had been introduced to his girlfriend he could understand why. She was the most beautiful, sensual woman he had ever seen. A streaked mass of hair, strong sexual face, burning green eyes, and a body that defied description. Carlos had professed himself honoured to meet her, and he had meant every word of it.

Now she sat next to him at the concert, but alas, on his other side sat his wife – a magnificent seventeen-stone lady.

Carlos sighed, and patted Dallas delicately on the leg. 'More champagne, my dear?'

She shook her head. Who needed champagne? She was high enough. And without any outside aids. Just Al. He had been so wonderful to her. So understanding and kind. They had talked until the dawn. Exchanged thoughts and feelings – rapped about themselves until she felt she knew him better than anyone she had ever known. And he certainly knew her. Yet he hadn't been disgusted. He had listened, and sympathized, consoled, and advised. He had understood.

She had always thought that if she ever told anyone the truth about herself they would back off. Al had stayed. He had given her a feeling of inner strength – a feeling she knew she could begin to build on.

And he had not touched her.

He had proved beyond doubt that he did not want her for her body. And yet they both knew it would happen, and when it did it would be clean and good and everything that she had ever imagined.

A sudden roar went up from the crowd as Al appeared. He stood in the middle of the platform holding both arms aloft in greeting, allowing the audience's adoration to pour over him.

Suddenly Dallas knew if there was such a thing as love – this was it.

She loved the man giving himself to the crowds. She loved him with her whole being.

'I changed my mind, I just don't want to go – that's all.'

Louis frowned. 'I just do not understand you, Cristina. For three weeks I hear nothing else but Al King this, Al King that. When is he coming? Where is he staying? Who is he with? Now comes the big moment – the concert at Maracana Stadium – we are on our way there – and you make me stop the car, and tell me you do not wish to go.'

Cristina attempted a gay laugh, although she did not feel at all gay.

'Louis – you know what I'm like. I get moods, sudden desires. I can't be conventional.'

He nodded resignedly.

'What I really feel like doing now is driving to the airport. Does that sound crazy?'

'The airport.' Louis was disgusted. 'Why the airport?'

Cristina shrugged. 'I don't know. I just *feel* like it. Maybe we could see Al King's plane – I heard your father say he has a *bedroom* in it. A bedroom! Can you imagine!'

'All our friends are at the concert, they will wonder what has happened to us.'

'Let them wonder. Who cares? We'll tell them we were making mad passionate love somewhere,' she moved her hand onto his knee – tiptoeing her fingers up towards his crotch. '*That* would make them all envious as anything. They're jealous of us anyway. Marie Therese is beside herself because *I've* got you.'

He let out a strangled groan. 'Don't do that, Cristina, you know what it does to me.'

Teasingly she replied, 'What does it do, Louis? Tell me, please tell me.' She felt him growing beneath her fingers.

'Oh God!'

'I know what, I'll make a bargain with you. If we can go to the airport I'll do what you begged me to do the other night. Remember? The mouth thing. Would you like me to do that to you?'

'Yes,' he agreed urgently.

'OK, drive somewhere quiet. Then after, do you promise we can go to the airport?

'I promise.'

He started the car, and Cristina took a deep breath. *One* hurdle accomplished.

He was out there for one and a half hours. Alone most of the time apart from his musicians, and joined on two occasions by 'Hot Fudge'.

The crowds were going mad, screaming for more. Carlos Baptista was beaming from ear to ear. Better than he had expected. A sensation in fact. Al King generated the most excitement he had ever seen.

Bernie was hustling around getting everyone together for the helicopter trip to the airport. Dallas, Evan, Paul, Luke. They would take the plane directly to Sao Paulo, and it would return for the others, plus all the equipment, in the morning. It was only a short hop.

Bernie assembled everyone while Al was still singing – got them all aboard the orange helicopter – so now all they needed was Al to be rushed straight on with Luke, and they would be away before the crowd stopped cheering.

All it took was a little organization.

Nino took a bus to the airport. He was early, but he had meant to get there early. Now that the wheels were in motion he felt pretty good. He felt important. He knew he *was* important.

He headed straight for the information desk where he had arranged to meet Juana – a plump girl who worked at the airport as a ground hostess.

She was duly waiting. He greeted her with a kiss, pinched her fat bottom. She gazed at him with adoring eyes. 'Last night was . . .'

'Shhh.' He quietened her with a kiss. 'Tonight will be better, my little carioca, much, much better. Did you find out what I wanted?'

'Naturally. I can show you exactly where the plane is, and where Mr King and his party will be boarding. Nino, tonight . . .'

'Later, we'll talk about it later. Did you get me the uniform?'

'Yes. Are you sure no one will know I helped you?'

'Of course not. And so what if they do. I'm only going to interview Al King, not shoot him.'

Juana giggled.

'Think of the money I will get for an exclusive interview,' Nino reminded, 'and think of who will benefit from it.'

Juana giggled again. 'Me?' she suggested coyly.

'Yes, you. Now quickly, where is the uniform? Where can I change?'

In the helicopter Al held Dallas by the hand.

'You really did it!' she said.

'My inspiration was in the audience,' he replied, squeezing her hand hard.

Sitting behind them Evan couldn't help eavesdropping. Horrible woman. How he hated her, taking up all his father's attention. Why, Al was virtually ignoring him now *she* was around. He hadn't even asked him how he liked the show, and he always did that.

Evan picked viciously at a spot and glared out of the window. He didn't even know what was supposed to be happening after South America. Were they going back to England? No one had bothered to tell him. He didn't matter. *He* was only Al's son – not his stupid girlfriend.

'I've got a confession,' Cristina said nervously, 'I promised someone I would do them a favour.'

'What favour?' asked Louis easily.

They stood in front of the newspaper and magazine stand at the airport.

'Remember Nino? Cristina asked.

'That rat bag,' replied Louis dismissively, 'why do you mention *him*?'

She bit deeply into the side of her lip. 'He's not so bad.'

'*You* hardly know him.'

Desperately she thought of what lie would make everything all right. 'I know his sister,' she stammered.

'How do you know his sister?' he asked curiously. 'I didn't even know he had one.'

'She works at the hairdresser I go to,' Cristina lied, 'my mother likes her – feels sorry for her. Sometimes she comes to the house.'

'Look, why don't we buy some magazines and go on home,' said Louis, suddenly bored by the whole thing. 'They have American *Vogue*, and look – a new edition of *Motor Sport*.' He took out his wallet. 'Anything else you want?'

'I'm doing this favour for my mother,' Cristina said quickly, '*she* asked me to help Nino's sister.'

'What *are* you talking about?'

'Nino's going to meet us here. I promised we would help him see Al King's plane.'

Louis stared at her. 'Are you mad? How would that help his sister?'

'It's a long story, very complicated. *Please* help me, Louis. Honestly it's *very important*. I *promised* my mother we would help, I *promised*.' She was near to genuine tears.

'This is crazy,' he said, completely bewildered.

'If you love me you'll help me.'

'But, Cristina . . .'

'Oh look, here comes Nino now. *Please*, Louis, *please*. I'll explain it all to you later, but *please* don't ask questions now.'

*

There were no press at the airport. Al's departure had been kept a secret. They were able to transfer from the helicopter to the plane with no fuss at all.

Holding Dallas' hand he strode through the jet to his private bedroom at the back, barely pausing to nod at his two stewardesses.

Bernie greeted them with his usual dirty jokes, and they laughed and asked about the show.

Paul sat down, opened up a table and laid out some contracts that he wanted to go over.

Evan strapped himself into an isolated window seat, and continued putting work in on the spot he was attacking.

Two key journalists had been invited along for the trip. They sat up near the front hopeful that Al would eventually emerge.

'Is that everyone, Mr Suntan?' stewardess Cathy inquired.

'That's it,' replied Bernie. 'We're empty this trip.'

'We'll close up then.'

As she spoke Cristina Maraco came running down the ramp leading onto the plane. She was flushed and breathless.

'Oh!' she gasped, 'we made it!'

The two journalists looked at her in surprise. Bernie waddled over. 'What do *you* want, girlie?' he asked, thinking she was a fan. 'And how the heck did you get on here?'

'The man at the desk let me through. He said it was all right. I'm Cristina Maraco – remember – we met at the airport when you arrived – and at the party last night. I'm Louis Baptista's fiancée. Louis, Carlos Baptista's son. Didn't Senor Baptista telephone you?'

'Should he have?'

'Oh yes – he said he would. You see he wants you to take us to Sao Paulo with you – he wants Louis to be there early to organize some things to do with the concert tomorrow.'

She spotted Evan and waved. 'Hi – good to see you again. Oh and there's Senor King's brother,' she called out desperately. 'Hello – remember me?'

Paul hardly glanced up.

Bernie scratched his head. 'So where is Louis?' He remembered him, a nicely spoken boy, and he vaguely remembered her. Hadn't she spent quite a time dancing with Evan the previous evening?

'He's just coming. It is all right then?'

'I don't see why not. Let me just check it.'

He walked over to Paul, who plainly did not want to be bothered.

'Carlos Baptista wants his son and fiancée to come with us. Is that Jake?'

'If Carlos says so.'

'So I'll tell them it's fine?'

'Yes. I suppose so.' Paul returned to studying the contracts.

Bernie waddled back to Cristina.

'Yes?' she asked anxiously.

'Yeah. Only hurry your boyfriend up, we're waiting to go.'

Cristina rushed off the plane to where Louis and Nino stood waiting in the tunnel which joined the embarkation point to the plane.

'It's okay,' she said.

Nino and Louis moved forward, Nino walking slightly behind Louis in his mechanic's uniform. In one hand he carried a shabby airline bag. The other hand was buried deep in his overall pocket clutching onto a gun which was pointing straight at Louis' back.

sixty-two

Van Howard glanced at his co-pilot and raised a questioning eyebrow.

'Five minutes,' Harry Booker assured him, removing his radio head set. 'The runway's clearing now.'

'Good,' Van was tired, and was looking forward to finishing off the short hop to Sao Paulo and getting some sleep. He had not slept at all the previous evening. Truth to tell he had had a lousy evening. The problem was Cathy, his wife.

At first the idea of captaining Al King's private jet across America, with the opportunity of taking Cathy along in a professional capacity – had just seemed heaven-sent. He had recently quit his job of seventeen years with a commercial airline, and he had been looking around wondering what to do, when a friend had mentioned the Al King job.

Van had attended two interviews, and been hired over eight other equally experienced applicants. Cathy being chief stewardess had been part of the deal.

What an opportunity it had seemed. The money was great, and it would get them out of the ten-year rut their marriage seemed to have become stuck in.

Everything had started off all right, but gradually Van noticed Cathy changing. He had married her when she was seventeen, and as far as he knew had been her only boyfriend. Their marriage had seemed quite stable -- the only black spot being the fact that they seemed unable to produce children. Privately Van knew it was her fault. At forty-seven years of age he had had more than his share of girlfriends with unwanted pregnancies. However, they had both subjected themselves to various undignified tests, and although there seemed to be nothing clinically wrong, still it had not happened.

Van had hoped that this trip might do the trick. Different environments. Different places to make love. But as they progressed across America Cathy became more and more withdrawn.

She had finally told him the previous evening. Told him after drinking a bottle of wine to give herself dutch courage.

She had fallen in love with one of the musicians on the tour. A twenty-four-year-old long-haired freak who made his living strumming a guitar.

'Are you mad?' Van had asked her.

'I'm leaving you,' she had replied. 'As soon as the tour is finished I'm leaving you.'

'All set, chief,' Harry Booker interrupted his thoughts, 'we just got clearance. Seems we've taken on three extra passengers. Shall I inform control?'

'Doesn't matter.' Van shook his head. It was impossible to keep a proper passenger list on these flights. People popped on and off from city to city. Journalists, photographers, groupies. Van never knew who was aboard. He glanced round at the navigator and flight engineer, men he had been allowed to pick personally.

'Are we ready?' he asked. A question he always asked before turning on the power.

Their nods were affirmative.

In his custom-built flying bedroom Al tossed Dallas a bathrobe.

'Make yourself comfortable,' he suggested, 'I'm going to.'

She looked around her. 'This is unbelievable!' she exclaimed.

'You like it?' he asked proudly.

'It looks like something out of *Macho* magazine! Even a hick like me can see it's in the worst taste possible! It's nothing but a travelling knocking shop!'

'I'll have you know I've caught up on a lot of sleep in this room.'

'I'll bet!' She shook her head in amazement at the circular bed covered in black silk sheets, the fake leopard padded walls, the thick pile carpet.

'Bathroom's over there,' he indicated a hidden door in the padded walls, 'what shall I order for you? A drink? Food? You name it – we've got it.'

'This whole thing must cost you a fortune!'

'Tax deductible.'

'I'll have a Bloody Mary. You *are* going to allow me to have alcohol, aren't you?'

He grinned. 'Bout as much as you allow me. I'm sweating like a pig – I'll have a shower as soon as we take off.' He threw off his clothes and put a bathrobe over his undershorts. Then he picked up an intercom phone and snapped, 'Cathy – two Bloody Marys right now. How long before take off?'

Cathy Howard hung up the intercom phone and made a face. She wished Al King could be like everyone else and *wait* for his drink. Didn't he realize she had other things to do just before take off? Besides that, she felt terrible. Telling Van the truth last night had been a tremendous strain. Why couldn't he have taken it like a man instead of dissolving into pitiful tears? She had been shocked. Van had never shown one ounce of emotion throughout their ten-year marriage. Perhaps if he had, things might have been different . . .

She busied herself in the small galley with tomato juice, vodka, and ice cubes. Al liked his drinks just so – he always insisted that she fixed them personally.

Wendy, the other stewardess, rushed in. 'Did you get a load of the mechanic with the Baptista party? she asked. 'Mmm . . . tasty. I wouldn't sling *him* out of bed!'

'*You* wouldn't sling *anyone* out of bed,' Cathy replied crisply.

Wendy had started the trip as Harry Booker's girlfriend. That had lasted all the way to Chicago, when they had both decided to go their own ways. Since that time Wendy had undertaken her own personal survey of the sexual habits of the American male.

'Who are the drinks for?' Wendy asked.

'Mr King of course.'

'You want me to take them?'

'I can manage, thank you.'

Wendy pouted, 'Why do *you* always have to do everything for him?'

'Because *I'm* chief stew. Anyway, he likes me.'

458

'Given half a chance he could like me,' Wendy muttered. 'Are you feeling OK? You look terrible.'

'Well enough to take him his drinks, thank you.'

The FASTEN YOUR SEAT BELTS NO SMOKING sign had flashed on.

Bernie was sitting up front rapping with the two journalists.

Paul was engrossed in the contracts, making notes on a separate piece of paper.

Evan had settled into a secluded seat at the back, near the door to Al's private bedroom, and he was studying his latest batch of girlie magazines, trying to decide between Elvira, who loved horses, and had the biggest knockers he'd ever seen, or Yana, whose widely spread legs displayed a healthy abandon for wide open spaces.

Cristina sat opposite Louis and Nino, a table separating them. She had paled beneath her suntan, and her eyes were wide and alarmed. Under her breath she whispered. 'Help me God – Please help me. I promise to be good. I promise to do everything my parents want. I promise to be the perfect daughter. But please please God help me out of this mess.'

And what a mess it was. Nino had turned up to meet them all right. He had smiled, his eyes blazing intently. And he had said, quite politely, 'How are you, Louis? How does it feel to have a gun pointing at your belly?'

And she had laughed, thinking it was a joke, thinking he was kidding. But he had moved insidiously towards her, pressing himself against her so that she could feel the pressure of the metal, and he had said, 'Tell your boyfriend to do as he is told, Cristina. Tell him or I'll blow his guts out.'

With a sudden fear she had known that this was no joke. 'Do as he says, Louis. He means it.'

Louis had stared at her with an expression of disbelief. 'What is this . . .' he began.

'Shut up and start walking,' Nino had interrupted. 'Walk ahead of me, I'll tell you where to go. *Both* of you ahead of me.'

She hadn't dared to argue. She hadn't dared to say another word. She had just followed Nino's instructions, and now here they were bound for Sao Paulo where she didn't know what would happen.

Louis hadn't looked at her once. He just stared straight ahead with a stony expression. He probably thought she was a part of it.

He probably thought she had tricked him. And the horrible truth was that she had – but she hadn't meant to, hadn't wanted to. And had certainly not been aware of the fact that Nino would have a gun.

The jet was taxi-ing down the runway, preparing for take-off. A stewardess touched Cristina on the arm, and she jumped.

'Sorry,' said the stewardess, 'did I startle you? Just wanted to check that you have your seat belt fastened.'

She smiled provocatively at Nino. 'All done up?' she asked, flashing admirable teeth.

He nodded, returning her smile, stripping her with his eyes.

'I'll be back to see what you'd like to drink as soon as we're airborne,' she said, instinctively smoothing down her skirt.

'You've got everything organized,' Dallas remarked.

'Sure,' agreed Al, 'I like my privacy.'

He had settled them both into a small couch with concealed seatbelts. He indicated a niche for her to place her glass in.

'How many ladies have you had on this plane?'

He grinned. 'No ladies.'

The jet began to pick up speed, thundering down the runway, then lifting up into the sky with a lyrical ease.

Al leaned over and kissed her, softly, insistently. She parted her mouth to accept his kiss, teased him with her tongue. 'I think,' he said gruffly, 'I'm going to like this flight.'

'I think,' she replied, 'we both are.'

Nino licked dry lips. His throat was parched, and he was dying for a glass of water. No time for that though. No time for anything except putting his plan into operation.

He glanced swiftly at Louis sitting silently beside him. He had been easy enough to handle. Rich boy frightened of getting a bullet in the stomach.

Cristina was staring at him with an accusing expression. He knew she was beside herself to speak to him – but she couldn't – didn't want to let her precious Louis know that she had been in on it.

Nino allowed himself a small, tight smile, and his hand caressed the gun in his pocket lovingly. What power it gave him. What wonderful incredible power.

The jet had stopped climbing and was levelling out. The SEAT BELT and NO SMOKING signs flashed off.

Out of the corner of his eye Nino saw the two hostesses spring into action bustling around taking drink orders. Rock music filtered through the speaker systems.

'I'll tell you what we are going to do,' Nino said in a low voice, 'lean forward and listen, Cristina.'

She did as she was told. Louis glared at him, wanting to speak but not quite sure if he dared.

'This plane has three bombs aboard. Only *I* know where they are. Shortly I will tell the rest of the passengers. If everyone co-operates with me no one will get hurt – if they don't' – he shrugged – 'too bad for all of us.'

Cristina gasped. 'Nino! Are you mad?'

Louis joined in. 'He's not mad, he's bluffing. I know for a fact that Al King's plane is searched by security guards before he boards it.'

'An hour, sometimes two hours before he boards. Plenty of time left for a mechanic with an authorized pass to come aboard and do what he has to do.'

Louis said, his voice strained, 'What are you doing this for?'

'Ask your girlfriend, she knows all about it. Now I want you two to sit here quietly while I go and have a word with the captain. I should advise you not to tell anyone – I shall do so soon enough. Should anyone attack me, try to knock me out – that would be very unfortunate. The bombs are due to go off at fifteen-minute intervals half an hour from now. Only *I* can stop them. And please don't forget the fact that I have a gun – a weapon that I am quite prepared to use.' He undid his seat belt and stood up. 'The safest thing for you two is to just sit tight. I wouldn't *want* to hurt either of you, but I can assure you I would.' He set off down the centre aisle of the plane towards the flight deck.

Cristina looked helplessly at Louis. 'I'm sorry . . .' she began, 'I didn't know . . . didn't realize . . .'

'Didn't know *what*?' hissed Louis, 'how much *did* you know? *You* arranged to meet him. *You* got us on the plane. This all must have been planned . . . you *knew* all along.'

'I didn't know what he planned. I didn't know he had a gun, bombs. Do you think I would have helped him if I'd known that?'

'So you *were* helping him?'

'I only . . .'

'Shh – he's talking to the stewardess. As soon as he's out of sight I must tell someone.'

＊

Wendy was fixing drinks for the journalists when Nino came up. She winked. 'Can't wait, huh? In that case what's your pleasure?'

'I'd like to talk to the pilot.'

'Sorry – forbidden ground. Now what do you want to drink?'

'I have a gun in my pocket,' Nino said pleasantly, 'it's pointing right at you.' He gestured with the outline of it. 'Shall we go?'

'Oh no!' said Wendy. 'Oh, Jesus, no!'

'Come on. Move. Walk in front of me and keep smiling.'

They were always trying to screw you.

Always trying to make points.

Always slipping in goddamn stupid clauses that a twelve-year-old would spot!

Angrily Paul made copious notes. Who the fuck did Lew Margolis think he was dealing with? A bunch of amateurs, for Crissake? A bunch of schoolkids?

Paul always checked the contracts before passing them on to the lawyers. He could spot things that the lawyers wouldn't even notice. What did they care? As long as their astronomical bills were paid.

And who did all the work? Who saved Al thousands of pounds by going through the small print? He did of course. Baby brother. The schmuck who never got any appreciation. The schmuck who was treated like a combination of Bernie and Luke. Chief gofer.

Linda was right. Linda had always been right. And where the hell had *she* been last night? It was difficult enough getting through to Los Angeles – but he had managed it three times – and three times her phone had rung and nobody had picked up. It was just too bad. He had told her he would probably be phoning. The least she could have done was stay in.

He had promised her marriage – wasn't that what she had been angling for? Wasn't that what she wanted?

It just wasn't good enough. She was playing games with him and he didn't *need* that crap.

Louis Baptista slid into the seat beside him. Christ! Conversation he didn't need either.

'Don't panic – don't panic—' Louis's voice was high-pitched and nervous – 'we're being hijacked – he's got a gun – bombs. He's with the pilot now.'

'Whhaat?'

'Nino. He's mad – quite mad. What shall we do? What shall we do?'

*

Van Howard knew at once what was happening. As soon as Wendy pushed her way onto the flight deck – every drop of colour gone from her face – the dark boy behind her – he knew.

Every pilot had imagined himself in the situation a thousand times. They even used to give lessons on what to do at the airline he had worked for. Stay calm. Don't panic. If it's not possible to disarm the hijacker/hijackers then go along with what they say. Reassure the passengers. Under no account put their lives at risk. Try and maintain radio contact with control. All of this flashed through Van's mind before the terrified Wendy uttered a word.

'He's – he's got a gun in my back,' she gasped.

Al finished showering and called out, 'You want to join me?'

'No thanks, I find showering in the middle of the sky absolutely crazy!' Dallas sat cross-legged in the centre of the bed and sipped her Bloody Mary.

'Don't knock it if you haven't tried it,' Al walked back into the bedroom knotting the cord of his bathrobe. He joined her on the bed and started to laugh.

'What's the matter?' Dallas asked.

'First time I ever shared a bed with a girl I haven't given one to.'

'Your English expressions are so cute!'

'Fuck you.'

'Another cute expression!'

'Now look . . .'

She smiled at him, stopping him in his tracks.

'I think . . .' he said.

'I think so too.'

He stared at her earnestly, 'Are you sure?'

'I'm as sure as I'll ever be.'

He reached for her, and she moved towards him willingly.

'I've waited a long time for this,' he whispered, shrugging off his bathrobe.

'Me too,' she whispered back, running her fingers lightly over his chest.

'Christ!' he muttered, 'you want to see what I've got for you?'

'I can see, I can see.'

'Just a minute,' he reached over to the panel surrounding the bed and pressed a few buttons.

'What are you doing?'

'Locking the door and turning off the intercom. Now nothing can disturb us.'

*

By the time Louis had garbled out a story that Paul understood, it was too late. Van Howard's voice was booming out through the speaker system. 'This is your captain speaking,' he said calmly, as if he was just about to give them a weather and altitude report. 'We seem to have a slight problem here.'

Cathy, busying herself with a tuna fish sandwich and a chocolate milkshake for Bernie, stopped to listen. What slight problem? It was a beautiful clear night, no turbulence, a short hop. What problem?

'It seems we have a gentleman on board who would prefer us to land elsewhere. He has asked me most persuasively, and for the safety of all of us I feel that I must comply with his wishes.'

'What the fuck?' said Bernie, who had been only half listening. 'Did I fuckin' hear right?'

One of the journalists nodded nervously. 'I think maybe we are being hijacked.'

'Hijacked!' Bernie boomed, 'the fuck we are.'

'There is absolutely no need for any kind of panic,' Van's voice continued, 'we have a full tank of fuel, and I would like you all to move to the back section of the plane and sit together. Please do that now. Cathy – please organize this procedure.'

She couldn't believe it was happening to her again. Two years previously she had been working a flight hijacked by three Arab guerillas. The passengers had panicked, and two of them had got shot. The plane had crash-landed in the desert, and there had followed two days of captive hell before they were rescued. The whole incident was a nightmare – the reason she had stopped working for a major airline.

'Cathy,' Van was repeating, as if he knew she would be rooted to the spot, 'please move all the passengers to the back of the plane, see they are strapped in, and sit with them yourself. If you all cooperate everything will be fine. Under *no circumstances* attempt to take matters into your own hands. I repeat – *under no circumstances*.'

Automatically Cathy sprang into action. Remember the rules. Don't panic. Appear calm and in control. Be reassuring but firm. 'Come along, everyone,' she said, 'let's make our way to the rear of the plane.'

Bernie and the two journalists were nearest the front. 'Bring your drinks with you if you want,' Cathy said. She could do with a drink herself. She took the female journalist by the arm. 'Come along now.'

Bernie said, 'Jeesus Chee-rist! What the fuck's happening?'

Cathy managed a wan smile. 'Think of the publicity, Mr Suntan.'

'Who's hijacking us, for Crissake? Al will go fuckin' nuts!'

'I think it must be the young man who came aboard in the mechanic's uniform. He seems to be the only one missing – he must be on the flight deck.'

'Well, let's rush him, for Crissakes.'

'No,' said Cathy firmly, 'if the captain says we should take no action then we must obey him.'

'The fuck we must!' Bernie turned as if to head for the front of the plane.

Quickly Cathy blocked his path. 'Mr Suntan. We are in an emergency situation. We must obey the captain. To disregard him would be foolish.'

'Aw – shit,' grumbled Bernie. But he allowed himself to be herded with the others towards the back of the plane.

Cristina sat rigidly in her seat.

Cathy shook her by the shoulder. 'Come along, miss,' she said softly. She could see the girl was in shock, 'there is nothing to worry about.'

'He forced me,' Cristina mumbled, 'he blackmailed me.'

'Yes,' agreed Cathy, 'come along now.'

Cristina allowed herself to be helped from her seat. 'Louis isn't talking to me,' she said sadly, 'Louis hates me.'

Paul was already standing in the aisle as Cathy encouraged her small group of passengers towards the back of the plane.

'What can I do?' he asked urgently. He knew about the previous experience Cathy had gone through, and considered her an expert on the subject.

She didn't feel like an expert, but she did know that they all had to do what Van said. 'Just stay calm,' she replied, 'and help everybody else to do the same.'

Evan, already seated at the back of the plane, was startled to suddenly be descended on by a whole group of people. He shut an obscene centrefold quickly, and took off the earphones attached to his portable radio – the reason why he had not heard what was going on. Quickly his uncle brought him up to date.

'Crikey!' he exclaimed, quite excited by the whole prospect. And he bundled his magazines together and dumped them under his seat.

•

'I'm going to tell you something,' Al said softly. 'All my life I've been fucking. This is what I call making love.'

'I know,' she whispered in reply.

They sprawled across the bed together, naked, exploring each other's bodies with their eyes, their hands, their fingers.

They had done no more than to stroke, to touch, to marvel. It was enough for the time being. In a way they were both nervous, neither of them wanted to rush things.

'You do have the most marvellous, beautiful, untouched body I have ever seen,' Al told her.

'Untouched?'

'Yeah. That's the way I feel about you. Do you know what I mean?'

She nodded. She knew exactly what he meant. It was the first time in her life she had felt like this. So peaceful, and warm, so soft and expectant. Climbing a mountain, slowly, lazily. Stopping to rest every so often. No rush to get to the peak.

'What about Al?' Bernie asked Paul, 'the shit'll fly when he finds out.'

'I don't think he's going to find out,' Paul replied, 'not until we land anyway. He's incommunicado. Doors locked. All speakers must be turned off. And you know his bedroom section is completely soundproofed from out here. There is no way we can reach him.'

'Thank God for small mercies,' Bernie snorted. 'But somebody's balls will get minced when we end up in some asshole communist dump. Cuba probably. How far away are we?'

Paul shrugged. 'What makes you think Cuba?'

'Isn't that where all hijacked planes go?'

'Cristina,' Paul leaned in to talk to the girl. They had sat her next to Evan. 'Do you know where this Nino character plans to take us?'

She was ashen-faced. 'I don't know,' she mumbled.

'But you were helping him, you *must* know,' Louis spat.

'I don't. I don't.' Tears started to trickle silently down her cheeks.

'Leave her alone,' said Cathy. 'Can't you see she's in shock.'

'Look – if she can help us . . .' Paul began.

He was interrupted by the crackle of the speaker.

'I am talking on behalf of my people,' Nino's voice announced, 'the oppressed, the sick, the poor. There are three bombs aboard this plane . . .'

466

'Aw – Jesus!' exclaimed Bernie, 'we're dealin' with a fuckin' commie psycho.'

'Three bombs that I can trigger off at any time. The captain has agreed to cooperate with me. I advise you for your well being to do the same. My organization – the P.A.C.P. – People Against Capitalistic Pigs – requires only money. We will land in a safe and secure place, and when the money is paid you will be released. If you behave you will not be hurt.'

The speaker shut off.

'Money,' muttered Bernie, 'we're the capitalistic pigs and *they* want the money. Assholes.'

'I have to contact flight control,' Van insisted, 'I have to get air clearance.'

'No. You will follow the course I have given you.'

'But we could be in another plane's flight path.'

'It has all been checked beforehand,' Nino intoned, 'just do as I tell you.'

'Is it an airport you want me to land at?'

'*I'll* ask the questions. You follow my instructions.'

'I have to know. I can't just land this plane anywhere. We need certain conditions – a proper runway.'

'You are a first-class pilot. I am sure you will manage.'

'We're flying blind without radio contact. You have taken us off the radar path – we're flying blind.'

'Follow the instructions I have given you.'

Van glanced in exasperation at Harry, and then turned around to his navigator and flight engineer. They both seemed quite calm. At least he had an experienced crew. But flying without radio contact, on a new flight path, in a strange country, at night, was dodgy to say the least.

'Can you let the girl go back in the cabin with the others?' Van asked. Wendy was huddled in a corner quite obviously terrified.

'She stays with me,' Nino said sharply, 'if anyone doesn't co-operate she will be the first to get a bullet.'

Cathy peered anxiously out of the window. They had been flying for quite some time, long past the time they should have landed at Sao Paulo. Since the two speaker announcements there had been silence. She wondered how Van was coping. He was a good pilot, a professional to his fingertips. He would stay calm, she knew that.

She had risked going to the galley and made everyone coffee, and she had brought a couple of bottles of brandy and some packets of biscuits back with her. It was getting cold, and she had pulled down blankets and pillows and told everyone to try and get some sleep.

Van would have been proud of her. She was very together and in control when she could so easily have lapsed into hysteria at the memory of the other time.

She thought about her long-haired musician, and wondered what he would do when he heard.

Sao Paulo must have realized the plane had left its flight path long ago. Perhaps other planes had already been sent out to search for them. After all it was Al King's plane, with the great superstar himself aboard. And Carlos Baptista's son was with them, although from what she could make out nobody knew he was aboard. Anyway – a major search would be launched immediately.

It had begun to rain – little driblets of water were trickling down the windows. She hoped she was mistaken, but she thought she heard thunder. She hated flying through storms. A stewardess friend of hers had been killed in a plane struck by lightning.

'Perhaps I should go up to the flight deck and ask if I can make them all coffee,' she suggested.

'I don't think you should,' warned Paul. 'If he has a gun he may be getting jumpy. You busting in could set him off.'

'You're right. But I bet they sure could use a cup of coffee.'

The weather conditions were worsening. What had started out as light rain had turned into a thunderstorm.

As far as Van could ascertain they were flying over the interior of Brazil – probably somewhere over the Amazon, heading in the general direction of Peru. Fortunately they had plenty of fuel, but it wouldn't last for ever.

'How soon can we expect to land?' Van asked. He was getting tired, the sleepless night had not helped.

'I told you – don't ask questions,' Nino replied.

Harry said, 'Weather conditions ahead are really bad. I suggest you tell us where and when we put this thing down.'

'Shut up,' snapped Nino. He had a blinding headache. If they read and studied the instructions he had given them they would *know* where to land. It puzzled him that they kept on asking questions – *he* didn't know. The organization had told him it was a disused airport somewhere – it was all in the instructions. When they landed other members of the organization would be waiting to take over. Nino would be flown out of there, back to Rio, where he had a new name and a new apartment waiting.

'Just follow the instructions,' he said grimly.

'Let's have the rest of them then,' snapped the navigator.

'You've got them.'

'Up to here I have, there must be another page.' He held up the paper to Nino.

'I gave you both pages.'

'Only one.'

'Both!' screamed Nino, suddenly panicky. The instructions – written out in navigational terms by a former airline pilot were on two sheets of white paper. He was sure he had handed them both over.

Van and Harry exchanged glances. They sensed a crisis.

'Look for it – you fool, perhaps you dropped it,' Nino raged.

'*You* look for it,' shouted the navigator, '*I* never bloody had it.'

'Is this some trick?' screamed Nino, and he pulled out his gun.

At that precise moment the plane hit an air pocket and plummeted several feet. It was enough to throw Nino off balance, enough to precipitate his trigger finger, and the gun went off, the bullet lodging firmly in Van Howard's right shoulder.

sixty-three

Cody was angered by Bernie Suntan's phone call. Dallas regrets she will not be able to make the studio until Monday. How on earth had Dallas known that the studio required her? For all she knew she was still out on her ear. And why had she not picked up a phone and spoken to him herself? Too cowardly no doubt. Frightened of the major blast she would get from him. And he *was* angry. His anger overshadowed the relief he felt at the fact that she was all right. She *knew* how concerned he must have been. How could she just vanish without so much as a word? He had spent a sleepless night imagining her raped or murdered or something equally horrific. Instead she had been unconcernedly shacked up with Al King. And now she was hopping off for a quick weekend in South America. Lew Margolis would love that. And *he* was the one stuck with telling him.

In fact Lew took the news surprisingly calmly. 'Oh,' was all he said. A resigned and weary 'Oh.'

'She'll be on the set bright and early Monday morning,' Cody assured him.

'Yes,' replied Lew vaguely.

Cody had expected fireworks. All he got was a damp squib. He was puzzled. Anyway – at least she was back on the series, that was the main thing. He just hoped that she wasn't going to turn up stoned on Monday morning, she had been in bad shape when she had set off for Palm Springs. He sighed. Well, of course he had known the first time he set eyes on her that it wasn't going to be an easy ride. But he had expected the traumas and temperaments when she had made it – not on the way there.

Thank God he was emotionally untangled. Getting involved in that way was suicide time. It was good it had been so brief.

Carol had worked as far as restoring his ego was concerned. But she had become too much of a good thing – and he had moved out and taken a short lease on a furnished house on Miller Drive. Nothing spectacular, but it would do to be going on with.

His business was going well. Apart from his English comedy actor signing for a major movie, he had just completed a very lucrative deal for his young stud actor to make a film in England. If things were sorted out with Dallas, and everything seemed to be going smoothly, then he saw no reason why he couldn't make a quick trip to Europe. He had never been there, it would be an experience.

His secretary came into the office. She was apologetic. 'Miss Cameron is *insisting* upon speaking to you. This is the fourth time she has called today.'

'Tell her I'm in a meeting.'

'I told her that three hours ago.'

'Tell her it's a long meeting.'

'Yes, Mr Hills. Oh, and your mother called again, said she was waiting for you to call her back.'

He made a wry face. 'I'll do that now.' Big agent or not you couldn't keep mother waiting. If he did she would nag the pants off him, and *that* he didn't need.

Linda peered at herself in the mirror. Here she was, thirty-two years old, living in California, and going out on a date, for Crissakes. She hadn't been on a date since she couldn't remember when. Her relationships had fallen into either the Paul or Rik categories. A commitment or a screw. Who went on dates any more?

She looked good. Black hair, clean and shining. Make-up not over emphasized. Figure, slim and enticing in a beige pants suit and matching shirt.

She decided she looked exactly what she was. A no-nonsense career girl who was prepared to meet anyone on equal terms. For a brief moment she wanted to kick her cool together image. Why couldn't she look wild and sensual like Dallas? Why couldn't she have a ripe luscious body that drove men to distraction?

She laughed softly at her thoughts. Might be all right for a night, but to be saddled with that kind of image? Forget it. Anyway, in her own quiet way she hadn't done too badly.

The afternoon she had spent indulging herself on a soothing shopping trip around Beverly Hills – purchasing the suit, and shirt, some boots, a slew of make-up, six new hardback books, and a new lens for one of her cameras. Pure extravagance. But she had enjoyed every minute of it. Anything to get her mind off that asshole Paul and the number he was giving her. Christ – but he must think she was an idiot. And that was the most insulting thing of all – to think that she would believe his crappy lies – with Melanie King and Manny Shorto plastered over every fucking paper in town.

She had stormed back to her apartment after her therapeutic shopping trip, still fuming. She had contemplated phoning Julio and making a quick appointment. But why waste him on a quickie? If he was as good as he was supposed to be – why rush?

So now she was hanging around waiting for her date to pick her up. She should have arranged to meet him at the restaurant – much better idea. Now she would have to offer him a drink, and make idle stilted chit-chat. *He* would probably want to talk about nothing but Dallas, and *she* would be bored stiff. She just wanted to forget about Dallas and that whole scene for a while. Images of Doris Andrews – wholesome idol of the American screen – kept on floating around her head. Doris naked. Doris kissing, biting, sucking . . .

She wondered if it was too late to phone Cody and cancel. Who needed a date? She needed a session with her parking boy or some such faceless male.

The doorbell buzzed, and ended *that* escape route.

Cody stood there washed and clean and nice looking. He had brushed his sandy hair forward, and wore a well-cut jeans suit. And he carried – Oh no! A box of ribbon-wrapped candy!

'You make me feel like I'm back in high school,' Linda grinned, accepting the box from him and dumping it on the small bar which divided the kitchen and living areas.

'This is nice,' said Cody, looking around.

'It's cheap, and I don't know how long I plan to make it home.'

'Why didn't you stay on with Dallas then?'

One minute and she was already a part of the conversation. 'I like my privacy. Can I fix you a drink?'

'Vodka would be fine – on the rocks.'

He prowled round the room. Perfect set-up for a bachelor girl who planned to move on. Nothing cutesy. Nothing personal. 'You got a place in New York?'

'A sleazy apartment which I love.' Why was she lying to him? She hated it. Paul hated it. It was a dump. It was in a lousy neighbourhood – but it had been home for quite a few years.

'Anyone living there while you're away?'

'Why? You want to borrow it?'

'No – I just er wondered.'

'Like you want to know if I live with a man – right?'

He looked embarrassed. 'No . . . I . . .'

'I have had an on/off relationship with Paul King – Al's brother, manager, general wet nurse and pimp – for one and a half *very* long years. At the moment – for reasons I wouldn't dream of boring you with – it's very definitely off. Apart from him, my other attachments are only momentary. How about you?'

'I told you about myself and Dallas . . .'

She handed him a vodka, swirling the ice cubes with her fingers. 'Yes. You told me.' Please don't tell me again, Cody. If you do I'll scream! She was not in the mood to listen to stories about other women.

'Since then I've spent a little time with Carol Cameron.'

'Carol *who*?'

'Cameron. She's an actress.'

'In this town they all seem to be actresses,' Linda remarked drily. 'In New York they are models. In Hollywood – actresses. I think those two phrases encompass a huge spectrum of professions!'

Cody laughed. 'You're a bright lady.'

'Am I supposed to curtsey and say thank you, kind sir?'

'I meant it as a compliment.'

'Why? What's complimentary about calling someone bright? How would you like it if I gave you a look of amazement and said – hey – you're really quite intelligent.'

472

He gulped his vodka. 'Point taken.'

'I'm not in a very good mood,' she confided, 'in fact I'm pissed off at the world. Maybe we should just forget about tonight.'

'I'm not in a very good mood either. What do you say to going out and getting good and plastered?'

'Man to man?'

'Whichever way you want it.'

'I'm on.'

They had a good time. They started off with a bottle of wine over dinner, then Irish coffees, then lethal tequilas at a jazz bar Cody knew, and finally Brandy Alexanders at a high-class strip joint.

'I'm having a *marvellous* time,' Linda revelled, 'hey – Cody. Don't they have any *guys* in this place?'

'What do you want – a sex show?'

She patted him on the shoulder, her voice attempting to register an even keel. 'No, buddy. No sex show. I mean jus' guys. I mean we got tits every way you look – tits over there – an' there – an' there.' She pointed out two topless cocktail waitresses, and a stripper, then unexpectedly she stood on her chair, rocking dangerously. 'How about a few dicks?' she yelled. 'How about it, fellas? Show us what you got!'

'Get down,' laughed Cody, 'you'll get us thrown out of here.'

'Equality!' Linda yelled. 'I want to see some great big joints!'

A few females sitting round about joined noisily in. 'Yeah!' 'Get 'em off fellas!' 'Let's see the great white wonder!'

The cocktail waitresses looked at each other and sniggered. The waiters, all three of them, backed warily towards the bar.

With a drunken leap Linda left the chair. 'Ladies united. Let's debag 'em.'

'Jesus . . . Linda . . . stop . . .'

Cody was choking with laughter.

Linda advanced on a waiter reaching for his fly. He socked her straight on the jaw. Because she was so drunk she fell with a delicate easy grace.

She woke up five minutes later in Cody's car.

'We got thrown out,' he solemnly informed her, 'but I screwed 'em. I refused to pay the cheque!'

'I'll sue that sonofabitch for assault,' she wailed. 'My jaw feels like a side of beef!'

'I'll take you home and put an ice pack on it.'

'*Your* home – not mine.'

'I thought this was a man to man evening?'

'I'm a bright girl – I can change my mind, can't I?'

Evita watched the Al King concert at the Maracana Stadium. She even enjoyed it in a detached sort of way. And after, at a small dinner for twenty-five people that Carlos Baptista had arranged, she danced and chatted, and admired the exotic cabaret of eight voluptuous samba dancers.

But all the while her thoughts were elsewhere. He thoughts were concentrated on the following morning when Doris Andrews was due to arrive.

How should she treat her? Should she be cool, warm, enthusiastic, distant?

Should she *say* anything? Or just try to pretend their sexual dalliance had never occurred?

Jorge was enthusiastic about the party he had insisted she should plan. It was to be on Sunday and everything was arranged. She had even purchased a new dress for the occasion, and requested Jorge to collect her emerald and diamond jewellery from the safety deposit box at the bank.

In one way she was dreading Doris' arrival. But in another way it had excited her to fever pitch.

She was dancing with Carlos. The portly, rotund man reeked of cigar fumes.

'A magnificent evening – heh – heh? What did you think of my American star – heh – heh?'

'I thought he was English.'

'He is, he is. But you know what I mean. He is an *international* great. They loved him, didn't they? Did you hear them scream?'

'My ears are still ringing.'

He gave her an intimate squeeze and wistfully sighed. 'If only Jorge and I weren't such friends . . .'

'Yes?' she teased, 'and what would you do, Carlos?'

'I would . . . *Merda!*' He was being summoned to the phone.

Evita drifted quietly back to the table where Jorge was involved in an animated discussion of politics.

She watched him, her handsome distinguished husband, and wondered why he wasn't enough. Wondered why the need had been there for Doris Andrews to find and take advantage of.

'Where do *you* think the children could have got to?' Carlos' wife, Chara, was asking – interrupting Evita's thoughts.

'I really don't know,' Evita replied politely. She didn't really like the fat, gossipy Chara.

'So impolite,' Chara complained. 'Carlos is furious. Louis will be in trouble when *he* gets home. Wasting expensive tickets – two empty seats for everyone to see. I can assure you *Louis* will be in trouble.' She waited for Evita to assure her that Cristina would also be in trouble, but Evita just smiled, nodded, and looked around for someone to rescue her.

'The young people today have no manners,' Chara continued, 'no discipline. Why – when I was a girl I wasn't allowed out of the house without a proper chaperone,' she waved fat bejewelled fingers in the air. 'Today all they have is freedom – freedom – and no respect.'

Idly Evita wondered why both Chara and Carlos used words in double sequence.

'Of course I blame the parents.' Chara continued, getting in a dig at Evita. '*We* have always been very strict with Louis – very strict.' She stuffed a candied grape into her mouth. 'He is a good boy—' she sighed regretfully, 'but easily influenced by others . . . Tell me, why does Cristina wear such funny clothes?'

Evita smiled sweetly. 'It's her style. Personally I think at seventeen it doesn't matter what you wear. As long as you are young and pretty . . . Chara, do please excuse me, but I've been meaning to ask you – does obesity run in your family?'

Linda woke up with a bearable hangover. It was a long time since she had been so drunk – in fact hadn't the last time been over some sort of job crisis?

She reached over and touched Cody who was still sleeping. She had broken one of her golden rules – stayed overnight. But who had been able to summon the strength to drive home? Anyway – come to think of it – who had wanted to?

Cody Hills as a lover had been a delightful unexpected surprise. They had started the evening as mates and ended up as lovers – and she didn't have one single regret. In fact the whole situation reminded her of the first time with Paul. But of course Cody had none of the complications. He wasn't married. He didn't have children. He lived in America. He didn't work for his brother – indeed he didn't even *have* a brother. What a plus *that* was.

She laughed softly to herself, and climbed out of bed.

Cody started to wake, stretched out his arms to her.

She blew him a kiss. 'Coffee for two,' she said, 'black, extremely strong and I'll bring it to bed so stay right where you are.' She turned at the door. 'Oh, and do you take sugar?'

'Three spoons. What's your name?'

She treated him to a rude gesture. 'Get lost!' and exited.

Cody bounded from the bed. He felt marvellous. He went into the bathroom, scrubbed his teeth, took a piss, and climbed expectantly back into bed.

Linda was the best thing that had ever happened to him. She was *very* attractive, witty, intelligent, warm, funny. She was *everything* he had ever wanted in a woman. And in bed she did not make him feel inadequate – she made him feel like a giant! She wasn't Dallas – lying limply there suffering his advances. She wasn't Carol Cameron waxing false enthusiasms over his every move and exclaiming like a hooker at a convention. 'Ohhh Marvie!!!' 'You can't go near me that that huge thing!!!' 'You're soooo fan-tas-tic – *really* you are!'

He couldn't wipe the wide smile off his face. To find a woman like Linda so soon after the débâcle with Dallas. It was wonderful. *She* was wonderful. Of course he still loved Dallas – but it was a protective love – a brotherly love – an *agent's* love.

Linda walked back into the room carrying a tray with two steaming cups of coffee, and the papers which she had picked up from outside the front door. How many girls would think of doing *that*?

'Can you cook?' he asked.

'No – but I open a mean can!'

'In that case what do you say about moving in?'

'I say let's give it some time. OK?'

'If I can have an option on your evenings.'

'I'll talk it over with my agent.'

Carlos Baptista didn't want to break up the party. He puffed on a giant Havana cigar and wondered what to do.

His wife was talking to Evita. The rest of his guests seemed to be enjoying themselves. What to do? Tell them? Tell them what? That he had just had a report that Al King's plane had failed to turn up in Sao Paulo. That all radio contact had been terminated shortly after the plane left Rio.

What had happened? No one seemed to know. The weather between Sao Paulo and Rio was good. It was a bright, clear night. The whole thing was a mystery.

Carlos was an optimist. He had every confidence that the plane would turn up, after all it couldn't just vanish.

He decided anyway to keep the news to himself. No point in breaking up a good party.

He caught the eye of his latest mistress, a lovely zoftic girl married to one of his minions. He winked at her. With a slight incline of her head she indicated the dance floor. He noted Chara still busily chatting away, and he nodded at his girlfriend.

Life was too short to worry – Al King had obviously for some obscure reason instructed his pilot to go elsewhere – these stars were very temperamental. As soon as he turned up at another airport Carlos would be notified. Frankly he didn't care *merda* what Al King did. As long as he turned up on time for the concert in Sao Paulo the rest of the time was his own.

Carlos beamed, and swept down on his girlfriend. 'Senora Jobin, my turn to dance with you I think.'

Linda spent the day in a daze. She was knocked for six. It was all so unexpected. One second she had been contemplating murdering Paul – the next he was out of her mind, a past memory, and she knew for a fact that she *didn't love him any more.* Just like that she was freed, and the relief was incredible!

Not that it was instant love with Cody. No – he was nice, she liked him a lot, but it was a relationship that would have to be gradually built up. She was quite prepared to give it a try and see what happened. If it worked out – great.

She got through the day, drove over to Cody's house, and they barbecued steaks and talked and talked and talked. It was good. It was meaningful.

When they fell into bed at 4 a.m. it was even better than the night before.

'Where'd you *learn* all this stuff?' Linda murmured appreciatively.

'Tonight. Now,' Cody replied.

'He knows all the right things to say too!'

'He's a bright boy!'

The word bright had become their own private joke.

When they finally slept Linda kept on waking up.

'Wassamatter?' Cody asked sleepily.

'I don't know. I feel kind of strange. I have the weirdest feeling. I keep on thinking of Dallas and Al . . . As soon as I drift into sleep I see them both clearly. It's like they are in some kind of trouble . . .'

'Do me a favour – go to sleep. You know what an analyst would say, don't you? He'd say you were really thinking of Paul.'

'Thank you very much.'

'Goodnight, Linda.'

'Goodnight, analyst.'

sixty-four

The sudden plummeting of the large jet frightened everyone. But no one was hurt as they were all strapped firmly into their seats. The only damage was some spilled drinks, and verbal hysteria from the lady journalist, 'Ohmigod! Ohmigod! We're going to crash! We're going to crash! Ohmigooooood!!' The last word developed into a panic-stricken wail.

'It's nothing to get excited about,' Cathy said as calmly as she could, 'we just hit an unexpected air pocket, nothing unusual.'

The plane was jumping around all over the place, and Cathy wondered what the hell was happening up front. For the first time she felt frightened.

'Stay calm, everyone,' she said in her most reassuring tone, 'we seem to be going through a rather turbulent patch.'

'Where the fuck are we?' demanded Bernie.

'I don't know,' Cathy replied, furious with Van for leaving her stranded back here with a bunch of soon-to-be-hysterical passengers. He must know they would be getting anxious, the least he could do was make some sort of announcement – anything. But maybe he wasn't allowed to.

The lady journalist was still wailing and screaming, whilst everyone else sat silent and white-faced as the plane lurched around the sky.

'Chree-ist,' exclaimed Bernie in disgust, 'this whole friggin' plane's gonna bust apart if this keeps up. His comment induced further hysteria from the lady journalist. 'Will you shut up, you douche bag!' Bernie shouted. 'Keep your fuckin' screams to yourself.'

She was shocked into silence.

'This plane is built to withhold any kind of turbulence,' Cathy assured them. 'No chance of it breaking up, Mr Suntan.'

'Bullshit,' he muttered.

Dallas and Al were being thrown around the bed giggling and laughing.

'Do you believe it?' Al asked. 'Do you believe we've waited all this time and just when we are about to finally do it we run into a storm!'

'It's a sign from above,' Dallas said jokingly.

'I'll give *him* a sign. Come on – haul yourself over to the couch and strap yourself in.'

Staggering and bumping around they managed to get into bathrobes and strap themselves into the couch.

'It's not dangerous, is it?' Dallas asked.

Al laughed. 'I've been through turbulence that makes this look sick.' He held her hand. 'Nothing to worry about – got the best pilot money can buy – anyway we'll probably be landing soon, and you know the first thing we're going to do?

'No, what?'

'I'll give you one guess.'

As the bullet entered his right shoulder Van Howard lost consciousness. He slumped over the controls, and for seconds everyone on the flight deck was immobilized. Then, as the big plane lurched and bucked, Harry Booker sprang into action. He hauled Van out of the cockpit as best he could, and took over flying the plane himself.

By this time Nino was on his feet and screaming a string of expletives. Wendy was sobbing hysterically, and the navigator had ripped off his jacket and placed it under Van's head. It was now extremely crowded on the flight deck, and the storm and general turbulence were rolling the plane in all directions.

'I'm going back,' Harry Booker yelled, 'I'm turning round.'

'No, you are not!' Nino shouted in excited frustration.

'There's no other way, you've lost the rest of the flight plan. If we don't know where we're going eventually we'll run out of fuel.'

'I have not lost anything!' Nino screamed. 'He is hiding it – it's him.' And he turned his gun on the navigator.

'I think one of us should go to the front of the plane and see what's happening,' Paul said, more worried than he cared to admit.

'I'll go,' volunteered Louis.

'No, I'll go,' said Cathy. 'I'm less likely to alarm them.'

'We need you here,' Paul replied. 'I can go.'

'Please . . .' Cristina spoke for the first time. 'Please let me go. After all it is partly my fault we are all here.'

'Partly!' snorted Louis.

'Nino knows me. He will tell me what is happening. Please let me go.'

'Let her go,' growled Bernie. 'If she knows the guy maybe she can talk some sense to the prick.'

Paul had to agree that Bernie was right.

'Be careful then,' he warned, 'don't upset him. Just try and find out how long it will be before we land, and where.'

'I'll do my best,' Cristina replied, unstrapping her seat belt and setting off down the rolling plane.

'We have no alternative,' Harry Booker said stubbornly. 'I'll try and make radio contact.'

'No!' screamed Nino, his gun wavering back and forth between the navigator and Harry.

'What do you suggest then?' said Harry, his temper beginning to snap. 'We're flying out here in the middle of nowhere, we don't know where we're supposed to be going. We're flying blind, the weather conditions stink, and apart from all those plus's – that man is probably dying.' He indicated Van lying on the floor, Wendy crouched over him attempting to stem the flow of blood from his wound. 'What's the penalty for murder in your country?' Harry sneered. 'Come on, let me turn back. We might just be lucky enough to make it. When we land you can keep me, the plane, whatever you want – as hostage.'

'I don't want you,' Nino said with contempt. 'I want a million dollars for Al King.'

'They'll give it to you,' Harry said persuasively, 'they'll give it to you for saving him.'

'Do you think I'm a fool?' spat Nino. 'Do you think you are dealing with a boy?'

As they argued Harry was putting the plane into a very slow unobtrusive turn. He didn't know where he was, but surely it would be better to head back from where they had come.

'I think you should listen to me,' Harry said. 'I think right now you're in a big mess, and I want to help you get out of it.'

Nino brought his free hand up to his head, and pressed his throbbing temple. He was confused. He didn't know what to do. He had the plane. He had Al King. Single-handed he had achieved that with only the help of a gun and three crude home-made bombs that were not even detonated.

Now they wanted him to go back. They said they didn't have the second page of the instructions. But they must be bluffing. They *had* to be bluffing.

He had given them *two* pages of instructions – or had he?

Yes. He was sure of it – or was he?

The constant buffeting of the plane didn't help him think clearly. The rain smashing into the windscreen. The roar of the thunder. The angry flashes of lightning.

*

'What is going on?' Al said suddenly, after a particularly sharp burst of turbulence. 'I hired a guy like Van Howard so I wouldn't have to go through this shit. If there's a storm he knows enough to avoid it. This is like a goddamn roller coaster – the fucker must be drunk.'

Dallas placed her hand on his knee. 'Don't get excited.'

He forgot the vibrating plane for a second. 'With you beside me . . .'

She leaned in to kiss him. Their lips met and were jolted apart.

'Fuck this!' said Al. He undid his seat belt and lurched over to the bed. He pressed a switch marked 'flight deck' and picked up the intercom. 'Howard!' he yelled. 'Howard!' He jiggled the switch – 'Great. Can't even answer the phone. Howard! What the fuck's happening?'

Paul glanced around at everyone. They were mostly silent, huddled in their own private thoughts. Bernie was the only one who seemed to have developed verbal diarrhoea, muttering vague obscenities and curses of prophetic doom.

'Shut up, Bernie,' Paul snapped, 'keep your thoughts to yourself.' He wished that Al would emerge from his private retreat. Christ! He couldn't be sleeping or even screwing through this. And surely he must realize they had been in the air hours too long.

But of course he never bothered checking schedules. He had no idea how long the trip to Sao Paulo was. And he had Dallas to distract him. The beautiful Dallas, who like all the others had fallen into the appropriate position – bed.

Paul scowled. He knew what would happen. When they landed at whatever Godforsaken place they were heading for, Al would emerge. 'Where are we?' he would demand. And wherever they were, he, Paul, would get full blame.

He knew it. Everything was always his fault – so why should this occasion be different from any others?

On the flight deck everything happened at once. As Al's voice boomed from the internal intercom demanding to know what was happening, Cristina pushed through behind Nino, startling him even further. Instinctively he pressed the trigger of his gun, and a bullet ricocheted round the cabin, grazing the side of Harry Booker's head. Blood started to drip from a superficial wound.

'Nino!' Cristina screamed, flinging her arms about him in an attempt to wrestle the gun from him, 'stop it! Give up . . . Give up – you can't win. You must give up.'

481

Nino tried to throw her off, tried to club her with the butt of the gun.

The navigator, seeing this as a good opportunity to disarm the madman, left his position and joined in.

Blood was dripping across Harry's eyes. He felt like he had been zonked on the side of the head with a hammer. He raised his arm to clear the blood with his sleeve. He never saw the lightning explode in a huge flash of white hot burning light straight in front of the plane.

He never saw it hit the right wing of the plane, which immediately burst into flames.

He only knew that the plane was out of control, plummeting crazily.

'Brace yourselves,' Cathy yelled as the plane rocked violently, 'bend your heads forward – clasp your ankles.'

'We're going to crash – we're going to crash,' shrieked the lady journalist hysterically.

Jesus God! For the first time Paul felt fear. A cold fear that gripped him around the stomach. A fear that said – 'This is it – this is the final curtain.' He thought of his children, their faces flashing before him. He thought of Linda – how disappointed she would be. Then ironically he thought of Al screwing happily away in his private soundproofed bedroom. How fitting that he should go on the job.

'Holy shit!' exclaimed Bernie, 'the fuckin' plane's on fire!'

Vainly Cathy pleaded, 'Please stay calm. Everything will be all right. We have a very experienced pilot.'

Silent Luke suddenly burst into loud prayer, his resonant voice somehow comforting.

'Cristina! Cristina!' Louis screamed, struggling with his seat belt, 'I must get to Cristina!'

'Please stay seated,' begged Cathy. But she couldn't prevent him from staggering off down the lurching sinking plane.

Cathy tried to peer out of the window, but there was only darkness and rain, and bright yellowy orange flames shooting over the wing. If Van could get them out of this . . . Oh God – if Van could save them she wouldn't leave him. She would stay with him. She would be a faithful wife. She would give up her long-haired musician. Oh God – please let Van save them.

Evan was throwing up. Vomiting in uncontrollable bursts all over himself. He had wet his pants also. But he didn't care. Didn't care at all. He wanted his mother. She would take care of him.

She would know what to do. Tears rolled down his cheeks. He wanted mummy.

Al was thrown violently across the padded bedroom.

He could feel the plane dropping, being buffeted around by the wind. He knew that something was terribly, dreadfully wrong.

He hauled himself across the floor and managed to belt himself in next to Dallas.

Her eyes were huge with fear. 'What's happening?'

'I wish I knew.' He wanted to go through to the passenger compartment, but the plane was plunging so crazily he didn't dare move. He was lucky to have made it back to his seat.

Somebody's head would roll for this. When they made firm ground, somebody was going to pay for putting them through a trip like this.

It did not occur to him for one moment that they might not make firm ground. The possibility of a crash was unthinkable.

He took Dallas' hand, and she clung on to him tightly.

'Don't worry,' he said, soothingly, 'we'll soon be landing.'

The plane hurtled blindly down.

Harry Booker wrestled helplessly with the controls but there was nothing he could do. He was trying to stabilize the plane, get it under some sort of control.

He knew he would have to put it down, blindly, wherever they were. But if only he could get hold of the bastard . . . He pulled back on the wheel with all the strength he could muster, and forced the thrust levers into full power. 'Come on, you mother . . . Come on . . .' Painfully, slowly, the nose of the plane started to climb. But it was much too slow, and the fire on the wing had unbalanced them, and there was a short in the circuit showing . . .

The plane started to bank, and Harry knew it was hopeless, knew there was nothing he could do.

They were enveloped in a sea of blackness in the middle of nowhere. Behind him Nino, Cristina, and the navigator were in a fighting, clawing mass on the floor. Van was unconscious. Wendy hysterical. And the young flight engineer transfixed in a state of shock.

Vainly Harry tried to throttle back, attempted to bring down the landing gear. They were dropping so fast. Sinking like a stone.

Blankly he wondered where they were. It didn't matter, in a few moments they would all be dead.

•

'Brace yourselves against the seat in front,' Cathy yelled vainly, 'head on your knees – clasp your ankles. *Don't panic!*'

Nobody was listening – they were all too busy throwing up, or screaming hysterically, or praying, or cursing.

Cathy kept repeating her instructions, whilst her stomach jumped into her mouth with fear.

They were going to crash. They were out of control. They were on fire.

She tried to remember crash procedure. Everyone off the plane as fast as possible. Emergency shutes down. How soon would rescue services reach them? It depended where they were, and she didn't know that.

Oh God! Why had she ever left Van? This was a punishment. This was God's way of telling her she was wrong. If only he would give her another chance . . . If only . . .

With a deafening crash the plane ploughed into something. The impact created even more chaos. Hand luggage came hurtling down from all the racks, seats were wrenched free from their moorings, windows smashed in. All the lights went out, plunging them into a murky blackness.

But the plane didn't stop. Caught up in the trees it hurtled onwards – shuddering and shaking – pitching and rolling.

And the noise. Deafening, unreal. A tearing metal noise, an exploding jagged noise, a roaring vibrating noise.

The plane was ripping through the gigantic trees, disintegrating in parts as it progressed.

First the right wing snapped off on impact – then the left wing was wrenched free.

The body of the plane careered onwards, smashing a path through the trees, and finally splitting neatly in half.

The back of the plane shuddered to a stop. The front half slid on further into the jungle, then it too finally stopped.

Miraculously both sections of the plane were still in one piece.

For a moment there was silence except for the sound of the driving rain and startled bird cries. Then a series of small explosions came from the front of the plane, and the engines burst into flames.

Next came the human sounds. Cries for help, groans, terrified screaming.

It was amazing that anyone was still alive.

The plane had come to rest somewhere in the Amazon jungle, hundreds of miles from anywhere.

After smashing through the giant trees it had slithered to a stop amidst the dense forest ground.

The storm was abating somewhat. But the rain still poured relentlessly down.

From the sky the plane could not be sighted, the huge trees, some as tall as two hundred feet, took care of that.

Al King, his plane and occupants, had vanished into the bowels of the jungle without a trace.

sixty-five

There was always a moment when Linda first woke when she wasn't sure where she was. It had happened to her since the tour, and she found it quite an enjoyable sensation.

Where am I? What city? What bed?

It was quite exciting waiting for the answers to come flooding in.

Home – schmuck. Or – with Robert Redford of course. Or – that beautiful beach bum who is quite the best lay in town.

Los Angeles. Cody. His house.

She was quite satisfied. She rolled across the bed and nuzzled his back. He wore pyjamas – very sweet. She slept nude – was there any other way?

She put her arms around his soft waistline. He was very cuddly. A strict diet could get rid of his excess flab in two weeks.

She moved her hands inside his pyjama trousers, gently holding his flaccid penis.

'Are you awake?' she whispered.

He groaned in his sleep.

She played with him. Rubbing, kneading, teasing.

He grew hard in her hands.

She slid down under the sheet and took him in her mouth. He felt so good. She used her tongue in a variety of ingenious ways.

He groaned again, this time with sleepy pleasure.

She took him deep into her mouth. Released him slowly. Took him again.

He came in lovely throbbing spurts, his liquid filling her mouth with joy.

She slid up from under the sheets.

He opened his eyes in delighted surprise.

'My morning protein,' she grinned. 'How are you this morning?'

'You're a very sexy person.' He reached for her small taut breasts. 'Very sexy indeed.'

'Oh. You think so?'

'I definitely think so. And in about half an hour I'll prove it to you.'

'*Half an hour?*'

'I'm not nineteen, you know.'

She snapped her fingers together, 'Aw – shit. And I thought you were.'

They both giggled.

'What shall we do today?' Cody asked.

'Hmmm . . . Saturday . . . Let me see . . . How about nothing? Does that grab you?'

'It really does.'

She climbed out of bed. 'I'll make the coffee. It's actually your turn – but I'll let you off today.'

She padded in the kitchen.

Saturday – when had Paul said he would be back? Four days. He had called her on Thursday, so Sunday, tomorrow . . .

She didn't even want to talk to him, it was as simple as that. Maybe if she stayed over at Cody's she wouldn't have to. Not a bad idea.

She poured hot water onto the instant coffee, contemplated squeezing orange juice, but felt too lazy. Then she remembered the papers and opened up the front door, scooping them off the mat.

'AL KING VANISHED PLANE MYSTERY' the headline screamed.

Jorge shook his wife awake.

'Where is Cristina?' he demanded.

She struggled awake. 'I don't know . . . In bed, it's early isn't it?'

'She hasn't been home all night,' his voice rose dangerously. 'Marie came running to me hysterically – "Miss Cristina's bed hasn't been slept in, has she had an accident, Senor?" I went to her room, it's true, she hasn't been home.'

Evita sat up, reaching for a swansdown bedjacket. 'Have you telephoned Carlos? Is Louis home?'

'I haven't done anything. I came straight to wake you.'

Evita picked up the bedside telephone, dialled quickly.

'Oh – good morning, Chara. So sorry to wake you this early – oh you were,' she made a gesture of impatience as Chara engaged her in conversation. 'My God, that's dreadful. Look, I know you are busy, but I must speak to Louis. Yes, I'll hang on while you fetch him.' She covered the mouthpiece and addressed herself to Jorge. 'The plane flying Al King to Sao Paulo is missing.'

'Is Louis there?' exploded Jorge, not at all interested in any other subject.

'I think so. Just a minute.' She uncovered the mouthpiece. 'Yes, Chara. Oh, I see. Are you sure? Well, do you have any idea where she might be?'

Jorge snatched the phone from her. 'Chara? I'll break his neck. He has Cristina with him.' Jorge paused to listen. 'I don't particularly *care* about Carlos' other problems. *I want my daughter back.* I *know* they are engaged, that makes no difference to me. If your son has *touched* her . . .'

He slammed the phone down.

'Chara will tell the whole of Rio,' Evita stated. 'I wish you hadn't told her.'

'What bothers you? The fact that your daughter is somewhere with the Baptista boy? Or that fat *Cona* gossiping?'

'*Both* things bother me. Does she know where they are?'

'No, she doesn't. They'll have to marry at once you know – *at once*.'

'But everyone will think she is pregnant.'

'By this time she might be,' Jorge growled. 'I never did trust that boy.'

'I thought you trusted Cristina. *You* are the one who allowed her so much freedom. *You* are the one who kept on assuring me she was such a good girl.'

'She is, she is. I don't blame her – I blame the Baptista boy. She warned me about him, warned me he had made advances towards her.'

'I'm sure Cristina can look after herself.'

Jorge stared at his wife intently. 'You can be a very hard woman, Evita – very hard.'

'Not hard, Jorge, just realistic. I told you a while ago that Cristina was a woman. She is no baby innocent being taken advantage of.'

'How can you say such things about your own daughter?'

'Making love is not a crime.'

'For children it is.'

'They are not children.'

'You can be an impossible person,' Jorge spat. 'Sometimes you are a stranger to me. I will be in my study – fetch me the moment Cristina returns – the instant.'

He marched from the room.

Edna could hear the doorbell ringing, even though she was right down the end of the garden – an outside extension took care of that. She must remind herself to have it disconnected.

It chimed continually, and she ignored it. She was busy picking tomatoes. Home-grown, red, hard tomatoes. How beautiful they were. How satisfying it was to watch something grow.

She filled a wicker basket and decided to take some with her to the pottery class that evening. She would distribute them amongst her friends there – the first friends she had ever possessed. Oh – being married to Al King had produced many acquaintances, but never one true friend. They had always been nice to her because of Al. Ingratiated themselves in the hope that it would do them some good. It never did, and they dropped away as soon as they realized this.

Now she had friends. Nice people who had no idea who she was – she had joined the pottery class under her maiden name and so far her secret was safe. Yes – they would enjoy the tomatoes – Carol and Mavis, Roger and John – especially John. She blushed at the thought of his name. She mustn't keep on thinking of him. It was too early for that sort of thing. He was a nice person, a gentle man.

She headed back towards the house. The house, she had decided, must be sold. She didn't want it. It was far too big and fancy. All she wanted was a small cottage with a little garden. A private place where she could live in peace. A place where she could invite her friends without feeling embarrassed.

Humming softly to herself, deep in thought, she didn't notice the two photographers come bounding round the side of the house. She didn't notice them until their cameras flashed, and then she shouted in anger. 'What are you *doing*? How dare you. This is private property. Go away or I'll call the police!'

'Just one more shot,' pleaded one of the photographers, 'we've been waiting for hours.'

'GO AWAY!'

'How about a quote then?'

She marched towards them, shielding her face, outraged at this invasion on her privacy. 'I'm phoning the police!' she warned. But then she realized it was an idle threat. She had had the telephone cut off, she had not required its services any more. At the same time she had cancelled all the newspapers, and disconnected the four television sets.

A couple of reporters had joined the photographers. They were *trespassers*. Edna ran towards the house.

'Do you think Al is dead?' one of them called. 'Who was the girl he was with? Did you know her? Is your son with them?'

Edna stopped short in her tracks. 'What are you talking about? What are you saying?'

The reporter who had yelled the questions ventured nearer. He sensed a story. 'Didn't you hear yet, Mrs King? Al's plane has disappeared somewhere in South America – he's missing – presumed dead.'

Carlos Baptista had enough problems. He certainly did not need Chara yelling at him about Louis.

He took no notice of her complaints. It was perfectly normal for a young man to stay out all night. And if he had a pretty girlfriend – well, so much the better. He should have made up some sort of excuse though. They both should. Silly children. Now he would have Jorge Maraco breathing down his neck insisting on an early marriage.

But he couldn't worry about that now. He had other problems. Major problems. A disaster in fact. And it seemed no one could help him.

Fact. Al King's jet had left Rio with the famous man aboard.

Fact. Shortly after take-off it had terminated radio contact and apparently vanished off the face of the earth.

But how could a large jet just vanish? It was impossible. It had to turn up somewhere. This wasn't the Bermuda triangle.

Spotter planes had been sent out to see if it had force landed or crashed anywhere. They had no idea where to start looking. The flight path between Rio and Sao Paulo was clear. So where to begin the search?

The big plane had carried enough fuel to travel a long way. Who knew which direction it had taken?

Airline officials were doing everything in their power to track it down. But they had nothing to go on. Investigations were only just beginning.

Who exactly was on the plane?

Nobody seemed to know.

Airport staff on duty the previous evening were being rounded up. What had they seen? Anything suspicious? Anything unusual?

An assistant of Carlos' came rushing into the temporary office set up for him at the airport.

'The boarding officer has been located,' he huffed, somewhat out of breath, 'he has a passenger boarding list.'

'Yes?'

'It seems, Senor Baptista, that your son was aboard with Miss Maraco.'

'Whaaat? That is impossible.'

'Not impossible, Senor. Unfortunately confirmed. They boarded the plane at the last minute saying that you had sent them.'

'I don't believe it!' raged Carlos. 'Impostors.' But then he remembered Chara's phone call. Remembered the fact that Louis had not returned home. Remembered that Cristina Maraco was also missing.

Carlos buried his head in his hands.

'Oh dear God!' he mumbled, 'Oh Christ above. *Filho da puta*. What can I do? What can I do?'

sixty-six

As the plane hurtled to its death Harry Booker lapsed into unconsciousness. On the initial impact the trees smashed through the cockpit pulping Harry to pieces. He died fairly quickly.

The flight engineer was not so lucky, half his face was gouged away, he was trapped in his seat, and death did not come until the plane finally stopped and he was slowly burnt to death.

Wendy also died in the fire. Wounded and trapped beneath Van's body, she could not move. She died screaming for help.

Van, unconscious, died with her.

Nino, Cristina, and the navigator were all hurled from the plane when it split in two. The fact that they were not strapped into seats probably saved them from being burnt to death.

Nino broke both legs, and suffered a lethal-looking gash to the head. Unable to move he lay groaning on the wet ground.

Cristina was miraculously unhurt. She was thrown out of the plane like a rag doll, and a bump on the head rendered her unconscious.

The navigator landed in a tree, and hung there limply. His neck was broken. Nobody found him, and he died after an agonizing three hours.

Louis Baptista was also unlucky – caught midway down the plane as it broke in half – he was crushed to death. His last scream of '*Cristina!*' went unheard.

At the rear of the plane things were only slightly better.

The two journalists, destined never to write their story, were hurled the length of the plane strapped side by side into adjoining seats, which had cut loose on impact. They were hurled straight into nothingness, and were dead by the time they hit the ground.

Bernie Suntan had been saved by his bulk. A deadly strip of jagged-edged fuselage had bayoneted him in the chest. If he had been a thinner man it would have reached his heart, but it was embedded in fatty tissue, and although blood poured from the wound, it did not seem to be lethal.

Paul was trapped by his legs under a concertina of seats. He was extremely white and had lost consciousness.

Cathy was covered in blood. She too was trapped next to Paul, but her face had impacted with something, and blood streamed from a broken nose, and a gaping cut on her mouth.

Evan was still strapped into his seat at a crazy angle. He had been bruised and shaken, and his arm was somehow crushed beneath him. But he was alive.

Luke, however, was dead, his massive body slumped on the floor – one of his legs nearly severed by a long shard of glass. Blood pumped from the wound forming a huge puddle. He had been smashed on the head and his skull was crushed.

The door to Al's bedroom remained closed. Twisted and crushed where the roof of the plane had given way, it would not have opened even if Al had unlocked it. It was firmly jammed.

The couch where Al and Dallas had been strapped in had been yanked from the wall. Together they had been buffeted crazily around the padded room.

The soft walls had saved them from any serious injury, and although they were covered in bruises they had both survived. The worst injury Al had was a cut on his leg. Dallas thought she might have broken a couple of ribs – the pain was intense. But the relief of being alive was unbelievable. When the plane had started its uncontrollable, dizzying, roller-coaster drop, she had known she was going to die. *Known it.* And she hadn't screamed or cried out, but just clung tightly to Al's hand, and wished that they could have had more time together, wished that she could have trusted him sooner. Now it was all over, and at least she was going to die with him. He had made her happy in the short time they had been together, and she was thankful for that.

'I love you,' she had whispered as the plane fell, 'love you – love you – love you.' And she had meant it.

At that moment in time Al had been trying to keep up with his thoughts. Goddamn it. His plane was crashing. *His* plane. He had paid for the best – paid a fucking fortune. *How dare they do this to him? How dare they?*

Where was Paul? Luke, Bernie? Why weren't they *doing* something. That's what he paid them for, wasn't it?

Christ! Who would believe it?

He could feel Dallas' nails digging into his hand. 'Don't worry, don't worry, everything's fine,' he managed to mumble.

Seconds later they hit the trees, and the goddamn couch came hurtling away from the wall, and he thought, Sweet Jesus don't let me die like this. I don't *want* to die. I've got too many things left to do.

And they were all over the place, bumping around, smashing from one side of the cabin to the other. And he could hear himself repeating, 'Don't worry – don't worry.' And he thought how inane that must sound, how stupid, because even *he* realized that death must be only moments away. And he thought, what about Evan? And he thought of the first girl he had ever screwed. And he remembered Edna on their wedding day. And he flashed onto a memory of his first stage appearance.

And all the time he was aware of Dallas close beside him. And he wondered why it had taken him thirty-eight years to find her. And he wondered why now that he had found her she was to be taken away from him. He wanted to scream, and shout, but he just kept mumbling, 'Don't worry, don't worry.' And when the plane finally shuddered to a stop he was still saying it.

It took him moments to realize that they had stopped. He was stunned.

He wanted to shake his head and wake up – because Jesus Christ – this had to be a nightmare – this couldn't be happening to him. Then he realized with a leaden feeling that this was no nightmare, this was *real*, it *was* happening to him. And his next immediate thought was fire – and wouldn't it be ridiculous to have made it to the ground and then to get *burned* to death.

Dallas was moaning softly. They were still strapped firmly into the leopard-skin couch – cleverly designed by some faggot designer whose balls Al would have for breakfast – the fucking thing hadn't even stayed fixed to the wall, it had come to rest against the side of the bed – and now *he couldn't get the fuckin' straps undone*. They were trapped.

He couldn't hear a thing. Shouldn't there be sirens and bells, for Crissake?

Shouldn't they be surrounded by rescue squads?

Why weren't they being saved?

What the fuck was happening out there?

The pain in her legs was excruciating. Cathy tried to struggle up, but it was impossible. A whole section of seats seemed to have concertinaed back into a tangled mass of wreckage, and her legs were trapped beneath it.

She struggled in vain. Had to get up. Had to get everyone out of there.

It was freezing cold, pitch dark. She reached out and touched Paul, unconscious beside her. She wondered if he was dead.

Bernie was screaming with pain. 'I've been stabbed! I've been stabbed!' he kept on repeating, 'help me – help me!'

She felt for Paul's pulse. He was alive. She bent forward, and by feeling around, realized that he was also trapped.

'Can anyone help us?' she called out – but her words sounded so funny – and she realized half her teeth were missing, and the thick sticky stuff pouring down her face was blood. It was about then that she fainted.

Evan was paralysed with fear. He didn't dare to move. Yet he couldn't remain hanging nearly upside down in his seat like an inanimate puppet forever.

Feebly he struggled to free his arm twisted beneath him, and upon doing that he fiddled with the seat belt, getting it open, and falling out of the seat with a thud. He fell near Bernie, and as his eyes adjusted themselves to the dark he could make out something terrible protruding from the fat man's chest.

'Pull it out,' Bernie screamed in panic and terror, 'pull the fuckin' motherfucker out!'

Evan backed away, stumbling along the littered aisle.

He wished he had a torch. Wished he could *see* something. He heard the stewardess ask for help – then silence. He edged towards the door of his father's section, and tripped over the body of Luke sprawled outside. Suddenly his hands were covered in

493

something hot and sticky, and with horror he realized it was blood. 'Luke?' he questioned desperately, '*LUKE?*' He pulled himself away from the body, tried to open the door to his father's room. It wouldn't budge. He threw his scrawny body against it, and started to scream hysterically. It was to no avail. Eventually he slumped to the floor, leaning his head against the door, and sobbing quietly. They were all dead. Even Bernie had stopped screaming. He was the only one left alive. He was all alone. *What was he going to do? Who would save him?*

'I'm all right,' said Dallas, 'I can't believe it, but I am.'

'We've got to get out of here,' Al replied tersely, 'can you *hear* anything?'

'Nothing. Just the rain. Where are we?'

'Well, we're sure as hell not in Sao Paulo. Probably on the outskirts somewhere – I'm worried about the others. *We're* OK – but what about them?'

'They're probably down the emergency chutes by now.'

'Look – when I count to three push as hard as you can against the friggin' seat belt. We can't just lie here waiting to get rescued – this whole thing could go up in flames any minute. Come on now – one – two – *three*.'

She strained with him, and a wave of sickening nausea engulfed her. 'Oh God, Al, I can't. I – I think I've broken something . . . It's my ribs . . . It hurts . . . It really hurts . . .'

He knew that every second must count. Planes always blew up. Always burst into flame. Why wasn't someone breaking in to get them out? Why wasn't anyone giving a fuck? Christ – some heads would roll for putting him through this . . . A lot of people would be out looking for new jobs . . .

'Can you help me get us over to the door – if we crawl . . .'

'I'll try.'

Together, like some monstrous snail, they managed to twist onto their bellies and inch their way towards the door, the couch still attached to them.

'Try and straighten up,' Al instructed.

She was biting her lip trying to stop from crying out. Al was so strong, so calm, she didn't feel at all afraid.

He managed to unlock the door, but it wouldn't open. If he had been able to see in the dark he would have known why – the frame at the top was crushed down – holding the door tight. It was completely jammed. 'It's no good, forget it.' If he wasn't trapped by the safety belt he could kick the goddamn door in. Thank Christ Dallas wasn't showing any signs of panic. Thank Christ the plane hadn't gone up in flames.

Then he had an idea. He would cut them free – he had a manicure case in one of the drawers – he also had a torch. If he could find both items he could cut them loose, then with the torch see their way out of the emergency exit – it was better than staying here and roasting to death.

Only one problem. The drawers had come out and splintered to pieces all over the room. On their hands and knees, with the lunatic couch attached to their backs, they would have to crawl around searching. Well, it beat the hell out of sitting around doing nothing.

At first light Cristina recovered consciousness.

Slowly she opened her eyes and stared up in surprise. For a moment she had no idea where she was. Her mind seemed utterly blank. Then slowly it all started to come back. Nino. Louis. The plane. The storm . . .

She was lying in what seemed like a forest, her clothes soaking wet and torn, every bone in her body aching. She couldn't summon the strength to move, so she just lay there for a while trying to collect her thoughts. It dawned on her that somehow she must have been thrown from the plane, and gradually, tentatively, she attempted to get up – marvelling at the fact that nothing seemed to be broken.

When she stood, the world spun round. She felt very giddy and sick, and there was an empty gnawing feeling in her stomach.

She sat down abruptly, leaning against the trunk of an enormous tree. She had never seen such giant trees before and wondered where she was. Then she wondered where the plane was, and Louis and Nino and all the others.

Oh God – surely she wasn't alone out here?

She stood again, her legs barely able to support her they were shaking so much. Her shoes had been ripped from her in the fall, and her bare feet were covered in small cuts and scratches, in fact every exposed inch of her body was bruised and battered. Fortunately she had been wearing jeans, and they were intact apart from being soaking wet, but the thin cotton shirt on her top half was ripped and torn. The sweater she had worn casually tied around her shoulders was gone.

The rain had stopped, but the ground was sodden and overgrown, and she was frightened to walk on it lest she stepped on any insects – she had always had a phobia about anything creepy crawly, and the air was alive with animal and bird chirpings.

But what else could she do? She had to look for the plane. Had to hope that she wasn't the only survivor.

Resolutely she set off.

Paul opened his eyes, and the pain in his legs was so intense that he shut them again and willed himself to lose consciousness. He wondered if he still *had* legs. What was the story about amputees still feeling pain in legs and arms that had long gone. 'Nurse!' he called sharply, 'NURSE!'

Cathy touched his arm. 'We're still on the plane,' she mumbled softly, 'nobody's come yet. We're trapped, can't move.'

He opened his eyes and groaned. He had thought he was in a hospital. An English country hospital.

He turned to look at Cathy. She was a horrible blood-caked sight.

It was just beginning to get light. 'How long have we been here?' he croaked. His throat felt dry, and there was a bitter taste in his mouth.

'Hours, I think. Evan's alive. Bernie was . . . I don't know if he still is. I don't know about the others . . . We're trapped. We'll just have to wait 'till the rescuers get here.'

'Al?' questioned Paul, his voice sounding unreal, '*where is Al?*'

Cathy shook her head.

Paul pushed desperately with his body, trying to shift the debris that was imprisoning them. He summoned every bit of strength he could muster, but it was to no avail.

He leaned out to look down the aisle, and was shocked to see the plane reach an abrupt and jagged end half way down. He could see Bernie slumped in his seat with the lethal-looking metal protruding from his chest. The fat man's face was deathly pale, his mouth hanging blankly open. But he was still taking shallow breaths.

Paul looked to the back of the plane. The door to Al's compartment was badly crushed. The body of Luke lying, as if still on guard, in front of it, surrounded by his own blood. And the inert huddled shape of Evan silent and unmoving.

'Evan!' croaked Paul. Cathy had said the boy was alive. 'EVAN!'

Cathy mumbled, 'He's in shock. I tried to get him to help us before. He's in shock . . .'

496

'EVAN!!' roared Paul.

The boy turned slowly and regarded his uncle blankly.

'Come here,' said Paul kindly. 'Are you hurt?'

Evan shook his head.

'See if you can get us out . . . Start pulling the metal away at the front of the pile. Come on Evan, hurry up.'

'I can't do it,' replied Evan, 'I can't do it. I have to wait here for my mother. If I don't she'll be angry with me.'

'Just try,' persuaded Paul, 'your father would want you to. If you can get me out, I can go and look for him.'

Evan turned his back, covering his ears and leaning his head against the compartment door.

'He's in shock,' repeated Cathy.

'I couldn't give a shit what he's in. He *has to help us*. Evan, goddamit – get over here and *help us*.'

Evan pressed his hands tightly over his ears and closed his eyes. He wondered how long it would be before his mother came for him. He hoped she wouldn't be cross, it wasn't *his* fault.

It seemed to take hours, but Al finally found the scissors, and started cutting through the thick webbing of seat belts. It took a long time, but the relief of getting that terrible contraption off their backs was worth it.

By the time he had completed the job it was beginning to get light.

Thank Christ the plane hadn't gone up in flames. If it had, they would have been finished. So much for the fast, efficient rescue teams in South America. When were they going to appear – tomorrow?

He lay Dallas on the bed. She was a mass of bruises which were starting to show up in purplish lumps.

'I'm all right,' she insisted, 'let's get out of here.' She shared his fear of fire.

He threw himself against the door in an attempt to shift it, but by this time he could see it was hopelessly jammed.

He hurried to the emergency exit.

'Christ!' he exclaimed. 'We're in some sort of jungle!'

Dallas struggled to sit up. 'What are you talking about?' Her ribs were throbbing with pain, but she had decided, after feeling them carefully, that they were only badly bruised.

'A jungle!' Al continued. 'Trees fifty friggin' feet tall! I don't believe it!'

Dallas joined him at the window.

'You're right,' she said in awe.

'How this plane made it in one piece . . .'

She nodded in agreement.

'How *we* made it . . .'

'Al – what about the others?'

He suddenly felt tired. He wanted to lie down, go to sleep, and wake up in a luxury hotel somewhere. He didn't want to start crawling out of the plane to discover – who knew what?

He wanted to pick up a phone and tell Paul or Luke or Bernie to find out what the fuck was going on.

He didn't need this whole frigging scene.

Dallas said quietly, 'At least we're alive.'

He put his arms around her and held her tightly, 'Jesus – Dallas – I don't think I can go out there . . . I don't want to find them . . . I can't . . . I just can't do it . . .'

'Sure,' she agreed soothingly. 'I know you don't *want* to go. But we have to. We have to see if they've radioed for help. We have to see if . . .' She trailed off. They both knew what they had to see. They had to see if anyone else was alive.

Cristina struggled through the heavy undergrowth, stopping to rest every few minutes.

She had shut every thought out of her head except finding the aircraft. Somehow she had persuaded herself that if she found the plane everything would be all right.

As the sun got higher in the sky it started to become very warm, and her clothes dried on her.

She had discovered a massive lump on the side of her head, and it throbbed painfully.

Her feet hurt as she squeamishly picked her way along, terrified of stepping on anything that moved. Occasionally she called out in the vain hope that there was someone to hear her. But the only noises were animal ones. A monkey howling in a tree somewhere, strange unusual bird cries, the buzz of flies and mosquitoes.

She was so hungry, her stomach making angry rumbling noises. There was a tree with delicious-looking red berries growing from it, but she was frightened to pick any in case they were piosonous.

She paused by the tree anyway, but screamed in terror as a huge spider landed on her bare arm. She shook it off, screaming hysterically, plunging on through the wilderness.

Then she heard the groans. Awful inhuman sounds.

*

They knotted the silk sheets from the bed together, and made a crude rope to lower themselves from the exit.

Dallas had dressed quickly in jeans and shirt. She went down the rope first, landing with a thud on the heavy ground.

Al followed her, having made sure the rope was secure enough to allow them back up again. If the worst came to the worst he figured they could at least wait in comfort until the rescuers came. Who else had the luck to crash out with a double bed at their disposal?

Deliberately he tried to keep his thoughts light. He didn't even want to consider what they might be about to find.

Almost at once they saw that only the back half of the plane existed.

They struggled around to the gaping, jagged, open edge.

'Anyone there?'

Paul's voice came back faintly, 'We're trapped. Help us.'

Jubilantly Al hugged Dallas. 'They're alive!' he enthused. 'Evan – Evan – can you hear me?'

Paul's voice weakly, 'Can you get us out of here?'

'I'll try and climb in,' Dallas volunteered, 'If I can stand on your shoulders . . .'

'Forget it. We'll get some more sheets – secure them, then we can both go up.' He shouted out: 'Hang on. Is everyone all right in there?'

Paul twisted uncomfortably in his seat. 'We're trapped,' he shouted back, 'Cathy and me. Bernie's hurt badly. Luke's dead, I think. Evan's all right. Hurry up.' He could hardly stand the pain any more. Cathy's eyes were closed, she seemed to be drifting in and out of consciousness. He could understand why. She was in a worse state than he. And that cruddy kid. Nothing wrong with him – but he couldn't even help. Couldn't even get them some water. When he got free he would break his scrawny little neck.

Flies had invaded the plane, it seemed like hundreds of them, and their main targets appeared to be Bernie and Cathy. Paul tried to keep them off her face, but every time he brushed them away they were back, settling onto her blood-soaked skin with relish. Luke was another prime target, forcing Evan to move away from his body.

'Your father is alive,' Paul croaked, 'he's coming to help. Get us some water – I can see the dispenser – it's not broken.'

Evan ignored him, huddling into an intact seat, and covering himself with a blanket.

Paul licked his dry lips. If only he was free. It was a miracle that Al was still alive. It was a miracle that any of them were.

He wondered about the fate of those at the front of the plane. He had heard the explosions last night – he didn't hold out too much hope.

It took another hour before Al was able to get a sheet-made rope and gain access to the plane. Then he climbed up.

'Oh God!' he murmured in despair, 'Oh Jesus Christ!'

Hurrying, he turned and hauled Dallas up after him.

Nino was sprawled on the ground, his legs bent beneath him at an impossible angle. Across his forehead the skin gaped open exposing a deep cut surrounded by dried blood.

He was making these awful noises – a heavy groaning sound which ended up as a despairing scream.

Ineffectually he beat at the flies which buzzed around him, but he was very weak, and as soon as his arms flopped down the flies descended once more.

At first Cristina was too scared to approach him. She stood partly hidden behind a tree just watching.

Nino, her lover, her invincible strong revolutionary. Look at him now – wracked with pain, screaming in agony.

It was *his* fault she was here. Why couldn't it have been Louis she had stumbled on?

Suddenly, from the corner of her eye, she saw a movement in the long grass. With horror she realized it was a snake – a long green and black monster slithering silently towards Nino.

Working feverishly with his bare hands Al pushed and pulled and tore at the debris trapping Paul and Cathy. He was covered in a film of sweat and had stripped down to his undershorts.

He had been at it for two hours, and his hands were cut and bleeding, but it didn't seem to bother him. He kept up a stream of bright conversation, making jokes, making light of their whole situation.

'We're getting there.' He paused for a moment. 'Jeeze Paul, if you think you're getting ten per cent of *this* gig – forget it!'

Dallas was busy too. They had laid Bernie out on the floor, a pillow under his head. He was in a bad way, and they both knew the jagged metal would have to be removed from his chest if he was to have any chance at all.

'We'll get Cathy and Paul free first,' Al had muttered, 'then we'll pull it out. We'll need their help. In the meantime fill him up with brandy.'

She was doing just that – sharing the one bottle that had survived the crash between Bernie, Cathy and Paul.

Evan was no use at all. Al had tried to slap him into shape, but he had merely burst into tears, and finally they had left him alone, huddled in a seat, staring into space.

Paul had told them about the hijack. Al was furious. Christ – what kind of idiots was he surrounded by? Didn't they know enough not to let strangers on his plane? He held his temper and didn't scream. What was the use of screaming? Who was he going to scream at? Paul – caught underneath a ton of fucking steel? Bernie – whose chances were about as good as Woody Allen fighting Mohammed Ali? Luke – mutilated and dead?

For once in his life he had no one to scream at. It didn't bother him. He had other things on his mind – like getting his brother free.

His hands were red and raw. But he didn't pause – he kept going. Had to get them free – had to get them out of there.

He clawed at the twisted metal – keeping up a stream of chat.

Here he was – the man who had everything. Money. Fame. Power.

Look where it got you – stuck in some asshole jungle trying to dig your brother out of the shit.

'Dallas,' he called urgently. 'I think we're getting there. Hold this back, I think I can get them out.'

She rushed to his assistance, holding on to the metal strut he had managed to lift. It was heavy, but she didn't flinch, although the pain around her ribs was agony.

Carefully Al pulled Paul free, dragging him out, leaving him on the floor, and going back for Cathy. She screamed as he moved her, and he could see why. One of her legs from the knee down was almost pulped. Blood and skin and bones. It was a dreadful sight.

He moved her into the aisle.

'It hurts, it hurts . . .' she moaned.

'Let it go,' Al instructed Dallas.

She dropped the strut and it clanged back into place.

At least they were out. He had managed that. Now all they had to do was wait for the goddamn rescue plane – and *why was it taking so long?*

•

Cristina stood rooted to the spot. She was unable to move, unable to breathe almost. With wide eyes she watched the huge snake slither and slide its way towards Nino. It seemed to move so slowly, and there was something almost hypnotically beautiful about its measured adulations.

She knew she should do *something*. But what? How did you frighten a snake away? And, anyway, if she intervened, it might attack *her*.

At least she had to warn Nino. His head was turned away from the approaching snake, she *had* to shout, do *something*.

He let out another of his inhuman yells, and the snake paused, its tongue flicking in and out. It was only about six feet away from its human prey now.

Cristina willed it to turn and go away. But it didn't. It slithered forward, raising its head with a hissing sound, and struck purposefully towards Nino's left leg.

Simultaneously Cristina screamed out a warning. Nino rolled over, but not quickly enough. The snake had bitten into his leg, and he let out a roar of pure agony.

The snake slid quietly away, vanishing into the undergrowth as silently as it had appeared.

'Oh mother of God!' Nino bellowed, 'save me – save me. Help me – please help me.'

Cristina stepped out from behind the tree. She was nauseous and hot, dizzy, and racked with stomach pains.

Nino saw her, and his eyes filled with tears. 'I'm going to die,' he said simply. 'Help me, Cristina. I'm going to die, and I don't want to be alone.'

She rushed forward and fell on him. She couldn't think about hate. She couldn't think about anything other than the fact that she wasn't by herself any more. 'I'll help you,' she promised, 'you won't die. I'll help you. What can I do?'

'Water. Do you have any?'

She shook her head. 'I've got nothing.'

He groaned. 'I can't walk. My legs are broken. You must suck out the snake venom. Do it now – do it now, please, I beg you.'

She stared at his leg in horror. The place where the snake had bitten him was already swelling into a vile purplish mound.

'I . . . I . . . can't . . .'

'If you don't, I'll die. You'll be alone out here. Suck the poison and spit it on the ground. Hurry, Cristina, it may already be too late.'

She bent her face to his leg, shushing away the flies which

seemed to be everywhere. There was a bone protruding where it shouldn't. There were cuts and scratches, and in the middle of it all was the obscene purple lump of puss. He pressed near and around it with his fingers. 'Now!' he urged, 'now!'

She put her lips over it, sucked and spat twice. Then turned away and vomited.

He let out a sigh. 'We'll know soon enough . . . soon . . . Maybe you'll end up alone after all, my little carioca – maybe . . .' He laughed bitterly. 'I nearly did it. I would have been a hero – you hear me . . .' His eyes closed.

Cristina began to sob. 'You'll be all right, Nino. I know you will. I know you will. You can't leave me. Promise. I want you to promise.'

He did not reply. He had passed out.

'How do your legs feel?' Al asked anxiously.

Paul nodded. 'Not bad. I think the circulation's coming back.' He was propped on the floor of the compartment, with Dallas massaging his legs. Miraculously they seemed to be only badly bruised. It was the pressure that had been causing him all the pain.

They had cut his trouser legs off at the knee, and applied hand cream to massage away the numbness.

Cathy, however, had not fared so well. Apart from her facial injuries, which Dallas had cleaned up as best she could, her shattered legs was quite obviously useless.

The flies had invaded the plane with a vengeance. Small ones, big horse flies, tiny stinging little tics. Infection would set in at once, and there was nothing to be done.

They had covered Cathy with a blanket, but she kept on pushing it off and complaining of the heat. It was unearthly hot and humid. They were all pouring with sweat.

'You must stay covered,' Dallas warned, 'the flies will only make it worse . . .'

Cathy moaned softly, 'It couldn't be any worse . . .'

Al took Dallas to one side. 'What do you think? Shall we try and get that thing out of Bernie, or shall we wait for help?'

She gave him a strange look. 'What makes you think help is coming?'

'Don't talk crap. Of course it's coming. I'm a million dollar property, kid. They'll be searching 'til they find me. I'm sure Van must have radioed our position before he crashed.'

'Why aren't they here then?'

'I shouldn't think this is the easiest place to reach. A plane couldn't land here. I suppose they'll have to get to us by land.'

She shrugged unbelievingly. 'I haven't heard any planes flying over here today . . .'

'They'll find us,' he said sharply.

'If you say so. In the meantime if we don't pull that chunk of metal out of Bernie he's going to die.'

'Let's do it then.'

'Paul will have to hold him down . . .' she hesitated, 'If Evan could help . . .'

'I don't think so. Look – I'll pull it out, you help Paul hold him. Can you take the blood?'

'Can you? I worked with animals when I was a kid, I'm used to it.'

'I haven't always been the world's favourite superstar, you know . . .'

She pushed the hair away from her face wearily. 'Let's do it, Al. We need a towel to stem the blood.'

He held her face briefly. 'I love you,' he said quietly, 'I just want you to know that. You're not only the most beautiful girl in the world, you're also the best one to get stuck in a plane crash with.'

'You and your quickie trips to South America. Why did I ever listen to you?'

Bernie moaned loudly.

'Give him the rest of the brandy,' Al said. 'I'll be right back.'

Paul was attempting to stand.

'All right?' Al asked.

'Shaky but nothing seems to be broken.'

'I'm going to get some towels.'

'Why don't we bust through the door? Is the bed still in one piece? Maybe we could put Cathy and Bernie on it.'

'Yeah,' Al contemplated the crushed door. 'If we could get some support – take the pressure off. Shit – it would beat the hell out of crawling in and out. We'll give it a try.'

Paul stared admiringly at his brother. Who would have thought that Al had it in him? His hands were cut and bleeding. His body dripping with sweat. He hadn't stopped for a moment. And yet he was still willing to go on. *He* wasn't hurt. He could have just sat tight in his bedroom waiting for help. He hadn't even touched the brandy, although he must have been dying for a swig. 'You all need it more than I do,' he had insisted.

'I think I can walk,' Paul said, trying a few steps.

'Let's give it a try then, boyo, let's do it. You and I together, we

504

always were a good team.' Al slapped his brother on the shoulder. 'Now, this is what we'll do . . .'

Night fell quickly in the jungle.

Cristina had bodily dragged Nino up against the trunk of a tree, arming herself with a hefty stick in case of further snake attacks. She was exhausted. She knew that without food or drink she could not last much longer.

'Tomorrow,' she told Nino, who drifted in and out of consciousness, 'I'll find the plane. It can't be far. I won't leave you for long, I'll get water and come back for you.'

'Yes,' he mumbled.

She cradled his head on her lap, brushing away a spider. Her mouth was so dry. Her body ached. She had been bitten to pieces by the flies. A wasp had stung her. Her head throbbed.

Now with the darkness came the frightening noises. What other animals apart from snakes lurked in the blackness?

She clung onto Nino and tried not to think.

'I'll find Louis tomorrow,' she crooned softly, 'he will save us. Tomorrow we'll be all right.'

'I could've been a hero,' Nino mumbled, shudders racking his body.

Eventually they both fell into an uneasy sleep.

On the plane, progress had been made. Between them Al and Paul had managed to get the door to the bedroom compartment open. They had half-carried, half-dragged Bernie in there, and laid him out on the bed.

Wrapping his hands in towels, Al had gripped the protruding jagged metal, and with a horrible suction sound, it had come out of Bernie's chest. Dallas had tried to stem the flow of blood with more towels. They were already soaked through, but at least Bernie seemed in less pain.

When the darkness came they were all exhausted. Their only sustenance had been water from the unbroken dispenser and a packet of dry biscuits. Al had not thought of rationing anything because he quite expected they would be rescued shortly. It occurred to him that he should have checked just how much water there was. It was too late now. Darkness had descended and the only thing to do was sleep.

Cathy and Bernie were on the bed. Evan was huddled in the seat he had not moved out of all day. Paul had chosen to sleep on the floor in the bedroom. Dallas and Al sat side by side in two intact seats near the break in the plane.

Night had brought a respite from the interminable flies, and that was a relief. But strange jungle noises were all around them, and the impossible heat of the day turned into icy cold at night.

Al slid his arm around her. 'I told you I'd take you somewhere romantic.'

She moved as near to him as she could get. 'You're not going to break into song, are you?'

'Only if you'll pay me.'

She tried to laugh, but it caught in her throat and emerged more like a sob.

'Hey – You're not going to break on me, lady? You've been pretty fantastic all day.'

'Al? We're in real trouble, aren't we? How are they ever going to find us? We're lost – even if planes *did* fly over, how would they spot us? We would be hidden from sight by the trees.'

'Don't worry,' he replied easily, much more easily than he actually felt. 'Tomorrow night we'll be at the Beverly Hills Hotel celebrating on fat juicy steaks and champagne. And if you're good – you know what?'

'What?'

'I'll take you to a party at Karmen Rush's. How does *that* hit you?'

'Like a ton of shit!'

'Oh, that's nice – really nice!'

This time her laughter stuck, and she fell asleep soon after.

Al didn't sleep. He stared out into the blackness thinking about the reality of it all.

They had been missing how long? At least twenty-four hours, and Dallas was right, not one plane had flown over, and she was also right about the trees shielding them from sight. Quite obviously the authorities did not know where to look. If they did there would have been some activity in the sky today.

The fact was it might take days before they were found. And how would they survive? There was no food, little water. Cathy and Bernie were both in a bad way . . . How long could they last without proper treatment?

Al swore softly under his breath. He was so used to picking up a phone and having a dozen people jumping at his every command. Somehow he felt cheated that this situation could not be taken care of in the same way.

Here he was, roughing it on a fucking aeroplane seat, whilst Bernie Suntan enjoyed the comforts of *his* bed. What a switch *that* was.

A monkey howled loudly nearby. Al jumped. Dallas mumbled something in her sleep. He stroked her hair. He loved her. For the very first time in his life he loved a woman. And he had to protect her, save her. And goddamn it he would.

Tomorrow he would find the other half of the plane, see if the radio was still working, get some action going.

Yes. And he would find some food, there must be fruit, berries . . . His eyes were closing, niggly little pains attacking every part of his body. Scratches, cuts, strains, bruises . . . He had used muscles he had forgotten existed.

'Tomorrow . . .' he mumbled. 'I'll get it together tomorrow . . .'

sixty-seven

By Saturday afternoon a passenger list of those aboard the missing Al King jet was published.

Linda read it through twice.

'I can't believe it,' she said to Cody, 'I just can't believe it.'

He was stunned himself.

'How can a huge jet like that just vanish?' Linda demanded for the hundredth time.

He shook his head. 'I can only think that it must have been hijacked. If it had crashed they would have found it by now.'

'Oh God!' Linda buried her face in her hands. 'It just doesn't bear thinking about. What can we *do*?'

He had been thinking the same thing himself. It was such an impossible situation to have to garner every little piece of news from television and newspapers.

'I'm going to place a call to Carlos Baptista. If anyone knows what's going on it's him.'

In New York, Melanie King licked dewey red lips, blinked baby blue eyes, and smiled into the television camera. 'Manny and I are in a dreadful state,' she said in reply to the interviewer's question. 'Paul and Manny are the best of friends. There has never been unpleasantness between any of us. After all, divorce is such

507

an everyday happening nowadays. Paul is like . . . well, he's like a much-loved brother.' She paused triumphantly, pleased with her choice of words.

Marjorie Carter, who was conducting the interview, leaned forward intently. 'How about Al, Melanie? You must know him as well as anyone. How do you think he would be able to cope if this is indeed a hi-jack?'

Melanie widened her eyes. 'Al King is a wonderful human being . . . kind and generous. I'm sure he would react in the appropriate fashion.'

'Thank you, dear, for being with us in your time of stress.' Marjorie faced the camera straight on. 'Well, that's all for now. We will be bringing you the news as it comes in. Meanwhile, Al King, wherever you are, our thoughts are with you. This is Marjorie Carter signing off.'

The red light on camera flicked off.

Melanie asked breathily: 'Was I all right?'

Gathering papers together, Marjorie threw her a cynical look. 'All right? You're kidding, aren't you? The sonofabitch should have you write his obituary for him! Since when has that prick been a "kind and generous wonderful human being"? Crap – pure crap. I've had him, I should know.'

Melanie dived into her bag and produced a small hand mirror. She studied her face. Petulantly she said: 'I hope I looked all right – If you need me again I'll be happy to come back.'

'Sure kid,' replied Marjorie, 'if they find the body you can come again! Oh – and give my best to Manny.'

'She is under sedation,' Jorge said, his face grey with strain.

'I'll just sit with her,' Doris Andrews replied softly, 'comfort her.'

'If you like . . .' agreed Jorge.

He led Doris through to the bedroom. Evita lay wanly in the centre of the bed, her face a pale mask, her eyes wide open and staring.

'Doris is here,' Jorge said quietly. 'She'll sit with you for a while.'

Evita's eyes flickered slightly.

Doris took her hand and sat on the side of the bed. 'It's terrible,' she said, 'dreadful. I have friends on the plane . . .'

Jorge walked quietly from the room. Bad enough that Evita knew about Cristina and Louis being on the plane, but he didn't dare to tell her the latest news he had received. Apparently when they had boarded the plane at the last minute, they had been accompanied by a third party. A young man dressed in a mechanic's overalls. From his description he sounded uncannily like Nino.

Lew Margolis said, 'What was the cunt doing on a plane with Al King in the first place?'

Cody gripped the phone tightly, trying not to lose his temper. 'She was having a rest.'

Lew snorted nastily. 'A rest? With that motherfucker? The cunt was supposed to be at the studio working for me. Remember?'

'You had fired her,' Cody reminded him.

'So I hired her again. Big fuckin' deal.'

'Will the studio release a statement or shall I?'

'We will. The publicity will give "Man Made Woman" a peachy send off. Trying to get it slotted on the tube earlier than planned. The cunt might have done us a favour.'

Cody's temper snapped. 'Don't keep on calling her that.'

'What you want I should call her? Princess?' He sniggered. 'Did I ever tell you, Cody, about how I first met your beautiful client?'

'No.'

Lew thought better of revealing the facts. 'Some other time – remind me. By the way – you got any other girls right for the part? Looks like we might have ourselves a vacancy.'

Edna sat in her kitchen sipping her fifth cup of tea in an hour. She was trying to sort out her feelings. She was grieved but not heart-broken. *And that was a horrible reaction. Why didn't she feel worse?*

Was it the uncertainty? The fact that nobody knew whether the occupants of the plane were dead or alive?

Her *husband* was on board. Her *son*. The two men she had devoted her life to. The two men who had prevented her from having any life of her own.

She had let go long ago . . . the night she had walked in on Al in Tucson. And the relief of not caring any more . . . The simple pleasure of living her life without having to put two other un-appreciative people before her.

Al first . . . then Evan. She had realized the mistake of clinging to her son. He would be better off with his father. *She* would be better off alone.

Now this . . .

The photographers and news media had descended like vultures. How happy they were that he was with another woman on the plane. They seemed to have forgotten the fact that she had previously announced she was divorcing him. That was an irrelevant fact now. It spoiled the dramatic suspense. Far better to have a 'left at home' wife while he had been gallivanting with a beautiful young girl across America.

She had sent them all packing. But they were still outside the house, waiting like birds of prey to pounce as soon as she appeared.

She had made her way across the garden and comforted Paul's two children. Nanny was in an awful state, sobbing and wailing.

'Is Mrs King returning from New York?' Edna asked.

'She can't,' snivelled nanny, 'she phoned to say it's impossible. Oh it's so awful . . . That poor, poor man . . . And to think I only spoke to him a few days ago . . . Oh it's dreadful . . . shocking . . . These poor little mites . . . What will happen to them?'

'We don't know the worst yet, nanny. The plane might be perfectly safe in some other country. Please try and calm yourself.'

'Yes,' sobbed nanny, 'yes.'

Edna phoned the telephone exchange and asked them to reconnect her phone. Then she went home and waited. It was all she could do – wait.

'You left Acapulco very suddenly,' Doris Andrews whispered, 'why was that? You didn't even say goodbye.'

Evita stared at her. 'Jorge had to get back . . . Unexpectedly.'

'Oh. I see.' Doris squeezed her hand, 'I was hoping it had nothing to do with what happened between us.'

'It didn't,' Evita replied shortly.

'Good.'

The two women were silent. Evita lying wanly on the bed. Doris sitting close by.

'I thought of writing many times,' Doris confided, 'but then I would change my mind.' She laughed nervously, 'I hate rejection, you know.'

'Don't we all,' agreed Evita, sitting up to sip from a glass of water.

Doris's eyes slipped hungrily to her breasts which were softly enclosed in a pink satin nightgown. 'You are as beautiful as ever,' she murmured.

'Please, Doris. What do you want? Why are you here?' Evita's low voice was pained.

'I had to see you. I waited a year. I told Lew that you had invited me. I knew he was too busy to accompany me. I have thought about you . . . about us . . . so many times.'

Evita sighed. 'Doris . . . what happened . . . It was a slip on my part. I like you, I really do. But you must understand, I love my husband, it could never happen again. Please – would you go now. I'm really too distraught to discuss anything.'

'I know. It was selfish of me to come today. But I want to comfort you. You'll allow me that small pleasure, won't you?'

'No one can comfort me. Not until I know where my daughter is.' Tears streamed down her face. 'This not knowing is a terrible thing . . .'

'They'll find her,' Doris assured. 'You'll see, she'll be all right. Have faith, Evita. I promise you she will be all right. I feel these things, I am very intuitive.'

'Are you?' Evita questioned hopefully, 'are you really?'

'Yes,' replied Doris soothingly, 'you wait, you'll see. Trust in me. Now why don't you try and sleep, I can come back later.'

Evita closed her eyes obediently, 'I'll try.'

Saturday night there was no further news. Linda had watched the Melanie King interview on television and she was disgusted and despondent. What kind of a woman went on television and gave an interview at a time like this? Why hadn't the bitch flown back to London to be with her children? How could she be away from them at a time like this?

'I think I'll go home tonight,' she told Cody. 'I feel like being alone.'

He understood. 'If I hear anything I'll come over.'

'Sure,' she nodded. It wasn't that she felt any differently about Paul . . . Or was it? The fact that he might be dead. The fact that she might never see him again . . . even if she wanted to. It was too awful . . . And Dallas, Bernie, Al . . .

She just wanted to be alone.

The not knowing was the worst.

The uncertainty.

'We'll know something tomorrow,' Cody assured her.

'Yes?' she answered listlessly.

'Yes,' he replied positively, although he was as unsure as she was.

It was going to be a long hard night, and one he was glad that he would spend alone.

He wanted to think about Dallas.

He wanted to pray for her.

sixty-eight

Dallas was the first to wake. She ached all over, and her neck hurt from sleeping in a sitting position. She glanced at Al. He was stretched out, mouth slightly open, snoring softly. She didn't want to disturb him, he had worked so hard the previous day.

It must be very early, the sun was only just beginning to rise, and it was still chilly. At least it was daylight; the nights were so dark it was impossible to see anything.

She had woken in the middle of the night and heard noises – frightening rustles and growls. Instinctively she had know that there was some kind of wild animal circling around what was left of the plane. She had waited in horror, wondering if it would attempt to climb up, but eventually it had padded away.

She had not been able to sleep properly since then.

Oh God! What she would give for a simple cup of coffee . . . A piece of toast . . . . A lump of dry bread – anything!

Quietly she left her seat, padding down the aisle to check out if anyone was awake.

Evan was asleep. They would have to do something about *him* today – It was wrong just leave him alone, he would have to join in, become part of the group. After all, he wasn't hurt, he could be useful.

In the bedroom compartment Bernie lay on his back, his eyes wide open. The towels wrapped around him were stiff with dried blood. Flies buzzed everywhere. Cathy and Paul slept.

'How are you feeling?' Dallas whispered to Bernie.

The day before he had been incoherent.

'What the fuck we still doin' here?' he croaked.

'I guess we're waiting to be rescued,' she replied.

He coughed, and she was dismayed to see a trickle of blood dribble from his mouth.

'How long we been here?'

'Today's Sunday, we crashed Friday night.'

'Jeeze . . . I don't remember a thing.'

Al was having a beautiful dream. He was playing backgammon with the Shah of Persia, and *he* was winning. 'Hey – Shah,' he was saying, 'I won her – *you* may have more bread – but *I* won her.'

Dallas shook him back to reality. 'Al – wake up. There are a couple of cupboards in the bedroom I can't open. What's in them? Any food?'

He opened his eyes wondering where he was. Then he remembered. 'Food? I don't know . . . which cupboards?'

She took his hand, 'Come and see.'

Evan sneaked a bar of chocolate out of his shirt pocket. It was his last one. He wolfed it down ravenously. Now all he had left was a couple of packs of chewing gum. If his mother didn't come soon she would be too late . . .

Cathy woke up and affirmed the fact that the two locked cupboards *were* used to store supplies. She looked worse than anyone, with her poor battered face, missing teeth and crushed leg. But she refused to give in, she was cheerful and bright, and kept on saying, 'Chin up, everyone, they'll be here for us soon.'

Al smashed the two cupboards in, and they came upon a bonanza. One cupboard contained stocks of Kleenex, toilet tissue, paper towels, soap, cleaning materials, fresh towels and sheets. There were also three plastic containers of hand cream, an atomizer of perfume, and the best discovery of all – a first-aid box.

The second cupboard revealed an even more exciting array of goods. Three jars of instant coffee. Two boxes of tea bags. Four boxes of lump sugar. Three giant cans of orange juice. Six packets of crisps. Four tins of mixed nuts. Two packets of water biscuits. Six tins of the best caviar. Twelve small bottles of Perrier Water. Six large bottles of champagne. A packet of paper napkins. A packet of toothpicks. A glass jar of maraschino cherries. A corkscrew, bottle and tin opener. And finally three cans of anchovies.

'We just hit pay dirt!' Al exclaimed triumphantly, 'we can last forever on this little lot!'

'Not quite ever,' Dallas warned, 'I think we should ration it carefully.'

'The hell with *that*. I'm starving.' He was already opening up the biscuits, stuffing them in his mouth.

'Al!' reminded Dallas sharply, 'share them out.'

'Don't get panicky – there's plenty here. Everyone help themselves.'

'Look,' interrupted Dallas angrily, 'we don't know how long we're going to be here . . .'

'She's right,' Paul joined in.

Reluctantly Al put the biscuits down. 'So what the fuck do you want to do?'

'We should just make it last,' Dallas said coldly. She picked up the packet of biscuits and handed one out to everyone.

Al returned his with a sheepish grin – 'I already had two.'

She smiled at him. 'Thanks.'

'You're right,' he replied. 'I'm not going to argue when I know you're right. We could sit here for fucking ever waiting for them to come and get us. I think I'll take a little trip – see what I can find. Maybe I'll come across the rest of the plane. You feel well enough to come with me, Paul?'

His brother nodded.

Cristina's own tears woke her. She had been crying in her sleep, and the tears were stinging the cuts on her face.

It was already hot. A humid stifling heat which filtered down through the tall trees.

Nino lay across her lap. He looked a very funny colour, a sort of greyish white. She tried to rouse him, but he muttered angrily and refused to wake.

They were both covered in flies and mosquitoes. The horrible aggravating things wouldn't go away. They buzzed and dived, inflicting nasty little bites on any exposed piece of skin. At least her legs were covered, but her arms were bitten all over.

She wanted to get up. She knew she *must* get up. But her strength seemed to have deserted her, and she wasn't sure if she was capable of moving.

If she stayed where she was they would both die.

That thought stung her into action, and she stumbled to her feet, letting Nino's head rest on the ground.

'I'll come back soon,' she whispered, but he wasn't listening. He was rolling around groaning.

She noticed that he still had his shoes on, running shoes with thick rubber soles. *She* was the one that had to do the walking, her feet were in such an awful state, surely he wouldn't mind . . .

She struggled to get the shoes off him and put them on herself. They were big and sloppy, but they were better than nothing.

Exhausted before she had begun, she set off to try and find the plane.

Al and Paul were ready to leave.

'You've got to be careful,' Dallas warned. 'This is the jungle, there are a million and one dangers.'

'My lady – an expert on jungles!' Al laughed.

'I'm not an expert – but the only thing I learned as a kid was

514

about animals. The big ones will leave you alone if they've eaten. It's the smaller ones you must look out for. Poisonous insects, ants, scorpions, snakes. And whatever you do – don't eat anything – no berries, plants, even flowers.'

'You know something – eating flowers just ain't my scene – and after that feast I had for breakfast – two water biscuits and some orange juice – how could I possibly think about food!'

She put her arms around him and kissed him. 'Love you,' she whispered. '*Please* be careful.'

'We will.'

She watched them set off. They had two bottles of Perrier water with them, some saccharin, and Luke's gun. They had found the gun in his jacket before burying him near the plane. They had also found a packet of chewing gum, and a hip flask of whisky. It had all been added to their supplies.

God, it was hot! How she longed for a bath, her clothes were sweat-stained and sticky. She wanted to rip them off and walk around naked, but the risk of exposing skin to the hungry mosquitoes was just not worth it. She remained resolutely covered as much as she could, and so far the only bites she had experienced were on her hands.

She had changed the towels around Bernie's wound. It did not look good at all, but he certainly seemed in better shape than the previous day. Cathy, however, was deteriorating. Her leg was an ugly open wound, and even to Dallas' inexperienced eye it seemed to be gangrenous.

There was nothing she could do for either of them, except be near when they needed her.

The first aid box had helped. She had dabbed everyone's cuts and bruises with antiseptic cream and wrapped all the open wounds in gauze bandages to keep the flies off.

She wished that she could have gone with Al, but he had insisted she stay on the plane. 'You and I are the only two with our heads together – we can't desert them, they'll think we're never coming back. Paul's likely to fall to pieces any minute.'

He was right. Paul was making a supreme effort, but anyone could see he was on the edge of hysteria.

She could not get over Al. Spoiled superstar. Supreme user. He was a tower of strength, combining just the right amount of jokey cynicism with a strong conviction that rescue was just around the corner. He alone was keeping everyone's spirits buoyant.

She had gone to him in Las Vegas for a night of sex. They

hadn't even had that, but she knew that he was the man she wanted to spend the rest of her life with.

She laughed bitterly. Perhaps she would. Perhaps the rest of her life would only be a matter of weeks ... days ...

Just as a feeling of despondency swept over her she heard a noise in the distance. A noise that was unmistakable.

She ran to the front of the plane, and there, as clear as possible, zooming like a bird high above the giant trees, was an aeroplane.

Frantically she waved and shouted.

'We're *here!* Down here! Can't you see us? We're HERE!'

Her yelling was in vain. The aeroplane zoomed smoothly past, a tiny dot in the sky that vanished into the distance as suddenly as it had appeared.

Al and Paul heard the plane as they trekked their way through the jungle. Paul started to yell, but Al stopped him. 'Forget it,' he said. 'You think they're going to hear us? Save your breath.'

'How *will* they find us then?' Paul demanded, his voice rising hysterically.

That was a good question. Al was damned if he knew. 'They will,' he replied airily. 'Don't forget it's me they're looking for.'

'You!' spat Paul, 'if it wasn't for *you* I wouldn't be here.'

'*You* wouldn't be anywhere.'

Paul stopped abruptly. 'I've *had* that shit!' he screamed, 'had it up to *here*. You – you – you. FUCK YOU. Where would *you* be without me? I *dragged* you up to where you are today. *I* grafted the contracts, negotiated more money, *pleaded* with them to use you at first. All you were interested in was getting pissed and laid – in that order. Without me you'd be singing shit in bar-rooms for the price of a pint. I have devoted my life to you – *and I want some respect*. I'm not some ass-kissin' fan. I'm your manager, your agent, your brother, for Crissakes.'

'What the fuck are you getting hysterical about? Calm down,' Al interrupted, startled at his brother's sudden outburst.

'Don't you fucking tell *me* to calm down. I've stood in the background and let you shit on me all your life. It's over, Al, it's over. You even screwed my wife – you banged Melanie. Didn't you? Didn't you?'

For the first time in his life Al was ashamed. He had never realized that Paul harboured such resentment. And what he said was true. It was a fact that at the beginning Paul had stage-managed his success.

'Yes,' Al replied defensively, 'I laid Melanie. She wanted it. She was after me until the day she left you. It wasn't my fault, Paul, you've got to believe me on that score . . .'

'You fucking bastard. I should kill you . . . You hear me? Kill you . . .'

'Look – if you think I was the only other man in her life you're wrong. It happened once – and don't think I haven't sweated over it. I hated myself for it.'

'My brother!' Paul spat, 'my dear brother.'

'I know it's a little late to say I'm sorry, but I am. I was sorry the moment it happened.'

'Have you any idea what it's been like having you for a brother? At parties I'm dragged around like exhibit A – I don't have a name – I'm the great Al King's brother. That's enough for me to be accepted. Not as myself – as your fucking brother.'

'That's not my fault. I didn't know . . .'

'Of course not. When have *you* ever given a shit about anyone else's feelings? What *you* want – when *you* want. A fuck. A meal. A massage. Call Paul – any time of the day or night – he'll arrange it.'

'Jesus, Paul – I never . . .' He stopped talking abruptly.

Staggering towards them was a semi-hysterical, ragged girl. 'Help me!' she cried out. 'Oh God! Please, please help me.'

A plane would never spot them. How could it? It would be like finding the proverbial needle in a haystack. And even if by some miracle they were seen – what then? A plane would never be able to land here, not even a helicopter. The trees took care of that. Majestic giant trees – some maybe as high as two hundred feet.

It occurred to Dallas that if they were to get out it would have to be by their own efforts – and that was impossible. They had no idea where they were. No idea how far from any settlement or community. They had no compass, map, suitable clothes, or adequate supplies. To survive in the jungle was difficult enough – even with the right equipment. But without . . . It was probably impossible.

Besides which Cathy and Bernie were in no shape to travel, and they couldn't leave them.

But if they just stayed put . . .

How long would their meagre supplies keep them going? A week . . . Two weeks . . . Who knew?

Al didn't understand. He seemed to think they would be rescued. How could they be rescued when nobody knew where they were?

Angrily she swotted a mosquito away, and made her way back down the plane.

Evan still huddled in his seat. She sat down beside him. He stunk, his clothes stained with vomit, sweat and urine. The flies were having a field day around him.

'Hi,' she said softly. 'Feeling OK?'

He ignored her, staring off into space.

'Listen,' she said gently, 'we have to get you out of those clothes – one thing we've got plenty of is clothes – a whole closet full. Come on, let's sort something out.'

He still didn't say anything.

'Did you see the plane?' she asked brightly. 'They'll be coming for us soon. You don't want them to see you like that, do you?'

'Is Nellie coming?' he mumbled.

A response at last! 'Sure she is.' Dallas took his arm. 'Come on, Evan, I'll help you choose something.'

He stood up and something fell off his lap. It was a portable radio. Dallas pounced on it. 'Does it work?'

'Don't know.'

She switched it on and was rewarded with a blurred crackle. Desperately she twiddled the tuner. Faintly she was able to receive a music station. What a find! She switched it off. Save the batteries. Maybe later, when Al returned, they would be able to tune into a news programme and find out if anyone *was* actually looking for them.

Greedily Cristina swallowed the contents of one bottle of Perrier water, and munched on the saccharin tablets they gave her.

'Christ!' Al kept on exclaiming, 'I don't know how you're still alive, it's a bloody miracle.'

At first he had thought the dark-skinned, wild-haired girl was part of some Indian tribe. But Paul had recognized her as she had stumbled exhausted into their arms. Incoherently she had told them her story, finishing off with a request about Louis' safety.

'We haven't seen him,' Paul replied. 'Maybe he was lucky like you.'

'Lucky?' the tears filled her eyes, 'I have been in hell. So alone ... so frightened. Please find Louis – *please*.'

Al glanced at Paul. They both knew she was asking the impossible.

'Let's get her back to the plane,' Al said.

'What about Nino?' she asked quickly. 'He's not far away. I can't leave him, I can't ... I promised ...'

518

'The bastard can stay where he is . . .' Paul began. 'If it wasn't for him . . .'

'Take us to him,' Al said quietly, 'I guess he's regretting the whole gig just as much as we are.'

By early afternoon Bernie was feeling a lot better. His huge bulk propped up in bed he was able to flick through Evan's collection of magazines.

'What the fuck . . .' he boasted, 'tomorrow I'll be up and about. Jeeze . . . I can see it now. Goddamn press gonna accuse me of engineering the whole shitbag. They know I'll do anything for a hot story!'

'You can't help having a reputation that goes before you,' Dallas replied jokingly.

'Yeah,' Bernie mused, 'you're right. I can name my price after this. Whatcha think? Think they're gonna come for us today?'

'I wouldn't be surprised.'

He slapped a spider, squashing it on his arm, 'Goddamn insects! Gonna drive me crazy!'

Cathy, lying beside him, groaned. She had been semi-conscious all day, and her leg was looking worse than ever. Dallas did not know much about medicine, but she did know if Cathy's leg was gangrenous it would have to come off if her life was to be saved.

She only hoped that Al had found the other half of the plane, and that maybe the radio had been working, and that maybe . . .

Pipe dreams.

She lifted Cathy's head and gave her a few sips of water.

It was hopeless and she knew it.

It was just beginning to get dark when Al and Paul arrived back at the plane. Between them they carried Nino, and Cristina stumbled along behind.

Dallas and Evan helped them haul Nino up into the plane, and then they assisted Cristina.

'Thought we'd never make it back,' Al gasped. He grinned at Evan. 'Hey, boyo – feeling better?'

Evan nodded.

'Did you find anything?' Dallas asked anxiously.

'Only these two. She needs taking care of – the kid's bitten and scratched to pieces. He's in a bad way. Snake bite.'

'Evan – get me the antiseptic lotion and bandages. Al, we've found a portable radio, I thought if we could tune into a news station . . .'

'Where?'

She showed him where the radio was and left him to it while treating Cristina. The girl was a mess. Dehydrated, confused, feverish. Dallas took her into the bedroom compartment, laid her on the floor, and gently got her clothes off. Then she dabbed at the scratches and cuts and bites with the antiseptic lotion. With horror she realized that whatever it was that had bitten the girl had laid eggs under the skin, and larvae were pushing their way up, horrible tiny black heads popping through the skin.

She didn't know what to do. So she just covered the girl with the antiseptic lotion and hoped that it would kill them off. Then she dressed her in a pair of Al's slacks and a shirt, and fed her a couple of water biscuits and some orange juice.

Nino was another matter. He was delirious, and seemed to be experiencing difficulty in breathing. The gash on his forehead was quite obviously infected, and his body twitched in desperate spasms of pain.

Dallas knew about snakes. They had kept them at the zoo in Miami. But there were so many different species, and she had no idea what type had bitten Nino. Without an anti-venom being administered immediately she did not hold out much hope for his chance of survival.

She fed him some water and covered him with a blanket. It was all she could do for him.

Al had managed to locate a news programme. He listened to the faint crackly newscaster intently. Paul and Dallas crowded around him.

The news was of a major earthquake in Europe, and a terrorist group holding hostages in New York. Finally the newscaster continued, 'The Al King mystery deepens. The singer and his nine passengers and five crew have still not been heard from. The jet plane missing since Friday night on a trip between Rio and Sao Paulo has apparently vanished without trace. The police and airport authorities are completely mystified. No ransom demands have been received, ruling out the possibility of a hi-jack attempt. Search planes sent out have failed to spot any sight of the missing jet. In India, the new government is calling for . . .'

Al clicked the radio off. 'I think we're lost,' he said bitterly. 'I think we're lost and nobody gives a fuck. You know what? I could easily become the Glenn Miller of the seventies. How does *that* grab you?'

sixty-nine

Juana fidgeted uneasily as she waited to be ushered in to see Carlos Baptista. It was the reward that had attracted her. Fifty thousand dollars! A fortune! Who could even imagine that amount of money. *Fifty thousand dollars!*

She glanced around the waiting room. It was crowded. Beside her sat a thin girl wearing spectacles, and next to her a young man who was not unlike Nino, only not so good-looking. He had the same untidy hair and intense eyes, but his face was longer – more horsey. No – side by side he would not be able to hold a candle to Nino.

Thinking of him she shuddered slightly. Where was he? The last time she had seen him had been at the airport when she had helped him. I'm just going to interview Al King – not shoot him – he had joked. But what *had* he done? Where had he gone? Because without doubt she knew that the disappearance of that plane with Al King aboard was Nino's doing. And she was going to tell Carlos Baptista all about it. She was going to pick up a fifty thousand dollar reward. Probably.

Didi adjusted her spectacles and edged away from the plump girl sitting next to her. The girl was fidgeting in a most aggravating way, squirming on her seat as if she had ants in her pants. Didi sighed and glanced at her watch. She had been sitting here waiting to see Carlos Baptista for one and a half hours. Her lunch hour was past, she would get back to her job as receptionist at the hotel so late that she would more than likely be fired. But if she collected the fifty thousand dollar reward who cared . . .

To think that she, an intelligent girl, had been taken in by a boy like Nino. She had given him everything. Her trust . . . Her body . . . She blushed at the intimacies they had shared together.

He had used her. He had wanted to get to Al King and he had used her. All that talk of love . . . Oh, what a fool she had been.

He had cleared out of his room, she had gone there on Sunday. He had vanished . . . What a *filho da puta!* But she would fix him. She would tell Carlos Baptista everything she knew. And she would get the fifty thousand dollar reward. Probably.

Jorge sat in a corner of the office smoking a long thin Havana cigar. He looked drawn and haggard. He had not slept since his daughter's disappearance.

Carlos was at his desk wearily interviewing the applicants who had answered his call for information. Fifty thousand dollars ap-

521

peared to have attracted every nut in Rio. They filed in, one by one, with their unbelievable stories.

One woman, apparently well-dressed and respectable, claimed that Al King was under her skirt at that very moment fucking the life out of her. 'If you want him I can open my legs and reveal him,' she confided. 'But you must hand me the cheque first.'

The young secretary, taking copious shorthand next to Carlos, blushed to the roots of her hair. The police chief sitting on Carlos's other side chewed complacently on a pencil stub and ordered, 'Next one in.'

In three hours they had not received one piece of relevant information.

Then the girl came in, thin, nervous, wearing spectacles. She stated her name and address and place of work. She told them her story.

Jorge leaned forward at the mention of Nino's name. The secretary took notes. The police chief chewed on his pencil. Carlos picked his teeth with a wedge of paper.

'Is that all?' the police chief asked when she had finished.

'It's all I know. But I can assure you that Nino will lead you to Al King.' She stood anxiously. 'Do I get the reward?'

'*When* we find this Nino, *if* he leads us to Al King, *then* you get the reward,' the police chief replied.

She looked disappointed. 'I'll probably be fired...'

Carlos intervened, 'I'm sure you've been most helpful. Stop by my secretary on the way out and she will give you fifty dollars for your trouble.'

'Fifty? But I thought the reward was fifty thousand?'

'For information leading to Al King. If your information finds him then you get the money.'

Didi shrugged and left.

The men looked around at each other. 'It looks like Nino is the one we want...' the police chief said, 'at least we have a lead on him now.' He reached for the phone and issued instructions to a minion on the other end.

Jorge was not surprised. As soon as he had heard the description of the 'mechanic' on the plane he had known it was Nino. He had known he was involved. But he had been unable to tell the police anything. He was ashamed to admit that he had allowed his daughter to keep company with a boy about whom he knew nothing. Now at least they had an address.

The next person was ushered in. A plump girl in a floral dress.

'My name is Juana Figlioa,' she said, 'and I work at the airport.

I helped a boy called Nino get aboard the Al King plane . . .'

Finally they were getting somewhere.

Of course the party in Doris Andrews' honour had been cancelled.

'I'm sorry . . .' Evita had apologized.

'Don't be silly,' Doris had replied, 'as if you could host a party at a time like this . . . And anyway I didn't come here for parties. I came to see you . . .'

She was by Evita's side constantly, comforting and sustaining her. It suited Jorge perfectly. He wanted to be alone with his own personal grief. He didn't want to share the misery and uncertainty he felt. He did not want to share the feeling that somehow it was all his fault . . . That if he had listened to Evita . . . taken more care of what Cristina was doing . . . who she was seeing . . . heeded Evita's intuition about Nino instead of laughing at her fears . . .

In the event the two women were left alone together, and by Monday Evita was convinced she had only got through the long weekend because of her friend's support.

'How is your husband?' she finally remembered to ask.

'I am divorcing him,' Doris announced simply. 'It's not enough that he has had me watched and followed throughout our entire marriage. It's not enough that he had been unable to engage in sex. I understood. I was the perfect wife. But last week he became frighteningly violent towards me. He came home from the studio one day and beat me up. Yes – physically beat me. I don't know why. I moved out immediately. Let him have the mansion and cars for now. My lawyer will see I do not suffer. My trip here was already planned, so I came here anyway.'

'I'm glad you did,' said Evita. They sat in the conservatory, a glass-walled, plant-filled room, overlooking the swimming pool. 'What will you do when you leave here?'

Doris shook her head. 'I don't know. Perhaps a trip to Europe. Would you like to come with me?'

'I can't make any plans.'

'Of course not.' She reached for Evita's hand and squeezed it gently. 'But when you can . . .'

Evita allowed her hand to remain in the older woman's. It was so comforting . . . It made her forget . . .

'Why don't you lie down?' Doris asked. 'You must be tired.'

Evita nodded. She *was* tired. The doctor had placed her on tranquillizers – a heavy dose.

Doris led her to the bedroom. 'Jorge told me he would be home late,' she remarked. 'He asked me to stay with you.'

'You don't have to . . .' objected Evita.

'I know I don't have to. I want to. We're friends . . . I want to help. Turn, let me unbutton your dress.'

Evita did as she was told. She knew what was going to happen but was powerless to stop it . . . She didn't want to stop it . . .

The dress slipped from her body, fell to the ground. She stepped over it and walked to her bed.

She closed her eyes and waited for Doris to join her.

She didn't have to wait long.

'Do you want to fly to Rio ?' Cody asked.

'No. What good would that do ?' Linda replied.

'I just thought it might help to be on the spot.'

'Would you come ?'

'If you wanted me to.'

'I can't eat this.' Linda pushed the salad plate away and stared around the restaurant. 'Look at them all stuffing their faces – as if they care.'

'They probably don't even know Dallas and Al.'

'Why do you always say Dallas and Al ?' Linda snapped. 'Paul's on that plane too, you know. Paul and Evan. Bernie and other people. You're as bad as the goddamn television – Dallas and Al – as if no one else is with them.'

'You don't have to get mad at me. You know how I feel . . .'

She was contrite. 'I'm sorry, Cody. I shouldn't be taking my feelings out on you. It's this not knowing . . . It's so awful. It would almost be better if they were all dead. If the plane *had* crashed and been found – at least we would *know*.' She touched his arm. 'I don't mean that. I don't know what I mean any more. I'm so mixed up. It's all such a shitty game. Do you know I am making more money out of this than I ever made in my life ? My pictures of Dallas are selling time and time again – the same with my stuff on Al. It doesn't seem right to make money on it.'

'That's the way it goes.'

'Oh, Christ, Cody, isn't there anything we can *do* ? I feel so helpless sitting here.'

'We can go to Rio. Say the word and I'll get the tickets.'

'I don't know . . . What do you think ?'

'I think we should go.'

'You're right. Let's do it. But I want to pay my own way. Understood ?'

'If you say so.'

*

Jorge went with the police to Nino's miserable one-roomed apartment. The two girl informants had been able to furnish them with the address.

They busied themselves taking fingerprints and searching for information. The only things Nino had left behind were a broken pair of black sunglasses, and a filthy T-shirt. The sordid room yielded few clues. A cracked ashtray overflowing with cigarette butts, hairpins scattered over the dirty grey sheet on the bed – obviously not his. And a single gold earring was discovered under the bed. A rough hoop for pierced ears – the kind Cristina used to wear.

'Does it belong to your daughter?' the police chief asked, thrusting it into his hands.

Jorge hesitated, weighing the earring gingerly. He was sure that it was Cristina's. 'I don't know,' he replied. 'I can't be certain.'

How could he admit that his daughter had been in this dirty little room? It was unthinkable that she might have lain on that filthy bed.

'Perhaps you can ask your wife,' the police chief said.

'Yes,' agreed Jorge. What did it matter anyway whose earring it was? The important thing was finding Cristina.

Alive or dead, he had to know.

seventy

Sunday night was the worst yet.

Nino kept everyone awake with his unearthly screams and agonized writhings. As if that was not enough, sometime before dawn, the rain started again. A heavy torrential rain that poured down spilling through the blown-out windows.

A meal of tinned caviar, maraschino cherries, and champagne seemed to have disagreed with everyone, and the toilet was occupied all night. Since the wastes could not be flushed away, a horrible stench was coming from the tiny bathroom off the bedroom.

'We'll all get sick,' Dallas told Al, 'we should never have used that bathroom.'

'So what else was there to do? Jump off the plane every time you wanted to pee?'

'Al. We've got to face facts. I don't think anyone's going to find us here.'

'I told you – tomorrow I'll search for the rest of the plane. With luck we'll be able to radio for help. If I hadn't have had to drag Cristina and Nino back I would have found it today.'

'And if you don't find it? If the radio doesn't work?'

'We'll think again.'

'We've been here two days and only seen one plane fly over. I don't think anyone's looking for us – not here anyway. We'll have to make an attempt to get out of here ourselves.'

He laughed drily. 'Are you kidding?'

'No, I'm not. I think it's our only hope. We'll all die if we stay here.'

'Worry about it when we can't use the radio.'

'But we're wasting time.'

He groaned and held his stomach. 'Christ! Remind me never to eat caviar again.'

'You don't want to listen to me, do you?'

'What makes you think you know what you're talking about?'

'I keep on telling you. I never had much education – the only kind I *did* get was about animals and survival. We have to find water – a river. If we do that and follow it, eventually we'll find people.'

'Tell me tomorrow.'

'We're not getting any stronger, we should set off soon.'

'What about the others?'

'We'll find help and send it back for them.'

'You're kidding. That lot alone out here wouldn't last five minutes.'

She sighed. 'Since when did *you* start thinking about other people?'

'Since I found you.'

By morning the rain was heavier than ever. Al had set out any receptacle they had to catch it in, and it enabled everyone to have a wash.

'Shit – I always did hate Monday mornings,' Bernie complained, as Dallas bathed his wound. It didn't look too bad. The skin was beginning to pucker and close up.

Cathy's leg was very infected and Dallas was convinced it would have to come off. Impossible. They didn't even have a knife. The only cure for gangrene was amputation. Cathy could barely open her eyes.

'What shall we do?' Dallas whispered to Al.

526

'There's nothing we *can* do. Even if we cut the leg off she'd die anyway.'

'Yes, but we would have tried.'

'And put her through a terrible scene – for what?'

'I know you're right, but I can't help feeling so helpless.'

He put his arm around her and held her close. 'I love you,' he whispered. 'Whatever happens I love you. I've been using women all my life – good for a fuck – nothing else. And then came you. I've waited for you thirty-eight years – don't feel helpless. You've made my life worth living.'

'For how long? Another week? Because if we stay put that's about all we'll have. Maybe two if we're lucky.'

'You ever tried positive thinking? I'm going to see if I can find the other half of the plane.'

'In this rain?'

'You wouldn't want me to just sit around.'

He found the front half of the plane two hours later. The vultures led him to it – huge, decadent scavengers, circling above the wreck, taking their time between sweeping down and pecking at the remains of their human victims.

There was a strong smell of petrol mixed with burnt flesh. So strong that Al found it difficult to approach.

He forced himself to do so in the hope that there would be something of use he could salvage. Certainly no radio could have survived, that was obvious. But he had to look.

The nose of the plane was dug deep into the ground. Al walked around it, peering through the front aperture. What he saw made him sick to his stomach. Something that had once been a human being, now a crawling maggotty mass of open flesh and bone. He moved closer – the interior was just a charred wreck, and more maggot-ridden bodies. Oh Christ . . .

He turned and threw up, retching on an empty stomach. Then suddenly he saw a huge snake. He backed away, still sick to his stomach.

No fucking radio. What next?

The image of the maggot-ridden bodies danced before his eyes. Christ! That was one hell of a way to go.

He stumbled on through the dense undergrowth, then sat down at the foot of a giant tree and tried to shut out what he had seen, but the image would not leave him. He closed his eyes, but that made the vision worse.

It was all so frigging hopeless. Dallas was right. The only way out was if they did it themselves. Nobody was going to find them. Nobody was going to rescue them. It was yesterday's news already.

Do you remember Al King?

Who?

The rain lasted until midday, crashing through the trees relentlessly, marooning the plane in a sea of mud. Then it stopped, quite suddenly, and the sun appeared almost immediately, and soon the heat was back – the humid, steamy jungle heat, which could render you exhausted in a matter of minutes.

Nino was in a bad way. His eyes and tongue protruding, his limbs stiffening, and all the while he was crying out and moaning.

Cristina sat on the floor next to him and fed him sips of water, but they all knew he was dying, and that there was nothing they could do to save him.

Since Dallas had persuaded Evan to change his clothes he seemed much brighter, and was eager to help out if he could. He didn't seem to realize where they were though, and addressed Dallas as either Nellie or Edna. He did whatever she told him, and another pair of hands was a great help.

Of course she knew he was still in shock, and suffering from some kind of amnesia along with it, but at least he was no longer huddling in his seat incommunicado.

Paul had become very morose. He woke up complaining of stomach pains and a headache, and he was indeed very hot. Dallas got out the thermometer from the first aid box and took his temperature. He had a fever of 105 degrees.

As if they didn't have enough problems.

She lay him down, covered him with blankets, and fed him three aspirin from their fast-dwindling supply.

How had she become den mother? She would have liked to have crawled into a corner and collapsed too – but now with Paul ill and Al away she seemed to be the one they all depended on. Not that Paul had been much help – it was Al who was keeping everyone's spirits up. He was incredible. She allowed herself a brief moment of pleasure to think about him. God, if anyone should have fallen to pieces it should have been him. So spoiled, so used to crooking a finger and having everything done for him. He had certainly come up trumps.

She remembered their time together on the plane before the storm. Lying next to each other. Exploring each other's bodies.

It had all been so beautiful. Touching his naked body had been like touching a man for the first time. At last she had known what Linda was talking about. Known a feeling of such tense expectant pleasure that she had never wanted to leave his side. She had *wanted* to do things to him that she had been *forcing* herself to do to other men all her life. They had been unable to do anything except look and touch. The plane had forced them from the bed into the safety of the couch. Safety – that was a laugh. And all the time, while they had been locked in, the plane had been heading for disaster.

She sighed deeply. If they were going to die at least they would be together.

If they were going to die she wanted to possess him at least once. But how could they . . . here . . . on the plane . . . with everyone watching.

'Hey – Dallas baberooney,' Bernie's voice boomed out, 'wacha all say to a little lunch? I am personally wasting away. Can you imagine *me* thin?'

'Never!' she laughed. At least he was recovering; it was more than she could say for Cathy who had lain silently all day – not even strong enough to moan. 'What's your choice, Bernie? Nuts, crisps, or a couple of lumps of sugar?'

'How many crisps?'

'Your share would be about six.'

'Sound like a feast.'

'Come on, Evan, help me prepare lunch!'

Al leaned back against the tree trunk and watched the wild life. As the rain stopped, insects, birds and animals seemed to pop out from everywhere. A beautifully coloured parrot perched on a tree branch and communicated with another amazingly plumed bird. All around him on the ground tiny insects scurried around. A school of very large ants marched past. An enormous spider weaved an elaborate trap.

Suddenly a whole troop of monkeys came skipping about amongst the trees, leaping from branch to branch. Al grinned. They were all managing to survive pretty well. If they could do it . . . He stood up, feeling better. What was it Dallas had said? We must find a river. Maybe if he followed the monkeys . . . Mustn't get lost . . . Mustn't forget which direction he had come from . . .

He took a lump of sugar from his pocket and sucked on it.

Instant energy. Try to forget the way your stomach really feels. The filthy taste in your mouth. The frigging flies and mosquitoes who had decided to become permanent companions. The wet clothes sticking to your aching body. Thank Christ he had been in good shape to start off with.

He thought of the others waiting at the plane, expecting him to come back with good news. He couldn't let them down. He set off after the monkeys, keeping a wary eye open for snakes. Didn't want to finish up like Nino. Dallas was right, in the jungle you had to keep your eyes open all the time.

Cathy died at four o'clock. She drifted silently away, and it wasn't until Bernie noticed she wasn't breathing that anyone realized.

'We'll have to move her,' Dallas said sadly. 'In this heat her body will decompose very quickly.'

'Bury her next to Luke,' Bernie suggested. Al and Paul had buried Luke some distance from the plane.

'Yes, but I can't do it alone.'

'I'll help you,' said Evan quickly.

'I don't know . . . It will be difficult. Maybe we should wait for Al.'

'Honestly, Nellie, I can help you,' Evan said earnestly.

'Yes I know you can. But I think the best thing is if we get her body off the plane, and then we can bury her tomorrow. It will be getting dark soon.'

Bernie said, 'Jesus Christ – she was a good kid. She handled the whole hijack caper magnificently – I'm gonna miss her.' His voice was all choked up. 'If they'd got us out of this piss hole she could have been saved . . . Jesus . . . maybe she's the lucky one . . . Maybe that's what's in store for all of us . . . Trash out in some friggin' jungle . . .' He slumped down on the bed.

Dallas wrapped the body in a sheet, and with Evan's help lowered it off the plane. She wished Al would get back. It was almost dusk, and the deadly blackness followed soon after.

Paul was hotter than ever, the fever seemed to be getting a grip on him.

Nino's screams of agony were getting weaker, it would be him next.

'I'd better take a look at your bites before it gets dark,' Dallas said to Cristina. The girl had stayed next to Nino all day, not moving at all.

'No . . . not now. Tomorrow.'

'How do you feel?'

Cristina nodded. Her face was a mass of dark purple bruises and cuts. 'Fine,' she mumbled.

'You don't look fine. I want you to have some orange juice.'

'Yes,' agreed Cristina.

Dallas walked to the gaping front of the plane and peered out. No sign of Al, and darkness was closing in. She shut her eyes tightly and said a silent prayer. If anything had happened to him she didn't want to go on. She just couldn't make it.

Evan came and stood beside her. 'Don't worry,' he said, as if reading her thoughts. 'He'll be back, really he will.'

She turned to the son of the man she loved and saw him as if for the first time. He had Al's eyes, widely-spaced pools of jet, and once his acne cleared up and he filled out a little he would be a good-looking boy.

'Thank you, Evan,' she said quietly, 'you've been a great help to me and I want you to know that.'

The darkness hid his blush. 'S'OK, Dallas, I want to help.'

He had called her by the right name. She smiled and took his hand. 'You and me and your dad, we're going to get out of this. Right?'

'Right,' he agreed.

The monkeys led him to a stream. A fast-running rush of clear water that filled Al with buoyancy. He waded in, revelling in the feel of the cold water. He drank some. It tasted fine.

Now if he followed the stream it must lead to a river. Had to. And according to Dallas a river would eventually lead to people.

He was exultant. It was a way out. As Dallas had said it sure beat the hell out of sitting around waiting for some kind of slow death.

He was tempted to start on the journey immediately, and waded some way down the stream. But then he realized it was getting late, and he must go back and tell them what he was going to do. Also he should get some supplies to keep him going – who knew how long it would take? A few cubes of sugar and a bottle of water would not get him far.

It occurred to him that he should have shot one of the monkeys – he had the gun – and they needed meat. Didn't the Chinese regard monkey as some great delicacy?

He had picked up a hefty stick which he used to beat his way through the heavy undergrowth. Sometimes he could hear animals scurrying away as he approached.

He was good at directions, and hoped to Christ he knew where

531

he was going. By the time darkness descended he knew he was not going to make it back to the plane in time, and he swore softly under his breath. Now Dallas would be worried. She would think something had happened to him.

There was nothing he could do. It would be stupid to travel in the dark.

He was mad at himself for having got caught like this. Underneath his anger he was scared. Who knew what jungle animals were kicking around out there. He leaned back against a tree and rested his hand comfortingly on the gun. He wouldn't sleep. It was too dangerous to sleep. Too fucking dangerous. Within minutes he was snoring.

The ants woke him, they were crawling all over him, biting his exposed flesh, eating him alive.

He jumped up cursing, and brushed them frantically off. They clung stubbornly. They were everywhere, they had even managed to crawl inside his clothes.

It was dawn, light enough for him to continue his journey.

He stripped off his clothes, shaking the little monsters out of them, brushing them from his flesh. He was a mass of tiny red bites. 'Fuckers!' he screamed, venting his anger and feeling better for it.

When he was sure his clothes were ant-free he put them on again, and set off. He was nearing the plane when he heard the noises. Animal noises of great ferocity.

He stopped, his blood chilling, and approached cautiously.

A few yards from the plane two jaguars tore at a human body, pulling it between them like a rag doll. Blood was everywhere as they picked and bit at the flesh.

Al's hand tightened on the gun, his only protection. He was immobilized with shock. Maybe it was Dallas . . . Evan . . . Paul . . .

Maybe they were *all* dead.

The animals could have leapt aboard the plane during the night. They could have picked off their human victims one by one . . .

He remained frozen to the spot until they finished, and strolled off fully satisfied.

Still Al couldn't move. He was paralysed with horror.

A monkey swung down off a tree, inspected the bones, squatted beside them.

Slowly Al stepped forward, the monkey skipped off. There was nothing human left to recognize.

Al hauled himself aboard the plane. Curled up in a seat at the front was Dallas. She was asleep. In the seat behind her Evan slept.

Further down the plane Nino lay on the floor, Cristina crouched beside him. Nino's eyes were wide open and staring in a sightless fashion. Al knelt, felt for his pulse. He was dead.

Cristina didn't say anything, but tears were falling down her face. She knew.

He continued through to the bedroom section where Bernie and Paul shared the bed. Cathy was no longer there. With a sick feeling he knew who the jaguars had been eating. He only hoped to God she had been dead when they had got her. Then he realized that she must have been – probably died yesterday, and been put off the plane without being buried. He couldn't help being angry. Who could have done a stupid thing like that?

He looked longingly at the bed. What wouldn't he give to just flop out and get a few hours' real kip. What was Paul doing on it anyway? Nothing wrong with him. Dallas should have the bed. She was working harder than anyone. He would soon sort *that* out today.

He went back down the plane and slid into the seat next to her. He touched her lightly on the arm. She woke with a jump, 'I knew you would come back,' she said softly. 'What happened? I was so worried. Cathy died.'

'I know.' He decided not to tell her what he had seen.

'Tell me what you found.'

'The plane. No survivors. No radio.'

'Oh . . .' Her face fell.

'But I found a stream. I was going to follow it but it was getting late. I was thinking about what you said. The only chance we've got of getting out is doing it ourselves. I'm going to do it . . . I'll find help and come back.'

'I'm coming with you.'

'No way. It's dangerous. You'll stay here.'

'Oh no, I won't. You think I can just sit around and *wait* in the hope that you'll make it. I'm coming too – there is no argument.'

'Oh yes there is . . .'

Her eyes became dangerously narrow. 'I know more about jungles than you do. I know about animals, plants. I know what's safe to eat . . . things like that. *I am not staying here.*'

'We'll talk about it.'

'Nothing to talk about. This is our fourth day here, nobody's going to come for us.'

'The others . . . We can't leave them alone.'

'We'll take them with us . . . They'll die here anyway when the food and water run out.'

'You're a stubborn bitch.'

'The hell I am. We're talking about survival, Al. *Our* survival. I want to make it – staying here means certain death. The other way there's a chance.'

'I don't know . . .'

'Well, I do.'

The rest of the day was not good for any of them. Nino had to be buried, and Cristina did not want to be parted from the body. 'He knows where Louis is,' she explained patiently to anyone who would listen, 'and I want him to tell me.'

Paul was still running a high fever, alternately hot and cold, sweating and shivering.

Bernie was coughing up blood, fat globules.

The heat was unbearable. The metal parts of the plane attracted the sun filtering through the trees like a magnet, until it was like being in the middle of a giant sun reflector.

Flies and mosquitoes were worse than ever, bothering everyone incessantly. And the larvae popping obscenely from Cristina's arms had to be dug out with a pair of tweezers while she screamed in pain.

Evan was sick and unable to stomach any food. As soon as he ate even the smallest thing he was beset with terrible cramps.

The plane's odour was getting worse, a sickening mixture of stale sweat and excrement.

'Staying here is making everyone ill,' Dallas told Al. 'The sooner we leave the better.'

He was forced to agree with her. Hellishly hot and stinking during the day. Freezing at night.

They had seen no more planes fly over. The portable radio had given one last crackle and stopped functioning.

'If everyone can walk we'll leave tomorrow,' he said.

Dallas prepared back packs for each of them to carry. A blanket, a towel, their share of food and a bottle to keep their water in. She organized a separate medicine bundle containing bandages, ointment, and the rest of the pain killers.

Wednesday Paul was not well enough to travel, so they lost another day. But by Thursday morning his temperature had receded, and although he was weak, he was able to walk.

Leaving the plane was like leaving home. They had slept there for six nights. At least it had been a base, a place of shelter. But it was now riddled with insects and unfit to spend one more night in.

They made a motley procession. Al in the lead, followed by Cristina, then Bernie, Paul, Evan, with Dallas bringing up the rear. 'If we meet any wild animals,' Al joked, 'we'll frighten them to death!'

Progress was slow, and it took them nearly the whole day to reach the stream, a journey that had only taken Al a few hours before. He detoured so that they wouldn't have to pass the nose of the plane with its maggot-ridden occupants, and for a while he thought they were lost. But his sense of direction had not deserted him, and eventually they arrived at the stream.

'We'll stay here overnight,' he said. They were all dripping with sweat and nobody argued. They dumped their back packs and collapsed on the mossy ground.

'Watch out for giant ants,' Al warned, 'and snakes, and anything else that moves.' He felt he was becoming quite an expert after having survived one night out in the open.

'I'm going to bathe,' Dallas said. She stripped down to her bra and panties and waded into the shallow water. It was heavenly. She lay down and let her hair loose and luxuriated in the tingling freshness of the water. If she closed her eyes she could imagine she was in Palm Springs playing about in the shallow end of a swimming pool. She tried it. It worked.

She felt Al watching her, and opened her eyes and grinned at him.

'Why don't you join me?'

She didn't have to ask twice. He stripped to his shorts and was beside her almost immediately.

Cristina, swallowing her shyness about taking her clothes off in front of these strangers, followed.

Evan thought about it a bit. Should he? Shouldn't he? Would they laugh at his skinny body? Would his jockey shorts reveal anything? It looked so inviting. So what if they did laugh. He took off his clothes and got in.

Bernie, red in the face from the exertion of the trip, waded to the side, rolled his trouser legs up, and stuck his legs in.

Paul watched. His head throbbed. He wanted to join them, but he couldn't muster the strength. The attack of fever had left him weaker than he cared to admit. He kept on thinking about his children – they were both so young – if anything happened to him . . . He lay on the ground and closed his eyes. It didn't bear thinking about.

The bathe in the stream raised everyone's spirits. For a few brief moments they could forget about where they were and just relax. A large frog stood on the bank and watched them. Tiny little fishes swam about in confusion.

'Maybe we could catch a few,' Al suggested, 'I could just fancy a fry-up.'

Evan tried, but they were too small and fast for him. Cristina giggled at his efforts. It was the first time she had smiled since they had found her.

'We had better get out now, the sun's going down . . .' Dallas said.

'Wish I was,' Al muttered.

'Huh?'

He pulled her close to him and whispered in her ear, 'You're never going to believe this but I'm feeling horny!'

'Just now you were hungry . . .'

'All my appetites seem to be at full tilt! Come on – let's take a walk.'

They got out of the stream, dried off and dressed.

'Dallas and I are going to survey the scene ready for an early start tomorrow,' Al said, 'we won't be long.'

'I'll come,' Evan offered.

'No, son. You stay here – keep an eye on things. I reckon as tonight's the first step of our journey we should celebrate and have anchovies for dinner. How about that?'

'One tin,' Dallas said sternly.

'Between six of us? We'll starve to death before we get to the other two tins. I say we open all three and have half a tin each.'

'No. We've got to save what food we have.'

'Shit – we'll probably be out of here tomorrow – let's go for broke and gorge on *all* the anchovies.'

'No,' Dallas objected.

'Yes! We'll put it to the vote. All those in favour shove your hands up.'

Bernie's hand shot up, so did Evan's. Hesitantly Cristina joined them by raising her arm.

'You're outvoted,' Al said, taking Dallas by the arm and picking up his blanket, 'hey, Paul, you going to eat?'

'He's asleep,' said Bernie. 'Don't worry, we'll save his share.'

'Yeah – well, save ours too. We'll be back soon.'

Bernie shook his head in amazement. Al King was certainly to be admired. Not content with getting them all together and marching them through the jungle like some kind of Messiah – he was now ready to knock one off! Unbelievable!

But Christ – he had met his match in Dallas. She was some woman. Some incredible lady.

He sighed, and reached for the anchovies. What the fuck ... If the two of them wanted to do it in the middle of the goddamn jungle then good luck to them. Where there was life there was hope – and God knows they could all do with a little bit of hope ...

Evan watched his father disappear off into the undergrowth with Dallas, and he didn't mind. For the first time in his life he felt he was seeing Al as he really was. A man who cared about other people. He thought about all the hate he had stored up towards this man. Hate and envy ... It all seemed to have dissolved away.

It would have been so easy for Al to have left them all. He was far stronger than any of them, and not wounded. If he travelled alone he would make much better time, have a better chance. But he wasn't leaving them ... He was sticking with them ... Helping them ...

Evan was proud of having Al King for a father. He turned to Cristina, her damp curls surrounded a pinched frightened face. She probably wasn't that much older than him, he hadn't realized that before. In fact he had not taken any notice of her at all, he had been too busy worrying about himself. But she was a girl. She was alone. It must all be a terrifying experience for her.

'How are you feeling?' he asked hesitantly.

'Not so good.' Her eyes were brimming over with tears.

He put a comforting arm around her, half expecting her to shove her away. But she didn't, she moved closer to him and the tears slid silently down her cheeks. 'It's all my fault,' she muttered. 'Louis is dead and it's all my fault.'

'No, it's not,' he said in a kindly fashion. 'You mustn't blame yourself, really you mustn't. Nino would have found a way to get on the plane with or without your help.'

Her eyes widened. 'Do you *honestly* think so?'

'Yes,' he comforted, 'I'm sure he would.'

She stopped crying. 'Can I tell you about it? I must tell someone, it's driving me crazy. You'll understand, I know you will. Can I tell you from the beginning?'

'Of course you can.' Evan replied, 'you can tell me anything you want.'

•

They didn't stray too far from the others. They just walked a few minutes downstream, and then Al lay the blanket on a soft mossy patch of ground and took off his clothes.

Silently Dallas did the same. She lay down on the blanket and stared at him expectantly. Her ribs were badly bruised, but apart from that she had suffered only a few bites.

'I'll be gentle,' Al said quietly, lowering himself on top of her. His lean body was a mass of bites, scratches, and little cuts that seemed to be healing.

'I love you,' she whispered, arching her body to meet his.

'Yeah?' he questioned. 'That's funny cos I love you too. Never thought I'd say that – to anyone.' He entered her, and slowly moved back and forth. She moved with him, welcoming him into her body with a passion she never knew she possessed.

'Tell me when you're ready,' he muttered, 'I'm not as strong as I used to be!'

'I love you.'

'Christ!' he shuddered, '*I love you too. Chriiist!* This must be a record! Son-of-a-beetch!' He climaxed, collapsing on top of her, his body ridden with spasms.

She came immediately after him, sighing his name, raking his back with her nails. They rolled across the blanket still joined together.

'God Almighty!' Al started to laugh. 'I haven't come that quickly since I was in *school*! I just blew my reputation in one fell swoop!'

She laughed with him. 'What reputation?'

He moved his hands appreciatively down her body, 'When you haven't eaten for a week I guess it's got to effect your sex life. I feel like . . .'

'Good I hope.'

'Pretty goddamn good. I've got sixteen flies dive bombing my ass – and hey – just a minute – how was it for you?'

'Pretty goddamn good!'

'I mean was it like you wanted it to be?'

'It was beautiful, incredible, everything I knew it would be with you from the first moment I ever set eyes on you. I'm not too mad about the setting – but the event . . . Well . . . What can I say?'

'I love you, lady. You know that? You know that's something I've never told anyone in my whole life. *NEVER*. Sex was sex. A fuck was a fuck. Women were just something to stick it into – get rid of the dirty water – a joke. Wow – I am here to tell you I have humped in a lot of strange places in my time – but this . . .'

'So have I.'

'Don't go trying to get one up on me.'

'Who's trying? I just am not very interested in hearing all about the places you've screwed in.'

'You're right. It's past news. Jesus!' He slapped ineffectually at his posterior. 'I am getting killed! I don't think these little mothers have had such a good meal in a long time. Come on, let's get dressed and back while I've still got the strength!'

They both stood up, shaking their clothes out before putting them on.

'Hey . . .' Dallas questioned, wriggling into her jeans.

'Yes?'

'If we ever get out of this . . .'

'Don't say if – say when.'

'*When* we get out of this . . . What do you want to happen with us, Al?'

'I want whatever you want. We'll be together – buy a house together – have fun together. You name it.' He knocked a spider out of his shoe before putting it on. 'What do *you* want?'

'I'll tell you if . . . *when* we get out of this.'

He stroked her neck, and said seriously, 'I want to know now. Do you feel like I do? Do you want to spend the rest of your life with me?'

She buttoned up her shirt. 'Yes, and the way we're going it looks like I will. Come on – the light is fading and I'm not walking in the dark.'

'Don't be flip. I'm trying to tell you something. I'm trying to give you words . . . I *need* you. I *love* you. Understand?'

She nodded.

He stared at her. 'As long as you understand . . . Christ! I could get another hard-on just looking at you!'

'I look horrible.'

'You'll never look more lovely.' He took her hand and they started to make their way along the side of the stream back to the others. When they were nearly there he stopped. 'I want you to know,' he said quietly, 'that was beautiful.'

She kissed him. 'Mutual.'

He grinned. 'And now I've got a tin of anchovies to look forward to. This could turn out to be the best day yet.'

Friday morning they set off early, everyone in quite good spirits.

By noon they were sweat-stained and exhausted, moving slowly through the ever-thickening undergrowth, finding it difficult to

539

breathe, under constant attack from the vicious horse flies and mosquitoes. To make matters worse, the stream, instead of getting bigger and leading them to a river, was diminishing in size, and becoming just a tiny trickle of water.

Al knew that the whole morning was wasted. They would have to go back the way they had come, and set off down the stream in the other direction. He was loathe to suggest it. But it had to be done.

'We'll have to turn around,' he said, 'we're getting nowhere fast.'

'Can't,' Bernie gasped, collapsing to the ground, 'can't take another fuckin' step.'

'Let's have a break,' Dallas suggested.

It was hours before Al could persuade them to move again, and then it was just a question of slogging back the way they had come earlier in the day. By dusk they were back at their original camping ground. This time none of them could summon the energy to bathe. They flopped out on their blankets after sharing a precious tin of caviar, and slept.

The expectation of getting out of the steamy jungle alive was slowly dying in each and every one of them.

Except Al. Nothing seemed to daunt him. 'We'll set off tomorrow at dawn,' he told them. 'It will be cooler then. OK everyone? Want to see you ready to go bright and early.'

'You missed your fuckin' vocation in life,' Bernie muttered grimly. 'You shoulda bin' a fuckin' sergeant major!'

seventy-one

By Wednesday Cody had booked himself and Linda on a flight to Rio. He picked her up at her apartment, and they drove straight to the airport.

Cody had not been sure how to handle the hotel reservations. Would Linda want to share with him? Or would she be furious if he booked them into the same room? In the end he had decided to play it safe, and reserved two separate rooms. He made sure they were adjoining – just in case.

He wasn't quite sure how to play it with Linda. He liked her tremendously – but she was so cool and independent – and he didn't want to blow it by behaving in a way she might misconstrue.

Since the plane's disappearance physical contact between them had terminated abruptly. He understood. He wasn't feeling exactly horny himself. But he hoped that eventually things could go back to the way they were. They had been at the beginning of what promised to be an exciting and maybe long-lasting affair. Relationships like that were few and far between. Hollywood was full of Carol Camerons. But how many Lindas did you come across?

The airport was crowded, people bustling back and forth – meeting, greeting, hiring cars, buying souvenirs, or just standing around. Cody saw a couple of people he knew – a fellow agent who a couple of months ago wouldn't have bothered to give him the time of day – and a minor actress who greeted him like an intimate friend. He could swear he had never met her before.

Linda walked over to the magazine stand to pick up the newspapers.

'Who's your friend?' the agent asked admiringly. 'I like her style.'

Proudly Cody followed Linda with his eyes. She *did* have a lot of style. She looked coolly chic in a white safari suit, her jet hair pulled severely back, and purple-tinted shades hiding her eyes.

'Linda Cosmo,' Cody replied, 'a photographer from New York.'

'Sure,' said the agent enthusiastically. 'I've seen her work – she's got a six-page spread in *People* this week. I never realized she looked like that . . . You want to trade numbers?' He indicated his actress, who, as if on cue, broke into a large toothy Californian grin and said in a flowing Southern accent, 'You all know if they've cast a new "Man Made Woman" yet? I don't usually test, but I got to thinking that maybe I might – you know – just for once. It's a perfect part for me.'

Cody had yet to meet an actress who didn't think every part written was the perfect one for them.

'I don't know,' he said. 'As far as I'm concerned it's a little early to start putting in a replacement.'

'Early?' hissed the agent. 'You don't think they're gonna *find* that Dallas broad do you?'

'As a matter of fact I am flying to Rio now.'

'Why – anything new happen?'

'No – but . . .'

The agent laughed. It was more of a rude sneer than a laugh. 'Chasing a dead client – come on – that ain't gonna put shekels in your pocket. She's dead, man – face it. That plane probably crashed into the sea – they'll never find it.'

It was not the first time that this sentiment had been expressed to Cody – although perhaps not in such harsh terms. His mother over a cold fish dinner the previous evening, had clutched him warmly by the hand. 'I think if she was alive they would have heard something by now,' she offered. 'Better she's dead than in the hands of those foreign maniacs.'

The two theories given wide news coverage were either that the plane had strayed off its flight path and crashed, or that some sort of terrorist organization had managed to hijack it.

The crash theory was now gaining the most strength. The plane had been missing five days. If a ransom demand was to be made it would have been done by now.

Cody bid a curt goodbye to the agent and actress, and joined Linda at the newstand.

She waved a newspaper at him. 'Page three,' she said in disgust. 'From headlines to page three.'

'It's old news,' replied Cody wearily.

'If only we knew . . . Oh God . . . If only we *knew* . . .'

Jorge did not want to show the earring to Evita. Did not want to be forced to admit that perhaps he had been wrong – that perhaps Cristina *had* been sharing Nino's bed. Evita's positive identification of the earring would prove facts that Jorge did not wish to face.

Wasn't it bad enough that his daughter was missing – probably dead. He couldn't even begin to come to terms with *that*. Cristina was the best thing that had ever happened to him – an extension of his love for Evita – more, really, because while Evita was his wife, she was also a separate entity – another human being – a person from an entirely different background. Of course that didn't bother him – never had – but Cristina was his own blood. She was all he had. She was the other children Evita had not been able to have. The son that was never to be.

Jorge swore softly under his breath and turned to look at his sleeping wife lying beside him. How beautiful she was, but he was glad that Cristina resembled him and not her. It would be somehow incestous to have a daughter the image of your wife – besides which, he was proud of Cristina's dark earthy looks. She was a born Maraco through and through. No one could dispute *that*.

He had returned to the house late the previous evening and slipped quietly into bed so as not to disturb his wife. Thank God Doris Andrews had arrived when she did. She had been a tower of strength, looking after Evita day and night, moving in to the spare room to be near her. What a magnificent friend she had turned out to be.

Evita stirred in her sleep, turning restlessly and pushing the covers from her. The beige satin nightgown she was wearing had slipped from one of her breasts. Ordinarily Jorge would have been instantly aroused. But not now – in fact it irritated him, and he pulled the covers over her and left the bed.

He knew he was not being supportive towards his wife. He knew he was rejecting her at the time she needed him most – but he had to go through this alone. Cristina was somehow more his than hers – maybe it was the strong resemblance – maybe it was the fact that she was his only child. Who knew? Whatever it was his grief was personal and could not be shared – with anyone.

He shaved and dressed, then went in his study and wrote a brief note to accompany the earring which he left on Evita's bedside table. He wanted to go straight to Carlos' office. Today might be the day they got some news.

Silently he left the house, climbed into his Maserati and drove quickly away.

Doris Andrews watched him from the guest bedroom window. She waited a few minutes, then smiling softly to herself she padded along to Evita's bedroom. She locked the door and climbed into the space that was still warm from Jorge's body. Confidently she waited for Evita to awaken.

Talia Antonios strode purposefully down the street. She was a tall, arrogant-looking girl clad in a smart brown linen suit. Her red hair was cropped close to her head, and she wore very little make-up.

She swept into the building that Carlos Baptista owned, and took the elevator to the eighth floor which housed his private suite of offices.

A secretary glanced up at her. 'Yes?'

'I have an appointment,' Talia said, 'ten o'clock.'

'Oh yes – Senor Baptista said for you to go right in.' The secretary indicated the way.

Talia strode through the door without bothering to knock.

Carlos, sitting behind his desk, was quite startled by the girl. For a start she was exceptionally tall, and secondly she bore down on him so intensely that he thought for a moment she was going to sweep right round his desk and hit him. She had that kind of look about her. Tough and uncompromising. Carlos was pleased that the chief of police and Jorge Maraco were stationed in an adjoining office with a tape recorder. She was only a woman – but there was something horribly violent about her – betrayed in her icy grey eyes. On the telephone he had sensed this. Known by instinct that here was someone who really did have some information for sale. She had requested that they meet alone. No police. Nobody official.

She paused at his desk and glanced around the office. 'Let's go for a walk,' she said. Hardly the opening line he had been expecting.

'A walk?' he blustered, 'what are you talking about? You said on the phone a private meeting – well, here we are alone in my office. What could be more private than that?'

'Plenty of places. The information I have for you is for your ears alone. After I've told you, then make your own decisions. For all I know this place is bugged – So we either walk – or forget the whole thing.'

Carlos hesitated. He wasn't sure what to do. But then he decided a walk would be all right – after all, as soon as he left the office the Police Chief would have his men watching his every move. The girl couldn't kidnap him – the hidden fear of every rich businessman in South America.

'If that's what you want we'll walk then,' said Carlos, getting up from behind the desk, 'but I hope what you have to tell me is worth the trouble.'

Talia nodded. 'I think you'll agree it is.'

The city of Rio de Janeiro was as beautiful as Linda had always expected it to be. She only wished that she was visiting under different circumstances. Her New York agency had suggested that she do a photo story on the trip as soon as she had told them she was going. 'No!' she had protested, 'it would be ghoulish.' But she had brought her cameras anyway – she never went anywhere without them.

Why had she and Cody come there? It wasn't as though they could *do* anything . . . But somehow it was comforting to be nearer. Someone would have to identify the bodies when they were found . . . If they were ever found . . .

For the first time, sitting on the plane earlier, she had finally faced the fact that Paul, Dallas, Al, Evan . . . were all dead.

She had desperately tried to remember the last time she and Paul had been together . . . Really together. But all she could come up with was Tucson, and Melanie bursting in on them. Before

544

that was just a blur of airports and hotels and parties.

She wanted to cry, but tears wouldn't come. And Cody was sitting beside her inquiring after her welfare every two minutes. He was starting to drive her mad with his niceness. It was too much. Right now she would have preferred a parking boy or a Rik – someone who was not personally involved and would act accordingly.

The phone in her hotel room buzzed. It was Cody. He had contracted Carlos Baptista and a car would be picking them up in an hour.

'He wants us to dine at his house,' Cody said.

'I didn't realize this was a social trip,' Linda replied coldly.

'It's not. Apparently something has come up and he wants to tell us about it.'

'They've found the plane?'

'I don't know. We'll find out soon enough. Is your room all right? Do you need anything?'

Yes – I need to be relaxed – I need to be fucked. 'Everything's fine,' she replied. She was tempted to tell him what she really wanted, but somehow she felt he wouldn't understand.

She sighed deeply. Men she could have relationships with would never understand her needs. They would be shocked at how strong her demands could be at times . . . Most men enjoyed sex. But no man enjoyed the thought that he might be used as a sexual object. Yet wasn't that the way men had treated women since time began?

She half thought that she might call Cody back . . . But no . . . he wouldn't understand.

Cody replaced the telephone. It was unfair of Linda to take her rattiness out on him. None of this was his fault. He was as destroyed as anyone about it. If he hadn't sent Dallas off to Palm Springs she might never have got it into her head to go chasing after Al King in Las Vegas. And if she hadn't gone to Vegas . . . then no South America . . . No plane crash . . . Maybe it *was* all his fault . . .

Anyway, he had thought he and Linda had something good going. Had was the operative word – it all seemed to have gone sour.

He thought of banging on the communicating door – but what for? To get another knock back.

Instead he picked up the phone again and placed a call to Los Angeles – better he should take care of business.

*

Evita examined herself in the mirror. The same ivory skin, smooth features, pale blond silky hair. Her eyes were still blue, her breasts voluptuously full.

She looked exactly the same. Glacial, proud, arrogant. A simmering iceberg.

She stared at herself for a while longer – and she hated what she saw – hated the cool blonde perfection that so betrayed her background.

It would all come as such a shock to Jorge. He had always thought of her as so utterly and absolutely his. The thought had probably never entered his head that she was capable of being unfaithful to him. He owned her, didn't he? He had rescued her from a life of poverty? At the best – if not for him – she might have become a waitress – a shopgirl – or because of her exceptional looks perhaps – and it was only a perhaps – a rich man's mistress or high-class call girl. At the start of their marriage he had often told her these pertinent facts. The thought of 'what a wonderful thing he had done for her' was instilled daily. After all she had so much to thank him for. He had bought her parents a house in Sao Paulo, and moved the entire family there. He still, even after seventeen years, paid them a monthly allowance.

Of course she never saw them. Jorge had thought it best that way. 'Forget about your beginnings,' he had told her. 'Your marriage to me is the beginning.'

'My poor little girl' was the pet name he called her as he instructed her in the intricacies of making love. 'Lie like that – legs spread – wider – wider – just like that, my poor little thing.' And he would sink his body into her, sighing with pleasure all the while.

Occasionally – if the mood took him, he would tweak her breasts for a minute at a time. But not enough to get her in the mood – never enough.

He liked her to kneel on all fours whilst he took his pleasure from behind.

He liked her to suck on his penis for hours on end.

In seventeen years of marriage he had never given her an orgasm. Oh, he was generous in other ways. Clothes, furs, jewels. She could have whatever she wanted.

But in all these years . . . Often she had wondered what it would be like with another man . . . But Jorge loved her – in his way. He trusted her . . . He *had* saved her. How could she do that to him?

And then Doris had happened . . . Doris who caressed her body into molten liquid. Seeking and finding with her tongue every pleasure spot ever invented.

Oh God ... Evita shuddered with joy at the very memory. And yet ... how could she feel anything at a time like this?

She continued to stare at herself until she felt a self-hate so strong that it overwhelmed her, and she had to turn away from her own reflection.

How could a woman whose daughter was missing – presumed dead – be so heartless as to embark on a new and frighteningly exciting affair?

It was an impossible situation. If ... when Jorge found out ... he would want nothing more to do with her. Nothing. And she could not blame him.

Her eyes filled with tears and spilled down her naked body.

The house was quiet. Jorge had gone to an important meeting at Carlos' house. Doris was out at a dinner.

Jorge had not suggested she accompany him. Doris had.

Evita's body shook with her own sobs. She kept on thinking of Cristina – her wilful fiery daughter – a woman – but no more than a child really. That child was lying dead somewhere. Dead because of her involvement with a boy called Nino. Evita was sure of *that*. If Jorge had been firmer. If ... If ... If ...

Slowly Evita opened the bathroom cabinet and extracted the bottle of sedatives the doctor had prescribed for her. She tipped them out – all of them. There were plenty. Everyone knew Evita. They knew she was a cool, calm, intelligent woman. It would never even enter the doctor's head to limit the amount of pills he gave her.

She picked up the pills, one by one – and swallowed them down with the help of a tumbler of water. When they were all gone she extracted another bottle from the cabinet. Jorge's sleeping pills – large turquoise capsules. Methodically she swallowed every one of those. Now she was feeling tired. Her body was aching, and she felt a strange sickness.

Unsteadily she walked into the bedroom, and climbed into bed. Her eyes were blurring, distorting everything around her. She closed them, peacefully aware that she would never have to open them again.

Talia Antonios had killed the hope that Al King and his plane were being held somewhere for ransom. In a brisk no-nonsense way, she had explained the situation to Carlos Baptista as they walked through the public park near his office. She had explained about the organization P.A.C.P. and Nino's involvement.

'We were expecting the plane,' she explained without emotion. 'We probably could have claimed that we did indeed have the plane, and collected the million dollars that was to have been our price. But what then? You would have paid the money – and we would not have been able to produce the goods. Not so hot for our reputation – who would have ever paid us ransom money again? We are a serious organization – dedicated to helping the oppressed and the poor. Our work is just beginning. Soon we will be famous for our deeds. We will deal honestly – and people will respect us. If we should kidnap – well – say *you* for instance – then we would demand a suitable ransom and if it was paid you would be returned unharmed. If it was not paid you would be returned anyway – in little pieces. But the point is you would be returned – either way. Are you understanding me?'

Carlos gulped. The woman was obviously mad and had to be handled with extreme caution. He glanced around, hoping that indeed the police were having him followed.

'So,' Talia continued, 'it is quite obvious what must have happened. Nino was able to seize the plane, but unfortunately it must have crashed before it reached us.'

'Perhaps Nino has taken the plane elsewhere,' Carlos suggested.

'Utterly impossible,' Talia snapped. 'Nino is – *was* – dedicated. Circumstances must have arisen to cause the plane to crash. They are all dead, Señor Baptista, and the reason I have come to see you is to know if you wish to pay for the privilege of recovering the bodies?'

'Do you *know* where the plane crashed?' Carlos asked incredulously.

'Not exactly. But for the reward money you have offered – fifty thousand dollars, isn't it? Then I could supply you with an exact flight plan. With that information it would merely be a matter of time before the plane was found.' She paused, then added meaningfully, 'I am sure that you would want to see your son have a proper burial.'

'You *cona*!' Carlos spat in her direction. 'What kind of a person are you? Do you have no feelings? Can you just talk about people being dead – my *son*. You *cona* – I will have you arrested!'

She shrugged. 'For what? You have nothing on me. I would of course deny this whole conversation. I didn't *have* to come and see you, did I?'

548

'I expect fifty thousand dollars was persuasion enough.'

'If you wish to accept our offer have the money in used notes by noon tomorrow. I will telephone you with further instructions. When the money is safely in our possession you will receive the flight plan.'

'I'm supposed to just trust you?'

'I told you,' replied Talia coldly, 'the P.A.C.P. is a very trustworthy organization. If we get the money – you get what *you* want.'

Carlos had related the entire conversation to the Police Chief and Jorge. They were all of the opinion that Talia knew what she was talking about.

'We will pay,' Carlos had finally decided.

'Yes,' Jorge had agreed. He wanted to recover his baby girl's body as soon as possible. Numb with shock he kept this new information to himself and did not even reveal it to Evita.

Talia had informed Carlos that Cristina had been working with Nino. Had helped to execute the whole stinking mess!

Of course Jorge did not believe it. Anyone who knew Cristina would see at once it was a bunch of lies. She had been an innocent party to a series of bizarre events. She was not to blame. No way could she possibly have been knowingly involved in any kind of terrorist plot.

'It looks like a movie set,' Linda muttered, as the chauffeured Mercedes drew up outside Carlos Baptista's palatial white mansion.

'A simple palace . . .' Cody observed.

'I wonder what he is like.'

'He sounds pleasant enough on the phone.'

A butler ushered them into an ornate room and poured them drinks. Then Carlos himself appeared. He greeted them both warmly, hugging Linda as if she was an old friend. She liked him immediately – although physical contact from a stranger would normally have repulsed her.

'The news is not good,' he told them both gravely. 'I think we have to assume beyond question they are all dead.'

Jorge Maraco arrived then, and they went into the dining room and struggled through a meal that no one was really interested in eating.

'Please excuse my wife for not joining us,' Carlos explained. 'As you can imagine . . . she is . . . Louis was her favourite . . .'

549

His voice broke. 'He was a very fine boy. Very good-looking, very intelligent—' he covered his grief with a gruff laugh, 'Not like his father, you know.'

During the course of dinner he explained the situation to them. Telling the story as he knew it, trying to piece together the bits he didn't know. 'So you see . . .' he finished off at last, 'I think we must believe this woman, and with the flight plan we will be able to trace the plane. Without the right information . . . Well – up to now our search planes have come up with nothing. Tomorrow we will pay the money. Tomorrow I think we will find them – God rest their souls.'

Linda was very depressed when the chauffeur dropped them back at the hotel. She wanted to cry, but tears again refused to come.

Cody had lapsed into his own silence.

They rode up in the elevator not saying a word to each other. Outside her door Cody kissed her absently on the cheek. 'Goodnight,' he said quietly.

Goodnight. What was so good about it? She marched into her room, slammed the door, and flopped down on the bed.

Why *had* they come here? What was the point?

Deep down she knew the point. When the plane was found – when the bodies were brought back . . . Well, she wanted to be sure that Paul had someone around who cared . . . It was silly . . . after all, he would never know . . . But all the same she felt that it was only right.

She sighed restlessly. She would never sleep. She felt strung out and tense.

The hell with it! Suddenly she didn't care *what* Cody thought of her. He could take her as she was or not at all.

She jumped off the bed and went to the communicating door. She released the lock on her side, and knocked loudly. 'Cody – hey, Cody – can you hear me?'

It was minutes before he unlocked his side and appeared, wearing a towel knotted around his middle.

'I was just going to take a bath,' he explained. 'What is it?'

'Why don't we bathe together? I've *had* being alone.'

Jorge stayed and drank brandy with Carlos into the early hours of the morning. He did not want to go home. He did not want to be alone. He did not want to face what were more than likely to be proved irrevocable facts.

He dreaded telling Evita, and decided not to tell her anything definite until the plane was actually found.

Dawn was already breaking when he let himself into the house. He went straight to his study and sat at his desk for a while staring at the various framed pictures of Cristina. A pictorial history of her short life. There she was a few hours old – then a saucer-eyed four – at ten, riding her pony – at twelve, reading a book – fifteen, a formal portrait. He had no recent photos – she had suddenly become camera-shy and refused to be photographed.

Wearily he made his way upstairs. Exhaustion was creeping over him, and he wanted to be up early – perhaps go out in one of the search planes.

Eivta was asleep in the darkened bedroom. He barely glanced at her. He threw his clothes off and walked in the bathroom. At first he didn't notice the two empty pill containers. Then he saw them and picked them up curiously. Wasn't one of them his . . . He read the label on the side – 'Jorge Maraco – sleeping tablets.' That was strange . . . He hadn't used them for weeks . . .

He picked up the other empty container. 'Evita Maraco – sedatives.'

He stood very still for a moment – the full implications slowly seeping through to his muddled brain.

Sleeping tablets . . . sedatives . . . empty . . .

He walked into the bedroom.

Evita lay very still, uncannily still.

He took her hand, it was extremely cold.

He felt for her pulse. There was none.

She was dead.

Carlos paid Talia. She kept her side of the bargain and within hours a duplicate copy of the two pages of neatly scripted flight plans were on his desk.

Search planes were in the air almost immediately. For two days they scoured the route, but could spot nothing. This was not surprising because the missing Al King plane had been flying over the dense interior of the Amazon jungle, and to spot a crashed plane beneath the thick foliage was virtually impossible. Even if the wreckage was found everyone knew that by this time there would be no hope of any survivors.

On the Monday the search was called off. Al King and his plane had been missing exactly ten days.

Carlos Baptista held a news conference and revealed the facts about a mystery woman and an organization named as the P.A.C.P. 'In view of the information received we must assume that Senor King's plane did indeed crash, and that he and his fellow travellers died as a result. It would seem futile to continue the search. Al King must be declared officially dead.'

Linda and Cody were on a plane back to Los Angeles the same day.

In New York, Melanie King – soon to be Mrs Manny Shorto – appeared once again on television. 'I am deeply saddened by the news,' she said. 'Manny and I will be praying for them all.' Later that evening Manny and Melanie were to be found hosting what appeared to be a celebration party, and she was joyfully heard to confide to practically everyone in sight, 'Now we can get married at once, don't have to go through all that divorce *shit*!'

In Los Angeles Lew Margolis signed a blonde amazon ex-tennis player to be the new 'Man Made Woman'. He also took a repentant Doris back and announced plans for her to star in a controversial new film about lesbianism.

In New York Aarron Mack announced his engagement to a sixteen-year-old German countess. 'She will be the new Mack girl,' he announced to the world, without so much as a word of condolence about Dallas.

At Malibu beach, Karmen Rush gave an exclusive interview to *Macho* magazine in which she revealed Al King was the most exciting lover she had ever had.

In New York Marjorie Carter snorted that Karmen Rush couldn't have had many lovers.

In London Edna King packed away the last of Al's clothes and sent them to a local charity. She was about to start on Evan's things when she realized she would be late for her pottery class – late for John . . .

Hurriedly she left the house.

In Chicago Van Valda threw a big party. '*In Memoriam Al King*', the quickly printed invitations read. 'Al wouldn't have wanted a wake,' Van puffed, his pipe lodged firmly in the corner of his mouth, 'he would have wanted all of his friends to have a good time.'

Of the two hundred and twenty-three guests, Al had personally known six – and they were only vague acquaintances.

In Long Island, Ed Kurlnik gazed out of his bedroom window overlooking the sea. He sipped at a heavy tumbler of neat scotch.

His hand was shaking. There would never be another Dallas – never. She had been the sexual realization of a lifetime of searching. He regretted ever letting her go.

Meanwhile, the immaculate Dee Dee entertained a senator and a foreign ambassador to a sumptuous lunch served on the terrace. While her twin daughters, Cara and Dana, entertained movie star Ramo Kaliffe on their speed boat.

In Philadelphia the ex-'Miss Miami Beach', now 'Miss Coast to Coast' sat down to write her memoirs. She devoted two whole chapters to Al King, and their 'lasting and meaningful' affair. She devoted one terse line to Dallas – claiming she had been stripped of her title for unseemly behaviour.

In Los Angeles, Glory and Plum hung around outside a rock concert hoping to score a little coke – their new kick. 'Hey – bad news Evan hadda trash out that way,' Plum said.

'Yeah, man,' Glory agreed, 'shame he never had an address for us – he mighta laid a little bread on us in his will.'

'You think he hadda will?'

'Yeah – all these rich dudes got wills.'

'Shit! You're probably right. What a bummer. I guess we really lost out.'

In a recording studio in Memphis, Rosa and Sutch of The Promises were cutting an album track.

'Mothafucker deserved to go that way,' Rosa spat, 'I hope he suffered!'

'Aw,' Sutch protested, 'don't be so hard – he had his good points.'

'Yeah – in bed. Superfuck. Super*prick* more like. Screw the motha. I'm *glad* he's dead.'

In Rio Jorge Maraco wept at his beloved wife's funeral and prepared to start his life afresh.

The past was finished.

You couldn't bring back the dead.

Headlines the world over stopped mentioning Al King.

He had been declared officially dead.

Dead people only made good headlines for one day.

His record slipped rapidly out of the number one slot.

Within days he was forgotten.

A decade later – if he was lucky – his records might be resurrected by a whole new generation. Boddy Holly. Otis Redding. Maybe Al King. Only maybe.

seventy-two

Saturday morning Dallas woke first. The pain woke her, niggly little nips of pain on her tender skin. For a moment she lay quite still, trying to get her bearings. Then she remembered – and it wasn't the nightmare she had hoped – it was real – horribly sickeningly real. Eight days of misery.

She leaped up in a hurry, and attempted to brush the giant ants from her body. They were crawling all over her – they had even managed to infiltrate under her clothes. She screamed in anger – waking the others. The ants were all over Al and Evan also. Soon everyone was standing and brushing off their clothes. Al stripped his off and doused his body in the stream. Dallas followed.

The sun was just beginning to rise, it was very early and still chilly.

Al shivered in the stream, and looked around at his travelling companions. What a motley group. Cristina with her poor bruised and cut face, her body covered in his clothes which were already tattered and torn.

Blood-soaked Bernie – the weight dropping off him at an alarming rate.

Paul – wild-eyed and feverish.

Evan – his skin red and peeling from the incessant sun of the previous day.

And Dallas – his lady – his woman. Nothing seemed to daunt her. She had screwed her luxuriant hair into a ball on top of her head. Her normally olive skin had turned a deep mahogany colour, and without any sign of artifice she still looked magnificent.

'Let's get moving,' Al said, getting out of the stream and drying off.

'What about something to eat?' Bernie demanded, his voice hoarse.

'We'll travel up stream a bit while it's still cool – then we'll take a break – eat something – and set off again.'

'What about him?' Bernie indicated Paul, who had slumped down on the ground.

Dallas knelt and felt his head. 'I think he's got the fever again,' she said earnestly.

Bernie sat down heavily. 'Aw – what the fuck . . . We're never gonna get out of this pisshole. Who the fuck we kidding? We shoulda stayed with the plane . . . We shoulda . . .'

554

'Shut up,' said Al, his voice ominously cold. 'Stop bitching and get on your feet. Our only chance is to keep going – and that's just what we're going to do – even if I have to carry Paul.'

'You're not the friggin' superstar boss out here,' Bernie shouted in a burst of fury. 'I don't have to jump for you here. I can tell you to get fucked. I can tell you what I want!' He laughed hysterically. 'We're all gonna die anyway – even *you*.'

'If that's what you think, Bernie, fuck off back to the plane. *I'm* getting out of this *alive* – and I don't want anyone trailing along who doesn't have faith. You want to go – then do it. We'll give you your share of what's left of the food.'

'Aw . . . shit . . . I didn't mean nothin' . . . course I'm with you . . .'

Evan stood silently watching his father and Bernie argue. He couldn't understand how the fat man could be so stupid. Al would get them all out of it. He had *said* so. Evan had complete confidence that he would do as he said.

'I feel dizzy,' Cristina whispered, 'these . . . *things* in my arms . . . Oh, Evan, they're driving me mad!'

Evan patted her on the shoulder reassuringly, 'Dallas will look at them, she'll put some cream on them.'

Cristina held out her arms. The larvae from the eggs the vicious blow flies had planted were emerging like tiny wriggling worms.

Evan felt his stomach turn over with horror. Her arms were alive with the obscene larvae, digging little holes. 'Dallas,' he croaked, forcing himself not to turn away, 'can you do something about Cristina's arms?'

Dallas was immediately sympathetic, getting out the tweezers, and the cream, prising the larvae out of the girl's arms, and then bandaging them with strips of material.

Al waited impatiently – knowing that every minute lost would mean the sun getting higher in the sky – and the inhuman heat forcing its way through the tree tops.

At last they were ready to set off. Paul was hauled reluctantly to his feet, mumbling incoherently – the fever was getting a grip again. Al supported him on one side, Evan on the other. Cristina and Bernie followed with Dallas at the rear.

Slowly they began the day's journey.

The stream meandered tortuously on, twisting and turning to such an extent that an hour's walking sometimes covered only a few yards.

The mosquitoes and flies followed them – perpetual tormentors – buzzing and stinging every step of the way.

A band of monkeys joined the parade for a while, chattering amongst themselves with avid interest.

Time passed in a confused haze as they staggered and stumbled on. The humidity was so bad that it became difficult to breathe. But gradually the stream began to widen, hardly noticeable at first, but soon developing into more of a river.

Exhausted as he was, Al felt exhilaration. What was it Dallas had said? If we find a river and follow it, eventually we'll find people. He kept that thought firmly in his head as he half-dragged Paul along with him. Evan had dropped back to help Cristina.

They were all getting weaker and weaker. If they didn't get something solid to eat soon there would be no more walking – no one would have the strength. Al thought about the monkeys that had been following them earlier. Roasted monkey sounded like a treat indeed. He had the gun . . . Next time he saw them . . . and then there were many birds, frogs, probably fish now the stream was bigger. When they stopped for the day he would do some hunting.

Paul groaned and nearly fell. Al hoisted him up, 'Come on, me old son, we're going to make it . . .' he said reassuringly – but Paul wasn't listening, he eyes were glazed and staring.

Al glanced back, in a straggly line behind him the others fought to keep up. Another hour, if he could just force everyone to keep going for another hour . . .

The sun burned down. The dense undergrowth along the river bank was changing. Hard roots rose up in ridges along the ground, deep beds of decaying leaves, strange palms and tree ferns. The gigantic buttress trees were becoming less dense, allowing the sun to burn down even more intensely. Al – like Dallas – had a naturally dark skin that tanned easily – but he knew that Evan would be in bad shape from so much sun. He had suffered from sunburn all his life – he took after Edna, who always turned a lobster pink.

Edna. The name stuck in Al's mind. How was she taking it? She must be beside herself. Poor cow. He felt sorry for her. How she must be suffering. The newspapers were probably driving her nuts. The publicity alone must be forcing her into a decline. He wondered if she thought he was dead. He wondered what the world thought. Had they already written him off as dead, or were they still looking and searching? It seemed funny that in eight days he had only heard one plane fly over. But of course, they probably had no idea where to look. He shoved an overhanging bough out of the way and shouted back to the others to watch out for it.

'Can we stop?' gasped Bernie, sweat coursing down his red face.

'Let's give it another half hour,' Al shouted back encouragingly.

Bernie merely groaned in reply. Each step forward was a nightmare. He wasn't sure if he *could* proceed any further. His heart was beating so fast, his mouth was so dry. He was starting to think in terms of death being better than this. To just lie down and die . . . It would be painless . . . just like going to sleep . . .

Al knew he *couldn't* keep going much longer. The extra weight of supporting Paul was draining all his strength.

Paul. There had been no chance to talk to him since his outburst. The hate that had suddenly come pouring forth from his younger brother had shocked Al completely. He had never realized the frustration bottled up inside Paul. He had always thought of him as so together and organized. In a way he had *envied* him. And God knows he had always depended on him. He would be the first to admit that without Paul to push and promote he would never have got anywhere. He *would* have been content to piss and screw his life away.

But surely Paul had known how he depended on him? Oh yes, they had their fights, but he had always listened to him in the long run. He had never argued with his final decision on anything career-wise.

Melanie was the bitch that had forged a barrier of hate. A hate that Al had never once suspected . . .

When they got out of this Al had made up his mind that one way or another he would make it up to his brother. He would show him a love and respect and thanks that Paul obviously did not know existed.

It was funny, really. He had always looked to Paul for everything, and now here he was making his own decisions. Dragging them all through the jungle in the hope of being rescued. Maybe they should have stayed with the plane. Yeah – stayed and starved. Which reminded him, he was going hunting. The next clearing they came to he would call a stop.

Cristina forced her legs to move. On and on, ignoring the cuts and blisters, and the horrible little eggs which were hatching out and eating her skin. *She was being eaten alive. Her arms were being eaten.*

She choked back a sob, and Evan tightened his grip on her. 'Can you keep going?' he questioned.

She nodded mutely. She had done enough harm, she wasn't going to hold anyone up. She would keep going until she dropped.

She thought of her mother. The beautiful blond Evita. The woman she had been so disdainful of – the woman she had sometimes hated.

'Don't question me, mama,' she would scream. And when her mother asked, pleasantly, 'Where are you going today, dear?' she would reply with an unfriendly sneer: 'Out.' She had thought her parents so stupid. Rich bourgois idiots. Nino had taught her that. But now she realized they had only been concerned for her welfare – they had loved her – they were worried about her. Or at least Evita had been. It was easy to fool Jorge – a little kiss on the cheek, a plaintive 'Don't you trust me, poppa?' and he was putty in her hands.

If only she had been honest with them. Told them about Nino at the beginning . . .

She thought with shame of the things she had done, and the tears rolled down her bruised cut face. If only she could wish time back, how different things would be. If only she could wish Louis back . . .

It was impossible.

Dallas heard the planes first, and she called out to Al to stop so that they could listen. They all gazed skywards, and suddenly there they were, two tiny specks far up in the sky.

Silently everyone watched them. There was no point in waving or screaming. Besides, who had the strength?

Like two far-off birds the planes vanished out of sight.

'We may as well rest here,' Al said. He didn't have to say it twice, they all flopped down immediately. 'Watch out for ants,' he warned. 'Dallas, you want to take a look at Paul?'

She came over immediately, putting her hand on Paul's fevered brow, feeling for his pulse. He was shivering in spite of the excessive heat, his body shaking, his teeth almost chattering.

'I thought he'd got over the fever,' Al said. 'He seemed much better yesterday.'

'I think it's more serious,' Dallas replied quietly, 'I think it's something like malaria.'

'Are you kidding?'

'Be quiet, don't let the others hear.'

'Malaria. But that's . . .' he trailed off hopelessly. 'How can we treat it?'

'We can't. I don't know much about it – but special medicine is necessary. Quinine, I think.'

'Jesus!' Al buried his face in his hands.

'I might be wrong,' Dallas said quickly, 'it's just that malaria apparently attacks in spells. In between the victim is weakened – but all right.'

'You mean he'll be OK?'

'No, I don't mean that. It depends what type of jungle fever he's got. I remember my father – he'd had malaria in the tropics at some time – anyway he still used to get occasional attacks – an ague fit, he called it. But he had medicine.'

'How the fuck did Paul get it?'

'Certain mosquitoes carry the germ – it's not difficult to pick up in this kind of climate.'

'Shit! This is all we need, isn't it?'

Dallas felt Paul's forehead again. 'If it is malaria the attack will probably be over by tomorrow – we'll be able to go on – if we can find help . . .'

'If . . . if . . . if we could have found help Cathy could have been saved. Even Nino. What makes you think we're going to find help for Paul?'

She sighed wearily. 'What can I tell you, Al? There's nothing we can do except keep going.'

'I know.'

They lay down in the heat, trying to find a shady patch. Al let his body relax. Dallas shared out the last of the nuts and cube sugar. Now all they had left were three jars of caviar. Fortunately the river water seemed drinkable, so liquid sustenance was no problem.

Paul couldn't eat anything – but Dallas was able to feed him some sips of water. His shivering had stopped and the skin on his body was now burning up with a dry heat. He was delirious and incoherent.

Al didn't know how long he had been resting. Like the others he lay in a sort of stupor – his eyes closed – his mind drifting uneasily.

He was beginning to feel so weak . . . a feeling of physical impotence so strong that to lift his arm was a major effort.

He knew they should be moving on, to stop while it was still light was stupid. Time was all important. Move in the daylight. Rest at night.

He opened his eyes and saw the monkeys – about eight of them. They were unconcernedly swinging and playing on some nearby trees.

Stealthily he reached for the gun and got up.

The monkeys moved on, and Al followed them.

They were moving away from the trees on the river bank and further into the thick foliage.

Christ! How long was it since he had fired a gun? Ten years? Twenty?

He flashed onto a memory of himself at seventeen. Battersea Park funfair, a girl on his arm, and a rifle in his hands. He had been shooting at a fixed target – a series of tin pigeons revolving in a circle. He had scored six out of six – won a mouldy pink teddy bear – and scored with the girl behind the bushes in the car park.

He could remember the scene vividly.

He raised the small gun and fired at the nearest monkey. It fell from the branch with an almost human cry, and the rest of the monkeys made off at full speed.

He hadn't killed it, merely wounded, and the small, almost childlike animal gazed up at him with bright inquisitive eyes.

He hated himself for doing it, but he finished it off with a blow to the head, and carried the still warm body back to the others.

Dallas was awake, so was Evan. They looked at him curiously.

'Did you kill it?' Evan asked.

'No,' snapped Al, 'it fell off a tree complete with bullet hole!'

'How can we eat it?' Evan continued. 'It's all covered in fur.'

'You're going to skin it,' Al said. 'You took biology at school didn't you?'

'Yes . . . But we never skinned monkeys.'

'So now's you chance to learn.'

Evan made a face, but he took out the penknife Al had given him, and squeamishly started the job.

Before nightfall they had feasted on monkey roasted over a fire Al lit with one of their precious matches. It wasn't bad at all – tasted somewhat like rabbit.

Paul still could not eat – but for the others, having a full belly was a luxury indeed.

Al looked around with a sort of pride. He had found them food. His son had prepared it – and they had eaten. It was a good feeling to know that his efforts were helping them to survive.

He slept well and woke very early to see more planes flying overhead. Three of them, in convoy, very fast and very high.

He didn't wake the others – why excite them for nothing? The planes couldn't possibly see them. But maybe at last they were searching. Maybe now search parties might come looking for them on foot.

He wondered for the thousandth time how far they were from

any type of human life. Dallas had mentioned that Indian tribes were supposed to live in the Amazon – and surely there were hunters and traders.

He felt better than he had in days. It was Sunday now. They had been in the jungle for nine days. It seemed like a lifetime – six days waiting for help in the goddamn plane – and three days travelling.

A parrot had settled itself on a tree and was watching him with beady black eyes. He wondered how parrot meat would taste . . .

In the distance a huge snake slithered along. He had learned to ignore them as long as they never came too close. The danger was in stepping on one by mistake.

The interminable flies and mosquitoes had ceased to bother him. They had become a part of everyday life. Cristina was the only one that seemed to suffer from their bites. Her arms were in a dreadful state.

Paul opened his eyes and mumbled, 'What happened? Where are we? I don't remember a thing.' He was emaciated, his eyes sunken into his gaunt face, his arms almost too weak to hold the cup of water Al offered him. But as Dallas had predicted, the fever had left him.

Al explained that he had been sick, but that they were nearing help.

'How'd I get here?' Paul asked.

'He carried you,' Evan said proudly, joining in the conversation, and indicating his father.

Paul looked at Al.

'I didn't *carry* him,' Al objected, embarrassed, 'I just helped him along a little.'

'My brother – the hero,' Paul said mockingly, his voice hardly more than a whisper. But he smiled when he said it, and reached and squeezed Al by the arm. 'Thanks, brother.'

Al looked away. 'I reckon I owed you a favour.'

Dallas was moving around getting everyone ready to set off on the day's journey. Her medicinal supplies were running low. The last of the antiseptic cream was shared between Cristina's arms and Evan's badly burned face.

Foot blisters and sores – which everyone was suffering with – were tied around with strips of material.

Bernie was the last to wake. He shoved Dallas away when she asked to inspect his wound. 'I feel fine,' he snapped. But he didn't look fine. He looked extremely flushed, and his eyes were runny and bloodshot. Dallas hoped that he wasn't coming down with the fever – Bernie there would be no chance of carrying.

They set off, struggling along the tortuous path – fighting their way through the tangled undergrowth until it was almost impassable. Finally Al suggested that they wade along the shallow edge of the river. It was cooler, and the mild current would help their progress.

They had been doing this for about an hour when Al spotted the alligators – huge mud-covered creatures sliding off the opposite river bank and moving lazily through the water towards them.

'Get out of the water!' Al screamed. 'Alligators – get out! For crissakes MOVE!'

The river bank was slime-covered and slippery – it had become much steeper than when they had first entered the water.

Al hauled himself out, grabbing hold of Paul and pulling him to safety.

At the same time Evan helped Cristina out, and followed quickly.

Dallas was also able to move fast, but Bernie – his fat body half encased in the water, seemed paralysed with fear.

'Come on, man!' screamed Al – struggling back along the muddy bank to help.

Dallas leaned over and grabbed Bernie by the arm, trying to pull him. 'Move, Bernie, MOVE!' she yelled, watching in horror as the alligators glided nearer and nearer.

Bernie, stung into sudden action, attempted to climb out. But the mud was so slippery that he fell back – nearly pulling Dallas in with him. The force of his efforts caused his chest wound to open up, and suddenly his shirt was soaked with blood as he tried to stagger to his feet and get out of the water.

By this time Al was at the side to help – grabbing Bernie's arm pulling . . . pulling . . . but the smell of blood had attracted the alligators to move faster, and as Al pulled at one end, the first of the huge reptiles attacked at the other, its massive jaws opening and clamping its ferocious teeth down on Bernie's leg.

He screamed in agony as the alligator tried to drag him deeper into the water. Al wasn't strong enough to hold on – and Bernie's arm was snatched out of his grasp.

They all watched in mute horror as the fat man was pulled struggling and screaming into the centre of the river.

'Isn't there anything we can *do*?' Dallas pleaded. 'God! We must do *something*!'

It was too late anyway. The other alligators had moved silently in on their victim – joining in the attack.

Bernie had disappeared under the water. He never surfaced again.

They waited at the same spot for hours, huddled together. Eventually the alligators slid lazily off, climbing and slithering on to the other side of the river bank and basking in the sun's rays.

No sign of Bernie. It was as if he had never even existed.

'There's no point in staying here any longer,' Al said at last – loath to point out the very obvious fact that there was only a small river separating them from the alligators. If they decided to cross over . . .

Cristina was crying. Evan put his arm around her, and she gazed up at him with very tired eyes. 'I want to be home,' she stated simply.

'We will be,' Evan reassured, 'don't worry.'

The rest of the day passed by in a haze. Blindly they followed Al, struggling along the densely overgrown river bank, too frightened to get back into the water. Driven mad by the mosquitoes and the intense burning sun. Fearful of stepping on snakes. Scratched and bruised by overhanging boughs, and sometimes being forced to wade into the water for a few yards to get round rotting tree trunks which occasionally blocked their way.

Al, in the lead, was more watchful than ever. He could only blame himself for what had happened earlier. It was he who had suggested they enter the water. If they had been on land the alligators would not have attacked.

Every bone in his body ached, and he knew that he should start to look for a suitable place to settle for the night. But when they stopped, while the others rested, he would have to look for food. All they had left was the caviar.

His head ached and his vision was blurring. Every so often he glanced behind. Paul was managing fairly well – dogging his footsteps in a dazed fashion. And behind him, Evan, half supporting Cristina, whispering encouragement to keep her going. And bringing up the rear, Dallas.

It was a horrible thought, but without Bernie they seemed to be moving faster. Had he been slowing them down? Or were they just escaping from the memory of his horrible death?

Eventually they stopped. Al was too exhausted to search for food – so silently they shared a jar of caviar and fell asleep.

In the middle of the night the rains came. Pelting great hailstones stinging them awake.

They couldn't travel, and they couldn't sleep. Huddled together they just had to accept the full brunt of the rain. It didn't stop. It was still falling heavily at the first sign of light, and they set off as soon as they could see, their path made even more hazardous by thick squelching mud.

By midday the rain turned into a storm. Ominous black clouds filling the sky, belching loud rumbles and luminous streaks of lightning.

For the very first time Dallas considered death as an alternative. Where were they going to? What were they struggling for? Perhaps Bernie was the lucky one . . .

To just lie down and sleep. Close your eyes and succumb to the temptation of never getting up again.

She thought she might suggest it to Al. If she could die in his arms . . .

She had lost all idea of time. Her clothes were soaked through, torn and tattered. Her shoes could not last much longer – soon she would have to walk barefoot. She was dizzy and nauseous.

When the rain stopped, they did also, and finished off the two remaining jars of caviar because they were quite literally starving.

Paul had the fever again. Cristina was screaming with the pain in her arms. Evan meticulously dug out the festering maggots and tried to calm her down.

Dallas moved over and lay next to Al.

He was staring up at the sky mouthing some kind of personal appeal.

She rolled close to him. 'We're going to die, aren't we?' Her voice rose hysterically. 'You can tell me, Al. I don't mind, honestly, I don't. *We're going to die . . .*'

He hit her across the face with a strength he no longer knew he possessed. 'The *hell* we are. We're going to *make it*. You understand me? *We're going to make it.*'

She understood why he had hit her, and she was glad he had. To lose control now after all they had gone through. She sobbed and he held her very close. 'I love you, babe,' he said over and over, 'and we're going to make it – you hear me – we're going to make it.'

She believed him, and once more she was calm. Held firmly in his arms she fell asleep.

Tuesday. Eleven days in the jungle. Cristina whimpering quietly to herself. Stomach racked with cramps. Soon they would lose all track of time, and each day would merge into the next – fused together by the rain and the mud – the insects and blistering heat.

Dallas sat up. Insects were crawling over her – she could hardly be bothered to brush them off.

'Where is Al?' she asked Evan.

'He left early, said he was going to find something to eat. I wanted to go with him, but he said I should stay with you.'

Evan was bearing up considerably well – in fact as far as Cristina was concerned he was a tower of strength. It was funny, really – he was hardly recognizable as the surly, bad-tempered boy of days ago.

Paul was still racked with fever, mumbling to himself – his normally good-looking features changed almost beyond recognition. His face was gaunt and flushed. His eyes sunken and surrounded by deep black circles. His arms twitched uncontrollably.

Dallas missed Bernie. He had complained a lot, but he had also managed to greet each day with a wisecrack. She tried not to think about him – it was too painful.

Her clothes were stiff with dried mud, and disgustingly itchy. She removed her shoes and socks, and regarded her swollen blistered feet. It didn't seem likely that they could carry her much longer. Painstakingly she tried to bandage them with strips of material torn from her shirt sleeves. The effort involved exhausted her, and she lay back – too tired to even examine Cristina's arms. What good could she do anyway? Subject the girl to the agony of digging more maggots out when the arms were already raw and infected?

She closed her eyes and drifted back into a sort of sleep. The thought of continuing the journey today was impossible – both Paul and Cristina were in no fit state to move anyway.

It wasn't fair. It just wasn't fair. Whatever Al might say they were all going to die out here. Die . . . Death . . .

She didn't really care any more. It would be a relief really . . . A blessing . . .

Al had been moving stealthily through the jungle for more than an hour. He had started off following some birds – but then he had seen the herd of wild hogs – about six or seven of them – and he had thought – Christ! If I can shoot one of those it will keep us going for days!

So he had trailed the snorting, grunting creatures, awaiting his opportunity.

They looked somewhat like ordinary pigs, only they were

bigger – with a higher back and coarse long bristles. And an incredibly strong smell issued forth from them.

Al wrinkled his nose in disgust – but somehow the hunting of food raised his spirits, and he felt fitter than he had for days. He suddenly understood what survival was all about. Pitting your strength against the elements and coming out on top. Adrenalin pumped through his body at an alarming rate. Now he could understand why men climbed mountains and sailed across oceans in little boats. The excitement of conquering nature. At thirty-eight years of age he was discovering there was more to life than climbing up on a stage and singing your guts out.

Slowly he raised the gun and pointed it at the nearest and smallest hog which had paused to sniff at something.

The bullet hit it right between the eyes. A clean shot which threw the animal to the ground in a writhing fury. It thrashed around for a few minutes, and finally rolled onto its back and died.

Al leaped forward. The stinking animal was going to be too heavy for him to carry.

But he was determined. People were depending on him. His son. The woman he loved. His brother.

He took off his belt which was made of leather, and slotted it around the animal's neck tightly. He was then able to drag the hog behind him, and make his way slowly back to the others. It took quite a while, but he made it, and in no time at all Evan was dismembering the animal, and Dallas was getting a fire together.

They roasted several portions, and picked at the hot greasy flesh ravenously. It wasn't the most tempting of meals – what with the smell and the unbearable heat and the flies. But it *was* food. They cooked more than they could eat and wrapped it in one of the blankets to take with them.

Strengthened, they set off once more on their journey. Supporting Paul between them – Dallas and Al led the way.

'We won't go far today,' Al said – he estimated it was already well past noon, 'but however little – it's something.'

The river was becoming wider and wider, and they were getting quite used to the sight of the crocodiles resting on small islands in the middle. Nobody was about to forget what had happened to Bernie – so they were extra careful. At one point they came across three or four baby alligators slouched on top of each other blocking their path. Quickly they detoured further into the forest unwilling to risk upsetting the mother.

It was hard work propelling Paul along – but Al encouraged

Dallas to keep going. She did so – moving one leg stiffly in front of the other. Tripping, being ripped and scratched by the overhanging boughs, allowing the filthy flies and mosquitoes to settle on the parts of her body that were exposed and lay their disgusting eggs. She was just too exhausted to brush them away.

She only kept going because of Al.

She couldn't let him down – he was so sure they would find help – so certain of being rescued. Soon he too would realize it was hopeless. Soon he would allow her to lie down and not get up again. Soon ... Soon ... Soon ...

'Sonofabitch!' Al exclaimed sharply, 'what the hell's *that*?'

Dallas looked ahead. She could see nothing but the river and jungle.

Al let go of Paul, his full weight came down onto Dallas, and the two of them fell to the ground.

'Wait there!' said Al excitedly.

Dallas closed her eyes. She couldn't get up again.

Evan and Cristina also sank to the ground, glad of the respite.

Al rushed ahead, spurred on by what he had thought he had seen around the next twist of the river.

He had not been mistaken. About fifteen yards from the bank of the river stood a hut. A primitive structure as he could see – but it was man-made.

He wanted to shout and scream. Yell out greetings. They had made it!

He hurried to the hut. It was empty. In fact it was hardly a hut – more a thatched roof supported on four posts, with a crude dried mud floor. There were no walls, and no sign of recent habitation. A vine was secured across part of the roof from which hung a large dead snake. Several spiders had spun their intricate webs and made their home there. A lizard stood stock still in one corner. A parade of ants marched to and fro up one of the posts.

Al squatted down on the floor, disappointment flooding through him. He had thought ... Aw – to hell with what he had thought ... At least it was a roof for the night, and at least it proved they were probably near some kind of human habitation. It proved above all that they weren't alone out here. That sometime – someone had built this shed.

He pulled the dead snake off the vine and slung it out into the jungle. It was completely dried up, must have been hanging there for quite a while. The lizard made a wild dash for safety before Al had even considered it as a possible source of food. Roast monkey – hog – why not lizard? Too bad he hadn't thought of it before.

Well, at least they would sleep with a roof over their heads tonight.

He went back for the others, and slowly they staggered to the refuge he had found for them.

'It ain't the Beverly Hills,' he quipped, 'but it beats the shit out of sleeping on the ground!'

It was sheer luxury. Ravenously they finished off the pieces of hog, and even Paul was able to chew some. Once more the fever was receding, leaving him weakened but intelligible.

They discussed the significance of finding the hut. It was a definite plus. It did mean that people had been here – in which case they must now be within travelling distance of human life.

By nightfall they settled down to sleep in comparative comfort. They even felt it safe to remove their shoes and socks and free their imprisoned feet.

In the middle of the night Cristina woke them all with some unearthly screams 'My foot – my foot!' she screamed, and a black shape fluttered away to escape her writhings. Al inspected her foot. It was spotted with blood and marked.

'Probably a vampire bat,' Dallas said dully. 'They suck out the blood . . . I don't think it's poisonous.'

They tried to calm the frightened girl, while Dallas soaked a rag in water, and wrapped it around her foot.

'Maybe we should all put our shoes back on,' she suggested, 'but shake them out first . . .'

Al couldn't sleep after that. His mind was racing. If he left them at the hut and travelled on alone he could make much better time. They had plenty of water. In the morning he could find some more food to leave with them. And the gun for their protection. Yes – it was the only way. He was the strongest . . . He could move fast . . . and speed was of the essence. If Paul didn't get medicine soon . . . and Cristina was in a bad way . . . even Dallas was in a weakened state. Only Evan seemed strong enough to continue.

Al swelled with pride at the thought of his son. What a man he had turned out to be. The King blood flowed strong in his veins. And to think how disappointed he had once been in him.

By morning Al was prepared to go hunting. Quietly he woke Evan, and told him where he was going. Evan wanted to accompany him – but Al suggested it was best he stay with the others.

He set off into the jungle, feeling quite at home, and confident of a kill. He soon came across some monkeys and approached them stealthily. He raised his gun ready to fire, and the thought occurred to him that what was he going to do when he ran out of bullets? It wouldn't be quite such an easy job then. He fired, reckoning he would face that problem when he came to it. One of the monkeys fell – this time it was a clean shot, and the animal was dead. He picked it up by the legs, and carried it back to the hut.

It was ridiculous – perverse really – but he was almost enjoying himself. The challenge of getting them all out of this mess . . . and he was doing it. Single-handed. He was providing shelter and food – and soon – he was *sure* of it – he would find them medical help.

It was a great source of achievement that he had been able to accomplish this. He – who in the past had been so spoiled that all he had to do was pick up a telephone and request anything he wanted – and get it. He could not honestly remember a time when he had had to do something for himself. Now four other people's lives depended on him – and if it was humanly possible he would save them.

He told Dallas of his plan to travel on alone.

She nodded, her beautiful eyes filled with defeat.

He squeezed her hand, and was suddenly overcome with a very tender love for her. 'If I don't find anything in the next two days – I'll come back. The monkey should last that long – and you've got plenty of water. You'll be fine – won't you?'

She managed a weak smile. 'If you say so.'

'I'll leave you the gun . . .'

'I love you,' she interrupted softly. 'Whatever happens, I love you.'

'We'll make up for lost time when we get out of here. Screw work – you and I, lady, are just going to laze around making love and having good times for at least a year. You like that plan?'

'I like it . . .'

He bent down and kissed her. A long insistent kiss. And he felt the beginnings of a hard-on, and he laughed – because – shit – if he could still feel horny after all they had gone through – well, jeeze – that meant he wasn't ready to give up yet. He was a survivor. They *all* would be.

He went over to Paul and said, 'Hang on in there, brother, I'll be back before you know it. We'll bung you full of medicine – you'll be in great shape – you'd better be – there's a lot of contract-breaking I want you to do for me. You know I'm lost without you.'

Paul grabbed him by the arm, his voice hardly more than a whisper, 'I want you to forget what I said the other day – I didn't mean it. Can you forget I said anything?'

'I don't remember a thing.'

Paul nodded, the muscles in his face twitching, his eyes more sunken than ever. 'If I die,' he said slowly, 'I want you to look after my children. I want . . .'

'Don't talk such crap. You'll be good as new once they stuff some medicine down you.'

'Sure,' agreed Paul weakly, 'I know that. But if I die . . . the children . . . promise me they'll live with you . . . I don't want Melanie to have them . . . she doesn't care . . . promise me, Al.'

'I promise – I promise. Big deal. You ain't goin' nowhere.'

'And Linda . . . take care of Linda . . .'

'Jesus!' Al threw his eyes upwards in mock despair, 'dictate me your will while you're at it!'

Paul hung on to his brother's arm even tighter. 'Take it easy,' he whispered.

Al nodded, frightened of the strong emotions he felt. 'I plan to, kid, I plan to.'

Cristina was sleeping, Evan by her side, swiping the flies away from her immobile body.

'*You* look after everybody,' Al said sternly, 'you hear me?'

'Yes, dad. You can depend on me.'

Al stared at his son, hardly recognizing him. The boy seemed to have thrived on the deprivations of the past twelve days. He no longer seemed scrawny – more thin and wiry – and now that his sunburn was clearing up and turning into a deep suntan, miraculously his acne appeared to have vanished.

Emotively Al hugged him. Then he was on his way – moving quickly along the sinuous river bank, making good time. He had to. They were all depending on him.

The day passed in a haze for those at the hut. They lay in a somnolent state, sweating through the day, and shivering at night.

Evan skinned and roasted some of the monkey. It didn't really matter what it tasted like, it was edible, and it filled their empty stomachs.

Paul was drifting in and out of a fevered state. He didn't want to eat. He didn't want to move. He was beginning to waste away.

Cristina, too, was in a bad way. She whimpered quietly to herself, moaning constantly about the pain in her arms.

Dallas felt incredibly weak and nauseous. She managed to eat the monkey, but after, she suffered very bad abdominal pains, and was forced to leave the hut and retch it all up.

Evan watched over everyone, clutching onto the gun, unable to help any of them, but ready to face any emergency.

Night brought relief from the heat, but it also brought frightening rustling noises and animal cries.

Evan wondered about his father, out there somewhere in the murky blackness alone. He had taken no food – no gun. How could he expect to survive and come back with help? What was going to happen to them all?

Evan tried, he tried his hardest. But all through the night tears rolled down his cheeks.

His father had left them alone. *They were all alone*. And one by one they would die.

Al was amazed at the speed with which he could travel now that he didn't have to consider four other people. He stuck to the river bank for a while, but then it occurred to him that it would make his going much easier if he swam. The wide river seemed to have a strong current which would carry him along nicely. Also being in the water would protect him from the fearsome heat. Of course there were dangers. The alligators would have to be watched out for at all times. But he figured if he stayed close to the bank and was careful . . . He slid into the delightfully cool water and allowed it to carry him along. It was a much easier way to travel. The current was strong and it was no effort for him to allow himself to be swept along. In fact it was rather pleasant. The first time he saw some alligators ahead he got out quickly. But they were merely lolling on an island and took no notice of him. The second time he risked staying in – they were on the opposite bank and didn't even notice him floating past. After that he stayed in the water unless they loomed ahead dangerously close.

By dusk he was starving hungry. He hadn't eaten all day, and there seemed no likelihood of any food. He looked longingly at a tree heavy with berries, but he remembered Dallas' warning about things being poisonous. It was stupid of him not to have provided himself with food, or at least the means to get some. He was no superman. He would not be able to keep going on water alone. He just hadn't thought. So sure was he of the fact that he was going to come upon human life.

He found a tree to curl up under for the night, and slept fitfully.

By dawn every bone in his body was aching, and muscles were hurting that he never knew existed.

He stood and stretched, tried to limber up. It didn't help, but he set off anyway, sticking to the bank of the river until the sun became warm, and then slipping back into the current to be carried along.

His thoughts were of food. Roast chicken. Sizzling bacon and eggs. Succulent veal. Steak and kidney pud.

He shut his eyes for a moment, imagining himself sitting down for a large slap-up meal. He would drink beer . . . Or perhaps champagne . . . yes – certainly champagne – for it would be a celebration meal . . . He grinned at the very moment his body slammed into a large tree trunk fallen across the river. He clung to it for support, his head whirling – lights flashing before his eyes. He had been knocked almost senseless.

With great effort he dragged himself from the river and crawled along the bank – collapsing in the mud.

He could feel his forehead beginning to swell where it had taken the force of the collision.

What next?

He lay very still, partially stunned. And after a while, as if in a dream, he heard voices – strange foreign sounds – and then it was all too much and he passed out.

Inevitably morning dawned. The insect and animal sounds filtered through to Dallas. And the smell of four people stuck together unable to wash or clean themselves. It was a sickening smell, but one you soon got used to. If she had the strength she would go to the river and bathe – to hell with the alligators – but she felt unable to move. Her stomach was still cramping, but she had nothing left to throw up. She felt so very weak, and there was this strange euphoric feeling. A lightness of the head, an immovability of the limbs. She tried to sit up, and fell back. If a snake had entered the hut at this point and headed towards her she would have had neither the strength nor the initiative to move out of its way.

Evan offered her water. 'Shall I make a fire and cook the rest of the monkey?' he suggested.

She sipped at the water. 'No food,' she mumbled, 'don't feel good.'

He placed a hand firmly on her head, and was alarmed to find her burning up. With dismay he realised that she too had some

572

sort of fever. He did not know what to do. Cristina was flushed and delirious. Paul was dehydrated and possibly unconscious and he had been unable to rouse him. And now Dallas.

A black terror swept over Evan. He had promised his father to look after them all. But how could he look after them if they were going to die on him one by one?

It was an impossible situation. And one that he was powerless to do anything about.

There was a moving sensation – not unpleasant. And still the strange mutterings – only clearer now – more excited.

Al opened his eyes to find himself being carried on some crude sort of stretcher – and for a moment he imagined he was being carried from the plane, and the thirteen days spent in the jungle had never happened.

His head was pounding, and he raised his hand to it, and felt something warm and sticky. He lowered his hand to find it covered with blood. He must have groaned aloud, because the stretcher was suddenly put down on the ground, and three faces were staring down at him. Three young Indian boys – perhaps sixteen years of age. They were of a deep mahogany colour, with wide, rather flattened faces, and jet black straight hair worn long and parted in the centre. They were totally naked apart from a small piece of cloth twisted around their loins. But they compensated for their lack of dress by being liberally decorated with painted symbols and designs.

They stared at Al and chatted amongst themselves in a language he had never heard in his life.

'English,' he said slowly, and then realizing he had been found, and remembering what had gone before, he raised his voice: 'English!' he yelled. 'You speak English?'

The boys jumped back in alarm.

'Christ! Am I glad to see *you*!' He raised himself on one arm.

The boys regarded him suspiciously.

'Plane,' Al said slowly, 'the sky,' he pointed to the sky, 'crashed.'

The boys exchanged glances.

'Other people,' Al enunciated carefully, 'back there.' He gestured behind him, and observed that they were travelling through the interior of the forest.

The boys jabbered excitedly together. They obviously did not understand a word he was saying. Finally one boy stepped forward and made a short speech – pointing and gesticulating ahead. Then he indicated that Al should lie down on the stretcher once more, and mimed a man much taller than himself.

Al understood it to mean that they were taking him to a person who would understand him. He complied with their wishes and lay back.

Effortlessly the boys picked up the stretcher and resumed their journey through the steamy forest. They moved quickly, weaving through the thick undergrowth at a fast pace.

Within minutes they were approaching a large clearing, where once more the boys placed the stretcher on the ground.

Al sat up, and realized that he was an expected guest. Almost an entire village of Indians had emerged from their huts to stare at him. Women, children, men – young and old. They pointed and stared and jabbered away in their incomprehensible tongue.

The women were entirely naked, the males were covered by loincloths. The huts they had emerged from were similar to the one Al had left the others at. Crude dwellings consisting of four supports and a thatched roof.

The boys, seemingly having done their part, stepped back and blended in with the onlookers. A few children ventured nearer for a closer look. Their eyes were as bright as buttons, and even they were covered in intricately painted designs.

Finally the taller man they had indicated appeared. He emerged from a hut, and everyone stood back to let him pass. He was indeed tall, and obviously someone important – for his hair was greased and coaxed into a fine tower – and some kind of stylish comb emerged from the top. Also his chest was covered by an intricately carved shield, and he wore more necklaces, bracelets and adornments than anyone else.

He approached the stretcher, regarded Al solemnly, and addressed him in a deep monotonous voice.

The only trouble was that English did not appear to be the language of the day.

'Hey—,' said Al – his initial relief at being found turning into slight anxiety – 'how about speaking a little *English* around here.'

The Chief – as Al had decided to christen him – replied in his own language, and stared – awaiting a reply to what was obviously a whole load of questions.

Al attempted to stand – realizing he must look as funny a sight to these Indians as they did to him.

He pointed to himself. 'English,' he said clearly, 'Al King.'

He was hoping that his name would cause at least a spark of recognition. After all, he was known throughout the world – his disappearance must have caused a lot of waves – maybe word had filtered through.

Suddenly he wanted to laugh. Who was he kidding? He was stuck in the middle of some dumb jungle and he actually expected a bunch of naked Indians to know who he was! It just showed how conditioned he was to his own fame. He could remember dreaming of going somewhere where no one would recognize him. Now here he was. Big fuckin' deal. Wrong place. Wrong time.

Christ! His head was throbbing, his stomach was one aching mass, and he was worried about getting back to the others. He proceeded to pantomime a series of events. A plane flying, falling from the sky, more people, a journey. He indicated strongly that they had to return down the river.

The Chief seemed to understand him – indeed he even started to mime a reply.

Al took it to mean that soon it would be dark, and they could not travel at nightfall. Early in the morning, the Chief seemed to be indicating. Then he was addressing members of his tribe, and two women came and shyly started to pull Al towards a hut.

He went with them, although there were still many questions he had to try and ask. The Chief had expressed to him that his head wound would be treated, and that then they would eat.

Al wondered how far they were from civilization. Radio contact? An air strip? When the others were rescued how long before they could all be out of here?

The women were peeling the clothes from his body, talking and giggling amongst themselves. They laid him on a rush mat, and other women appeared with an earthen pot filled with some sort of milky liquid. They proceeded to dab his cuts and scratches. It was cool, and had an almost numbing effect. His head wound they treated particularly carefully.

He tried to lie back and relax, but he was so worried about the others, and wished that they could be on their way back for them.

The Indian girls were similar in appearance. Stocky, smooth bodies, with firm jutting breasts. Greased hair. Much ornamentation. They wore beads around their necks and arms, and their lower lips were pierced and had little strings of white beads inserted. The delicacy with which they attended him reminded him of a trip he and Paul had once made to a Japanese whorehouse.

They took his filthy torn clothes away to wash, and offered him a loincloth to put on. He felt stupid in it – but what the heck – it seemed to be the thing to wear.

Dinner with the Chief was the next event. They sat on the ground in a semi-circle with other men of the tribe, and the women served them a series of tasty dishes in earthenware pots.

Al did not know what he was eating, and he didn't much care. He wolfed everything down ravenously – from a mushy stuff which tasted like bananas – to a sort of sour dough bread. Not steak and champagne – but it beat the shit out of nothing!

The Chief launched into a friendly discourse about what he seemed to regard as flying birds and the stupidity of men who went up in them. He shook his head in amazement a lot – and Al noticed that the other members of the tribe copied everything he did.

'Telephone,' Al kept on repeating in pidgin English, illustrating the act of making a phone call.

The Chief nodded and smiled, but did not appear to understand.

Then it was dark, and Al was guided to a hut – where for the first time in thirteen days he had a proper place to sleep – a most comfortable hammock. As he rocked back and forth he thought of Dallas, and the others, and could not wait until morning when he would be on his way to fetch them.

Evan thought he should eat, even if the others didn't want to. He uncovered the remains of the monkey which he had carefully wrapped in a towel – and was horrified to find it crawling with maggots. He threw it out of the hut in disgust. Now there was no food at all, but he did have the gun. He fingered the weapon lovingly. He too would be able to go out in the forest and hunt like his father. He would have to.

The thought excited him. It spurred him to get up and stretch his cramped limbs. The stench in the hut was awful, even though there were no walls. He tried not to look at the others. He was frightened that one of them might be dead.

He had no idea what time it was, but maybe if he was able to kill some fresh meat he could persuade them all to eat. If they ate they would get better.

Thinking that way at least gave him something to aim for. At least he would be doing something constructive instead of just sitting there.

He set off into the jungle, filled with a sudden sense of adventure. He was like his father – strong. A survivor.

He saw some monkeys, but he decided that something different might whet the appetities of the others, he didn't know what – but it would be silly to just shoot the first animal he came across. That would be the easy way – why take the easy way?

He continued on into the interior of the forest – not at all frightened – and not taking much note of the direction he was travelling in.

The foliage was becoming sparse – the ground clearer. The area appeared to be changing in character. He noticed a huge black and green snake coiled around a tree trunk. It was a real monster, and he stepped well away from it.

Suddenly, with no warning, a large black jaguar appeared no more than fifteen yards ahead of him.

Evan froze to the spot, as did the animal. For moments they stood and stared at each other. Then simultaneously they moved – Evan reaching for his gun, and the jaguar tensing itself ready to spring.

The Indians woke Al before it was light. They were anxious to be on their way.

He wondered how they were planning to bring back the four others he had told them about. He had made them understand they would be too sick to walk. They did not seem bothered. They kitted him out in a pair of thonged sandals such as they wore, and still clad in his loin cloth he was beginning to feel almost like one of them.

They set off, trotting through the jungle, expecting Al to keep up with them. It was impossible for him, and they made faces and laughed as they had to slow down for him. Eight young men had been sent on the mission, and they talked excitedly together in their native tongue – enjoying the break in their usual routine.

Al had explained, as best he could, about the hut he had left the others at. The Indians seemed to understand him, and the Chief had indicated that it was no more than one day's journey away. It had taken him *two* days to reach them, but he didn't argue. They obviously knew best.

They journeyed to the river, where Al was shown the reason he had been found by them. The tree trunk blocking the river was a trap – set by the Indians. Nobody passed their section of the river without them knowing about it.

They set off in three canoes kept concealed in the undergrowth going against the current, but making good time anyway. The Indians were very proficient in their use of the small wooden paddles used to propel the boats along. They ignored the alligators – navigating around the islands and rocks with great skill.

The sun burned down, but Al noticed how the flies and mosquitoes seemed to have left him alone ever since his body had been bathed in the white lotion. They certainly didn't bother the Indians.

Half way through the day they stopped and rested for no more than half an hour, chewing on raw fruits they had brought with them.

Then they were off again, the flimsy canoes moving exceedingly fast.

The knew exactly where to stop – pullling the boats up on the bank – and skipping curiously over to the hut.

Al followed. He had been gone three days and two nights – a lifetime in the jungle. But he had left them with food, water, and Evan to protect them. They shouldn't be too bad.

The Indians stood in a silent circle around the hut. Al pushed his way through them. He was horrified at what he saw. Three silent heaps – insects crawling all over them.

He went to Dallas first, feeling urgently for her pulse. She was alive, and so amazingly were Cristina and Paul. But all three of them were very sick.

There was no water left in the two leather flasks they had used to carry their supplies, and they were parched with thirst and dehydrated.

Al shoved the Indians into action – and instead of standing and staring they began to help. Running to fill the flasks with water, beating the insects off the three inert bodies.

'Evan,' Al shouted, 'where is Evan?'

He looked through the hut, there was no gun, and it occurred to him that perhaps his son had gone off hunting. But would he have left them with no water? It didn't seem likely.

Al bent to Dallas. Her face was covered in bites. So much so that her eyes and lips were swollen to a horrible degree. 'Can you hear me?' Al whispered, 'hey – beautiful – can you hear me?'

She mumbled something incoherent. She was in the grip of a raging fever.

Al turned to one of the Indians and by a series of actions tried to explain that someone was missing.

The boy nodded. He appeared to understand. He turned to one of his friends and jabbered away in the native tongue. Then the two of them rushed off into the forest.

There was nothing to do but wait. Nothing to do but feed water to Dallas, Paul and Cristina – and hope that they could stay alive another day.

One of the Indians sat quietly beside Cristina digging the maggots from her raw infected arms. She was too weak to even cry out in pain.

Another one produced the magic white lotion and dabbed it on Dallas' face.

They talked amongst themselves all the time, obviously discussing the accident, and how these people had come plummeting down into the jungle.

They went to the river and caught fish with their bare hands for dinner, which they skinned and prepared over an open fire. It was quite delicious. Al only wished that the others could taste it. He saved a piece in the hope that Evan would shortly emerge from the forest. He didn't.

It was after dark when the two Indians returned. They shook their heads and lowered their eyes. In their hands they carried the gun Al had left with Evan, and the boy's shirt – torn to shreds and covered with blood.

'Where *is* he?' Al screamed, frustrated in his efforts of not being able to understand their language.

The Indians tried to explain. With gestures they drew a picture of a large fierce animal. 'Onca,' they kept on saying, 'onca nigra.'

It meant nothing to Al. Then as they continued to try and explain to him he realized what they were telling him. Evan was dead. Evan had been killed by an 'onca nigra' whatever that was.

He could not believe it. To have gone through so much . . . it couldn't be true . . .

'The body,' he said, 'where is the body?'

They understood him. They glanced at each other and opened their arms to the sky. It was a very final gesture.

Al knew what they meant. Cathy. Bernie. The law of the jungle devoured bodies that were not immediately buried.

For the first time in his life Al cried. He could not claim to have ever been particularly close to his son – but in the past days they seemed to have developed a deep bond of mutual trust and love that had never been apparent before. The future had promised a fine relationship between them. He held his head in his hands and sobbed like a baby.

The Indians looked away in confusion.

And so the night passed.

In the morning they carried Dallas, Cristina, and Paul to the canoes and set off as fast as possible.

The journey took much less time as the river current was with them, and the boats fairly whipped along at an alarming speed.

Al travelled in the canoe with Dallas, cradling her head on his lap. He couldn't help blaming himself for Evan's death – if he hadn't left them . . . He knew the answer to *that*. If he hadn't left them to fetch help they would all have died.

But it seemed so cruel and unnecessary. If only Evan had stayed where he was he would have been all right. Obviously he had gone to hunt for food . . . He had died trying to keep them all alive.

Returning to the Indian village was almost like returning home. The Chief himself came to the river to greet them and peer at the other white people. He clucked his tongue at their condition, and issued orders. Three of the boys were dispatched off into the jungle, three more sent off on up the river in their canoe.

Then Dallas, Cristina, and Paul were carried to the village, and whisked off by the womenfolk.

There was nothing Al could do except sip strange herb tea with the Chief, and attempt to carry on a conversation by mime.

He was weary. The strain of the past fourteen days was finally taking its toll. How long before they could get out of here? How many more had to die before they saw the light of civilization?

He tried to ask the Chief – who merely nodded and smiled.

It was unreal – the whole thing was some sort of nightmare.

He finished his tea and went to see Dallas. The women had her stripped off and were bathing her bruised, cut, scratched, and bitten body with the white liquid.

People wandered in and out of the hut to stare at her, and Al was suddenly filled with an uncontrollable jealous fury. 'Get the fuck out of here!' he screamed at two Indian males, who merely smiled politely in return, had a good look, and wandered in to stare at Cristina next door.

Goddamn savages! How many days before they could get out of this pisshole? How many fucking days?

It took three. Long enough for Dallas, Cristina, and Paul to be well enough to travel.

The medicines the Indians employed were amazing. They calmed the fever in both Dallas and Paul, and treated Cristina's arms with some sort of raw plant wrapped around them.

The three of them were exhausted and weak, but no longer next to death.

Cristina was able to understand a very little of the Indians' language – it seemed several of the words were close to Brazilian or Portuguese. They were able to ascertain the fact that the only way out of this village was by river, and when they were well enough to travel a three-day journey would take them to a larger jungle settlement – and from there a day's journey would take them to a trading village which had a small airstrip. From there it was only a few short hours to the outside world.

'I guess we'll be a big surprise to everyone,' Dallas managed weakly. She was growing stronger every day. But the stronger she grew physically the more she clung to Al. He never left her side, and they talked about Evan and Bernie and why it had all happened and why they had been saved.

Paul was in a very weak state and seemed to have lost any kind of lust for life. He lay in his hammock – eating listlessly, accepting the medicines the Indians persuaded him to take.

Cristina could talk of nothing but her parents. How wonderful they were – and how she would make everything up to them. She had cried for Evan. But now her tears were dry and she was anxious to get home.

They were all anxious to get home. But where was home for Al? He kept on shutting Edna out of his head – but she was still his wife. What a shock it would be for her – she had probably resigned herself to the fact that Evan and he were dead. Now he would come strolling out of the jungle alive. What would she expect from him?

He would have to go to her, explain about Evan. Tell her what a hero her son had been. Dallas would go with him. One thing he was sure of – and that was that he and Dallas were not going to be parted – no long absences – in fact no absences at all. They had talked it over and decided that that was what they both wanted.

Thank God she seemed to be recovering. But he was still worried about Paul, and couldn't wait to get him into a proper hospital.

The Indians had been wonderful – kind and helpful – they couldn't do enough. But as soon as Al felt everyone could travel – they set off.

The Chief came to the river to bid them farewell. He seemed genuinely sorry to see them go, and in a strange way Al had grown fond of him and his tribe of gentle people. Untouched by civilization they seemed to have got human relationships together very nicely indeed. Al would have liked to have done something for them. But what did they need? They were self-sufficient – they needed none of the artifices of modern society.

The Chief and Al solemnly exchanged hand clasps – and on impulse Al took the heavy gold chain from around his neck and gave it to the Chief, who appeared delighted. He examined the various medallions and charms excitedly. A St Christopher. A small gold spoon. Brazilian hand. Solid gold tag inscribed 'Al is King', and a gold and onyx dice.

The Chief then removed his own necklace – a fearsome combination of ivory, quartz stone and animal teeth, and placed it ceremonially around Al's neck.

'I'll be back,' Al smiled. 'When I want to get away from it all I'll know where to come.'

Then they were off, in a convoy of three canoes – and their journey back to the outside world had really begun.

seventy-three

Twenty-two days after vanishing on the trip between Rio and Sao Paulo Al King reappeared in the outside world.

Headlines screamed hysterically –
AL KING ALIVE – SUPERSTAR SURVIVES PLANE CRASH – AMAZING JUNGLE RESCUE OF AL KING.

None of the newspapers had the facts – just news of his survival through the wire services. Journalists from all corners of the world were rushed to Rio where Al was expected to arrive from some obscure jungle trading village.

Nobody had much information – only that he was alive, and had apparently survived an air crash, trekked through dense jungle, and was on his way back.

The excitement was intense. Who was with him? How had the plane crashed? How had he managed to make his way through unmapped wastes of treacherous jungle for twenty-two days?

It was the story of the year.

The world waited with bated breath.

*

Linda was in bed when she heard. Alone. Idly watching television, flicking between 'Charlie's Angels' and an old Joan Crawford movie. A newsflash informed her that Al King had been found alive, and she sat rigidly up in bed not knowing what to do. The newsflash was so brief – it told nothing.

She leapt from her bed and frantically switched channels – nothing – commercials, soap operas, game shows, comedy, singers. No news.

Christ! Her hand was shaking as she reached for the telephone. If Al had been found alive somewhere . . . What about Paul? And Dallas, and the others.

She dialled Cody's number. He would know. She had not spoken to him since they had returned from Rio twelve days previously. She had given him the speech, 'I like you a lot but . . .' Somehow she had not felt it was quite the right time to go falling head first into a heavy affair. If Cody had been a casual lay it would have been OK. But he wasn't. He was a kind, interesting, funny man – the sort of man she could quite consider spending the rest of her life with. And somehow . . . with Paul missing – probably dead – it just wasn't the right timing.

'If you still want to we can get together in a couple of months,' she had told a puzzled Cody.

He had not understood. 'But why?' he had kept on asking over and over.

She had shrugged. 'It just doesn't seem right. Oh I know I had planned to split with Paul – but I hadn't *told* him. To be with you now . . . how can I explain it? It would just be disloyal.'

'That's a load of crap – you're just opting out of what could be a very good relationship.'

'It's the way I *feel*.'

So they had not spoken to or seen each other since the Rio trip.

His phone did not answer. She kept ringing until the service picked up. 'Cody Hills,' she requested breathlessly. 'One moment, please,' the operator replied, leaving her hanging for what seemed like an endless two minutes – then – 'I'm sorry, Mr Hills is out of the country.'

'Out of the country?' Linda repeated in a dazed voice.

'He'll be in Europe for the next ten days. Would you like to leave a name and number?'

'How . . . how long has he been gone?'

'I'm sorry. I don't know. Would you like me to check for you?'

'If you would.' How could he just go away like that? Without even calling her. But she had specifically requested that he did not call her. Yes ... but Europe. He *should* have called.

'Mr Hills has been gone three days,' the operator returned to inform her. 'Is there any message?'

'Do you have a number I can reach him at?'

'Sorry, Mr Hills is moving around. I'm sure he'll be calling in.'

'When?'

The operator was getting impatient. 'I really don't know that. Now – can I take your name or not?'

Linda left her name. A lot of good *that* would do. Where the hell *was* he? And why hadn't he told her? She felt strangely hurt, although he was only doing what she had asked him to do.

Shit! She kicked the side of the bed in sudden anger. Then – remembering what the phone call had been all about in the first place – she rushed to her purse. Somewhere, written on a slip of paper, she had Carlos Baptista's number. If anyone would know what was happening – he would.

Cody was in London when he heard. He had just arrived back at his hotel after a pleasant dinner at Mr Chow's with his stud actor, the director of the picture his actor had just begun, and a young stoned model that the actor and director appeared to be sharing.

As he collected his room key from the desk the clerk remarked, 'Did you hear Al King's been found?'

The clerk had been volunteering this piece of information to hotel guests all evening – and reaction had varied from vague interest to an avid desire for details. Cody's reaction was the best yet. He stood stock still, went very white, and through clenched teeth muttered, 'You mean they've found his body?'

'*Him*,' the clerk elucidated, 'apparently he came walking out of the jungle. Can you imagine that?'

'Alive?'

'Well, he must have been alive if he was walking.'

'Where did you hear this?'

'Here – did you *know* him?'

'Was there anyone with him?' Cody did not realize it but he was shouting, 'Was there anyone with him?'

The clerk backed away. '*I* don't know. They didn't say.'

Cody grabbed his key and raced to the elevator.

It was amazing – a miracle. If Al King was still alive ... What about Dallas?

He had to place a call to Carlos Baptista immediately.

*

Edna was sitting in the front room with John and his elderly mother when she heard. She was at their house, where she had been a guest in their tiny spare bedroom for three days – ever since moving out of the big mansion she had shared with Al. She had moved out in a hurry because the Arab who had bought the house wished immediate occupation with his wife, eight children, and numerous relatives. Leaving all furniture had been part of the deal. Edna had not minded. There was nothing she wished to keep. In fact the relief at leaving the big house had been immense.

John had been so understanding and kind. She had been forced to tell him who she was because of the fact that her picture was all over the newspapers. It had been *his* idea that she move in with him and his mother.

'Nothing improper,' he had hastened to add when first mentioning the idea, 'but you will have privacy – no one will bother you.'

She had jumped at the idea – and living with them was like returning to the kind of life she had always yearned for. The kind of life she had hoped that she and Al would share. A proper cooked breakfast to see John off to his work in the morning. Housework. Tea. Six o'clock dinner, and John and his mother *loved* her cooking. Then togetherness in front of the telly before an early bedtime.

She knew that as soon as he felt a suitable amount of time had elapsed John would ask her to marry him. She was ready to say yes.

Now this. A sudden jolting newsflash that Al was *still alive*!

A newsflash that made the blood drain from her face, and sweat break out all over her body.

John was wonderful. He was calm and did not panic. 'I think,' he announced slowly, 'that this calls for a nice cup of tea.'

Melanie was in Las Vegas when she heard.

'Shit!' she exclaimed, 'that's impossible.'

She was sitting in the Noshorium coffee shop in Caesar's Palace Hotel with Manny Shorto, three of his permanent entourage, two hangers-on and four interchangeable showgirls.

She was on her honeymoon, having married Manny five days previously in a much publicized midnight ceremony.

'Manny, you hear that?' she shrilled.

Manny was not hearing much of anything. He was into his sixth – or was it seventh – scotch, and he was working out the strategy he would employ in the poker game he planned to join at any minute. Meanwhile he was concentrating on a bagel – liberally spread with lox and cream cheese. 'God's food,' he called the combination – his only gesture in the direction of religion.

Melanie flapped her hands in a mild panic. 'Al King's alive!' she screeched, repeating what an alert reporter had just whispered in her ear.

'So?' munched Manny.

'If he's alive ... well maybe ... well ... what about *Paul*?'

'He alive?'

'*I don't know.*'

'So worry about it when you know.'

'But Manny ...'

'Be a good broad and cool it with the *kvetching*.'

'*Kvetching?* Are you kidding? This could be *serious*. This could mean you and I are not even married!'

Manny gazed expansively around the table – bagel hovering near his lips. 'Let's hear it for instant divorce! Think I made myself a *record* here!'

His audience laughed appreciatively.

Melanie stood up, quivering with fury. 'Fuck *you*!' she shrieked.

'Name the place, kid,' replied Manny, 'I'll be there!'

The journey back to civilization was a nightmare. But a minor one compared to what they had already suffered.

The three day journey by boat to the next village was a difficult one. As they progressed in their parade of canoes the river became wider and far more difficult to navigate. There were innumerable bends and turns, and rocks and islands abounded. The water was sometimes calm, and sometimes strong currents led the flimsy boats into whirlpools and rapids.

All the time alligators were present – lounging on their islands, sliding sinuously into the water – ready to pounce at any opportunity. And the sun blazed unmercifully down.

Al did not mind the heat any more. His body was burned a deep mahogany colour, and he wore the native Indian costume which allowed him to sweat freely. Like the Indians he accepted the heat as a fact of life. They had learned to live with it, and so would he. It bothered Cristina and Paul, though. They lay in the bottom of the little boats, uncomfortable, sweating, and weak.

Dallas had rallied wonderfully. Her swollen feet were almost better, as was her face. She had lost a lot of weight with the fever though, and her once voluptuous body was painfully thin. 'Who needs a health spa,' she joked. 'This is instant diet.'

Al knew that a couple of weeks of proper eating was all she needed to regain her strength. The primitive medicine the Indians had given her to cure the fever seemed to have worked wonders.

After three days they had arrived at the next village – and they were left there surrounded by more Indians who came running out of their huts to form a circle and stare. Then a man had appeared dressed in shorts and a shirt. A white man – well, half white, as Al had discovered later.

He stared at them in amazement, and then in faltering English shook his head and exclaimed, 'I can hardly believe it. How long?' He gestured out into the jungle.

'Twenty-one days,' Al replied, 'and are we glad to see you!'

The man's name was Pucal. He was of mixed Indian and white blood. He was a trader who lived a nomadic existence amongst the Indians – only occasionally travelling to civilization to fetch supplies for himself and Indian family.

'I have a signal you coming,' he explained. 'Cannot believe you come from jungle. Tonight we rest. Tomorrow I take you trading village – one day's journey. I radio them now you here. Small plane take you nearest city.'

He took them to his house. A more civilized affair than the Indians' habitations. It had walls, a thatched roof and a raised floor. There he gave them steaming hot coffee, mashed banana, and a sort of maize bread.

Al decided it was probably the best meal he had eaten in his entire life.

Pucal could not seem to get over the fact that they had trekked through the jungle alone and practically unarmed – and emerged still alive. He kept on staring at them unbelievingly and muttering: 'A miracle . . . God sends a miracle . . .'

The next morning they set off early – Pucal and five sturdy Indians accompanying them. Another river journey. More sun. More mosquitoes to plague them.

But nobody minded. They were on their way home. They were on their way out of the jungle.

Late afternoon they left the river and travelled overland for an hour. The terrain was smooth and flat, and rose steadily. Eventually they reached a cluster of run-down houses, and beyond them the land was more cultivated and the people that ran from the houses to stare were dressed in ragged trousers and shirts. Civilization.

A small twin-engined plane was waiting to fly them to the nearest city. The pilot, a weather-beaten American regarded them with

587

the same amazement as Pucal. He chain-smoked cigarettes and chewed vigorously on gum. 'I gotta message hadda fly some people out . . . Where the hell you all *come* from?'

Al tried to explain, but the American just shook his head in disbelief. 'Nobody could survive an air crash and come through that jungle alive.'

'We did,' said Al, 'I'm Al King. Maybe you read about me . . .'

'Holy mackerel!' The American peered at him intently. 'Jee . . . sus! You're that singer fella – the one the papers were full of a few weeks back . . .' Within minutes he had radioed in the news, and by the time they were airborne the rumour that Al King was still alive and had been rescued from the jungle was spreading all over the world.

Carlos Baptista was as stunned as everyone else. Everything seemed to have happened so quickly. One minute Al King was dead and forgotten – the next – alive and on his way back to Rio.

The information filtering through was vague, and it had not yet been established exactly who was with him – but there were, apparently, three other survivors. And they had been transferred off the rescue plane, and were now on their way to Rio via a jet due to arrive at any minute.

Carlos waited at the airport with Jorge. Both men were silent and tense. Both men were hoping that their children were amongst the survivors.

Two ambulances waited on the tarmac ready to whisk Al and whoever was with him to a private clinic where Carlos had arranged for the best doctors to be standing by. Now that the singer was alive Carlos felt that he was his responsibility – besides which Al still owed him a concert – and what a concert it would be! Magnificent! The best ever! A giant tribute to Al King's return to life! Carlos' business brain was ticking over. He would use the Maracana Stadium again – but this time he would be able to charge *double* the price for the tickets. Everyone would want to see Al King. Everyone. It would be the most exciting concert ever staged.

Carlos sighed. If only Louis was alive . . .

Beside him Jorge stood stiffly to attention. He appeared to have aged ten years – his black hair – once tinged with attractive grey sideburns – had turned suddenly white. His face sagged, his whole body sagged. He was a lost and lonely man. All the money in the world could not buy back his lovely wife or return his daughter to him.

At fifty-eight years of age he found himself with nothing but an abundance of material possessions and wealth. He did not want to return to his former empty life. A different woman every week. A different party every night. A different city every month. That kind of life was for young men – men who had nothing more on their minds than how many women they could seduce in a year. Jorge had lived that life. Lived it to the hilt until Evita. Evita . . . Evita.

The jet coming into land was his last chance. Perhaps God would be kind and give him back Cristina. Although how a young girl could have survived the ordeal they must have gone through . . .

He closed his eyes and muttered a fervent prayer.

Dallas held Al's hand tightly. 'What do I look like?' she whispered.

He hugged her. 'Alive. That's what you look like.'

'I never thought we would make it. I really didn't.'

'Come *on*. If it wasn't for you we would still be sitting in the wreck – dead. It was *you* who said we had to find a river . . .'

'Yes, and *you* who took us down it. Al, I'm so sorry about Evan, so very, very sorry. He was a terrific boy. I just don't know what happened that day . . . It's all a blur . . . a nightmare . . .'

'He went to find food. The funny thing is none of you could have eaten anyway.' He shook his head in despair. 'I don't know . . .'

They had discussed it back and forth for days. How was he going to tell Edna? He just didn't know . . .

The plane touched the ground and roared along the tarmac.

'This is not going to be easy,' Al said. 'The press are going to be after us like vultures. Say nothing – whatever you let slip will be twisted – so silence. Right?'

'You make it sound as if we've done something wrong.'

'I just don't want a lot of bullshit fairytale stories hitting the papers.'

'And no Bernie to protect us . . .'

'Just remember I love you,' he squeezed her hand. 'We've come through one jungle – here we go again. Just watch out for the snakes!'

'I don't understand.'

'You will. The media is out there waiting. The real savages. They want me – they want you. We're news – the best goddamn news they've had for a long time. They'll try to tear us into shreds – so watch out, lady – they'll claw each others' balls to be the first with the story. You understand me now?'

She shuddered. 'Yes.'

'So – stay silent, and I'll protect you.'

The plane taxied to a stop.

The doors opened.

Chaos.

They were back.

Six months later

seventy-four

The gates to the huge Bel Air estate opened at exactly 12 a.m. and the cluster of journalists and photographers entered impatiently.

They followed a laconic security guard up a long winding path which led them to the main house. 'Don't know why we couldn't have *driven* in,' one woman complained.

'We're lucky to be here at all,' a black girl, dressed in a jump suit and aviator shades replied. 'I mean this is the *first* interview Al King has given in *six* months. The first since his *crash*.'

'Who cares about Al King,' sniffed the woman reporter, 'it's Dallas *I'm* here to see. *She's* the star as far as *I'm* concerned.'

'Yeah,' agreed a lanky male photographer. 'Man – she is the greatest. Hottest TV star of the season. Beeee-utiful! I am glued to my set when *she* is on – but *glued*.'

'So is every other man in America,' intoned a languid blonde, 'and who can blame them? I wouldn't throw her out of *my* bed – and *I'm* into guys!'

'Hey – Marlene – that stud you 'bin running with a guy – I thought he was a gay!' interrupted the photographer.

'Go stick it up your own ass!' Marlene replied, 'since when did *you* even know what to do with that noodle you've got hanging between your legs!'

Linda, walking at the back of the crowd, was only half listening.

Had it really only been six months since Al had come walking out of the jungle. And Dallas . . . the girl Cristina . . . and Paul.

It seemed years away. Was it really only months?

She could remember the night she had heard. The phone call to Carlos Baptista. The suspense of waiting to find out who the other three survivors were.

When she had heard that one of them was Paul she had rushed to the airport and boarded the next plane to Rio.

Seeing him lying in bed in the private clinic she had thought that he would die. He looked like a man teetering on the edge of death.

She had sat at his bedside, held his hand, and willed him to get better.

Gradually he had recovered. Gradually he had begun to look human again.

Cody had been in Rio too, and if they happened to bump into each other they smiled politely and exchanged stilted conversation. They referred to nothing personal. That's the way she had stated it should be, and Cody had respected her wishes. He was still respecting her wishes. She had neither seen nor heard from him.

So – what happened? She had spent five weeks with Paul before telling him it was all over. Five weeks of having Paul behave towards her the way she had always dreamed about. But it wasn't working. It just wasn't there any more as far as she was concerned, and finally she had told him.

He had been shocked and surprised. 'But this is what you always wanted,' he had insisted, 'for us to be together, to get married. There is no Melanie to bug you any more – I'm totally yours.'

Sure he was totally hers. Melanie had publicly humiliated him. Choked when he had turned up alive making her a bigamist, she had rushed to Mexico for a quickie divorce, and married Manny Shorto all over again. The newspapers enjoyed every minute of it.

Al was not pleased when he heard Linda was taking off on baby brother. He had summoned her into his presence and screamed at her a lot. She had told him to go fuck himself – it was none of *his* business.

So she had left – returned to New York for a few months and worked and played – hard – very hard. But the playthings were not as beautiful as the ones on the coast – the bodies were not as bronzed – the muscles not as taken-care of – the faces not facsimiles of Ryan O'Neal and Warren Bearry. I mean if playthings are going to be your thing – then go for the shiniest toys.

So she had returned to California, rented an apartment in the same building as before – and thought about calling Cody. It was only a thought – she had her pride – if he didn't care enough to contact her in all these months . . . Instead she had called Julio – male hooker supreme – and they had made a businesslike appointment.

He had turned up at her apartment – white Ferrari parked rakishly outside, white teeth gleaming like a toothpaste ad in his incredibly good-looking very black face.

'Hi – I'm Julio,' he had announced very properly, very politely. Then he had removed his French trousers, silk shirt, Gucci loafers, and come into her life with such energy and expertise that she had been quite breathless.

He had been worth every cent of his exorbitant fee.

But she couldn't help thinking about Cody. Funny, sweet, kind Cody . . .

Occasionally she read about him in *Variety*. He was doing very well businesswise – and sometimes his name would appear in the gossip column linked with this girl or that. She hated them all – whoever they were.

She also read about Paul in the trades. Read that he had returned to England and was concentrating on his management company while the great Al remained in solitary exile with only Dallas for company.

Had Al King retired permanently? That's what everyone wanted to know. After his miraculous escape from the plane crash and jungle he had given one short press conference on his arrival in Rio. It was a one-liner, 'I want to thank everyone for their concern . . .' And the world waited impatiently for the story of what had really happened.

They waited in vain. No one was talking.

Cristina Maraco was offered fabulous amounts of money to tell her story. Through her father she refused. She had spent a great deal of time in and out of hospital having skin grafts on her damaged arms. In between times she devoted herself to her father – the two were inseparable.

Paul, of course, was not talking.

And Dallas had gone with Al into his self-imposed exile. The two of them had not been seen by anyone except the small group of loyal employees who worked for them. And *they* had to sign statements that they would not write or give interviews or do anything that would infringe the privacy of their famous employers.

Of course the fact that Al and Dallas were inaccessible made everyone want them all the more. Especially since Dallas was now as big a star as Al – this due to the fact that her six hour-long segments of 'Man Made Woman' had been shown on television – and repeated almost immediately because of public demand. Suddenly she was the hottest lady on television – and nobody could get to her. Lew Margolis was tearing his hair out in frustration.

Sackloads of fan mail arrived at the studio daily. A poster of Dallas wearing nothing but a miniscule leopardskin bikini and a smile had broken all sale records. It would seem that half the homes in America wanted Dallas on their wall.

Now – finally – the two of them had agreed to have a press conference. Public interest was to at last be sated.

Linda could not resist attending. Why not? She was press. She was entitled.

She trailed behind the others, and wondered what it was they were coming out of exile to say.

Cody Hills had arrived at the Bel Air house an hour earlier. The guard at the gate had greeted him in a friendly fashion and waved him through in his car. The car was comparatively new – a sleek silver Mercedes – not rented – bought and paid for. His mother had had a fit when she had seen it – 'A *German* car!' she had exclaimed, 'I always knew you would let the family down!'

'The war was a long time ago,' Cody had patiently pointed out. He spent a lot of his time patiently pointing things out to his mother.

'So?' she replied sarcastically, 'tell your Uncle Stanley that. *He* remembers like it was yesterday!'

Cody drove right up to the main house – a sprawling building of Tudor design. He rang the front doorbell, and a thin girl, in owl-like glasses and a man's business suit, answered.

'Hi, Tilly,' Cody said. 'Are we all set?'

'Getting there, I think,' Tilly replied in clipped tones. She was the English secretary that Paul had sent over with all of Al's papers, and she had stayed on to work exclusively for Al. Paul no longer managed Al's affairs. Mutually they had agreed that it would be better for Paul to concentrate on doing his own thing. Besides which he wanted to stay in England to be with his children, and his health was not what it was – although he was better – the doctors said he could get a recurrence of fever at any time.

Al had chosen Cody to represent him. If Dallas liked and trusted him that was good enough recommendation.

Not that there had been anything to do as yet – except get out of contracts and free Al from every commitment.

Cody found himself in the position of having the two most wanted clients in show business – and not – until now – being able to set up one deal for them.

They had both wanted to do exactly nothing. They were happy just to lounge around their huge house – swimming, watching television, playing tennis, reading, listening to music – and most of all laughing, giggling, and making love.

Cody thought he had never seen two people so happy in each other's company. They glowed when they were together. They were insular – they needed no one else. He was about the only friend they allowed into their lives.

It had not been easy for Al after the crash. The newspapers had made much of the fact that his wife Edna had sold their house and *all* of his personal possessions and moved in with some nobody – all within weeks of his supposed death. She had even got rid of his *clothes*! It was a shock. But he had never made one public comment about it. He had made a short private trip to London to talk to Edna about Evan – tell her what had really happened and how proud she could be of her son.

Throughout their meeting she had clung nervously onto her friend John's arm, and she had refused to look Al in the eye. It was almost as if she wished he *had* died. She was not enjoying him intruding into her life again – she had found what she wanted and now she just desired to be left alone.

Al wasn't bitter. She had put up with a lot throughout the years. He had wished her luck, and shortly after, a divorce had been arranged, and Edna had since married John.

'Can I fix you a drink?' Tilly was asking.

'Not at this time of day – I never indulge until after dark.'

'How about a coffee then?'

'That would be nice.'

Tilly went off to get his coffee, and Cody wandered into the huge comfortable living room.

The press conference had been *his* idea. It had taken him weeks to talk them into it. It had taken him even longer to talk them into doing a film together.

Lew Margolis and every other major producer in Hollywood had been bugging him to try and put a deal together. They were offering the earth. Name it. Have it. Dallas and Al King together would be the dynamite package of all time. It was too good an opportunity for both of them to blow.

'You can do whatever you want,' Cody had told them, 'brief the best screenwriter in town to do what *you* like. Choose your own director. You will have *complete* control – plus a sizeable chunk of the action.'

At first they hadn't even bothered to listen to him. Then Dallas' phenomenal success on the television series fired her ambitious streak. 'Why not?' she began to ask Al, 'it would be fun – we would be together.'

'Because . . .' Al had replied, 'this business stinks. It's a grinding cut-throat bag of shit.'

'I know that – I didn't just get off the bus, you know. But Al . . . to do something together . . . anything we want . . . It *is* a great opportunity.'

Eventually she had talked him into it. She was young, excited by her success, she had no idea what real fame was all about . . .

If that was what she wanted Al wasn't about to stand in her way. But he wondered if she realized how soul-destroying becoming public property was . . . You gained a lot. You also sacrificed your right to privacy.

Of course he could protect her. He had taken the trip before.

Against his better judgement he gave Cody the go-ahead.

Dallas was ecstatic, 'It will be wonderful!' she enthused. 'I love you, Al, I love you – love you – love you!'

He was glad it made her happy – but he was wondering what the cost would be for both of them.

The six months alone together – away from people – pressures – hassles. It had been the happiest time of his life.

Shortly after returning from Rio he handed Dallas an envelope. It was a private investigator's report on her family in Miami. Her mother, father, husband . . . Al knew that one of her main hang-ups was the fact that her family had never come looking for her when she had run away. It had made her feel worthless and un-wanted. Secretly Al had decided to find out *why* they had never looked for their daughter – even when she was on magazine covers all over the country they had never stepped forward. And that *was* unusual – even the husband had never come sniffing around.

The reason was in the envelope.

The day Dallas had left the zoo there had been a fire. Arson was suspected, but nothing proved. Her mother, father, husband . . . all dead. And the police were looking – or had been at the time according to the press report – for a young black couple.

'After you ran off there must have been some kind of fight,' Al explained. 'The black stud you told me about must have burned the place down. Now you know why they never came looking for you.'

Dallas was numb with shock. But when the shock wore off she began to understand that perhaps after all she hadn't been abandoned – perhaps if they had been alive her parents *would* have come looking for her.

595

'You're not a married lady any more,' Al had joked later.

'Oh yes I am ... Cody ...'

A discreet annulment was arranged. Cody was just as shocked as she was. He still loved Dallas – but as a sister. Somehow it was Linda he couldn't get out of his head ...

Tilly came back in the room carrying a cup of coffee. 'Here you go.'

Cody took it. 'Thanks. What are they doing?'

'Dallas is fiddling around with her hair, and Al's watching her. Do I have to tell *you* what they're like? Togetherness at all times. If it wasn't so sincere it would be positively sick-making!'

'Yeah.' Cody grinned. He knew what she meant. It made anyone else in the room feel like an outsider.

He thought with satisfaction of his recent conversation with Lew Margolis. Rumour had flown all over town as soon as he had put out the word that Al and Dallas were looking for the right property.

Lew Margolis had phoned him.

'So the cunt finally came around to my way of thinking,' he had bragged. 'Knew she would – and that sonofabitch she's shacking up with. You want to come over and talk terms. I can get the contracts up this week. How long before they choose a property? I'd like to start shooting as soon as possible.'

I bet you would – thought Cody. Lew had recently had a monster flop with a film on lesbianism starring his wife. '*Doris Andrews a dyke*', one of the reviews had hooted, '*it's like casting Warren Beatty as a fag!*'

'They've found the property they want,' Cody said evenly.

'Great!' enthused Lew, 'it can be the biggest piece of crap in the world – what do I care – with them in it we're going to clean up – friggin' clean up! Get your ass over here, Cody – let's hear what the cunt wants.'

Cody took a deep breath. It wasn't in his own interests to screw a man like Lew Margolis – but Jesus – if anyone deserved it ... 'Sorry Lew,' he said smoothly, 'but "the cunt" decided to go elsewhere. Jordan Minthoff's producing.'

He hung up on Lew's explosion. It was a satisfying moment.

Linda was impressed by the house. It was big and lavish – but at the same time lived-in. There was no sign of any plastic interior decorator here.

They were led through the living room out to a large tented area

596

beside the pool. A long table was set out as a bar with two virile young bartenders. Maybe later . . . Then she saw Cody. He was suntanned, his sandy hair bleached lighter and combed carefully across his forehead to hide his balding hairline. He was wearing white slacks and a blue blazer with bold brass buttons; the obligatory Hollywood tinted shades covered his eyes. He was smiling and talking to a busty blonde strung with too many cameras.

Linda hung back. She didn't want him to see her . . . and yet . . . Oh shit – they could be friends, couldn't they?

She moved nearer to him – was going to change her mind and back off – but then he saw *her*. He left the blonde mid-sentence and was by her side. 'Good to *see* you.'

'You too.' They grinned foolishly at each other.

'So . . . what are you doing here?'

'I'm a photographer, aren't I? Thought I'd see what all the excitement was about.'

'I thought you were in New York.'

'I was.'

'When did you get back?'

'Few weeks ago.'

'Can I get you a drink?' he asked anxiously, leading her towards the bar.

'No, I'm fine.'

'You look fine. I mean you look terrific.'

She laughed self-consciously. 'I cut my hair.'

'Looks nice, really nice.' He paused, at a loss for words. 'Well . . .'

'Well . . .'

'I keep on seeing your work in every magazine I pick up.'

'And I keep on reading about you – this gossip column – that gossip column – you've really been getting around.'

'Gotta fill my time.'

'Oh sure.'

'You mean *you* sit home?'

'Not exactly.'

'I didn't think so.'

They were both suddenly serious, staring at each other.

'I am here to tell you I have really missed you,' Cody volunteered, 'like *really*.'

'Yes?'

'Yes.' He fumbled for a cigarette, dropping the pack and picking it up quickly. 'I'm not nervous – really I'm not.'

She laughed softly.

'I heard about you and Paul.'

'Al was furious. You would think it was him I was walking out on. I don't know how he'll feel about me being here today.'

'I'm sure he's forgotten all about it. Paul's doing very nicely in London – I hear he's got himself a girlfriend.'

She didn't feel at all jealous. 'That's nice.'

'Why didn't you call me?' Cody asked intently.

'Call *you*? Why didn't *you* call *me*?'

'You told me not to.'

'*Screw* what I *told* you. Oh, Cody – the trouble with you is you're too goddamn *nice*.'

'You wouldn't have said that if you'd heard me on the phone to Lew Margolis the other day. I shafted him right between the goolies. It felt good.'

Linda laughed. 'You don't have to defend yourself for being nice. I love you for it!'

'Do you realize what you just said? I think a remark like that calls for dinner tonight. I'll pick you up at eight. Where?'

'Same place, different apartment number.'

Again they both found themselves grinning foolishly.

'Hey – I've got a press conference to get on the road here,' Cody said at last. 'You're taking my mind off everything!'

'So sorry – what's it all about anyway?'

'Announce the movie . . . you know Dallas has become some huge star from that one TV series.'

'You don't have to tell me. I have made a small fortune from my pictures of her. They sell again and again and again.'

'A fortune, huh? You mean you're rich?'

'Well, you always did say I was a bright lady!'

'Ouch! You never forget.' He kissed her lightly on the cheek. 'Time to bring on my two superstars. How about you staying on after and getting some exclusive shots?'

'If you don't think they'll mind . . .'

'Mind! Dallas will be delighted, she's always talking about you.' He didn't want to confess that so was he. 'See you in a minute.'

He vanished inside the house, and Linda couldn't wipe the smile off her face. She felt ridiculous really, standing there grinning like an idiot, but there was nothing she could do about it. Seeing Cody again just made her feel *so* good.

She glanced around at her fellow photographers and journalists. They were chatting, drinking, setting up tape recorders and cameras.

Suddenly a hush fell over the gathering. Framed in the patio doorway stood Al and Dallas.

What a couple they made. Somehow Dallas was softer than before – more glowingly beautiful. She was wearing a very simple white dress which emphasized her suntanned body. Her luxurious wild hair cascaded down over her shoulders, and her huge green eyes gleamed with a hidden danger. She looked incredibly sensual and vulnerable all at the same time. An irresistible combination. That was the new ingredient – Linda decided – the vulnerability. It had every man in the room falling instantly in love. They didn't know whether they wanted to rape or protect her. She had them bewitched.

Linda also noticed a change in Al. A big change. The arrogance had gone and had been replaced with a look of deep satisfaction. For the first time since she had known him he looked like a contented man. And who could blame him? The two of them sparked off enough electricity to light up the house. Al was thinner than she remembered, and very darkly tanned. Also he had stuck to the beard he had grown in the jungle, and it gave him the look of a gypsy. His jet hair was long and unruly, and on his forehead there was a thin scar – a souvenir of the jungle.

Whereas before Linda had always thought his sex appeal somewhat manufactured – now he looked like the real thing.

The photographers and journalists surged forward – and was it her imagination or did most of them surge in Dallas' direction? She wasn't sure but she could have sworn a look of resignation swept over Al's face.

'Ladies and gentlemen of the press,' Cody announced proudly, 'I give you Dallas, and Al King.'

Jackie Collins
Hollywood Wives £3.99

'Behind the electric gates of Bel Air mansions and the towering walls of Beverly Hills panic reigns. The film capital of Hollywood is buzzing with rumour, midnight phone calls and wicked whispers. The reason is a sizzling new book ... close-up look at life among the ladies who owe their carefully preserved figures, matching Mercedes and palatial homes to the men who make the movies' DAILY EXPRESS

Sinners £3.50

Sunday Simmons and Charlie Brick live off their looks and rely on their agents. Today they're stars but tomorrow, who knows? In the fast-moving, hard-hitting Hollywood movie world sinning and winning can be one and the same.

'Scandalously sexy ... a racy tale of two celebrities in Hollywood's celluloid-and-sex race' NEWS OF THE WORLD

Chances £3.99

From the penthouses of New York and the bedrooms of Beverly Hills to the casinos of Vegas and the villas of the South of France – *Chances* was the name of the game. Gino Santangelo was the slum kid who carved an empire out of bootlegging, gambling, extortion, even murder; his daughter Lucky was as deadly as her father – she accepted crime as a business and power as an aphrodisiac. And Lucky Santangelo was too much like her father not to challenge him for an empire ...

'Ferociously entertaining ... outrageously uninhibited saga of sex and ambition' SUNDAY EXPRESS

All Pan books are available at your local bookshop or newsagent, or can be ordered direct from the publisher. Indicate the number of copies required and fill in the form below.

Send to: **CS Department, Pan Books Ltd., P.O. Box 40,
Basingstoke, Hants.   RG21 2YT.**

or phone: 0256 469551 (Ansaphone), quoting title, author
and Credit Card number.

Please enclose a remittance* to the value of the cover price plus: 60p for the first book plus 30p per copy for each additional book ordered to a maximum charge of £2.40 to cover postage and packing.

*Payment may be made in sterling by UK personal cheque, postal order, sterling draft or international money order, made payable to Pan Books Ltd.

Alternatively by Barclaycard/Access:

Card No.

Signature:

Applicable only in the UK and Republic of Ireland.

While every effort is made to keep prices low, it is sometimes necessary to increase prices at short notice. Pan Books reserve the right to show on covers and charge new retail prices which may differ from those advertised in the text or elsewhere.

NAME AND ADDRESS IN BLOCK LETTERS PLEASE:

....

Name ——————————————————————————

Address ——————————————————————————

——————————————————————————

——————————————————————————

——————————————————————————

3/87